PENGUIN TWENTIETH-CENTURY ~~~~~

IVY COMPTON-BURNETT: A ~~~~~ IBUS

Ivy Compton-Burnett wa~~~~~ ond marriage; her father ~~~~~ ad five children by his fir~~~~~ classics at Royal Holloway, ~~~~~ vel, *Dolores*, in 1911. The effects of ~~~~~ y – the death of a brother, the probable s~~~~~ broke her health and spirits; she did not pub~~~~~ 1925, when *Pastors and Masters* appeared and was ~~~~~ the *New Statesman* as 'astonishing, amazing. It is like nothi~~~~~ se in the world.' There followed *Brothers and Sisters*, *Men and Wives*, *More Women Than Men*, *A House and Its Head*, *Daughters and Sons*, *Elders and Betters*, *Manservant and Maidservant*, *Two Worlds and Their Ways*, *Darkness and Day*, *Mother and Son* (which won the James Tait Black Memorial Prize), *A Father and His Fate*, *A Heritage and Its History*, *The Mighty and Their Fall*, *The Last and the First* and the three novels collected in this omnibus edition.

Ivy Compton-Burnett's novels are set in a claustrophobic late-Victorian world, in the decaying mansions of the landed gentry; they concern power struggles within families, repressed hatreds and desires so strong that they break the bonds of convention. Pamela Hansford Johnson has said of her: 'Writing of a dying age she stands apart from the mainstream of English fiction. She is not an easy writer, nor a consoling one. Her work is an arras of embroidered concealments beneath which the cat's sharp claws flash out and are withdrawn, behind which the bitter quarrels of the soul are conducted "tiffishly", as if cruelty and revenge and desire, the very heart itself, were all trivial compared with the great going clock of society, ticking on implacably for ever behind the clotted veilings.'

Ivy Compton-Burnett continued to write until her death in 1969. From 1919 she shared a house with the scholar Margaret Jourdain. After Margaret died in 1951 she lived alone in her Kensington flat, and gave tea parties for her admirers. Robert Liddell has called her work 'a source of intense and peculiar intellectual excitement and pleasure ... one of the things we live by: a standard for our own conduct (in spite of shortcomings and backslidings) and a support in bad times.'

Hilary Mantel's latest novel is *A Change of Climate* (Viking, 1994). Her previous five novels, all published by Penguin, include *Fludd* and *A Place of Greater Safety*, winner of the 1992 *Sunday Express* Book of the Year Award.

A FIRST OMNIBUS

A FAMILY AND A FORTUNE
A GOD AND HIS GIFTS
PARENTS AND CHILDREN

IVY COMPTON-BURNETT

with an introduction by
HILARY MANTEL

PENGUIN BOOKS

PENGUIN BOOKS

Published by the Penguin Group
Penguin Books Ltd, 27 Wrights Lane, London w8 5tz, England
Penguin Books USA Inc., 375 Hudson Street, New York, New York 10014, USA
Penguin Books Australia Ltd, Ringwood, Victoria, Australia
Penguin Books Canada Ltd, 10 Alcorn Avenue, Toronto, Ontario, Canada m4v 3b2
Penguin Books (NZ) Ltd, 182–190 Wairau Road, Auckland 10, New Zealand

Penguin Books Ltd, Registered Offices: Harmondsworth, Middlesex, England

A Family and a Fortune first published by Victor Gollancz 1939
Published in Penguin Books 1962

Copyright 1939 by Ivy Compton-Burnett

A God and His Gifts first published by Victor Gollancz 1963
Published in Penguin Books 1983

Copyright © Ivy Compton-Burnett, 1963

Parents and Children first published by Victor Gollancz 1941
Published in Penguin Books 1970

Copyright 1941 by Ivy Compton-Burnett

This omnibus edition, with an Introduction by Hilary Mantel, first published 1994
1 3 5 7 9 10 8 6 4 2

All rights reserved

Filmset by Datix International Limited, Bungay, Suffolk
Printed in England by Clays Ltd, St Ives plc
Set in 10/12 pt Monophoto Baskerville

Except in the United States of America, this book is sold subject
to the condition that it shall not, by way of trade or otherwise, be lent,
re-sold, hired out, or otherwise circulated without the publisher's
prior consent in any form of binding or cover other than that in
which it is published and without a similar condition including this
condition being imposed on the subsequent purchaser

Contents

Introduction by Hilary Mantel   vii

A Family and a Fortune   1

A God and His Gifts   251

Parents and Children   395

Introduction

It is breakfast time, *c.* 1890; we are somewhere in England, and our class is upper middle. The family assembles. Coffee cups are passed; a letter arrives, perhaps from a treacherous lawyer, or a spouse believed seven years dead. A manservant stands by, ready to relish the night's disasters. Has there been a suicide attempt, perhaps? Or a cast-off nightgown (incriminating, monogrammed) found in a room where it should not be?

Assume that for once the night has been uneventful. No uncles have disappeared into a snowstorm; no one has a sudden marriage to announce. Breakfast conversation proceeds: formal, dignified, polite. Between the lines you can hear the sound of knives being sharpened.

The usual setting of Ivy Compton-Burnett's novels is a country house. It is large, shabby, costly of upkeep. The date is between 1885 and 1910. The estate is encumbered, and the family exercise stringent economy. So does the author. The scene moves – from dining-room to drawing-room to servants' hall; perhaps, even, to the garden. When the characters travel – or, as one might say, escape – they do so off the page. Calls are made on neighbours, who have similar domestic arrangements, and similar barbed conversational habits. Luncheon and tea provide the occasion for the family to indulge in ritual humiliation of the victims selected that day. Feast-day or fast, their diet is each other.

Ivy Compton-Burnett is one of the most original, artful and elegant writers of our century. To read her for the first time is a singular experience. There is almost no description or scene setting; the writing is pared to the bone, the technique is a gavotte on needles. The story unfolds in page after page of spiked dialogue. It is not always clear who is speaking; the words themselves are unlike any you have come across before. The manner of narration is so odd that some readers are unnerved, and cannot continue. Those who keep their nerve may quickly find themselves addicted. They give her scope to explore most human passions, especially the base ones.

She was born in 1884. When she was old, she found it entertaining to rearrange for interviewers the facts of her life and ancestry; she understood how to protect herself. Her background was not quite like that of her characters. She was the daughter of a homoeopath, and grew up in Hove. The family was large, and her father had married twice; her books are evidence that she thoroughly understood the position of the step child. She attended Royal Holloway College and took a degree in classics. Holloway was not like the austere women's colleges of the day. It was housed in a building of the utmost frivolity: an ersatz *château*, white and rose-red, set on rolling Berkshire lawns. The pupils picked orchids and wild strawberries in the grounds, and dressed for a (good) dinner; the founder had stipulated that each of them was to be provided with a large looking-glass. One of the girls' favourite occupations was sliding down the carpeted stairs on tea-trays.

Photographs show a beautiful, serious girl, with her hair tucked into a band. The face aged, the hairstyle remained the same: through Hitler's war, through the 1960s. Her world-view froze. She could not, she said, write with authority of anything that had happened after 1910.

Yet in no sense are her novels period-pieces. Because they are of one time, they are of no time. They deal in verities, in the old law of dog eat dog. Unity of place and narrowness of aim add to their sharpness and power. The themes are universal: jealousy, lust, greed, betrayal. The tone is that of high comedy, and sometimes that of stark tragedy. Self-interest is the ruling principle, and the weak receive no quarter.

Within Ivy's own large family there were marked groupings, age-constellations of the type one finds in her books. She was close to two brothers, both of them interesting and capable young men; Guy died at twenty, of pneumonia, and Noel was killed on the Somme. Ivy belonged to that generation of women whose lives were devastated by the Great War. 'Smashed up,' she would say. 'Smashed up.' In 1917 two of her sisters committed suicide. Survivors, with no men to marry, became independent women whether they liked it or not.

INTRODUCTION

She had written an early novel called *Dolores*, perhaps in collaboration with Noel. Then, for fourteen years, nothing: the succession of family disasters left her physically and spiritually incapacitated. In 1925, when she was forty-one years old, she produced *Pastors and Masters*. It was followed by eighteen other novels. Of these, *A Family and a Fortune* and *Parents and Children* belong to the middle period of her work, and were published respectively in 1939 and 1941. *A God and His Gifts*, published in 1963, was her last completed book.

In later years she lived in Cornwall Gardens in Kensington with the antiquarian Margaret Jourdain. She read her contemporaries, but they did not influence her. She wrote in pencil, in penny exercise books, and like Jane Austen she left none of her work about to be seen by casual visitors – though anyone who called on her casually would have needed an iron nerve. Incident is crowded into her early years; latterly, it seems, she ate chocolates, gave tea-parties and increased in wisdom.

The course of her life is told very well by Hilary Spurling in two volumes of biography, *Ivy When Young* and *Secrets of a Woman's Heart*. Ivy became one of those old ladies who is described as formidable. She was baffled by the modern world, or pretended to be. Yet some of her attitudes were so liberal that they startled her friends; and her oblique, ironic sensibility was of the kind that always seems ahead of the fashion. She enjoyed gossip, and liked to know about people's financial affairs. She had no time for religion, and did not change her opinion as death approached. Her chief interest was what it had always been: power, how to get it, how to abuse it. I imagine her as an extraordinarily intelligent woman, who never made less of her intelligence to any person, in any circumstance. And for a woman, even now, that is a good deal to say.

During her lifetime she had a devoted group of admirers, but her work was often misread and misinterpreted. As her typist Cicely Greig put it, she 'escaped the perils of popularity'. Her themes, it was commonly said, were those of Greek tragedy. But when the furnishings of tragedy are silver teapots and joints of ham, when butlers and nursery maids form the chorus, does tragedy become melodrama? Melodrama is a pejorative term, of

INTRODUCTION

course. It implies a wilful rejection of reality, an irresponsibility on the author's part. Compton-Burnett's novels were criticized because their events did not seem to bear relation to the events of ordinary life. But this was life as experienced, narrowly perhaps, by metropolitan book critics. In conversation with the novelist and critic Kay Dick, Ivy said darkly, 'I think there are a great many more deeds done than most people know.' We are perhaps readier to accept this nowadays. Inquire closely into the life of any 'ordinary' family, and you may find more material of the Compton-Burnett variety than you can bear.

It is strange that though in most people's lives money and love have roughly equal importance, writers tend to concentrate on love. Ivy's characters are often consumed by sexual passion – off the page, of course – but incest and illegitimacy do not terrify them so much as the prospect of penury. While the former cannot be frankly discussed, the latter can and indeed must be. As one of her characters put it, 'It seems absurd to say that money is sordid, when you see the things that really are.'

A Family and a Fortune is all about money; you might say that money is the main character. The opening scene of the Gaveston family at breakfast gives the author the opportunity to describe each of them. Ivy's descriptions of her characters are seldom memorable, but they are done to a formula which has meaning in itself. She is interested in how ancestry shows in face and figure; how, and in what proportion, the features of parents and grandparents are blended in each individual. Ivy is a Darwinian. Descent has its logic and its laws. Like those animals who live in groups, her characters fit into a hierarchy, and at crisis points they jostle for position.

Unusually, the family here consists of only two generations. Edgar is the head of it, married for thirty years to Blanche, who has her harmless vanities, and who is easily drawn into the conversational traps set by her two elder sons. Edgar is devoted to his brother Dudley, who lives with the family; he does not love his children, though he is unaware of this.

Mark, the eldest boy, helps his father run the estate he will inherit. He is accordingly a relaxed character, by the author's bracing standards. Clement, two years younger, is sharp and cold, a would-be escapee with no resources to finance his flight. Justine is like other elder sisters who appear in the novels: good-hearted, bossy and tactless. There is a younger brother, Aubrey, considered too dim-witted to go to Eton and taught at home by one of the fussy tutors who bumble through the books. Ivy's families often have one misfit child who is the target of others' wit; he is often witty or perceptive in himself, and just as frequently pathetic.

Though the family fortunes have declined, there is still a grand other-worldliness among its members. Having suddenly inherited a fortune, Edgar's younger brother Dudley is able to think of giving to charity for the first time:

'I suppose I shall subscribe to hospitals. That is how people seem to give to the poor. I suppose the poor are always sick. They would be, if you think. I once went round the cottages with Edgar, and I was too sensitive to go a second time.'

Early in the narrative, which occupies fourteen months, other members of the family come to live at the lodge on the estate. They are Blanche Gaveston's old father, her sister Matilda, and her sister's companion Miss Griffin. They no longer have the means to maintain the family home. Ivy is not sympathetic. In her novels, homosexuality barely merits a shrug, incest is an everyday occurrence, and murder not especially a thing to mention outside the family; but Aunt Matty and her father have committed the unforgivable sin. Failing to make ends meet on the interest from their investments, they have spent their capital. 'We should not kill the thing we love,' as the butler says in *A God and His Gifts*.

A Family and a Fortune contains one of the author's most memorable tyrants. 'Poor Aunt Matty,' Justine says. 'One can feel so sorry for her when she is not here.' In middle age Aunt Matty was crippled in a riding accident. Before this, she was a popular girl, with suitors; but she had declined to marry. 'She had never met a man who she saw as her equal, as her conception of herself was above any human standard.'

Matty treats Miss Griffin, her companion, with a shocking emotional and physical brutality. Unable at times to rise from her chair without aid, Matty is capable when she likes of trekking miles across the park to give a hard time to her niece and nephews. There is a scene in which, having driven Miss Griffin out of doors, at night and in freezing weather, Matty chuckles over the thought of her dying of exposure. It often happens, in reading a Compton-Burnett novel, that the reader blinks, does a sort of double-take: am I really reading this? Oh yes, Ivy will tell you with gentle insistence: people do behave badly, very badly indeed. Just as badly as you have ever dreamed. Just as badly as you yourself . . .

Having promised to do something for the children, the newly rich Dudley has to break his promise; he falls in love and means to marry, and will need his inheritance to establish himself. Expectations have been raised only to be disappointed. Then – in a typical Compton-Burnett manoeuvre – Edgar steals his brother's fiancée. Comedy gives way, for a moment at least, to compassion. Dudley's emotional isolation is movingly portrayed, and when Ivy writes of his illness and near-death, she seems to recall her own struggle to survive the influenza epidemic that followed the Great War.

Technically, this is a very good book. Transitions – the passage of fallow time – are handled with impressive briskness. Never, here or elsewhere, does the author misjudge her effects or lose her sureness of tone. There is nothing natural in her art; her books are a product of supreme contrivance. But she is never self-conscious. Cicely Greig said that Ivy concurred with Hemingway's advice: 'All you have to do is write one true sentence. Write the truest that you know.'

The book also contains Ivy's most shocking bedroom scene; it offers a spectacle at which even her hardened characters must pause, aghast, and revise their view of what it is to be English, and gentlepersons, and living in 1901.

Parents and Children introduces a much larger family, with the typical Compton-Burnett stratification. At the head of it are Sir Jesse Sullivan and his wife Regan; her father named her after Lear's daughter, having heard that Shakespeare's women were strong types. Their son Fulbert, married to Eleanor, is a failed barrister; because his elder brother has died he has 'a place to which he had not been born'. He is the father of nine children.

INTRODUCTION

They are divided into three groups – the young adults, Daniel, Graham and Lucia; the schoolroom children, Isabel, Venice and James; the nursery children, Honor, Gavin and Nevill.

Nevill is three years old, 'with an ambition to continue in his infancy': he is one of the most winning of Compton-Burnett's children. James is twelve, with 'features regarded as pretty and childish, and vaguely deprecated on that ground'. But the author's especial sympathy – such as it is – goes to the two young men. Sir Jesse has no education and does not feel the lack of it; he resents the fact that his two grandsons must be kept at Cambridge so that they can be turned into schoolmasters. He accuses them of 'grinning and chattering like apes and costing like dukes'. Only inheritance will deliver such young men – who appear throughout Ivy's work – from a harsh world in which money must be earned at a humiliating trade. But they are the third generation; they have to wait for their grandfather to die before they can reasonably start hoping for their father's decease.

The teeth-grinding tensions of family life are examined with particular care in this novel. As usual in Compton-Burnett's world, the characters are willing to say out loud what gentler people would hardly permit themselves to think; and if advantage is offered, her characters grasp it. Honor may be a child of ten, but she is not lowest in the pecking order, for she is expecting a new governess. 'I know the tricks of the trade,' she says, ominously ... 'And the nature of the beasts.'

In a cottage on the estate lives another family, the Marlowes, maintained on a pittance by Sir Jesse. They keep up the appearance of gentility, but are forced to sneak out and gather firewood, like medieval peasants. The astute reader will soon guess why the old man maintains them – and why he does it so meanly. No one would read Ivy Compton-Burnett for her plots, which are often perfunctory. The point is not what happens, but who knows about it, who tries to conceal it, who cooperates in delusion; the books are full of willing dupes. Ivy is an exact psychologist, and practises on her reader as well as her characters. The fact that we usually know what is going to happen makes her books more powerful, not less. When we watch an archetypal human drama – by Sophocles, let us say – we wait in horrified suspense for the inevitable to occur, for the characters to learn and admit as much about themselves as we know about them. But – quite unlike Sophocles – Ivy suspends us between horror and laughter. The most usual emotion of her books is a stifled, indecent mirth. No one has written so well about one of humanity's most puzzling characteristics: the disposition to break into a grin at life's most hideous or solemn moments.

A God and His Gifts is a complex work, with a time span of many years. In this novel, conventional morality is everted, and tapped on its base till the cracks appear.

The book begins with the family home endangered: 'the creditors have no pity'. But Hereward, the son of the family, is a popular novelist, and is able to help the estate with his own money. The butler Galleon has a jaundiced view of his calling, admitting that though shameful, the trade can be tolerated: '... if there happens to be necessity it does not involve anything manual ... not to the point of soiling the hands'.

Hereward marries Ada, his second choice of woman: 'There is much that I like about her,' he says coolly. Ada has a pretty younger sister, with whom Hereward seems likely to enjoy a warmer relationship: 'I expect that you will have little interchanges of your own,' Ada says indulgently. As a result of the little interchanges, the young sister has to leave the district. This is only the beginning of Hereward's career. He will go on to greater things: all his 'interchanges' are half-recognized by the family and condoned by the person closest to him, his sister Zillah.

In this novel, the family seems unable to help itself as the pattern of outrageous events unfolds, repeats, unfolds again. The words 'innocent' and 'helpless' are often coupled, but Ivy reminds us that 'guilty' and 'helpless' also make a pair. For years, whilst maintaining a front of propriety and rectitude, Hereward seduces any young woman who comes within the family's orbit; but this is not the only repeating pattern in the book. Time after time, individuals are cheated and bullied out of their own thoughts and opinions by other members of the family. When Merton, Hereward's son, finds out that his fiancée is pregnant, his instinct is to break off with her; the other members of the family persuade him that what he wants is to marry her, and let them adopt the child. Later, Hereward's forlorn wife Ada says that she has no course but to leave her husband; the others persuade her that she has no course but to stay with him. *A God and His Gifts* has moments of intense feeling, of real tragedy; what is most interesting is that characters are denied the right to their own pain. Seeking a comparable study in manipulation and control, one thinks of the tape-recordings R. D. Laing made of his schizophrenic patients and their families. Laing's view of madness has gone out of fashion now, but his work told us a great deal about the mechanisms by which families victimize weaker members and confiscate their identities and self-belief. Ivy Compton-Burnett had made the same discoveries years before, without recording aids or research grants.

This late work found Ivy Compton-Burnett as clear-sighted as ever, free from illusions about the human condition. 'The truth has come out, and few of us are wise, and no one better for it.' She is worth reading, and celebrating, for the integrity of her vision, and because she is unique. She invented her own way of writing a novel; form and content (unlike her characters) make the happiest of marriages. C. P. Snow – an author who made small demands on his readers – said that Ivy Compton-Burnett asked too much of hers. Some people have found it too much; yet Robert Liddell said that she offered 'intense and peculiar intellectual excitement and pleasure'.

It is possible to be more specific about the nature of the addict's delight. Because it requires an effort of concentration to read the books they offer a respite from ordinary, nagging preoccupations. They offer respite without comfort, if such a thing can be: a relief from the quotidian and the trite. Ivy Compton-Burnett is an enemy of the easy, the unexamined life. She is not a cynic, but a tough-minded moralist; having anatomized the world's nonsense, she offers a bleak sense of her own. She returns her reader to the ordinary world equipped with skinned sensibilities, an educated ear and a fleeting ability to address his or her own loved ones in clipped, peculiar, deeply distressing sentences.

Hilary Mantel

A FAMILY AND A FORTUNE

Chapter 1

'Justine, I have told you that I do not like the coffee touched until I come down. How can I remember who has had it, and manage about the second cups, if it is taken out of my hands? I don't know how many times I have asked you to leave it alone.'

'A good many, Mother dear, but you tend to be rather a laggard. When the poor boys sit in thirsty patience it quite goes to my heart.'

'It would not hurt them to wait a few minutes. Your father and your uncle are not down yet. There is no such hurry.'

Mrs Gaveston dealt with the coffee with small, pale, stiff hands, looking with querulous affection at her children and signing in a somewhat strained manner to the servant to take the cups. She had rather uncertain movements and made one or two mistakes, which she rectified with a sort of distracted precision. She lifted her face for her children's greetings with an air of forgetting the observance as each one passed, and of being reminded of it by the next. She was a rather tall, very pale woman of about sixty, who somehow gave the impression of being small, and whose spareness of build was without the wiriness supposed to accompany it. She had wavy, grey hair, a long, narrow chin, long, narrow, dark eyes in a stiff, narrow, handsome face, and a permanent air of being held from her normal interest by some passing strain or distraction.

Her only daughter and eldest child was shorter and stronger in build, with clear, light eyes, a fuller face, pleasant features which seemed to be without a plan, and a likeness to her mother which was seen at once to overlie a great difference. She looked as much less than her thirty years as her mother looked more than her double number. Strangers often took Blanche for her children's grandmother, a fact which she had not suspected and would not have believed. She considered that she looked young for her age, or rather assumed that she did so, as she also took it for granted that she was successful, intelligent and admired, an attitude which came from a sort of natural buoyancy and had little meaning. She really gave little thought to herself and could almost be said to live for others. Her children had for her a lively, if not the deepest affection, and she was more than satisfied with it. She would hardly have recognized the deepest feeling, as she had never experienced or inspired it.

The three sons kissed their mother and returned to their seats. The eldest was a short, solid young man of twenty-eight, with large, grey eyes, the dark, curly hair his mother had had in her youth, a broader, blunter but perhaps more attractive face, and an air of being reasonably at peace with himself and his world. The second, Clement, was taller and thinner, with straight hair and darker skin, and looked the same age as Mark, although two years younger. He had cold, dark eyes, a cold, aloof expression, and a definite resemblance in feature to his mother. He seemed to look what he was, and neither to require nor repay observation. Aubrey, the youngest by eleven years, was a boy of fifteen, small and plain to the point of being odd and undersized, with a one-sided smile which often called for the abused term of grin, an indefinable lack of balance in movement, and a reputed backwardness which did not actually extend beyond his books. They had all been named after godparents from whom their mother had vague expectations for them. The expectations had not materialized, but Blanche had been too indefinite about them to resent it, or even actually to imagine their doing so, and felt less disappointment than vague appreciation that they had been possible.

Justine and Mark conversed with goodwill and ate with an ordinary appetite; Clement did not converse and showed an excellent one; Blanche watched her children's plates and made as good a meal as she could without giving her attention to it; and Aubrey sat and swung his feet and did not speak or eat.

'Are you not enjoying your breakfast, my dear?' said Blanche, in a faintly outraged and incredulous manner, which was possibly due to surprise that this should happen again after so many times.

Aubrey gave her a smile, or gave a smile in her direction. The smile seemed to relate to his own thoughts, and did so.

'Wake up, little boy,' said Justine, leaning across to tap his shoulder.

Her brother gave a smile of another kind, intended to show that he was at ease under this treatment.

'If I have some toast, perhaps I shall grow tall enough to go to school.'

Aubrey's life at home with a tutor was a source of mingled embarrassment and content, and the hope that he would eventually go to Eton like his brothers was held by everyone but himself. Everyone knew his age of fifteen, but he alone realized it, and knew that the likelihood of a normal school life was getting less. Blanche regarded him as a young child, Justine as a slightly older one, Mark as an innocently ludicrous exception to a normal family, and Clement as a natural object of uneasiness and distaste. Aubrey saw his family as they were, having had full opportunity to know them, and made his own use of it.

'This omelette is surely a breach with tradition,' said Clement.

'It is not,' said Blanche, instantly and without looking at it or following the words beyond recognizing a criticism. 'It is very good and very wholesome.'

'Clement speaks from experience,' said Aubrey, glancing at his brother's plate.

'Why do you eat it, if you don't like it?' said Mark, with no sting in his tone.

'I am hungry; I must eat something.'

'There is ham,' said Justine.

'Clement will eat the flesh of the pig,' said Aubrey.

'It is certainly odd that civilized people should have it on their tables,' said his brother.

'Do uncivilized people have things on tables?'

'Now, little boy, don't try to be clever,' said Justine, in automatic reproof, beginning to cut the ham.

'Justine understands Clement,' said Aubrey.

'Well, I know you all in and out. After all, I ought, having practically brought you all up.'

'Well, hardly that, dear,' said Blanche, looking at her daughter with the contraction of her eyes which marked her disagreement. 'You were only two when Mark was born. It is I who have brought up the four of you, as is natural.'

'Well, well, have it your own way, little Mother.'

'It is not only Mother's way. It is the way of the world,' said Mark.

'Would some ham make me grow?' said Aubrey. 'I am afraid my size is really worrying for Clement.'

'What does it matter on what scale Aubrey is?' said the latter.

'I should always be your little brother. So you do not mind.'

'Always Mother's little boy,' said Blanche, taking Aubrey's hand.

'Mother's hand looks lily-white in my brown, boyish one.'

'Don't let us sit bickering all through breakfast,' said Justine, in an absent tone.

'We are surely not doing that, dear,' said Blanche, her eyes again contracting. 'We are only having some conversation. We can't all think alike about everything.'

'But you do all agree that I am hardly up to my age,' said Aubrey. 'Not that there is anything to take hold of.'

'I thought the conversation was tending to a bickering note.'

'I don't think it was, dear. I do not know what you mean.'

'Well, then, neither do I, little Mother. I was only talking at random.'

'Suppose Justine's voice was to be stilled!' said Aubrey. 'What should we feel about it then?'

'Don't say such things,' said his mother, turning on him sharply.

'I am not so very late,' said a voice at the door. 'You will be able to feel that you had me in the first hour of your day.'

'Well, Uncle dear,' said Justine, accepting the normal entrance of a member of the house.

'Good-morning, good-morning,' said another voice. 'Good-morning, Blanche; good-morning, Justine; good-morning, my sons. Good-morning.'

'Good-morning, Father dear,' said Justine, leaning forward to adjust the cups for her mother.

The two brothers who entered were tall, lean men in the earlier fifties, the elder being the squire of the neighbourhood, or rather the descendant of men who had held this title together with a larger estate. He had thick, straight, speckled hair, speckled, hazel eyes, vaguely speckled clothes, a long, solid nose and chin, a look of having more bone and less flesh than other men, a face and hands which would have been called bronzed, if there had been anything in the English climate of his home to have this effect on them, and a suggestion of utter honesty which he had transmitted to his daughter. The younger brother, Dudley, was of the same height and lighter build, and was said to be a caricature of the elder, and was so in the sense that his face was cast in a similar mould and had its own deviations from it. His nose was less straight; his eyes were not entirely on a line, and had a hint of his youngest nephew's; and his skin was rather pale than bronzed, though the pair had lived in the same place, even in the same house all their lives. It was a question in the neighbourhood which brother looked the more distinguished, and it was thought a subtle judgement to decide for Dudley. The truth was that Dudley looked the more distinguished when he was seen with his brother, and Edgar by himself, Dudley being dependent on Edgar's setting of the type, and Edgar affording the less reward to a real comparison. The butler who followed them into the room, bearing a dish to replace the cold one, was a round-featured, high-coloured man about thirty, of the same height as his masters but in other respects very different.

'Good-morning, sir; good-morning, sir,' he said with a slight, separate bow to each.

'Good-morning,' said Dudley.

'Good-morning, good-morning,' said Edgar, taking no longer over the words.

Blanche looked up in a daily disapproval of Jellamy's initiative in speech, which had never been definite enough to be expressed.

'It is a very unsettled day, sir.'

'Yes, it appears to be,' said Edgar; 'yes, it is unsettled.'

'The atmosphere is humid, sir.'

'Yes, humid; yes, it seems to be damp.'

Edgar seldom made a definite statement. It was as if he feared to commit himself to something that was not the utter truth.

'I love a conversation between Father and Jellamy,' said Justine, in an undertone.

Blanche looked up with an expression which merely said that she did not share the feeling.

'The plaster is peeling off the walls in the hall, sir.'

'I will come some time and see. I will try to remember to come and look at it.'

'I meant the servants' hall, sir,' said Jellamy, as if his master would hardly penetrate to this point.

'That room you all use to sit in? The one that used to have a sink in it?'

'The sink has been removed, sir. It is now put to the individual purpose.'

'That will do, Jellamy, thank you,' said Blanche, who disliked the presence of servants at meals. 'If we want you again we will ring.'

'It would be a good plan to remove all sinks and make all rooms into halls,' said Dudley. 'It would send up the standard of things.'

'In this poor old world,' said Aubrey.

'How did you sleep, Father?' said Justine.

'Very well, my dear; I think I can say well. I slept for some hours. I hope you have a good account to give.'

'Oh, don't ask about the sleep of a healthy young woman, Father. Trust you to worry about the sleep of your only daughter!' Edgar flinched in proportion to his doubt how far this confidence was justified. 'It is your sleep that matters, and I am not half satisfied about it.'

'The young need sleep, my dear.'

'Oh, I am not as young as all that. A ripe thirty, and all my years lived to the full! I would not have missed out one of them. I don't rank myself with the callow young any longer.'

'Always Father's little girl,' murmured Aubrey.

'What, my son?' said Edgar.

'I still rank myself with the young,' said Aubrey, as if repeating what he had said. 'I think I had better until I go to school. Anything else would make me look silly, and Clement would not like me to look that.'

'Get on with your breakfast, little boy,' said Justine. 'Straight on and not another word until you have finished.'

'I was making my little effort to keep the ball of conversation rolling. Every little counts.'

'So it does, dear, and with all our hearts we acknowledge it.'

Blanche smiled from her eldest to her youngest child in appreciation of their feeling.

'Aubrey meets with continual success,' said Mark. 'He is indeed a kind of success in himself.'

'What kind?' said Clement.

'Too simple, Clement,' said Justine, shaking her head. 'How did you sleep, Uncle?'

'Very well until I was awakened by the rain. Then I went to the window and stood looking out into the night. I see now that people really do that.'

'They really shut out the air,' said Clement.

'Is Clement a soured young man?' said Aubrey.

'I had a very bad night,' said Blanche, in a mild, conversational tone, without complaint that no enquiry had been made of her. 'I have almost forgotten what it is to have a good one.'

'Poor little Mother! But you sleep in the afternoon,' said Justine.

'I never do. I have my rest, of course; I could not get on without it. But I never sleep. I may close my eyes to ease them, but I am always awake.'

'You were snoring yesterday, Mother,' said Justine, with the insistence upon people's sleeping and giving this sign, which seems to be a human characteristic.

'No, I was not,' said Blanche, with the annoyance at the course which is unfortunately another. 'I never snore even at night, so I certainly do not when I am just resting in the day.'

'Mother, I tiptoed in and you did not give a sign.'

'If you made no sound, and I was resting my eyes, I may not have heard you, of course.'

'Anyhow a few minutes in the day do not make up for a bad night,' said Mark.

'But I do not sleep in the day, even for a few minutes,' said his mother in a shriller tone. 'I don't know what to say to make you all understand.'

'I don't know why people mind admitting to a few minutes' sleep in the day,' said Dudley, 'when we all acknowledge hours at night and indeed require compassion if we do not have them.'

'Who has acknowledged them?' said Clement. 'It will appear that as a family we do without sleep.'

'But I do not mind admitting to them,' said Blanche. 'What I mean is that it is not the truth. There is no point in not speaking the truth even about a trivial matter.'

'I do not describe insomnia in that way,' said Mark.

'Dear boy, you do understand,' said Blanche, holding out her hand with an almost wild air. 'You do prevent my feeling quite alone.'

'Come, come, Mother, I was tactless, I admit,' said Justine. 'I know people hate confessing that they sleep in the day. I ought to have remembered it.'

'Justine now shows tact,' murmured Aubrey.

'It is possible – it seems to be possible,' said Edgar, 'to be resting with closed eyes and give the impression of sleep.'

'You forget the snoring, Father,' said Justine, in a voice so low and light as to escape her mother's ears.

'If you don't forget it too, I don't know what we are to do,' said Mark, in the same manner.

'Snoring is not a proof of being asleep,' said Dudley.

'But I was not snoring,' said Blanche, in the easier tone of one losing grasp of a situation. 'I should have known it myself. It would not be possible to be awake and make a noise and not hear it.'

Justine gave an arch look at anyone who would receive it. Edgar did so as a duty and rapidly withdrew his eyes as another.

'Why do we not learn that no one ever snores under any circumstances?' said Clement.

'I wonder how the idea of snoring arose,' said Mark.

'Mother, are you going to eat no more than that?' said Justine. 'You are not ashamed of eating as well as of sleeping, I hope.'

'There has been no question of sleeping. And I am not ashamed of either. I always eat very well and I always sleep very badly. There is no connection between them.'

'You seem to be making an exception in the first matter to-day,' said her husband.

'Well, it upsets me to be contradicted, Edgar, and told that I do things when I don't do them, and when I know quite well what I do, myself,' said Blanche, almost flouncing in her chair.

'It certainly does, Mother dear. So we will leave it at that; that you know quite well what you do yourself.'

'It seems a reasonable conclusion,' said Mark.

'I believe people always know that best,' said Dudley. 'If we could see ourselves as others see us, we should be much more misled, though people always talk as if we ought to try to do it.'

'They want us to be misled and cruelly,' said his nephew.

'I don't know,' said Justine. 'We might often meet a good, sound, impartial judgement.'

'And we know, when we have one described like that, what a dreadful judgement it is,' said her uncle.

'Half the truth, the blackest of lies,' said Mark.

'The whitest of lies really,' said Clement. 'Or there is no such thing as a white lie.'

'Well, there is not,' said his sister. 'Truth is truth and a lie is a lie.'

'What is Truth?' said Aubrey. 'Has Justine told us?'

'Truth is whatever happens to be true under the circumstances,' said his sister, doing so at the moment. 'We ought not to mind a searchlight being turned on our inner selves, if we are honest about them.'

'That is our reason,' said Mark. '"Know thyself" is a most superfluous direction. We can't avoid it.'

'We can only hope that no one else knows,' said Dudley.

'Uncle, what nonsense!' said Justine. 'You are the most transparent and genuine person, the very last to say that.'

'What do you all really mean?' said Edgar, speaking rather hurriedly, as if to check any further personal description.

'I think I only mean,' said his brother, 'that human beings ought always to be judged very tenderly, and that no one will be as tender as themselves. "Remember what you owe to yourself" is another piece of superfluous advice.'

'But better than most advice,' said Aubrey, lowering his voice as he ended. 'More tender.'

'Now, little boy, hurry up with your breakfast,' said Justine. 'Mr Penrose will be here in a few minutes.'

'To pursue his life work of improving Aubrey,' said Clement.

'Clement ought to have ended with a sigh,' said Aubrey. 'But I daresay the work has its own unexpected rewards.'

'I forget what I learned at Eton,' said his uncle.

'Yes, so do I; yes, so to a great extent do I,' said Edgar. 'Yes, I believe I forgot the greater part of it.'

'You can't really have lost it, Father,' said Justine. 'An education in the greatest school in the world must have left its trace. It must have contributed to your forming.'

'It does not seem to matter that I can't go to school,' said Aubrey. 'It will be a shorter cut to the same end.'

'Now, little boy, don't take that obvious line. And remember that self-education is the greatest school of all.'

'And education by Penrose? What is that?'

'Say Mr Penrose. And get on with your breakfast.'

'He has only had one piece of toast,' said Blanche, in a tone which suggested that it would be one of despair if the situation were not familiar. 'And he is a growing boy.'

'I should not describe him in those terms,' said Mark.

'I should be at a loss to describe him,' said Clement.

'Don't be silly,' said their mother at once. 'You are both of you just as difficult to describe.'

'Some people defy description,' said Aubrey. 'Uncle and I are among them.'

'There is something in it,' said Justine, looking round.

'Perhaps we should not – it may be as well not to discuss people who are present,' said Edgar.

'Right as usual, Father. I wish the boys would emulate you.'

'Oh, I think they do, dear,' said Blanche, in an automatic tone. 'I see a great likeness in them both to their father. It gets more striking.'

'And does no one think poor Uncle a worthy object of emulation? He is as experienced and polished a person as Father.'

Edgar looked up at this swift disregard of accepted advice.

'I am a changeling,' said Dudley. 'Aubrey and I are very hard to get hold of.'

'And you can't send a person you can't put your finger on to school,' said his nephew.

'You can see that he does the next best thing,' said Justine. 'Off with you at once. There is Mr Penrose on the steps. Don't keep the poor little man waiting.'

'Justine refers to every other person as poor,' said Clement

'Well, I am not quite without the bowels of human compassion. The ups and downs of the world do strike me, I confess.'

'Chiefly the downs.'

'Well, there are more of them.'

'Poor little man,' murmured Aubrey, leaving his seat. 'Whose little man is he? I am Justine's little boy.'

'It seems — is it not rather soon after breakfast to work?' said Edgar.

'They go for a walk first, as you know, Father. It is good for Aubrey to have a little adult conversation apart from his family. I asked Mr Penrose to make the talk educational.'

'Did you, dear?' said Blanche, contracting her eyes. 'I think you should leave that kind of thing to Father or me.'

'Indeed I should not, Mother. And not have it done at all? That would be a nice alternative. I should do all I can for you all, as it comes into my head, as I always have and always shall. Don't try to prevent what is useful and right.'

Blanche subsided under this reasonable direction.

'Now off with you both! Off to your occupations,' said Justine, waving her hand towards her brothers. 'I hope you have some. I have, and they will not wait.'

'I am glad I have none,' said Dudley. 'I could not bear to have regular employment.'

'Do you know what I have discovered?' said his niece. 'I have discovered a likeness between our little boy and you, Uncle. A real, incontrovertible and bona fide likeness. It is no good for you all to open your eyes. I have made my discovery and will stick to it.'

'I have always thought they were alike,' said Blanche.

'Oh, now, Mother, that is not at all on the line. You know it has only occurred to you at this moment.'

'No, I am bound to say,' said Edgar, definite in the interests of justice, 'that I have heard your mother point out a resemblance.'

'Then dear little Mother, she has got in first, and I am the last person to grudge her the credit. So you see it, Mother? Because I am certain of it, certain. I should almost have thought that Uncle would see it himself.'

'We can hardly expect him to call attention to it,' said Clement.

'I am aware of it,' said Dudley, 'and I invite the attention of you all.'

'Then I am a laggard and see things last instead of first. But I am none the less interested in them. My interest does not depend upon personal triumph. It is a much more genuine and independent thing.'

'Mine is feebler, I admit,' said Mark.

'Now, Mother, you will have a rest this morning to make up for your poor night. And I will drive the house on its course. You can be quite at ease.'

Justine put her hand against her mother's cheek, and Blanche lifted her own hand and held it for a moment, smiling at her daughter.

'What a dear, good girl she is!' she said, as the latter left them. 'What should we do without her?'

'What we do now,' said Clement.

'Indeed we should not,' said his mother, rounding on him at once. 'We should find everything entirely different, as you know quite well.'

'Indeed, indeed,' said Edgar in a deliberate voice. 'Indeed.'

Edgar and Blanche had fallen in love thirty-one years before, in the year eighteen hundred and seventy, when Edgar was twenty-four and Blanche thirty; and now that the feeling was a memory, and a rare and even embarrassing one, Blanche regarded her husband with trust and pride and Edgar his wife with compassionate affection. It meant little that neither was ever disloyal to the other, for neither was capable of disloyalty. They had come to be rather shy of each other and were little together by day or night. It was hard to imagine how their shyness had ever been enough in abeyance to allow of their courtship and marriage, and they found it especially the case. They could only remember, and this they did as seldom as they could. Blanche seemed to wander aloof through her life, finding enough to live for in the members of her family and in her sense of pride and possession in each. It was typical of her that she regarded Dudley as a brother, and had no jealousy of her husband's relation with him.

Edgar's life was largely in his brother and the friendship which dated from their infancy. Mark helped his father in his halting and efficient management of the estate, and as the eldest son had been given no profession. Clement had gained a fellowship at Cambridge with a view to being a scholar and a don. Each brother had a faint compassion and contempt for the other's employment and prospect.

'Mother, dear,' said Justine, returning to the room, 'here is a letter which came for you last night and which you have not opened. There is a way to discharge your duties! I suggest that you remedy the omission.'

Blanche held the letter at arm's length to read the address, while she felt for her glasses.

'It is from your grandfather,' she said, adjusting the glasses and looking at her daughter over them. 'It is from my father, Edgar. It is so seldom that he writes himself. Of course, he is getting an old man. He must soon begin to feel his age.'

'Probably fairly soon, as he is eighty-seven,' said Clement.

'Too obvious once again, Clement,' said Justine. 'Open the letter, Mother. You should have read it last night.'

Blanche proceeded to do so at the reminder, and Edgar gave a glance of disapproval at his son, which seemed to be late as the result of his weighing its justice.

His wife's voice came suddenly and with unusual expression.

'Oh, he wants to know if the lodge is still to let. And if it is, he thinks of taking it! He would come with Matty to live here. Oh, it would be nice to have them. What a difference it would make! They want to know the lowest rent we can take, and we could not charge much to my family. I wish we could let them have it for nothing, but I suppose we must not afford that?'

There was a pause.

'We certainly should not do so,' said Mark. 'Things are paying badly as it is.'

'It opens up quite a different life,' said Justine.

'Are we qualified for it?' said her brother.

'I don't see why we should not ask a normal rent,' said Clement. 'They would not expect help from us in any other way, and they do not need it.'

'They are not well off, dear,' said Blanche, again looking over her glasses. 'They have lost a good deal of their money and will have to take great care. And it would be such an advantage to have them. We must think of that.'

'They think of it evidently, and intend to charge us for it. I wonder at what they value themselves.'

'They ought to pay us for our presence too,' said Mark. 'I suppose it is worth an equal price.'

'I believe I am more companionable than either of them,' said Dudley.

'Oh, we ought not to talk like that even in joke,' said Blanche, taking the most hopeful view of the conversation. 'We ought to think what we can do to help them. They have had to give up their home, and this seems such a good solution. With my father getting old and my sister so lame, they ought to be near their relations.'

'Do you consider, Mother dear, how you and Aunt Matty are likely to conduct yourselves when you are within a stone's throw?' said Justine, with deliberate dryness. 'On the occasions when you have stayed with each other, rumours have come from her house, which have been confirmed in ours. Do remember that discretion is the better part of many another quality.'

'Whatever do you mean? We have our own ways with each other, of course, just as all of you have, and your uncle and your father; as brothers and sisters must. But it has been nothing more.'

'Edgar and I have not any,' said Dudley. 'I don't know how you can say so. I have a great dislike for ways; I think few things are worse. And I don't think you and your sister ought to live near to each other, if you have them.'

'What an absurd way to talk! Matty and I have never disagreed. There is no need for us to treat each other as if we were strangers.'

'Now, remember, Mother dear,' said Justine, lifting a finger, 'that there is need for just that. Treat each other as strangers and I will ask no more. I shall be utterly satisfied.'

'What a way to talk!' repeated Blanche, her tone showing her really rancourless nature. 'Do let us stop talking like this and think of the pleasure they will be to us.'

'If they bring any happiness to you, little Mother, we welcome them from our hearts. But we are afraid that it will not be without alloy.'

'I think – I have been considering,' said Edgar, 'I think we might suggest the rent which we should ask from a stranger, and then see what their not being strangers must cost us.' He gave his deliberate smile, which did not alter his face, while his brother's, which followed it, seemed to irradiate light. 'We must hope it will not be much, as we have not much to spare.'

'I suppose the sums involved are small,' said Justine.

'We are running things close,' said Mark. 'And why should they put a price on themselves when other people do not?'

'Oh, my old father and my invalid sister!' said Blanche. 'And the house has been empty for such a long time, and the rents in this county are so low.'

'We shall take all that into account,' said Edgar, in the tone he used to his wife, gentler and slower than to other people, as if he wished to make things dear and easy for her. 'And it will tend to lower the rent.'

'Then why not just ask them very little and think no more about it? I don't know why we have this kind of talk. It will be so nice to have them, and now we have made it into a subject which will always bring argument and acrimoniousness. It is a great shame.' Blanche shook her shoulders and looked down with tears in her eyes.

'They want us to write at once, if Mother does not mind my looking at the letter,' said Justine, assuming that this was the case. 'Dear Grandpa! His writing begins to quaver. They have their plans to make.'

'If his writing quavers, his rent must be low, of course,' said Mark. 'We are not brutes and oppressors.'

Blanche looked up with a clearing face, as reason and feeling asserted themselves in her son.

'Yes, yes, we must let them know,' said Edgar. 'And of course it will be an advantage to have them – any benefit which comes from them will be ours. We cannot dispute it.'

'We do not want to,' said his daughter, 'or to dispute anything else. This foretaste of such things is enough. Let us make our little sacrifice, if it must be made. We ought not to jib at it so much.'

'Let us leave this aspect of the matter and turn to the others,' said Mark, keeping his face grave. 'Do you suppose they really know about Aubrey?'

'I don't see how they can,' said Clement. 'He was too young the last time they were here, for it to be recognized.'

'I don't know what you mean,' said Blanche, who fell into every trap. 'They will be devoted to him, as people always are.'

'Yes, Aubrey will be a great success, I will wager,' said Justine. 'We shall all of us pale beside him. You wait and see.'

'I shall have the same sort of triumph,' said Dudley. 'They will begin by noticing my brother and find their attention gradually drawn to me.'

'And then it will be all up with everyone else,' said Justine, sighing. 'Oh, dreadful Uncle, we all know how it can be.'

'And then they will think – I will not say what. It will be for them to say it.'

'Well, poor Uncle, you can't always play second fiddle.'

'Yes, I can,' said Dudley, his eyes on Edgar. 'It is a great art and I have mastered it.'

Edgar rose as though hearing a signal and went to the door, resting his arm in his brother's, and a minute later the pair appeared on the path outside the house.

'Those two tall figures!' said Justine. 'It is a sight of which I can never tire. If I live to be a hundred I do not wish to see one more satisfying.'

Blanche looked up and followed her daughter's eyes in proper support of her.

Mark took Clement's arm and walked up and down before his sister.

'No, away with you!' she said with a gesture. 'I don't want an imitation; I don't want anything spurious. I have the real thing before my eyes.'

'I like to see them walking together like that,' said Blanche.

'Well, I do not, Mother. It is a mockery of something better and I see nothing about it to like.'

'I am sure they are very good friends. We need not call it a mockery. It illustrates a genuine feeling, even if the action itself was a joke.'

'Genuine feeling, yes, Mother, but nothing like the feeling between Father and Uncle. We must face it. You have not produced that in your family. It has skipped that generation.'

Blanche looked on in an impotent way, as her daughter left the room, but appreciation replaced any other feeling on her face. She had the unusual quality of loving all her children equally, or of believing that she did. If Mark and Aubrey held the chief place in her heart, the place was available for the others when they needed it, so that she was justified in feeling that she gave it to them all. Neither she nor Clement suspected that she cared for Clement the least, and if Dudley and Aubrey knew it, it was part of that knowledge in them which was their own. Edgar would not have been surprised to hear that her second son was her favourite.

Jellamy came into the room as his mistress left it, and carried some silver to the sideboard.

'So we are to have Mr Seaton and Miss Seaton at the lodge, sir?'

'How did you know?' said Mark. 'We have only just heard.'

'The same applies to me, sir,' said Jellamy, speaking with truth, as he had heard at the same moment. 'Miss Seaton will be a companion for the mistress, sir. The master and Mr Dudley being so much together leaves the mistress rather by herself.' Jellamy's eyes protruded over a subject which was rife in the kitchen, and had never presented itself to Blanche.

'She is never by herself,' said Clement. 'We all live in a chattering crowd, each of us waiting for a chance to be heard.'

Luncheon found the family rather as Clement described it. Edgar sat at the head of the table, Blanche at the foot; Dudley and Justine sat on either side of the former, Mark and Clement of the latter; and Aubrey and his tutor faced each other in the middle of the board. Mr Penrose was treated with friendliness and supplied with the best of fare, and found the family luncheon the trial of his day. He sat in a conscious rigour, which he hardly helped by starting when he was addressed, and gazing at various objects in the room with deep concentration. He was a blue-eyed, bearded, little man of forty-five, of the order known as self-made, who spoke of himself to his wife as at the top of the tree, and accepted her support when she added that he was in this position in the truest sense. He had a sharp nose, supporting misty spectacles, and neat clothes which had a good deal of black about them. He was pleasant and patient with Aubrey, and made as much progress with him as was possible in view of this circumstance, and had a great admiration for Edgar, whom he occasionally addressed. Edgar and Dudley treated him with ordinary simplicity and never referred to him in any other spirit. Justine spoke of him with compassion, Mark with humour, Blanche with respect for his learning. Clement did not speak of him, and Aubrey saw him with the adult dryness of boys towards their teachers.

'Well, Mr Penrose, a good morning's work?' said Justine.

'Probably on Mr Penrose's part,' said Clement.

'Yes, I am glad to say it was on the whole satisfactory Miss Gaveston. I have no complaint to make.'

'I wish we could sometimes hear some positive praise of our little boy.'

'He is before you,' said Mark. 'Consider what you ask.'

'Don't talk nonsense,' said Blanche. 'None of you was perfect at his age. If you tease him, I shall be very much annoyed. Have you done well yourself this morning, Clement?'

'Well enough, thank you, Mother.'

'We hear some positive praise of Clement,' said Aubrey.

'Clement ought to have a mediocre future before him,' said Dudley, 'and Aubrey a great one.'

'I don't agree with this theory that early failure tends to ultimate success,' said Justine. 'Do you, Mr Penrose?'

'Well, Miss Gaveston, that has undoubtedly been the sequence in some cases. But the one may not lead to the other. There may be no connection and I think it is probable that there is not.'

'Dear little Aubrey!' said Blanche, looking into space. 'What will he become in time?'

Mr Penrose rested his eyes on her, and then dropped them as if to cover an answer to this question.

'That is the best of an early lack of bent,' said Clement. 'It leaves an open future.'

'The child is father of the man,' said Mark. 'It is no good to shut our eyes to it.'

'I cannot grow into anything,' said Aubrey, 'until I begin to grow. I am not big enough to be my own son yet.'

Edgar laughed, and Blanche glanced from him to his son with a mild glow in her face.

'We were talking of the growth of the mind, little boy,' said Justine.

'I am sure he is much taller,' said Blanche.

'Mother dear, his head comes to exactly the same place on the wall. We have not moved it for a year.'

'I moved it yesterday,' said Aubrey, looking aside. 'I have grown an inch.'

'I knew he had!' said Blanche, with a triumph which did not strike anyone as disproportionate.

'If we indicate Aubrey on the wall,' said Clement, 'have we not dealt sufficiently with him?'

'Why do you talk about him like that? Why are you any better than he is?'

'We must now hear some more positive praise of Clement,' said Aubrey.

'It need not amount to that,' said his brother.

'I don't want to have him just like everyone else,' said Blanche, causing Aubrey's face to change at the inexplicable attitude. 'I like a little individuality. It is a definite advantage.'

'A good mother likes the ugly duckling best,' said Justine, coming to her mother's aid in her support of her son, and with apparent success, as the latter smiled to himself. 'How do you really think he is getting along, Mr Penrose?'

'Mr Penrose has given us one account of him,' said Edgar. 'I think we will not – perhaps we will not ask him for another.'

'But I think we will, Father. The account was not very definite. Unless you really want to leave the subject, in which case your only daughter will not go against you. That would not be at all to your mind. Well, have you heard, Mr Penrose, that we are to have a family of relations at the lodge?'

'No, I have not, Miss Gaveston. I have hardly had the opportunity.'

'Grandpa and Aunt Matty and Miss Griffin,' said Aubrey.

'How did you know, little boy? We had the news when you had gone.'

'Jellamy told me when he was setting the luncheon.'

'Father, do you like Aubrey to make a companion of Jellamy?'

'Well, my dear, I think so; I do not think – I see no objection.'

'Then there is none. Your word on such a matter is enough. I shall like to see poor Miss Griffin again. I wonder how she is getting on.'

'Do I understand, Mr Gaveston, that it is Mrs Gaveston's family who is coming to the vicinity?' said Mr Penrose.

'Yes, Mr Penrose,' said Justine, clearly. 'My mother's father and sister, and the sister's companion, who has become a friend.'

'My father is an old man now,' said Blanche.

'Well, Mother dear, he can hardly be anything else with you – well, I will leave you the option in the matter of your own age – with a granddaughter thirty. Mr Penrose hardly needed that information.'

'And my sister is a little older than I am,' continued Blanche, not looking at her daughter, though with no thought of venting annoyance. 'She is an invalid from an accident, but very well in herself. I am so much looking forward to having her.'

'Poor little Mother! It sounds as if you suffered from a lack of companionship. But we can't skip a generation and become your contemporaries.'

'I do not want you to. I like to have my children at their stage and my sister at hers. I shall be a very rich woman.'

'Well, you will, Mother dear. What a good thing you realize it! So many people do not until it is too late.'

'Then they are not rich,' said Clement.

'People seem very good at so many things,' said Dudley, 'except for not being quite in time. It seems hard that that should count so much.'

'Mother will be rich in Aunt Matty,' said Aubrey.

'I shall,' said Blanche.

'Really, you boys contribute very tame little speeches,' said Justine. 'You are indifferent conversationalists.'

'If you wish us to be anything else,' said Clement, 'you must allow us some practice.'

'Do you mean that I am always talking myself? What a very ungallant speech! I will put it to the vote. Father, do you think that I talk too much?'

'No, my dear – well, it is natural for young people to talk.'

'So you do. Well, I must sit down under it. But I know who will cure me; Aunt Matty. She is the person to prevent anyone from indulging in excess of talk. And I don't mean to say anything against her; I love her flow of words. But she does pour them out; there is no doubt of that.'

'We all have our little idiosyncrasies,' said Blanche. 'We should not be human without them.'

'It is a pity we have to be human,' said Dudley. 'Human failings, human vanity, human weakness! We don't hear the word applied to anything good. Even human nature seems a derogatory term. It is simply an excuse for everything.'

'Human charity, human kindness,' said Justine. 'I think that gives us to think, Uncle.'

'There are great examples of human nobility and sacrifice,' said Blanche. 'Mr Penrose must know many of them.'

'People are always so pleased about people's sacrifice,' said Dudley; 'I mean other people's. It is not very nice of them. I suppose it is only human.'

'They are not. They can admire it without being pleased.'

'So I am to write – you wish me to write to your father, my dear,' said Edgar, 'and say that he is welcome as a tenant at a sacrifice to be determined?'

'Yes, of course. But you need not mention the sacrifice. And I am sure we do not feel it to be that. Just say how much we want to have them.'

'Father dear, I don't think we need bring out our little family problems before Mr Penrose,' said Justine. 'They concern us but they do not – can hardly interest him.'

'Oh, I don't think that mattered, dear,' said Blanche. 'Mr Penrose will forgive us. He was kind enough to be interested.'

'Yes, indeed, Mrs Gaveston. It is a most interesting piece of news,' said Mr Penrose, relinquishing a spoon he was examining, as if to liberate his attention, which had certainly been occupied. 'I must remember to tell Mrs Penrose. She is always interested in any little piece of information about the family – in the neighbourhood. Not that this particular piece merits the term, little. From your point of view quite the contrary.'

'We shall have to do up the lodge,' said Blanche to her husband. 'It is fortunate that it is such a good size. Matty must have remembered it. The back room will make a library for my father, and Matty will have the front one as a drawing-room. And the third room on that floor can be her bedroom, to save her the stairs. I can quite see it in my mind's eye.'

'Drawing-room and library are rather grandiloquent terms for those little rooms,' said Justine.

'Well, call them anything you like, dear. Sitting-room and study. It makes no difference.'

'No, it makes none, Mother, but that is what we will call them.'

'We need not decide,' said Clement. 'Aunt Matty will do that.'

'Aunt Matty would never use exaggerated terms for anything to do with herself.'

'There are other ways of exaggerating,' said Mark.

'Mrs Gaveston,' said Mr Penrose, balancing the spoon on his finger, to show that his words were not very serious to him, 'it may interest you to hear how Mrs Penrose and I arranged rooms on a somewhat similar scale, as I gather, as those you mention.'

'Yes, we should like to hear indeed.'

'Thank you very much, Mr Penrose,' said Justine, warmly, sitting forward with her eyes on Mr Penrose's face.

'We selected large patterns for the carpets, to give an impression of space, though it might hardly be thought that the choice would have that result. And we kept the walls plain with the same purpose.'

'We can have the walls plain,' said Justine, 'but we must use the carpets at our disposal, Mr Penrose. We are not as fortunate as you were.'

'We shall not be able to write in time for them to hear by the first post,' said Blanche. 'I hope it won't seem that we are in any doubt about it.'

'About the sacrifice,' said Dudley. 'I hope not. I said that people were pleased by other people's sacrifice. They would not like them to have any hesitation in making it.'

'It would be an unwilling sacrifice,' said Aubrey.

'Another point to be made,' continued Mr Penrose –

'Yes, Mr Penrose, one moment,' said Justine, leaning to her father and laying a hand on his arm, while glancing back at the tutor. 'It is very kind and we are so interested, but one moment. Would it not be better, Father, to send the letter into the town to catch the afternoon post? Things always get to Grandpa in the morning if we do that.'

'It might be – it probably would be better. I will write directly after luncheon, or as soon as we have decided what to say. What is Mr Penrose telling us?'

'It does not matter, Mr Gaveston. I was only mentioning that in the experience of Mrs Penrose and myself – it is of no consequence,' said Mr Penrose, observing that Justine had turned to her mother, and resuming the spoon.

'Indeed it is of consequence,' almost called Justine, leaning towards Blanche over Aubrey and giving another backward glance.

'You have one of our seventeenth-century spoons?' said Edgar.

'Yes, Mr Gaveston, I was wondering if it was one of them. I see it is not,' said Mr Penrose, laying down a spoon which his scrutiny had enabled him to assign to his own day. 'You have some very beautiful ones, have you not?'

'They are all put away, Mr Penrose,' called Justine, in a voice which seemed to encourage Mr Penrose with the admission of economy. 'We are not allowed to use them any more. They only come out on special occasions.'

'Do go and write the letter, Edgar,' said Blanche.

'Poor Father, let him have his luncheon in peace.'

'He has finished, dear. He is only playing with that fruit and wasting it.'

'Waste not, want not, Father,' said Justine, in a warning tone which seemed to be directed to Mr Penrose's ears.

Edgar rose and left the room with his brother, and Justine's eyes followed them.

'Are they not a perfect pair, Mr Penrose?'

'Yes, indeed, Miss Gaveston. It appears to be a most conspicuous friendship.'

'What are you doing?' said Blanche, suddenly, as she perceived her elder sons amusedly regarding the youngest, whose expression of set jauntiness told her that he was nearly in tears. 'You are teasing him again! I will not have it. It is mean and unmanly to torment your little brother. I am thoroughly ashamed of you both. Justine, I wonder you allow it.'

'I merely did not observe it, Mother. I was talking to you and Father. Now I certainly will not countenance it. Boys, I have a word to say.'

'It is unworthy to torment someone who cannot retaliate,' said Blanche, giving her daughter the basis of her homily.

'I have managed to get my own back,' said Aubrey, in an easy drawl, depriving her of it.

'We were only wondering how to keep Aubrey out of Grandpa's sight and Aunt Matty's,' said Mark. 'A shock is bad for old and invalid people.'

'You are silly boys. Why do you not keep out of their sight yourselves?' said his mother.

'That might be the best way to cover up the truth,' said Mark, looking at his brother as if weighing this idea. 'It would avoid any normal comparison.'

'Suppose either should come upon him unawares! They have not seen him since we could hope it was a passing phase.'

'A phase of what?' said Blanche. 'I do not know what you mean and neither do you.'

'We thought a postscript might be added to the letter,' said Mark. 'So that they might be a little prepared.'

'Prepared for what?'

'Just something such as: "If you see Aubrey, you will understand."'

'Understand what?' almost screamed his mother. 'You don't understand, yourselves, so naturally they would not.'

'Mother, Mother dear,' said Justine, laughing gently, 'you are pandering to them by falling into their hands like that. Take no notice of them and they will desist. They are only trying to attract attention to themselves.'

'Well, that is natural at their stage,' said Aubrey.

'We did take no notice and they had reduced poor Aubrey

nearly to tears,' said Blanche, too lost in her partisanship of her son to observe its effect upon him.

'They are naughty boys, or, what is worse, they are malicious young men, and I am very much annoyed with them. I did not mean that I was not.'

'Then speak to them about it,' said Blanche, standing back and looking with expectance born of experience from her daughter to her sons.

'Boys, boys,' said Justine gravely 'this will not do, you know. Take example from that.' She pointed to the garden, where Edgar and Dudley were walking arm-in-arm. 'There is a spectacle of brotherhood. Look at it and take a lesson.'

'So your father has not written the letter!' said Blanche.

'If you will excuse us, Mrs Gaveston, Aubrey and I should be thinking of our walk,' said Mr Penrose, who had been uncertain whether the family had forgotten his presence.

'Yes, of course, Mr Penrose, please do as you like,' said Blanche, who had forgotten it, and even now did not completely recall it. 'If he does not write it soon, it will have no chance of the post.'

Aubrey went up to his brothers and linked their arms, and taking a step backwards with a jeering face, took his tutor's arm himself and walked from the room.

'Dear, dear, what a little boy!' said Justine. 'I think Mr Penrose carried that off very well.'

'Edgar!' called Blanche from the window. 'You are not writing that letter! And it has to go in an hour.'

'We are deciding upon the terms – we are discussing the wording, my dear,' said her husband, pausing and maintaining the courtesy of his voice, though he had to open his mouth to raise it. 'It needs to be expressed with a certain care.'

'Indeed,' said Mark. 'There is no need to employ any crudeness in telling Grandpa that we can't do him too much charity.'

'Oh, that is all right then,' said Blanche, turning from the window. 'There is no question of charity. That is not the way to speak of your grandfather. It is the coachman's day out. Who had better drive the trap into the town? I have seen Jellamy drive. Would your father mind his driving the mare? I wish you would some of you listen to me, and not leave me to settle everything by myself.'

'Mother, come and have your rest,' said Justine, taking Blanche's arm. 'I will take the trap myself. You need have no fear. I also have seen Jellamy drive, and if Father does not grudge him the particular indulgence, I do.'

Blanche walked compliantly out of the room, relaxing her face and her thoughts together, and her husband and his brother passed to the library.

'I think that will express it,' said Dudley. 'You are to drop a sum every year and not refer to it, and feel guilty that you take money from your wife's relations for giving them a bare roof.'

'I think it should be good for Blanche to have them. I hope we may think it should. I fear there may be – I fear –'

'I fear all sorts of things; I am sick with fear. But we must think what Blanche is facing. I always think that women's courage is hard on men. It seems absurd for men and women to share the same life. I simply don't know how we are to share Blanche's life in future.'

'I am never sure how to address my father-in-law.'

'When we speak to him, we say "sir". I like saying "sir" to people. It makes me feel young and well-behaved, and I can't think of two better things, or more in tune with my personality. What a good thing that Blanche will not ask to see the letter! I have a great respect for her lack of curiosity. It is a thing I could never attain.'

Dudley drafted and dictated the letter, and Edgar wrote it and submitted it for his inspection, and then suggested a game of chess. When Justine came for the letter, the brothers were sitting silent over the board. They played chess often, Dudley playing the better, but Edgar playing for the sake of the game, careless and almost unconscious of success. Justine tiptoed from the room, mutely kissing her hand towards the table.

Chapter 2

'Is this a house or a hutch? It is meant, I suppose, for human habitation,' said Blanche's father, walking about his new home. 'It is well that I shall soon be gone and leave you alone in it. For it is better for one than for two, as I cannot but see.'

'Come, Father, pluck up heart. You are an able-bodied man and not a crippled woman. I must not be given any more to bear. You must remember your poor invalid, though I never remind you that I am that.'

'If that was not a reminder, I need not take it as one. I grant that that fall made a poor thing of you, but you want a chair to sit upon, all the more. And I don't see where we are to put one, on a first sight.'

'There are plenty of chairs, Father. Let us sit down in two of them. Come, I think they have done their best. It only needed a little best for such a little home, but such as it had to be, I think it is done. And we must be as grateful as they will expect us to be.' Blanche's sister put back her head and went into mirth. 'This room is quite a pretty little place. So we must try to feel at home in it. We are not people to fail in courage.'

Matilda Seaton was two years older than Blanche, of the same height as her sister, but of the suppler, stronger build of her niece, Justine. She had hair less grey than her sister's, a darker skin less lined, and the same narrow, dark eyes looking out with a sharper, deeper gaze. A fall from a horse had rendered her an invalid, or rather obliged her to walk with a stick, but her energy seemed to accumulate, and to work itself out at the cost of some havoc within her. Her voice was deeper than her sister's and had some sweeter tones. She appeared handsomer, though she also looked her age and her features were of the same mould. Her father admired her the more, and believed her maidenhood to be due to her invalid state, though her accident had not happened until she was middle-aged. It had done him a service in a way, as he had been at a loss to account for the position. The truth was that Matty had had many chances to marry and had not accepted them. She had never met a man whom she saw as her equal, as her conception of herself was above any human standard. She may also have had some feeling that a family would take her attention and that of others from herself. The idea that anyone could pity her found no place in her mind; there was no place there for such a feeling. Even her lameness she saw as giving a touch of tragic interest to an already remarkable impression. Oliver knew of her offers, or rather had been told of them, as his daughter kept nothing which seemed to exalt her, to herself, but he thought it normal self-respect in a woman to invent proposals if they were not forthcoming. Matty did not guess that she had not justice from her father, as he thought it wise to keep his doubt to himself, indeed knew it was. The father and daughter were less alike than they had been, for Oliver's face, once the original type, was fallen and shrunk from age. His figure was of the same size for a man as his elder daughter's for a woman, and had a touch of the awkwardness of the younger's, which was something apart from the stiffness of the old. When he was seen with Blanche and her youngest son, this lack of balance became a family trait. His wife had been some years his senior and had herself lived to an advanced age, and at her death he had been old enough to accept his daughter in her place.

'Yes, I am sure they have done what they can,' said Matty, still looking round. 'It is a funny little pattern on the paper. Suitable for the funny little room, I suppose. We are not to forget how we are placed. They thought it was better for us to take the plunge at once. Well, I daresay they are right. We will try to think they are. That is a lesson we shall have to learn.'

'You seem to be failing at the moment,' said Oliver, as Matty wiped her eyes. 'I can't see that the scrawl on the paper makes much odds. And the room seems to hold two people, which is what we want of it. What are you crying about? Aren't you thankful to have a home?'

'I am not so very at the moment. I can't help thinking of the one we have left. Perhaps it shows the feeling I had for that,' said Matty, putting her handkerchief away with a courageously final movement. 'I shall soon be able to be myself, but it is rather a sudden difference, the little paper and all.' She put her hand to her mouth in her sudden laughter. 'Well, shall we say that we appreciated our old home so much? I think we may say that without being unthankful.'

Oliver was silent. He had suffered from leaving his home as well as his daughter, almost feeling that he left his youth and his prime and his married life behind in it, but the lessening grasp of his age had saved him the worst. He had lived all his life on private means, and his capital had dwindled, partly in the natural course – his investments suffering from age like himself, and even in some cases succumbing like his wife – and partly because he had annually spent a portion of it. The eventual result struck him as a sudden misfortune, and he and his daughter faced their retrenchment in this spirit.

'Is that commotion to continue?' he said, as sounds of adjusting furniture came from the hall. 'No one would guess that we left our possessions behind. I should not have thought that the place was large enough to allow of it.'

'We must have a few necessities even in a little home. But there is less to be done than if we were to have what we have always had. That is one bright side to it.'

'And you see it, do you? When did you get your glimpse?'

'Things will soon be done, and you can have your dinner,' said Matty, retaliating on her father by explaining his mood. 'Miss Griffin will come and tell us.'

'You will eat as well as I, I suppose, and so will she. Will she be able to put up with the corner in which she finds herself?'

'It is the only home we can give her. We have to be content with it.'

'I meant what I said, her corner of it,' said Oliver, with a grin which recalled his youngest grandson. 'I still mean what I say.'

'We cannot help having had to leave our house for this one. It is not a pleasure for us.'

'No, my dear, you give no sign that it is. I grant it to you. Well, Miss Griffin is a good woman not to leave us. She has indeed been a remarkable person not to do that. I cannot say what she gets out of serving us.'

'Of course you can. It is quite clear. We give her a home when she has no other.'

'Sell it to her for herself, I should say. I would not congratulate her on her bargain.'

'It is better to stay with people who are fond of her, than to start again with strangers.'

'Strangers would treat her as a stranger. That was rather in my mind. And fond of her! You may be that; I am myself. But I shouldn't be proud of your way of showing it. Indeed I am not proud of it.'

'It would take her a long time to get to the same stage with another family.'

'Why, that is what I meant; this stage could not come at once. But I suppose women understand each other. I can only hope it. I don't see what I can do more. But it doesn't seem enough to keep a human being at my beck and call.'

'They have not come down to see us,' said Matty, glancing at the time. 'They have not run across from their big house to see how we are faring on our first evening in our small one. Well, I suppose they have many other claims: we must think they have.' She looked again at the clock and tapped her knee with her hand, making a simultaneous movement with her foot, as if she would have tapped the ground if she had been able.

'Well, I cannot tell. But we have not been in the house above two hours.'

'They are long hours when you have to sit still and hear other people about and doing, and feel how much better you could do it all, if you were as they are. They have been long ones.'

'Why, so they have, child, for me as well as for you.'

'Well, we must be still and go on a little longer.'

'Why, so we must, and for how much longer we cannot say. But it will not help us for you to cry about it. And what is your reason? You have a home and a bed and women to wait on you, haven't you?'

'Yes, I have, and I am going to feel it. I have more than many people. But it did seem to me for a moment that people who have more still – and we must say much more – might spare a thought to us in our first isolation. It was just for the moment.'

'Then it doesn't seem to you so any longer.'

'No, it must not,' said Matty, again concealing her handkerchief. 'There shall be nothing in our minds but bright and thankful thoughts.'

'Well, that will make a difference. And here is someone in the hall. So if you want to hide your handkerchief, find a place that serves your purpose. It is well that you are what you say in time.'

'Well, Matty dear, well, Father dear!' said Blanche's voice, the unconscious order of the names telling its tale. 'Well, here is a red letter day for us all!'

'Red letter day, when we have left our home and all we have, behind!' said Matty in a rapid aside to her father, pressing her handkerchief to her face in another spirit.

Blanche entered with outstretched arms and stumbled slightly over nothing apparent, as she hurried forward.

'Well, how do you like coming here amongst us? We like to have you so much. How are you both after your journey? I could not wait another minute to come and see.'

Blanche gave her father and sister a long embrace, stooping to the latter, as she remained in her seat, and then stood back to receive her response.

'Well, how do you feel about coming to share our life?' she said, as something more was needed to produce it.

'We shall be happy in it, dear. We shall,' promised Matty, rapidly using her handkerchief and hiding it. 'We see that now. We did not feel quite amongst you until this moment. But we do now indeed.' She took her sister's hand and lifted it to her face, as Blanche often did her daughter's.

'Sit down, my dear, sit down,' said Oliver. 'You give us a welcome and we do the same for you. I think there is a chair; I think there is room for three.'

'Of course there is. It is a very nice little room,' said Blanche, sitting down and looking round. 'How do you like the little paper? Don't you think it is just the thing? It is the one the boys have in their study.'

'Yes, dear, is it? Yes, it would be nice for that,' said Matty, following her sister's eyes. 'Just the thing, as you say. For this room in my house, and for a little, odd room in yours. It is the suitable choice.'

'Don't you like it in this room, dear?' said Blanche, evidently accustomed to answering her sister's meaning rather than her words.

'Yes, yes, I do. It is best to realize that we are in a little room, and not in a big one any longer. Best to leap the gulf and have a paper like the one in the boys' study.' Matty began to laugh but checked herself at once. 'Far better not to try to make it like the room at home, as we might have done by ourselves. We might have tried and failed, and it is so much wiser not to do that. Yes, it was best for people to deal with it, who saw it from outside and not from within. And it was so good of you to do it for us, and it is kindly and wisely done.'

'I thought you would like it so much; I did not know that you would want it like the drawing-room at home. That was so much larger that I thought it would be better to start afresh.'

'So it was, dear; that is what I said.'

'No, you said other things, child,' said Oliver.

'That is what we are doing, starting afresh, and finding rather a task at the moment,' said Matty, not looking at her father. 'But we shall manage it. It is only hard at first, and we can't help it that you find us in the first stage.' She touched her eyes and this time retained the handkerchief.

'Keep it, my dear,' said Oliver, offering her another. 'It is more convenient to you at hand.'

Matty held up the handkerchief to her sister with a smile for its size, and went on as if she had not paused.

'We shall make a success of it, as you have done with the room.'

'The room serves its purpose, my dear,' said Oliver to Blanche. 'The paper covers the walls and the plaster would not look as well without it, and what more should be done? You have managed well for us, and so we should tell you, and I do so for us both.'

'Yes, if we have seemed ungrateful, we are not,' said Matty, not explaining the impression. 'We both thank you from our hearts. So Edgar did not come with you to see us?'

'He came with me to the door and left me. He thought we should like our first meeting by ourselves.'

'He is always so thoughtful, and we have liked it indeed. And we shall like one with him as well the next time he is at our door. We have come to a place where we hope there will be so many meetings.'

'Blanche is enough for us,' said Oliver. 'We do not want her man. Why not say that you want the whole family? You almost did say it.'

'Well, I did have a thought that they might all come running down to greet the old aunt on her first night. I had almost imagined myself the centre of a family circle.'

'You imagined yourself the centre! So that is what is wrong. No wonder you wanted a room like the one at home. I don't know where you would have put them.'

'They could have got in quite well,' said Blanche. 'No doubt they will often do so. But to-night we thought you would want to be spared.' She paused and seemed to yield to another impulse. 'I am glad that you are so little depressed by the good-bye to the old home. We thought you might be rather upset by it.' Her way of speaking with a sting seemed an echo of her sister's in a lighter medium.

'We are too affected by that to show it on the surface,' said Matty. 'That is not where the feeling would appear. Is that where you would look for it?'

'Then what can we see there?' said Oliver. 'Your sister can find something, and does so. If that isn't where it ought to be, put it in its place.'

'Edgar is coming to fetch me in an hour,' said Blanche, resuming her normal manner. 'You will see him then and he will see you. He is looking forward to it.'

'You are only staying an hour, dear? I thought that you might have dinner with us, or we with you, on our first night.'

'Why pack so much into it?' said Oliver. 'There are other nights and others after those. And your sister is right that we are not fit for it. You were certainly not when you were crying into a rag. And why did you order dinner here, if you wanted to eat it somewhere else?'

'We had to have it somewhere, Father, and we did not hear.'

'Oh, we thought you would be tired,' said Blanche. 'And there are so many of us. It would not be restful for you. And we are not prepared for you to-night. We shall be so delighted to see you when it is arranged, and we hope that will be very often.'

'I did not make anything of extra guests, when I ran a large house,' said Matty, with a simple wonder which was not entirely assumed, as her housekeeping had played its part in her father's debts.

'And that may be partly why you are now running a small one,' said the latter, with a guess rather than a glimpse at the truth.

'We are hoping to see you constantly,' said Blanche. 'We can't quite manage our home so that people can come without notice, but we hope to plan so many things and to carry them out.'

'We can't run in and out, as if we were of the same family? We felt we were that when we came. That indeed is why we are here. You can do so in this little house. You will remember and tell the children?'

'I hope she will not retain any of this talk,' said Oliver, looking at his elder daughter, nevertheless, with his own admiration. 'I will ask her to forget it. Well, Miss Griffin, have you done enough of putting away what we have, in a space that cannot hold it?'

'We shall have to get rid of some furniture, dear,' said Matty to her sister, with a vague note of reproach.

'My dear, you have not brought all the furniture of that big house?'

'No, no, we remembered the size of this one, and only brought the things we knew and loved. I daresay you would not remember some of them. But we did not realize that it was quite such a cot. I expect our thoughts of it were tinged with memories of you and your large one, as that is how we have seen the life here. Never mind, we shall call it our cottage home, and be quite happy in it.'

'Then pray begin to be so,' said Oliver. 'Happiness is too good a thing to put off. And I am not at the age for doing that with anything.'

'How do you do, Miss Griffin?' said Blanche, shaking hands with her sister's attendant and companion. 'I hope you are not too tired with all your efforts?'

'How do you do, Mrs Gaveston? No, I am not so very tired,' said Miss Griffin, a short, thin woman of fifty, with a long, sallow face, large, hazel eyes, features which might have been anyone's except for their lines of sufferance and kindness, hands which were more developed than her body, and a look of being very tired indeed. 'It is very good of you to come to welcome us.'

'Mrs Gaveston came in to see her father and sister, of course,' said Matty, in a tone which said so much more than her words, that it brought a silence.

'Yes, indeed, dear,' said her sister. 'And when you want me to go and leave you to your dinner, you must tell me.'

'The dinner is not – the dinner will not be ready yet,' said Miss Griffin, in a stumbling tone, glancing at Matty and away. 'The maid does not know where anything is yet. She is quite new.'

'Of course she is, as we did not bring her with us,' said Matty, with her little laugh. 'Couldn't you show her where the things are, as you have just unpacked them?'

'She put everything together – I put it all together – we have not sorted them yet. She is just finding what she can.'

'I should have put all the things in their places as I took them out. I should not have thought of any other way.'

'We couldn't do that. The men were waiting to take the cases. We had to put them all down anywhere.'

'I should have known where anywhere was. I often wish I were able-bodied, for everyone's sake.'

'We wish you were, child, but for your own,' said Oliver.

'I think Miss Griffin has managed wonders from the look of the house,' said Blanche.

'We have all done that to-day,' said her sister. 'I almost think I have managed the most, in keeping still through all the stir and turmoil. I hope we shall never have such a day again. I can't help hoping it.'

'I know I shall not,' said her father.

'I remember so well the day when you came to us, Miss Griffin,' said Blanche. 'It was thirty-one years ago, a few days before my wedding. And you were so kind in helping me to pack and put the last touches to my clothes. I wished I was taking you with me.'

'I remember thinking that you were using my companion as your own,' said Matty, smiling from one to the other.

Miss Griffin turned her face aside, finding it unsteadied by ordinary kindness.

'Sit down, Miss Griffin, and rest until dinner,' said Matty. 'There is no need to stand more than you must, though I often wish I could do a little of it. That may make me think other people more fortunate than they are.'

Miss Griffin sat down in the sudden, limp way of someone who would soon have had to do so.

'There is Edgar,' said Blanche. 'He will come in and say a word, and then we will leave you all to rest.'

'Why, Edgar, this is nice,' said Matty, rising from her seat as she had not done for her sister, and showing that she stood tall and straight, in spite of disabled lower limbs. 'I did not think you would forget us on our first night. We had not forgotten you. No, you have been in our minds and on our lips. Now what do you say to our settling at your very gates?'

'That it is – that I hope it is the best place for you to be,' said Edgar, putting out all his effort and accordingly unable to say more.

'And your brother! I am never quite sure what to call him,' said Matty, putting round her head to look at Dudley. 'Come in and let us hear your voice. We have been cheered by it so many times.'

'I am glad you have. I have always meant you to be. I am in my element in a chat. My strong point is those little things which are more important than big ones, because they make up life. It seems that big ones do not do that, and I daresay it is fortunate.'

'Yes, it is indeed. We have been involved in the latter to-day, and we see that we could not manage too many. Now it is so good to hear you talk again. We see we have not given up our home for nothing.'

'Indeed you have not. You have left it to make a new one with all of us,' said Blanche, relieved by the turn of the talk and not disturbed that she had been unable to produce it.

'Such a lot of happiness, such a lot of affection and kindness,' said Matty, in a tone charged with sweetness and excitement. 'It is so good to know that we are welcome.'

'It is indeed,' said Oliver; 'for a moment since I should have thought that we could not be.'

'How are you, sir?' said Edgar and Dudley, speaking at one moment but obliged to shake hands in turn.

'I am well, I thank you, and I hope that both of you are better by thirty odd years, as you should be.'

Oliver put a chair for his son-in-law and settled down to talk. He gave his feeling to his daughters but he liked to talk with men.

'How are you, Miss Griffin?' said Dudley, turning from the pair. 'I hope you are not hiding feelings of your own on the occasion.'

'No, I am not; it all makes a change,' said Miss Griffin, admitting more feeling than she knew into the last word. 'And we did not want that large house for so few people. It is better to be in a little one, where there is less work and more comfort. And I don't mind the small rooms. I rather like to be snug and compact.'

'Now I would not claim that that is just my taste. I confess to a certain disposition towards the opposite,' said Matty, in a clear tone. 'It is not of my own will that I have changed my scale of life. I admit that I felt more at home with the other. It is all a matter of what fits our different personalities, I suppose.'

'I hope I do not make cosy corners wherever I go,' said Dudley. 'I don't want too many merely lovable qualities. They are better for other people than for oneself.'

'Well, there will always be such a corner for you here. I shall be grateful if you will help me to make one, as it is rather outside my experience and scope. But once made, it will be always hospitable and always ready. If we can't have one thing we will have another, or anyhow I will. I am not a person to give up because I can't have just what I should choose, just what fits me, shall we say.'

'I don't know why we should say it, child,' said Oliver. 'And anyhow you should not.'

'I wish my parents were not dead,' said Dudley. 'I should like to be called "child" by someone. It would prove that there were people about who were a generation older than me, and it will soon want proof.'

'Welcome, welcome to your new home!' said Justine's voice. 'Welcome to your new life. I know I am one too many; I know you are tired out; I know your room is full. I know it all. But I simply had to come to wish you happiness, and to say to you, Welcome, well come.'

'So you had, dear, and it gives us such pleasure to hear it,' said

Matty, raising her face from her chair. 'I did hope that some of you would feel that and come to tell us so. It seemed to me that you would, and I see I was not wrong. One, two, three, four dear faces! Only three left at home. It is such a help to us in starting again, and it is a thing which does need help. You don't know that yet, and may it be long before you do.'

'Well, I judged it, Aunt Matty, and that is why I am here. Of course, you must need courage. You can't start again without a good deal of looking back. That must be part of it. And I did feel a wish to say a word to help you to look forward.'

Blanche looked at her daughter in simple appreciation; Edgar threw her a glance and withdrew it; and Oliver surveyed the scene as if it were not his concern.

'You help us, dear, indeed,' said Matty. 'It was a kind and loving wish, and as such we accept it and will try to let it do its work.'

'I know you will, Aunt Matty dear; I know your inexhaustible fund of courage. You know, I am of those who remember you of old, straight and tall and proud, as you appeared to my childish eyes. My feeling for you has its ineradicable root in the past.'

The words brought a silence, and Justine, fair in all her dealings, broke it herself.

'How are you, Miss Griffin?' she said, shaking hands with great cordiality, and then sitting down and seeming to render the room at once completely full. 'Now this is a snug, little, cottage parlour. Now, how do you take to it, Aunt Matty?'

'We shall be content in it, dear. We mean to be. And where there is a will there is a way. And it should not be difficult to come to like it, our little cottage parlour. Those are good and pretty words for it. They give the idea without any adding to it or taking away.'

'It is not a cottage, dear,' said Blanche, looking at her daughter.

'Isn't it, Mother? Well, no, we know it strictly is not. But it gives all the idea of one somehow. And I mean nothing disparaging; I like a roomy cottage. When I am a middle-aged woman and Mark is supreme in the home, I shall like nothing better than to have perhaps this very little place, and reign in it, and do all I can for people outside. Now does not that strike you all as an alluring prospect?'

'Yes, it sounds very nice,' said Miss Griffin, who thought that it did, and who was perhaps the natural person to reply, as the arrangement involved the death of most of the other people present.

'I don't think it gives the idea of a cottage at all,' said Blanche, looking round with contracting eyes. 'The rooms are so high and the windows so broad. One could almost imagine oneself anywhere.'

'But not quite,' said her sister, bending her head and looking up at the men from under it. 'We can't, for example, imagine ourselves where we used to be.'

'Well, no, not there, dear. We must both of us leave that. It was my old home too, as you seem to forget.'

'No, dear. You do at times, I think. That is natural. You have put too much over it. Other things have overlaid the memory. I chose to keep it clear and by itself. There is the difference.'

'Well, it *is* natural, Aunt Matty,' said Justine. 'I don't think Mother must be blamed for it. There *is* a difference.'

'Yes, dear, and so you will not blame her. I have said that I do not. And is the old aunt already making herself tiresome? She must be so bright and easy as an invalid in a strange place?'

'Come, Aunt Matty, invalid is not the word. You are disabled, we know, and we do not underrate the handicap, but your invalidism begins and ends there. Now I am not going to countenance any repining. You are in your virtual prime; you have health and looks and brains; and we are going to expect a good deal from you.'

'My dear, did Aunt Matty ask you to sum up her position?' said Blanche, a faint note of triumphant pride underlying her reproof.

'No, Mother, you know she did not, so why put the question? I did not wait to be asked; it is rather my way not to. You need not put on a disapproving face. I have to be taken as I am. I do not regret what I said, and Aunt Matty will not when she thinks it over.'

'Or forgets it,' said her aunt. 'Yes, I think that is what Aunt

Matty had better do. She has not the will or the energy to think it over at this juncture of her life. And forgetting it will be better, so that is the effort she must make.'

'Now I am in disgrace, but I do not regard it. I have had my say and I always find that enough,' said Justine, who was wise in this attitude, as she would seldom have been advised to go further.

'How very unlike Edgar and Justine are, dear!' said Matty to her sister. 'They have not a touch of each other, and they say that daughters are like their fathers. They are both indeed themselves.'

'Well, that is as well,' said Justine. 'Father would not like me to be a copy of him. He would not feel the attraction of opposites.'

'Opposite. Yes, that is almost the word,' said her aunt.

Miss Griffin gave the sudden, sharp breath of someone awaking from a minute's sleep, and looked about with bewildered eyes.

'Poor Miss Griffin, you are tired out,' said Blanche.

'I am so glad you got off for a minute, Miss Griffin,' said Justine.

'I did not know where I was; I must have dropped off with all the voices round me,' said Miss Griffin, with a view of the talk which she would hardly have taken if she had heard it. 'I don't know why I did, I am sure.'

'Being overtired is quite enough reason,' said Justine.

'So Miss Griffin is the first of us to make it one,' said Matty, in an easy tone.

'It is a stronger reason in her case.'

'Is it, dear?' said Matty, so lightly that she hardly seemed to enunciate the words.

'Why, Aunt Matty, she must have done twice as much as you – as anyone else. You know that.'

'Twice as much as I have, dear? Many times as much, I daresay; I have been able to do hardly anything. And of course I know it.' Matty gave her little laugh. 'But what we have mostly done to-day, is sitting in the train, and we have done it together.'

'Yes, but the preparations before and the unpacking afterwards! It must have been overwhelming. The time in the train must have been quite a respite.'

'Yes, that is what I meant, dear.'

'But it was only one day, only part of one. The work must have begun directly you reached this house. I can see how much has been achieved. You can't possibly grasp it, sitting in a chair.'

'So sitting in a chair has become an advantage, has it?'

'Poor, dear Aunt Matty!' said Justine, sitting on the arm of the chair, as if to share for the moment her aunt's lot. 'But it cannot contribute to the actual weariness, you know. That is a thing by itself.'

'So there is only one kind of weariness,' said Matty, putting her hand on her niece's and speaking in a tone of gentle tolerance towards her unknowing youth.

'Dear Aunt Matty! There must be times when to be hustled and driven seems the most enviable thing in the world. You are more unfortunate than anyone,' said Justine, indicating and accepting her aunt's lot and Miss Griffin's.

Miss Griffin rose and went to the door with an explanatory look at Matty. Dudley opened it and followed her.

'How do people feel on a first night in a new place? I have never had the experience. I have lived in the same house all my life.'

Miss Griffin lifted her eyes with a look he had not expected, almost of consternation.

'It does make you feel uncertain about things. But I expect you soon get used to it. I was in the last house thirty-one years. Miss Seaton had never lived in any other.'

'And are you sorry to come away from it?'

'No, not very. It makes a change. We shall see different people. And it will be nice for Miss Seaton to have her sister and her family. It was the wisest plan.'

'The best plan, not the wisest. It was very unwise. But a great many of the best things are that.'

Miss Griffin looked at him with a hint of a smile.

'You agree with me, do you not?'

Miss Griffin checked her smile and looked aside.

'You and I must be very much alike. We both live in other people's houses; we are both very kind; and I am very good at playing second fiddle, and I believe you are too.'

'Oh, I never mind doing that,' said Miss Griffin in a full tone.

'I have minded in my weaker moments, but I have conquered my worse self. You have no worse self, have you?'

'No,' said Miss Griffin, speaking the truth before she thought. 'Well, I don't know. Perhaps everyone has.'

'You have to think of other people's. So I see that you have not. And as I have suppressed mine, it is another point we have in common.'

Miss Griffin stood with a cheered expression.

'Has Miss Seaton a better self?' said Dudley.

Miss Griffin gave him a half smile which turned to a look of reproach.

'Yes, of course she has. Everyone has.'

'So it was her worse self we saw this evening?'

'I did not mean that she had a worse self. You know I did not. She was very tired. It must be so dreadful not to be able to get about.' Miss Griffin's voice died away on a note of pure pity.

'Well, good-night, Miss Griffin; we shall often meet.'

'Good-night, Mr Dudley,' said Miss Griffin, turning towards the kitchen with a lighter step.

Dudley returned to the parlour to find the family dispersing. Matty was on her feet, talking with the lively affection which followed her difficult moods, and which she believed to efface their memory.

'Good-bye, dearest; good-bye, my Justine; you will often come in to see the cross old aunt who loves you. Good-bye, Dudley; where have you been wandering? It was clever to find enough space to lose yourself. Good-bye, Edgar; my father has so enjoyed his masculine talk. It is a thing that does him so much good.'

'And how have you enjoyed your feminine one?' said Oliver, who had caught snatches of this dialogue. 'Upon my word, I daresay a good deal. You look the better for it.'

'Good-bye, Aunt Matty dear,' said Justine. 'I have seemed a brute, but I have meant it for your good, and you are large enough to take it as it was meant.'

'Good-bye,' said Edgar at once. 'We shall often meet; I hope we shall meet very often.'

'Well, of course, people are only human,' said Dudley to his brother, as they walked to the house behind the women. 'But it really does not seem much for them to be.'

'Yes, we must do what we can in our new life,' said Edgar, as if in reply. 'I think we may call it that. It may be a better life for Blanche. I think – I trust it may.'

'Is her present life so bad?'

'She may be lonely without knowing it. I fear it may have been the case. I feel – I fear I have little to be proud of in my family life.'

'It is I who have the cause for pride. It is wonderful, the way in which I have put myself aside and kept your affection and won your wife's. But I think the things we suffer without knowing are the best, as we are born to suffer. It is not as if Blanche had suspected her loneliness. And she can't be with her sister and be unconscious of it.'

'Neither can any of us,' said Edgar, with the short, broken laugh which was chiefly heard by his brother. 'I could see – I saw that she realized it to-day.'

'I saw that Justine did too. The sight became too much for me and I had to escape.'

'What were you doing all that time?'

'Why do people say that they do not like having to account for their every action? I do like it. I like telling everything about myself and feeling that people take an interest. I was saying a kind word to Miss Griffin. They say that a kind word may work wonders; and I saw that something had to work wonders for her; and so I said the word and it did.'

'Poor Miss Griffin! I mean that we cannot judge of other people's lives.'

'Of course we can. We all have lives and know about them. No one will have it said that he has no knowledge of life; and it could not be true.'

'She has been with Matty and her father for a long time. I am not sure how long.'

'I am. She told me. But there are things which cannot pass my lips.'

'It must be over thirty years.'

'You are a tougher creature than I am. I wonder if people know that you are.'

'It is difficult to form a picture of all those years.'

'Edgar, you do sometimes say the most dreadful things. You should remember my shrinking nature. I shall have to see a great deal of Miss Griffin. Will seeing her take away that picture before my eyes?'

'Come along, you two,' called Justine, turning with beckoning hand. 'If you wait every minute to argue, we shall never get up the drive. Mother does not like to keep stopping.'

This was true of Blanche, and therefore she had not stopped, but was proceeding towards the house, with her short, unequal steps carrying her rapidly over the ground. When she came to the porch she paused, as if waiting there affected her differently.

'There is that little brick house beyond the trees,' said Justine, turning to look back as they all met.

'Your eyes do not deceive you,' said her father, with a smile.

'Now don't try to snub me, Father; that is not like your dealings. There it is, and it is good to think of Grandpa and Aunt Matty snugly sheltered in it. I shall call up the picture to-night when I am in bed.'

'At night,' murmured Dudley, 'and in bed! In those hours when things rise up before us out of their true proportion!'

'What are you murmuring about to yourself, Uncle?'

'About the picture which you will call up in the night.'

'You like to share it with me? It is a pretty picture, isn't it? Dear Grandpa, with his white hair and fine old face; and Aunt Matty, handsome in the firelight, vivacious and fluent, and no more querulous than one can forgive in her helpless state; and dear, patient Miss Griffin, thinking of everyone but herself. It is a satisfying sight.'

'Perhaps it is healthier to bring it out into the light.'

'You were the one who did not forgive your aunt,' said Edgar, smiling again at his daughter.

'Now, Father, don't think that your naughty little thrusts are atoned for by your especial smile for me, dear to me though it is.' Edgar's expression wavered as he heard it defined. 'Aunt Matty and I are the firmest friends and very good for one another. We never mind looking at ourselves through each other's eyes and getting useful light on our personalities. I do not believe in putting disabled people on one side and denying them their share in healthy human life. It seems to me a wrong thing to do, and in the end bad for everyone. So I sound my bracing note and snap my fingers at the consequences.' Justine illustrated what she said.

The scene in the lodge was as she saw it, except that Matty's querulousness was missing. The latter was sitting at dinner, talking with a great liveliness, as if her audience were larger than it was, almost as if in practice for greater occasions. She often threw herself into the entertainment of her father and her companion, with or without thought of imaginary listeners.

'And then those funny, little, country shoes! Dear Blanche, still full of her quaint, little, old touches! I had to laugh to myself when I saw her coming tripping and stumbling in, such a dear, familiar figure!'

'No one would have known you had,' said Oliver. 'It might have been better to give some sign. It seemed the last thing to expect of you.'

Matty was indifferent to her father's criticism and knew that her talk diverted him.

'And then her own little, charitable ways, a mixture of daughter and sister and lady bountiful! So full of affection and kindness and yet with her own little sharpness, just our old Blanche! And her dear Justine' – Matty put her hand to her lips and fell into mirth – 'so sure of her right to improve us all and so satisfied with it! So pleased with her effort to influence her aunt, who has faced so much more than she could conceive! Dear child, may she never even have to attempt it. Well, we are not all alike and perhaps it is as well. Perhaps it is good that we are all on our different steps in the human scale. And there are good things on each level. In some ways we might take a leaf out of her book.'

'We might, but I do not think of it, and I do not ask it of you.'

'It is naughty to say it, but does she remind you of that church worker at home? Someone so good and useful that everyone loved her and no one admired her? Now how unkind and malicious! I am quite ashamed.'

'Have I met a person of that kind?'

'You must remember poor Miss Dunn at home.'

'Why should I single her out of all that I remember? And how could I guess her employment?'

'The coat and the collar and the shoes,' said Matty, again in mirth.

'They both wear such things, I grant you. I do the same and shall do it still for a short time.'

'Poor Miss Griffin, you were the target. You might have been a little dark slave or a wee beastie in a trap, from the way she spoke. We do not move every day, do we? It has only been once in thirty years.'

Miss Griffin felt that there was some reproach in the rareness of the step, though she would willingly have taken it oftener.

'She meant to be very kind, I am sure.'

'She meant to be a little stern with me, just a tiny bit severe. But I did not mind. She is my dear, good niece and wants to improve the world and the people in it, Aunt Matty into the bargain.'

'They might be the better for it,' said Oliver, 'but it is not her business.'

'She feels it is, and so we must let her do it. We must take it up as a funny little cross and carry it with us.'

'Why do that? Why not close her mouth upon things which are not her concern? That is a thing you can do. I have observed it.'

'Edgar is a handsome man,' said Matty in another tone. 'He was very tall and distinguished in this little room. Oh, wasn't it funny, the way they kept talking about it? Calling it snug and cosy. We might be cottagers.'

'That is what we are, though your sister did not allow it.'

'And Justine said that she was glad we were safe in it. We had no other refuge, had we?'

'I cannot tell you of one. So we have our cause for thankfulness. But it is not for her to point it out. She seems to me to have greater cause.'

'Mr Gaveston and Mr Dudley are not so much alike when you get to know them,' said Miss Griffin.

'They are of the same type, but Mr Gaveston is the better example,' said Matty, who maintained the full formal distance between herself and her companion, in spite of her habit of frankness before her.

'I like Mr Dudley's face better.'

'Do you? It is not the better face. It has not the line or the symmetry. It is a thought out of drawing. But they are a fine pair of brothers.'

'There is something in Mr Dudley's face that makes it quite different from Mr Gaveston's. I hardly know how to say what I mean.'

'That might be said, of any two people. They are not just alike, of course.'

'Mr Dudley's face has a different kind of attraction.'

'There is only one kind, of the one we were talking of,' said Matty in a tone which closed the subject.

'Miss Griffin has found another,' said Oliver, 'or has fancied it. But why talk of the fellows' looks? They are not women. And both of you are, so it is wise to leave the matter.'

'Was Mr Dudley talking to you outside?' said Matty in a sudden, different tone to Miss Griffin.

'No – yes – he just said a word, and then went out to look at the night, into the porch,' said Miss Griffin, who told a falsehood when she could see no other course.

Oliver had heard the voices in the hall, but he did not speak. He never crossed the barrier into the women's world. If he had done so, he would have had to protect Miss Griffin and anger his daughter; and he felt unequal to either of these things, which would have tried the strength of a younger man.

'Did you notice the way they set off home?' said Matty, with a return of mirth. 'I saw them from the window. My eyes are still alert for what they can see, though I am tied to my chair. Blanche leading the way, and Justine trying to keep up and to keep step, and failing in both in spite of her youth and her strength! And the two men walking behind, as tranquil as if they were unconscious of the feminine creatures in front! Blanche leading a group is one of my earliest memories. Her stiff, little legs marching on, how they come back to me! And they are so little different, the active, determined, little legs. How much of her height is in her body! Well, my legs are not so much to boast of now. I have not my old advantage. Dear, dear, it is a funny thing, a family. I can't help feeling glad sometimes that I have had no part in making one.'

'Why try to help it? It is well to be glad of anything, and you do not too often seem so. Though some people might not choose just that reason.'

'Well, mine is not a lot which calls for much gladness. It needs some courage to find any cause for it.'

'So courage is the word for your talk of your sister. We could find others.'

'Blanche and I are the closest friends. I am going to rejoice in being the elder sister again. You and she are the only people who see me as I was, and not as I am, the poor, baffled, helpless creature who has to get her outlet somehow. Yes, I was bright and young once. Even Miss Griffin remembers part of that time.'

'Yes, indeed I do; indeed you were,' said Miss Griffin.

'Miss Griffin was even younger,' said Oliver, bringing a new idea to both his hearers as he rose to leave them.

'Yes, I was a naughty, sprightly person,' continued Matty after a moment's pause, during which the idea left her. 'Always looking for something on which to work my wits. Something or someone; I fear it did not matter as long as my penetration had its exercise. Well, we can't choose the pattern on which we are made. And perhaps I would not alter mine. Perhaps there is no need to meddle with it, eh, Miss Griffin?'

Miss Griffin was standing with her hand on her chair, thinking of the next step in her day. She gave a faint start as she realized her plight and saw the look on Matty's face. The next moment she heard her voice.

'Don't go dragging away from the table like that. Either move about and get something done, or don't pretend to do anything. Just posing as being a weary drudge will not get us anywhere.'

'Perhaps the things which have made me that, have got us somewhere,' said Miss Griffin, in an even, oddly hopeless tone, with little idea that the words on her lips marked a turning point in her life.

'You need not answer like that. That is not going to begin, so you need not think it is. I do not expect to have my words taken up as if I were a woman on the common line. I am a very exceptional person and in a tragic position, and you will have to grasp it, or you are no good to me. And going off in that way, pretending not to hear, taking advantage of my helplessness! That is a thing of such a dreadful meanness that no one would speak to you if he knew it; no one would go near you; you would be shunned and spat upon!'

Matty's voice rose to a scream, as her words did nothing and Miss Griffin passed out of hearing. She rocked herself to and fro and muttered to herself, with her hands clenched and her jaw thrust forward in a manner which would have made a piece of acting and really had something of this in it, as she did not lose sight of herself.

Miss Griffin went along the passage and paused at the end where the wall made a support, and looked to see that Matty had not followed.

'It is all I have. Just this. I have nothing else. I have no home, no friends. I go on, year after year, never have any pleasure, never have any change. She feels nothing for me after I have been with her for thirty years. All the best years of my life. And it gets worse with every year. I thought this move might make a change, but it is going to be the same. And my life is going; I may never have anything else; and no one ought to have only that.' She shed some tears, scanty through fear and furtiveness, and lightening her face and throwing off a part of her burden, went into the kitchen to the maid, glad of this degree of human fellowship.

Matty, left to herself, relaxed her body and her mind and hoped that her father had not heard her voice, or rather recalled that he would behave as if he had not done so. When Oliver came from his study to bid her a good night, she rose to meet him, hiding what she could of her lameness, and led him to a chair, amending both his and her own conception of herself.

'I come to take my leave of you, my dear, in case I do not see you again. My end may come at any time and why not to-night? The strength ebbs after dark and I have used too much of mine to-day. So good-night and more, if that is to be.'

'Come, Father, you are overtired and depressed by being in this funny little place. Cosy we are to call it, and we will do our best. We have to try to do so many things and in time we shall succeed. We are not people who fail. We will not be.'

'I am almost glad that your mother is not here to-night, Matty. This would not have been a home for her. It will do for you and me.'

'I don't know why we should be so easily satisfied,' said Matty, unable to accept this view of herself in any mood. 'But we shall have another outlook to-morrow and it will seem a different place, and we shall wish Mother back with us, as I have wished her many times to-day.' Her father must pay for using such words of his daughter. 'But we can't do anything more to-night. We have striven to our limit and beyond. It is no wonder if we fail a little. I daresay we have all had our lapses from our level.'

Oliver, who was in no doubt of it, left her and mounted the stairs, bringing his feet together on each. In his room above the step became stronger, and Matty listened and put him from her mind. She understood her father. A good deal of him had come down to her.

Miss Griffin came in later with a tray, to find Matty in an attitude of drooping weariness, with a pallor which was real after her stress of feeling.

'Will you have something hot to drink?' she said in a tone which seemed to beseech something besides what it said. 'It will do you good before you go to bed.'

'It will do us both good. It was a sensible thought. If you will bring up that little table and move that chair' – Matty indicated with vivacious hand this further effort for Miss Griffin – 'we will have a cosy time together and feel that we are doing what we should, as cosy is what we are supposed to be.'

'It really is rather cosy in here,' said Miss Griffin, looking round with a faint air of surprise.

'Yes, it is foolish to fret for the might-have-beens. Or for the have-beens in this case.'

Miss Griffin did not fret for these.

'Now do not shirk drinking your share,' said Matty, replenishing the cups. 'You need it as much as I do. Being up and doing is as tiring as sitting still, however much one may envy it. Mr Seaton has gone to bed. He was overtired and sorry for himself, but I did not take much notice. It was wiser not to sympathize.'

'Oh, I expect he was very tired,' said Miss Griffin, sitting up as if to put her full energy into her compassion.

'He begins to feel his age, but he is very well and strong. And we are all tired.'

'Yes,' said Miss Griffin, speaking in a mechanical tone and suddenly enlivening it. 'But it is a healthy tiredness.' She had been so often told of the beneficial effects of weariness on the human frame, that she felt she should know them.

'It has gone a little beyond that to-day. But it is only once in a lifetime. We must not complain.'

Miss Griffin was not going to do this, but her nod had something besides agreement.

'Come, come now, we must go to bed,' said Matty, keeping her eyes from the other as if in fear of what might meet them. 'We shall be a couple of sleepy old maids in the morning, if we do not take care.'

Miss Griffin's eyes opened wide and held themselves on Matty's face.

'We owe it to ourselves and to other people not to sink to that. We must not quite lose our self-respect. This is a matter in which considering ourselves is best for everyone. Has Emma gone to bed?'

'Yes, hours ago,' said Miss Griffin, only realizing her implication when she had spoken.

Matty did not comment on it, possibly for the reason that Emma had only been half a day in her service and had not yet learned the benefits of exhaustion.

'Well, then she can be up bright and early to wait upon us,' she said with an effort which did not say nothing for her will. 'We will not be down until ten o'clock. We have had a nice little chat. Good-night, and mind you sleep.'

Matty went to her room, feeling that she had made her companion ample amends, and the latter, waiting to turn out the lamps, wondered that she did not feel the same, as she had felt it so many times. This was the reason for her not feeling it again.

Chapter 3

'I am ready for Aunt Matty,' said Aubrey.

'Are you, little boy? And very nice and trim you look. I wish I could feel the same. I am done with village dressmakers. I am not much of a woman for personal adornment, but there are stages beyond even me. I ought to think of my family; it was selfish and lazy of me. I certainly can't expect to rejoice their eyes.' Justine sighed over her conclusion.

'Won't smoothing it make it better?'

'No, it will not, impertinent child. It will leave it as it is.' Justine aimed a blow in her brother's direction without moving towards him.

'Mark, are you ready for your aunt?' said Aubrey.

'As far as the outward man can count. But her eyes may pierce the surface and pounce on what is beneath.'

'Now I won't have Aunt Matty laughed at for her penetration,' said Justine. 'It is a valuable quality and one which deserves to be reckoned with.'

'And is more than any other.'

'She has none,' said Clement. 'She attributes motives to people, whether they are there or not. That gets us further from the truth than anything. Mother has really a sounder penetration.'

'Dear little Mother,' said Justine, giving a pitying tenderness to the same quality in Blanche.

'Clement, are you ready for your aunt?'

'Nothing would prepare me for the manners, the morals and the methods of such a woman. She is at once super and subhuman. I always wonder if she is goddess or beast.'

'Clement, Clement, that is neither gallant nor kind,' said Justine. 'A man does not speak of a woman like that, you know. And can't you brush the collar of your coat? Not that I have any right to speak.'

'But I think both the boys look very nice Justine,' said Aubrey.

'How does Justine appear?' said Clement. 'I will hear the accepted view before I express my own.'

'Oh, you are right; it is hopeless. It deserves anything you like to say. You need not be afraid that I shall rise up in its defence like a mother with her young.'

'You might help to smooth it, Clement,' said Aubrey. 'It is all that can be done now.'

'Why don't you change it?' said Mark. 'What about that one you generally wear?'

'No, I will stick to it now. I will remain in it and face the music. Mother is expecting to see me in something different, and I daresay she will like it. I won't take refuge in some old one which does not catch the eye. It will teach me a lesson that I deserve.'

'It is not a matter of such mighty import,' said Clement.

'Indeed it is! It should be a point of great interest to you all, how your only sister looks. I will not have it in any other way. I have no patience with that kind of high-and-mightiness. It is the last thing that exalts anyone.'

'Clement, are you listening to Justine?' said Aubrey.

'He does not know how true quality is shown,' said Mark. 'That is a thing which cannot be taught.'

'All Clement's learning will stand him in but poor stead.'

'Here are the guests! And Father and Mother are not down!' said Justine, in a tone of consternation.

'They are remedying the position,' said Clement, showing that he did not recommend the feeling.

Blanche led the way into the room, in an old-fashioned gown of heavy material and indifferent cut, which had been altered to show successfully how it should have been made, and which in its countrified quality and stiffness became her well.

'Well, dear ones, how nice you look! Justine, it is a very pretty colour. I do want Aunt Matty to see you all at your best. And dear Grandpa has seen so little of you for so long.' Blanche spoke to her children of their relations either from their point of view or her own.

'Mr and Mrs Middleton,' said Jellamy.

'How are you, Mrs Middleton? It is kind of you to adapt yourselves to our early hours,' said Blanche, who observed the formalities with guests with sincerity and goodwill. 'My father and sister will be here in a moment. It is a long time since you have met.'

'Whose idea was it that they should come to live here?'

'It was their own. But we welcomed it with great delight. My sister and I have missed each other for so many years.'

'Isn't the lodge rather small after their old home?'

Sarah Middleton's questions seemed to come in spite of herself, as if her curiosity were stronger than her will.

'Yes, it has to be that. They have lost money lately and are obliged to live on a small scale. And it is a nice little house.'

'Very nice indeed,' said Sarah, with the full cordiality of relief from pain, which was the state produced in her by a satisfied urge to know.

Sarah Middleton was a tall, upright woman of seventy, strong and young for her age, with a fair, rather empty face and an expression at once eager and soured and kind. Her grey hair was done in some way which seemed to belong to a world where men and women were more different, and her cap had been assumed in her prime in tribute to matronhood, though to Justine and her brothers it was a simple emblem of age. She looked about as she talked, as if she feared to miss enlightenment on any matter, a thing which tried her beyond her strength and which happily seldom occurred. Her husband, who was ten years younger and in the same physical stage, was a tall, spare, stooping man, with a good head, pale, weak eyes, a surprisingly classic nose, and an air of depression and an excellence of deportment which seemed to depend on each other, as though he felt that the sadness of life entitled people to courtesy and consideration. He had wanted to write, and had been a schoolmaster because of the periods of leisure, but had found that the demands of the other periods exhausted his energy. After his marriage to a woman of means he was still prevented, though he did not give the reason, indeed did not know it. Neither did he state what he wished to write, and this was natural, as he had not yet decided. Sarah felt that the desire gave him enough occupation, and he almost seemed to feel the same.

'Yes, say what you like, Uncle,' said Justine, standing before Dudley and holding out her skirts. 'It merits it all and more. I have not a word to say. This will teach me not to waste my time and energy on going backwards and forwards to poor Miss

Spurr. She has not an ounce of skill in her composition.'

Blanche looked at the dress with mild, and Sarah with eager, attention.

'It could be made into a dressing gown,' said Dudley, taking a sudden step forward. 'I see just how it could be done.'

'My dear, that beautiful material!' said Sarah, holding up her hands and turning her eyes on Justine to indicate the direction of her address.

'I am sure it is a very pretty colour,' said Blanche, implying and indeed feeling that this was a great part of the matter.

'I knew I could count on a word of encouragement from you, little Mother.'

'Dressing gowns are always the best colours,' said Aubrey. 'I go in and look at them sometimes.'

'You little scamp,' said Justine. 'You are happy in being young enough for that sort of thing.'

'Dear boy!' said Sarah.

'What is the matter with the dress?' said Edgar, with careful interest. 'Do you mean that it ought to be better made?'

'Yes, Father, I do mean that. Everyone means it. We all mean it. Don't go unerringly to the point like that, as if it were almost too obvious to call for comment.'

'I don't think it calls for so much comment,' said Clement.

'Well, I daresay it does not. Let us leave it now. After all, we all look ourselves in whatever we wear,' said Justine, deriving open satisfaction from this conclusion, and taking Aubrey's chin in her hand. 'What are you meditating upon, little boy?'

'I was expecting Aunt Matty,' said Aubrey, reluctant to explain that he had been imagining future daughters for himself and deciding the colours of their dressing gowns.

'Well, dear ones all,' said Matty, almost standing still on the threshold, partly in her natural slowness and partly to be seen. 'Well, here is a happy, handsome' – she rapidly substituted another word – 'healthy family. So much health and happiness is so good to see. It is just what I want, isn't it?'

Blanche looked up with narrowing eyes at the change of word, though she knew that it was prompted by the sight of more and not less handsomeness than her sister had expected.

'Is not Father coming?' she said in a cool tone, putting down her embroidery before she rose.

Sarah looked from sister to sister with full comprehension and the urbanity which accompanied it.

'Yes, dear, he will not be a moment. He is only rather slow. I came on to get a start of him, as I am even slower.' Matty kissed Blanche with more than her usual affection in tacit atonement for what had passed, but seemed to feel rather soon that atonement had been made. 'It seems that I know him better in these days and have to tell you about him. Perhaps he has always belonged to me a little the most. Why, Mrs Middleton, how are you both? So we are to be neighbours as well as friends.'

'It did not take you long to make up your mind to the change,' said Sarah, her tone leading up to further information.

'No, I am a person of rapid decision. Fleet of foot, fleet of thought and fleet of action I used to be called in the old days.' Blanche looked up as if in an effort of memory. 'And I have retained as much of my fleetness as I can. So I made my resolve and straightaway acted upon it.'

'My dear, you have retained so much of what you had,' said Sarah, shaking her head.

'Mr Seaton,' said Jellamy.

'Now I can barely walk forward to greet you,' said Oliver, pushing his feet along the ground, 'but I am glad to find myself welcome as I am. There have come moments when I thought that we might not meet again. So, Middleton, I am pleased to see you once more on this side of the grave.'

Thomas shook hands with an air which accepted and rejected these words in the right measure.

'Why are people proud of expecting to die soon?' said Dudley to Mark. 'I think it is humiliating to have so little life left.'

'They are triumphant at having made sure of more life than other people. And they don't really think they will die.'

'No, of course, they have got into the way of living. I see it is a lifelong habit.'

'Have we no relations who can enter a room in the usual way?' said Clement.

'None in the neighbourhood,' said his brother.

'Now, Grandpa, that is naughty talk,' said Justine, leading Oliver forward by the arm as if no one else would think of the office. 'Now which chair would you like?'

'Any one will serve my purpose; I ask but to sit in it.'

'Dear Grandpa!' said Justine, keeping her hands on his arms as he sat down, as if she were lowering him into it.

'That is a fine gown, my dear,' he said, as he let go the chair and sank back.

'It is the most fearful thing, Grandpa; I forbid you to look at it. It will be my shame all the evening.'

'You know why you put it on, I suppose. I should have thought it was intended to catch the eye, as it has caught mine.'

'I think it is such a nice colour,' said Blanche.

'Beautiful,' said Sarah, shaking her head again.

'Why, so it is, my dear,' said Oliver, relaxing his limbs. 'Your girl looks well in it, and what more would you have?'

'But the shape of it, Grandpa!' said Justine, withdrawing her strictures upon his looking, to the extent of disposing herself that he might the better do so. 'The cut, the hang, the balance, the fit!'

'Well, I do not see any of those, my dear; I do not know if you are trying to show them to me.'

'I am trying to show you the lack of them.'

'Then you do so, child; I see it,' said Oliver, lifting one leg over the other.

'Well, if anyone received a snub!' said Justine, looking about her at the success of her effort.

'What is the colour?' said Matty, her easy tone revealing her opinion that enough had been said on the matter. 'Magenta?'

'No, dear,' said Blanche. 'It is a kind of old rose.'

'Is it, dear?' said Matty, contracting her eyes on the dress and looking almost exactly like her sister for the moment. 'A new sort of old rose then.' She smiled at her niece, taking her disparagement of the dress at its literal value.

'Oh, come, Aunt Matty, there is nothing wrong with the colour. It is the one redeeming point.'

'Yes, dear?' said Matty, in questioning agreement, her eyes again on the dress.

'Oh dear, this garment! Is it destined to be a bone of contention in addition to its other disadvantages?'

'I tremble to think about its destiny,' said Clement, 'as its history up to date is what it is.'

'Why is magenta an offensive term?' said Mark. 'It seems to be.'

'It is odd how colours seem to owe their names to some quality in them,' said his aunt.

'Their names come about in quite a different way.'

'Now we don't want a philological lecture,' said Matty, showing her awareness of this.

'Magenta can be a beautiful colour,' said Sarah, in a tone of considerable feeling. 'I remember a dress I once had of a kind of brocade which we do not see now. Oh, it would have suited you, Mrs Gaveston.'

'Those old, thick brocades were very becoming,' said Matty.

'Aunt Matty does not restrict the application of her words,' said Aubrey, seeming to speak to himself, as he often did when he adopted adult phrase.

'I can imagine you looking regal in one of them, Aunt Matty,' said Justine, in a tone of saying something that was expected.

'Dinner is ready, ma'am,' said Jellamy.

'And not too soon,' said Clement. 'I hope that food will be a better subject for our attention than clothes.'

Edgar gave his arm to Sarah and led the way in conventional talk, which he maintained at whatever happened to be the cost to himself. Dudley adapted his step to Matty's with an exactness which involved his almost standing still, and kept up a flow of conversation at no personal expense at all. Matty was known to prefer Dudley to a son of the house, and her nephews supported her choice. Blanche and her father walked together, as the result of his suggestion that it might be their last opportunity, which was proffered to Thomas as an excuse and duly repudiated and accepted. They were assisted by Justine to link their arms and take their first steps – and indeed there might have been a less perilous association – and checked by her serious hand from a too precipitate advance. Justine herself went with Thomas, placing her free arm in Mark's.

'Now I do not require four partners, but I may as well use up one superfluous young man. Follow on, you other two. Aubrey can be the lady.'

'I place my delicate hand on Clement's arm and lean on his strength.'

Thomas gave a laugh and Clement shook off the hand and walked on alone.

'What a really beautiful room, dear!' said Matty to her sister, with appreciation brought to birth by the lights and wine and the presence of Dudley and Edgar. 'It is like a little glimpse of home, or if I may not say that, it is like itself and satisfying indeed to my fastidious eye. And my own little room seems to gain, not lose by the comparison. This one seems to show how beauty is everywhere itself. I quite feel that I have taken a lesson from it.'

'And one which was needed, from what I hear,' said Mark.

'Is that how happiness does not depend on surroundings?' said Aubrey.

Mark and Aubrey often talked aside to each other. Clement would join them when inclined to talk, Justine when inclined to talk aside. Aubrey also talked aside to himself.

'Naughty boys, making fun of the poor old aunt!' said Matty, shaking her finger at them without interest in what they said.

'What was it, Mark?' said Edgar, with a hint in his tone that his eldest son should speak for the ears of the table.

'I was agreeing with Aunt Matty, sir.'

'Yes, yes, we may praise our own home, may we not, when it is as good as this?' said his aunt.

'I was doing the same, Father – the same, sir,' said Aubrey, who had lately followed his brothers in this mode of address.

'Dear boy!' said Sarah, moved by the step towards maturity.

Edgar had come as near the reproof as he ever did. His hints were always heeded, and if it was not true that they were followed more than if he had raised his voice or resorted to violence, it was as true as it ever is. To Justine he never hinted a reproof, partly because of her sex and partly because he might have had to hint too much. Edgar did not love his children, though he believed or rather assumed that he did, and meted out kindness and interest in fair measure. He had a concerned affection for his wife, a great love for his brother and less than the usual feeling for himself. Dudley spent his emotion on his brother, and gave any feeling which arose in him to any one else. Justine believed that she was her father's darling, and Edgar, viewing the belief with an outsider's eye, welcomed it, feeling that it ought to be a true one, and made intermittent effort to give it support. Other people accordingly accepted it, with the exception of Dudley and Aubrey, who saw the truth. Clement would have seen it if he had regarded the matter, and Blanche liked the belief and accordingly cherished it.

'Does Jellamy manage by himself in this room now?' said Matty to her sister. 'It seems rather much for one person.'

'Yes, he has to, dear. It makes us slower, of course, but it cannot be helped. We have to be very economical.'

Matty glanced about the room with a faintly derisive smile.

'No, indeed, Aunt Matty,' said Justine, answering the look, 'you are quite wrong. Mother is speaking the simple truth. Strict economy is necessary. There is no pose about it.'

Matty lifted her brows in light enquiry.

'Now, Aunt Matty, you made the comment in all good faith, as clearly as you could have made it in words, intending it to be so taken. And that being the case, it must be so answered. And my answer is that economy is essential, and that Jellamy works single-handed for that reason.'

'Is it, dear? Such a lot of answer for such a little question.'

'It was not the question. It was the comment upon the reply.'

'No one is to make a comment but you, dear?'

'Justine does make them,' murmured Aubrey.

'Now, little boy, how much did you follow of it?'

'Upon my word, I do not follow any of it,' said Oliver.

Sarah leaned back almost in exhaustion, having followed it all. Her husband had kept his eyes down in order not to do so.

'Well, we mustn't get too subtle,' said Justine. 'They say that that is a woman's fault, so I must beware.'

Aubrey gave a crow of laughter, checked it and suffered a choke which exceeded the bounds of convention.

'Aubrey, darling!' said Blanche, as if to a little child.

'Now, little boy, now, little boy,' said Aubrey, looking at his sister with inflamed cheeks and starting eyes.

'Now, little boy, indeed,' she said in a grave tone.

'Poor child!' said Sarah.

'What shall I do when there is no one to call me little boy?' said Aubrey, looking round to meet the general eye, but discovering that it was not on him, and returning to his dinner.

'Aubrey has a look of Father, Blanche,' said Matty.

'I believe you are right, Aunt Matty,' said Justine, with more than the usual expression. 'I often see different likenesses going across his face. It has a more elusive quality than any of our faces.'

'I meant something quite definite, dear. It was unmistakable for the moment.'

'Yes, for the moment. But the moment after there is nothing there. It is a face which one has to watch for its fleeting moods and expressions. Would not you say so, Father?'

Edgar raised his eyes.

'Father has to watch,' said Aubrey, awaiting the proceeding with a grin.

'What a gallant smile!' said Clement, unaware that this was the truth.

'There, Uncle's smile!' said Justine.

The quality of the grin changed.

'And now Grandpa's! Don't you see it, Aunt Matty?'

'I spoke of it, dear. Yes.'

'And don't you, Father? You have to look for a moment.'

Edgar again fixed his eyes on his son.

'There, it has gone! The moment has passed. I knew it would.'

Aubrey had not shared the knowledge, the moment having seemed to him interminable.

'Father need not watch any longer,' he said, and would have grinned, if he had dared to grin.

'The process does not seem to be attended by adequate reward,' said Mark.

Clement raised his eyes and drew a breath and dropped his eyes again.

'Clement need not watch any longer either,' said Aubrey.

'Now, little boy, you pass out of the common eye.' Oliver turned his eyes on his grandson.

'The lad is getting older,' he said.

'Now that is indubitably true, Grandpa,' said Justine. 'It

might be said of all of us. And it is true of him in another sense; he has developed a lot lately. But do take your eyes off him and let him forget himself. This is all so bad for him.'

'He could not help it, dear,' said Blanche, expressing the thought of her son.

'Now are our little affairs of any interest to you?' said Matty, who had been waiting to interpose and at once arrested Sarah's eyes. 'If they are, we have our own little piece of news. We are to have a guest, who is to spend quite a while with us. I am looking forward to it, as I have a good deal of time to myself in my new life. There are many people whom I miss from the old one, though I have others to do their part indeed. And this is one of the first, and one whose place it would be difficult to fill.'

'We have found a corner for her,' said Oliver, 'though you might not think it.'

'She will have the spare room, of course, Father,' said Blanche. 'It is quite a good little room.'

'Yes, Mother, of course it is,' said Justine, in a low, suddenly exasperated tone. 'But it is to be like that. The house is to be a hut and the room a corner, and there is an end of it. Let us leave it as they prefer it. People can't do more than have what they would choose.'

Matty looked at the two heads inclined to each other, but did not strain her ears to catch the words. Sarah did so and controlled a smile as she caught them.

'Well, are you going to let me share this advantage with you?' went on Matty. 'It is to be a great pleasure in my life, and I hope it will count in yours. There is no great change of companionship round about.'

'Well, no, I suppose there is not,' said Justine. 'We are in the country after all.'

'So I am not a host in myself,' said Dudley.

'It is known to be better for the country to be like itself,' said Sarah, who found this to be the case, as it was the reason of her acquaintanceship with the Gavestons.

Thomas looked up with a faintly troubled face.

'This is a very charming person, who has been a great deal with me,' continued Matty, as if these interpositions did not signify. 'Her parents have lately died and left her at a loose end; and if I can help her to gather up the threads of her life, I feel it is for me to do it. It may be a thing I am equal to, in spite of my – what shall I call them? – disadvantages.'

'I always tell you that your disadvantages do not count, Aunt Matty,' said Justine.

'I feel that they do, dear. They must to me, you see. But I try not to let them affect other people, and I am glad of any assurance that they do not.'

'Do you mean Maria Sloane?' said Blanche. 'I remember her when we had just grown up and she was a child. She grew up very pretty, and we saw her sometimes when we stayed with you and Father.'

'She grew up very pretty; she has remained very pretty; and she will always be pretty to me, though she is so to everyone as yet, and I think will be so until she is something more.'

'It is odd to see Aunt Matty giving her wholehearted admiration to anyone,' said Justine to Mark. 'It shows that we have not a complete picture of her.'

'It also suggests that she has one of us.'

'It is pleasant to see it in a way.'

'We may feel it to be salutary.'

'She has only seen one or two of my many sides,' said Dudley.

'Miss Sloane has not married, has she?' said Blanche.

'No, she is still my lovely Maria Sloane. I don't think I could think of her as anything else. A rose by any other name would smell as sweet, but it seems that marriage might be a sort of desecration of Maria, a sort of plucking of the rose.' Matty ended on an easy note and did not look into anyone's face.

Sarah regarded her with several expressions, and Blanche with an easy and almost acquiescent one.

'Mrs Middleton has been plucked,' murmured Aubrey. 'Mr Middleton has plucked her.'

Thomas gave a kindly smile which seemed to try to reach the point of amusement.

'Is she well provided for, Aunt Matty?' said Justine in a clear tone.

Sarah nodded towards Justine at the pertinence of the question.

'I think so, dear; I have not heard anything else. Money seems somehow not to touch her. She seems to live apart from it like a flower, having all she needs and wanting nothing more.'

'Flowers are plucked,' said Aubrey.

'They look better when they are not, dear.'

'Money must touch her if she has all she needs,' said Clement. 'There must be continual contact.'

'Well, I suppose she has some, dear, but I think it is not much, and that she does not want any more. When you see her you will know what I mean.'

'We have all met people of that kind, and very charming they are,' said Justine.

'No, not anyone quite like this. I shall be able to show you something outside your experience.'

'Come, Aunt Matty, think of Uncle Dudley.'

'I could not say it of myself,' said her uncle.

'Yes, I see that you follow me, dear. But there is no one else who is quite as my Maria. Still you will meet her soon, and I shall be glad to do for you something you have not had done. I take a great deal from you, and I must not only take.'

'Is she so different from other people?' said Blanche, with simple question. 'I do not remember her very well, but I don't quite know what you mean.'

'No, dear? Well, we shall see, when you meet, if you do know. We can't all recognize everything.'

'Would it be better if Mother and Aunt Matty did not address each other in terms of affection?' said Mark. 'Is it supposed to excuse everything else? It seems that something is.'

'Well, perhaps in a way it does,' said Justine, with a sigh. 'Affection should be able to stand a little buffeting, or there would be nothing in it.'

'There might be more if it did not occasion such a thing,' said Clement.

'Oh, come, Clement, people can't pick their way with their intimates as if they were strangers.'

'It is only with the latter that they attempt it.'

'Father and Uncle behave like friends,' said Aubrey, 'Mother and Aunt Matty like sisters, Clement and I like brothers. I am not sure how Mark and Clement behave. I think like strangers.'

'No, I can't quite subscribe to it,' said Justine. 'It is putting too much stress on little, chance, wordy encounters. Our mild disagreement now does not alter our feeling for each other.'

'It may rather indicate it,' said Clement.

'We should find the differences interesting and stimulating.'

'They often seem to be stimulating,' said Mark. 'But I doubt if people take much interest in them. They always seem to want to exterminate them.'

'I suppose I spend my life on the surface,' said Dudley. 'But it does seem to avoid a good deal.'

'Now that is not true, Uncle,' said Justine. 'You and Father get away together and give each other of the best and deepest in you. Well we know it and so do you. Oh, we know what goes on when you are shut in the library together. So don't make any mistake about it, because we do not.'

Edgar's eyes rested on his daughter as if uncertain of their own expression.

'Do you live on the surface, Aunt Matty?' said Aubrey.

'No, dear. I? No, I am a person who lives rather in the deeps, I am afraid. Though I don't know why I should say "afraid", except that the deeps are rather formidable places sometimes. But I have a surface self to show to my niece and nephews, so that I need not take them down too far with me. I have a deal to tell them of the time when I was as young as they, and things were different and yet the same, in that strange way things have. Yes, there are stories waiting for you of Aunt Matty in her heyday, when the world was young, or seemed to keep itself young for her, as things did somehow adapt themselves to her in those days. Now there is quite a lot for Aunt Matty to talk about herself. But you asked her, didn't you?' Matty looked about in a bright, conscious way and tapped her knee.

'It was a lot, child, as you say,' said Oliver.

'Aubrey knew not what he did,' said Clement.

'He knew what he meant to do,' said Mark. 'Happily Aunt Matty did not.'

'We both used to be such rebels, your aunt and I,' said Blanche, looking round on her children. 'We didn't find the world large enough or the time long enough for all our pranks and experiments. I must tell you all about it some time. Hearing about it brings it all back to me.'

'Being together makes Mother and Aunt Matty more alike,' said Mark.

'Suppose Mother should become a second Aunt Matty!' said Aubrey.

'Or Aunt Matty become a second little Mother,' said Justine. 'Let us look on the bright side – on that side of things. Grandpa, what did you think of the two of them in those days?'

'I, my dear? Well, they were young then, as you are now. There was nothing to think of it and I thought nothing.'

'We were such a complement to each other,' continued Blanche. 'People used to say that what the one did not think of, the other did, and vice versa. I remember what Miss Griffin thought of us when she came. She said she had never met such a pair.'

'Miss Griffin!' said Justine. 'I meant to ask her to come in to-night and forgot. Never mind, the matter can be mended. I will send a message.'

'Is it worth while, dear? It is getting late and she will not be ready. There is not much left for her to come for. We will ask her to dinner one night and give her proper notice.'

'We will do that indeed, Mother, but there is still the evening. And she is just sitting at home alone, isn't she, Aunt Matty?'

'Why, yes, dear, she is,' said Matty with a laugh. 'When two out of three people are out, there must be one left. But I think she enjoys an evening to herself.'

'I see it myself as a change for the better,' said Oliver.

'Now I rather doubt that,' said Justine. 'It is so easy, when people are unselfish and adaptable, to assume that they are enjoying things which really offer very little. Now what is there, after all, in sitting alone in that little room?'

'Cosiness, dear, perhaps,' said Matty, with a change in her eyes. 'I have asked that same question and have had an answer.'

'The size of the room is well enough for one person,' said Oliver. 'That is indeed its scope.'

'Mother dear, I have your permission to send for her?' said Justine, as if the words of others could only be passed over.

'Well, dear, if you have your aunt's. But I don't know whom we are to send. The servants are busy.'

'There is no problem there; I will go myself. I have eaten enough and I will be back before the rest of you have finished.'

'One of the boys could go,' said Edgar.

'No, Father, I will leave them to satisfy their manly appetites. No one else will understand the exigencies of Miss Griffin's toilet, and be able by a touch and a word to put things right, as I shall.'

'Certainly no one else will undertake that,' said Mark.

'Should I come to help with the toilet?' said Aubrey.

'One of you should walk with your sister,' said Edgar, without a smile.

Aubrey rose with a flush, stood aside for Justine to pass and followed her out of the room.

'Oh, my baby boy has gone,' said Blanche, not referring to the actual exit.

'He has developed very much, dear,' said Matty. 'We shall have him like his brothers after all.'

'Why should he not be like them?'

'Well, he will be. We see that now.'

'He has always seemed to me as promising as either of them. A little less forward for his age, but that is often a good sign.'

'It must be difficult to judge of children,' said Mark, 'when their progress must count against them.'

'I can't think of a childhood with less of the success that spells failure,' said Clement.

'Slow and steady wins the race,' said Oliver, without actually following.

'He is not particularly slow. He is only different from other people, as all individual people are,' said Blanche. 'No one with anything in him is just like everyone else.'

'That cannot be said of anyone here, can it?' said her sister. 'We are an individual company.'

'Yes, but no one quite so much so as Aubrey. He is without exception the most individual person I have ever met.'

'Without exception, dear?' said Matty, bending her head and looking up from under it. 'Have you forgotten the two young rebels we were talking about just now?'

'No, but even you and I did not quite come up to him in originality. He is something in himself which none of the rest has been.'

'I think that is true,' said Mark.

'Now what do you mean by that? If you mean anything disparaging, it is very petty and absurd. I wish Justine were here to take my part. I can only repeat that there is something in Aubrey which is to me peculiarly satisfying. Edgar, why do you not support me?'

'You do not seem — you hardly seem to need my help.'

'But what do you think yourself of the boy? I know you always speak the truth.'

Edgar, who had lately hoped that his son might after all attain the average, broke this record.

'I see there is much — that there may be much in what you say.'

'Aubrey is the one with a touch of me in him,' said Dudley. 'I wish Justine were here too.'

'Hark! Hush! Listen,' said Matty. 'Do not make so much noise. Is it Maria's voice in the hall? Blanche, do ask your boys to stop talking. Yes, it is my Maria; Justine must have brought her. She must have arrived this evening. It is a full moment for me, and I am glad for you all to share it.' Matty broke off and sat with a listening expression and set lips.

'What a pity for her to come like this,' said Blanche, 'with dinner nearly over! I hope she has had something to eat, but Miss Griffin will have seen to that.'

'Yes, Miss Griffin will have cared for her, but I am here to give her welcome. And I cannot get my chair away from the table; I cannot manage it; I am dependent upon others; I must sit and wait for help. Yes, it is her voice. Sometimes patience is very hard. Thank you, Dudley; thank you, Edgar; I knew I should not wait long. No one else, Jellamy; too many cooks spoil the broth. I am on my feet now, and I can arrange my lace and touch my hair and make myself look my best, vain person that I am; make myself look like myself, I should rather say, for that is all my aim.'

'What relation is this friend to you all?' said Sarah, leaning towards Blanche.

'No relation, only an old friend. She lived near to our old home and my sister saw a good deal of her.'

Sarah gave a grateful nod and leaned back, ready for the scene. Justine spoke in the doorway.

'Now, I am simply the herald. I claim no other part. I found Miss Sloane already in the lodge and Miss Griffin at a loss how to manage the situation. So I took it into my own hands. And I feel a thought triumphant. I induced Miss Sloane, tired as she was, travel stained and unwilling as she was, harassed and mothered by crossing letters and inconsistent trains, to come and join us tonight. Now do you not call that a success? Because it was a hardly earned one. And now you can all share the results.'

A tall, dark woman of fifty entered the room, came towards Matty with a swift but quiet step, exchanged a natural embrace and looked round for her hosts. Blanche came forward in the character; Matty introduced the pair with an air of possession in each; Miss Griffin watched with the open and almost avid interest of one starved of interest and accordingly unversed in its occasions, and Justine took her stand at her side with an air of easy friendship.

'I do not need an introduction,' said Blanche. 'I remember you so well, Miss Sloane. I am afraid that my daughter has asked rather much of you, but we do appreciate your giving it to us.'

'Miss Sloane has made a gallant capitulation, Mother, and does not want credit for it any more than any other generous giver.'

'It is more than we had a right to expect,' said Edgar.

'It is certainly that, Father. So we will take it in a spirit of simple gratitude.'

'Well, stolen waters are sweet.'

'Bravo, Father!' said Justine, smiling at Miss Griffin. 'He comes up to scratch when there is a demand on him.'

'I have less right to expect what I am having,' said the guest, in a voice which did not hurry or stumble, shaking hands with several people without hastening or scamping the observance. 'I am a travel-worn person to appear as a stranger.'

'It is only a family gathering, Miss Sloane,' said Justine. 'We honestly welcome a little outside leavening.'

'We are glad indeed to see you, my dear,' said Oliver, who had got himself out of his chair. 'You are a good person to set eyes on. I do not know a better.'

'For heaven's sake sit down, Miss Sloane,' said Justine, when they reached the drawing-room. 'I shall feel so guilty if you continue to stand.'

'Now I am dependent upon help to get into a place by my guest,' said Matty, in a clear tone. 'I cannot join in a scramble.'

'Poor, dear Aunt Matty, the help is indeed forthcoming. And, boys, you must see that Miss Griffin has no chair. Thank you, Uncle; I knew you would not countenance that.'

Maria Sloane was a person who seemed to have no faults within her own sphere. She had a tall, light figure, large, grey eyes, features which were good and delicate in their own way rather than of any recognized type, and an air of finished and rather formal ease, which was too natural ever to falter. Matty had said that money seemed not to touch her, and that when they saw her they would understand; and Edgar and Dudley and Mark saw her and understood. Justine and Sarah thought that her clothes were of the kind of simplicity which costs more than elaboration, but she herself knew that when these two qualities are on the same level, simplicity costs much less. Blanche simply admired her and Miss Griffin welcomed her coming with fervid relief. She had lost a lover by death in her youth, and since then had lived in her loss, or gradually in the memory of it. Her parents had lately died, and she had left the home of her youth with the indifferent ease which had come to mark her. She believed that nothing could touch her deeply again, and losing her parents at the natural age had not done so. Her brothers and sisters were married and away, and she now took her share of the money and went forth by herself, seeing that it would suffice for her needs, rather surprised at herself for regretting that they must be modified, and welcoming a shelter in the Seatons' house while she adapted herself to the change. She had rather felt of herself what Matty said of her, that she lived apart from money like a flower, but she had lately realized that not even the extreme example of human adornment was arrayed as one of these.

'Confess now, Miss Sloane,' said Justine. 'You would rather be in this simple family party than alone in that little house. Now isn't it the lesser of two evils? I think that nothing is so hopeless as arriving after a long journey and finding the house empty and a cheerless grate, and everything conspiring to mental and moral discomfort.'

'Has Justine had that experience?' said Mark. 'If so, we are much to blame.'

'That could hardly have been the case, dear,' said Matty, 'with Miss Griffin and Emma in the house.'

'I meant metaphorically empty and cheerless. We all know what that means.'

'We are even more to blame,' said Mark.

'Make up the fire, Aubrey dear,' said Blanche, following the train of thought.

'It is metaphorically full,' said her son from a chair.

There was laughter, which Aubrey met by kicking his feet and surveying their movement.

'Get up and make up the fire,' said Clement, who found these signs distasteful.

His brother appeared not to hear.

'Get up and make up the fire.'

'Now that is not the way to ask him, Clement,' said Justine. 'You will only make him obstinate. Aubrey darling, get up and make up the fire.'

'Yes, do it, darling,' said Blanche.

'Now I have been called darling twice, I will. Why should I be obliging to people who do not call me darling or little boy or some other name of endearment?'

There was further laughter, and Aubrey bent over the fire with his face hidden. This seemed a safe attitude, but Clement observed the flush on his neck.

'Don't go back to the best chair in the room.'

Aubrey strolled back to the chair; Clement intercepted him and put a leg across his path; Justine came forward with a swift rustling and a movement of her arms as of separating two combatants.

'Come, come, this will not do: I have nothing to say for either of you. Both go back to your seats.'

'Will one of you help me to move the chair for your mother?' said Edgar, who did not need any aid.

'Yes, sir,' said Aubrey, with almost military precision.

'Now I think that Aubrey came out of that the better, Clement,' said Justine.

'The other fellow doesn't seem to be out of it yet,' said Oliver, glancing at his second grandson. 'I am at a loss to see why he put himself into it.'

'Miss Sloane, what must you think of our family?'

'I have belonged to a family myself.'

'And do you not now belong to one?'

'Well, we are all scattered.'

'I do not dare to think of the time when we shall be apart. It seems the whole of life to be here together.'

Thomas lifted his eyes at this view of a situation which he had just seen illustrated.

'Do you belong to a family, Miss Griffin?' said Dudley.

'I did, of course, but we have been scattered for a long time.'

'I have lived in the same house all my life, and so has my brother,' said Edgar.

'I have lived in two houses,' said Blanche.

'I am just in my second,' said Matty, 'and very strange I am finding it, or should be if it were not for this dear family at my gates. The family at whose gates I am, I should say.'

'Why should you say it, Aunt Matty?' said Justine.

'What difference does it make?'

'I too have just entered my second,' said Oliver, 'though it hardly seemed worth while for me to do so. I had better have laid myself down on the way.'

'And you, Miss Sloane?' said Edgar.

'I am on my way to my second, which must be a very tiny one. It will be the first I have had to myself.'

'And you have not had your road made easier,' said Oliver. 'You have been dragged out of it in the dead of night, when you thought that one of your days was done. The way you suffer it speaks well for you.'

'I have an idea that a good many things do that for Miss Sloane,' said Justine. 'But you make me feel rather a culprit, Grandpa.'

'You have done a sorry thing, child, and I propose to undo it.

Good-night, Blanche, my dear, and good-bye I hope until to-morrow. If it is to be for ever, I am the more glad to have been with you again.'

'Father is tired,' said Blanche, who would never admit that Oliver at eighty-seven might be near the end of his days.

'I am tired too,' said Matty, 'but after such a happy evening with such a satisfying end. I thank you all so much, and I am sure you thank me.'

'We do indeed,' said Justine. 'You are tired too, Miss Griffin, and I am afraid after a very brief taste of happiness. But we will make up for it another time.'

'Oh, I am not tired,' said Miss Griffin, standing up and looking at Matty.

'Be careful, both of you, on this slippery floor,' said Blanche. 'I always think that Jellamy puts too much polish on it. Do not hurry.'

'We shall neither of us be able to do that again,' said Oliver.

Blanche followed her father and sister with her eyes on their steps, and perhaps gave too little attention to her own, for she slipped herself and had to be saved. Justine moved impulsively to Maria.

'Miss Sloane, I do hope that you are going to spend some time with them? It comes to me somehow that you are just what they need. Can you give me a word of assurance?'

'I hope they will let me stay for a while. It is what I need anyhow, a home and old friends at this time of my life.'

'And there are new friends here for you. I do trust that you realize that.'

'I have been made to feel it. And they do not seem to me quite new, as they are relations of such old ones.'

'Dear Aunt Matty, she does attach people to her in her own way.'

'We have enjoyed it so much, Mrs Gaveston. We shall have a great deal to think and talk of,' said Sarah, able to express her own view of the occasion.

'We need not thank you,' said Thomas, uttering the words with a sincere note and acting upon them.

'You did not mind the inclusion of Aubrey?' said Justine. 'It is so difficult to keep one member of the family apart, and we know Mr Middleton is used to boys.'

'Can that give him only one view of them?' said Mark.

'Oh, come, he would not have given his best years to them, if they had not meant something to him. I daresay he often finds his thoughts harking back to the old days.'

'His best years!' said Sarah, laughing at youth's view of a man in his prime.

'Mr Middleton, what do you think of the little boy?' said Justine in a lowered tone. 'Don't look at him; he is enough in the general eye; but would you in the light of your long experience put him above or below the level?'

Thomas was hampered in his answer by being forbidden to look at the subject of it, a thing he had hardly done.

'He seems to strike his own note in his talk,' he said in a serious tone, trying to recall what he had heard.

'Yes, that is what I think,' said Justine, as if the words had considerable import, 'I am privately quite with you. But quiet; keep it in the dark; tell it not in Gath. Little pitchers have long ears. You see I feel quite maternally towards my youngest brother.'

Thomas was able to give a smile of agreement, and he added one of understanding.

'Do you think that we are alike as a family, Miss Sloane?' said Blanche, willing for comment upon her children.

'Really, Mother, poor Miss Sloane! We have surely had enough from her to-night.'

Maria regarded the faces round her, causing Aubrey to drop his eyes with a smile as of some private reminiscence.

'I think I see a likeness between your brother-in-law and your youngest son.'

'A triumph, Miss Sloane!' said Justine. 'That is a great test, and you are through it at a step. Now you can turn to the rest of us with confidence.'

'But perhaps with other feelings,' said Mark. 'Miss Sloane will think that we have one resemblance, an undue interest in ourselves.'

'In each other, let us say. She will not mind that.'

'I think there are several other family likenesses,' said Maria.

'And they are obvious, Miss Sloane. Quite unworthy of a discerning eye. You have had the one great success and you will rest on that. Well, I think that there is nothing more fascinating than pouncing on the affinities in a family and tracing them to their source. I do not pity anyone for being asked to do it, because I like so much to do it myself.'

'Must it be a safe method of judging?' said Clement.

'Now, young man, I have noticed that this is not one of your successful days. I can only assure Miss Sloane that you have another side.'

It now emerged that Matty and her father had reached the carriage, and the party moved on with the surge of a crowd released. Justine withheld her brothers from the hall with an air of serious admonishment, and assisted Edgar and Blanche and Dudley to speed the guests.

'Good-bye, Miss Griffin,' she called at the last moment. 'That is right, Uncle; hand Miss Griffin into the carriage. Good-night all.'

The family reassembled in the drawing-room.

'Now there is an addition to our circle,' said Justine.

'Indeed, yes, she is a charming woman,' said Blanche. 'I had not remembered how charming. It is so nice to see anyone gain with the years, as she has.'

'I believe I have been silent and unlike myself,' said Dudley. 'Perhaps Justine will explain to her about me, as she has about Clement.'

'Indeed I will, Uncle, and with all my heart.'

'I find that I want her good opinion. I do not agree that we should not mind what other people think of us. Consider what would happen if we did not.'

'Miss Sloane behaved with a quiet heroism,' said Mark.

'Under a consistent persecution,' said his brother.

'Oh, things were not as bad as that,' said Justine. 'She did not mind being asked to look at the family. Why should she?'

'She could hardly give her reasons.'

'And she was not actually asked to look at Aubrey,' said Mark. 'If her eyes were drawn to him by some morbid attraction, it was not our fault.'

'Don't be so silly,' said his mother at once.

'I really wonder that she was not struck by the likeness between you and Uncle, Father,' said Justine.

'We may perhaps accept an indifference to any further likeness,' said Edgar with a smile.

'We have to make conversation with our guests,' said his wife.

'I am glad that my look of Uncle flitted across my face,' said Aubrey.

'Little boy,' said Justine, pointing to the clock, 'what about Mr Penrose to-morrow? He does not want to be confronted by a sleepy-head.'

'Good-night, darling,' said Blanche, kissing her son without looking at him and addressing her husband. 'I do hope Matty enjoyed the evening. I could see that my father did. I am sure that everything was done for her. And Miss Sloane's arrival was quite a little personal triumph.'

'I could see it was,' said Mark, 'but I did not quite know why. It seemed that it had happened rather unfortunately.'

'Yes, dear Grandpa was quite content,' said Justine. 'He does like to be a man among men. We cannot expect him not to get older.'

'We can and do,' said Mark, 'but it is foolish of us.'

'I was sincerely glad of Aunt Matty's little success. It was something for her, herself, apart from what she was taking from us, something for her to give of her own. It seemed to be just what she wanted.'

'I think Miss Griffin will enjoy having Miss Sloane,' said Blanche, guarding her tone from too much expression.

'And I am glad of that from my soul,' said Justine, stretching her arms. 'I would rather have Miss Griffin's pleasure than my own any day. And now I am going to bed. I have enjoyed every minute of the evening, but there is nothing more exhausting than a thorough-going family function.'

'You need not work so hard at it,' said Clement.

'Clement has a right to speak,' said Mark. 'He has followed his line.'

'Yes, anyhow I have done my best. I could spare myself a good deal if I had some support.'

'Yes, that is true, Clement dear,' said Blanche. 'You ought to come out of yourself a little and try to support the talk.'

'Is it worthy of any effort?'

'If it is worthy of Justine's, it is worthy of yours. That goes without saying.'

'Then why not let it do so?'

'I had not realized that we were indebted to Clement for any regard of us,' said Edgar.

'I believe I had without knowing it,' said Dudley. 'I believe I felt some influence at work, which checked my spirits and rendered me less than myself.'

'Really, Clement, you should not do it,' said Blanche, turning to her son with a scolding note as she learned his course.

Clement walked towards the door.

'We will follow – perhaps we will follow our custom of parting for the night,' said his father.

'Good-night, Mother,' said Clement, slouching to Blanche as if he hardly knew what he did.

'Good-night, dear,' said the latter, caressing his shoulder to atone for her rebuke. 'You will remember what I say.'

'Father is sometimes nothing short of magnificent,' said Justine. 'The least said and the most done. I envy his touch with the boys. Good-night, Father, and thanks from your admiring daughter.'

Edgar stooped and held himself still, while Justine threw her arms about his neck and kissed him on both cheeks, a proceeding which always seemed to him to take some time.

'I was so proud of them all,' said Blanche, when her children had gone. 'I do see that Matty has much less than I have. I ought to remember it.'

'You ought not,' said Dudley. 'You ought to assume that she has quite as much. I am always annoyed when people think that I have less than Edgar, because he has a wife and family and an income and a place, and I have not. I like them to see that all that makes no difference.'

'Neither does it to you, because you share it all.'

'That is not the same. I like it to be thought that there is no need for me to share it, that that is just something extra. I hope Miss Sloane thinks so.'

'Has Miss Sloane as much as Blanche?' said Edgar, smiling.

'Yes, she has,' said his wife, with sudden emphasis. 'She is such a finished, satisfying person that anything she lacks is more than balanced by what she has and what she gives. I am not at all a woman to feel that everyone must have the same. I am prepared to yield her the place in some things, as she must yield it to me in others. And I think she will be such a good example for Justine.' Blanche put her needle into her work without alluding to her intention of going to bed, and observing Dudley retrieving her glasses and putting them into their case, seemed about to speak of it, but let the image fade. 'I mean in superficial ways. It is the last thing we should wish, that the dear girl's fundamental lines should be changed. We are to have breakfast half an hour later: did I remember to tell Jellamy? I must go and see if Aubrey is asleep. Good-night, Edgar; good-night, Dudley. I hope my father has got to bed. He seemed to be feeling his age to-night. If you are going to talk, don't sit up too long. And if you smoke in the library, mind the sparks.'

'We must be a little later than Blanche means,' said Dudley, as he brought the cigars to his brother and sat down out of reach of them himself. 'I want to talk about how Matty behaved. Better than usual, but so badly. And about how Miss Sloane behaved. Beautifully. I do admire behaviour; I love it more than anything. Blanche has the behaviour of a person who has no evil in her; and that is the rarest kind, and I have a different admiration for it.'

'I fear we cannot say much for Clement on the point.'

'We will not say anything. The less said about it, the better, and it is silly to say that and then talk about it.'

'Do you think he is developing on the right lines?'

'People don't alter at his age as much as older people think.'

'How old is he?' said Clement's father, wishing to know at this stage.

'Twenty-six the month before last. The change now must be slow. Perhaps the lad ought to be a grief to me, but I don't suffer a great deal; I hardly even think of him as the lad. To tell you the truth, I feel so young myself that I hardly feel I am any older than he is; but you will not tell anyone that. And now I have made one confession, the ice is broken and I should be able to make another. But do not look at me or I could not make it. You are looking at me, and for the first time in my life I cannot meet your eyes. Why don't you tell me to sit down quietly on that little stool and tell you everything?'

'Well, do that.'

'You know my old godfather?'

'The one who is ninety-six?'

'Yes, that one; I have no other. At least, of course people have two godfathers, but the other is dead. And now this one is dead too. I hope he was not feeling his age, but I expect he felt as young as Clement. You know he had no children?'

'Yes, I had heard it, or I think I had. Has he left you any money?'

'Edgar, is it possible that your thoughts have run on sordid lines?'

'I had not thought of it until this moment.'

'I am glad of that. I should not like to feel that I had lost my brother. It would be quite different from losing a godfather.'

'It would in the matter of money,' said Edgar, with his short laugh. 'Is it surprising that a childless man should leave money to his godson?'

'Yes, very. People have not any money. And they always have a family. It is very rare to have the first and not the second. I can't think of another case, only of the opposite one. We see that Matty has relations.'

'I did not know that he had much money.'

'I see you will feel the shock as well. I am not alone in my distress.'

'Why is it distress? Why not the opposite feeling?'

'Edgar, you must know that money is the cause of all evil. It is the root of it.'

'How did he get so much?'

'He speculated and made it. I knew he speculated, but I thought that people always lost every farthing. And it is wrong to speculate, and he has left the fruits of his sin to me.'

'The sins of the father are visited upon the children. And in default of them there is a godson.'

81

'Unto the third and fourth generation. But I expect they have generally lost it all by then.'

'Can you bring yourself to tell me how much it is?'

'No. You have only brought yourself to ask.'

'Is it very much?'

'Yes.'

'How can I help you?'

'I must leave it to you. You have never failed me yet.'

'Shall we wait and look at *The Times*?'

'No, that would imply a lack of confidence. There have never been secrets between us.'

'Is it as much as a thousand a year?'

'Yes.'

'As much as fifteen hundred?'

'Yes.'

'As much as three thousand?'

'No. How easy it is after all! It is about two. I am glad you have not failed me. Now our danger point is past, and we know that we can never fail each other.'

'Those letters you have had in these last days? That one you went away to answer?'

'I see there has been no secret between us.'

'It will make a great deal of difference, Dudley.'

'Yes, it will. I am not going to pretend that I don't think much of it. I think too much, as is natural. And I am not going to refer to it as a nice little fortune. I think it is a large one, though I am rather ashamed of thinking it. I don't know why people do such aggravating things. It must be because money brings out the worst in them. I shall never even say that I am a comparatively poor man. I have actually begun to push the thought from me.'

The door opened and Blanche appeared with a lamp, pale and different in the half light, her loose, grey hair and straight garments giving her the look of a woman from another age.

'What are you talking about all this time? I had no idea that you had not come up. I went to get something from Edgar's room and thought he must be asleep. I can never get to sleep myself while I know that other people are about. I am so afraid of fire. You know that.'

'Indeed I did not, Blanche,' said Dudley. 'At least, I thought that you slept in spite of your fear, like everyone else.'

'I thought the same, assumed it,' said Edgar.

'I cannot sleep when I feel that people are doing their best to set the house in a blaze every moment. How could I?'

'I don't see how you could. I did not know that Edgar did that when he sat up. It seems sly somehow, when he never does it in the day. And it does show that he ought to be in bed. But I do my best with quite different things. You can sleep in peace when you know that I am about.'

'You will accept our excuse when you hear it, Blanche. Dudley has been left a fortune – a sum of money by his godfather.'

'He hasn't,' said Blanche in a petulant tone. 'Not large enough to make all that talk and keep you up half the night. I know he was quite a poor man; I did not know why anyone had him for a godfather. Now come upstairs, both of you, and put out the lamps and push back the coals, as Dudley implies that he does it, and let us hear about it in the morning.'

The brothers occupied themselves with these measures.

'How much is it?' said Blanche, shading her lamp with her hand and speaking as if she might as well hear while she waited.

'It is a large sum, my dear, really very large. You must be prepared.'

'How much is it? It is very nice if it is large. I saw his death in the papers, and meant to speak about it and forgot. He was over a hundred, wasn't he?'

'He was ninety-six,' said Dudley, 'but that is old enough to make it excusable to forget his death.'

'How much is it? Why do you not tell me? Is there some mystery?'

'No, there is not; I wish there were; I hate having to manage without one. Edgar, you are failing me at last.'

'It is two thousand a year,' said Edgar, 'or probably about that sum.'

'Two thousand pounds a year?'

'Yes, yes. About that, about two thousand pounds.'

'Two thousand pounds a year or two thousand pounds?'

'Two thousand pounds a year.'

'Why, how very nice!' said Blanche, turning to lead the way from the room, with her hand still over her lamp. 'When did you hear? Dear Dudley, I do congratulate you. It is just what you deserve. I never was so glad about anything. And you were wise not to talk about it before Matty. It sometimes upsets her to hear that people have much more than she has. We might be the same in her place. Well, no wonder you stayed up to talk about that. We must talk it all over in the morning; I shall quite look forward to it. Well I shall sleep very soundly after hearing this.'

Blanche, meaning what she said and about to act upon it, went upstairs, guarding her lamp, and the brothers followed, pausing to whisper outside their doors.

'We have seen things out of their true proportion,' said Dudley. 'How is it that our outlook is so material? I was prepared to toss on my bed, and really we ought to sleep particularly well. I thought when I saw Miss Sloane, that she and I lived apart from tangible things. And really we have only been kept apart from them. Well, you can't separate yourself from me on the occasion. All that I have is yours.'

A flash from Blanche's door sent Edgar into his room and Dudley on tiptoe to her side.

'Blanche, I am only waiting for the morrow, to come and pour it all into your lap. And I am sure the house is not in a blaze.'

'Good-night, dear Dudley,' said Blanche, smiling and closing her door.

Chapter 4

'Well, has your uncle told you his news?' said Blanche at breakfast, as she moved her hands uncertainly amongst the cups. 'I heard it last night and I found it quite a tonic. I was feeling so very tired and it quite pulled me up. I slept so well and I still feel quite stimulated. I have been looking forward to talking about it.'

'What is it?' said Mark. 'Is Uncle going to be married?'

'No, of course he is not. What a thing to ask! There are other kinds of news.'

'Well, I must say, Mother, it occurred to me,' said Justine. 'What interpretation do you want put upon your words? That would be quite a natural one. I was already feeling a mingled sense of excitement and coming blank. And people were springing to my mind as likely candidates. As you have created the void, you owe it to us to fill it.'

'Perhaps your uncle would like to tell you himself.'

'No, I should not; I do not talk about my own affairs. I have come down early on purpose to hear you do it.'

'Or perhaps they would like to guess?'

'Really, Mother, we are not so young. And there is nothing to put us on the track. If Uncle has neither become engaged nor been left a fortune, we clearly cannot guess.'

'I think you can,' said Edgar. 'Indeed you have almost done so.'

'Have I? Oh, dear Uncle!' said Justine, springing up and hurrying round the table to Dudley. 'Dear, dear Uncle, who have given all your mind and your life to other people, to think that you have something for yourself at last! I would rather it were you than anyone else in the world. Far, far rather than that it were me.'

'I would rather it were me too.'

'I know you wouldn't. You would rather it were anyone and everyone. But it isn't this time. You are the hero of this occasion. And utterly rejoiced we all are that it is so.'

Blanche glanced from her daughter to Dudley with eyes of modest but irrepressible pride.

'We should like to know just at what we are to rejoice,' said Clement.

'I should not; I am quite indifferent. I just like to know that a piece of luck has crossed Uncle's path; and what it is and how much it is can stand over while I savour the main truth. It is what I have always waited for.'

'I suppose we all wait in case we shall be left a fortune,' said Dudley. 'But I never heard of anyone's waiting for other people to be left one. Because why should they be? They have no claim. And we should spend part of ours on them, and what can they want more?'

'Yes, that is what you want it for,' said Justine, sighing. 'To spend it on other people. And we shall all share in it evenly and equally. It was idle to hope that you would have anything for yourself. It hardly becomes us to ask how much it is. Oh, what am I saying? What a pass your dealings with us have brought us to! Somebody say something quickly to cover my confusion.'

'Perhaps someone who does not assume that it is his as much as Uncle's, may put the question,' said Clement. 'Our interest in Uncle may lead us to that.'

'Well, who will do it?' said Mark.

'I cannot,' said Justine, leaning back. 'Leave me out of it.'

'You were hardly anticipating that fate.'

'They all feel sensitive about it,' said Blanche, smiling at Dudley. 'This is something outside their experience.'

'But why should they feel like that? I do, of course, because I have something which I have done nothing to earn, and which makes me one of those people who have too much, when some people have not enough to live on; and anyone would be sensitive about that. I expect that is partly why rich people say they are poor. But only partly: they really think they are poor. I begin to understand it and to think I am poor myself, really to see that I am. So no one need feel sensitive for my sake. There is no reason.'

'I need not say how I feel for my own,' said Justine. 'Oh yes, Father, you may look as if your only daughter could do and say no wrong. I crossed the bound that time.'

'I don't see how we are to hear the main thing,' said Clement.

'Can we ask who has left the money?' said Mark.

'My godfather,' said his uncle.

'The man who was nearly a hundred?'

'Well, he was ninety-six.'

'Well, we need feel no sorrow; that is one thing,' said Justine, as if further complication of feeling would be too much.

'Is it a million pounds?' said Aubrey.

'Now, little boy, you are not as young as that.'

Aubrey fell into silence as he found what he did by words.

'What proportion of a million is it?' said Clement.

'A terribly small one,' said Dudley. 'About a twentieth, I should think. It is really very small. I have quite got over my sensitiveness and am afraid that people will think I am better off than I am. I see now how that happens. I am sorry I have so often said that people can surely afford things, when they are so well off. I feel so much remorse. I really don't like inheriting so little, except that now I suppose I should starve without it.'

'Oh, we shall not find it so very little. Make no doubt about that,' said Justine, meeting the general laughter with her own. 'Well, why should we not speak the truth after all?'

'You have seen no reason why you should not speak it,' said Clement. 'I mean, as you see it. Don't sit grinning at me, Aubrey. It makes you look more vacant than usual.'

'It is an immense family event,' said Mark. 'I mean a great event for Uncle. It seems that we can not speak without tripping, that all words mean the same thing.'

'I hope you are not all forgetting your breakfast,' said Blanche.

'I am so ashamed of being excited and toying with my food,' said Dudley. 'And all about my own little affairs! I have explained how little they are. I am grateful to Justine for taking the matter as concerning us all. It makes me feel less egotistic, sitting here chasing morsels round my plate.'

'Would you like something fresh and hot, sir?' said Jellamy, who had stood behind the table with prominent eyes, and now spoke as if any luxury would be suitable for Dudley in his new situation. 'Shall I give the word to Cook, ma'am?'

'No, you may go now. We have not really needed you all this time. We will ring if we want anything.'

'No, ma'am; yes, ma'am,' said Jellamy, going to the door with a suggestion of coat-tails flying.

'Jellamy has had a good half-hour,' said Mark, 'and will now have another.'

'Well, we have all had that,' said his sister.

'You have had the best,' said Clement. 'No one has been left anything but you and Uncle, and he has had his hour already.'

'That is unworthy, Clement. And there is something I do not like in the tone of the speech. Father, are you not going to say a word on the great occasion? We know it is greater to you in that it concerns Uncle and not yourself. And we seem to want your note.'

87

'Father said all that he felt last night,' said Blanche, unsure of her husband under the demand.

'What did the godfather die of?' said Clement, with a retaliatory note, as if to add a touch of trouble and reproach.

'Of old age and in his sleep,' said Dudley.

'He has shown us every consideration,' said Mark, 'except by living to be ninety-six.'

'I have been kept out of my inheritance too long, I might have saved by now, and then I should not have had so little. But I must conquer any bitterness.'

'There is little Mr Penrose,' said Justine. 'Aubrey, you can put all this excitement out of your head.'

'Perhaps I can have a full-sized tutor now.'

'Now, now, none of that. This makes no difference to you, except that you rejoice with Uncle. Apart from that you can just forget it.'

'He can indeed,' said Blanche, looking up. 'Are you paying attention, Aubrey?'

'Good-morning, Mrs Gaveston; good-morning, Mr Gaveston. May I offer you my congratulations upon the piece of news which has just come to my ears? Good-morning, Mr Dudley; I feel that I should have addressed you first on this occasion.'

'So you meet an occasion when you do not find me second to my brother.'

'Oh, I do not know that, Mr Dudley,' said Mr Penrose, laughing. 'I have never had any feeling of that kind. One naturally comes to the elder brother first. That has been all the distinction in my mind.'

'So good news runs apace,' said Edgar.

'How did you hear, Mr Penrose?' said Justine.

'From your manservant at the door. I do not generally talk to the man, but to-day he addressed me and volunteered the information. And if I may say so, he was full of the most pleasant and spontaneous goodwill towards the family.'

'I think we could not expect him to be silent upon such a piece of news.'

'Indeed no, Miss Gaveston,' said Mr Penrose, laughing. 'Not upon the accession of a quarter of a million to the family. It would indeed be much to expect.'

'It is about a twentieth of a million,' said Dudley.

'Well, well, Mr Dudley, putting it in round numbers.'

'But surely numbers are not as round as that. What is the good of numbers? I thought they were an exact science.'

'Well, taking the bearing of the sum upon ordinary life, shall we say?'

'No, we will not say it. We will say a twentieth.'

'Well, we may as well be numerically accurate,' said Mr Penrose, not pretending to appreciate any further difference. 'Come, Aubrey, we must be setting out. I suppose, Mr Gaveston — I suppose this modification of your affairs will not affect your plans for Aubrey's education?'

'No, no, not at all. As far as I can see, not at all.'

'Oh, no, Mr Penrose, not in the least,' said Justine. 'There is no difference in Aubrey's prospects.'

'Thank you, Miss Gaveston, thank you. You do not mind my asking? It is best to be clear on such a matter.'

'Poor, little Mr Penrose, he went quite pale,' said Justine. 'It would be sad if our rise in fortune should spell disadvantage for him.'

'Let us talk of something else,' said Dudley. 'We have had enough of me and my affairs. Of course I don't mean that. I am so worried about the confusion in people's minds. Mr Penrose has thoroughly upset me. You don't think he has any influence on Aubrey?'

'None,' said Mark.

'Oh, I am sure he has,' said Blanche, who had half heard.

'Well, that would be rather much to expect,' said Justine, 'that a tutor should be accepted as an influence by a pupil. But dear Uncle! I don't think I have seen you so much engaged with your own experience in all my life.'

'There, wealth has already ruined me. And I have not got wealth. I must be in the stage where I only have its disadvantages. I have heard of that. Do you think that people will think more of me or less?'

'More of you,' said Clement.

'Yes, well, I think we can hardly expect them not to do that in a way,' said Blanche.

'So they have not thought as much of me as they could?'

'I am sure they have in one sense, in any sense that matters.'

'Little Mother, you are coming out very nicely on this occasion,' said Justine. 'We could not have a better lead. And the occasion is something of a test.'

Blanche gave her daughter a rather absent smile, put her needle into her work and rose and went to the window.

'Father and Matty, Edgar! I thought I caught a glimpse of them. Coming up the drive! Both of them and on foot! It must have taken them half an hour. What can it be?'

'I will go out and help them to come in,' said Justine.

'What can Justine do?' said Clement. 'Carry them in, in her strong young arms?'

'It would be a useful piece of work,' said Mark. 'They can hardly be fit to take another step.'

'Oh, I am not at all ashamed of being strong!' called his sister. 'I have no wish to be the other thing. It would seem to me a very odd ambition. I like to be a good specimen physically, as well as in every other way.'

'I think we might all like that,' said Edgar, smiling and at once changing his tone. 'If arms are needed we all have them.'

'I will go,' said Dudley. 'I must keep my simple ways. I must not let myself become different. That sounds as if I have admired myself, and in a way I have.'

'Now, Grandpa dear, come in,' said Justine, keeping her eyes on Oliver as if to see that he followed her direction. 'We will have you established in a minute. Don't have any misgiving.'

'Thank you, my dear, you take it all off me; I have none.'

'Well, dear ones all,' said Matty, pausing in the door as if she could go no further, 'so here is a great occasion. I am come to share it with you, to rejoice in your joy. I could not remain in my little house and feel that so much had come – so much more had come to you in your big one, without coming to add my sympathy to all you have. For your happiness is mine. It shall be. And I shall have plenty if I can find it like that. And it is a lesson I have learnt, one that has come my way. And it isn't a hard lesson, to rejoice in the good of those so dear.'

'My dear, nothing has come to us. It is to Dudley,' said Blanche, emerging from her sister's embrace.

'Yes, and there is a difference, isn't there?' said Matty in an arch manner. 'And we are all to see it? Well, we can't, and that is flat, as the boys would say. And that is a great compliment to him and to you.'

'When do we say it?' said Mark.

'You can take that view too readily, Aunt Matty. Of course there is a difference,' said Justine.

'But Justine ought to sympathize with Aunt Matty in the idea,' said Aubrey.

'Of course, yes, of course,' said Matty, looking at Dudley. 'And you will let them say so? Well, I will not, I promise you. I will guard your reputation, I who know you almost as a brother. My sister's brother must be partly mine, as Blanche and I have always shared our good things. Now let me get to a chair and have my share of the news.'

'How did you hear?' said Clement.

'Well, well, little birds flit about the chairs of people who are tied to them. And it would be rather a sad thing if they did not, as they would be the last to hear so much, when it seems that they ought to be the first. So the news came, I won't say how.'

'I will do so,' said her father. 'It came through a tradesman's lad, who comes to our house after yours, or who comes to it on the way to yours and to-day chose to come again on his way back.'

'So Jellamy was the bird,' said Mark.

'Well, anyhow we heard,' said his aunt. 'But I should have liked to hear it from one of you, coming running down to tell me.'

'We should have been down in a few minutes,' said Justine.

'Would you, dear? But the minutes passed and nobody came. And so we came up to hear for ourselves.'

'A bold step for anyone tied to a chair,' muttered Clement.

'And came on foot!' said Blanche. 'Whatever made you do that?'

'Well, dear, what were we to do?' said her sister, laughing and glancing at Edgar.

'You could have waited a little while.'

'Well, it is true that that occupation palled,' said Oliver.

'I expect Miss Griffin was very interested,' said Justine.

'Well, now, let us settle down to hear the story,' said Matty, in a tone of leaving a just annoyance, smoothing her dress in preparation for listening. 'The full news of this happy quarter of a million. Let us hear it all from the first.'

'My dear, it is not as much as that. It is not a quarter as much; it is about a fifth as much,' said Blanche. 'It is barely a fifth. It is about a twentieth of a million.'

'Is it, dear? I am afraid they do not convey much to me, these differences between these very large sums. They have no bearing upon life as I know it.'

'But it is just as well to be accurate.'

'Well, you have been so, dear. So now tell me all about it. The exact sum makes no difference.'

'Of course it does. The one is precisely four times the other.'

'Well, but we don't have to think of proportions, after people have everything that they can have,' said Matty, giving a glance round the room as if this appeared to her to be already the case.

'But you can't have everything you can have, from a moderate fortune belonging to somebody else.'

'Oh well, dear, moderate. Your life has altered you more than I thought. Altered your attitude: of course you yourself are always my old Blanche. But a quarter of a million or some other proportion of one! We were not brought up to differentiate between such things. And belonging to somebody else! Dudley and I know better.'

'It is not a quarter of a million or some proportion of one. I said it was barely a twentieth,' said Blanche, her voice unsteady.

'You might say that fifty pounds is a proportion of one,' said Mark.

'I had better go and lie down,' said Dudley. 'I may feel better when I get my head on the pillow.'

'I don't care which it is,' said Justine. 'A simple life for me.'

'Yes, and for me too, dear,' said her aunt. 'I always feel that in my heart.'

'And keep it in your heart then,' said her father.

'Well, let me hear all about it,' said Matty, tapping her knee. 'I have asked more times than I can count.'

'Calculation does not seem to be Aunt Matty's point,' said Mark.

'I want to hear the beginning, the middle and the end. Not the exact sum; I won't press that; but the romance of it from the first. That would be a small thing to deny your invalid, who is dependent on you for the interest of her life.'

'Oh, how is Miss Sloane this morning?' said Justine, reminded of her aunt's other interests.

'That is another question, dear. Thank you, she is well and rested. And now for my own answer.'

'My godfather died and left no heir. That is the romance,' said Dudley.

'Left no heir!' said Matty, with a roguish look. 'He has left an heir indeed, and very much we all rejoice with him. There is the romance in truth.'

'That very old fellow,' said Oliver, 'who lived not far from us?'

'Yes, dear Grandpa, he was ninety-six,' said Justine, smoothing Oliver's sleeve in tender recognition of an age that was approaching this.

'He must have seen a lot,' said Oliver, making his own comparison.

'I remember him,' said Matty. 'Edgar and Dudley were staying at his house when Edgar and Blanche first met. I don't know why you object to the word, romance. It all seems to me to fit together in quite a romantic way. So now tell me all about it. When you heard, what you heard, how you heard. How you felt and what you said. You must know all the things that I want to be told.'

'They must by now,' said Oliver. 'I agree.'

'We heard at breakfast this morning. Mother and Father had heard from Uncle last night,' said Justine, in a running tone with a faint sigh in it. 'It is only an hour or two ago. And what did we feel? I declare it already eludes me.'

'That is really not fair on Aunt Matty,' said Mark.

'Then I heard nearly as soon as you,' said Matty, turning her eyes from her niece and nephew. 'But my feelings do not play such tricks on me; no, they were too strong and eager for you for that. But I want to know how Dudley felt when the truth broke upon him. That is the main issue of the story.'

'We heard last night, Edgar and I,' said Blanche. 'Edgar and Dudley sat up late, and when I came down to scold them, I was met by this piece of news. I told them it was quite a tonic. I slept so well after hearing it.'

Matty looked at her sister and simply turned to other people.

'But what did you feel, Dudley? That is the main point.'

'Uncle, gratify Aunt Matty's curiosity,' said Justine. 'She has every right to feel it.'

'Well, dear, more than a right, I think, and curiosity is an odd word. It is natural and sympathetic to feel an interest in an important change for a friend. It would not even be quite affectionate not to feel it.'

'No, no, Aunt Matty, you are all on the safe side. So now, Uncle.'

'I heard a few days ago and kept the matter in my heart.'

'Ah, that shows how deep it went.'

'Oh no, does it? If I had known that, I would have brought it out. I thought it showed that I did not attach enough importance to it, even to mention it. I meant it to be showing that.'

'Ah, we know what that kind of indifference means. Keeping the matter in your heart, indeed! And at last it got too big even for your big heart' – Matty gave Dudley a smile – 'and you revealed it to your second self, to Edgar. And didn't you have the tiniest feeling of interest? Not the least spark of excitement?'

'I had all the natural feelings. Shock, delight, excitement; compunction at having so much; worry lest I should be thought to have more than I had, though I did not know then how much reason there would be. Pleasure in what I could do for people; fear lest they should take it all for granted, or think I was conferring favours, and it does seem unlikely that they should avoid both. And then I told it all to Edgar, and the matter assumed its just proportions – you will remember that the sum is a twentieth of a million – and I went to bed feeling that my little affairs had a small place in the general scheme, and that it would all be the same a hundred years hence; which is not true, but it was right for me to feel it. And now I ought to say that that is the longest speech I have ever made, but I never know how people can be sure of that.'

'There, Aunt Matty, there is a proper effort,' said Justine.

Matty's swift frown crossed her face.

'You don't any of you seem to feel quite what I should have expected.'

'Well, no, child, I am rather of your mind,' said Oliver.

'We have not inherited anything,' said Blanche. 'It is Dudley who has had the good fortune.'

'A good fortune in two senses. And what do the two young men feel, whose prospects are now so different?'

'They are nothing of the kind,' said Blanche, with both her voice and her needle rising into the air. 'This had nothing to do with them, and they are not giving a thought to it, except to rejoice in their uncle's happiness.'

'I am not as bad as that,' said Dudley. 'Happiness depends on deeper things. Love in a cottage is the most important kind of love; no other kind is talked about so much. I can only hope to be allowed to share what I have with other people, and of course I shall feel that the generosity is theirs.'

'I am sure you will,' said Matty. 'And now what about the unchanged prospects of the two young men? Was I right or wrong in saying what I did?'

'You were wrong in saying it,' said her father. 'It was not a thing to say.'

'Well, was I wrong – incorrect in thinking it?'

'Your sister says that you were, her brother-in-law that you were not. You must decide.'

'Well, I decide that it was a true and natural thing to think, and therefore to say. And most heartily do I rejoice with them in the truth of it.'

'Clement and I have all we need,' said Mark. 'We should have no right or reason to ask for more.'

'And the people who do not ask for things, are the people who have them, I have heard. You would not ask, I am sure. Yes, I must not be denied my little bit of excitement for you. It is the one kind I have left, to let my spirits soar for other people, and I must be allowed to make the most of it. It is the best kind.'

'I suppose it is, Aunt Matty. Anyhow it is nice of you to feel it,' said Justine, 'but there doesn't really seem to be much need. I am with the boys there. We have our home and our happiness and each other, and the simple tastes and pleasures which are the most satisfying. We do not ask or need anything more. I am quite sorry for Uncle that it is so, because he would like nothing better than to pour out his all upon us. But our simple lot suffices us, and there it is.'

'They are all so self-reliant,' said Blanche, with mingled apology and pride. 'They have been brought up to be independent of things outside themselves.'

Matty gave her glance about the room, this time with an open smile.

'Yes, I see what you are thinking,' said her niece at once. 'We have been brought up in a beautiful and dignified home; that is the truth. I should be the last person to deny it. But it has become our background, and that means that we are independent of it in a way. Not that we do not love it; I do from the bottom of my heart. And that brings it to my mind that I should be glad for something to be done for the dear old house, to prevent its falling into decay. I have long wished that its faithful service could be repaid. It would be a relief to Father, who sees it as a life trust and not as his own in any personal sense, so that he would not really be taking anything for himself. And Mark feels about it in the same way. Yes, I think I may say that we should all be grateful for succour for the fine old walls which have sheltered us and our forebears.'

'Well, there is one bright spot in the darkness,' said Matty to Dudley, changing her tone as she spoke. 'I cannot but support my niece, though I must admit that my gratitude would have a personal quality.'

'But the house has sheltered me and my forebears too,' said Dudley. 'Perhaps it does not count.'

'Well, well, it may count a little. And anyhow it will cost a little. That must be your comfort.'

'What do you say, Father?' said Justine.

'I must say what you do, my dear; I cannot but say it. It is a thing that your uncle and I could do together.'

'Ah, that strikes the right note. That clinches the matter. You and Uncle can do it together. It stands that it will be done.'

'Better and better,' said Matty to Dudley with a smile.

'We can scarcely say that Father and Mark — that as a family we take nothing,' said Clement. 'The house hardly belongs to Father the less, that it will go to his descendants.'

'No, I do not feel that I can say it,' said Mark.

'No, you will not shirk your part as a benefited and grateful person,' said Matty, in a tone of approval and sympathy.

'That is hardly straight, Aunt Matty,' said Justine. 'I wish you would not let these touches of unfairness creep into your talk. It gives to all our response that little undercurrent of defensiveness. We are not ungrateful because we want something beautiful preserved, which will be of advantage to future generations as well as ourselves, and because we realize that that is the case. You have admitted to the same feeling.'

'I have it indeed, dear, but then I feel definitely grateful. It is a great thing in my life, this lovely background that I see behind you all, and feel behind myself at stated intervals. I should feel unthankful indeed if I did not appreciate it. And I ask your uncle to accept my gratitude for any service that he does to it.'

'The east walls are crying for attention,' said Edgar, as if his thought broke out in spite of himself. 'I have hardly dared to look at them, but they must be sinking. I can almost feel it; I know it must be the case. You and I might go round, Dudley, and sketch out a plan for the work. This — I find this one of the days of my life.'

Blanche looked up at her husband as if uncertain what she should feel.

'There, Uncle!' said Justine. 'I congratulate you. That is what you want. You have what you would ask.'

'Better still,' said Matty to Dudley. 'There is progress. I don't think you need fear.'

'Justine dear, will you fetch my silks from my room?'

'No, Mother, I can't be sent out of the room like that, even if I have been a little frank and definite and may be so again. You must know me by now, and if you want me you must take me as I am.'

'And as we cannot do without her, she has us in a tight place,' said Matty, retrieving her position.

'It is half past eleven,' said Blanche, relinquishing her work as if her thoughts had not returned to it. 'Matty dear, would you like anything? Or would Father? It is surprising how the time goes.'

'Well, I really don't think it is today,' said Justine. 'I should not have been surprised to find ourselves at the last stroke.'

'Well, dear, some coffee for me, and for Father a glass of wine and a sandwich,' said Matty, somehow implying that in the risen fortunes of the house such requirements would hardly count. 'I hope you are going to join us.'

'Yes, we will all have something; I think our nerves need it,' said Justine.

'Are you feeling guilty?' said Matty, in a low, mischievous tone to Dudley.

'Will Miss Seaton and Mr Seaton be staying to luncheon, ma'am?' said Jellamy.

'Yes. You will be staying, won't you, Matty? Father won't find it too much? He can have his rest.'

'We will quarter ourselves upon you,' said Oliver. 'You will put up with what comes to you to-day. I take it that you wouldn't alter it.'

'Yes, they will both be here for luncheon, Jellamy.'

'And Miss Sloane and Miss Griffin, Jellamy,' said Justine, throwing a glance from her chair.

'My dear, have you heard that?'

'No, Mother, I have just decided it. I think we need the effect of their presence.'

'But are they free, dear child?'

'Well, we can soon find out. If they are not, they cannot come, of course. But I fail to see what engagements they can have in a place where neither knows anyone.'

'But Miss Sloane may not care to come. What does Aunt Matty say? Miss Sloane is her guest.'

'Well, for that reason I should like to have her with me. It is a kind thought of Justine's. I was wondering if I could leave her alone, and how to send a message. But Miss Griffin finds it a change to be without us.' Matty's tone quickened and her eyes changed. 'And I find a certain relief in being only with my relations. So I will say what I mean in my family circle and feel it is said.'

'You will be better apart, if I may still depend on my eyes and ears,' said her father. 'I do not know what Maria makes of it all. I do not ask. She could not give a true answer and a false one would be no help. You forget the size of the house, though you talk of it.'

'Well, I am not used to it yet.'

'You would do well to become so.'

'Let me have my own way, Aunt Matty,' said Justine, sitting on the arm of her aunt's chair. 'Don't deny it to me because we have got a little across. Give it to me all the more for that.'

'Well, well, take it, dear. You know how I like you to have it.'

'You have your own way a good deal, Justine,' said Blanche.

'Oh, well, Mother, a mature woman, the only sister amongst three brothers, Father's only daughter! What can you expect?'

Edgar looked up as if to see how his own name had become involved.

'Everyone must rejoice with me to-day,' said Dudley. 'That always seems to me an absurd demand, but I am going to make it.'

'And if there is anyone for selfless rejoicing for other people, Miss Griffin is that person, if I know her,' said his niece. 'And I shouldn't be surprised if Miss Sloane has a touch of the same quality.'

'Suppose we keep people apart, dear,' said Matty in a light tone.

'Oh, Aunt Matty, Miss Sloane has not a touch of that feeling. She would not mind being coupled with Miss Griffin. Even being with her once told me that. I should think it is not in her.'

'But keep her apart, nevertheless, dear,' said Blanche, in a low voice that was at once reproving and confidential. 'She has nothing to do with anyone else.'

'I am not sure that she would say that,' said Justine audibly. 'She has the connection with Miss Griffin of a long friendship. I should say that she would be the first to recognize it.'

'Well, well, dear, are you going to run down and ask them?'

'No, no, not I this time,' said Justine, shaking her head. 'I am not always going to present myself as the bearer of such messages. It would mean that we thought too much of them altogether.'

'Clement and I will go,' said Mark. 'That will give a trivial air to the errand. And we can imply that we think little of it.'

'That should be easy,' said his brother. 'We have only to be natural.'

'Ah, that is not always so easy as you seem to think,' said Justine.

'Perhaps you find it too much so.'

'Well, run along, dears,' said Blanche, in a neutral manner. 'You can wait and bring them back.'

'If they consent to come, Mother,' said Justine, with a note of reproof.

'Well, you thought they had no other engagements, dear. Let the boys go now. It will be a breath of fresh air for them after their exciting morning. We can't have – nothing but excitement.'

'Do you know where to look?' said Matty to Dudley, in a mischievous aside.

'Mother talks as if we were guilty of some excess,' said Clement to his brother as they left the house. 'Our excitement has been for Uncle. Nothing has come to most of us.'

'A good deal has come to Father, and in a certain sense to me.'

'A good deal to you both. A house handed on intact is different indeed from one gaping at every seam, and sucking up an income to keep it over our heads. You are full of a great and solemn joy.'

'And my happiness is not yours?'

'Any satisfaction of mine must come out of my own life, not out of other people's. But I ought to have some of my own. Father's money will be set free and Uncle has no one to spend on but us.'

'What are your personal hopes?'

'Much as yours, except that they are on a smaller scale and yours are already fulfilled. I don't want a place or could not have one. But I do want a little house of my own in Cambridge. I hate the college and I am obliged to live in the town. And a little income to add to what I earn. Then I should not need to spend my spare time at home. I cannot suffer much more of Aubrey and Justine.'

'And I can?'

'Your prospects are safe. You have no right to speak.'

'I shall have nothing until Father dies, but the life which you must escape.'

'Your future is bound up in the place. Mine has nothing to do with it. The house is a halting place for me.'

'And for Justine and Aubrey what is it?'

'Aubrey is a child and Justine is a woman. There is no comparison.'

'Aubrey will not always be a child and Justine not always a young and dependent woman. I can imagine her in her own house as well as you.'

'Mine is the need of the moment.'

'So is mine. I could do with many things. But I don't know if we can make the suggestions to Uncle.'

'They may occur to him.'

'Images will have to come crowding on his mind.'

'I don't see why they should not. He must have seen our straitened life.'

'He must have lived it,' said Mark.

'You can make a joke of other people's needs, when your own are satisfied. He can hardly go on for ever, spending all he has on the house. All sorts of demands must arise. We have been held very tight and insensibly the bonds will be loosened.'

'When Father dies, you will have your share of what there is. Both he and Uncle must leave what they have to us.'

'And how long will that be to wait?'

'Clement, what manner of man are you?'

'The same as you, though you pretend not to know it. You can go in here and offer this invitation. Explain that we observe a piece of good fortune for one of us as a general festival.'

'I am in command of such a situation. You are right to imply that you are not.'

'There is Miss Griffin at the window. She is there whenever we come.'

'She sees the shadows of coming events. Such a gift would develop in her life.'

In due course the four emerged from the lodge and set off towards the house. Mark was ready to discuss the event; Clement was inclined to glance at Maria to judge of her view of it, and to try to talk of other things; Maria was lively and interested and Miss Griffin was alternately reflective and disposed to put sudden questions.

'Here is a fairy-tale piece of news!' said Maria, as she met the family. 'I shall always be glad to have heard it at first hand. We must thank you for our experience as well as congratulate you on yours.'

'Thank you, Miss Sloane. That is a pleasant congratulation indeed,' said Justine, turning to her brothers to continue. 'What a contrast to poor Aunt Matty's! What a difference our little inner differences make!'

'A quarter of a million pounds!' said Miss Griffin, standing in the middle of the floor. 'I have never heard anything like it.'

'Neither have I,' said Dudley. 'It is about a twentieth of a million.'

'A twentieth of a million!' said Miss Griffin, in exactly the same tone.

'About fifty thousand pounds.'

'Fifty thousand pounds!' said Miss Griffin, with the fuller feeling of complete grasp.

'We ought not to keep talking about the amount,' said Blanche. 'We value the thought and the remembrance.'

'But if we leave it out,' said Dudley, 'people will think it is so much more than it is.'

'I think it is better than that,' said Maria. 'It will not eliminate planning and contrivance from your life, and it will keep you in the world you know.'

'Sound wisdom,' said Justine. 'How it falls from unexpected lips!'

'I feel very comforted,' said Dudley. 'People may realize my true position after all.'

'It was deep sagacity, Miss Sloane,' said Justine. 'I daresay you hardly realize how deep. Words of wisdom seem to fall from your lips like raindrops off a flower.'

'Justine dear, was that a little frank?' said Blanche, lowering her voice.

'Well, Mother, pretty speeches always are,' said Justine, not doing this with hers. 'But I don't think that a genuine impulse towards a compliment is such a bad thing. It might really come to us oftener. And Miss Sloane is not in the least embarrassed. It is not a feeling possible to her. I had discerned that, or I had not taken the risk.'

'The impulse has come to Justine again,' said Mark to his brother.

'And embarrassment is a feeling possible to the rest of us.'

'Well, I have not been saying words of wisdom, perhaps,' said Matty, in a tone that drew general attention. 'But I have done my best to show my joy in others' good fortune. Though others is hardly the word for people with whom I feel myself identified. Contrivance had not struck me as one of the likely results, but if they like to enjoy the poverty of the rich, we will not say them nay. It is only the poverty of the poor which we should not welcome for them. We have that enough in our thoughts.' Matty's voice died away on a sigh which was somehow a thrust.

'I shall have to give to the poor,' said Dudley. 'It is a thing I have never done. It shows how nearly I have been one of them. I have only just escaped being always in Matty's mind.'

'A dangerous place to be,' said Mark.

'I suppose I shall subscribe to hospitals. That is how people seem to give to the poor. I suppose the poor are always sick. They would be, if you think. I once went round the cottages with Edgar, and I was too sensitive to go a second time. Yes, I was too sensitive even to set my eyes on the things which other people actually suffered, and I maintain that that was very sensitive. Now I shall improve things out of recognition, and then I can go again and not recognize anything, and feel no guilt about my inheritance.'

'No one can help being left money,' said Miss Griffin.

'That is not on any point,' said Matty lightly.

'I don't know, Aunt Matty; I don't think I agree with you,' said Justine. 'But I have disagreed with you enough; I will not say it.'

'Well, it may be as well not to let it become a habit, dear.'

'Justine dear, come and sit by me,' said Blanche.

'Oh, you mean to be repressive, Mother. But I feel quite irrepressible this morning. Uncle's good fortune sets my heart singing even more than yours or Father's would. Because he has been the one rather to miss things himself and to see them pass to other people, and to see it in all goodwill. And that is so rare that it merits a rare compensation. And that the compensation should come, is the rarest thing of all. "My heart is like a singing bird, whose nest is in a water'd shoot."'

'Are we all going to stay in the whole morning?' said Blanche. 'Justine, it is not like you to be without energy.'

'Surely an unjust implication,' said Mark.

'Well, we can hardly bring Miss Sloane and Miss Griffin up here, Mother, and then escort them out again at once.'

'They might like to join us in a walk round the park. I sleep so much better if I get some exercise, and I expect we shall sit and talk after luncheon.'

'An indulgence which can be expiated in advance by half an hour in a drizzle,' said Clement.

'Well, what do you feel, Miss Sloane?' said Justine.

'I should like to go with your mother.'

'And you, Miss Griffin?'

Miss Griffin opened her mouth and glanced at the fire and at Matty.

'Miss Griffin prefers the hearth. And I don't wonder considering the short intervals which she probably spends at it. So you set off with Miss Sloane, Mother, and the rest of us will remain in contented sloth. I believe that is how you see the matter.'

Blanche began to roll up her silks without making much progress. Justine took them from her, wound them rapidly round her hand, thrust them into the basket and propelled her mother to the door with a hand on her waist. Maria followed without assistance, and Blanche shook herself free without any change of expression and also proceeded alone. Matty at once addressed the group as if to forestall any other speaker.

'Now I must tell you of something which happened to me when I was young, something which this occasion in your lives brings back to me. I too might have been left a fortune. When we are young, things are active or would be if we let them, or so it was in my youth. Well, a man was in love with me or said he was; and I could see it for myself, so I cannot leave it out; and I refused him – well, we won't dwell on that; and when we got that behind, he wanted to leave me all he had. And I would not let him, and we came to words, as you would say, and the end of it was that we did not meet again. And a few days afterwards he was thrown from his horse and killed. And the money went to his family, and I was glad that it should be so, as I had given him nothing and I could not take and not give. But what do you say to that, as a narrow escape from a fortune? I came almost as near to it as your uncle.'

'Was that a large fortune too?' said Miss Griffin.

'It was large enough to call one. That is all that matters for the story.'

'You ran very near the wind, Aunt Matty,' said Justine. 'And you came out well.'

'I shall be obliged to take and not give, if no one will accept anything from me,' said Dudley. 'Because I am going to take. Indeed I have taken.'

'You have not been given the choice,' said Miss Griffin.

'Well, well, we all have that,' said Matty. 'But there is not always reason for using it. There is no obligation to seek out connections when there is no immediate family. This friend of mine had brothers.'

'I wish you would not put such thoughts into words,' said Dudley.

'I can't help wishing that he had not had them, Aunt Matty,' said Justine. 'You might have had a happier life or an easier one.'

'An easier later chapter, dear, but I do not regret it. We cannot do more than live up to the best that is in us. I feel I did that, and I must find it enough.' Matty's tone had a note of truth which no one credited.

'I find it so too,' said Dudley. 'My best is to accept two thousand a year. It is enough but I do wish that people would not think it is more.'

'Two thousand a year!' said Miss Griffin.

'Well, it is between a good many,' said Matty. 'It is so good when a family is one with itself. And you are all going to find it so.'

'To accept needs the truest generosity,' said Dudley. 'And I am not sure that they have it. I know that people always underrate their families, but I suspect that they only have the other kind.'

'It is that kind which is the first requirement,' said Clement.

'Clement, that remark might be misunderstood,' said Justine.

'Or understood,' said Mark.

'I don't think I should find any difficulty in accepting something I needed, from someone I loved. But I am such a fortunate person; I always have all I need.'

'There, what did I say?' said Dudley. 'An utter lack of true generosity.'

'I will go further,' said his niece. 'I will accept an insurance of the future of my little Aubrey. Accept it in my name and in that of Father and Mother. I think I am justified in going so far.'

'It is all very well to laugh, Clement,' said Dudley, 'but how will you look when it appears that your brothers have true generosity, and you have none?'

'I can do as they do and without having it. It seems to me to be the opposite thing that is needed.'

'Clement, be careful!' said Justine, in an almost stricken tone.

'People are always ashamed of their best qualities and describe them in the wrong way,' said Dudley. 'Clement will accept an allowance from me and let me forget that my generosity is less than his.'

'Then he is a dear, sensible boy,' said Matty.

'Sensible certainly,' said her nephew.

'Well, Clement, I don't know what to say,' said Justine.

'You can say what you will say to Mark and Aubrey.'

'Well, I suppose that is fair in a way, but it does seem that there is a difference. But I will say nothing. The matter is taken out of my hands.'

'It was never in them.'

'Now don't take that line with your sister. That does not make matters better.'

'I have no wish to improve them. I find them well enough.'

'I am afraid you do, Clement.'

'Now that is not sensible, dear, and perhaps not even quite kind,' said Matty.

'It seems fair that all three brothers should have something, if two have,' said Miss Griffin.

'Well, it is really a matter for the family.'

'Aunt Matty, don't snub Miss Griffin in public like that,' said Justine. 'That is certainly not quite kind.'

'My dear, you may have a way of coming between people, but between Miss Griffin and me there is our own relation.'

'I am afraid there is, Aunt Matty.'

There was a long silence.

'Dear, dear, money, money, money!' said Justine, leaning back and locking her hands above her head. 'Directly it comes in, away fly dignity, decency, everything.'

'Everything but true generosity,' said Mark.

'Dignity and decency depend up to a point on money,' said Clement.

'Indeed that is true,' said Dudley. 'You have only to go round the cottages. It seems absurd to say that money is sordid, when you see the things that really are.'

'And that come from the lack of it.'

'Why should it be sordid any more than any other useful thing?' said Matty.

'They say that it is a curse,' said Dudley, 'but I do not find it so. I like being a person to confer benefits. There, that is the worst.'

'Dear Uncle!' said Justine. 'Enjoy your money and your generosity and all of it. You have never had a chance before.'

'So you don't think that the things I gave, were more valuable than money. I knew that people never really did.'

'To talk about money's having no value is a contradiction in terms,' said Clement.

'Now I think that is honest, dear,' said Matty.

'Aunt Matty, you are going rather far in your implications,' said Justine.

'You do not go in for such things, dear, I know.'

Justine put back her head in mirth, the action so familiar in her aunt somehow throwing up her unlikeness to her.

'That may be fair, but we won't start another skirmish. And I don't take it at all as an insult, however it was meant. I am one for the direct and open line. Now here are the other elders, come in the nick of time to prevent our discussion from becoming acrimonious.'

'They are running it fine,' said Clement.

'Well, have you made up your minds how to spend your uncle's money?' said Oliver.

'Yes, we have,' said Clement, pausing a moment to get the plan of his speech. 'The house is to be put in repair for Father and Mark; there is to be an allowance for me; and something is to be done for Aubrey's future.'

'Oh!' said Blanche. 'Oh, it is too quick. I did not think it would all be arranged at once like that.'

'Would it be better for being delayed?'

'I don't know what to say. It does not seem right somehow. I really feel almost ashamed.'

'To tell you the truth, Mother, so do I,' said Justine. 'But I could not help it. I plead guilty to the suggestion about Aubrey's future, but otherwise I can hold myself apart.'

'As a benefited person, I feel that my tongue is tied,' said Edgar. 'The mention of me was adroit.'

'It was simply true,' said Clement.

'Dudley, I don't know what to say,' said Blanche. 'What can you think of them all?'

'I feel that we are drawn closer. They will not spoil things for me by letting me feel alone. I don't think Clement and I have ever been so close before. And I expect them to share my joy, and people ought not to share a feeling without sharing the cause of it. I should not think it is possible. And I should be ashamed of feeling joy over a thing like money, if no one felt it with me.'

'There is something in that, I suppose,' said Justine.

'Well, it is nearly time for luncheon,' said her mother. 'I suppose I must not say any more. We have had such a nice walk. I feel all the better for it and Miss Sloane has quite a colour. It was so kind of her to come with me. Father did you get your sleep?'

'I slept like a child, my dear, as is well for a person approaching his second childhood.'

'That is not the speech of someone doing that, Grandpa,' said Mark.

'Father, what a way to talk! Well, I must go and take off my things. Perhaps Miss Sloane would like to come with me. And then we should open these windows. You have all been in here all the morning.'

'With all our selfish hopes and desires,' said Clement. 'But I wonder that Justine has not been like a breath of fresh air in herself.'

'I expect she has,' said Blanche, patting her daughter's cheek.

'I have certainly been a breath of something, Mother, but I believe it has been felt to be more like a draught. But it may have been fresh and wholesome.'

'We did not talk about the good fortune all the time,' said Matty. 'We had our glimpse of other things. I gave them an early experience of my own, which amused them with its likeness to this one. Its likeness and its difference, shall we say? Well, what do you think of your aunt's varied history? I see you are not to be allowed to dwell on it. Your mother is directing our attention to more material things.'

'The luncheon will not improve by waiting, dear, and I like it to be nice for you all. Let the boys help you out of your chair.'

'Thank you, dears, Miss Griffin will do it. I am more used to her,' said Matty, forgetting that she had objected to Miss Griffin's presence. 'But she seems to be having a little nap. Wake up, Miss Griffin; even our pleasure days have their little duties, you know.' Matty's tone of rallying reproof changed as she found herself alone with her companion. 'You appear to have fallen into a trance. You can't come out just for enjoyment when you come with me. There is some thought of your being of a little use. You are not quite in the position of Miss Sloane.'

'I did not know that you wanted any help.'

'Of course I want the help you always give me. I cannot be deprived of the few little things I have, just because other people suddenly have so much. You need not lose yourself in their experience. It will affect no one but themselves. It will anyhow make no difference to you.'

'You so often get out of your chair by yourself. I can hardly know when you want help.'

'Well, understand that I always want it, when you are standing by doing nothing. It would not be suitable for me to manage alone, when it is easier for me with help, and you are there to give it. I wonder you do not see it. But then I suppose you see nothing.'

'Just fancy all that money!' said Miss Griffin, who was used to meeting attacks as if she were unconscious of them. 'I can hardly grasp it.'

'You won't have to. That is the last thing you will have to do. So that is what you have been doing instead of keeping your eyes open for my convenience. I see that a break from routine does not suit you. I must remember it.'

'When a break comes very seldom, it does sometimes upset people,' said Miss Griffin, in a lower tone.

'Oh, you are going to be like that! That is to be the result of a little change and pleasure. I must see that you do not have it. I see that it does not work. I must take counsel with myself and arrange for your life to be nothing but duty, as that is what seems to suit you.' Matty, as she spoke, was accepting Miss Griffin's ministrations as if they were rendered by a machine, and indeed the latter could only perform them in this spirit. 'Well, are we going in to luncheon, or am I going in alone? Perhaps you had better go straight home and be by yourself. That would probably make the best of you.'

Miss Griffin followed Matty without reply, and seemed consciously to change her expression to one of anticipation.

'Come in, Miss Griffin,' said Justine, as if Miss Griffin needed this encouragement and her aunt did not, an attitude more supported by fact than she knew. 'Come in and sit by me. And Aunt Matty, take the seat by Father. And Miss Sloane on his other side, if she will.'

'The seats are all arranged, dear,' said Blanche.

'Yes, Mother, but a word of help is not amiss. They were all standing about like lost souls. A large family party is the most baffling thing.'

'I will sit on the other side of Miss Sloane,' said Dudley, 'and go over everything from the beginning. She can hardly check me; she does not know me well enough.'

'Do not abuse her indulgence, Uncle. Well, Mr Penrose, what sort of a morning?'

'Well, to be frank, Miss Gaveston, not up to our standard. I am not disposed to make any complaint, as I think the family news is responsible. It is natural and perhaps not wholly undesirable that it should be so. And I hope we shall atone for it to-morrow.'

'Now, little boy, what sort of hearing is this? And when Uncle has been thinking of you and your future! What kind of return is this to make?'

'He did not know about that, dear,' said Blanche. 'He has been excited about his uncle, as you all have. And any difference for him will not be for a long time. We must allow him his share of the pleasure, so I think he might have a holiday this afternoon. We must not expect him to settle down so much sooner than anyone else. You have all been shaken out of yourselves, and no wonder. What do you say, Edgar?'

'What you do, my dear. It is – it seems to me the thing to be said.'

'And you, Mr Penrose?' said Justine. 'We should not dream of upsetting the routine without your sanction.'

'Well, I should be disposed to be indulgent upon the occasion, Miss Gaveston.'

'There, little boy, there is your holiday assured.'

'Half holiday,' said Aubrey.

'I am afraid it is nearer a whole one than it should be.'

'They will be able to go for a long walk,' said Blanche, 'instead of having to be back by four.'

'Well, really, Mother, I think Mr Penrose might have his share of the celebration. I should guess that he is inclined to shake the dust of this house off his feet. He has his own private life as much as we have.'

'Well, Mr Penrose will do as he likes, dear. Aubrey can play by himself.'

'It is very considerate, Mrs Gaveston.'

'Am I big enough to play alone?' said Aubrey.

'No, you are not,' said his sister. 'You are incapable of managing your time. I will see that we both spend a pleasant and profitable afternoon.'

'You have all stopped talking about my inheritance,' said

Dudley. 'Does it mean that you think enough has been said about it? Miss Sloane does not seem to think so. But she may not know how much has been said.'

'I have thought of nothing else since I heard of it, Uncle.'

'Neither have I,' said Aubrey. 'I have a witness.'

'Neither have I,' said Dudley.

'I should like to hear what your uncle is going to do for himself,' said Blanche.

'I doubt if we shall have that satisfaction, Mother,' said Justine, 'great as it would be. Uncle is a man of few and simple desires. Unless he has a house of his own, which heaven forbid as long as we are all in this one, it is hard to see how he is to spend so much on himself. He has his interests and occupations and his brother. More he does not ask of life.'

'He has all of us as well,' said Mark. 'That cannot be left out of account. Anyhow it has not been.'

'Our desires have a way of getting bigger with our incomes,' said Matty. 'Just as they have to get smaller with them. I have had the latter experience, and rejoice the more that all of you are to have the first.'

'Miss Sloane shows a great patience with our family drama,' said Mark. 'I am too enthralled by it myself to wonder.'

'I have come on your family at a dramatic moment. Patience is the last thing that is needed.'

'That is what I should have thought,' said Dudley. 'I am wounded by Mark's speech.'

'Wait a moment, Miss Sloane, I am going to ask it,' said Justine. 'It is not a crime, if it is a little unconventional. Which do you consider the better to look at, my father or my uncle? Do not hesitate to say; they will not mind.'

'I am afraid I do hesitate,' said Maria, laughing. 'And I had not thought of making a comparison.'

'Oh, come, Miss Sloane, that is not quite ingenuous. People always think of it; it seems inevitable. They can't see the one by the other, without summing up their respective characteristics and ranging them on different sides.'

'Dear Justine, Miss Sloane had not thought of it,' said Blanche. 'She has told us.'

'Well, she will think of it now, Mother, as I ask her to. I am sure she has never denied anyone without more reason.'

'I have never met two people whom I should see less in terms of each other.'

'Ah, now that is subtle, Miss Sloane. And I believe you are right. Now I come to consider, neither have I. It is simply superficial to talk as if one were a feeble copy of the other.'

'It is worse than that,' said Dudley. 'It is too bad.'

'They should give more attention to the comparison,' said Edgar, smiling at the guest. 'My daughter seems only to have grasped the essence of it at this moment.'

'Oh, now, Father, you would like me to be perfect, wouldn't you? Well, I am not, so you can make the best of it.'

'Father may claim to have done so,' said Clement.

'I think we are better when we are greedy than when we are clever,' said Mark. 'The one quality is natural to us; the other is not.'

'And your uncle can satisfy the one, but he can do nothing for the other,' said Edgar, with another smile.

'They might all do so much, Miss Sloane, if they would only apply themselves,' said Blanche, pursuing the line of her children's ability.

'I suppose – have the arrangements you spoke of taken any form?' said Edgar.

'Not definitely, Father,' said Justine, 'but they are taking their course. Uncle has opened his purse in the way that I knew he would, as I indeed foretold, though my doing so raised an outcry. Clement is to have an allowance; Aubrey's future is secure; the house benefits in whatever way you have arranged; and what your private and personal benefits are to be, we do not know. They are between you and him and will be left so.'

Blanche took something from a dish which Jellamy handed, as if it were no good to interpose.

'And what is my Justine to have from the open purse?'

'Oh, trust you to ask that, Father. My position is safe with you. Well, I am having peace of mind about Aubrey. It is what I asked and what was at once granted to me. I could think of no other need.'

'Who was to depend on Father to that extent?' said Clement to his brother.

'Perhaps Justine did. If so, we see that she was right.'

'Justine holds herself apart from my easy generosity,' said Dudley, 'so that to her I am what I have always been, simply her uncle.'

'But you shall be more than that!' said his niece. 'I will not stand aside a moment longer. You shall be generous to me. I will take a yearly subscription to my pet charity, to my old men and women in the village. Yes, I think I can ask that, without feeling that I am piling up a life already loaded. And you need not tell me that it is forthcoming, because I know it is. Actually, for myself I ask nothing, holding myself already too rich.'

'And I have only felt that about myself for a few days. How much better you are than I am! And I already think I am poor.'

'You will soon be right,' said Mark.

'You know I meant that a twentieth of a million was poor.'

'One thing I say!' said Justine, suddenly raising her hand. 'One stipulation I make. Uncle shall feel free to break off these undertakings at any time, to stand as fully apart from them as if they had never been made. And this at any hint of demand from his own life. In one moment, at one fell swoop – at one swoop, what is his own is in his hands, to be deflected to his own purposes. It is on this understanding and this alone, that I subscribe to the engagements, and rejoice for other people and accept for myself.'

'Well, that goes without saying, dear,' said Blanche.

'Oh, no, it does not, Mother. And therefore it shall not on this occasion. I am not quite without knowledge of life, though you probably believe me to be. I know how to safeguard the future or how it should be safeguarded. And as no one else made the move, I did it myself; and I am glad to have done it and glad to have it behind.'

'It is well to have it said once,' said Edgar. 'We will all remember it has been said.'

'Thank you, Father. If I could not depend on you, where should I stand?'

'It is wise to say it for another reason. Your uncle can only use the income from his money. The capital is held in trust and cannot be touched.'

'I can only will it,' said Dudley. 'So other people will have the use of it in the end. I am not in at all a selfish position. My godfather must have been afraid that I should rush to ruin. He did not mind if other people did. I do appreciate his special feeling for me. Indeed I approve of all his feeling.'

'It may be a wise condition,' said Maria. 'You would be checked in any headlong course. I daresay you will live to be glad of it.'

'I have done that already,' said Dudley, lowering his voice. 'We began to consider the repairs to the house, and I was checked almost at once. To do them all would take all my income and leave me as I was before, and I could not bear to be that. I think that fifty-three years must have made me tired of it.'

'One thing I ask!' said Aubrey, raising his hand in imitation of his sister. 'And that is that Mother shall have a new dress to celebrate the event.'

'Yes, well, I think I can accept that,' said Blanche, 'as it is for that reason.' She turned to her son with more feeling than she had yet shown. 'My little boy does not like his mother to be shabby.'

'And so can I,' said Justine, 'and with all my heart. And rejoice in other people's pleasure in it, which will be greater than my own.'

'Justine's advantages will not cost any less, that she gets no personal benefit from them,' said Clement to Mark.

'And so can I,' said Matty, smiling at Dudley. 'And so I will, to show that I rejoice as heartily as anyone in your access to the world's good things. We will all have one good thing for ourselves, to show our wholehearted approval of them.'

'Now that is nice of you, Aunt Matty, and nicely put,' said Justine.

'They are all too kind,' muttered Clement.

'I am so pleased with you all,' said Dudley. 'No one wants me to feel any misery because I have more than he has. I wish I had never said that anyone had more than was right for any one person. I see now what a revealing thing it is to say.'

'It will not be true of you, Uncle,' said Mark.

'I will have a new suit,' said Aubrey.

'Now, now, little boy, no making a mock of what is serious in itself. There *is* a certain generosity in accepting, as Uncle recognizes.'

'He has plenty of practice,' said Clement.

'Miss Griffin will have a dress too,' said Dudley. 'She does not grudge me my inheritance any more than anyone else.'

'Indeed I do not. Indeed I will, if it is to prove that,' said Miss Griffin, flushed and conscious and cordial.

Matty gave her a friendly smile.

'Will Miss Sloane be allowed to escape?' said Mark.

'Shall we have Grandpa decked out for the occasion?' said Clement.

'Miss Sloane, it may be asking too much of you,' said Justine. 'But if it is not, you will give my uncle the privilege? It will be accepted as such.'

'I think I will ask to have my congratulations accepted without any proof of them.'

'And being denied does not form a large part of your experience? You will not be in this case. We should not dare to attempt it.'

'We must not ask Maria to become one of us quite so soon,' said Matty.

'I have seldom felt so much one of a family.'

'Never at a loss for a graceful response!' said Justine, turning aside and sighing. 'I wonder what it feels like.'

'Miss Sloane turned her whole mind on my affairs,' said Dudley. 'I have never seen anyone do that for anyone else before.'

'No, Uncle, you have rather been the one to do it for people yourself. But I daresay it has brought its own reward.'

'It has,' said Mark.

'Did you hear my mean little speech?' said Dudley to Maria. 'I believe I think that I ought to be taken more seriously because I have money. Well, I suppose it had to make me deteriorate in some way.'

'You are going to leave us, Blanche, my dear?' said Oliver.

'You and the other women. I should like to have my smoke and talk while I have the strength for them.'

'Grandpa is a privileged person, you observe, Miss Sloane,' said Justine. 'Things are permitted in him which would not be in other people.'

'You know it is only for a short time, child, and show me that you do.'

Aubrey rose with a glance at Clement and passed out of the door as if unconscious what he did. He disliked remaining with the men and facing his brothers' banter more than he disliked the status of a child. He sometimes wondered how he would fill any role but this.

'Now, Mr Penrose, off with you; out of our house,' said Justine. 'You do not want to be with us a moment longer, and we do not want you, will not attempt to detain you. So off to keep your holiday in your own way.'

'I am more than glad of the cause of it, Miss Gaveston.'

'So am I,' said Dudley.

The five men settled at the table, Edgar and Dudley to talk to Oliver, and Mark and Clement by themselves. It was at this stage that the latter would have turned their attention to their brother. Dudley presently pointed to Oliver, who had fallen asleep.

'Here is my chance to say something else. Would it be right to give some money to Matty? Would she dislike me more for keeping it or giving it? Both are such disagreeable things, and I must do one of them. No one can carry off either.'

'We need not make a suggestion,' said Clement. 'We have shown the course we prefer.'

'You have tried to make me happy. But your aunt may not really desire my happiness. She may wish me to pay for it.'

'Well, you are proposing to do so.'

'I mean pay with discomfort.'

'She would rather you paid for it with money.'

'Such simplicity is seldom the whole truth,' said Edgar, without hesitation. 'Your aunt has come on evil days, or days which she sees as such, and your uncle on good ones; and if she is struck by the difference it may not mean so much.'

'It would make the difference less, if I gave her a little of the money and went without it myself. Or is it true that people want more, the more they have? Of course, she is not my real relation and others have a nearer claim. I am beginning to get the outlook of the rich. Do you hear me talk in their way? You would know how terrible it would be, if she wanted more, the more she had, if you had just inherited money.'

'It would have to be a moderate, settled sum. It would be a pleasure to Blanche, Dudley. May I suggest — I will suggest an allowance of about two hundred a year.'

'Thank you; that is real help. It is not too much or too little. I think that is the way rich people talk. Fancy saying that two hundred a year is not too little, when you have two thousand a year yourself!'

'That is no longer true,' said Mark.

'Yes, you won't have so much more left than you can do with,' said Oliver, raising his head. 'We shall all be busy relieving you of it. I find I am doing my part, and I do it willingly. Why shouldn't I have my last days made easy? They are my very last. And my daughter has had enough ill fortune to render it worth while to make it less. Thank you, my boy, you are a pleasant person to take it from, and I pay you a compliment.'

'Of course the generosity is yours. We have decided that.'

'No, it is yours, which pleases me better and serves its purpose. Such a quality in me would serve none.'

'What are the other allowances?' said Edgar. 'I am still in the dark. It does not do to be shy about these things, if we can take them.'

'What dreadful speeches reticent people make!' said Dudley. 'I suppose it is want of practice.'

'The lads are only like the rest of us,' said Oliver.

'We do not know,' said Clement, something in his tone showing that he was in suspense.

'I thought three hundred a year for Clement, and two hundred for Mark, as he has an interest in the house. And a hundred for Justine, as she will not spend it on herself and I am mean to a woman and good works. And Aubrey's future to be provided for as it develops. And any bitterness to be at once considered and the cause rectified. Causes of bitterness are always so just. And the rest to be for myself, to dole out as I please and earn gratitude and be able to call the tune. How despicable it sounds, and how I do like it!'

'So do we. Do not worry about our part,' said Oliver, rising to his feet. 'I will tell my daughter and spare you the scene. And having got what I can get, I will take my leave. Do not come after me. I can walk to the next room, where the women will busy themselves.'

'I believe it was too little,' said Dudley. 'Unless I have reached the stage of expecting extravagant thanks for the least thing. I hope that is what it is. Of course it is a mean sum. Two hundred a year is a tenth of two thousand, and it must be mean to offer anyone a tenth of what you have. It sounds as if I were keeping nine times as much for myself. I hope Matty will not hear before she goes. People don't resent having nothing nearly as much as too little. I have only just found that out. I am getting the knowledge of the rich as well as their ways. And of course anyone would resent being given a tenth.'

'I do not,' said Mark. 'I have the opposite feeling.'

'I am overpowered,' said Clement.

'I must not forget to thank you for your true generosity. Mine is the other kind and we begin to see what that is. Justine is to have a twentieth and she will appreciate it, which is true generosity indeed. I find myself actually looking forward to it, I am deteriorating so fast. There is her voice. The very sound of it ought to be a reproach.'

'Well, so the occasion is at an end,' said the voice. 'Or the moment has come when it would cease to be a success. We really are seeing something of each other. It is such a good thing when those things don't fail to materialize. There is always the touch of risk. It is a tribute to us all that the risk has not even hinted itself in this case. Miss Griffin and I have had a talk to ourselves. We settled down as two women and made the most of each other.'

'So we take our leave after hours so full of happiness,' said Matty. 'It is a pleasant weariness that follows a long rejoicing for others. I only wish I could call it by some other name, that there was some different word for cramped limbs and aching head. But the happiness outweighs it, and that is all I ask.'

'Here is the carriage, dear,' said her sister. 'You won't have to take the walk a second time.'

'Well, I could not do that, dear. We cannot go beyond our strength. Up to it willingly but not beyond. I shall be so glad when you have a second carriage, and it should not be long now. It is a thing I have wanted for you. We get into the way of planning things for other people when we must not imagine them for ourselves. And it is a good and satisfying substitute. We can be grateful for it. The cushion into the carriage, Miss Griffin. It won't walk in by itself.'

'Jellamy will take it,' said Justine, putting her arm in Miss Griffin's. 'It will be safely in its place.'

Edgar took the cushion and went to the carriage, and Miss Griffin stood within Justine's arm as if she would linger in its safety.

'Come, Uncle,' said Justine, 'tear yourself away from Miss Sloane. She gives no sign of relief in her escape from us, and most heartily do we thank her. But the moment has come for her release.'

'Matty cannot know of my meanness,' said Dudley, looking after the carriage. 'She could not show her view of it as openly as that.'

'Does Mother know of all your other meanness?' said Mark.

'Oh, I don't like to think of it,' said Blanche, when she had heard the truth. 'I cannot bear to feel that you have all taken so much. I ought to blush for my family.'

'I don't think you need, Mother,' said Justine. 'I should be more ashamed if I could not take Uncle's bounty openly and generously, as it is offered. It would show a smaller spirit. It is not for us to hold ourselves above the position of grateful people. We have to be able to accept. Anything else shows an unwillingness to grant someone else the superior place.'

'Uncle must feel well established in that,' said Mark.

'I have done what I can to help him. I have been able to take more pocket money,' said Aubrey, kicking a rug with his eyes upon it.

'Aubrey looks down to get the advantage of the ostrich,' said Clement.

'Which is very real,' said his brother, instantly raising his eyes.

'Oh, is that what you and Uncle have been talking about?' said Blanche. 'I don't know what to think of you all. I feel that I did not know my children. I am glad I am taking nothing for myself.'

'Well, it is all for you in a way, Mother,' said Justine. 'You can't dissociate yourself from the benefits of your family.'

'Poor Mother, that is rather hard,' said Mark.

'No, that is why I feel as I do,' said Blanche to her daughter in a tone of simple rejoinder. 'And Grandpa and Aunt Matty too! Well, I cannot do anything. Here is the carriage coming back. The coachman is bringing a letter.'

'For Uncle from Aunt Matty,' said Justine, handing it to Dudley. 'We should not read the envelopes of letters, but this is an exceptional occasion.'

'We can be sure that it will not repeat itself,' said Mark.

'It would be very bad for us all,' said Blanche.

'I will read it aloud,' said Dudley, 'and have the general protection. Suppose I have patronized Matty, or presumed on my connection, or thought that money meant something to her. I have taken a foolish risk.'

'Read away, Uncle,' said his niece. 'We are all ranged on your side. But I shouldn't be surprised if Aunt Matty comes out well on this occasion.'

'Is it an extreme test?' said Clement.

'MY DEAR DUDLEY,

I cannot wait to give you my thanks and my father's for your thinking of us as part of my sister's family. We feel that we are related to you, and we can take from you what we would take from a son and a brother. And we thank you as much for being that to us, as for the help that sends us forward lighter of heart. And we rejoice with you in your joy.

Your affectionate and grateful

MATILDA SEATON'

'I did not know that I was as near to them as that, and I have not given in that measure. I have kept nine times as much for myself. That in a son and a brother does seem dreadful. Riches are a test of character and I am exposed. And Matty still thinks that I have joy in having money, instead of pleasure in giving and other decent feelings. She may know me better than I know myself. People do have a terrible knowledge of sons and brothers.'

'Mrs Middleton is in the carriage,' said Aubrey.

'My dears!' said Sarah, emerging on to the gravel with hands upraised. 'What you must think of us! Your coachman picked us up as we were coming to hear your news. And I waited while you read your letter: I did not want to interrupt.' Sarah spoke the truth; she had wished to hear to the end. 'A quarter of a million of money! What a thing for you to face!'

'And to put to other purposes,' said Thomas, appearing in his turn and using a tone of kindliness and pleasure.

'It is so good of you to be interested,' said Blanche. 'It has been a great event for us all. We are still quite excited about it.'

Sarah met Blanche's eyes.

'Poor Mrs Middleton!' said Justine. 'Do satisfy her curiosity.'

'Yes, I want to hear, dear,' said Sarah, almost with pathos. 'I want to know how it came about, before we talk of it.'

'My godfather's lawyer wrote to say that my godfather had died and left me all he had,' said Dudley. 'He died a few days ago as a very old man. I am so glad that you would like to hear; I was afraid that people might be getting tired of the subject.'

'He had no children, Mrs Middleton,' said Justine, in a benevolent tone. 'Indeed he seems to have had no relations.'

'Then it was natural that he should leave his money to your uncle?' said Sarah, her face lighting at this clearance of her path.

'Quite,' said Dudley. 'I have every right to it. But I did not know that he had any. I heard a few days ago and told my brother last night, and to-day we all discussed it at breakfast.'

'You did not tell them all at once?'

'No, I waited to get confirmation. It was not needed, but I felt that I wanted to have it.'

Sarah bowed her head in full understanding.

'And my father and sister came in to learn all about it,' said Blanche, 'and have just gone. I found the news such a tonic yesterday I thought I was too tired to sleep, and I had the best night I have had for months.'

'That is right, both of you. Tell Mrs Middleton succinctly all she wants to know,' said Justine.

'We are indeed glad to know that,' said Thomas, putting a sincere note into his tone.

'How had they heard?' said Sarah, her eyes just crossing Justine's face. 'They came quite early, didn't they?'

'They came soon after breakfast,' said Justine with indulgent fluency. 'They had heard from one of the tradesmen, who had heard from Jellamy. We had discussed it at breakfast in the latter's hearing.' She gave a little laugh. 'And already it seems quite familiar knowledge. How did you hear?'

'My dear, it is all about everywhere,' said Sarah, now able to follow a lead into the drawing-room. 'And what a sum! A quarter of a million!'

'A twentieth of a million,' said Dudley. 'No more to do with a million than with any other amount. I do not know why people mention a million. Everything is a fraction of one.'

'And this is really a twentieth?' said Sarah, pausing with a world of knowledge in her tone. 'Well, I don't know whether to congratulate you or the rest of them. I expect they have already made their wishes known.'

Her voice asked for further enlightenment, and Mark sat down by her side and gave her as much as he chose.

'A little house in Cambridge for Clement,' she said, as she rose at the moment of her satisfaction. 'And this house to be put in order for your father. Ah, that will be a joy to you all. This beautiful inheritance! And Aubrey to have what he needs as time goes on. And your dear sister to be helped in her useful work. Well, I will leave you to rejoice with each other. It is pretty to see you doing it together.'

'Let us send you in the carriage,' said Blanche, who had resumed her work.

'No, we will walk and perhaps drop in on your sister. My husband will like a chat with your father. The men like to talk together.'

'The women may not object to it on this occasion,' said Thomas, with a smile. 'I may say how very pleased I am.'

'Now do you feel fully primed, Mrs Middleton, with all that

you want to discuss?' said Justine, as she went to the door with the guests.

'Yes, dear, I know it all, I think,' said Sarah, resting her eyes once more on Justine's face. 'I don't like things to pass me by, without my hearing about them. We are meant to be interested in what the Almighty ordains.'

'Mrs Middleton gives as much attention to the Almighty's doings as he is supposed to give to hers,' said Mark.

'I am glad the Almighty has given half a million to Uncle,' said Aubrey.

'Half a million!' said Dudley. 'Now I am really upset.'

'What did you think of Mrs Middleton's account of her curiosity, Justine?' said Clement.

'Poor Mrs Middleton! We can't call it anything else.'

'She can and did,' said Mark.

Sarah went on to the lodge, desiring to know the Seatons' share in the fortune and hoping that it was enough and not too much. The matter was not mentioned and her compunction at overhearing the letter vanished. She saw that she could not have managed without doing so.

Chapter 5

'Uncle is walking with Miss Sloane on the terrace,' said Aubrey to his sister.

'Well, that is a normal thing to do, little boy. I notice that Uncle is often with Miss Sloane of late. It may be that it gives Aunt Matty a chance to talk to Father.'

'He has been helping her up the steps. She goes up them by herself when she is alone.'

'Well, when you are older you will learn that men often do things for women which they can do for themselves. Uncle is a finished and gallant person, and there has been a late development in him along that line. He seems to be more aware of himself since he had this money. I hope it does not mean that we took him too much for granted in the old days. But the dear old days! I can't help regretting them in a way, the days when he gave us more of himself, somehow, though he had less of other things to give. I could find it in me to wish them back. I don't take as much pleasure in my new scope as I did in the old Uncle Dudley, who seems to have taken some course away from us of late. Well, I have taken what I can get, and I am content and grateful. And I hardly know how to put what I mean into words.'

Blanche looked up at her daughter as if struck by something in her speech, and rose and went to the window with her work dropping from her hand.

'Mother, what is it? Come back to the fire. Your cough will get worse.'

Blanche began automatically to cough, holding her hand to her chest and looking at her daughter over it.

'It is true,' she said. 'They are walking arm-in-arm. It is true.'

'What is true? What do you mean?' said Justine, coming to her side. 'What is it? What are we to think?'

'We are spying upon them,' said Aubrey, his tone seeming too light for the others' mood.

'Yes, we are,' said his sister, drawing back. 'No, we are not. I see how it is. Uncle is choosing this method of making known to us the truth. We are to see it and grasp it. Well, we do. We will let it stand revealed. So that is what it has meant, this strange insight I have had into something that was upon us, something new. Well, we accept it in its bearing upon Uncle and ourselves.'

'Dear Dudley!' said Blanche, picking up her work.

'Dear Uncle indeed, Mother! And the more he does and has for himself, the dearer. And now go back to the fire. You have grown quite pale. It cannot but be a shock. Aubrey will stay and take care of you, and I will go and do as Uncle wishes and carry the news. For we must take it that that is what his unspoken message meant.'

'We must beware how we walk arm-in-arm,' said Aubrey.

Blanche extended a hand to her son with a smile which was absent, amused and admonitory, and remained silent until her other sons entered, preceded by their sister.

'Standing at the landing window with their eyes glued to the scene! Standing as if rooted to the spot! Uncle chose his method well. It has gone straight home.'

'My Justine's voice is her own again,' said Blanche, looking at her sons as if in question of their feeling.

'Well, Mother, I am not going to be knocked down by this. It is a thing to stand up straight under, indeed. I found the boys in a condition of daze. I was obliged to be a little bracing, though I admit that it affected me in that way at first. This is a change for Uncle, not for ourselves. It is his life that is taking a new turn, though ours will take its subordinate turn, of course, and we must remember to see it as subordinate. But dear Uncle! That he should have come to this at his age! It takes away my breath and makes my heart ache at the same time.'

'Are we sure of it?' said Mark.

'Let us build no further without a foundation,' said his brother.

'Look,' said Justine, leading the way to the window. 'Look. Oh, look indeed! Here is something else before our eyes. What led me to the window at this moment? It is inspiring, uplifting. I wish we had seen it from the first. We should not have taken our eyes away.'

Edgar was standing on the path, his hands on the shoulders of Maria and his brother, his eyes looking into their faces, his smile seeming to reflect theirs.

'Is it not a speaking scene? Dear Father! Giving up his place in his brother's life with generosity and courage. We see the simplicity and completeness of the sacrifice, the full and utter renunciation. It seems that we ought not to look, that the scene should be sacred from human eyes.'

'So Justine stands on tiptoe for a last glance,' said Aubrey, blinking.

'Yes, let us move away,' said his sister, putting his words to her own purpose. 'Let us turn our eyes on something fitter for our sight.' She accordingly turned hers on her mother, and saw that Blanche was weeping easily and weakly, as if she had no power to stem her tears.

'Why, little Mother, it is not like you to be borne away like this. Where is that stoic strain which has put you at our head, and kept you there in spite of all indication to the contrary?

Where should it be now but at Father's service? Where is your place but at his side? Come, let me lead you to the post that will be yours.'

Blanche went on weeping almost contentedly, rather as if her resistance had been withdrawn than as if she had any cause for tears. Aubrey looked on with an uneasy expression and Clement kept his eyes aside.

'I am quite with Mother,' said Mark. 'It is all I can do not to follow her example.'

'Has the carriage been sent for Aunt Matty?' said Aubrey.

'Ought it to be?' said Blanche, sitting up and using an easier tone than seemed credible. 'We must ask Miss Sloane to stay to luncheon, and I suppose your aunt must come too. It is she who first brought her to the house. We little knew what would come of it. But not Miss Griffin, Justine dear. We had better be just a family gathering. That is what we shall be, of course, now that Miss Sloane is to be one of us.'

'We will have it as you say, little Mother. I will send the message. And I commend your taste. It is well to be simply as we are. And in these days there is no risk of the promiscuousness and scantiness which did at intervals mark our board.' Justine broke off as she recalled that her uncle's open hand might be withdrawn.

'Are we to take it as certain that Miss Sloane and Uncle are engaged?' said Mark. 'The evidence is powerful, but is it conclusive?'

'Conclusive,' said Justine, with a hint of a sigh. 'Would a woman of Miss Sloane's age and type be seen on the arm of a man to whom she stood in any other relation? Uncle is not her father or her brother, you know.'

'Unfortunately not,' said Clement. 'That should be a certain preventive.'

'Come, Clement, it is in Uncle's life that we shall be living in these next days. He has had enough of living in ours.'

'It is odd that we are surprised by it,' said Mark.

'I suppose we are,' said Justine, with another sigh. 'But we have had an example of how to meet it. Father has given it to us. Don't remind me of that scene, or I shall be overset like Mother.'

'You were unwise to call it up, but I admit the proof.'

'Wait one minute,' said Justine, going to the door. 'I will be back with confirmation or the opposite. I shall not keep you long.'

'I must go and make myself fit to be seen,' said Blanche in her ordinary tone. 'I have been behaving quite unlike myself. I suppose it was thinking of your uncle, and his having lived so much for all of us, and now at last being about to live for himself.'

'It is enough to overcome anyone,' said Clement, when his mother had gone. 'It puts the matter in a nutshell.'

'You mean that Uncle may want his own money?' said Mark.

'It seems that he must. Nearly all the balance after the allowances are paid has gone on the house. It seemed to need all but rebuilding. Houses were not meant to last so long. Can things be broken off at this stage?'

'They can at the end of it. I suppose they will have to be. Uncle had very little money of his own. There is so little in the family apart from the place. He was a poor man until he had this money. And he can only use the income; the capital is tied up until his death. And he will want to give his wife the things that go with his means. And she will expect to have them, and why should she not?'

'Because it prevents Uncle from giving them to us,' said Aubrey.

'We do not grudge Uncle what is his own.'

'We only grudge Miss Sloane what has been ours.'

'How about your extra pocket money?' said Clement.

'I grudge it to her. And I thought she liked Father better than Uncle. She always looks at him more.'

'I did not think about which she liked better,' said Mark. 'I thought of her as Aunt Matty's friend.'

'Perhaps she did not find Aunty Matty enough for her,' said Aubrey. 'I can almost understand it. Well, we shall have her for an aunt and she will be obliged to kiss Clement.'

'Well, I bring confirmation,' said Justine, entering the room in a slightly sobered manner. 'Full and free support of what we had gathered for ourselves from the full and frank signs of it. It was not grudged or withheld for a moment. I was met by a simple and open admission such as I respected.'

'And did they respect your asking for it?' said Clement.

'I think they did. They saw it as natural and necessary. We could not accept what we could not put upon a definite basis. They could not and did not look for that.'

'So you did not have much of a scene?'

'No – well, it was entirely to my taste. It was brief and to the point. There was a natural simplicity and depth about it. I felt that I was confronted by deep experience, by the future in the making. I stood silent before it.'

'That was well.'

'Are we all ready for Aunt Matty?' said Aubrey.

'Yes, we are not making any change,' said Justine. 'That would imply some thought of ourselves. We are meeting to-day in simple feeling for Uncle.'

'Just wearing our hearts on our sleeves.'

'Now, little boy, why are you not at your books?'

'Penrose is not well. He sent a message. And directly his back was turned I betrayed his trust.'

'Well, well, it is not an ordinary day. And I suppose that is the carriage. Are we never to have an experience again without Aunt Matty? Now what a mean and illogical speech! When we may owe to her Uncle's happiness! I will be the first down to welcome her as an atonement.'

'So you are not too absorbed in the new excitement to remember the old aunt. That is so sweet of all of you. And I do indeed bring you my congratulations. I feel I am rather at the bottom of this. So, Blanche, I have given you something at last. I am not to feel that I do nothing but receive. That is not always to be my lot. I am the giver this time, and I can feel it is a rare and precious gift. And I do not grudge it, even if it may mean yielding up a part of it myself. No, Dudley, it is yours and it is fully given. You and I are both people who can give. That is often true of people who accept. And you find yourself in the second position this time.'

'There have to be people there or giving would be no good.'

'We are all there together,' said Blanche, who looked excited and confused. 'Edgar's sister will be a sister to me, as his brother has been my brother.'

'We have always valued the relation,' said Matty, taking Blanche's hand. 'And now we are to be three instead of two, we shall have even more to value. I must feel that I also am accepting. I shall try to feel it and not dwell upon what I relinquish.'

'I do not feel that I am losing anything. I know Dudley too well.'

'Well, if I feel I am giving up a little, I yield it gladly, feeling that others' gain is more than my loss, or more important. For I have been a dependent person who has had to make demands; and now there has come a demand on me, I am glad to meet it fully. I have had my share of weakness and welcome a position where I have some of the strength.'

'I need not talk about what I am accepting,' said Maria, 'in this house where it is known. I am giving all I have in return.'

'Simple and telling, Miss Sloane, as we should have expected,' said Justine. 'But we did not need you to say it, and hope that it was not at any cost. And we will all give you on our side what is right and meet. And rest assured, Aunt Matty, that we are not unmindful of your sacrifice. If we seem to be a little distant to-day, it is because the march of affairs is carrying us with it. Let us make our little sally and return in course.'

'Edgar, we must have a word from you,' said Matty. 'It may seem hard when you are giving up the most, but you are a person from whom we expect much.'

'Surely not in that line,' said Clement.

'Well, Aunt Matty, I think it *is* hard,' said Justine. 'And you have given the reason. Well, just a word, and then we must make a move. We must eat even on the day of Uncle's engagement. Uncle's engagement! Who could know what the words mean to us?'

'I think that will do for my speech,' said Edgar.

'Then that is enough,' said Justine, taking his arm and setting out for the dining-room.

'Dudley must sit by Miss Sloane,' said Blanche, 'and then that is the whole duty of them both.'

'Shall I say my little original word?' said Aubrey.

'Now, little boy, silence is the best kind of word from you.'

'I should like to see Clement come out of himself.'

'You go back into yourself and stay there.'

'Does Miss Sloane know how bad notice is for Clement?'

'You must forgive him, Miss Sloane; he is excited,' said Justine, giving an excuse which both satisfied the truth and silenced her brother.

'Blanche, your cough is worse,' said Matty. 'I believe you ought to be in bed.'

'I could not be, dear, on a day like this. What would happen to them all? I am indispensable.'

'You are indeed, my dear. That is what I mean.'

'Mother was condemned to remaining in one room,' said Justine, 'but I had not the heart to carry out the sentence. Our little leader shut up alone, with the rest of us observing this celebration! My feelings baulked at it.'

'It is a mistake to be all heart and no head,' said Clement.

'I am quite well,' said his mother. 'I am only a little worked up. I cannot sit calmly through a day like this. I was never a phlegmatic person. I feel so keenly what affects other people. I get taken right out of myself. I almost feel that I could rise up and float above you all. I don't know when I have felt so light all through myself. I don't believe that even your uncle feels as much lifted above his level.'

'I see that people really do rejoice in others' joy,' said Dudley.

'You have done your share of it, Uncle,' said Justine. 'And it is well that something else has come in time. A spell of natural selfishness will do you good. Give yourself up to it. We have schooled ourselves for the experience. It will be a salutary one. And a proportion of your thoughts will return to us, supported by someone else's.'

'So for the time I have no uncle,' said Aubrey.

'You will have a second aunt, dear,' said Matty. 'Come and sit by your first one. Aunts can be a compensation, and you shall find that they can.'

'Perhaps I shall be Miss Sloane's especial nephew.'

'You do not deserve it, but I have an idea that you may be,' said Justine. 'Naughty little boy, to have a way of being people's favourite and knowing it! Confess now, Miss Sloane, that you already look upon him with a partial eye.'

Maria smiled at Aubrey but was not in time to check a glance at his brothers.

'Ah, now, you may not be so much the chosen person this time. You can take it to heart and retire into the background,' said Justine, as Aubrey did both these things.

'Mother, you don't seem to know what you are doing,' said Mark. 'You keep on beginning to eat and forgetting and beginning again. You have not accomplished a mouthful in the last ten minutes.'

'I am a little wrought up, dear. I can't treat this as an ordinary day. Your uncle has never been engaged before.'

'Never and may not be again,' said Clement. 'He will not spoil Mother's appetite many times.'

Blanche began to laugh, pursuing something with her fork and continuing her mirth as she had continued her tears, as if she had not the strength to overcome it.

'Mother, you are over excited,' said Justine. 'You are on the point of becoming hysterical. Not that that is any great matter. It is pleasant for Uncle in a way to see how you feel yourself involved in his life. It is not your own interest that looms large to you, is it?'

Blanche looked up as if she did not follow the words.

'You are faint from want of food, Blanche,' said Edgar. 'You ate nothing at breakfast. You must make an effort.'

'I can't make an effort,' said his wife, in another tone. 'I don't feel well enough. And I do not like being told what I am to do. I am used to doing what I choose. I am able to judge for myself.' She thrust her plate against her glass, and sat watching the result in a sort of childish relief in having wreaked her feeling.

'Mother is not herself,' said Justine, rising to deal with the damage, and speaking for her mother's ears, though not directly to her. 'She is at once more and less than herself, shall we say?'

Blanche watched the process of clearing up with vague interest.

'That is one of the best table napkins,' she said, reaching towards it. 'That wine does not stain, does it? I only put them out last week.' Her voice died away and she sat looking before her as if she were alone.

'We must take – it would be well to take her temperature,' said Edgar.

'That was in my mind, Father. I was waiting for the end of luncheon.'

'Send Jellamy away,' said Blanche suddenly. 'He keeps on watching me.'

'Jellamy can fetch a thermometer,' said Mark, giving an explanatory smile to the man. 'That will kill two birds with one stone.'

Jellamy vanished in complete goodwill towards his mistress, and Blanche gave a laugh which passed to a fit of coughing, and sat still and shaken, with her eyes moving about in a motionless head.

'Mother's breathing is very hard and quick,' said Clement.

'She must have been feverish all day,' said Mark.

'We all see that now,' said Justine sharply. 'It is no good to wish that someone had seen it before. That will not help. We can only deal with things as they are.'

'I thought perhaps no one would notice, if I did not speak,' said Blanche, as if to herself. 'Sometimes people don't see anything.'

Edgar had come to his wife's side. Dudley and Maria had risen and were talking apart. Matty sat with her eyes on her sister, her expression wavering between uneasiness and irritation at the general concern for someone else. Aubrey looked about for reassurance. There was the sudden stir and threat of acknowledged anxiety.

The thermometer told its tale. Blanche lost her patience twice and delayed its action. Matty and Dudley talked to amuse her while she waited. She was interrupted by her cough, and they all realized its nature and its frequency. Her sister's face became anxious and nothing else.

'I heard Mother coughing in the night like that,' said Aubrey.

'Then why did you not say so?' said Clement.

'That is no good, Clement,' said Justine. 'We all wish we had taken earlier alarm. It was not for Aubrey to give us the lead.'

Blanche was found to be in high fever, and seemed to take pleasure and even pride in the discovery.

'I never make a fuss about nothing,' she said, as she sat by the fire while her room was warmed. 'I have always been the last to complain about myself. When I was a child they had to watch me to see if I was ill. I never confessed to it, whatever I felt.'

'That was naughty, dearest,' said Matty. 'And you are not a child now.'

'An ignorant and arrogant boast, Mother,' said Mark.

'Poor Uncle!' said Justine, in a low tone, touching Dudley's sleeve. 'On your engagement day! We are not forgetting it. You know that.'

'I am oblivious of it. I am lost in the general feeling.'

'I often kept about when people less ill than I was, were in bed,' continued Blanche, her eyes following this divergence of interest from herself. 'I remember I once waited on my sister when my temperature was found to be higher than hers. I daresay Miss Sloane remembers hearing of that.'

'Don't tell such dreadful stories, dear,' said Matty.

'But I often think that not giving in is the best way to get well,' said Blanche, putting back her hand to a shawl that was round her shoulders, and glancing back at it as a shiver went through her. 'Staying in bed lowers people's resistance and gives the illness a stronger hold. Not that I am really ill this time, though a bad chill is something near to it. I shall not give in for long. I am a person who likes to do everything for herself.'

'It is not always the way to do anything for other people, dear.'

'You will do it once too often, Mother,' said Clement, glad that his words were broken by the opening door.

The room was said to be ready. The doctor was heard to arrive. It seemed incredible that an hour before the household had been taking its usual course, even more incredible that the course had been broken as it had.

Blanche sat still, with her eyes narrower than usual and her hands and face less than their normal size, stooping forward to avoid the full breath which brought the cough.

'I think people know what suits themselves. I have never done myself any harm by keeping about. I shall not stay in bed a moment longer than I must. The very thought of it makes me feel worse. I am worse now just from thinking about it. People's minds do influence their bodies.' Her tone showed that she was accounting for her feelings to herself.

The doctor gave his word at a glance. Blanche was wrapped up and taken to her room. Her sons returned with the chair which had carried her, and glanced at each other as they set it down.

'What a very light chair!' said Clement, giving it a push.

'People who are light are often stronger than heavier ones,' said his brother.

Aubrey began to cry.

'Come, come, all of you,' said Justine. 'Mother can't have got any lighter in the last days. She can never have weighed much. I always feel a clodhopper beside her.'

'When is the nurse coming?' said Mark.

'As soon as she can,' said Matty, who had returned from seeing the doctor. 'That is good news, isn't it? And I have some better news for you. We are sending for Miss Griffin. Your uncle and Maria have gone to fetch her, and she is the best nurse I have ever known. That is why I am yielding her up to you. So Aunt Matty provides the necessary person a second time.'

Miss Griffin arrived with her feelings in her face, concern for Blanche and pleasure in the need of herself, and settled at once into the sickroom as her natural place. She had more feeling for helpless people than for whole ones, and it was Matty's lameness rather than the length of their union, which made the bond she could not break. She began to talk to Blanche of Dudley's engagement, feeling it an interest which could not fail, and making the most of the implication that Blanche was bound up with ordinary life.

But Blanche had taken the news more easily than Miss Griffin, and had a lighter hold on the threads of life, though she seemed to have so many more of them. Her lightness of grasp went with her through the next days, working for her in holding her incurious about her state, against her in allowing her less urge to fight for life. With petulance and heroism, childishness and courage she lived her desperate hours, and emerged into peace and weakness with remembrance rather than realization of what was behind.

Her family was new to such suspense and lived it with a sense of shock and disbelief. After the first relief they accepted her safety and resented that it had been threatened.

When Matty and Maria came to share the rejoicing, they found it took the form of reaction and silence. The first evening after the stress might almost have been one at the height of it.

Justine extended a hand to her uncle as though she had hardly strength to turn her eyes in the same direction.

'We must seem selfish and egotistic, Uncle, in that we do not remember your personal happiness.'

'Just now we are sharing yours,' said Maria.

'And I am afraid we cannot be showing it,' said Dudley.

'We can all share each other's,' said Matty. 'I can give my own illustration. My joy for my sister to-night only gives more foundation to my joy for my friends. Yes, that other happiness which I feel here, is very near to my heart.'

'You are fancying it,' said Dudley. 'Maria and I have laid it aside.'

'You have pushed it deeper down. Into a fitter place.'

'I am appalled by the threat and danger of life,' said Mark.

'It may be good for us to realize that in the midst of life we are in death,' said his sister.

'What benefit do we derive from it?' said Clement.

'Oh, don't let us talk like that on this day of all days. It is not suitable or seemly. Our nerves may be on edge, but we must not hold that an excuse for crossing every bound.'

'We may have no other excuse,' said Edgar, 'but our guests will accept that one. We have been tried to the end of our strength and I fear beyond.'

'We are not guests, dear Edgar,' said Matty. 'As a family we have been in darkness, and as a family we emerge into the light. And perhaps it is a tiny bit ungrateful not to see the difference.'

'We do not find the light dazzling,' said Clement.

'No, so I see, dear. Now I do find it so, but to me the darkness has been so very dark.' Matty was easily tried by depression in others, being used to support and cheer herself. 'You see, my sister and I are so very near. From our earliest memories our lives have been bound in one. And not even the mother's tie goes back so far.'

'Really, Aunt Matty, that is too much,' said Justine. 'Or I should say it was, if it were not for the occasion.'

'It is that which makes it so,' said Mark.

'So the occasion does mean something, dears?'

'Aunt Matty, if you do not beware, you will have us turning from you with something like shrinking and contempt,' said Justine, allowing her movement to illustrate these feelings.

'Something very like,' said Clement.

Edgar looked up as if weariness held him silent.

'Well, well, dear, perhaps I betrayed something of such feelings myself. We are all wrought up and beyond our usual barriers. We must forgive each other.'

'I do not see why,' said Clement.

'And I am indulging in personal joy all through this,' said Dudley. 'And Matty said that she shared it. So I suppose this is what joy for others is like. No wonder people rather avoid feeling it.'

'Miss Sloane, come to our rescue,' said Justine. 'We need some sweetness and sanity to save us from ourselves.'

'It is the anxiety that is to blame. A happy ending does not alter what has gone before.'

'That is what I say,' said Clement. 'Why should we hold a celebration because Mother's life has been threatened and just saved?'

'Poor little Mother! Are we in danger of losing her experience in our own?'

'Surely not, dear,' said Matty. 'No, I do not think that you and your brothers would find yourselves coming to that.'

Justine gave a laugh which was openly harsh in its acceptance of her aunt's meaning.

Matty raised her brows in perplexed enquiry.

'Come, come,' said Edgar.

'No, I shall not come, Father. I shall not rise to that bait any more. I shall not rise to those heights. I will not be forbearing and tolerant through any strain. It is not a fair obligation on anyone. I shall be hard and snappish and full of mean and wounding insinuation like anyone else. Oh, you will find a great difference. You will find that I mean what I say. I feel the strain of temper and malice which is in the family, coming out in me. I am a true daughter of the Seatons, after all.'

'Well, you are your mother's daughter, dear,' said Matty. 'And we will ask nothing better, if you can be that.'

'But I cannot. I am not even now saying what I mean. I am not Mother's daughter as much as your niece. That is what I should have said; that is what I did say in my heart. I have nothing of Mother in me. That strain of heroism and disregard of self is wanting in me, as it is in you, as it is in all of us.'

Edgar made a sound of appeal to Maria, and she rose and came to his daughter and allowed her to throw her arms round her neck and weep.

'I hope I am not the cause of this,' said Matty.

'What is your ground for hope?' said Clement.

Edgar threw his son a look of warning.

'I am not surprised to hear that heroism is not one of my qualities,' said Mark, trying to be light. 'I have always suspected it.'

'Heroism and disregard of self,' said Matty, giving a little laugh. 'Has my poor little sister had to show such things?'

'Oh, what will you all think of me?' wept Justine. 'What of my poor little boy who is looking at me with such baffled eyes? What is he to do if I fail him?'

'We think you have had more strain than other people, and been of more use,' said Maria.

'Indeed, indeed,' said Edgar. 'The chief demand has fallen on Justine and Miss Griffin. My wife is not happy with strangers, and the actual nursing is a small part of what has been done.'

'Father has surpassed himself,' said Justine, sitting up and using a voice which became her own as she spoke. 'There, I am myself again. I have had my outburst and feel the better for it. And I don't suppose anyone else is much the worse.' She wiped her eyes and left Maria and returned to her place.

'I am very shaken,' said Aubrey, speaking the truth.

'You have all been very good,' said Miss Griffin, who had

witnessed the attack on Matty with consternation, pity and exultation struggling through her fatigue, and now lifted eyes that seemed to strive to see.

'You are very tired, Miss Griffin. You had better go home and rest,' said Matty, somehow betraying a desire to deprive the family of Miss Griffin's service.

Miss Griffin looked up to speak, assuming that words would come to her and finding her mistake.

'It cannot be good for you or for anyone else, for you to go on in that state.'

'It is the best thing for Mother,' said Justine. 'She will be happier if she knows that Miss Griffin is sleeping in the next room. We shall see to-night that it is real sleep.'

'Well, that is a good way of feeling indispensable. Too sound a way to be given up. We shall all be useful like that to-night. I shall be able to sleep for the first time, and I shall be glad to feel that I am doing some good by doing it.'

'Well, I think you will be, Aunt Matty,' said Justine, who was right in her claim that she was again herself. 'Doing what we can for ourselves does make the best of us for other people. And not sleeping is the last thing to achieve either.'

'We are certainly more useful – have more chance of being of use when we are not tired out,' said Edgar, 'though it is only Miss Griffin who seems to be indispensable at the moment of sleep.'

'Then she is continually useful,' said Matty, glancing at Miss Griffin and using a tone at once light and desperate.

Miss Griffin rose with a feeling that movement would be easier and less perilous than sitting still.

'I will go and take Mrs Gaveston's temperature. That was the doctor's bell. I will bring it down so that she need not be disturbed again to-night.'

'You see us all human again, Dr Marlowe,' said Justine.

'He would hardly have a moment ago,' said Clement.

'We could not be more human than we have been in the last week,' said Dudley. 'We have sounded the deeps of human experience. I am very proud of all we have been through.'

'Father, you were going to say some formal words of gratitude to Dr Marlowe,' said Justine. 'But there is no need. He is no doubt as skilled in reading people's minds as their bodies.'

'Then it is well that he was not here just now,' said Aubrey.

'So, little boy, you have found your tongue again,' said Justine, stooping and putting her cheek against his.

'Weren't you glad to hear my authentic note?' said Aubrey, glancing at the doctor.

'I meant to sound mine too,' said Dudley.

'We heard it, Uncle, and happy we were to do so. But you have had your own support in the last days.'

'My feelings have been too deep for words like anyone else's.'

'I think we hear our Justine's voice again,' said Matty, with an effort to regain a normal footing.

Justine crossed the room and sat down on the arm of her aunt's chair.

'What a thing affection is, as exemplified between Aunt Matty and Justine!' said Mark.

'A thing indeed but not affection,' said Clement.

'I think this thermometer must be wrong,' said Miss Griffin, in the measured tones of one forcing herself to be coherent in exhaustion. 'I used it myself and it has gone up like this. I don't know what can be wrong with it. It has not had a fall.'

The doctor took it, read it, shook it, read it again and was suddenly at the door, seeming to be another man.

'Come with me, anyone who should. There may be no time to be lost. The temperature has rushed up suddenly. I hoped the danger was past.'

The family followed, at first instinctively, then in grasp of the truth, then with the feelings of the last days rushing back in all their force. The late hour of reaction might have been an imaginary scene, might have been read or written.

They reached the bedroom and Edgar took his daughter's arm. Justine pushed Aubrey back into the passage and then walked forward with her father. Her brothers stood with them, and Dudley a step behind. Maria drew back and waited with Aubrey on the landing.

'You feel hot, Blanche, my dear?' said Edgar.

'Yes – yes, I do feel hot,' said his wife, looking at him as if she barely saw him and hardly wished to do more. 'What have you all come for?'

'To say good-night to you, Mother dear,' said Justine.

'Yes, I am better,' said Blanche, as if this accounted for their presence. 'I shall soon feel better. Of course it must be slow.'

'Yes, you will be better, Mother dear.'

'But I don't want Miss Griffin to go,' said Blanche, with a sharpness which was her own, though her voice could hardly be heard. 'I don't want to have to get well all at once. I am not going to try.'

'Of course you are not,' said her husband. 'You must just lie still and think of nothing.'

'I don't often think of nothing. I have a busy brain.'

Edgar took her hand and she drew it away with a petulance which was again her own.

'Is Aubrey in bed?'

'He will be soon. He wanted to come and see you, but we thought you were too tired.'

'Yes, I am very tired. Not so much tired as sleepy.'

'Shut your eyes, Mother, and try to sleep,' said Mark.

Blanche simply obeyed but opened her eyes again.

'I want Miss Griffin to be where I can see her. You make her go away.'

Miss Griffin drew near and Blanche gave her a smile.

'We are happy together, aren't we? My sister does not know.'

'I am very happy with you.'

'My bed is right up in the air. Are you all up there too?'

'We are with you, dear,' said Edgar. 'We are all here.'

'It is too many, isn't it?' said Blanche, in a tone of agreement. 'Has Matty been here to-day?'

'She is downstairs, waiting to hear how you are.'

'She cannot come up here,' said his wife, with a note of security.

'No, she will wait downstairs.'

'Her brain is not really so much better than mine.'

'No, we know it is not.'

'Father does not know that I am really a nicer person. But it does not matter, a thing like that.'

'We all know it, Mother,' said Mark.

'But you must be kind to Aunt Matty,' said Blanche, as if speaking to a child.

'Yes, we will be, Mother.'

'She wants too much kindness,' said Blanche, in a dreamy tone.

'Shut your eyes, dear, and try to sleep,' said Edgar.

'Are you that tall man who asked me to marry him?' said Blanche, in a very rapid tone, fixing her eyes on his face.

'Yes, I am. And you married me. And we have been very happy.'

'I did not mind leaving Father and Matty. But I don't think that Father will die.'

'No, not for a long time.'

'Dr Marlowe is watching me. A doctor has to do that. But I don't like it when Jellamy does it.'

'He shall never do it again,' said Edgar, stumbling over the words.

The doctor moved out of her sight, and Dudley felt his brother's hand and came to the bed.

'They are not really so alike, when you get to know them,' said Blanche to Miss Griffin.

'Mother, try to rest,' said Mark.

'Try to rest,' echoed his mother, looking before her.

'Perhaps you are a little near to the bed,' said the doctor.

They moved away.

'Where have you all gone?' said Blanche at once.

'We are here, dear,' said Edgar. 'You are not alone.'

'Alone? That would be an odd thing, when I have a husband and four children.'

'We are all here, Blanche, all with you.'

'Matty does not mind not having any children. Some women do not mind.'

Justine came closer and her mother saw her face.

'Are you my beautiful daughter?' she said, again in the rapid tone. 'The one I knew I should have? Or the other one?'

'I am your Justine, Mother.'

'Justine!' said Blanche, and threw up her arms. 'Why should we want her different?'

'I am here, dear,' said Edgar, bending over her, and saw that his wife was not there.

For another minute they were as silent as she.

Then Miss Griffin spoke.

'I got to love her so much. She was so good. She never made a murmur and it must be dreadful not to be able to breathe. We could hardly wish her to linger like that.'

The speech, with its difference of thought, of word, of class, seemed to shock them back into life. Edgar turned from the bed as if forcing himself to return to the daily world. Clement moved towards the door. Dudley turned to speak to the doctor. Mark tried to lead his sister away. Aubrey met them in the passage and stood with the expression of a man before he broke into a child's tears. Maria went down to tell Matty the truth. The day which had been at an end was ending again. Another end had come.

'We must go down and say good-night to Aunt Matty,' said Justine, as if feeling that normal speech and action were best. 'And then Miss Griffin must go to bed. Uncle, you have Father in your charge. Dr Marlowe will understand us. We cannot say much to-night.'

Matty was sitting in her chair, waiting for them to come. She held out her arms to them, one by one, going through an observance which she had had in her mind, and which seemed to suggest that she offered herself in their mother's place.

'My poor children, your mother's sister is with you. That is the light in my darkness, that I am here to watch over you. It must have been put into my thoughts to come to your gates that you might not be alone when your sorrow came.'

They stood about her, heedless of what she said, and her voice went on on the same note, with another note underneath.

'There is one little comfort I can give you, one poor, sad, little comfort. You have not suffered quite the worst. You have not sat still and felt that you could not go to her side. You were able to obey your hearts.'

They did not answer, and as Matty's face fell from its purpose a look of realization came. Her world would be different without her sister; her place in it would be different. She rose to go and found that she must wait while Dudley and Maria took their leave.

'Come, dear, I must get home to my father. I have more to go through to-night. And if I do not face it now, my strength may fail. I feel I have not too much.' She broke off as she remembered that Blanche would not hear and suffer from her words. They would fall on other ears and she must have a care how they fell.

'Well, I must leave you to take care of yourselves, of yourselves and Miss Griffin and each other. I must believe that you will do it. And I will go home and take some thought for myself, as there is no one else to do that.'

'There is not, Aunt Matty,' said Justine, in a clear, slow, almost ruthless voice. 'We cannot tell you that there is. We have all lost her who watched over us. We are all desolate. We cannot tell you that that place will be filled.'

Chapter 6

'Well, my son,' said Oliver, as he entered Edgar's house on the day after his daughter's funeral. 'I hope I may always call you that. It is what she has left to me. It is the wrong thing that she is taken and I am left. No one feels it more than I do.'

Edgar was silent before the difference made by death. His father-in-law had never used the words before.

'No, Grandpa, you must not feel that,' said Justine, walking with her arms about him. 'We do not take one person in terms of another. She never did and we do not.'

'It is kind of you, my dear, but I cumber the ground in her house.'

'If Grandpa had had the choice of sacrificing himself for Mother,' said Mark to Clement, 'I should have taken it ill if he had not done so.'

'I wonder if he would have. There are only records of the opposite feeling.'

'Mrs Middleton, this is kind,' said Justine, 'and I ought to have greeted you. But I instinctively waited for someone else to do it.'

'My dear, if kindness could do anything!'

Thomas stood aside, as if he would suppress a possibly unwelcome presence.

'Well, dear ones,' said Matty, looking at her nephews as though uncertain of her new position with them. 'Now is anyone good and brave enough to say that he has had a good night?'

'Brave in what sense?' said Clement.

'I am not going to admit that I have no heart and no feeling,' said Mark. 'I think that is the sense.'

'So you slept well, dear?' said Matty.

'They are still in a daze,' said Sarah with compassion.

'I wish I could have taken refuge for longer in that first numbness. But it has passed and left me without defence. I have nothing left to me but courage, and I am sure my boys and girl have that. Is it enough for them to tell me that they are better and brighter this morning?'

'We seem to have told her,' said Mark.

'Because I have not been able to summon mine as yet,' said Matty, lowering herself into a chair with a weakness at once assumed and real. 'No, I cannot give a very good account of myself. I am not much of an example.'

'We none of us are,' said Justine. 'It is rather soon to expect it.'

'Yes, it is, dear, but I catch a return of spirit in those words, a note of hope and resolve for the future. I fear that I have not got so far. I feel to-day as if I may never do so. There is a confession to make. That is not much of an aunt to boast of.'

'We should be out of sympathy with any other feeling.'

'That is kind, dear. And I must try to sympathize with your hope and looking forward.'

'We must be allowed to live in the moment, Aunt Matty.'

'But I must be in sympathy with your moment. I must not feel that it is like my eternity.'

Justine gave her aunt a glance and turned away, and Matty sank lower in her chair, in apprehension and remembrance.

'Can't you occupy yourself, little boy?' said Justine.

Aubrey began to cry. Matty looked up and held out her arms, and he faltered towards her and stood within them. Justine did not speak; she would take no more on herself. Sarah sent her eyes from face to face and then put up her hand to steady them.

'What will Father do without either Mother or Uncle?' said Clement to Mark. 'I can't imagine his life.'

'I shall have to spend more time with him.'

'And that will fill the double blank?'

'It will be doing what I can. More than you will do by living your time for yourself.'

'If I had it carried on for me, as you have yours, I could be more free with it.'

'Boys, boys!' said Justine, with a hand on their arms. 'It is a dreadful day, a day which puts more on us than fits our strength, but we shall gain nothing by being conquered by it.'

'Will you come into the library?' said Edgar to his father-in-law. 'We can do no better than keep to our old ways.'

'I will do what you tell me. I have not come here, seeing any good in myself. I must take what is done for me. And who but you will do anything?'

'Whatever is done, is really done by Mother, Grandpa,' said Justine, accompanying him to the door.

'I am in no doubt about the bond between us, child.'

'Are we to hear your uncle's voice to-day?' said Matty. 'Is he to give us anything of himself?'

'He is in the garden with Miss Sloane,' said Aubrey. 'Perhaps he has given all of it.'

'Little boy, I like to see you try to do that with yourself,' said Justine in her brother's ear. 'We know who would have liked it.'

'We do not grudge them to each other,' said Matty. 'I do not, who gave them. But it seems that they might spare a little of what they have to-day. I might feel now that I went almost too far in giving. I must rise above the feeling, but to-day it seems far to rise.'

'They may hesitate to intrude their happiness on our sorrow,' said Justine.

'They might give us a little of the one, dear, and share a little of the other. Your uncle lived with your mother for thirty years. It might be that he missed her. If he knew how I envy him those years!'

'Oh, Aunt Matty!' said Justine, shaking her head and turning away, and then turning impulsively back again. 'Poor Aunt

Matty, you are old and helpless and alone, and we give ourselves to our own sorrow and forget your greater need. For your need is greater, though your sorrow is less.'

'Yes, that is how you would see me, dear. That is how I should seem to you all, now that my sister is gone. I must thank you for trying to feel kindly towards what you see.'

Clement gave a faint laugh, and Matty looked at him as if in surprise at such a sound.

'They keep on passing the library window and looking in,' said Mark.

'Oh, I know,' said Justine. 'They are waiting for Grandpa to go, so that Uncle may go in to Father. Their minds are full of us, after all. Miss Sloane is waiting to yield up Uncle to his brother. They say that sorrow makes us sensitive to kindness, but I am touched by that.'

Matty sat with her lips compressed and her hands on her chair, as if trying to face the effort of rising. Sarah watched her but did not offer her aid, knowing that it would not be welcome.

'Well, we will go, dear, if they are waiting for that, if that is what we can do to help you. We came to try to give our help.'

'Dear Aunt Matty, I believe it would be doing what you can. Grandpa has had his word with Father, and can go, strengthened by it. And Father can have the support of Uncle's companionship. He is hardly in a state to give virtue out himself to-day.'

Matty turned and went to the door, hardly looking at her niece.

'Where is Miss Griffin?' she said, in a tone of asking for something that went as a matter of course.

'I don't know. She may not be up yet. We leave her to sleep late. She may not know that you are here.'

'Well, no dear, not if she is not awake. If she were, she would know that I should not have stayed away.'

'I will go and see if she can come down.'

'She can come down, dear.'

'Well, I will go and see.'

'Send her down, and then your grandfather can come with me. Until she comes he had better stay with your father.'

'She may not be ready, Aunt Matty. Would not Miss Sloane go home with you?'

'We are talking about Miss Griffin, dear,' said Matty, with a smile and a sigh.

'We may have to keep you waiting.'

Matty turned and went back to her place, loosening her cloak and drawing off her gloves in preparation for this period.

She sat down with her nephews, and began to distract their thoughts with lively accounts of their mother's youth, which neither saddened them nor required them to suppress their feelings, seeming to forget her own trouble in her effort to help them in theirs. When Justine returned she hardly looked up, and maintained her talk as if fully occupied with it.

'Miss Griffin will be ready quite soon. She has only to put her things together.'

Matty gave two bright nods in her niece's direction, as if in reference to something that went without saying, and continued to talk.

Miss Griffin came down, a little abashed, a little out of heart, a little the better for her time under another roof. Matty just threw her a glance and gave herself to ending a tale. Then she looked round in faint question, as if expecting something to be taking place.

'Are you ready for Grandpa, Aunt Matty?'

'Yes, dear, I have been ready since we talked about it, since you said that things would be the better for our going. But I don't think my nephews were quite so inclined for me to leave them.'

'Shall I fetch him for you?'

'Yes, dear,' said Matty, in a tone of full encouragement. 'But I see that Aubrey is going for you. He is better and brighter in the last half hour.'

'Mrs Middleton, I feel that we are dismissing you,' said Justine. 'And it has been so kind of you to come.'

'We have had our glimpse of you, dear,' said Sarah, in an unconsciously satisfied tone, having had a full sight of the situation.

Thomas departed with a bare handshake, as though he would impose the least demand. He uttered no word as a word would have required an ear.

'Well, it becomes easier for me to leave you all,' said Oliver. 'I have those who belong to me on both sides. It gets to make less difference to me on which side I am.'

His grandsons looked at him with incredulous eyes, startled by the faith of a man who was in other respects a normal being. They had no grasp of the mental background of Oliver's youth.

'I suppose Grandpa is saved,' murmured Aubrey.

'People always are,' said Clement. 'That is the plan. It is specified that sins may be of any dye and make no difference.'

'There are arrangements for those who are not,' said Mark, 'permanent ones. They seem indeed to err on the side of permanency.'

'I suppose Aunt Matty is saved,' said Aubrey. 'Sins being as scarlet —'

'Boys dear,' said Justine, 'isn't this rather cheap jesting upon subjects which are serious to many people? Do you know, at this moment I could find it in me to envy Grandpa his faith?'

'I see that he has the best of it,' said Mark.

'We should like to have some comfort,' said Aubrey, his grin extending into the grimace of weeping, as he found himself speaking the truth.

Justine stroked his hair and continued to do so while she addressed her aunt.

'Aunt Matty, as you are taking Miss Griffin and you also have Grandpa, will you leave us Miss Sloane? I feel we need someone to break down the barriers of family grief. And I begin to find it much, this being the only woman in the family.'

'Yes, dear, take anything from me; take anything that is mine,' said Matty, proceeding on her way. 'I am willing to be generous.'

Justine ran after her and flung her arms round her neck.

'Dear Aunt Matty, you are generous indeed. And we do value the gift.'

Her aunt walked on, perhaps not wishing to go further in this line.

Justine sighed as she looked after her.

'I believe I have put something definitely between Aunt Matty and me. That is what I have done in the first days without Mother. Well, we can't expect to do so well without her.'

'Is Miss Sloane remaining with us in simple obedience?' said Mark.

'I should like to stay with you all.'

'I will give her to you for a time,' said Dudley. 'I must learn to talk like a husband.'

'And Aunt Matty has given her,' said Aubrey.

'Father, she is yours, if you will have it so,' said Justine. 'No one counts with us as you do.'

'Justine has also given Miss Sloane,' said Aubrey.

'Then I will talk to your father,' said Maria. 'And you can have your uncle.'

Justine waited for the door to close.

'Uncle, I don't think it is too soon to broach a subject which Mother would wish to be dealt with. This does not seem the wrong day to carry out what may have been her last wish. You know what I would say?'

'Can't you try to say it? Because I cannot. And if your mother would have wished it, you must.'

'It goes without saying,' said Justine, with a casual gesture. 'It is yours, that which you gave us in your generosity when it was yours to give. Now it belongs to another, and we are glad that there is the nearer claim. The lack of it was the shadow over your good fortune. Mother felt it for you and just had time to know that it was lifted. You must have known her feelings.'

'What about your old men and women in the village?'

'I shall give them what I gave them before, the work of my heart and head. They like it better, or rather I like it as well for them, as it does not touch their independence. Do not fear, Uncle. There is no sacrifice in rendering to you the things that are yours.'

'It seems that there must be sacrifice in rendering things. What does Mark feel about the house?'

'Am I so much worse than Justine?'

'I should think you must be rather worse. Anyone would be. And it is on the weaker person that the greater sacrifice falls.'

'Sacrifice? Faugh!' said Justine. 'What Father can bear, Mark can, and with as good a grace, I hope, as someone who is less affected and matters less.'

'I did not know all that about Mark. And I am still ill at ease. To give a thing and take a thing is so bad that I cannot do it. It must be done for me. And I am glad that a beginning is made.'

'We can go on,' said Clement, quickly. 'Everything in your hands. Have you anything to tell us of your future home?'

'Do you remember,' said Justine, 'how I almost foresaw the need of some readjustment like this, and made a stipulation to meet it? Everything was to be as it had been. That is how it is.'

'Mark has not told me that he will like to see the house decay. I wish he would.'

'I can tell you how glad I am to have parts of it saved, and the parts in most danger. And how glad to feel that you will have a home of your own.'

'Here is a little man who is as ready as anyone to make what you will call his sacrifice,' said Justine. 'He is too shy to say so, but he feels it none the less.'

'I am ready indeed,' said Aubrey at once, showing his sister's rightness and her error.

'And it is not really a sacrifice,' said Dudley. 'He will tell me that it is not.'

'There is no need to do that, Uncle.'

'Haven't you enjoyed the money I gave you? It is dreadful to want you to enjoy it and then to give it back. But am I the only person in the world who really likes money?'

'We have savoured it to the full,' said Justine, 'but not as much as we shall savour the sense that you are using it for yourself.'

'I do not like the sound of that. I want to eat my cake and have it. I had better let Aubrey keep his pocket money. Then I shall feel that I am letting my brother's family have all I can. That is all I can let them have. Five shillings a week.'

'Well, the little boy will appreciate it, Uncle. And he will feel that he has shown himself willing to fall into line.'

'Aubrey will eat his cake and have it,' said Clement.

'So he will,' said Dudley. 'And I shall keep my cake and give away the smallest morsel of it. I think that is what people do with cakes. I shall have to be like people; I cannot avoid it.'

'You cannot,' said Justine. 'You are caught in the meshes of your own life. It has come at last, though it has been so long delayed.'

'You don't think I am old, do you?'

'No, not at all. You are in time to give your full prime to her who has won it. Accepted it, you would like me to say. And I think it may be the truer word.'

'And some people always have a touch of youth about them.'

'Yes, and you are indeed one of them.'

'Thank you, I think that is all. And yet I feel there is something else. Oh, Clement has not told me that he is pleased to give up his allowance.'

'It goes without saying, Uncle.'

'I see it will have to. And I am taking everything and giving nothing. That is terribly like people. I have so often heard it said of them.'

'The tables are turned on you at last,' said Justine. 'Brace up your courage and meet the truth.'

'Of course people never can really part with money. You seem to be the only ones who are different from them. I am getting to know myself better. I knew people before.'

'You will have a larger charity.'

'Is it larger? It is certainly not the same. Perhaps it is what people have when they give their sympathy and nothing else? I am more and more as they are. I shall have to face it.'

'Well, I don't think it does us any harm to look at that straight. I have always regarded it squarely myself.'

'But you have never given a thing and taken a thing. You may not really be like people. You can cling to that in your heart.'

'I wonder if I do,' said Justine, in a musing tone.

'I am going,' said her uncle. 'I may be told that I am like people and you are not. Saying a thing of yourself does not mean that you like to hear other people say it. And they do say it differently.'

'Well, we have come to it quickly,' said Clement. 'I wonder that Uncle liked to bring another change to our life at once.'

'It was Justine who chose the time,' said Mark.

'I liked the way he did it,' said Justine, still musingly. 'It was the way I should have chosen to see him carry it through. My heart ached for him as he tried to keep his own note throughout. And he succeeded as well as anyone can, who attempts the impossible. And I think that I spared both him and us by grasping the rope in both hands.'

'You could not have helped him more,' said Mark.

'Miss Sloane and I are to share his money,' said Aubrey. 'It should knit us closer.'

'I am glad you are not to make a sacrifice, little boy. You are young to take that sort of part in life.'

'I regret that I have to make one,' said Clement.

'I would rather that Uncle had the money than I. I am only so glad that he wants it.'

'I can't understand his wanting it all at once like this. Our little allowances can't make so much difference.'

'He has spent too much on the house,' said Mark. 'It has taken much more than we foresaw. He has overdrawn his income and the capital he cannot touch. He must actually be in debt. If he did not have this money, he would have nothing for the time. If he had not inherited it, he could not have thought of marrying.'

'He would have had to see Miss Sloane quite differently,' said Aubrey. 'We see the power of wealth.'

'He could easily borrow money,' said Clement.

'You talk as if you did not know him,' said Mark. 'He would not do that; he would hardly dare. You must allow for the effect of his life upon him and for his own character. And it may be less easy to borrow when your securities are in trust.'

'The income would soon accumulate. He is not going to be married to-morrow.'

'Let us face the truth,' said Justine suddenly. 'Uncle has lost himself heart and soul in Miss Sloane. Nothing counts beside her and his desire to lavish all he has upon her. His old feelings and affections are for the time in abeyance. We must face it, accept it, welcome it. Anything else would be playing a sorry part.'

'And he has to take a house and do the part of an engaged man,' said Mark. 'He will have expenses.'

'We shall have to see that we have none,' said Clement.

'And quite time too,' said Justine, 'if it makes us feel like this. It is a good thing that the change has come before we are quite ruined.'

'You are all ruined but me,' said Aubrey.

'Make an end to your selfish complacence,' said Clement to his sister. 'You are giving up nothing.'

'Justine has spent what she had on other people,' said Mark. 'Her old men and women are the sufferers.'

'Oh, I have spent on them very wisely, very circumspectly. I have seen to it that they should take no risk. They will feel no sudden change. I have had a care for them.'

'Is Aunt Matty to give up her money?' said Clement.

'No. Uncle indicated to me in an aside that there would be no question of that. It is to remain as it is.'

'He should have had an aside about Clement,' said Aubrey.

'Mother has left her money to Father, hasn't she?' said Clement.

'Yes, most of it. A small legacy to Aunt Matty. She had very little.'

'Will Aunt Matty be ruined, Justine?' said Aubrey. 'What will she be like then?'

'Poor Aunt Matty!'

'Rich Aunt Matty!'

'Oh, come, she is an invalid woman, living in a small way. It is not for us, in this house and in comparative luxury, to grudge her any extra that she has. And it will make a difference to Grandpa's last years.'

'Grandpa is not an old man in the village. Only in the lodge.'

'And you are a naughty little boy. We must have Mr Penrose back. We must make an end of this doing nothing because of our sorrow. We have lost our leader, but we are in no doubt about her lead. We shall get into the way of hiding a good deal of laziness under our grief. I am in her place and I must represent her.'

'Your own place entitled you to direct Aubrey,' said Mark.

'We must take up our burdens and go forward.'

'People say that kind of thing so cheerfully.'

'I am at a standstill,' said Clement.

'Things go deep with people of Clement's saturnine exterior,' said Aubrey, glancing at his brother with a wariness which was not needed, as the latter's demeanour showed that he had not noticed his words and would notice no other words from him.

'I do see his point,' said Justine. 'But it will not hurt him to show a little grit in his youth.'

'Things like that ought to be guaranteed or not given,' said Clement. 'People can't have credit for giving things just while they do not want them.'

'Uncle asked no credit.'

'No, but he had it, and we shall have none for giving them up when we are becoming dependent on them. People's outlook alters a great deal in a few months.'

'Really, Clement, I don't see that you deserve any praise for your kind of relinquishment. We have not had enough giving up in our lives. We see it as a thing which has to be learnt. I am not quite so pleased with my part in it as I perhaps implied; but in a way I welcome it and look forward to getting my teeth into it and going forward without a sign. We may look back on this early lesson and be grateful.'

Aubrey looked at his sister in surprise at the place she gave the lesson in her life.

'What will Father do now?' he said. 'There will be no one to be with him.'

'Ah,' said Justine, shaking her head, 'is that ever out of my mind? Does anything matter beside our real problem? We can snap our fingers at any other.'

'Yes, we see you can,' said Clement.

'We must all do our best,' said Mark.

'Mark has confidence in himself as a substitute for Mother and Uncle,' said Clement, irritated by this attitude towards problems.

'Now I don't think what he said suggested that, Clement.'

'We can't help fate,' said Mark.

'We can't help it,' said his sister, sighing, 'in any sense.'

'I suppose all problems solve themselves.'

'Why do you think that?' said Clement. 'Yours does. My problem and Father's have no solution. We shall have to cut the knots, and the result will be the usual mess and waste.'

'Come,' said Justine, beckoning with a slow hand and moving to the window. 'Come. Perhaps the answer to our question is here.'

Maria and the brothers were walking together below.

'Is that our solution? May it be.'

'May it,' said Clement. 'It has served so far for several seconds.'

'Come,' said his sister, beckoning again. 'Is it unfolding itself before our eyes?'

Dudley had left his place in the middle and taken Maria's other arm, leaving the one he relinquished, for his brother.

'There may be the lifting and laying of our fear, the final token of the future.'

'You build rather much on it,' said Mark.

'I feel it is symbolic, emblematic, whatever you call it. I cannot feel that the future will be left to itself, with Uncle's eyes upon it, with Uncle's hand to steer its way. And by the future I mean Father's future, of course.'

'No one else has one,' said Clement. 'But it is natural that Father should not escape Uncle's thoughts at this time. He has just lost his wife, and his brother is leaving him after fifty years. It is not an average situation.'

'Well, I feel that we have had a sign. But you are determined to be contrary until your own little share in the change becomes familiar.'

'Why is it little? Because yours is? There is no other reason.'

'Look at that and keep it in your heart,' said Justine, pulling the curtain further. 'Of what do you consider that a sign? What kind of an omen?'

Dudley had gone, and Edgar and Maria were walking together.

'Is not Uncle sharing everything even as Father has shared it?'

'Uncle has his own ways of sharing. He may withdraw it at his pleasure.'

'Even their married lives are at the disposal of each other. It is a sobering and cheering thing.'

'Boys,' said Aubrey, blinking and pointing to the window, 'what of the lesson of another pair of brothers?'

'And they are walking in step,' pursued Justine, bending over the sill, 'Uncle's brother and future wife. Is not that prophetic? I choose to see it so.'

Clement came to her side and stood looking down with her.

'May you be able to abide by your choice.'

'Away now,' said Justine, resuming her ordinary voice. 'Away to your daily employment. We must not go on dreamily, self-indulgently, deaf to the normal demands of life. Father has set us the example. He is up and about and turning his eyes on the future. At who knows what cost to himself? We must not be behind him, who has so much more to face. He hears the call of life and obeys it.'

Edgar looked up as if feeling eyes upon him.

'They are watching us, those four who are my charge and whom I know so little. My brother has taken too much of my life, and you will not find that hard to understand. I must use the time I shall have to myself, to get to know my children. It may be too late to do anything except for myself.'

Maria did not realize the unusual freedom of his words.

'You may find that you know them better than you think. It must be difficult to live with people and not know them, anyhow young people. I think we seem to know them when anything brings them out. Have you often been surprised by these?'

'I think perhaps I have not. I think they are themselves under any test. And if I have not served them much, I have made little demand. I have not much debt to pay. It might speak better for me if I had. I have not set myself apart from the normal relations of life, and I should have done better in them.'

'Justine will solve many problems for you and will make none.'

'Perhaps that in itself may be a problem.'

'You do not often find people good all through as she is.'

'You like my Justine?' said Edgar, with what he felt should be his feeling.

'I like good people,' said Maria, with the simplicity which in her had its own quality, something which might have been humour if she could have been suspected of it. 'I never think people realize how well they compare with the others.'

'You have thought about people?'

'I have been a great deal alone and perhaps thought more than I knew. I should have learned more by meeting them.'

'You must help me, if Dudley will let you. And I see that he will.'

'I will if I can. I have been afraid of coming between you.'

'You can hold us together from there. Dudley has put you between us. I do not know what I should do if he had not. It helps me to face the future, to face my double loss. I feel there is something – someone in the place.'

Justine turned from the window as her uncle entered.

'Uncle!' she said, extending her hand towards the scene below.

'Perfect. To think that I am the possessor of all that!'

'It is all yours. Your full meed was delayed to come at last. When I look at those two tall figures, walking in step as if they would walk so all their lives, I see you between them, still walking somehow self-effacingly, there to do your part by both. I take it as an augury.'

'Perhaps I am marrying for the sake of others. I could not think of myself at such a time. If I could, I might feel that I was doing so, or other people might. I don't suppose we ever feel that we are thinking of ourselves.'

'Do you think we do not know you, Uncle?'

'I have been afraid you were getting to know me.'

'Go your way, Uncle. Set your heart at rest. Forget yourself and go forward. If there is any little thing on which you do not like to turn your eyes, turn them from it and pass on. Take your life in your own hands. It is yours.'

'You are certainly getting to know me.'

'I declare this is the first time that I have felt cheerful since Mother left us. But the sight of Father with you and Maria – yes, I will say the name – has helped me to it. I feel I can emulate you and go forward.'

'I can't be so very bad, if you are going to be the same.'

Justine walked out of the room as if carrying out her words, and passed her brothers on the landing.

'Yes, it is a fascinating spectacle. I don't blame you for standing with your eyes riveted to it. But do not let it be a snare to lure you from righteousness. Life will be rushing by and leaving us in a backwater. Father has embarked upon the stream. We must not be behind him.'

'Is that what has happened to Father?' said Clement to his brother. 'Or has the stream sucked him in unawares? It has taken him already some distance. I wonder if he knows.'

'Knows what?'

'Is it like Father to wander about alone with a strange woman?'

'It is like very few of us, but that is not what he is doing.'

There was a pause.

'When is Uncle going to be married?'

'I don't know. I suppose not too soon after Mother's death.'

Clement remained at the window after his brother had left him. He was to stand there several times in the next two months. At the end of them he came to the room where his sister was alone.

'Are not Father and Uncle going away in a few days?'

'Yes. Uncle has to see his godfather's lawyer, who manages his money. It may be about settlements or something. I have not asked. It is between him and Miss Sloane.'

'Then they are going near Grandpa's old home. It was when he and Father were visiting the godfather, that Father and Mother met.'

'Yes, so it was. Yes, they must be going there. It will do Father good to get away alone with Uncle.'

'But surely this will not be the suitable change for him. Are we simply passing over Mother's death and expecting him to do the same?'

'Oh, I had not thought. Of course he must not go there. I had forgotten the place. I will speak to Uncle. Poor Father, no wonder he was not very eager over the plan.'

'Grandpa and Aunt Matty are more and more anxious to sell their house and the furniture they left in it,' said Clement, strolling to the window and twisting the blind cord round his hand, while his eyes went down to what was beneath. 'The agent who is supposed to be doing it, seems to need some pressure and supervision. Could not Uncle try to put it through and come home a little later? It would put an end to Aunt Matty's talk.'

'Does she talk so much about it? She must talk to you and not to me. It suggests that I am in disgrace. I daresay Uncle could do it. It is a good idea. We will ask him.'

'And I believe that Miss Sloane wants something done in her old home.'

'Well, he will certainly be glad to do that. She can ask him herself; I will remind her. And I will also remind Aunt Matty. It will make a good approach and help to bridge the rift. What a thoughtful boy you grow!'

Clement still twisted the cord.

'You seem tied to the window in every sense. What is there to be seen from it? If we light upon any uplifting scenes, we are only concerned with them as onlookers. For us there remains the common task.'

Chapter 7

'I am just the person who should not be going away,' said Dudley.

'Courage, Uncle,' said his niece. 'Absence makes the heart grow fond. And we will all keep an eye on her for you.'

'Do you want to give me any instructions as the person in charge?' said Matty.

'I have not had my own yet. I am waiting to be told to take care of myself and to come back as soon as I can. I must take the will for the deed, though that always seems to be giving people too much credit.'

'Come away from the hall,' said Justine. 'Leave the engaged pair to enact their little scene in privacy and peace. They do not want eyes upon them at every moment. Someone give an arm to Aunt Matty.'

'I think I may stay here, dear. I am not so able-bodied as to keep running away on any pretext. And I am to take Maria home as soon as your uncle has gone.'

'I think it would be better to forget your office for once. Too duenna-like a course is less kind than it sounds.'

'It did not sound kind, dear. And the words are not in place. There is nothing duenna-like about me. I have no practice in such things. I have been a person rather to need them from other people.'

'Yes, I daresay, Aunt Matty. I did not mean the word to be a barbed one. Well, come along, Father. Leave Aunt Matty to carry out her duty in her own way. It would not be my way, but I must not impose my will on hers.'

'You can only do your best,' said Mark. 'And that you have done.'

'Come, let the engaged couple have anyhow only one pair of eyes upon them.'

'They are still accustomed to being apart,' said Edgar, as he moved from his place. 'Their life together is not to begin yet.'

'No, but common sense will hardly play much part in their feelings at this time. Whatever they feel, logic will not have much to do with it.'

'If they don't want people's eyes they may not want their tongues,' said Clement.

'Father, protect me against this unchivalrous brother.'

Edgar edged by his daughter and walked down the hall. She misinterpreted his abruptness and followed and put her hand through his arm. He shook it off and went on, giving one backward glance.

'Father's look at Uncle goes to my heart,' she said, as she joined her brothers.

Clement looked at her and did not speak. He also had followed his father's eyes.

'Some things are too sacred for our sight,' said Aubrey. 'They can only bear Aunt Matty's.'

'Yes, that is the inconsistence I can't quite get over,' said Justine. 'It does not seem fair, but we are not allowed to prevent it.'

'They have all their lives to be alone with each other,' said Mark.

'Oh, why can't people see that the whole of their lives has no bearing on this moment?' said his sister, beating her hands against her sides. 'All those moments added together will not make this one. It is one of the high water marks of life, the first parting after an acknowledged engagement. Why must we be so uncomprehending about it all?'

'We need not grasp more than is there,' said Edgar, who had returned and now spoke with a smile. 'The parting is to be a short one. Your uncle is hardly making so much of it.'

'A fortnight or more. You don't know how long a fortnight can be in certain circumstances, Father.'

Edgar again turned away, and Justine was after him in a moment, putting her hand in his.

'Oh, Father, what a crass and senseless speech! Why do I talk about people's want of comprehension? Why do I never take a lesson myself? Well, I have had one this time. I hope I shall never again take a fall like that. I hope there is one self left behind.'

'It is hard on the people who assist Justine's rise on her dead selves to higher things,' said Clement.

Edgar stood with his hand in his daughter's, silent in service to his duty.

'Come, Father, and just wave farewell,' she said, as if she thought heroism the best course. 'And then we will go and look at the work that was done before the men left. There is one piece of security for the future.'

Edgar went with her, without taking the first step, and Mark spoke to his brother.

'Father does not miss Mother more than he will miss Uncle.'

'He will miss someone else as much as either.'

'Has he fallen in love with Miss Sloane?' said Aubrey.

'Get away,' said Clement. 'Why do you think we want you here?'

'I don't think so, but why should that make any difference?'

'You should not be always listening to grown-up talk.'

'I wasn't. Only you two boys were talking.'

'That is too childish even for you.'

'Well, I am Justine's little boy. And she likes me to be with other boys as I do not go to school.'

'Go and hang on to her apron strings. No one else in the house wants you.'

Aubrey recoiled, glanced about the room and burst into sudden tears.

'What is the matter?' said Mark.

Neither of his brothers gave the answer they both knew.

'Boys, boys!' said Justine, appearing with a promptness which struck her brothers as natural, but which was caused by her father's wish to be alone. 'What is all this? Can I not leave you for a moment without coming back to find disturbance and tears?'

'You have not contrived to this time,' said Mark.

'I shall have to learn to be in several places at once.'

Aubrey gave a laugh to indicate that his emotion was of an easy nature.

'Tell me what it is.'

'It seems to be nothing,' said Mark.

'Nothing,' Aubrey supported him with a sob.

'Well, I refuse to be left in the dark.'

'It appears that you will be,' said Clement.

'Clement, what is it?' said Justine, her voice deep with suspicion.

'Nothing at all. We told Aubrey to go out of the room, and he refused and some words resulted.'

'You did not touch him?'

Clement raised his shoulders in contempt of her thought, and Aubrey supported him by a derisive laugh at it.

'Am I to conclude that it is absolutely nothing?'

'It is my own conclusion,' said Mark.

Justine cast a glance at Clement and another at Aubrey, as though to trace some connection between them.

'Well, little boy, when are you going to show your face?'

Aubrey did not reply that this would be when he found the courage.

'Are you going to cry all day?'

Aubrey saw the awkwardness of the prospect but no means of averting it.

'Tell me what it is, Clement. I can see that you know.'

'I told him to hold on to your apron strings and produced this result.'

'Poor little boy, he has no others to hold on to. Oh, that is what it is.' Justine held out her arms to her brother as his renewed crying gave her the clue. 'You must be more careful. And what a silly thing to say! A child is always in the charge of women. You were yourself not so long ago.'

'I told him that we were all boys together,' said Aubrey, with tears and mirth. 'That is what he did not like. He tries to think he is a man.'

'Is anyone hurt?' asked Edgar at the door.

'No, Father, only someone's feelings. And they are already soothed,' said Justine, encircling Aubrey's head in a manner which for once he welcomed, as it hid his face. 'So we need not worry you with it.'

Edgar looked at his eldest and youngest children, as they went together from the room.

'There is a good deal on your sister. I hope you will be a help to her. I will ask you both to do your best. A house like this goes ill without an older woman. It will run for a time of itself as it has been set on its lines. But if any part goes off, the whole must follow. We must support that one of us who may be destined to strive and fail.'

'I hope that Uncle will live near to us,' said Mark.

'I hope so; I think he will do his best. But a separate household will not keep this one to its course. I trust the lines may run together; I trust they may.'

Edgar left the house and walked on the path where he was used to walking with his brother. He held his head upright and his hands behind his back, as if seeking a position to replace the old one. His face was still and set, as though he would not yield to any feelings that would cause a change. He looked at his watch, surprised by its slowness, and at once replaced it and walked on.

Justine, watching from a window, left her place and hastened to her room. Coming downstairs in outdoor clothes, she passed her brothers with a sign.

'Do not ask me where I am going. Do not see me. Do not remember I have gone. Go on with what you are doing and leave me to do the same.'

'Where is she going?' said Mark. 'What is the mystery?'

'I suppose to see Aunt Matty. She may be about to make some scene. It is a good thing to be out of it.'

'Is Aunt Matty very lonely without Mother?'

'She must miss the concern which it had taken sixty years to work up. I should think it could not have been done in less. It is no good for anyone else to begin it.'

'It is a pity that Grandpa is too old for a companion to Father.'

'You are less sure of yourself in that character?'

'That aspect of me does not seem to strike him,' said Mark, with his easy acceptance of the truth. 'And I hesitate to bring it to his notice.'

'We shall be a wretched household if Uncle – when Uncle goes. And I shall be obliged to spend more time in it.'

'You take your usual simple attitude.'

'What would happen to me if I did not?'

'You might devote yourself to doing a mother's part by Aubrey.'

'You might have more success in that part yourself than as a wife for Father.'

'Successful!' called Justine's voice, as her rapid feet bore her though the hall. 'Successful and you need not ask in what way. That is in my own heart and I do not need to reveal it. I am content with my own sense of satisfaction.'

Clement paced up and down, silent and as if preoccupied. When Maria came up the drive he glanced through the window, and continued pacing as if unaware of what he had seen.

Three weeks later Aubrey came to the others.

'I saw Father and Miss Sloane saying good-bye.'

'Did you?' said his sister. 'Well, that was not much of an event. They must meet and part every day.'

'Do people – do men kiss the women their brothers are going to marry?'

'Oh, that is what you saw? So that is what it has come to. Well, I am glad it has. They can carry that off, being the people they are. I don't know whether it is conventional between brothers and sisters-in-law, but that does not matter with these two. No doubt they felt that. They must know themselves as they are.'

'Father will miss Miss Sloane when Uncle marries,' said Clement.

'And shall we not all miss several people? A great part of our life will be a blank. This is something to be a help to him until the break comes. It is sad that we should think in that way of the consummation of Uncle's life, but we can hardly help it. I question indeed whether I have been wise in throwing Father and Maria so much together. I meant it for the best; God knows I did; but it will be something else to be relinquished. And I have been so glad to see him brighter and hear the old spring in his step. Well, we will not anticipate trouble. It will be on us soon enough.'

'He must be better for being helped through the first stage. When that is over, he will have himself in hand and can look to his future. He must be used to his loss, before he is master of his own life.'

'And people get used to anything,' said Mark. 'Even if he never gets over it, he must get used to it.'

'He will get over it,' said Justine. 'To be honest, we know he will. His feeling for Mother was sound and true, but it was not that, not the kind to live by itself when its object was gone. You do not misunderstand me?'

They did not, and she stroked Aubrey's hand to help him over this initiation into the truth of life.

'We are all leaving our loss behind,' said Clement. 'And it is the better for us and for other people, the sooner it is done.'

'I hope it does not mean that our little mother is drifting away,' said Justine, frowning as she tried to think of another meaning. 'But what dear, good boys you are in these days! You will not leave your sister alone at the helm. It is only Father whose future troubles me. He does seem to be separated by a wide gulf. Mark and I hoped that we could bridge it, but we found our mistake. That is why I am glad if Maria can get even a little way towards the self which is hidden. Somehow he seems to want to keep it so. Somehow I feel that there is a higher barrier between us than there was. There is something which I can't put into words about it.'

'Does Father like Miss Sloane better than Mother?' said Aubrey.

'Now, little boy, you know better than to ask such questions. It is not worth while to answer them. But Father's life is not my affair, if he does not wish it to be. I was presumptuous to feel that I could in any way take Mother's place. I am content that Maria should do so to any extent that she can. The trouble is that it cannot be for long.'

'Then Father likes Miss Sloane better than you, Justine.'

'Oh, come, I am Father's only daughter, since Mother died the only woman in his family. You will know better when you are older, what that means. He may not want to mix up other relations with it. He has a right to have it by itself, simple and intact, if he wishes.'

'Uncle is coming back to-morrow,' said Clement.

'And Father's life will be full for the time. And we will not look further.'

'Uncle has written to Miss Sloane every day,' said Aubrey. 'I saw the pile of letters on Aunt Matty's desk.'

'Really, little boy, I don't know what to say to that. I hope they remained in a pile; I am sure they did; but even then I don't know what has become of my training.'

'I don't think she writes to him as often,' said Mark. 'I took their letters to the post one day, and there was not one from her to him.'

'My dear boys, what has come to you? I suppose you must have your little curiosities, but this goes too far. People must have their private lives and you must leave them. In some ways convention is a good thing. Mark, you are too old not to be quite certain about it.'

'It is a wonder that the young are not worse than they are, when everything is condoned in them,' said Clement. 'We do all we can to prevent their improvement.'

'Do you think Clement is softened lately, Justine?' said Aubrey.

'He has been more at home,' said Mark. 'I hoped, Justine, that our combined influence might do something for him. And I am not wholly disappointed.'

'Don't talk nonsense. It will only end in a quarrel. And one thing I want to say. When Uncle comes back and meets Miss Sloane, don't all stand round in a circle, gaping at them. Let them have their moment.'

'I do not remember grouping ourselves in that manner or with that self-indulgence. It was not a conscious effect.'

'Well, you know what I mean. Anyhow you all seem to know a good deal. Talk about the curiosity of women! I seem to have much the least. Keep away and allow them their first hour. I expect even Father will do that. And it will be more to him, a foretaste of the time when he will be deserted. For that is what I fear he will feel in spite of his children. Dear, dear, I hardly dare to look at the future.'

Edgar did not do as his daughter foretold. He met his brother, standing at Maria's side, and shook hands with his eyes on his face, as if he felt it was his duty to meet his eyes. Dudley took a step towards them, but stopped short, warned by some instinct that things were not as they had been. He drew back and waited for them to speak, feeling with his natural swiftness that this imposed on them the most demand and gave him the fullest chance. Maria's letters came to him, and he saw in a flash that this was not how she wrote. He waited to hear that she wanted release and had enlisted his brother's support. What he heard was always to return to his mind, each word sharp and heavy with all its meaning.

'Dudley, I must say what I must. Everything comes from me. You must hear it from my lips. Maria wishes to be released from you and has consented to marry me. We would not continue in a lie to you for a day. I cannot ask you to wish us happiness, but I can hardly believe, with my knowledge of you, that you will not wish it. And I can say that I wished it to you, when it seemed that things were to be with me as they are with you.'

Dudley looked at his brother with motionless eyes, and in an instant recovered himself and met the moment, seeming to himself to act a part over unrealized feeling.

'So I am to be a hero. Well, it will suit me better than it would most people, much better than you, Edgar. I see how unheroic you are. And I return to my life of living for others. I don't think that they have really liked my doing anything else. And I see that it is nicer for them. And I shall keep you both instead of giving up one for the other. I expect that is what you have been saying. It sounds an improvement, but I shall not let you think it is. I must have some revenge for being put in this position. I shall look so foolish, standing aside in simple renunciation.'

'You will indeed keep us both,' said Edgar, in so low a voice that he seemed to feel it unfitting that he should speak.

'I ought to have thought of this myself. It would have come

better from me. It does not come at all well from you, Edgar. I wish I could have the credit of suggesting it. I suppose I can't have it? We can't pretend that it did come from me?'

'It did in a way, Dudley. You gave us so full a share of each other.'

Dudley recoiled but in a moment went on.

'And you have both taken a larger share than I meant. That is the worst of kindness; people take advantage of it. You really have done so. It will give me a great hold on you both.'

His words, and his voice more than his words, laid a spell on his hearers and kept them still. Maria did not speak. She had nothing to say, nothing to add to what Edgar had said. Dudley looked at her, aloof and silent, and over his tumult of feeling continued to speak. He felt that he must get through the minutes, get them behind, that he must meet his brother's children and break the truth, before he went away alone to face the years. He could not face them with anything more upon him.

'I will go and tell Justine and the boys that I am to remain in their home. I suppose you do not wish me to leave it? You don't feel as guilty before me as that. They will betray their pleasure at the news, and I suppose that will be balm to my sore heart. I may be fortunate that I have never needed any balm before. They would rather have me than you, Edgar. I suppose I have really been the only father they have known. It is a good thing that you have not to face this ordeal. You would be quite unequal to it. You have been very awkward in this last scene. I see what people mean when they say that I am the better of the two.'

'So do I, Dudley.'

Dudley left them with a light step and they still stood apart. But as he paused to get his grasp on himself, he saw them move to each other and lift their eyes. Their ordeal was over: his had begun.

He paused at the door of the upper room and listened to the sound of voices. Justine and Aubrey and Mark were playing a game. Clement was standing on the hearth, as he had stood while the scene went on below. Dudley had not thought to dread this moment as much as he dreaded it. It had seemed that his main feeling must drown any other, and a thought just came that he could not be suffering to the last. He stood just inside the door and said the words which he felt would be his.

'I bring you a piece of good news. You are not going to lose me. I am to remain the light of your home. You thought that my gain was to be your loss, but I am not going to have the gain. It seemed impossible that I should be going to marry, and it is impossible.'

'What do you mean, Uncle?' said Justine. 'Have you changed your mind?'

'No, I am better than that. I have been rejected in favour of my brother and I have risen above it. I am the same person, better and finer. The last little bit of self has gone. It was rather a large piece at our last interview, but that does not matter, now it has gone.'

'Tell us what you mean,' said Mark.

'I don't think I can be expected to say plainly that Maria has given me up and is going to marry your father. Surely you can save me from the actual words. I shall soon have said them. Surely, you have taken the hint.'

'It is really true, Uncle?'

'Yes, you have taken it,' said Dudley, sinking into a chair as if in relief.

'We are to accept this as definite and acknowledged? It affects us as well as you.'

'It does, doesn't it? I had not thought of that. I am glad that you are to share the embarrassment. A burden is halved if it is shared, though it almost seems that it would be doubled. And you must be very uncomfortable. It is very soon for your father to want to marry.'

'But Father can't marry Miss Sloane,' said Aubrey. 'He is married to Mother.'

'No, dear,' said Justine, in a low tone. 'Mother is dead.'

'But she would not like him to have another wife.'

'We do not know, dear. Hush. Mother might understand.'

'So that is what it has meant,' said Mark, 'their being so much together.'

'Is that what it was,' said Aubrey, 'when I saw them —'

Justine put her hand on his to enforce his silence.

Yes,' said Dudley, 'all of it was that. It is bad enough to bring out the best in me, and it has had to be the very best. And your position is not so good. Your father is losing no time in filling your mother's place. I must make one mean speech; I can't be the only person to suffer discomfiture. But of course you see no reason why I should suffer it, and of course I see that your mother would have wished this to happen, and that your father is simply fulfilling her wish.'

'We cannot but rejoice that we are to keep you, Uncle,' said Mark.

'Yes, we must feel that for ourselves,' said Justine.

Clement and Aubrey did not speak.

'I don't wonder that you are ill at ease. And I must embarrass you further and tell you that you will have your money back again. I want you to feel some awkwardness which is not caused by my being rejected. No doubt you see that I do. But you will have the money after you have proved that you could give it up. It is just the position one would choose. And I have simply proved that I could take it back. My situation would not be chosen in any way. What do you think people will think of me? Will they despise me for being rejected? I do not say jilted. A vulgar word could not pass my lips.'

'They will think what they always have of you, Uncle,' said Justine.

'That I am second to my brother? Well, they must think that. Do you think a vulgar word could pass their lips?'

'I am sure it could not in connection with you.'

'That is a good thing. Perhaps I am a person who can carry off anything. I must be, because that is what I am doing. You will have to support me and not show it. I should not like it to be thought that I needed help from others. And as I am still well off, people won't entirely despise me.'

'You are many other things, Uncle.'

'They are not the kind of things that people would see. People are so dreadful. I am not like them, after all.'

'When will Father marry Miss Sloane?' said Aubrey.

'We do not know, dear. No one knows,' said his sister. 'Some time will have to pass.'

'That seems so unreasonable,' said Dudley. 'Why should people wait to carry out their wishes? Of course they should not have them. I see that; I like to see it. I am not a man without natural feelings. I could not rise above them if I were without them. And that seems the chief thing that I do.'

'Will you be taking up the repairs to the house again?' said Justine, in a practical tone, as if to liberate her uncle from the thrall of speech.

'Your father will think of that. It will be to his advantage. Oh, I must not let myself grow bitter. People are ennobled by suffering and that was not the speech of an ennobled man. And I thought of my advantage when my turn came. That came as a shock to people; I like to remember that it did. I was not a person who could be trusted to think of himself; they actually hardly expected it. If I had not become engaged, my true self would never have emerged. And now I shall never be thought the same of again. But I suppose nobody would be, whose true self had emerged.'

'Is Father's self made manifest now?' said Aubrey.

'Yes, it is, and we see that it is even worse than mine.'

Justine rose and shook out her skirt with a movement of discarding the traces of some pursuit.

'People's weaker side is not necessarily their truer self,' she said, in a tone which ended the talk and enabled her uncle to leave the room.

A silence followed his going.

'Are men allowed to marry someone else as soon as they like after their wives are dead?' said Aubrey.

'How many weeks is it?' said Mark.

'I do not know. We will not say,' said his sister. 'It can do no good.'

'It may have been the emotion of that time which prepared the way for the other.'

'It may have been. It may not. We do not know.'

'Is it often like that?' said Aubrey.

Justine sat down and drew him to her lap, and as he edged away to save her his weight, suddenly raised her hands to her head and burst into a flood of tears. Her brothers looked on in silence. Aubrey put his knee on the edge of her chair and stared before him.

'Well, that is over,' she said, lifting her face. 'I have to let myself go at first. If I had not, it would only have been bottled up and broken out at some inopportune time. Witness my passages with Aunt Matty. Well, I have betrayed my feelings once and am in no danger of doing it a second time. I can feel that Uncle will be able to face his life, and that I shall be able to face seeing him do it.'

'Shall we all be able to, or must we all cry?' said Aubrey, who was himself taking the latter course.

'Well, women look into the depths more than men. But you need not fear that I shall reveal myself again.'

'Shall we all follow Justine's example?' said Aubrey, glancing at his brothers to see if they had done so.

'Uncle did a difficult thing well,' said Mark.

'I wondered when he was going to stop doing it,' said Clement.

'Clement! Ah well, it is your feeling that makes you say it,' said Justine.

'Justine helped him to stop,' said Mark. 'I wonder what would have happened if she had not.'

'He would have managed for himself. I had no real fear. I only wanted to spare him all I could.'

'It seems that we have been blind,' said Clement.

'Have we?' said his sister. 'Did we see anything? Did we foresee it? Shall we ever know?'

'Of course we shall,' said Mark. 'We know now that we have had a shock.'

'It seems that there must have been signs, even that there were. Well, then, so it was.'

'I wonder what the scene was like between Uncle and Father,' said Clement.

'We need not wonder. We know that it was an exhibition of dignity and openness on the one side and generosity and courage on the other.'

'Miss Sloane was there,' said Aubrey. 'I saw them all go into the library together.'

'And what quality did she contribute?' said Mark. 'But there was surely no need of any more.'

'I wonder which of them one's heart aches for the most,' said Justine.

'For Uncle. Mine only aches for him.'

'I don't know. If I know Father, he has his share of the suffering.'

'I think it is clear that we did not entirely know him. And Uncle is reaping the reward.'

'Yes, yes, that in a way,' said Justine, putting her hands round her knee and looking before her. 'That, indeed. And yet there is something so stimulating in the thought of Uncle's course. It is such a tonic sadness. One wonders if such things are ever not worth while.'

'Not for Uncle, I am afraid. The benefit is for other people.'

'Do you know, I don't know?' said Justine, beginning again to gaze before her but checking herself. 'Well, I must go and pursue the trivial round. Even such things as these bring duties in their wake. Miss Sloane will be staying to dinner, and I suppose Aunt Matty must come to preside at this further involvement of her fortunes with ours.'

'Is that the best thing?' said Mark.

'Yes, my dear,' said Justine, simply. 'It saves Uncle the most. He gets it all over in one fell swoop and has his path clear. Let him go to bed to-night, feeling that his hard time is behind, that he has finished with heroism and has only to look forward in his old way to the happiness of others.'

'Finished with heroism!'

'Well, begun it then, begun the real part. Begun to serve his sentence, even if it is for life. That is not so foreign to Uncle. We are not on his level. We can trust him to go further than we could.'

'And fare worse, it seems.'

'And fare as he may,' said Justine with a sigh. 'Now we have to take our thoughts from him and think of Father.'

'A less elevating subject.'

'No, no, Mark. We will not cross our proper bounds. Though Father is changing his life and ours, we are none the less his children.'

'Will Aunt Matty be any relation of Father's now?' said Aubrey. 'It was because of Mother that he was her brother.'

'Oh, what a muddle and mix-up it all is! Well, we must leave the future. We have no right to mould or mar it. Aunt Matty is Mother's sister and has a right in our home. And she is also Miss Sloane's friend. It is strange that I do not feel inclined to say Maria now. But I daresay that is littleness and perhaps, if I knew, self-righteousness. She has brought this happiness into Father's life, and we must not forget it, though we have counted the cost. Let me see bright faces now. It is due to Father and to her, yes, and to Uncle too, that we should show a pleasant front to those who are managing their lives in their own way.'

'Certainly not ours,' said Mark.

'The whole point is the feeling between Father and Miss Sloane,' said Clement. 'It is best for things to happen according to the truth underneath.'

'We can't help resenting the truth; that is the trouble,' said his sister. 'We shall have to hide our feelings, and we shall not be the only people doing that. It is surprising how little we are in control of our minds. I found myself wishing that Mother were here, to help us out of the muddle which has come through her death.'

'Well, she is not, and Father has to make his life without her. And he would be a more tragic figure alone than Uncle, if only for the reason that he would be lonely and Uncle will not.'

'Not on the surface. We shall all see to that. But there is such a thing as being alone in a crowd. And perhaps we had some feeling that Father ought to be lonely at this time. Well, if we had, we had; I don't know what it says for us. Now will you walk across to Aunt Matty, and break the news cheerfully, gently – oh, how you please, and come back and tell me if she is coming tonight? To see her friend taking her sister's place may be a thing she can face, and it may not. Only she can know. Dear, dear, I don't see how things are to straighten out.'

'I believe that you are a contributing cause of all this,' said Mark to Clement as they set off. 'It was your idea that Uncle should stay away to serve Aunt Matty. That is how things had the chance to turn themselves over. They could hardly have done it otherwise.'

'It was a good thing they had it, with all this working underneath. It would not have done for the future to go on without any root in the truth.'

'Have you had any base thoughts in your mind?'

'What do you mean?'

'Have you begun to think of having your money?'

'Oh, that. Uncle said something about it.'

'He said the one significant thing.'

'I suppose I shall come to it: I see you have done so.'

'I was wondering if my mind were baser than anyone else's. I see it is baser than yours.'

'Oh, all our minds are alike,' said Clement. 'Everyone is base in a way.'

Dudley came across the grass behind them, raising his voice.

'Are you going to see your aunt? Then I will come with you and get the last piece of my ordeal over. I have shown you how a person should bear himself under a reverse, and now I will give the same lesson to Matty. We do seem to feel that she needs lessons, though I begin to see that her failings are not so bad as such things go.'

Matty's voice came to their ears, raised and almost strident.

'Of course I should not be treated like this. You seem to be devoid of any knowledge of civilized life. Here have I been sitting alone all day, imagining everything, anxious about everyone, yearning for some word or sign! And here I am left as if I were nothing and nobody, and had nothing to do with the people who are the nearest in my life. I have lost my sister, but her children are my charge, and the woman who is to take her place is my friend. I am deeply involved in all of it and it is torment to be kept apart.'

'I only said that they must have had a shock, and may not have thought of sending anyone down.'

'Then don't say it; don't dare to say it. Sending anyone down! As if I were some pensioner to be cast a scrap, instead of what I am, the woman who stands to my sister's children in the place of a mother! You have never felt or had any affection, or you could not say such things.'

Miss Griffin looked at the window, opening her eyes to prevent any other change in them, and Matty broke off, touched her hair, laid her hands on her flushed cheeks and leaned towards the door.

'Come in, whoever you are, and find a poor, wrought-up woman, tired of knowing nothing, tired of being alone. You have come to put an end to that. I am not quite forgotten. And do I see three dear faces? I am not forgotten indeed. But I have been feeling quite a neglected, sad person, and I am not going to sympathize with anyone. I have used up that feeling on myself. I know how the day was to go; I had my place behind the scenes; and I am just going to congratulate two of you on keeping your uncle. I know that I am striking the right note there.'

The three men greeted the women, Mark guessing nothing of the scene, Clement part of it, Dudley the whole.

'Well, so I am to hear what has happened, all of it from the beginning. You tell me, Dudley. You are too interested in the whole panorama of life to be biased by your own little share. You know that I use the word, little, in its relation to your mind, not to mine. So tell me about it, and when it is all to take place, and what you will do with your wealth, now that it has come back into your hands. You won't think there is anything I do not want to hear. I include all human experience in my range. You and I are at one there.'

'I think you have got me over my first moment better than anyone,' said Dudley, reminded of Blanche by her sister and catching the deeper strain in Matty's nature. 'I can really pretend that I feel no embarrassment. We ought not to feel any when we have done nothing wrong, but there are so many wrong things people do without feeling it, and so few they can have done to them. And being rejected in favour of a brother is not one of those. People will say that I am behaving well, but that I shall keep the most for myself by doing so, and how wise I am. They said it thirty-one years ago, and I remember it as if it were yesterday, and now it is happening again to-day. And you just said that my wealth had come back into my hands. And that is one of those words which we carry with us. I have never heard anyone say one of those before.'

Matty flashed her eyes over his face and touched the chair at her side.

'Now you and I have to suffer the same sort of thing. I feel that my sister's place will be filled, and that I have not quite the same reason for being here as I had, and not quite the same claim on her family. And people will say the things of me, as you say they will of you.'

'Do you really think they will? I like someone else to have things said, but I expect we can depend on people.'

'Miss Griffin, suppose you run away and find something to do,' said Matty, in such a light and expressionless tone that she might almost not have spoken.

Miss Griffin, whose eyes had been fastened on the scene, withdrew them and went to the door, with her face fallen and a step slow enough to cover her obedience to a command. Matty turned to her nephews.

'Well, you thought that you were to have a new aunt, and you are to have a new – what can we say? Well, we can't say it, can we? You and I can't. So we will just say that you are only to have one aunt after all. We do not want to cloud other people's happiness, and we will not; we shall be able to steer our way; we will keep to the strait and narrow path. But now we have made our resolve, we will get what we can out of it for ourselves. Let us have our gossip. That is much less than other people are getting, and if we do not grudge them their big share, they must not grudge us our little one. So when did you see the first hint of change, the cloud no bigger than a man's hand?'

'We saw no cloud until it broke,' said Mark.

'Let me get my word in at once,' said Dudley, 'or I shall feel more awkward. It is best to take the bull by the horns. That is a good figure: it shows that we are talking of a terrible thing. Well, the cloud fell on me, sudden and complete, and I lifted my head and went forward. I told people myself; I went through my strange task, shirking nothing, and adding my own note with what was surely the most heroic touch of all. I am sure you would not dare to pity me. If you would, I must just face the hardest part.'

'Well, you know, I do not feel that about pity. I often feel that I deserve it and do not get my share. People so soon forget to give it.'

'That is another kind thing to say. But is pity really better than forgetfulness? Then I have still to suffer the worst indeed.'

'Justine wants to know if you will join us at dinner, Aunt Matty,' said Mark. 'We can send the carriage when you like.'

'Mark thinks I am talking too much about myself. Forgetfulness is already coming, and I see how bad it is. And coming so soon too! It is the only thing that could do that.'

'What time, Aunt Matty? Justine was firm on the point. She wants an exact answer.'

'Dear Justine! A time is always exact, I should have thought. Well, a quarter to seven, if that is not too early, if she can do with me so soon. She is still the regent in the house.'

'I suppose Mark wanted to save me from myself. He is afraid that I may run on and not dare to stop, for fear of the silence that may follow. He has noticed that is my tendency. So will someone speak at once?'

'Well, perhaps half past six,' said Matty, with immediate and smiling response. 'Half past six and brave, bright faces. We have all made up our minds. So good-bye for the moment and good luck to our resolve. And tell Justine exactly half past six.'

'You go on and take the message,' said Dudley to his nephews. 'And I will have a word with Miss Griffin. I find her regard for me very congenial. This trouble has come from someone's being without it.'

Miss Griffin was lingering in the hall with almost open purpose.

'Well, you and I have more than ever in common, Miss Griffin. People think too little of both of us. I have been rated below my brother, and I am wondering if it will add to me to accept the view. Everyone feels that that ought to be done for me just now, and keeps trying to do it. And we ought to do what we can for ourselves.'

'We don't all think you are below him.'

'Most people do, and I expect I shall accept the judgement of the many, though it is known to be a silly thing to do. I am glad you are not so foolish.'

'I am not indeed; I mean, I don't accept it.'

'Of course I may be inferior to him. It is true that when I inherited money, I thought it put me on a pedestal. And when I gave it away, I thought it was wonderful. To give away money that cost me nothing to gain. But between ourselves I am still inclined to think it was. And I am not sure that he would have done it.'

'Anyhow it was unusual.'

'So now I am going to give it back, because if you can part with money, you can do something that very few people can do.'

'I suppose people could do it if they liked,' said Miss Griffin, in sincere thought.

'No, they could not. They are the slaves of money, not its masters.'

'It seems funny, doesn't it?'

'I used not to understand it. But when I had money myself, I understood. I had to act quickly in case I became a slave. I nearly became one.'

'But you did not quite.'

'No, but soon afterwards I did. I feel I must speak so that you can only just hear. I asked for the money back again.'

Miss Griffin smiled as if at a child.

'Did you not know that?'

'No.'

'Isn't it extraordinary that such news does not spread? I should like so much to hear that about anyone. I did not know that people were so unimportant. And they are not: everyone is important.'

'Of course everyone is.'

'Do you feel that you are?'

'Everyone ought to be.'

'I am afraid I am thought important because of what I can do. And it may be the same with you.'

'I cannot do much for anyone.'

'I thought you did everything for Miss Seaton.'

Miss Griffin looked aside.

'It is extraordinary how people put things to themselves. I daresay my nephews will take back their money with a sense of doing something to improve my position. And Miss Seaton probably thinks that you lead the same life as she does. And my brother may say to himself that he is saving me from a loveless marriage, when everyone knows that it is wise to found a marriage on other feelings. And Miss Sloane must have those for me now, when everyone makes such a point of it. And I will tell you something that I have told to no one else. I think it is ordinary of her to prefer my brother to me. It already makes me like her less. Our marriage might not have been loveless, but I think our new relation may be. It seems so obvious to choose the eligible brother.'

'Is he more eligible? A widower with a family? Everyone would not say so.'

'Perhaps he is not. Perhaps she really does prefer him to me. Then that makes me like her less still. I am glad if she is making a bad match. I wonder if people will recognize it. People have such average minds. It is something that I can speak of her in this detached way. I wish she knew that I could. Do you like her?'

'I did very much, until –'

'Until you heard that she had rejected me. So she has lost some of your affection and mine in the last hours. There is no gain without loss. And I shall make the loss as great as I can. That sounds unworthy, but it is natural. We really only want one word for natural and unworthy.'

'There is Miss Seaton!' said Miss Griffin.

Matty came towards them with her slow step, her deep eyes fixed on their faces. Dudley caught a footfall on the stairs and looked up to address her father.

'We have been waiting for you to come down, sir. Miss Griffin said it would be soon. Are you going to join us to-night and be a witness of my courage?'

'Your virtues are your own, my boy, and will be no good to me. So I do not look for a chance to enter my daughter's house, and see her husband cheating himself that he can forget two-thirds of his days. Perhaps you will remain a moment and let me hear a human voice. And then you can take my poor Matty to do what she must in the home that was her sister's.'

'Isn't it nice that we are all in trouble together?'

'It is better than being in it alone. It is the truth that we find it so. We will remember it of each other.'

'We are sure to do that,' said Dudley. 'I shall not deny myself anything at such a time.'

Miss Griffin and Matty had gone to the latter's room in silence. During Matty's toilet they hardly spoke, Miss Griffin fearing to be called to account and Matty uncertain whether to probe the truth. Matty maintained an utter coldness, and feeling for the first time an answering coldness in Miss Griffin, resented it as only someone could who had wreaked her own moods through her life. She left her attendant without a word, appearing unconscious of her presence. As she reached the hall and heard her step moving lightly above, she paused and raised her voice.

'Miss Griffin, will you bring my shawl from the bed? You did not give it to me. I am waiting for it.'

Miss Griffin appeared at once on the landing.

'What did you say, Miss Seaton?'

'My shawl from the bed! It was under your eyes. You can run down with it in a minute.'

Dudley took less than this to run up for it, and more to receive it from Miss Griffin, and Matty turned and walked to the carriage in silence.

'Oh, my shawl; thank you,' she said, taking it as if she hardly saw it.

Dudley took his seat beside her, indifferent to her mood, and she felt a familiar impulse.

'Well, how are things to be to-night? Is it to be an evening of rejoicing or of tactful ignoring of the truth? In a word, are we to consider Edgar's point of view or yours?'

Dudley read her mind and felt too spent to deal with it.

'Well, are we not to have an answer to an innocent question?'

'It was a guilty question and you will have no answer.'

'Well, we will try to do better. Let us take some neutral ground. Justine remains safe and solid. How does she feel about yielding up her place? Dear, dear, these are days of relinquishment for so many of us.'

'Justine thinks very little about herself.'

'Then I know whom she is like,' said Matty, laying her hand on Dudley's.

Dudley withdrew his hand, got out of the carriage and assisted Matty to do the same, and, leaving Jellamy to hold the door, went upstairs to his room. Matty passed into the drawing-room, unsure of her own feelings.

Maria was sitting alone by the fire. The others had gone to dress, and it was not worth while for her to go home to do the same. And it seemed to her that any such effort for herself would be out of place.

'Well, Matty, you see the guilty woman.'

'I see a poor, tired woman, who could not help her feelings any more than anyone else. I began by liking Edgar the better of the brothers, and Blanche liked him better too; so if you do the same, both she and I ought to understand. And I feel she does understand, somehow and somewhere, my dear, generous Blanche.'

Maria looked up at Matty, sensing something of her mood.

'I am not troubled by its being a second marriage. That has its own different chance. Nor about having made a mistake and mended it. But I wonder how things will go, with me at the head, and Edgar's children living under a different hand. It does not seem enough to resolve to do my best.'

Matty regarded her friend in silence. So she did not disguise her own conception of the change. Her simplicity came to her aid. She saw and accepted her place.

'Perhaps Justine will take most of it off you. She may remain in effect the head of the house. And things will not go far awry while she is there.'

Maria met the open move with an open smile. She knew Matty better since she had lived in her house.

'She will not do that. Her father would not wish it, and she is the last person to feel against him. And I must set her free to enjoy her youth.'

'My poor sister! How ready people are to enjoy things without her! But you will not have much freedom for yourself.'

'I shall give up my freedom. I have had enough and I have made no use of it.'

'It is dead, dear, the old memory?' said Matty, leaning forward and using a very gentle tone.

'It is not dead. But the cause of it is. I ought to have realized that before.'

'You knew it at the right moment. Dear, dear, what a choice you had! Your understanding of yourself came in the nick of time.'

'That can no longer be said. We must forget that I had a choice, as both of them will forget it.'

'Stay there, stay there,' said Justine, entering and motioning to Maria to keep her seat. 'That is the chair which will be yours. Remain in it and get used to your place. Father will sit opposite, as he always has. There has to be the change and we will take it at a stride. It is best for everyone.'

'Yes, you do welcome it, dear,' said Matty.

'Now, Aunt Matty!' said Justine, sinking into a chair and letting her hands fall at her sides.

'Now what, dear?'

'Already!' said Justine, raising the hands and dropping them.

'Already what? Already I face the change in the house? But that is what you said yourself. You called out your recommendation from the door.'

There was silence.

'Well, it is the replacement of one dear one by another,' said Matty.

There was silence.

'It is good that they are both so very dear.'

There was still silence. Maria lifted a fan to her face, screening it from the fire and from her friend. A current seemed to pass between her and Justine, and in almost unconscious conspiracy they held to their silence. Matty looked at the fire, adjusted her shawl with a stiff, weak movement, saw that it stirred a memory in her niece, and repeated it and sat in a stooping posture, which she believed to be her sister's in her last hours downstairs.

'No, no, Aunt Matty,' said Justine, shaking her head and using a tone which did not only address her aunt. 'That is no good. Conscious acting will do nothing.'

Matty altered her position, and instantly resumed it, a flush spreading over her face. Justine held her eyes aside as if she would not watch her.

As Edgar's sons entered, Maria rose and went to a bookcase and Justine took her seat.

'What a long day this has seemed!' said Mark, speaking to avoid silence.

'Yes, I expect it has, dear,' said his aunt with sympathy. 'It has taken you from one chapter of your life into another. We cannot expect that to happen in a moment. It generally takes many days. This has been a long one to me too. I seem to have lived through so much in the hours I have sat alone. And it has not been all my own experience. I have gone with you through every step of your way.'

'Yes, we have taken some steps,' said Justine, 'and in a sense it has been an enlarging experience. I don't think Miss Sloane minds our talking about it. She knows what is in our minds, and that we must get it out before we leave it behind.'

'And she knows she is fortunate that it can be left,' said Matty.

'It will fall behind of itself,' said Maria.

'The first touch of authority!' said Justine. 'We bow to it.'

'It was not meant to be that. I am here as the guest of you all.'

'It was just a little foretaste of the future,' said Matty. 'And quite a pleasant foretaste, quite a pretty little touch of the sceptre. I think we must hurry things a little; I must be taking counsel with myself. We must not leave that capacity for power lying idle. Now this is the sight I like to see.'

Edgar and Dudley entered, at first sight identical figures in their evening clothes, and stood on the hearth with their apparent sameness resolving itself into their difference.

'This is what I used to envy my sister in her daily life, the sight of those two moving about her home, as if they would move together through the crises of their lives. I used to feel it was her high water mark.'

'And they have just gone through a crisis and gone through it together,' murmured Justine. 'Yes, I believe together. Miss Sloane, it must be trying for you to hear this family talk, with my mother always in the background as if she still existed, as of course she must and does exist in all our minds. But if it is not to your mind, put a stop to it. Exert your authority. We have seen that you can do so.'

'I should not want to do so, if I had it. I know that I have not been here for the last thirty years. I shall begin my life with you when I begin it. That is to be the future.'

'And we will share with you what we can of ours.'

'I hope you will. I should like it.'

'Is Justine glad that Father is going to marry Miss Sloane?' said Aubrey to Mark.

'She is glad for Father not to be alone. It is wise to make the best of it. We can do nothing for people who are dead.'

'It is a good thing that Mother does not know, for all that,' said Aubrey, with an odd appeal in his tone.

'Yes, we are glad to be sure of it.'

Aubrey turned away with a lighter face.

'Edgar,' said Matty in a distinct tone, 'I have been thinking that I must be making my plans. Come a little nearer; I cannot shout across that space; and I cannot get up and come to you, can I? The wedding will be my business, as Maria's home is with me. And I think I can make the cottage serve our needs. You will like a simple wedding, with things as they are? And it cannot be for some months?'

'I shall know about such things when I am told.'

'I thought we ought to save you that, Aunt Matty,' said Justine, sitting on her aunt's chair and speaking into her ear. 'It does not seem that it ought to devolve on Mother's sister.'

'Why, you are not sparing yourself, dear, and you are her daughter. And that is as close a tie, except that its roots are of later growth. I shall be doing what I have done before for your father. It is fortunate that I am so near. And I think we need not be troubled for your mother. If we feel like that, this should not be happening. And she will go forward with us in our hearts.'

'No,' said Edgar, suddenly. 'She will not go forward. We shall and she will not.'

'Her wishes and her influence will go on.'

'They may, but she will not do so. She has had her share, what it has been.'

'I can see her in all her children,' said Maria. 'I shall get to know her better as I get to know them.'

'And yet Edgar can say that she does not go on.'

'She does not, herself. It will make no difference to her.'

'We cannot serve the past,' said Mark, 'only fancy that we do so.'

'Only remember it,' said Justine, looking before her.

Maria and Edgar exchanged a smile, telling each other that these days had to be lived. Matty saw it and was silent.

'I shall be best man,' said Dudley. 'I think that people will look at me more than at Edgar. I shall be a man with a story, and he will be one who is marrying a second time, and the first is much the better thing.'

'You need not worry about any of it,' said Matty, with apparent reassurance. 'People's memories are short. They too will feel that they cannot help what is gone, and they will not waste their interest. You will soon be a man without a story again.'

'Do you resent a tendency to look forward?' said Clement.

'No, dear, but it seems to me that people might look back sometimes. Not for the sake of what they can do for the past, of course; just for the sake of loyalty and constancy and other old-fashioned things. My life is as real to me in the past as it is in the present, my sister as much alive as she was in her youth. But all these things are a matter of the individual.'

'Aunt Matty,' said Justine, in a low tone, bringing her face near to her aunt's, 'this house is moving towards the future. It is perhaps not a place for so much talk of the past.'

'They are a matter of age, I think,' said Mark. 'The young are said to live in the future, the middle-aged in the present, and the old in the past. I think it may be roughly true.'

'And I am so old, dear? Your old and lonely aunt? Well, I feel the second but hardly the first as yet. But I shall go downhill quickly now. You won't have to give me so much in the present. I shall be more and more dependent upon the past, and that is dependent upon myself, as things are to be.'

'People are known to be proud of odd things,' said Dudley, 'but I think that going downhill is the oddest of all.'

'Yes, you forget about that, don't you?' said Matty, in a sympathetic tone. 'About that and the past and everything. It is the easiest way.'

'Miss Sloane, what has your life been up till now?' said Justine, in a tone of resolutely changing the subject. 'We may as well know that piece of the past. You know our corresponding part of it.'

'The man whom I was going to marry died,' said Maria, turning to her and speaking in her usual manner. 'And I did live in the past. It may not have been the best thing, but it seemed to me the only one.'

'Then long live the future!' said Justine, slipping off her aunt's chair and raising her hand. 'Long live the future and the present. Let the dead past bury its dead. Yes, I will say it and not flinch. It is better and braver in that way. Mother would feel it so. Aunt Matty, join with us in a toast to the future.'

'Aunt Matty raises her hand with a brave, uncertain smile,' said Aubrey, as he himself did this.

Chapter 8

'Now all to the fore,' said Justine, 'and in a natural way, as if you were thinking of Father and not of yourselves. It is his occasion, not ours, you know. People do not return from a honeymoon every day.'

'It is not the first time for Father,' said Mark. 'And Maria planned it for herself before.'

'I wonder if Father will think of last time,' said Aubrey.

'Now I should not wonder that sort of thing,' said his sister. 'Just take it all simply and do what comes your way. The occasion is not without its demand. I do not find myself looking forward with too much confidence.'

'Boys, can you look your father straight in the eyes?' said Aubrey.

'Will he want just that?' said Mark. 'Will he be able to do it with Uncle?'

'Oh, why should he not?' said Clement. 'He need not hang his head for behaving like a natural man.'

'That is a thing I never thought to see him do.'

'I can still only think of Uncle as he was at the wedding,' said Justine. 'Easy, self-controlled, courteous! It was a lesson how to do the difficult thing. We have only to think of that example, if we find ourselves at a loss.'

'Is Father in love with Maria?' said Aubrey in a casual tone.

'Yes, we must say that he is. The signs are unmistakable. We could not be in doubt.'

Aubrey did not ask if the same signs had been seen between his father and mother: he found he could not.

'Come, Mr Penrose,' said Justine, as the latter edged through the group. 'If you want to slip away before the arrival, we will not say you nay. We know that it is our occasion and not yours.'

Mr Penrose responded to this reminder by hastening his steps.

'Were you wondering about me?' said Dudley, approaching from the stairs. 'The scene would lose its point if I were not here. I shall not try to acquit myself as well as I did at the wedding. There are not enough people here to make it worth while. I hope the memory of me then will remain with them.'

'It remains with us, Uncle.'

'Justine spoke quietly and simply,' said Aubrey.

'That is not what I meant. Does it remain with Mr Penrose?'

'Yes, indeed, Mr Dudley. Mrs Penrose and I found it a most enjoyable occasion. We have several times spoken of it.'

'Oh, away with you, Mr Penrose,' said Justine, with a laugh. 'Your heart is not in the occasion as ours is. And indeed why should it be?'

Mr Penrose did not admit that he saw no reason.

'I am most interested, Miss Gaveston.'

'Of course you are, most interested; and what a feeling compared with ours! Away with you to the sphere which claims your feeling.'

Mr Penrose obeyed, but with some feeling over for the sphere he left.

'Oughtn't Aunt Matty to be here?' said Mark.

'No,' said his sister. 'No. I decided against it. You do not suppose that I have not given the matter a thought? We must break the rule that she is to be here on every occasion. We must not hand on such rules to Maria, ready made. Things cannot be quite the same for Aunt Matty here in future. Maria has a debt to her and doubtless will repay it, but the manner and method thereof must be her own. It may not be her choice to be confronted by her husband's sister-in-law on her first homecoming. Aunt Matty will be with us at dinner, and that is as much as I felt I could take on myself.'

'You and I are wasted on this occasion, Justine,' said Dudley. 'It must be enough for us if we have our own approval. My trouble is that I only care for other people's.'

'Uncle, you know you have enough of that.'

'Is Maria very old to be a bride?' said Aubrey.

'Not as old as Father to be a bridegroom,' said Mark.

'Well, men marry later than women,' said Justine.

'Welcome to the bride and bridegroom,' said Aubrey raising his hand.

'Welcome to your father and his wife,' said his sister, gravely.

'Welcome to my brother and the woman who preferred him to me,' said Dudley. 'I am equal to it.'

'I should not be, Uncle,' said Justine, in a gentle aside. 'I should put it out of my mind, once and for all. That is the way to gain your own good opinion and mine. Oh, here are the travellers! I feel we ought to raise a cheer.'

Aubrey gave her a glance.

'I should suppress the impulse,' said Clement.

'Oh, you know what I mean.'

'Well, so would everyone else.'

The scene was over in a minute. Maria was simple and ready, kind and natural; Edgar was stilted and sincere; and both were themselves. Dudley shook hands with both as if after an ordinary absence. His natural spareness and the flush of the occasion covered his being worn and pale. Maria kissed her stepchildren as if she had thought of nothing else, and took the head of the tea table without demur. She made some reference to Blanche in the course of supplying her family, and joined in the talk of her which followed. They felt that the situation was safe, and had a sense of permanence and peace. They had begun to talk when a trap drove up to the door.

'Aunt Matty!' said Aubrey.

'That high trap!' said Justine.

'Is she not expected?' said Edgar.

'Not until dinner, Father. I thought it was all arranged. And that fidgety horse! Will she ever get down?'

Dudley and Mark and Jellamy were perceived to be approaching the scene, and Matty was set upon the ground.

'Perhaps she has come to welcome me,' said Maria.

'She has come for no other reason,' said Clement.

'She comes!' said Aubrey.

Matty came in and went straight up to Maria, her eyes seeking no one else.

'My dear, I was so sorry not to be here to welcome you. The trap I had ordered did not come in time, and Miss Griffin had to go for it. I would not have had you arrive without a familiar face from the old world. You have so many from the new one.'

'I have had a very good welcome.'

'Yes, they are good children and mean to continue to be so. They are my own nephews and niece. But I feel that I am the bridge between the old life and the new, and I could not let you cross the gulf without it. The gulf is so much the widest for you.'

'I am safely on the other side, with the help of them all.'

'So you are, dear, and I will sit down and see it. I will have a chair, if I may. Thank you, Dudley; thank you, Mark; thank you, my little nephew. You are all ready and willing; you only want a little reminder. I will sit near to Maria, as it is she who is glad of my presence. Do not let me displace you, Edgar; that is not what I meant. We will sit on either side of her and share her between us. We are used to that sort of relation. I want to feel that this second time that I give you your life companion, is as much of a success between us as the first.' Matty gave Edgar a swift, bright look and settled her dress.

There was a pause.

'We did not know you were coming,' said Justine, 'or we would have sent for you.'

'You asked me to come, dear. I should have done so, of course, but you did remember the formality. But it was for dinner that you said. I did not know that they were expected so early. I only found it out by accident.'

'We did not mean to give a wrong impression.'

'No, dear? But you said for dinner, I think.'

'I did not know you expected – that you would want to be here for their arrival. We thought they would have a rest, and that you would see them later.'

'Have a rest, dear?' said Matty, with a glance round and a twitch of her lips.

'Well, stay with us for a little while, and then go upstairs by themselves and meet everyone at dinner.'

'Maria never rests in the day, even after a journey,' said Matty, in the casual tone of reference to someone completely known to her.

'I am finding all this a rest,' said Maria.

Matty looked round again, with her mouth conscientiously controlled, but with a gleam in her eyes.

'Well, can it be true?' said Clement.

'I am finding it a great strain,' murmured Aubrey.

'Hush, don't whisper among yourselves,' said their sister.

'I think I will have some tea, Justine dear,' said Matty. 'Or am I to remember that I was only asked to dinner?'

'Really, Aunt Matty, I shall not reply to that.'

'I am afraid I am pouring out the tea,' said Maria, laughing and taking up the pot.

'Are you, dear? I thought you were having a rest, and that Justine would still be directing things. I have had no directions except from her.'

'You could not have them from me until I returned.'

'You did not write to me, I thought you would want to arrange your first day yourself.'

'I did not think of it. I was content just to come home.'

'No, no, Aunt Matty. You will not make bad blood between Maria and me,' said Justine, shaking her head.

'Bad blood, dear?' said her aunt, in a low, almost troubled tone. 'I did not think there was any question of that. I had put the thought away. I am sure there is none any longer. I am sure that all the little pinpricks and jealousies have faded away.'

'Justine does not know what such things are,' said Edgar.

'Well, I said they had faded away, and that amounts to the same thing.'

'It is on the way to the opposite thing.'

'Dear Father, he has come back to his only daughter,' said Justine.

'Incontrovertibly,' said Aubrey, looking down.

'Well, am I to have any tea?' said Matty.

'When you stop holding everyone rooted to the spot,' said Clement. 'As long as they are petrified, they cannot give you any.'

'Well, I must lift my spell. I did not know it was so potent. Some people have more power than others and must be careful how they wield it. Thank you, Dudley, and a penny for your thoughts.'

'I was thinking that I had never made a speech which carried a sting.'

'I was wondering when we were going to hear your voice. I have never known you so silent.'

'I recognize the sting. I almost think that the gift of speech is too dangerous to use.'

'What should we do without your talent in that line?'

'I believe that is a speech without a sting.'

'Oh, Aunt Matty, if you would only do it oftener!' said Justine, sighing. 'You don't know how far you could go.'

'Don't I, dear? I sometimes think I should be left in a backwater. I admit that I sometimes feel driven to apply the goad.'

'Aunt Matty, how wrong you are! If only you would realize it!'

'It must be a trying obligation,' said Maria.

'If you can manage without it in your ready-made family, you are fortunate.'

'I see that I am.'

'And we all see that we are,' said Mark.

'I am sure – I hope we have many happy days before us,' said Edgar.

'Rest assured, Father, that we are not poaching on your preserves,' said Justine. 'Maria is yours, root, barrel and stock. We claim only our reasonable part in her.'

Aubrey looked at his sister.

'You don't understand my wholehearted acceptance of our new life, do you, little boy? When you get older you will realize that there is no disloyalty involved.'

'It is a rich gift that I have brought you,' said Matty, smiling at Edgar. 'So do you think I may have it in my own hands for a time, while you and Dudley go and make up your arrears, and the young ones play at whatever is their play of the moment.'

The word was obeyed before it was considered. Edgar withdrew with his brother and his children found themselves in the hall.

'If I were Maria,' said Clement, 'I would not let Aunt Matty order the house.'

'She will not do so for long; do not fear,' said his sister. 'There are signs that she is equal to her charge. I am quite serene. And I was glad to see Father and Uncle go off in their old way. Uncle still has his brother. I don't think anything has touched that.'

Edgar and Dudley were sitting in their usual chairs, their usual table between them, the usual box of Dudley's cigars at Edgar's hand.

'The young people have given no trouble?'

'None.'

'You have not lavished too much on them?'

'Nothing. They keep to what they have.'

'Is there anything to tell about the house?'

'The work goes on. Mark and I have had our eye on it.'

'Dudley,' said Edgar, keeping his voice to the same level but unable to control its tones, 'I have always taken all you had. Always from the beginning. You did not seem to want it. Now, if I have taken something you did want –'

'Oh, I am a great giver. And giving only counts if you want what you give. They say that we should never give away anything that we do not value.'

'It is the rarest thing to be.'

'Well, I don't wonder at that. It seems to be one of those things which may end anywhere. We see that it has with us. But I had to follow my nature. It may have been my second nature in this case. It would be best to hide a first nature quickly, and I was very quick. I hope people admire me. To be admired is one of the needs of my nature; my first nature that would be. But I should only expect them to admire the second. It would not often be possible to admire first natures. I used to think that you and I only had second ones, but now we have both revealed our first, and it gives us even more in common.'

Edgar looked at his brother, uncertain whether to be cheered or troubled by the tangle of his words.

'You find you are able – you can be with Maria and me?'

'Yes. There is not so much of my first nature left as you fear. And I daresay it is best that I should not marry. If a man has to forsake his father and mother, he ought to forsake his brother, and I find I could not do that. I suppose you have forsaken me in your mind? You should have.'

Edgar looked up with a smile, missing what lay behind the words, and the cry from his brother's heart went unanswered.

When Edgar's children came down to dinner they found their aunt alone.

'Well, here is the first evening of our new life,' said Justine. 'I feel easy and not uncheerful.'

'Yes, I think so do I, dear,' said Matty. 'I think I can see my Maria over you all, as I could not see anyone else.'

'I already see her taking her place at the table in my mind's eye,' said Justine, leaning back and closing her other eyes to give full scope to this one. 'Easily and simply, as if she had always had it.'

'Well, perhaps not quite like that, dear. That might not be the best way. I think she can do better.'

'That would be well enough,' said Mark.

'I daresay she will take her place like anyone else,' said Clement.

'I think the boys admire their young stepmother, Justine,' said Aubrey.

'Well, we are at a difficult point,' said Matty. 'We are the victims of a conflict of loyalties. We must be patient with each other.' She smiled at them with compressed lips, seeming to exercise this feeling.

Maria took her seat at the table as if she were taking it naturally for the first time.

'The place is taken,' murmured Aubrey.

'And as I said it would be,' said Clement.

'Well, I want a little help in taking my place,' said Matty. 'I am not able to take it quite like that. Thank you, Edgar.'

'I shall so enjoy shelving the household cares tomorrow,' said Justine. 'No housewife ever parted with her keys with less of a pang.'

'You will give what help you can?' said Edgar.

'No, I shall not, Father. I know it sounds perverse, but a house cannot do with more than one head. Nothing can serve two masters. I go free without a qualm.'

'I only serve one master,' said Aubrey. 'Penrose.'

'Do you feel you would like a change?' said Maria.

'No, no, don't pander to him, Maria; he will only take advantage. I mean, of course, that that is what I have found. You will form your own conclusions.'

'Perhaps I shall find that I have learnt more from Penrose, than many another lad at a great public school.'

'I don't know what ground you have for the view,' said Mark.

'It was just one of my little speeches. What would the house be without them?'

'It would be better with Uncle and no one to copy him,' said Clement.

'Now, Clement, come, there is a real likeness,' said Justine.

'Clement is jealous of my genuine touch of Uncle.'

'Does Dudley see the likeness?' said Matty, with a faint note of sighing patience with the well-worn topic.

'I should think it is the last thing anyone would see, a likeness to himself,' said her niece.

'Should you, dear? The opposite of what I say. We are not all like your uncle.'

'I make no pretence of lightness and charm. I am a blunt and downright person. People have to take me as I am.'

'Yes, we do, dear,' said Matty, seeming to use the note of patience in two senses.

'Clement thinks that I try to cultivate them,' said Aubrey, 'and it makes him jealous.'

'You may be wise to save us from taking you as we take Justine,' said Clement.

Aubrey gave a swift glance round the table, and sat with an almost startled face.

'Maria, what do you think of our family?' said Justine. 'It is full experience for you on your first night.'

'It is better not to have it delayed. And I must think of myself as one of you.'

'This is the very worst. I can tell you that.'

'I have often been prouder of my sister's children,' said Matty.

Edgar and Dudley turned towards her.

'I believe the two brothers are so absorbed in being together that no one else exists for them.'

There was a pause and Matty was driven further.

'Well, it is a strange chapter that I have lived since I have been here. A strange, swift chapter. Or a succession of strange, swift chapters. If I had known what was to be, might I have been able to face it? And if not, how would it all be with us? How we can think of the might-have-beens!'

'There are no such things,' said Edgar.

'We cannot foretell the future,' said Mark. 'It might make us mould our actions differently.'

'And then how would it all be with us?' repeated Matty, in a light, running tone. 'Maria not here; Justine not deposed; nothing between your father and uncle; everything so that my sister could come back at any time and find her home as she left it.'

'Is it so useful to have things ready for her return?'

'It is hardly a dependable contingency,' said Clement.

'No, no,' said Justine, with a movement of distaste, 'I am not going to join.'

'So my little flight of imagination has fallen flat.'

'What fate did it deserve?' said Edgar, in a tone which fell with its intended weight.

'Did you expect it to carry us with it?' said Mark.

Matty shrank into herself, drawing her shawl about her and looking at her niece almost with appeal. The latter shook her head.

'No, no, Aunt Matty, you asked for it. I am not going to interfere.'

'What do you say to the reception of a few innocent words, Dudley?'

'I have never heard baser ones.'

Matty looked at Maria, and meeting no response, drew the shawl together again and bent forward with a shiver.

'Have you a chill, Matty?' said Dudley.

'I felt a chill then. There seemed to be one in the air. I am not sure whether it was physical or mental. The one may lead to the other. I think that perhaps chills do encircle you and me in these days.'

'That is not true of Uncle,' said Justine. 'He is safely ensconced in the warmth of the feeling about him.'

'And I am not? I am a lonely old woman living in the past?

I was coming to feel I was that. Perhaps I ought not to have come to-day, sunk as I was in the sadness of this return.' Matty ended on a hardly audible note.

'It was certainly not wise to come with no other feeling about it,' said Mark.

'No, it was not, because that was how I felt. So perhaps it is not wise to stay. I will make haste to go, and lift the damper of my presence. I feel that I have been a blight, that your first evening would have been better without me. I meant to come and join you in looking forward, and I have stood by myself and looked back. I am glad it has been by myself, that I have not drawn any of you with me.' Matty kept her eyes on Mark's, to protect herself from other eyes. 'But I have been wrong in not hiding my heart. My father sets me an example in avoiding the effort destined to fail. I thought I could follow your uncle: I meant to take a leaf out of his book. But I can't quite do it to-day. To-day I must go away by myself and be alone with my memories. And I shall not find it being alone. And that is a long speech to end up with, isn't it?'

'Yes, it is rather long.'

'Very well, then, go if you must,' said Justine.

'What does my hostess say?'

'Oh, of course, I should not have spoken for her,' said Justine, with a little laugh.

'Justine has said the only thing that can be said. But the carriage cannot be here at once.'

'Well, I will go and sit in the hall. Then I shall have left the feast. There will no longer be the death's head at it. I shall be easier when I am not that. That is the last thing I like to be, a cloud over happy people. We must not underrate happiness because it is not for ourselves. It ought to make us see how good it is, and it does show it indeed.'

'Who is going to see Aunt Matty out?' murmured Aubrey.

'Perhaps Dudley will,' said Matty, smiling at the latter. 'Then he and I can sit for a minute, and perhaps give each other a little strength for the different effort asked of us.'

Dudley seemed not to hear and Maria signed to her husband.

'Aunt Matty would have been burned as a witch at one time,' said Clement.

'Does Clement's voice betray a yearning for the good old days?' said Aubrey.

'Witches seem always to have been innocent people,' said Mark.

'That will do. Let us leave Aunt Matty alone,' said Justine. 'She may merit no more, but so much is her due."

'What does Maria say?' said Dudley, in an ordinary tone.

'We are all moving forward. And if Matty does not come with us, she will be left behind.'

'She may pull herself up and follow,' said Justine.

'She will probably lead,' said Clement.

'She will not do that,' said his father, returning to the room.

'Has Aunt Matty gone already, Father?' said Justine.

'No. She asked me to leave her, and I did as she asked.'

After dinner it was the brothers' custom to go to the library. Blanche had had her own way of leaving the room, pausing and talking and retracing her steps, and any custom of waiting for her had died away. Dudley put his arm through Edgar's, as he had done through his life. Edgar threw it off with a movement the more significant that it was hardly conscious, and waited for his wife, giving a smile to his brother. Dudley stood still, felt his niece's hand on his arm, shook it off as Edgar had done his own, and followed the pair to the library. He sat down between them, crossing his knees to show a natural feeling. Edgar looked at him uncertainly. He had meant to be alone with his wife and had assumed that his brother understood him. This withdrawal of Dudley's support troubled him and shook his balance. Something was coming from his brother to himself that he did not know.

'Does Maria mind smoke?' said Dudley, knowing that she did not mind, knowing little of what he said.

'No, not at all. I am used to it.'

'I do not smoke; I never have; I get the cigars for Edgar.'

'I could not afford them for myself,' said Edgar.

'I must give you some as a present,' said his wife, feeling at once that the words would have been better unsaid.

Dudley looked at her and met her eyes, and in a moment they seemed to be ranged on opposite sides, contending for Edgar. Edgar sat in a distress he could not name, moving his strong, helpless hands as if seeking some hold.

'They come from some foreign place,' said Maria, taking up the box. 'We shall have to depend on Dudley for them.'

Dudley lifted eyes which looked as if he were springing from his place, but held himself still. The silence held, grew, swelled to some great, nameless thing, which seemed to fill the space between them and press on their hearing and their sight. Edgar rose and showed by his rapid utterance as well as by his words how he was shaken out of himself.

'What is this, Dudley? We cannot go on like this. We should not be able to breathe. What is it between us? It is not fair to give me everything, and then turn on me as an enemy.'

'Not fair to give you everything?' said Dudley, rising to bring his eyes to the level of his brother's. 'Do you think it is fair? Does it sound fair as you say it? For one person to do that to another? For the other person to take it? Or do you take it all, as you always have, you who know how to do nothing else? And turn on you as an enemy. What have you been to me but that? If you have never thought, think now.'

'So it has come to this, Dudley. It has all been this. This has been before us, and so between us, all our lives. You have given me nothing. You wanted to have me in your hands in return. No one can give really, not even you; not even you, Dudley. I shall not think that any more of you. You are not different. Why did you let me think you were? I would not have minded; I could have taken you as you were; I did not want anything from you. And now I have lost my brother, whom I need not have lost if I had known.'

Edgar turned his face aside, and the simple movement, which Dudley knew was not acting, pierced him beyond his bearing and flung him forward. His pain and his brother's, the reproach which he suffered in innocence and sacrifice, flooded his mind and blurred its thought.

'You have lost your brother! Then know that you have lost him. Know that you speak the truth. You may be glad to be left with your wife, and I shall be glad to leave you. I shall be glad, Edgar. I have always been alone in your house, always in my heart. You had nothing to give. You have nothing. There is nothing in your nature. You did not care for Blanche. You do not care for your children. You have not cared for me. You have not even cared for yourself, and that has blinded us. May Maria deal with you as you are, and not as I have done.'

Maria stood apart, feeling she had nothing to do with the scene, that she must grope for its cause in a depth where different beings moved and breathed in a different air. The present seemed a surface scene, acted over a seething life, which had been calmed but never dead. She saw herself treading with care lest the surface break and release the hidden flood, felt that she learned at that moment how to do it, and would ever afterwards know. She did not turn to her husband, did not move or touch him. The tumult in his soul must die, the life behind him sink back into the depths, before they could meet on the level they were to know. She felt no sorrow that she had not shared that life, only pity that his experience had not found cover as hers had found.

Dudley went alone from his brother's house, taking nothing with him but his purse and covering from the winter cold. He went, consciously empty of hand and of heart, almost triumphant in owning so little in the house that had been his home. As he passed Matty's house, forming in his mind some plan for the night, he heard a sound of crying behind the hedge, which seemed to chime with his mood. He followed the sound, thinking to find some unfortunate who would make some appeal, and willing for the sense of being met as a succourer, and came upon Miss Griffin bent over the bushes in hopeless weeping. She raised her head and came forward at once, spreading her hands in abandonment to the open truth.

'Miss Seaton has turned me out. I have been out here for some time. I haven't anywhere to go, and I can't stay here in the dark and cold. And I can't go back.' She looked round with eyes of fear, and something showed that it was Matty in relenting mood, with an offer of shelter, that she feared.

Dudley put his arm about her and walked on, leading her with him. She went without a word, taking her only course and trusting to his aid. Her short, quick, unequal steps, the steps of someone used to being on her feet, but not to walking out of doors, made no attempt to keep time or pace, and he saw with a pang how she might try the nerves of anyone in daily contact.

The pang seemed to drive him forward as if in defiance of its warning.

'You and I are both alone. People have not done well by us, and we have done too well by them. We should know how to treat each other. We will keep together and forget them. We had better be married, and then we need never part. We have both been cast out by those who should have served us better. We will see what we can do for ourselves.'

'Oh, no, no,' said Miss Griffin, in an almost ordinary tone, as if she hardly gave Dudley's words their meaning. 'Of course not. What a thing it would be! We could not alter it when it was done, and of course you would want to.' Her voice was sympathetic, as if her words hardly concerned herself. 'And what would people think? You can help me without that.' The words stumbled for the first time. 'If you want to help me, that is, of course.'

'I was trying to serve myself,' said Dudley, too lost in his own emotions to feel rebuff or relief. 'I must serve you in some better way. You can think of one yourself. And now we must hurry on and get you under a roof.'

He walked to Sarah Middleton's house, seeing his companion's thinly covered feet and uncovered head, and the scanty shawl snatched from somewhere when she was driven into the cold. On the steps of the house she looked up to explain the truth, that he might know it and express it for her.

'She came back from the house very early and very upset. I could hardly speak to her. Nothing I said was right. And she did not like it if I did not speak. It was no good to try to do anything. Nothing could have made any difference. Mr Seaton had gone to bed and we were alone. At last she flew into a rage and turned me out of doors. She said it drove her mad to see my face.' Miss Griffin's voice did not falter. She had felt to her limit and could not go beyond.

Dudley asked to see Sarah and told her the truth. She heard him in silence, with expressions of shock, eagerness, consternation, delight and pity succeeding each other on her face. When at last she raised her hands, he knew that his task was done. He saw her hasten into the hall and bring the hands down on Miss Griffin's shoulders. Her husband rose and put a chair for the guest, keeping his face to the exact expression for the action.

'You will be safe, my dear; we will see that you are safe,' said Sarah, showing that Miss Griffin was not the only person in her mind.

Miss Griffin parted from Dudley with eager thanks, and he saw her go in to food and fire with greater eagerness.

He left the house, feeling soothed and saner, and found himself imagining Sarah's experience, if she had known his own solution for her guest. He went to the inn to get a bed for the night, indifferent to surprise or question, finding a sort of comfort in the familiar welcome. He slept as he had not slept since his brother's engagement, the sense of suspense and waiting leaving him at last. He found that his mind and emotions were cleared, and that his feeling for Edgar had taken its own place. He had been lost in the tumult of his own life, and the hour passed in another's had done its work. Edgar stood in his heart above any other. The knowledge brought the relief of simplified emotion, but fed his anger with his brother, and confirmed his resolution to remain out of his life.

He went to Miss Griffin in the morning in almost convalescent calm, prepared to live his life without hope or eagerness. She came into the hall to meet him, wishing to see him without Sarah, as her sympathy with curiosity did not lessen the trial of response.

'Oh, it was everything to be warm and safe. I shall never forget that waiting in the cold. I don't know what would have happened if you had not come.'

'What would you like to do now? And in the future?'

'I should like to get away from Miss Seaton,' said Miss Griffin, meeting his eyes in simple acceptance of his knowledge. 'It seems a dreadful thing to say after all these years, but every year seems to make things worse. I should like to have some peace and some ordinary life like other people, before I get old.' Her voice broke and her eyes filled, both actions so simple that she did not heed or disguise them. 'I don't feel I want to have had nothing: it doesn't seem right that anyone should go through life like that. You only get your life once. Of course, if people were fond of you, that would be enough; but Miss Seaton seems to hate me now, and I don't know what to do to make it different. I only want to be peaceful somewhere, and not always driven and afraid, and to be able to do something for someone else sometimes.' Her eyes went round the hall as if its narrow comfort satisfied her soul.

'You would like a cottage of your own, and a little income to manage it on, and perhaps a friend to live with you, who needed a home.'

'Oh, I know two or three people,' said Miss Griffin, in gladness greater than her surprise. 'I could have them in turn, to make a change for me and for them. Oh, I should like it. But I don't know why you should do as much for me as that.' Her voice fell more than her face. She depended on Dudley's powers, and would have liked so much to do this for someone, that she hardly conceived of his not feeling the same.

'I shall like to do it, and I can do it easily. I shall be the fortunate person. We will arrange for the money to come to you for your life. I shall not be living here, but that will make no difference.'

Miss Griffin hardly heard the last words. She stood with a face of simple joy. She believed that Dudley would not miss the money, would have been surprised by the idea of his doing so, and saw her life open out before her, enclosed, firelit, full of gossip and peace.

'What will Miss Seaton say?' she said, in a tone which was nervous, guilty, triumphant and compassionate. 'Well, she will soon get used to it and settle with someone else.' A spasm crossed her face but did not stay. She had been tried to the end of her endurance, and knew that she could not continue to endure. 'Perhaps you could come and tell Mrs Middleton. Then I need not talk about it, and other people will hear.'

Sarah was startled, incredulous, rejoiced, desirous that Miss Griffin should have enough for her ease, anxious that she should remain a much poorer person than herself, relieved when it was apparent that she would; and betrayed her feelings partially to Dudley and completely to Miss Griffin, without surprising or estranging either. Miss Griffin's thought followed hers. She did not want a whit more than she needed, felt that the money would have more significance if every coin had its use, looked for the pleasures of contrivance, and allowed for a touch of laxness in herself, which Matty had combated with bitterness, with an open self-knowledge which to Sarah was sensible, and to Dudley comic and touching. She did not stress her gratitude, almost betrayed a faint sense of envy of anyone who could give so much without sacrifice. If she had not forgotten the offer of marriage, she behaved as if she had, and he saw that in effect they would both forget it, that she saw it simply as an impulsive offer of rescue. If she divined that it had some root in his own life, she saw the life as too far removed from her own to be approached.

Dudley left her with the natural sense of elation, and as it fell away, walked on with the single intention of going further from his brother, thinking and caring for nothing beyond.

Chapter 9

Edgar and his wife were left looking at each other. Maria was the first to speak.

'We must go on as if nothing had happened. We could not help it. I do not think we could. We might have seen it had to come. But I thought it would not come, with Dudley. Did you think that?'

'I thought it,' said Edgar, hardly parting his lips. He was summoning up his brother's experience, grasping at its meaning as his brother had lived it. He had taken from him the thing he had asked, taken and held it for himself, and let him move aside to walk alone, but near him that he might give his support. The demand was exposed, and he felt that he could not believe in the sight. Maria saw that it was useless to be with him, that each was alone.

By common consent they remained apart that night. When they met in the morning they felt it was a new meeting, that it came after a sudden separation and brought them to a new future. It almost made a fresh bond between them, giving them a common knowledge out of all they knew.

'Well, this is a sobering morning,' said a voice, which seemed to be neither Aubrey's nor Justine's, but was really the former used in imitation of the latter. 'But we shall be stimulated by it. We must live in Father's life and not allow ourselves to cross the bound. I will take it all at one fell swoop and lead the way into the room.'

'You both look tired after your long day,' said Mark.

His father felt that his words should cover that part of the day he did not know.

'Maria is tired,' he said.

'She will soon be rested in her own home,' said Justine. 'I already enjoy a personal sense of relief. I am a mere unimportant child of the house again.'

'Will you wait breakfast for Mr Dudley, ma'am?' said Jellamy.

'No. He is not coming back so early.'

'Where has he gone?' said Clement.

'Away for a time, I am afraid,' said Edgar. 'He felt he wanted a change. I fear that he found the sight of the two of us together too much.'

'Well, I think it is a thoroughly good idea,' said Justine at once. 'Uncle has been attempting altogether too much of late. He can't go on being superhuman. Even he is subject to the rules of mortal life. I wanted to suggest his having a break, and would have done so if I had dared.'

'He has done his duty in giving you a welcome, and feels he is free,' said Mark, realizing the false impression he gave.

'He has taken no luggage, ma'am,' said Jellamy.

'And does that prevent your bringing in the breakfast?' said Edgar.

'He will be sending for what he wants, I expect,' said Maria. 'He had to get away at once. Yes, bring in the breakfast.'

'I thought it might imply that he would be back this morning, ma'am.'

'You heard that he was not coming back,' said Edgar.

'Bring in the breakfast, Jellamy, and make no more ado,' said Justine. 'You will forgive me, Maria; the words slipped out. I can't keep my tongue from leaping out at that man sometimes.'

'I feel with Jellamy,' said Mark to Clement, as they followed the others to the table. 'He wants to know why Uncle has suddenly gone, and so do I. And the luggage is a point. Either he is coming back at once or he has left in storm and stress.'

'Don't whisper, boys,' said Justine, turning and lowering her own voice. 'Things are difficult and we must do our part. Pull yourselves together and remember that we are mere pawns in the game of skill and chance which is being played.'

'Are we as essential to the game as that? I feel a mere spectator. And it is really a simpler game.'

'Well, don't look as if we were making some mystery.'

'We could hardly contrive to do so. It is clear on what lines the break came, if break there has been.'

'Shall I remove Mr Dudley's place, ma'am?'

'No,' said Edgar, as he saw the traces of his brother about to be obliterated. 'Leave it as it is. It is likely – it is possible that he may come back.'

'We will all take our own places,' said Justine. 'Then Uncle can return and find his place ready for him, and the others occupied round him, as will be right and meet.'

'Not a gap in the circle,' said Aubrey, flushing as he realized his words.

'No one can be expected to show himself in Uncle's place,' said Mark.

'Yes, to take it would be even less easy – would be almost as difficult,' said Justine – 'oh, what a time this is for innocent and inapposite speeches!'

'No one tries to take anyone's place,' said Maria. 'Empty places remain and new people make their own.'

'Of course. Why cannot I put things as you do?'

'If you knew the reason,' said Clement, 'I am sure you would deal with the matter.'

'Well, that comes well from you. We don't see much sign in you of a gift for words.'

'Should we have said that silence was golden, if we had only known Clement?' said Aubrey.

Maria laughed, and Edgar looked up and smiled more at the sound than at his son's words.

'Yes, cheer up, Father,' said Justine. 'You have not lost everything with Uncle. And he will come back and everything will be as it has always been – everything will be straight and well.'

'Silence is golden,' murmured Aubrey.

'Oh, I don't know. I believe I would give all the silence in the world for a little healthy, natural speech.'

'Well, you have always done so,' said Clement.

'And I do not regret my choice.'

'Clement raises his brows,' said Aubrey.

'Aubrey is readier with his words than you will ever be, Clement.'

Aubrey looked at the window.

'Can you see through the curtain?' said his brother. 'If you can, it is still dusk outside.'

'I can see the wide, wintry expanse with my mind's eye.'

Edgar looked up, with his mind following his son's, and meeting the picture of his brother with no refuge before him or behind. He turned to his wife and knew that she saw the same.

'Did Uncle say anything?' said Justine. 'Did he – oh, I will take the bull by the horns, as he does. Has he any plans? Did he leave any address?'

'He had none to leave. He went suddenly,' said her father. 'He may – it will be possible for him to send one later.'

'We know all,' murmured Mark to Clement.

'You know all we can tell you,' said Edgar.

'A flush mantles Mark's cheek,' said Aubrey.

Maria was again amused, and her stepson showed his nonchalance by rising and walking to the window and pulling the curtain aside.

'Aunt Matty! Coming across the snow!'

'Across the snow? Aunt Matty?' said Justine.

'She must be coming across the snow if she is coming,' said Mark.

'Did you know she was coming, little boy? Why did you go to the window?'

Aubrey did not give his reason.

'Boys, get your coats and go to meet her. Perhaps she has some news of Uncle.'

Edgar rose.

'I hardly think so,' said Maria. 'She would not be coming herself.'

Matty was approaching with her halting step, holding a wrap

across her breast, holding something to her head in the wind, pressing forward with a sort of dogged resignation to her slow advance. She gave a faint smile to her nephews as she suffered them to lead her in.

'You have come alone, Aunt Matty?'

'Yes, I have come alone, my dears. I had to do that. I shall be alone now. My dear father has left me, and left me, as you say, alone.' Matty sank into a chair and covered her face. 'I must be content alone. I must learn another hard lesson after so many.'

She kept her hand to her brow and sat without moving, as the family gathered about her.

'Yes, I have had a life of deep and strange experiences. It seems that I ought to be used to them, that I ought to have that sad protection.'

There was silence.

'Losing her father when she is over sixty herself is not a startling one,' said Clement.

'Is Grandpa dead?' said Aubrey.

'That is a better way of putting it,' said Mark.

'Well, his life was over,' said Justine. 'It was not hard to see that.'

Matty was continuing to Edgar and his wife.

'He had gone to bed early as he was very tired. And I sent up something, hoping that he would eat before he slept. And it was found that he was already sleeping, and that he would not wake again.'

'We cannot improve on that,' said Mark.

'Yes, it was a good way to go,' said Matty, misinterpreting his words. 'He was full of years. His harvest was gathered, his sheaves were bound. For him we need not weep. But I must grieve for myself, and you will grieve for me a little.'

'Dear Aunt Matty, we do indeed,' said Justine. 'And Mother would have suffered equally with you.'

'Yes, dear. That is my saddest thought, that I have no one to do that. But I will be glad that yours is the lighter part. I had thought that my sister and I would sorrow together in this natural loss. But so much was not to be for me.'

Maria took the seat by Matty, and Matty gave her her hand,

putting the other over her eyes, but in a moment laid both hands on her friend's and looked about with a smile.

'Well, I must not fail in resolution. I must be myself. I must be what I always was to my father. I must not be lonely when I am not. I will not be.'

'Look round and see the reason,' said her niece.

'Yes, I see all my reasons,' said Matty, looking about as if to discover the truth. 'All the dear reasons I have for clinging to life, the dear faces which I have seen growing into themselves, the dear ones whose link I am now with one side of their past. Well, it should forge the link strongly. We shall go forward closely bound.'

'How was dear Grandpa found? Did Miss Griffin go in to him?'

'No, dear, the maid went in and found him as I say. As she thought at first, sleeping; really in his last sleep.'

'Poor Emma, it must have been a shock for her. Was she very much upset?'

'Well, dear, I was the more upset, of course. She was troubled in her measure. And I was sorry for her, and glad that she only had her natural share of the shock. Your grandfather had been always good to her. But she is not a young woman. There was nothing unsuitable in her being the one to find him. One of us had to do so, and I am not in the habit of going up and down stairs, as you know.'

'And now Miss Griffin is managing everything?'

'No, dear; Dr Marlowe is seeing that everything is done for me. He is a good friend, as you have found. There would not have been much for Miss Griffin to do.'

'She will feel it very deeply. I daresay she is too upset to be of much use. It is a long relation to break.'

'Yes, well, now I must tell you,' said Matty, sitting up and using an open tone. 'You will think that I have had a stranger life than you thought, that I seem to be marked out for untoward experience. Well, I was sitting in my little room alone, waiting for the shadows to close in upon me. It seems now that I must have had some presentiment; I had been so wrought up all day; you must have had your glimpse of it. And it was found that Miss

Griffin had left me, that my old friend with whom I had shared my life for thirty years, had vanished and left me alone in my grief. Well, what do you think of that for an accumulation of trouble, for what the Greeks would have called a woe on woe? I seem to be a person born for trial by flame. I hope I may emerge unscathed.'

There was silence.

'When did Miss Griffin go?' said Justine. 'Did anyone know when she went? Did she suddenly disappear?'

'Well, I must try to answer all those questions at once. But I only know what I have told you. I was sitting alone in the parlour, as you call it, finding the time rather drag as it moved on towards my trouble. I see that the boys are smiling, and I should not have wished to hasten it, if I had known. And I seemed to need the sound of a human voice, and I opened the door of the house – Miss Griffin had run into the garden on some pretext that I had sent her out, or something. You know I left you rather out of sorts; things here had upset me – and I found – Well, you find my tale amusing? I am making a mountain out of a molehill? It is a trifle that I am exaggerating because I am personally involved? Well, we have all done that. You will not find it hard to understand.'

'Then Miss Griffin did not leave you after Grandpa died? She had gone before? Yes, I know you implied that she had. But you said that you were alone in your grief. I did not quite follow.'

'I meant my grief for your mother, dear. I happened to be remembering. But it was not the time for you to do so, as I had found. Well, I will get on with my story. So I found that was how it was, that my old friend had left me – well, we won't say alone in my grief – alone in a dark hour. And what do you say to that for a sudden revelation? I won't say that I have nourished a viper in my bosom; I won't say that of Miss Griffin, who has been with me through so many vicissitudes, and whom I have spared to you in yours. I will just say – well, I will say nothing; that is best.'

'I don't think we can say anything either. We must find out where she has gone unless she returns very soon. But in the meantime tell us how you are yourself, and if you are staying here for the time.'

'Well, it is to Maria that I must answer that question,' said Matty, turning to her friend. 'Answer it as a matter of form, because I must remain with you. I cannot go back to that house alone. So the formal question is answered, and I can settle down in as much content as I can, in as much as will prevent my being a damper on other people.'

'Would you like anything fetched from your house?' said Maria.

'No, dear, no; Justine can lend me things of her mother's. I need not trouble you for anything.'

'I hope you will trouble anyone for anything you need.'

'Yes, dear, I know it would not be a trouble,' said Matty, with a faint note of correcting the term. 'But I am a person of few wants, or have learned to be. Now shall we leave me as a subject and go on to all of you? Or would you like to hear more of the old friend, or old aunt, or old responsibility, or whatever you call me to yourselves?'

'We should like to know all we can. Have you given any thought to the future? You clearly have not had time. But will you settle down in your house or will you be too much alone? Did you mean to stay there after your father died?'

'One moment, Maria. One thing, Aunt Matty,' said Justine, leaning forward with a hand on Maria's arm. 'Is Emma alone in that house? Let us get that point behind.'

'No, dear, she has a sister with her. You have not reached the stage of arranging such things for other people as a matter of course. And that being so, it was a natural anxiety. Well, what was Maria saying? Yes, I was to stay here after my father died. He meant me to, and so did my sister. And I shall follow what I can of their wish. It will seem to bind me to them closer, to carry out our common plan. So I shall be too much alone: I must answer "yes" to that question. But I shall not be too proud to accept any alleviation of my solitude.' Matty smiled at the faces about her. 'I have no false notions about what exalts people. I have my own ideas of what constitutes quality.'

'We will do all we can for the sake of the past, for your sake,' said Edgar. 'Maria will do it with us, as she will do everything.'

'Thank you. So we shall all have helped each other. We have

done our best with Blanche's place in filling it and finding that we cannot fill it.' Matty turned the smile on Maria. 'And now we must do what we can with another, and I know you will do your part. We are used to striving together to meet a common loss.'

'I read Aunt Matty like a book,' murmured Aubrey. 'I wonder if it is suitable for Justine's little boy.'

'And we hope that Miss Griffin will come back and be with you, Aunt Matty,' said Justine. 'I cannot imagine the two of you apart.'

'It is a relief not to have to think of them together,' said Aubrey, turning to meet his brothers' eyes. 'Yes, I am sure that is what Uncle would have said. You can see that I am trying to prevent your missing him.'

'Cannot you, dear?' said Matty to her niece. 'I have had to go a little further. You see I am having the experience. But shall we leave my prospects to the future, as we cannot in the present say much for them? I am holding you up in your breakfast. I will sit down and try to go on with it with you. I must make as little difference as I can.'

'Here is a place all ready for you.'

'Is there? How does that come to be? Had any news reached you? No, you were unprepared. Did you expect me to stay last night and order a place for the morning? Well, I must be glad that I went home to my father. Something seems to guide us in such things.'

'The something took a clumsy way of doing its work,' said Mark.

'So it was to be my place?' said Matty, seeming pleased by the thought. 'Perhaps you hoped that the truant guest would return and expiate her sins?'

'It is Dudley's place,' said Maria, knowing that the truth must emerge. 'We thought that you would not be here. But he has followed Miss Griffin's example and left us for the time.'

'Has he? Dudley? Has he run away and left you? Do we all manage to make ourselves impossible to those near and dear to us?' said Matty, her voice rising with her words. 'Is it a family trait? Well, we can all assure each other that our bark has quite wrongly been taken for a bite.'

'Barking may be enough in itself,' said Mark. 'It may not encourage people to wait for the next stage.'

'Our Dudley? Has he found things too much? Well, I can feel with him; I find things so sometimes. But running away is not the best way out of them. They will not get the better of him, not of Dudley. I should have been glad to get a sight of him, and borrow a little of his spirit. It seems that people who show the most have the most to spare. Theirs must be the largest stock. Well, I must have recourse to my own, and I have not yet found it fail. It is not your time to need it, but you may look back and remember your aunt and feel that you took something from her.'

'Why had Aunt Matty not enough spirit to give some to Miss Griffin?' said Aubrey.

'She gave her a good deal, or she got it from somewhere,' said Mark.

'Yes, it is Miss Griffin, is it?' said Matty, with a different voice and smile. 'Miss Griffin who takes the thought and takes the interest? That is how it would be. The person who has suffered less makes less demand. And we who suffer more must learn it. Well, we must not make a boast of spirit and then not show it.'

There was silence.

'I think we ought to find out where Miss Griffin has gone,' said Justine. 'I do really think so, Aunt Matty.'

'Yes, dear, I said she would be in your minds. And I think as you do. I shall be so glad to know where she is, when you can tell me.'

'I suppose we have no clue at all?'

'That I do not know, dear; I have none.'

'You have no idea where she may have gone?'

'None as she has not come here. I had a hope that she might have. I am so used to finding the house a refuge myself' – Matty gave her niece another smile – 'that I did not think of her being perhaps struck by it differently. Especially as she has spent her time in it in another way.'

'We are all very grateful to her. I am very hurt that she has not come here.'

'Yes, dear? She has hurt us all.'

'Has she any home?' said Mark.

'Her home has been with me. I know of no other.'

'She has no relations she could go to?'

'She has relations, no doubt. But, you see, to them she would be, as you say, a relation. It is to you that she is the person outside the family.'

'She has no friends in the neighbourhood?'

'She has those to whom you may have introduced her. She can have no others.'

'Aunt Matty, I know that you think we might have introduced you to more people,' said Justine. 'But the truth is that when the house was running at full pressure, with all of us at home and you and Grandpa coming in, Mother could manage no more. It worked out that your coming here to meet our friends meant that you could not meet them. It implied nothing more and I am sure you know it, and Maria may manage better; but as concerns the past that is the truth. It seemed to be a rankling spot, and so I have let in a little fresh air upon it.'

'No, dear, that is not the line on which my thoughts were running,' said Matty, lifting her eyes and resting them in gentle appraisement on her niece. 'They were on the death of my father, as they hardly could not be. And friends and houses and Miss Griffin all came second to it. Indeed only Miss Griffin came in at all.'

'We have no clue either to my brother's whereabouts,' said Edgar, taking the chance of opening his mind. 'It is a strange fashion, this silent disappearance. We must try to get on the tracks of them both. Was Miss Griffin prepared for going? It is very cold.'

'As far as I know, she went out of the garden without hat or coat or anything. The action was sudden and unpremeditated and she will probably be back at any time. She may be back now, in which case my father's death will have been a great shock to her.'

'Did she wander in the garden without hat or coat in this weather?' said Clement.

'Take care; Aunt Matty must have driven her out,' said Mark. 'And she did not wait to be called back, but went on her own way. And if she freezes or starves or dies of exposure, and it seems that she must do all those things, she will be better off than she has been.'

'Had she money, Aunt Matty?' said Justine.

'I do not know – yes, dear, more than I have at the moment.'

'And had she it with her?'

'I can only know that, when you find out and tell me. That thought has been in my own mind from the first.'

'She cannot have gone far,' said Maria, who had listened in silence. 'We could send someone to drive about the country and look for her. We had better do it at once.'

'May I interpose, ma'am?' said Jellamy.

'Yes, if you have anything to tell us.'

'Mr Dudley and Miss Griffin were perceived to be walking together last night, ma'am.'

'Oh, they were together. That is a good thing. How did you hear?'

'The information came through, ma'am.'

'You are quite sure?'

'The authority is reliable, ma'am.'

'Well, that is the worst off our minds about both,' said Justine. 'We need not worry about anyone who is in Uncle's charge, or about anyone in Miss Griffin's. Each is safe with the other. They both have someone to think of before themselves, and that will suit both of them.'

'It is a mercy that their paths crossed,' said Mark. 'What would have happened to Miss Griffin if they had not?'

'She would have gone home, dear,' said Matty, with a change in her eyes.

'Well, they did cross, so we need not think about it,' said Justine.

'We can hardly help doing that,' said Maria. 'It was the purest chance that your uncle passed at the time.'

'There are inns and other shelters,' said Edgar, glancing at the window.

'For people who have money with them. She seems to have gone out quite unprepared.'

'I told you that the action was unpremeditated,' said Matty. 'But they would have trusted her as she is known to live with me.'

'People might not trust a person who was leaving the house where she was employed.'

'Maria, it is a great feat of courage,' whispered Justine, 'and I honour you for it. But is it wise? And is it not an occasion when indulgence must be extended?'

'Your aunt had not lost her father when she turned Miss Griffin out of doors.'

'Oh, you have your own touch of severity,' said Justine, taking a step backwards and using a voice that could be heard. 'We shall have to beware. It may be a salutary threat hanging over us.'

'Well, what of Dudley?' said Matty. 'Are we to hear any more about him, now that Miss Griffin is disposed of? Have you any room for him in your minds? Do you take as much interest in his comings and goings? Did he go out prepared for the weather? Had he any money? Did you have notice of his going? Tell me it all, as I have told you. We must not deal differently with each other.'

'We will tell you, Aunt Matty. We admit that he went suddenly,' said Justine. 'And that we do not know the manner or the wherefore of his going.'

'Mr Dudley was sufficiently equipped for the weather, ma'am,' said Jellamy. 'Miss Griffin was perceived to be wearing his coat when they were observed together.'

'Was she? Then he was no longer in that happy state,' said Matty, going into laughter rather as if at Jellamy and his interruption than at Dudley's plight. 'We can keep our anxiety to him. Miss Griffin no longer requires it. What about scattering some coats and hats about the road, for people to pick up who have fared forth without them? It is really a funny story. Somebody from the large house and somebody from the small, running away into the weather without a word or a look behind! Well, people must strike their own little attitudes; I suppose we are none of us above it; but I cannot imagine myself choosing to posture quite like that. And if I had had to pick out two people to scamper off into the snow with one coat and hat between them, I should not have pitched on Dudley and Miss Griffin.' Matty bent her head and seemed to try to control her mirth. 'It was a good thing that the coat belonged to Dudley, if they were to wear it in turn. He could not have got into hers.'

No one joined in the laughter, and Matty wiped her eyes and continued it alone, and then stopped short and adjusted her skirt as if suddenly struck by something amiss.

'I have heard better jokes,' said Mark. 'The weather is icy cold and one coat is not enough for two.'

'I wonder who was wearing the hat,' said his aunt in a high voice which seemed to herald further laughter.

'Miss Griffin was perceived to be wearing a shawl about her head, ma'am.'

'Oh, what a picture! It sounds like a gipsy tableau. I wonder if they intended it like that. I wonder if they had a caravan hidden away somewhere. I know that Miss Griffin has plenty of hats in her cupboard. Some of them I have given her myself. What can be the reason of this sudden masquerade?'

'Perhaps she had none in the garden,' said Clement.

'We know they have not a caravan,' said Mark. 'And it is hard to see how they are to manage without one.'

'There is the inn,' said his father, in a sharp tone.

'Of course there is, Edgar,' said Matty in a different manner. 'They all seem to think that the scene is staged on a desert island. But the scene itself! I can't help thinking of it. I shall have many a little private laugh over it.'

'But no more public ones, I hope,' muttered Mark.

Maria rose from the table, and Justine, as if perceiving her purpose, instantly did the same. Matty followed them slowly, using her lameness as a pretext for lingering in Edgar's presence. She came to the drawing-room fire in a preoccupied manner, as if the cares of her own life had returned.

'Well, you are well in advance of me. I came in a poor third.'

'We know you like to follow at your own pace,' said Justine.

'I do not know that I like it, dear. My pace is a thing which I have not been able to help for many years.'

'Well, we know you prefer people not to wait for you. Though Father and the boys have waited. I suppose they saw that as unavoidable.'

'Yes, I expect they did, dear. I don't think we can alter that custom.'

'No, naturally we cannot and we have not done so. But poor Aunt Matty, of course you are not yourself.'

'No, dear, of course I am not,' said Matty, with full corroboration. 'And it has been silly of me to be surprised at seeing all of you so much yourselves. This morning is so different from other mornings to me, that it has been strange to find it so much the same to other people. You have not had days of this kind yet. Or you have put them behind you. Sorrow is not for the young, and so you have set it out of sight. And you have filled your empty place so wisely and well, that I am happy and easy in having helped you to do it. Any little shock and doubt and misgiving has melted away. But my father's place will be always empty for me, and so I must remain a little out of sympathy – no, I will not say that – a little aloof from the happiness about me. But I am glad to see it all the same. I must not expect to find people of my own kind everywhere. They may not be so common.'

'I should think they are not,' said Clement.

'You mean you hope not, naughty boy?' said Matty, shaking her finger at him in acceptance of his point of view.

'You do not want to think they are.'

'I only found myself noticing that they were not.'

'We might – perhaps we might see ourselves in other people more than we do,' said Edgar.

'We all have our depths and corners,' said Justine.

'And we all think that no one else has them,' said Mark.

'Dear, dear, what a band of philosophers!' said Matty. 'I did not know I had quite this kind of audience.'

'Do you see yourself in us more than you thought?' said Clement.

'No, dear, but I see a good many of you at once. I did not know you were quite such a number on a line. I had thought of you all as more separate somehow.'

'And now you only see yourself in that way?'

'Well, dear, we agreed that I was a little apart.'

'I don't think we did,' said Mark. 'You implied it, but I don't remember that you had so much support.'

'I am going to end the talk,' said Maria, rising. 'Your aunt is more tired than she knows and must go and rest. And when I come down your father and I will go to the library, and you can have a time without us.'

'How tactless we have been!' said Justine. 'We might have thought that they would like an hour by themselves. But what were we to do while Aunt Matty was here?'

'What we did,' said Mark. 'No one could have thought that the scene was to our taste.'

'I do admire Maria when she gives a little spurt of authority.'

'She did not like to think of Miss Griffin wandering by herself in the snow,' said Aubrey, bringing this picture into the light to free his own mind.

'Little tender-heart!' said Justine, simply evincing comprehension.

'Without a coat or hat, and I suppose without gloves or tippet or shawl,' said her brother, completing the picture with ruthlessness rather than with any other quality.

'It is odd that we feel so little about Grandpa's death.'

'Aunt Matty's life puts it into the shade,' said Mark.

'Well, he was old and tired and past his interests, and we really knew him very little. It would be idle to pretend to any real grief. It is only Aunt Matty who can feel it.'

'And it does not seem to drown her other feelings.'

'Perhaps that is how sorrow sometimes improves people,' said Aubrey.

'No, no, little boy. No touch of Uncle at this moment. It is too much.'

'We might all be better if our feelings were destroyed,' continued Aubrey, showing that his sister had administered no check.

'Poor Aunt Matty! One can feel so sorry for her when she is not here.'

'You do betray other feelings when she is,' said Mark.

'I suppose I do. We might have remembered her trouble. Even Father and Maria seemed to forget it.'

'Well, so did she herself.'

'She will be very much alone in future. I don't see how we are to prevent it.'

'Will grief' be her only companion?' said Aubrey.

'Well, she has driven away her official one,' said Mark.

'She will be confined to rage and bitterness and malice,' said Clement.

'So she will be alone amongst many,' said Aubrey.

'No, no, I don't think malice,' said Justine. 'I don't think it has ever been that. I wonder what Miss Griffin and Uncle are doing. But their being together disposes of any real problem. I think Uncle may safely be left to arrange the future for them both.'

'Uncle has been left to do too much for people's futures,' said Mark. 'And not so safely. We can only imagine what happened last night.'

'You are fortunate,' said Clement. 'I cannot.'

'Or unfortunate,' said Aubrey, who could.

'I have been keeping my thoughts away from it,' said Justine.

'They have had enough to occupy them,' said Mark. 'But they will return. Grandpa's death, Miss Griffin's flight, even Aunt Matty's visit will all be as nothing. We may as well imagine the scene.'

'No, my mind baulks at it.'

'Mine does worse. It constructs it.'

'Maria was there,' said Aubrey.

'Yes, poor Maria!' said Justine. 'What a homecoming! It never rains but it pours.'

'I think it nearly always rains. We only notice it when it pours.'

'Yes, it is Uncle. Clear, natural and incontrovertible,' said Justine, with a sigh, as if this fact altered no other. 'Well, you may be clever boys, but you have a depressed sister to-day.'

'How would it all have been if Maria had kept to Uncle?' said Aubrey.

'That is not Uncle,' said Clement.

'Little boy, what a way of putting it!'

'Miss Griffin would still have run away; Grandpa would still have died; Aunt Matty would still have paid her visits,' said Mark. 'Only it might have been Father instead of Uncle who met Miss Griffin. And that might not have worked so well. He would have been more awkward in offering her his coat. So perhaps it is all for the best. That is always said when things are particularly bad, so there could hardly be a better occasion for saying it.'

'Look,' said Justine, going to the door and holding it ajar. 'Look at those two figures passing through the hall, as two others used to pass. What an arresting and almost solemn sight! Do we let our hearts rejoice or be wrung by it?'

'We will take the first course if we have the choice.'

'Which is better, the sight of two beautiful men or of a beautiful man and a beautiful woman? I do not know; I will not try to say.'

'I am letting my heart be wrung,' said Aubrey, grinning and speaking the truth.

'Will they ever be three again? Ought we to wish it? Or ought we just to hesitate to rush in where angels fear to tread?'

'We might be imagining them four,' said Aubrey, in a light tone.

'How I remember Mother's slender figure moving in and out between the two taller ones! That is a different line of thought, but the picture somehow came. And it brings its own train. Mother would have wished things to come right between them. And it may be that they will do so, and the three tall figures move together through life. But I fear it cannot be yet. Uncle was heading for trouble, and at the crucial moment it came. He could not go on too long, keyed up to that pitch. The strain of the last months can only be imagined. None of us can know what it was.'

'Is Justine transfigured?' said Aubrey.

'Well, I am affected by the spectacle of intense human drama. I do not deny it.'

'It were idle to do so,' said Clement.

'It would have been better to go away at once,' said Mark, 'and not attempt the impossible.'

'I don't know,' said his sister, gazing before her. 'It was a great failure. Surely one of those that are greater than success.'

'I never quite know what those are. I suppose you mean other kinds of success. The same kind involves the same effort and has a better end.'

'And a much more convenient one,' said Clement.

'Yes, yes, more convenient,' said Justine. 'But what we have seen was surely something more than that.'

'Something quite different indeed,' said Mark.

'Surely it was worth it.'

'Well, in the sense that all human effort must achieve something essential, even if not apparent.'

'Well, now the human drama goes on in the snow,' said Aubrey.

'Oh, surely they have got under shelter by now,' said Justine, laughing as she ended. 'Oh, what intolerable bathos! You horrid little boy, pulling me down from my heights!'

'You could not have gone on too long any more than Uncle.'

'I don't know. I felt I was somehow in my element.'

'That may have been what Uncle thought. I believe it was,' said Mark.

'A greater than Uncle is here,' said Aubrey.

'And they are different heights,' said Clement.

'I think Clement is making an effort to conquer his taciturnity, Justine.'

'Oh, don't let us joke about it. Do let us turn serious eyes on a serious human situation.'

'Miss Griffin and Uncle walking through the snow, with Miss Griffin wearing Uncle's coat and hat!' murmured Aubrey.

'She was not wearing his hat. She – she –' said Justine, going into further laughter – 'had a shawl round her head. Oh, why are we laughing? Why cannot we take a serious view of what is serious and even tragic in itself? Miss Griffin's long relation with Aunt Matty broken! Because I suppose it is the break. And her life at sixes and sevens, because that must be the truth. And we cannot see it without being diverted by silly, little, surface things which in themselves have their tragic side, just because they touch our superficial sense of humour.' Justine's voice quavered away as this again happened to her. 'I suppose we are half hysterical; that is what it is.'

'That is the usual explanation of unseemly mirth,' said Mark.

'Well, happiness is a good thing,' said Edgar, smiling in the door, his voice as he said Matty's frequent words, illustrating the difference between them. 'Maria and I are going to walk outside – that is, we are going for a walk before Mark and I begin to work. Your aunt is resting upstairs.'

'Oh, Father, it seems that we ought not to be in spirits on the day of Grandpa's death and Aunt Matty's desolation, and all of it,' said Justine, taking hold of his coat. 'But we are in a simple, silly mood. We have agreed that we must be hysterical.'

'Your grandfather's death can only seem to you the natural thing it is. He has not been much in your life and he has had his own.' Edgar's voice was calm and almost empty, as if his feelings on one thing left him none for any other.

'But Aunt Matty's loneliness and all that has happened,' said Justine, standing with her face close to the coat and bringing the lapels together. 'You do feel that you have an anchor in your children?'

Edgar turned and walked away.

'Oh, I suppose I have said the wrong thing as usual. I might have known it was hopeless to attempt to do anything for him. In my heart I did know.'

'It is good to follow the dictates of the heart,' said Clement.

'Yes, you can be supercilious. But what did you attempt after all? I did try to show Father that he had something to depend on in his home.'

'And he showed you that he could not take your view.'

'I suppose Maria has taken my place with him. Well, it would be small to mind it. I have never done much to earn the place. And it is better than her taking another. She does not feel she has taken that. We can think of that little place as open and empty, free for Mother's little shadow.'

Aubrey turned and slouched out of the room, kicking up his feet. He came upon Maria, who had been to fetch a cloak and was following her husband.

'Are you going upstairs?' she said. 'What is the matter? Come back a minute and tell me.'

Aubrey threw back his head, thrust his hands into his pockets and turned and sauntered back.

'Odd days these.'

'Yes, they are strange and disturbed. But they will pass.'

'Days have a way of doing that. It is the one thing to be said for them.'

'Too much happened yesterday indeed.'

'Indeed.'

'Your grandfather had had his full share of everything. And there is no greater good fortune than sudden death.'

'No,' said Aubrey, his face changing in a manner which told Maria her mistake.

'And he knows nothing now,' she said, 'not even that he is dead. And that can be said of all dead people.'

There was a pause.

'You have had your share of things,' said Aubrey, with terse and equal understanding.

'We have all had that and found it enough.'

'Too much for me. Quickly up and quickly down at my age. But if I am thought callous one minute, I am thought sensitive the next.'

'We need not mind being thought callous sometimes,' said Maria, seeing the aspect preferred.

'No. The heart knoweth,' said her stepson, turning away.

Chapter 10

'Shall I say what I can see?' said Mark. 'Or does it go without saying?'

'Let us not go to meet her,' said Clement. 'Let us begin differently and hope so to go on.'

'Your aunt is already in the hall or we should meet her,' said Edgar with a vision of his brother going swiftly to such a scene.

Matty came forward without exhibition of her lameness or of anything about herself.

'Now I am afraid you must see me as the bearer of ill tidings. And I may deserve to have to bring them. I have made myself the harbinger of sadness and now I am not to come without it. But you will make my hard task easy. You will know that the tidings are sad for me as well as for you.'

'What is it?' said Edgar at once. 'Is it my brother?'

'Yes, you have helped me. And now I can help myself and tell you that it is not the worst, that all is not lost. There is still hope. He is lying ill at a farmhouse twenty miles away. He walked for days when he left this house, and got wet and got weary, and ate and slept where he could; and came at last to this farm one night, hardly able to say who he was or whence he came.' Matty dramatized what she had to tell, but spoke without actual thought of herself. 'And the next day they fetched Miss Griffin to nurse him, and a message came from her to me this morning, to say that there is trouble on the lungs and that she does not dare to hide the truth. She has a doctor and a nurse, and the woman at the farm is good. So all we have to do is to go to him at once. All that you have to do. What I have to do is to stay here and keep the house until your return. And if it seems to me the harder part, I will still do it to the best that is in me. I will do what serves you most and what saves you anything.'

Edgar had already gone, followed by his wife. Matty suggested some things which might be of use, and before they were ready he had set off on horseback by himself.

'Someone should go with Father,' said Justine. 'But it is too late.'

'Is Uncle a strong man?' said Mark.

'He has seemed to be in his own way. But the troubles must have lowered his resistance, and the wet and cold have done the rest.'

'He saved Miss Griffin,' said Aubrey; 'himself he could not save.'

'My dear, think what you are saying. What makes you talk like that?'

'Excess of feeling and a wish to disguise it,' said Aubrey, but not aloud.

'Where has Miss Griffin been?' said Mark.

'At the Middletons' house, where your uncle took her on the day when your grandfather died,' said Matty, stating the fact without expression. 'I know no more.'

'We must go. Good-bye, Aunt Matty,' said Justine. 'Maria is in the hall. Keep Aubrey with Mr Penrose, and the house to its course. We can't say yet just what we may require of you.'

'Command me, dear, to any service,' said Matty, with a hint of dryness in her tone.

'You can send me word,' said Aubrey, 'and I will command my aunt.'

Edgar was in advance of his family and was the first to enter his brother's room. Miss Griffin met him at the door, and the way she spoke of Dudley, as if he could not hear, warned him of his state.

'He is very ill. He must have been ill for days. He will have me with him; he will not be left to the nurse.' She stood, stooping forward, with her eyes bright and fixed from want of sleep. 'He is like Mrs Gaveston in that. The doctor says that his heart is holding out and that he may get well.'

Dudley was raised a little in his bed, the limpness of his body showing his lack of strength to support himself, his breathing audible to Edgar at the door. His eyes were still and seemed not to see, but as his brother came they saw.

'What is the time?' he said in a faint, rapid voice between his breaths. 'They do not tell it to me right.'

'It is about twelve o'clock.'

'No, it is the afternoon,' said Dudley, with a cry in his tone. 'I have been asleep for hours.'

'Yes, you have had a sleep,' said Miss Griffin, in a cheerful, ordinary voice, which she changed and lowered as she turned to Edgar. 'It was only for a few minutes. He never sleeps for more.'

'It will soon be night,' said Dudley.

'Not just yet, but it is getting nearer.'

Dudley lay silent, his expression showing his hopeless facing of the hours of the day.

'Does the time seem very long to him?' said Edgar.

'Yes, it is so with very sick people. It is as if he were living in a dream. A minute may seem like hours.'

Dudley fell into a fit of coughing and lay helplessly shaken, and under cover of the sound Miss Griffin's voice became quicker and more confidential.

'Oh, I am glad I could come to him; I am glad that he sent for me. It was a good thing that I was not with Miss Seaton. She might not have let me come. She said she would never let me nurse anyone but her again. But I don't expect she would have kept to that.'

'I am sure she would not,' said Edgar. 'Is there anything my brother would like?'

'If only it would stop!' said Dudley, looking at Edgar as he heard the word of himself.

Edgar turned to him with so much pain in his face, that he saw it and in the desperation of his suffering tried to push it further.

'If only it would stop for a second! So that I could get a moment's sleep. Just a moment.'

'He is not like himself,' said Edgar. 'It seems – it reminds me of when my wife was ill.'

There were the sounds of the carriage below and Miss Griffin spoke with appeal.

'Is anyone coming who can help? I have been with him all day and all night. He cannot bear to be with strangers, and he should not be nursed by anyone who is too tired.'

'My wife and daughter are here,' said Edgar, the word of his second wife bringing the thought that he could not replace his brother. 'And any help can come from the house at once. In the meantime my sons and I have hands and ordinary sense, and can be put to any service.'

Maria came into the room and Dudley saw her.

'It is the afternoon,' he said, as if she would allow it to be so.

'Not yet,' she said, coming up to the bed. 'You did not send for us, Dudley. That was wrong.'

'I sent for Miss Griffin.'

'Yes, but you should have sent for Edgar and me.'

'I only want to have someone here. I don't think you are different from other people,' said Dudley, in a rapid, empty tone, which did not seem to refer to what she said, looking at her with eyes which recognized her and did no more. 'It doesn't matter if we are not married. I like Edgar best.'

'Of course you do. I knew it all the time. And he feels the same for you.'

'If I could get to sleep, the day would soon be gone. And this is the longest day.'

Maria turned to speak to her husband and Dudley's eyes followed her, and the moment of attention steadied him and he fell asleep.

Justine entered and kept her eyes from the bed, as if she would fulfil her duty before she followed her will.

'I have come to take Miss Griffin to rest, and then to wait upon anyone. The boys have gone on some messages. Father, the doctor is here and can see you.'

Dudley was awake and lay coughing and looking about as if afraid.

'Is it another day? Shall I get well?'

'Of course you will,' said the nurse. 'It is the same day. You only slept for a little while. But to sleep at all is a good sign.'

'People are here, are they? Not only you?'

'Justine and I are here,' said Maria.

'Why are you both here?'

'We both like to be with you.'

'Is it the afternoon?'

'It will be soon. Would you like me to read to you?'

'Will you put in any feeling?'

'No, none at all.'

'Who is that person who puts in feeling? Matty would, wouldn't she? And Justine?' Dudley gave a smile.

'What book will you have?'

'Not any book. Something about –'

'About what?' said Maria, bending over him.

'You know, you know!' said Dudley in a frightened voice, throwing up his arms.

The movement brought a fit of coughing, and as it abated he lay trembling, with a sound of crying in the cough. Edgar and the doctor entered and seeing them broke his mood, though he did not seem to know them.

'Well, I haven't much to live for,' he said to himself. 'I am really almost alone. It isn't much to leave behind.' He tried to raise himself and spoke almost with a scream. 'If I die, Miss Griffin must have some money! You will give her some? You won't keep it all?'

'Yes, yes, of course we will. She shall have enough,' said Edgar. 'But you will not die.'

Something in the voice came through to Dudley, and he lay looking at his brother with a sort of appraisement.

'You don't like me to be ill,' he said, in a shrewd, almost knowing tone. 'Then you should not make me ill. It is your fault.'

'He does not know what he is saying,' said the nurse.

'I do,' said Dudley, nodding his head. 'Oh, I know.'

'How long will it go on?' said Edgar to the doctor.

'It cannot be quick. He is as ill as he can be, and any change must be slow. And the crisis has yet to come.'

The crisis came, and Dudley sank to the point of death, and just did not pass it. Then as he lived through the endless days, each one doubled by the night, he seemed to return to this first stage, and this time drained and shattered by the contest waged within him. Blanche's frailer body, which had broken easily, seemed to have stood her in better stead. But the days which passed and showed no change, did deeper work, and the sudden advance towards health had had its foundation surely laid. The morning came when he looked at his brother with his own eyes.

'You have had a long time with me.'

'We have, Dudley, and more than that.'

'Do they know that I shall get better?'

'Yes, you are quite out of danger.'

'Did you think I should get well?'

'We were not always sure.'

Dudley saw what was behind the words, but was too weak to pursue it.

'Shall I be the same as before?'

'Yes. There will be no ill results.'

Dudley turned away his head in weakness and self-pity.

'You can go away if you like. There is nothing you can do. Where is Miss Griffin?'

Miss Griffin was there, as she always was at this time. The lighter nursing of this stage was within her powers. Dudley reached out his hands and smiled into her eyes, and Edgar watched and went away.

These moments came more often and at last marked another stage. Then the change was swift, and further stages lay behind. Dudley was to be taken to his brother's house to lie in his own bed, but before the day came even this stage had passed. The change was more rapid in his mind than in his body. In himself he seemed to be suddenly a whole man. The threat of death, with its lesson of what he had to lose, had shown him that life as he had lived it was enough. He asked no more than he had, chose to have only this. His own personality, free of the strain and effort of the last months, was as full and natural as it had been in his youth.

His return to the house as an essential member of it was too much a matter of course to be discussed. It was observed with celebration, Dudley both expecting and enjoying it. Maria went home in advance to get order in the house and Edgar and Miss Griffin were to manage the move and follow.

Matty had been an efficient steward, but the servants did not bend to her simply autocratic rule, and Jellamy was open in his welcome. She seemed to be oppressed by her time of solitude, and kept to the background more than was her habit, seeming to acknowledge herself as bound less closely to the house. She knew that Maria realized her effect on its life, and was trying to establish a different intercourse, welcoming her as a family connection and her own friend, but keeping the relation to this ground.

The family waited in the door for the carriage to appear.

'Well, what a moment!' said Justine. 'To think that our normal life is to be restored! It seems almost too much. It shows us what rich people we are.'

'That has hardly been true of us of late,' said Mark.

'Yes, it is partly the force of contrast. The sharp edge of our appreciation will blunt. So we will make the most of it.'

'I deprecate the method of enhancing our feeling.'

'Our worst chapter is behind, our very worst. And I mean what I say; I use the words advisedly. You need not all look at me. You see, our grief for Mother was unsullied. This would have had its alloy.'

'Relief from anxiety gives the impression of happiness,' said Clement.

'Then let us have that impression,' said his brother.

'Here they come! We must set our faces to disguise our emotion,' said Aubrey, doing as he said.

'I don't want to disguise it,' said his sister, wiping her eyes. 'I do not care how much of it is seen by Uncle or anyone else. I should not like to go away and nearly die, and come back to unmoved faces.'

'Neither should I,' said Dudley's voice. 'I could not bear it. I do not like people not to show their feelings. If they do not, they are no good to anyone but themselves, and they don't enjoy them nearly so much as the people who cause them. And it is better to have proof of everything, anyhow of feelings.'

'Oh,' said Justine, with a deep sigh, 'the old touch.'

'I must pay great attention,' said Aubrey. 'I have been a long time without an example.'

'Stay,' said his sister, thrusting a hand behind her as she strode forward. 'I am going to help Uncle out. I am going to use my feminine privilege in an unusual way.'

'She looks equal to it,' said Matty, smiling at Maria.

'Oh, someone else is to come out first,' said Justine, turning and ruefully raising her brows. 'Oh, it is Miss Griffin. Uncle does not forget to be himself. Well, it will give me great pleasure to help them both.'

'How do you do, Miss Seaton?' said Miss Griffin, as she set foot upon the ground, embarking on her ordeal at once.

'How do you do, my dear?' said Matty, shaking hands with cordial affection. 'We owe a great deal to you.'

'What a good thing it is that I am spared!' said Dudley, descending on his niece's arm. 'It is generally the valuable lives that are cut off, but I can feel that a real attempt was made on mine.'

'You helped yourself a great deal,' said Miss Griffin.

'And heaven helps those who do that. But I really don't remember any help but yours.'

'Now up to your room. No more talking,' said Justine, bringing her hands together. 'Not another moment in this chilly hall. Maria, you do not mind my taking matters into my own hands. You see, Uncle has been bound up with the whole of my life.'

'It is well that Maria feels as you say,' said Clement.

Justine's words brought a sense of what was behind, and Edgar cleared a way through the hall. Dudley was assisted by his nephews to his room. He would have been able to walk with Edgar's help, but the brothers shrank from following their natural ways, as yet unsure of their footing. The uncertainty had come with Dudley's return to health.

'Well, what are we to do to celebrate the occasion?' said Matty, with something of her old tense touch.

'Go into the drawing-room and sit quietly down,' said Justine, in a rather loud tone, 'and give ourselves to thankfulness.'

'Yes, dear, that is what we feel inclined to do. So we are to indulge ourselves,' said Matty, putting her niece's inclinations on their right level, and taking her seat by the fire in silence.

'Uncle will come and join us for an hour when he is rested.'

'Well, I will wait for that, if Maria will let me.'

'You will wait for it, of course, with all of us,' said Maria.

Mark and Clement returned.

'Uncle is resting in his own room and Miss Griffin in another.'

'Not in the same room?' said Aubrey.

'Now, little boy, no foolishness on this occasion.'

'Those two great, clumsy lads carried Uncle up with hands as gentle as a woman's,' said Aubrey, blinking his eyes.

'Poor Miss Griffin, I am shocked by her appearance,' said Justine. 'She looks more worn than Uncle.'

'Yes, dear, I am troubled too,' said Matty. 'It seems sad that her connection with us should bring her to this. I have never seen her looking in this way before.'

'You must have, Aunt Matty, at the times of your own illnesses.'

Matty gave a smile and a sigh, as if it were no use to make statements doomed to rejection.

'This was arduous nursing,' said Maria. 'It could not be helped.'

'Of course not, dear. If it could have been it would have. That is the thing that makes us sorry.'

'The nursing has not been much for some time,' said Edgar. 'Miss Griffin is looking fairly well. She was upset by the motion of the carriage.'

'And Father behaved with simple chivalry,' said Aubrey. 'Well, it would have been no good for Clement to be a witness.'

'Oh, I believe she always is!' said Justine, sitting up straight.

Matty gave a laugh.

'That sort of thing does make people look ill for the moment,' said Maria.

'And Miss Griffin is not used to driving,' said Justine.

Matty put back her head in mirth.

'Did you know, Aunt Matty, that she was to have a little house of her own?' said Justine, driven to the sudden announcement. 'Uncle is to make it possible.'

'No, dear,' said Matty, with her eyes dilating. 'I did not know. How could I when I was not told? When was that arranged?'

'When they met after – before Uncle was ill.'

'Well, I am glad, dear; glad that our long relation is ending like this; glad that I brought her to a family who were to do this for her. It is good that our friendship should have this culmination.'

'It was not the one which Aunt Matty planned when she turned her out of doors,' said Mark to his brothers. 'There was no question of any alternative roof.'

'I am sure you are glad, Aunt Matty,' said Justine.

'Are you, dear? So you accept something that I say.'

'And I am sure it will be the beginning of a new relation with Miss Griffin.'

Matty gave a little trill of laughter.

'Now, Aunt Matty, what exactly amuses you?'

'My relation with her, when you have all used her as a sick nurse and nothing else!' said Matty, bending her head and speaking in an impeded voice.

'Maria, would you advise me to move out of hearing of my aunt?'

Matty sat up and looked from her niece to her friend.

'If you think there would be anything gained,' said Maria.

Justine rose and went to a distant seat, and her aunt looked after her with open mockery.

'So I am too dangerous a tinder for my niece's flint and steel. Or is it the other way round?'

'Either account will serve,' said Clement.

'Well, well, then we must try not to come against each other. Perhaps we are too much alike.'

'No, I don't think that is it, Aunt Matty,' called Justine. 'Oh, what is the good of my moving to a distance if I must communicate from it?'

'No good,' said her brother.

'I should move back again, dear,' said Matty, easily. 'I don't think it does achieve anything.'

Justine returned and sat down even nearer to her aunt, raising her shoulders.

Matty looked at her for a moment and turned to Maria.

'You have the whole of your family at home?' she said, stooping as if unconsciously to free her dress from contact with her niece.

'They are all at home as a usual thing. Clement is away for the term, but he gives us a good deal of time.'

'He hasn't the house of his own yet?'

'I don't want it yet; I am putting it off,' said Clement, in a quick, harsh tone. 'I am thinking about it. I shall have it before long.'

'I have rather an uncompromising nephew and niece.'

'Well, we say what we mean, Aunt Matty,' began Justine. 'Oh, it is not worth while to waste a thought on us. Here is the person who matters! We might be twice as good or twice as bad and still be as nothing. And Father in attendance, after hovering about upstairs until he should wake! So that is why he crept away. I need not have wondered.'

'Can we all quite agree that we are as nothing?' said Matty in a low, arch, rapid tone, looking up at Dudley as he passed. 'I have never felt it of myself, or had it felt of me, if I can judge by the signs. So I must hold myself apart from that generalization, though it is not a thing that matters on this occasion.'

'This is the occasion in question,' said Clement.

'I have not had any sleep,' said Dudley. 'I could not lose myself. I may be better down here amongst you all. If you see me dropping off, you could all steal quietly away. Perhaps your talk will lull me to sleep unawares.'

Edgar followed his brother, looking as if he had no connection with him and holding his face to prevent an encounter of their eyes. Dudley sat down by the fire and signed for a cushion. His niece was at his side in an instant, settling the cushion behind him and thrusting a rug down on either side of his knees.

'I think Justine is a little more than nothing,' said Matty, with a smile.

'I am Uncle's willing slave. That is all I ask to be.'

'Well, I would ask nothing better, if I were permitted such a character. But, as I have said, it has not been the one assigned to me.'

'Well, you have been an invalid,' said Justine, making a sally towards the rug where it was working up.

'Justine explains it,' said Aubrey.

'Not always, dear. Not when I was your age, for instance.'

'I don't think this talk will lull me to sleep,' said Dudley.

'Well, I may not be a slave,' said Matty, holding up a piece of needlework for his eyes, 'but I have been willing in your service. A little bit of something made by a friend means more, I hope, than the same thing bought out of an ample purse.'

'Is every stitch in it worked by loving hands?'

In an instant Justine had the work out of her aunt's hands and before Dudley's eyes.

'Gently, dear, the stitches will unravel,' said Matty, leaning forward.

'Barely an inch or two. Nothing compared to the satisfaction of proving to Uncle that the work is all your own.'

'He would have taken Aunt Matty's word,' said Mark.

Matty retrieved the work and, placing it on her knee, set herself to remedy the damage.

'Not much harm done, is there?' said her niece.

'A piece to be worked again, dear. It does not matter. I have all the time to do it, as no doubt you thought.'

'Let me do it, just the piece that came undone. Then you will have worked the whole of it once.'

'I only want loving thoughts stitched into it,' said Dudley.

'You shall have them,' said Matty, in a full tone. 'Every thought shall be loving and every stitch mine, some of them doubly done.'

'Oh, we forgot to ask, Aunt Matty, how you have been managing without Miss Griffin,' said Justine, recalled by her aunt's industry to the fact that she was used to aid.

'Forgot to ask!' said Mark to Aubrey. 'I would have died rather than do so.'

'I think I shall die, now it is done. If I don't, I don't know how to manage.'

'Don't talk about dying in that light way,' said Dudley. 'You have no right. You have no idea of what it is to hover between life and death.'

'No experience of the valley of the shadow,' said Aubrey.

'None at all. I suppose there will be something in my face now that there is not in yours.'

'Don't let us talk about that time,' said Justine, with a shudder. 'Let us only remember it enough to be thankful that it is past.'

'And to feel the value of my presence in your home.'

The words recalled the other way in which Dudley might have been lost to them. Justine moved to her uncle and stood stroking his hair, and her father's eyes followed her hand.

'Father might like to help Justine to smooth Uncle's hair,' murmured Aubrey, 'to help his only daughter.'

'Well, Aunt Matty, what have you to tell us about yourself?' said Justine, putting more energy into her hand. 'We have been too lost in our own troubles to give a thought to things outside.'

'Your aunt has been in similar case,' said Edgar.

'Now there is a nice, understanding word,' said Matty. 'And it is indeed a true one, even though in my case the things were not outside myself.'

'Aunt Matty threw Father a grateful glance,' said Aubrey.

'So I did, dear. I do not get too much understanding since Mother died, and Grandpa,' said Matty, adapting her words to her nephew. 'So much of it went with them. I do not mean that I expect more than I have. It would be idle indeed to do so. But I am the more grateful when it comes.'

'Well, let us all emerge from that stage and take more interest in each other,' said Justine. 'You tell us of your plans and we will hear them.'

'Well, dear, I have none as yet, as your father would know. Plans need thought and attention, and they have not been forthcoming.'

'Try to do what you can about them at the moment,' said Maria.

'Shall I, dear? I have been wondering when I should hear your voice. All these loquacious young relatives of mine seem to overwhelm you.'

'I have never been a talkative person. Perhaps I have not much to say.'

'Don't be afraid, Aunt Matty; Maria can hold her own,' said Justine.

'Well, now, I have been asked for my plans. So I must make them and make them at once, so as not to keep people waiting. Well, as Miss Griffin is no longer to depend on me for a home, I must look for someone else who will find it a help to do so. For I cannot rely upon a maidservant for the greater part of my companionship.'

'Indeed no,' said Justine, 'though it would not be the greater part. You are wise to fill Miss Griffin's place, in so far as you can do so.'

'Yes, dear, we all have to deal like that with places, or we all do. And, you know' — Matty gave her niece a different smile — 'I do not make a sorrow of a friend's good fortune.'

'Ought the next person who is to depend on Aunt Matty for a home,' said Aubrey, 'to be told that it may be in the garden?'

'I have heard that snow is a warm covering,' said Mark. 'I don't know if Aunt Matty had.'

'Uncle had not, or he need not have given Miss Griffin, his coat.'

'Depend does not seem a word to use of Miss Griffin,' said Justine. 'She earned her independence, if anyone did.'

'It is clear what your aunt means,' said Edgar.

'Father, I believe you are jealous of me for my proximity to Uncle,' said Justine, hastening away from Dudley with no idea that her words had any real truth.

Edgar, who only knew it at the moment, put a chair for his daughter and smiled at her as she took it.

'Dear Father, with his one ewe lamb!'

'Suppose Father had more than one,' said Aubrey.

'Well, Miss Griffin has certainly earned her independence in these last weeks,' said Matty. 'And she is to have it. That is so good to hear.'

'Uncle had arranged to give it to her before he was ill,' said Justine.

'Had he, dear? Well, that does not make it any less good. And if she had not earned it then, she has now. Or if she had earned it then, she has now earned it doubly. Let us put it like that. So she has a right to it. And I shall like so much to see her in her own home, as she has always seen me in mine.'

'I really believe you will, Aunt Matty.'

Matty appeared once more to strive with her laughter.

'Where is Miss Griffin?' she said, looking round as she overcame it. 'Does she not want to be with you all? Or is she afraid of so many of us?'

'She is afraid of one of us,' said Mark. 'And so am I.'

'Where has Clement gone?' said Edgar.

'I expect to his room,' said Aubrey. 'He is always slinking away by himself.'

'Well, he has seen me,' said Dudley, 'and satisfied himself that I am on the mend.'

'And to do him justice, Uncle, he did not go until he had done that,' said Justine. 'And he has his work. And we shall have someone else disappearing to-morrow. These holidays are at an end and they come too often. Maria and I are agreed.'

'Aubrey could not work while he was gnawed by anxiety.'

'Well, the relief will be a tonic now.'

'I may wish to give myself to thankfulness for a time,' said Aubrey.

'We all feel inclined for that, but the world has to go on.'

'I suppose it would have gone on if I had died,' said Dudley. 'That is what we hear about the world. I think the world is worse than anything. Even Aubrey's lessons stopped.'

'They are about to begin again,' said Justine, with resolute descent to daily life. 'There are many things in Clement which he might emulate.'

'And Clement might take many lessons from his quiet little brother,' said Aubrey, looking to see his stepmother smile and inconsistently looking away as she did so.

'I suppose you will all understand each other better now,' said Dudley. 'People do that after anxiety. I can feel that I have not been ill in vain.'

'It seems that there ought to be more understanding,' said Matty, with a faint sigh.

'Oh, people are not often as ill as I was.'

'How does it feel to be so ill that you might die?' said Aubrey, with a desire to know.

'I can hardly say. Perhaps I was ready. I really don't understand about people who are not. When you are delirious and do not recognize people, it is hard to see how you can feel remorse for a lifetime and prepare yourself for eternity. I cannot help thinking that even people who die, are not as ill as I was. I think they are sometimes surprisingly well, even perhaps at their best.'

'It is the few lucid moments at the last,' said Justine.

'Well, I did not have those, of course. It is odd to think that we are all to have them. It does make me respect everyone. But long conversations and meetings after years of estrangement must be so difficult when you cannot recognize people. And it hardly seems worth while for a few moments, even though they are lucid. And I see that they must be. When people's lives are hanging by a thread, it seems enough to break the thread. And I think it must do so sometimes, if people die when they are equal to so much, more perhaps than they have ever been before.'

Justine looked at Dudley uncertainly, and Matty with a smile.

'Have you been reading the books in the farmhouse, Uncle?' said Mark.

'Yes, I read them while I was getting well. And if I had known I was to be so ill, I would have read them at first.'

'I love to hear him talk like his old self,' said Matty, glancing at her niece.

'Don't you notice that a new note has crept in? Perhaps it marks me as a person who has looked at death. I think that Justine has noticed it.'

'Yes, I have, Uncle,' said his niece quietly. 'It is the weakness of convalescence.'

'Convalescence seems to be a little like the lucid moments at the last. I may not have got quite far enough away from them.'

'You will soon forget it.'

'I shall not. You will. I see you are doing so.'

'I know what you mean,' said Matty, keeping her eyes on Dudley's face. 'I too sometimes feel rather apart, as I live in my memories and find that other people have lost them. But I would not have them oppressed by what I can carry alone.'

'I would; I had no idea that I should have to do that.'

'I thought that people would always be as they were at my sickbed. They were so nice then; I thought a great change had come over them, and it had. They must have been expecting the lucid moments and getting themselves up to their level. And now they have returned to their old selves, as you were saying of me. But they have really done it.'

'Are you joking, Uncle, or not?' said Justine.

'I am joking, but with something else underneath, something which may return to you later. If it does, remember that it is only convalescence. And now I will go and have another rest. Being here with you has not lulled me to sleep.'

'Mark had better go up with you,' said Maria. 'You are not quite steady on your feet.'

Dudley crossed the room, touching something as he passed and letting Mark take his arm at the door. His brother rose the next moment, adjusted something on the chimney piece, went to the door and swung it in his hand and followed.

'Father cannot keep away from Uncle and I cannot either,' said Justine. 'I am going to follow at a respectful distance, more to feast my eyes on him than to be of any use. I am not going to grasp at the privilege of waiting on him. I bow to Father's claim.'

'I will bring up the rear,' said Aubrey, 'and feast my eyes on Justine.'

'And Maria and Aunt Matty can have the hour together for which I suspect Aunt Matty has been pining.'

'I shall enjoy it, dear, but so I hope will Maria. It is a thing which depends on us both.'

'Yes, have it your own way. Enjoy it together. Forget us; agree that we are in the crude and callow stage; anything; I am quite beyond caring. Oh, I am so happy that I could clap my hands; I could leap into the air.' Justine proved her powers. 'I am in such a mood that it would be idle to attempt to contain myself.'

Aubrey gave a grin towards his stepmother, and opening the door for his sister, followed her with his head erect.

'Quite a finished little man,' said Matty. 'You should not have much trouble with him. In what order do they come in your affections? They are already there, I can see.'

'I hardly know the order. There will be one, of course. I think perhaps Mark comes first; then Justine; then Aubrey and then Clement. I hardly feel that I know Clement yet.'

'I think I would put them in the same order,' said Matty, who had lost her tenseness. 'Except that perhaps I would put Mark after Justine. Yes, I think that my niece comes first, even though we try to quarrel with each other. We never succeed and that says a great deal.'

'Why do you make the effort? It seems to be a rather constant one.'

'Ah, you are catching the note of my nephews! You are to be a true Gaveston after all. You are not going to be left behind.' Matty broke off as a noise came from the stairs.

Dudley had mounted the first flight, and coming to the second, had shaken off his nephew's hand and gone on alone. His limbs gave under him and he fell forward. Edgar sprang after him; Justine gave a cry; Mark turned back and raised his voice; Aubrey ran up the last stairs; Clement broke from his room and hurried to the scene. Dudley was helped to his nephew's bed, hardly the worse. Edgar stood by him, looking as if his defence had broken before this last onset. Clement made a movement to cover something on his desk, stumbled and made a clutch at the desk and sent a mass of gold coins in a stream to the floor.

Justine started and glanced at them; Aubrey paused for a longer moment and stared at his brother; Mark left the bed as he saw that no harm was done, and stood looking from the floor to the desk. Clement touched the coins with his foot, kicked a cloth towards them and thrust his hands into his pockets.

'How nice you all looked!' said Dudley, who had seen what they all saw. 'Just as you did when I was ill.'

'And we felt like it for a minute,' said Justine, turning from her uncle as she spoke.

Edgar sat down and looked at his son, as if he ought to have some feeling over for him.

'Father looks paler than Uncle,' said Mark.

'But anyone can see that I am the one who has been ill,' said Dudley.

Maria appeared at the door with Jellamy behind, and Clement

had the eyes of the household turned on the secret corner of his life.

'Is Dudley hurt?' said Maria. 'Was it Dudley who fell?'

'Yes, it was me. It was a silly thing to do. You will get quite tired of all my disturbances and think less of them. It never does to wear out people's feelings.'

'Is that money, Clement?' said Justine.

'If it is not, I will leave you to guess what it is.'

'Have you been saving?'

'I have been putting by something to spend on my house. You know that I am going to have one, and that I do not spend what I have.'

'Why do you keep it in that form?'

'It is like that at the moment. Or some of it is. I have to have some in hand for various things. And I don't care about having interest up to the last moment.'

'Clement is a miser,' said Aubrey, who accepted this account and did not know how the words struck other ears.

'Well, are you going to leave me?' said his brother, who was strolling up and down, enabled by the smallness of the space to turn round often and hide his face. 'Or are you going to settle in my room? Perhaps you forget that it is mine.'

'You can allow Uncle time to recover,' said Mark.

'He does not need to do so, as you know.'

'And the rest of us to get our breath.'

'I admit that I took that away from you,' said Clement, with a laugh.

'Clement, that is no good,' said Justine. 'It is not a pretty thing that we have seen, and you will not make it better by showing us anything else that is ugly.'

'I have no wish to show you anything. I don't know why you think so. It is your own idea to pry about in my room. I don't know what you keep in yours.' Clement turned to Aubrey, who was touching things on the table. 'Stop fingering what is not your own and get out of the room. Or I will throw you out.'

'Don't do that,' said Dudley. 'If anyone else has a fall, I shall not be the centre of all eyes. And if you won't share things with Aubrey, why should I?'

'Is anyone of any use to Uncle? And ought not Maria to be in the drawing-room, giving tea to Aunt Matty?'

'The king is in his counting house, counting out his money;
The queen is in the parlour, eating bread and honey,'

quoted Aubrey in the door.

Clement took one step to the door and kicked it to its latch, indifferent to what he kicked with it. It opened smoothly in a moment.

'Miss Seaton wished to be told if any harm was done, ma'am,' said Jellamy.

'None is done in here,' said Mark. 'I don't know about outside.'

'Master Aubrey has knocked his head, sir.'

'Oh, I had better go,' said Justine.

'We will come with you,' said Maria. 'Clement did not ask us in here.'

Edgar followed his wife, and Dudley got off the bed and strolled to the desk.

'I am glad that you value your money, Clement. I like you to take care of what I gave you. And it shows how well you behaved when I asked for it back. I can't think of that moment without a sense of discomfort. We all have a little of the feeling at times. To know all is to forgive all, but we can't let people know all, of course. Does it give you a sense of satisfaction to have money in that form?'

'I don't know. Some of it happened to be like that.'

'I wish you would tell me. Because, if it does, I will have some of mine in it.'

'I suppose some people sent it in that form, and I put it all together. It will not remain so for long.'

'Of course I am not asking for your confidence.'

'I hope you have not killed Aubrey, Clement,' said Mark.

'Justine would have come back and said so if I had. She would think it worthy of mention.'

'I should not like Aubrey to die,' said Dudley. 'I only nearly died, and it would give him the immediate advantage.'

'You must come to your room, Uncle,' said Mark. 'It was my duty to see you there.'

'I am not going there,' said Dudley on the landing. 'I am going downstairs again. I have lost my desire for rest. I can't be shut away from family life; it offers too much. To think that I have lived it for so long without even suspecting its nature! I have been quite satisfied by it too; I have had no yearning after anything further. Matty is going and the gossip can have its way. It will be a beautiful family talk, mean and worried and full of sorrow and spite and excitement. I cannot be asked to miss it in my weak state. I should only fret.'

'You won't find it too much?'

'I feel it will be exactly what I need somehow.'

Matty waved her hand to Dudley and continued her way through the hall, as if taking no advantage of his return.

'Now I feel really at ease for the first time,' he said as he entered the drawing-room. 'I do not mind having fled from my home in a jealous rage, now that Clement is a miser. It was a great help when Matty turned her old friend out into the snow, but not quite enough. Now I am really not any worse than other people. Not any more ridiculous; I don't mind if I am worse.'

'You know you are better,' said Justine, 'and so do we. Now, little boy, sit down and keep quiet. You will be all right in an hour.'

'You need not change the subject. I really am at ease. I don't need Aubrey to take the thoughts off me. I don't even like him to.'

'Clement believed that I had attained his size before I had,' said Aubrey, assuming that thoughts were as his uncle did not prefer them.

'Well, are we to talk about it or are we not?' said Justine.

'Of course we are,' said Dudley. 'You know I have already mentioned it. I hope you do not think that it would have been fairer to Clement if I had not. If you do, I shall never forgive myself, or you either. But of course you would forgive me anything to-day; and what is the good of that, if there is nothing to forgive?'

'It is fairer to Clement to talk of it openly, reasonably and without exaggeration.'

'Justine speaks with decision,' said Aubrey.

'It may be better still just to forget it,' said Maria. 'We came upon it by accident and against his will. And it may not mean so much. We all do some odd things in private.'

'Do we?' said Dudley. 'I had no idea of it. I never do any. As soon as I did an odd thing, I did it in public. I am so glad that life was not taken from me before I even guessed what it was.'

'How much money was there in gold?' said Aubrey.

'Now, little boy, that is not at all on the point.'

'If Clement is to have a house, it will take all he has,' said Edgar.

'A less simple speech than it sounds,' said Justine. 'There is the solution, swift, simple and complete.'

'Perhaps he will starve behind his doors,' said Aubrey, 'and put his gold into piles at night.'

'Someone deserved to have his head broken,' said Edgar.

'He may suffer from reaction and be driven into extravagance,' said Dudley. 'We shall all mind that much more. It must be difficult for young people to strike the mean.'

'The golden mean,' murmured Aubrey. 'Clement may like to strike that.'

'He will have a good many expenses,' said Mark. 'A house-keeper and other things.'

'We already detect signs of extravagance,' said Dudley.

His nephew strolled into the room.

'Well, am I to flatter myself that I am your subject? I am glad that you can take me in a light spirit. I was fearing that you could not.'

'We were wondering if you could afford to run a house,' said Maria.

Clement stopped and looked into her eyes.

'Well, I shall have to be careful. But I think I can manage with the sum I have saved. I am keeping part of it in money for the first expenses. They are always the trouble.'

'Do you think of having the house at once?' said his father.

'Well, very soon now. I shall be going to Cambridge to see about it. I have enough put by for the initial outlay.'

Clement went to the window and stood looking out, and then pushed it open and disappeared.

'Is it wise for a young man to spend all he has?' said Mark. 'Let us now transfer our anxiety.'

'So it is over,' said Dudley. 'Clement is a victim of the rashness of youth. I hope he will not waste his allowance.'

'And all our thought and talk about it are over too,' said Justine, rising. 'We are not saying another word. Come, Aubrey; come, Mark. Come, Maria, if I may say it; we are really following your lead. We know you want us to leave Father and Uncle alone.'

Edgar looked at the door as it closed, and spoke at once.

'The boy has hardly had a father.'

'No, you have failed in one of the deepest relations of life. And you are faced by one of the results. Because there is more in this than we admit. I am not going to get so little out of it. I am sure people got more out of my running away from home.'

'I hope he will go along now. This may be the result of too little to spare all his life. Your help may be a godsend in more than one sense.'

'It seems to have been the cause of the trouble. You can't be a miser with no money.'

'You can be with very little, when it is scarce.'

'I rather liked Clement to be a miser; I felt flattered by it. It was taking what I gave him so seriously.'

'We may be making too much of the matter.'

'Maria would not let us make enough. I will not give up the real, sinister fact. Why should I not cling to the truth?'

'Maria will be a help to us with all of them.'

'To us! You knew the word that would go straight to my heart. But you ought to be a success as a brother, when as a father you are such a failure. What can you expect but that the tender shoots should warp and grow astray? They had no hand to prune or guide them. I don't believe you even realized that Clement was a shoot. And he was so tender that he warped almost at once. I think you are very fortunate that he was the only one.'

'How much has happened in the last fourteen months!'

'Yes. Matty came to live here. I inherited a fortune. I was engaged to Maria. Blanche fell ill and died. You became engaged in my place. You and Maria were married. Matty's father died. Matty drove her old friend out into the snow. I ran away from my home. I am not quite sure of the order of the last three, but they were all on the same night, and it was really hard on Matty that it happened to be snowing. On a mild night she would not have been blamed half so much. I rescued Miss Griffin and took her into my charge. It was hard on us that it happened to be snowing too. I decided to provide for her for her life. It seemed the only thing in view of the climate. At any time it might snow. I was sick almost to death, and was given back to you all. In more than one sense; I must not forget that. Oh, and Clement was gradually becoming a miser all the time. You would have thought he had enough to distract him.'

There was a pause.

'Dudley, I can ask you a question, as I know the answer. Maria does not mean to you what she did?'

'No, not even as much as you would like her to. I cannot see her with your eyes. I have returned to the stage of seeing her with my own. I nearly said that to me she would always be second to Blanche, but it would be no good to echo your own mind. And of course to both of us she is only just second to her. But I think that you married her too soon after Blanche died, and that you may never live it down. You can see that I am speaking the truth, that I feel it to be my duty. I know that Blanche had a good husband, but it would never be anyone's duty to say that.'

'I was carried away. I had not been much with women. And I think that emotion of one kind — I think it may predispose the mind to others.'

'Why do some people say that we are not alike? We seem to be almost the same. But grief for a wife is a better emotion than excitement over money. Your second feelings had a nobler foundation and deserved success. But no wonder there are no secrets between us. I only have one secret left. But it shows me what it was for Clement, when his only secret was exposed.'

'Are you going to tell me?'

'Yes, I am, because it is proof that I have lost my feeling for Maria. I have already proposed to someone else.'

'What?' said Edgar, the fear in his tone bringing final content to his brother. 'You have not had time. You were ill a few days after you left this house.'

'Well, I proposed to her a few minutes after. You see that I lost my feeling for Maria very soon. And she refused me. Women do not seem to want me as the companion of their lives.'

'Miss Griffin?' said Edgar, with incredulity and perception.

'How affection sharpens your wits! But you should have said: "I want you, Dudley."'

'I think – I see that the sun is coming out.'

'So we can go out and walk as we have all our lives. The only difference will be that I must lean on your arm. I have had to say it for you. Saying it in your own way does not count. I said it in anyone's way. I am the better of the two.'

'I think you might for twenty minutes, for a quarter of an hour.'

The pair went out and walked on the path outside the house, and Justine, catching the sight from a window, rose with a cry and ran to fetch her brothers.

A GOD AND HIS GIFTS

Chapter 1

'I will ask you once more. It is the last time. Will you or will you not?'

'I will not. It is also the last time. It must be the last.'

'You will not give me your reasons?'

'I will give you one. You have too much. Your house and your land. Your parents and your sister. Your sister who is also your friend. Your work and your growing name. I like things to be on a moderate scale. To have them in my hands and not be held by them.'

'That is not the only reason. There must be a deeper one.'

'There is. And it may be deep. I do not want to marry. I seldom say so, to be disbelieved.'

'You don't feel that marriage would mean a fuller life?'

'I don't want the things it would be full of. Light words are sometimes true.'

'Then there must be a change. I do want to marry. I want to have descendants. I want to hand down my name. I could not keep up our relation under a wife's eyes. It has escaped my parents.'

'Your father I daresay. What about your mother?'

'I am not sure. It is hard to know.'

'It has not escaped her, or you would know. Silence has its use.'

The speaker's indifference to convention appeared in her clothes, her cottage, and her habit of looking full at her companion and voicing her thought. She was a short, fair woman of about thirty, with a deep voice, a strongly cut face, and calm eyes that were said to see more than other people's, and sometimes did. Her companion was a large dark man, with solid, shapely features, heavy, gentle, nervous hands, strong, sudden movements and a look of smouldering force. He ignored convention in another way, and in one that was his own. A consciousness of being a known and regarded figure showed in his dress and his bearing, and was almost undisguised. The breach of family tradition involved in his leading a writer's life in addition to a landowner's, enhanced him in his own eyes and supported his conception of himself.

'Well, this is a last occasion. It becomes one. It is what you choose.'

'And what you do. I think you will be happy. And I hope she will. That is where the question lies.'

'If I marry her, she should be. I will do my part.'

'It will be easier than hers. I wonder if you know it.'

'Hers cannot be what yours would be. I am helpless there.'

'So am I. I am not fitted for an ordinary domestic life.'

'So I must live with someone who is. And I shall not see the life as ordinary. None is so to me.'

'How do you see your own life? It is even less so to you?'

'It is as it is. As I am what I am. I know I am a man of full nature. I know I am built on a large scale. I am not afraid to say it.'

'It is true that most people would be. If I thought it of myself, I should. So you can't know if I think it. But do you know anyone who thinks he is built on a small scale?'

'I know many people who are. It is part of their interest to me.'

'But not of their interest to themselves. Do they know on what scale they are?'

'I am to marry someone who is on a moderate one, and who knows it.'

'Then I guess who it is. There is someone of whom it is true. And there would not be anyone else.'

'My father perhaps?'

'But you can hardly marry him, Hereward.'

'In effect I have done so. We are all wedded to each other. My wife must fit into a human framework. It is a demand I have to make.'

'And you feel you can make it. You know the woman who is to meet it. You are not in doubt.'

'I am not. I have my own knowledge of Ada Merton. Her qualities are many. I would not marry a woman I could not depend on and trust. I know I have had my early time. But in her own way she has had hers.'

'Well, there is the attraction of opposites. Though I never quite believe in it. It is safer to depend on qualities held in common. What will your parents feel about your marriage?'

'They will be glad to hear of it. They will welcome the thought of grandchildren. It is the natural, usual thing.'

'What of your sister? There is the touchstone. I will not speak of her scale. We do not question it.'

'She has always helped me. She will help me now. I have imagined her as your sister. I thought she would be.'

'But then I should be a sister too. And I have not a sister's qualities. I don't even know what they are. No doubt you can tell me.'

'I can, and they are great ones. I have seen some of them in you.'

'If you and I were married, think of the scale of our children! With both of us on such a considerable one. A house with such a brood! It could not stand.'

'It would have stood. But it was not to be. I wonder if you will regret it. People may see you as a disappointed woman.'

'They will. And I shall wish they knew I was not. I may be on a small scale after all.'

'You may be, Rosa. You are,' said Hereward with sudden force. 'You are content with too little. My wife will have more than you. To have a thing we must accept it. You could be the first person in my life. You choose to be nothing and it is what you will be. I cannot play a double part.'

'Not with me. But I should have thought you could. I fear you will, and I think you fear it. I know you, and you know yourself.'

'I do. I wish I did not. I know the forces within me. I know they may rise up at any time. As you have found, they have sometimes risen. I don't exhaust them on my work. They are not easily spent. The effort seems to give them strength, to set them free. You have been my safeguard. You could always be.'

'No, the forces would be there. You are not for the single path.'

'Rosa, I shall be a good husband.'

'You may be what you mean by the words.'

'I will see that Ada finds me what she should.'

'In time she must find what you are. There is no escape.'

'Do I not offer a good deal?'

'What do you ask? Your home is your father's. She will not be its mistress.'

'I did not know you considered such things.'

'I may not. We are not talking of me.'

'She is a good daughter and sister. She does not ask much for herself.'

'But now she may ask more. Will she marry to have the same?'

'She will have what I give her,' said Hereward, again with force. 'She will take it and be content. What is the good of your rejecting me yourself, and bringing all this against my marrying someone else? You know the way to prevent it.'

'There is nothing against your marrying her. There is everything in its favour. I was saying what there was against her marrying you. Does she know what it is?'

'She knows nothing. She will know nothing. And there may be nothing to know.'

'Let there be nothing, Hereward. Let there always be nothing. It will help you both. And there are many of you, and there may be more. It will help you all.'

Chapter 2

'My wife, there may be trouble coming. We will meet it with a brave heart. We have faced too much together to fail in these our latter days.'

'What have we faced, Michael? I don't think I can remember anything.'

'Ah, Joanna, our home is in danger. This old roof over our heads. It has sheltered our fathers, and may not pass to our son. Hand-in-hand we came in, in our youth and hope. Hand-in-hand we would go out, depending on each other, and the knowledge that we had harmed no one. Ah, no one is the worse for our downfall. That must be our stay. Without it we were poor indeed.'

'It sounds as if we should be poor with it. And some people must be the worse, if you mean we are in debt.'

'Ah, debt presses on us, Joanna. And the creditors have no pity. The old words mean nothing to them: "Blessed are the merciful". But our courage will not fail us. If our home passes to other hands, we will witness it, dumb and dry-eyed. If strangers cast on it appraising eyes and utter belittling words, we will stand aside and be silent.'

'Are they really as bad as that? When the house was in danger before, they said such nice things about it. And about what they would make of it, when it was theirs. I hardly knew its possibilities. I was quite sorry they could not have it.'

'Well, I was not,' said Sir Michael Egerton. 'I was glad we could keep it. Because what would happen to us without it I am at a loss to say. It would be the end of our world.'

The old house in question was large and beautiful and shabby, but only the last to any unusual degree. It had the appeal of a place where lack of means had prevented the addition of new things, and ensured care of the old. The land about it stretched to a fair distance, and in the past had provided its support.

'The end of the world never comes. And there are always people who expect it.'

'Well, it may not come, my wife. Matters may adjust themselves. They have done so before.'

'I don't think they have. It has had to be done for them. It will be done for them again. I can't say that Hereward will do it. It might seem that I was taking it as a matter of course.'

'I hope we are not, Joanna. I hope we have not sunk so far. What would you say, Galleon? I know you have not missed a word.'

'Well, Sir Michael,' said the butler, who had not done so, 'would it not be giving credit where credit is due?'

'Rendering to Caesar the things that are Caesar's. Well, I suppose it would. It has come to be our part.'

'And it must be nice to be Caesar,' said Joanna. 'I think Hereward must like it. I am sure I should.'

'Ah, Joanna, I am forced to lean where once I led. It goes against the grain. It would be at once better and worse to have no dear ones.'

'For us it would be worse. I don't know what to say about them. I suppose we are their dear ones. We have to assume we are. Well, they say that all love has its sad side.'

'Ah, ha, well, I suppose it has. We are looking to them, I admit. Well, we must be worthy of them. We must not bring faint hearts to the stress of life. We must face our indebtedness, shoulder the burden and carry it with us. We will not bend beneath it, heavy in its way though it be. Is not that our own victory?'

'Yes, it is. We can be sure it would not be anyone else's.'

'What would you call it, Galleon?'

'I can hardly say, Sir Michael.'

'Ah, the humble part is the hard one. Gratitude is the rare thing to give. In a sense it is a gift. If we can give it, nothing is beyond us. To render it is the way to be unvanquished by it.'

'It must be difficult to be vanquished,' said Joanna. 'I hardly see how anyone could be.'

'Ah, you can smile to yourself, Galleon. That is always your line. You don't know the cost of some of the stresses of life. I can only think you have escaped them.'

'These would hardly arise in my situation, Sir Michael.'

'They come from things that are common to us all.'

'It is the degree in which those are held, that is not common to us, Sir Michael. But I have no claim to them. It falls to me to observe them in other hands. And I think there may be news of some of them. The post is here, and, if I am right, a lawyer's letter. I am familiar with their aspect.'

'Yes, no doubt you are. And so am I. I am sure I wish I was not. You are right. I wish you were wrong. It is a lawyer's letter. And from Messrs Blount and Middleman, names that strike a chill to my soul. Middleman! It is the right word. Something between ourselves and human good. Now what a profession to choose! One that brings trouble and anxiety to innocent people. And does little else as far as I can see. Except cause threats and mysteries where there is none. It must be an odd man who wants it. I would rather bring a little peace and goodwill myself. Well, Messrs Blount and Middleman, and what have you to say? Is it my fault that tithes and rents fall, and expenses rise? What have I done to cause it? Nothing but lead a simple life and harm no one. Well, let us read your letter. The courage it needs! I declare I am without it. Strong man that I am, I have not enough to open it.'

'Perhaps her ladyship could be of help to you, Sir Michael.'

'No, she could not. I should not ask it of her. I am not a man who talks about the courage of women. It is for a man to show courage himself. So here is the moment. My Joanna, be prepared. It is the last straw that may break us. But we will show our mettle. We come of stock that has it. Come here and read it with me. I can't put a hand on my glasses.'

'Your hand happens to be on them, Sir Michael.'

'Yes, so it does. So I can read it myself. And I don't care what it is. It cannot be laid to my account. – So the land by the river is sold. The piece that has been on the market. The figures of the sale are here. And the expenses and the agent's commission. They would not be left out. Come and look at them, Joanna. Figures are out of my line. I have come to be afraid of them. Messrs Blount and the other have frightened me. I shudder at the thought of them. – What? Is that what it is? Money and a real sum of it! Enough to mean something! I don't know how to believe it. I will not believe it for the time. I will let it soak in. I will savour it. I will have some moments of relief. They do not come too often. Well, if money is the root of all evil, it is the root of other things too. There is no evil here that I can see. This delivers us, Joanna. This opens up our path. Forward can be our watchword. Forward, with heads up, eyes on the future, strong in heart.'

'If I may say so, Sir Michael, the money is capital, and should be seen and used as such.'

'Well, you may not say so. Who do you think you are? Messrs Blount and Middleman? One example of them is enough. A douche of cold water is not what we want at the moment. You should know that at your age. A man of forty should be equal to it. And money is money, capital or not. You can't get away from it.'

'Is capital exactly money?' said Joanna. 'If it was, it could be spent. It is a large amount, that brings in small ones without getting any less. And the small ones are spent; and their being so small leads people into debt. But it seems kind and clever of capital. We should not ask any more.'

'True, my lady,' said Galleon. 'We must not kill the thing we love.'

'Do I love capital? I suppose I do. It is dreadful to love money. I did not know I did. But capital is so kind to us. I am sure anyone would love it. And it is sad if it is sometimes killed. It makes me love it more.'

'Well, what I love is a little ease,' said Sir Michael, leaning back as if to enjoy it. 'I am a man of sixty, and it is time I had it. And I want it for you as much as for myself. More, of course; I want it chiefly for you. And for all the people in whose debt we are. Ah, I have thought of them, Joanna. My mind has not been only on myself. I have pictured them in want of what was theirs. I have not been blind to their claims. Because what is owed to them is theirs in a way. I have recognized it.'

'They have recognized it too. You and they seem to be alike. But it seems somehow inconsistent of them. Thinking it is theirs, when it is spent! They seem to love money as much as I do. And not to be ashamed of it. It makes me quite ashamed for them. They might have behaved nobly, and they have not.'

'Ah, we do not meet that, Joanna. We must not look for it, my wife. Self is what it is in their minds, self and little else. But they have been in mine. In it and on it, day and night. Sleeping and waking, I have had them in my thought. I have had to hold myself from dwelling on them. It was all I could do.'

'Well, if you did all you could! It is known that no one can do more.'

'Well, it is in the past. Our way is clear. My heart sings at the thought. It leaps for them and for ourselves. Let us celebrate it, Joanna. This renews the days when our yoke was easy and our burden light.'

The pair moved together and executed movements reminiscent of these days, while Galleon's large, pale eyes surveyed them from his large, pale face, his large, pale, skilful hands perhaps more usefully employed.

Sir Michael and his wife were both grey-haired and dark-eyed, tall and upright and active for their age. They were distant cousins, and a likeness was sometimes discerned in them. Sir Michael's broad features had a look of having failed to mature, while Joanna's, of similar type, were strongly formed and marked with lines of mirth. His hands, inert and solid and somehow kind, seemed a part of himself; and hers, spare and active and also kind, had a life of their own. Their common age of sixty was acknowledged by Joanna openly, and would not have been owned by Sir Michael at all, if his wife could have been depended on.

'Well, here is a scene,' said their daughter's voice. 'Shall we find ourselves equal to it? We have put away childish things.'

'Come, it is too soon for such a pose. Come and join your mother and me. Try to be as young as we are. We are celebrating good news. Good for ourselves and others; that is the happy part. Joy for ourselves is not true joy for us. This is the real thing.'

'Say what has happened,' said Zillah to her mother, as though taking the shortest line to the truth.

'Some money has fallen in. Some land is sold. We could pay what we owe, if the money was not capital. Or if capital was money, as your father thinks it is. He feels so kindly to creditors. And people so seldom do. I never speak of them myself. It might sound as if we were in debt.'

Zillah Egerton was shorter than her mother, and seemed to be darker, as she was not grey-haired. She had Joanna's definite features, but not Sir Michael's look of ease. She gave an impression of controlled energy, as Hereward gave one of effort to keep his under control. The gravity and perception of her face seemed the complement of the force in his. At thirty-two and thirty-four they had the air and poise of middle age.

'The land by the river!' said Hereward, guided to the letter by a sign from Galleon. 'Of course the money is capital. It must be invested. It is an appreciable part of the estate. Debts must be paid out of income. They were contracted in the ordinary course. They would be incurred again, if this method of payment were followed. You suggested that we should be as young as you are. It is a good thing we are not.'

'Now come, think again,' said Sir Michael. 'Let your thought go below the surface; let it go a little deep, pass beyond ourselves.

The money is not ours to invest. Others have the prior claim. Money that is owed belongs to the people it is owed to. We must be just to them, before we are generous to ourselves and our own ideas.'

'Papa, you deceive no one,' said Zillah. 'I suppose you don't really deceive yourself.'

'I really try to,' said Joanna. 'I don't understand money matters, and I keep my eyes from them, in case they are really easy to understand. It is best not to listen to Hereward, when clever people make everything clear in a few words.'

'I hardly seem to do so,' said her son. 'But I must ask my father to hear me. He cannot keep his eyes from the truth. I have no choice but to force it upon him. He is not a woman.'

'Force it upon me! There is a way to talk. Am I or am I not your father? And not a woman! Why should I be one? Are you a woman yourself?'

'Neither of us is a child. And you are not an old man. You may have a future before you. And you are on a road that has no turning. You must simply retrace your steps.'

'I will have no trouble for your mother,' said Sir Michael, in a warning tone. 'If anything you mean involves that, leave it unsaid. If other people suffer, she suffers with them. That is a thing I will not have, and there is an end of it.'

'There is an end of it all,' said Hereward, after a pause. 'There need have been no beginning. I will not waste my words. It is a waste of what is behind them, and that would mean another end. I will let you have the money, and replace it from what I earn. I can't see the place bled to death.'

'Well, no, we can't. I feel it as much as you do. There is the future to consider. We have to think of other lives. There may be descendants in the end. Of course we feel there will be. You are a good son, Hereward. We have reason to be grateful to you. We are not afraid of the word.'

'It is the natural one,' said Zillah. 'I wonder if you know how little you should be afraid of it.'

'I don't dare to know,' said Joanna. 'I shut my eyes to the truth. It does seem that we are eating our cake and having it. And I should have thought we were, if it was not known to be impossible.'

'It is, unless someone supplies another cake.'

'Yes, well, that is true,' said Sir Michael, on a rueful note. 'Yes, well, that is what it is. And we must be thankful for it. And thankful that the money comes in. It is strange that it should come just from writing books like novels. It seems such a light sort of thing. But of course people do earn by it, even more than by serious books they say. Well, if it is so, we are the better for it.'

'It is one of the most exacting of the arts,' said Zillah. 'Few people can go far in it.'

'Is it? Is that so? Well, you know best. But I always feel I could write a novel, if I tried. But I am a bad person for trying, and that is the truth.'

'You may be a bad person for achieving. Anyone can try.'

'Is that really true?' said Joanna. 'Could we all settle down and make an effort? Then I will just forget it.'

'Well, so will I,' said her husband. 'I don't know what I could have done, if I had been able for that. I often feel possibilities welling up within me. But it is late for them to get out. The time is past.'

'You are both talking of what you don't understand.'

'Well, otherwise should we not talk too little?' said Joanna. 'And not to either of you at all?'

'Well, I think I can understand a novel,' said Sir Michael. 'It would be odd if I couldn't manage that. It is not as if it had thought or learning in it. It is just about ordinary experiences that anyone might have. There is no question of not understanding.'

'They are imaginary,' said Zillah. 'And imagination is the highest kind of thought.'

'Well, writers must imagine something, if they haven't any knowledge. They must put something into a book. And they put in actual events and people; even the great ones; it seems to be accepted. I never know why they are great myself. It seems an easy thing to do. And it can't be called imagination, whatever kind of thought it is.'

'We can mistake Hereward's silence. It is his way of being patient,' said Zillah, showing she had found no way herself.

'Patient, is he? Well, I think other people have to be that.

Why, he can't be approached about anything, and is put out, if his door is opened twice in a day. He can't have a room without a door, and it has to be put to its natural use. He says it drives things out of his head. But he can think of something else. It can't be so hard, or he could not write all those books. Long ones too; I give him credit there. The mere writing must be a task, even if there isn't much more to it. But I wonder he did not work on a man's line, while he was about it.'

'What do you do on what you call a man's line yourself?'

'Now that shows how much you know about my life. Problems arise, and questions are asked, and complaints pour in. And can I say a word to Hereward about the place that will be his? No, I must wait until he emerges, dazed and dumb and vacant-eyed. I should like to tell him to wake up sometimes. And I would, if I dared.'

'No one should dare to tell anyone that,' said Joanna. 'It is too simple to have so much courage.'

'Well, I haven't it. So you need not fear. I am quite without it. If a father can be afraid of his son, that father is before you.'

'Hereward is absorbed in the lives he imagines,' said Zillah. 'He can't be so alert to this one.'

'Is he? Is that what it is? Well, things are not what they seem. Of course we know they are not. It has become a saying. Well, I am blind to it all. He has chosen a line apart from me.'

'And one more apart than you know. One where many are called, but few chosen.'

'Well, put like that, I have no choice but to accept it. If that is so, it is. So Hereward is one by himself. Well, of course we know he is. And we look up to him. We are grateful to him. We realize where we should be without him. We are thankful for every word that falls from his pen. And other people are grateful too. Look at the things that are said of him. Why, my heart swells with pride. Tears come into my eyes, and I am not ashamed of it. I quite tremble to think I am his father.'

'I expect he trembles at it too,' said Joanna. 'But people are always ashamed of their parents. So it hardly matters if they are more ashamed than usual.'

'Ashamed of us, are they? Well, it is a feeling I don't return.

I am proud of them. Proud of my son for what he achieves, and of my daughter for the help she gives him. I look up to my children. And if they look down on us, well, it can happen, as you say. And they have a right to look down on us. We are not equal to them. I mean, of course, that I am not. No man would look down on his mother. It need not be said.'

'Only part of my work is of use to you,' said Hereward. 'It is the part that should not mean the most to me.'

'Well, it means it to me. I should be ungrateful if it did not. Why, it is the part that gives us something. I don't see much point in work for its own sake. It is an odd, conceited view. And it is a wrong kind of conceit. The labourer is worthy of his hire. That would not be stated where it is, if it was not true.'

'My books are read for different reasons. We should be willing to write for the few.'

'Well, I am glad you write for the many too. It is natural that I should be. I am one of the many myself. And it gives the whole thing its meaning. The few have too much done for them. To serve the many is a larger aim. And it is best from your own point of view. Why should you toil and get nothing out of it? Or nothing in your own time. I often wonder how poets and painters feel, if they know about things in an after life. And novelists too. They are artists too in a way. Oh, I think about these things more than you know.'

'I am sure Hereward did not know,' said Joanna. 'I believe I hardly knew myself. I am proud of you, Michael. And I see that our children must be more and more ashamed.'

'Well, I talk and think in my own way. We all have our ways of doing everything. And of course mine is not theirs. I often wonder how my children came about. It escapes me. I can't explain it.'

'Something may have come to them through me. Not from me. It has passed me over.'

'Yes, it has missed a generation. That is a thing that does happen. I know there were unusual people in your family, and that they had no recognition in their time. It rather bears out what I have said. Well, Galleon, and what do you say to my son's manner of life? What is your opinion of it?'

'Well, Sir Michael, if there happens to be necessity, it does not involve anything manual,' said Galleon, making this clear.

'Well, I am not so sure. Scratching and scribbling and shuffling papers! It does that into the bargain.'

'Well, not to the point of soiling the hands, Sir Michael.'

'The ink and dust are equal to it, I should think.'

'Well, they may have their own suggestion, Sir Michael.'

'Would you like to write a book, Galleon?'

'Well, I have often thought of it, Sir Michael. The simplicity of it is before one's eyes, as it might seem.'

'Yes, it puts it into people's heads. I wonder I have never set my hand to it. It is a thing I shall never explain.'

'No doubt there is explanation in both cases, Sir Michael.'

'You mean you have not the time, and I have not the talent? Ah, I can read your thought, Galleon. I can often read people's minds. That might be useful to me, if I wrote. But the time is past. And one writer in a house is enough.'

'And the other pursuits are necessary, Sir Michael. To enable the writing to take place and the results to ensue.'

'Ah, you are indispensable, Galleon. Mr Hereward's work depends on yours, and so we all depend on it,' said Sir Michael, again using his gift of reading minds. 'Ah, we give you your due. Yes, you can go to your work, and so can he. Yes, your sister will go with you, Hereward. Ah, you have a helpmate in my Zillah. You have your comrade there. And I am glad to know it. It is a solace to me. I don't always feel you have sympathy in your home. I sometimes think we fail you there. And you do not fail us. You don't indeed. You have lifted a weight from us to-day. We respect work that does so much for us. If we have given another impression, it is a wrong one. My Joanna, our future is safe. We need not hide our joy. Galleon, can you imagine our son and daughter celebrating matters in this way?'

'It may not need such a feat of imagination, Sir Michael,' said Galleon, who knew that the pair in question were indulging in mimicry of the activity, as they went upstairs.

'Which of our parents is the greater character?' said Zillah, when they reached her brother's room.

'Pappa. Mamma is the greater person. How you protect me

from them! From those arch enemies of the artist, parents and home. Where should I be without you? Where should any of us be?'

'So many of your readers must be parents, and more must live in a home. It is no wonder that your best work is too little known.'

'Ah, Zillah, I am content. All my work is my own. If I serve many thousands of people I am glad to know I serve them. It is no ignoble task. What comes from my brain comes from myself, and I would not disown it. My best work, as it is called, is no more deeply mine. And its serving fewer gives it no higher place. Everything springs from the same source. I feel it is the same. But we can't control our brains as we control our movements. When I am in the power of mine, I don't belong to myself. Well, you will be on guard to-day. No one must come to my door. Meals can be sent up, if there is need.'

The need arose, and Sir Michael heard the order given. 'So the force is at work,' he said, as he came to the luncheon table. 'But it must need fuel like anything else. And that could be supplied down here.'

'It breaks a train of thought to take part in ordinary talk,' said Zillah.

'Hereward does not take part in it. He sits like a stork with his mind elsewhere. And eats as if he was doing something else, as I suppose he is. But he has a life apart from his thought. He can't feed himself with a pen. And we must use a knife and fork, as he does. I don't see there is all that difference. You will say that he feeds us all with his pen. Ah, ha, I forestalled you there. I took the words out of your mouth. There is not such a gulf between us.'

'It is natural that the words should be in our mouths. The thought must be in our minds.'

'Well, well, it is in yours, I know. It may be too seldom in mine. But it does not lessen my pride in my son. Why, I read things about him that quite take me aback. And I say to myself: "I am the father of this man. I gave him life. Whatever he has done, I have done myself in a way." It is a serious thought. I am sobered by it.'

'You knew not what you did,' said his daughter.

'Well, no, it is true in a sense. And yet it is not, you know. Why, sometimes I understand him as well as anyone. Parts of his books have brought tears to my eyes. And I have not been ashamed of it. And I have laughed too. Why, I have thrown back my head and laughed until tears came of another kind, and I was quite glad no one was there to witness it. I have been lost to anything outside myself. I don't deny it.'

'That was when anyone might have witnessed it.'

'Oh, well, was it? So the funny parts are the best. Well, I should hardly have thought it. They seem more on anyone's level. And yet I am not sure, you know. I sometimes see light on things in a way. I might make more of myself, if I tried.'

'People would not like you to try,' said Joanna. 'They think we make enough of ourselves. And they would see you trying and despise you.'

'Well, I should not care if they did. I don't always think as much of them as they believe. Why, when Hereward and Zillah talk, I often glimpse their hidden meanings, though I don't try to get the credit. It is as I have said. Indolence is my trouble. I might have been a different man without it.'

'We should all be different without our distinguishing qualities,' said Zillah. 'Not that our meanings are probably so deeply hidden.'

'Well, not from your father. There are games that two can play at. It does not do to forget it.'

'They are a good son and daughter,' said Joanna. 'We would not have them changed. Ought not one of us to say it?'

'Joanna, if I saw a hint of change in either of them, I should be distressed. It would be a grief to me. I would not alter one jot or one tittle of their qualities. I am not equal to them. I look up to them. My heart swells at the thought of them. They are superior to their father. If ever a man was thankful for his wife and children, I am that man. Well, Galleon, do you not feel I do well to be thankful?'

'No one could take exception to the feeling, Sir Michael.'

'I daresay you could see some cause for discontent.'

'No real one, Sir Michael. There are perhaps circumstances that might be found unexpected.'

'My son's doing work that you find so? You feel we should be mildly ashamed of it?'

'I should not use that word, Sir Michael. I see no disgrace in honest work. I need only adduce my own case. But in some we may look for a difference.'

'And you don't see it in this one? Well, I am a proud father, whether you believe it or not.'

'There seems no room for doubt of it, Sir Michael.'

'But you would not be proud in my place?'

'It is the place that might prevent it, Sir Michael.'

'Galleon, my son is a household word.'

'I have gathered that that is the position, Sir Michael.'

'And you hardly like to refer to it?'

'I do not often find it necessary, Sir Michael.'

'You would not betray us, unless you were obliged to?'

'I respect any private circumstance in the family, Sir Michael.'

'This has surely become public.'

'It could hardly fail to in the end, Sir Michael.'

'So it would be no good to deny it.'

'It is hardly a case for actual suppression, Sir Michael,' said Galleon, as he moved away.

'Ah, Joanna, "a prophet is not without honour". We can see that Hereward has too little in his home. I caught a glimpse of myself in Galleon. And I felt ashamed and resolved to do better.'

'He sees the disgrace in honest work, though he had to deny it. And how did the saying arise, if no one saw it? And how can it be seen, if it is not there? I wonder if I could see it, if I dared.'

'Well, I cannot and will not see it. If I were not proud and grateful, I should be less than a man. And I wish I did some honest work myself. I have come to wish it. I should be glad to be of help to someone. I envy Galleon, and he can hear me say it. Do you hear me, Galleon? I envy you for doing useful work in the world.'

'Work can only be done in the world, Sir Michael. There is no other locality for it. And you would envy a good many people, the larger number. Myself among them, as you say.'

'I see you don't believe me.'

'I know you believe yourself at the moment, Sir Michael.'

'Do you ever envy anyone?'

'Envy is one of the seven deadly sins, Sir Michael,' said Galleon with a smile. 'I hope I should not yield to it.'

'Do you like to be envied yourself?'

'I might like a position that involved it, Sir Michael. It has not fallen to me. I have remained below it.'

'I have always felt that people below me must envy me,' said Joanna, in an undertone. 'Of course I know they are not below. I wonder who ever thought they were. Again I think someone must have.'

'Do you take any interest in our actual life?' said Zillah, as though her own interest in the other matters had failed.

'Oh, in Hereward's marriage?' said her father. 'The hint of it has come before and meant nothing. And now there is no word of the woman. He can't be married without a wife, any more than the rest of us.'

'That is true. It is why it will make a difference.'

'Ah, it would to you, my poor girl. Your father knows it would. You would be the first to suffer.'

'Or the last,' said Joanna. 'Or the one not to suffer at all. Hereward will marry without a wife as far as anyone can.'

'Well, I hope he will marry in one way or another. It would be a step forward for him and all of us. I should welcome his wife as a daughter. I should rejoice in his fulfilment. I have not got so little out of marriage myself, that I should regret it for my son. And it would be good to have descendants, Joanna, to have our own kind of immortality. I know you think we have no other. I leave the question myself as something beyond me.'

'I should be glad to have the descendants. I don't mind about the immortality. It is not of a kind that matters.'

'Well, well, the generations pass. We have to play our part. What do you feel about these questions, Galleon? Do you ever wish you were a married man?'

'Well, I see there is something to be said for it, Sir Michael. Perhaps more on the other side.'

'You would not like to have descendants?'

'I hardly know what they would do for me, Sir Michael. And I should have to do much for them. More than my resources warranted.'

'Why, they would grow up and work for you, Galleon.'

'They would grow up at my expense and work for themselves, Sir Michael. There would be no alternative. And so it would go on.'

'To think that we are all descendants!' said Joanna.

'I am sure I am above the average. I have never worked for myself. It does sound egotistic.'

'Well, I have worked for myself and others in managing things,' said Sir Michael. 'I think it is a just claim.'

'Yes, Sir Michael. Though most work is for others,' said Galleon, leaving the matter there.

'I think all claims are just,' said Joanna. 'That is why they are made. I have never met an unjust claim. I suppose it is because there are not any.'

Chapter 3

'Now would Aunt Penelope approve of this idleness, Emmeline?'

'No. Nor approve of anything. She cannot feel approval.'

'She wants you to get on. She is thinking of your future. With such neighbours as the Egertons we must keep our wits alive. Or we shall not hold our own with them.'

'I don't know what my own is. And it is better not to know. Then I shall not have to come into it.'

'You know Father wants you to be educated.'

'But then I should be different. And he seems to like me as I am.'

'So do we all. We don't want our little one altered. We want her to grow into her full self.'

'I believe I am that already. But it is best for people not to know it. They think more of me.'

'Oh, I can't think what to say to you. You must be a changeling. And you will have to live in the world, like everyone else.'

'No, not like everyone. Only like myself. That is all I shall try to do.'

'It may not be so easy. You won't always be sixteen.'

'I feel as if I should. And I think in a way I shall.'

'I am sometimes afraid you will.'

'You set me a good example. You won't always be twenty-five. You have already ceased to be it.'

'I forgot my age when Mother died. It was the only thing, if I was to remember yours. Oh, I know Aunt Penelope came to take her place. And has done so with Father, as far as it could be done. But it ended there, and other things devolved on me. Oh, I don't mean I am not grateful to her. She takes Father off my mind. She does for him what I could not do. He does not see me as on his mental level. How can he, when I am not? We must be content to be ourselves. I did hope to be his right hand in other ways, and to be seen by him as such. But it was not to be. Aunt Penelope loomed too large. Not of set purpose; as the result of the difference between us. I am the first person to recognize it. Though Father's recognizing it so soon made me a thought rueful I admit.'

'It was Aunt Penelope who recognized it. He never thinks of the difference between her and me.'

'He does not, you fortunate elf. The difference is too great. So in a sense it might not be there. But I was a step on the way. I tried and failed. I aspired to be what I was not. And so I remained what I am.'

'Aunt Penelope says I should improve myself. All she sees in me is room for improvement.'

'She is not quite right there. And I confess I don't mind her being a little wrong sometimes.'

'She and Father are not alike, are they?'

'Heaven forbid!' said Ada, lifting her hands. 'If there is a more disparate brother and sister, I have yet to meet them. But she serves Father's purpose. And so serves ours in a way. She may have saved us from a stepmother. So I am grateful to her, or feel I should be, which is much the same thing.'

'I think it is quite different.'

'So it is, you perceptive sprite. I was making a false claim. I can't go the whole length with her, and that is the truth. I see her qualities; I see the scale she is built on; I recognize my second place. But I can't whole-heartedly go the full way. It is a thing I can't explain.'

'I think you have explained it.'

'So I have. And I have explained myself as well. And a poor figure I cut, in my own estimation anyhow. I hope it is disguised from other people. I think I have a right to that. For it is not my true level. I shall rise above it. I am determined, and that is half the battle. I will not lose hold of myself.'

'A strong resolve,' said a resonant voice, as Miss Merton entered the room, a tall, spare, elderly woman, with an experienced expression, resigned, grey eyes and an untypical but definite face. 'But one we can keep, if we will. We have ourselves in our own hands.'

'So we have, Aunt Penelope. And it is a power I am resolved to use. It does not matter along what line. We need not pursue it.'

'We will not, as we are not invited to,' said her aunt, smiling. 'Our dealings with ourselves are our own.'

'Is Father in his study? Is he happy by himself? I thought he seemed harassed at breakfast.'

'That was natural, as he was harassed. He is at the end of some work, and beset by the final troubles.'

'I wish I could be of some help. How impotent I feel!'

'You wish you were older and more erudite. It is natural that you are not.'

'I don't wish she was either,' said Emmeline.

'No, I wish I had the nameless thing that you have, Aunt Penelope. I don't think it depends on age and erudition. Those might come to me in the end; and one of them must come; but that will not. I am in no doubt about it. And neither are you.'

Miss Penelope smiled again on her brother's girls, her expression suggesting that she accepted them as they were. Ada was tall and strong and upright, with an opaque, clear skin, thick, brown hair, slightly puzzled, blue eyes and features that were pleasant and plain. Her sister was short and plump and fair, with a pale, full face and uneven, childish features that somehow attained the point of charm. She suggested the confidence in her own appeal, that her family accepted and encouraged.

The house they lived in was book-lined and not without grace, and seemed like a home from an old university moved to the country, which in its essence and life it was.

'Well, is my pupil prepared for me? I have given her time.'

'I fear she is not,' said Ada. 'And I fear the fault is mine. Other subjects arose, and I admit I myself was one of them.'

'Well, they may have had their claim. Certainly the last one had.'

'A little learning is a dangerous thing,' said Emmeline. 'And I should never have much. So perhaps I am better without it.'

'Better than many of us, I believe,' said her aunt, smiling.

'You are right, Aunt Penelope,' said Ada. 'It is large of you to see it. Ah, the old sayings are the best. Their wisdom never wears out. "A little learning" and the rest. "He does much who does a little well". They hold the truth.'

'Perhaps the surface of it. I think not always more. When someone does a little well, that is what he does. And very little it can be. Is there more truth in the theory of the great failure?'

'There may be. And perhaps a little truth in that of the small one. I must hope there is, as that is what I shall be. I feel it more when I talk to you, and glimpse the something beyond myself. But I remain an advocate of sayings. They give us wisdom in a nutshell. And that is what we need.'

'There can't be room for much in one,' said Emmeline.

'I think there is not,' said her aunt. 'Real knowledge must have depth and scope. I say nothing for the condensed or more likely the reduced form of it.'

'Well, it is better than nothing,' said Ada. 'Though again I glimpse the gulf between us. Half a loaf may be better than no bread.'

'Half is a good deal,' said Emmeline. 'And is it much good for a thing to be great, when it is failure?'

'Well, what is the talk?' said a deep voice, as Penelope's brother entered the room, a tall, handsome, grey-haired man, whose features suggested his sister's controlled to a better form. 'Let me know the matter in hand.'

'The great failure, Father,' said Ada. 'Aunt Penelope pleads ably for it. I was content to take a humbler stand.'

'If by great, you mean on a considerable scale, I would hardly plead for it. I am involved in one.'

'Oh, no, you are not, Father. It is the exhaustion after a prolonged effort. You need not fear. I do not for you.'

'I share people's fears for themselves,' said Penelope. 'They have the true basis.'

'But we need not encourage them. We can render a better service. I do feel my line is right there.'

'Mr and Miss Egerton,' said a servant at the door.

'Now you have come at an opportune moment,' said Ada. 'You find my father out of heart, and can say a word to cheer him. You can be no strangers to the reaction after endeavour. You have a twofold knowledge of it, as your two lives are one.'

'It is true,' said Hereward. 'But reaction may not come by itself. It tends to carry a sense of unsuccess. You are right that I am no stranger to it. I can offer nothing better than sympathy.'

'But that may be the best thing. To feel that someone suffers what you do, that it is not an isolated experience, may lift the heart more than anything. You may have said the word that was needed. I somehow felt you would.'

'We are helped in trouble by knowing we are not alone in it,' said Penelope, with a note of condoning the truth.

'Yes, Aunt Penelope. If either was flushed with success, the other might feel the contrast, would be bound to feel it. As it is, each is uplifted. I am sure I am right.'

'You may be,' said Zillah. 'It does sound like knowledge of our nature.'

'Well, that is a thing I have. It is a fair claim. It is my own peculiar province, natural to me. It comes to me not out of books, but from something in myself. Human life goes on all round me; human nature is exemplified in it. I have watched it and drawn my own conclusions, weighed them in the balance and not found them wanting. I am a companion for anyone on that ground.'

'Then will you be my companion, Ada?' said Hereward, moving towards her. 'My province is the same as yours. We need the same companionship. My sister and I have it, and would give it to you. And be grateful if you would take and return it.'

There was the moment of silence. Ada's father came to her side. She was the first to find her words.

'Why, I did not know that proposals took place in public like this.'

'They do not. This is not a usual one,' said Hereward. 'It offers what is usual, but it asks more. You would share a home with my parents and my sister. Share me with her, and give her a part of yourself. You see why I make it in your father's hearing. It seemed that he should know the whole.'

'Dear Sir Michael and Lady Egerton! It would be a privilege to share a home with them. And I have always wanted Zillah's friendship, and felt it was presumptuous of me. There is only advantage for me there.'

'Then if you will share even more with me, and share it always, may I feel our word is pledged?' said Hereward, taking her hand and looking at Alfred.

'Yes, there is something to be done there. My father's consent must be sought and gained before we go any further. Father, you have no objection to Hereward as a son?'

'None to him as a son. As my daughter's husband it is hard to be sure. He asks, as he says, more than other men. Is he to give any more? You have a stable nature; I have valued it, my dear. He is more uncertain, and, as I should judge, could be carried away. If there are risks in the future, are they his or yours?'

'They are mine, Father. I face them with open eyes. I am prepared to give some quarter. I don't feel I am so much in myself. I am hardly on the level of Hereward and Zillah, and am not unwilling to redress the balance.'

'As your father I can hardly support that account.'

'Nor can I,' said Hereward. 'I accept it even less than you. I don't ask you to trust me with your daughter. That is asking much. If she will trust herself to me, I will accept and fulfil the trust. I think it is for her to judge.'

'I have judged, Father,' said Ada.

'Then I have no more to say. But I have meant what I said. I hope you will never have to remember my saying it. Well, so the change is to come. And I am not to lose my daughter. And to welcome the son I have not had. I can say with Ada that there is only advantage for me there.'

'You are to have more than a son, Father. You will have a fellow-worker. There will be a healthy rivalry. The scholar and the novelist pitted against each other. With me as the intermediary, ensuring that it remains healthy. Well, it is a character I can fill. It is the sort of secondary one that fits me. Indeed all the parts I am to play will be suited to myself. I need feel no qualm.'

'How you think of yourself, Hereward!' said Emmeline. 'You forget that Ada has a sister. She does not like you any better than me, and you will not have the whole of her. I shall often be with her, whether you want me or not.'

'And with me too, Emmeline,' said Hereward, drawing her to him. 'You will be with both of us. I shall be your brother. Don't you know that is part of it to me?'

'Oh, what a sister to have!' said Ada. 'If our places were reversed, should I have had this welcome? I doubt it. Indeed, I can imagine the difference. It may be a salutary exercise for me. Oh, I expect you will have little interchanges of your own. Well, I will not grudge them to you.'

'Then you and I will have them,' said Zillah. 'We will have as many, and they will both grudge them.'

'Ah, the kind of word I was waiting for! I hesitated to say it myself, in case it should not come first from me. But coming from you, it is the very one for me. I am the last person to put the man before the woman. I am a staunch upholder of my own sex. You may not be sure if I justify my own opinion. In the case of this little sprite there will be no doubt.'

'It is the life before you and me, that is in my mind, Ada,' said Hereward. 'And I hope in yours.'

'Yes, it is in mine. Too deep down to take form in words. Not that we can enter on it on quite equal terms. That is a thing that cannot be. Mine is an open sheet, with everything written on it plainly for your eyes. Yours will have its spaces and erasures. A man's life is not a woman's. I am not a woman to expect it. Oh, they are metaphorical sheets, little Emmeline, but none the less real for that. As you will understand, when you have things written on your own. At present it must be a blank.'

'She and I will write on it,' said Hereward, smiling. 'We shall find our words.'

'Oh, I expect you will,' said Ada, with a sigh. 'I shall be out of it sometimes. I am prepared. It is no new thing. She and Father indulge in companionship that I do not share. I have learned to accept it.'

'I scarcely knew it,' said Alfred. 'And she and Hereward will not. The companionship will be between you and him.'

'Yes, in another sense, Father. As it has been between you and me. Oh, I have understood. I have been content with my place. It is a content that is natural to me. I am even content with my own face, with the example of yours before me. And when mine should resemble it by right of inheritance.'

'Your mother reproached me for not transmitting my looks to my daughters. She had little value for them in my case.'

'Yes, it was a strange stroke of fate. I often think of the first impression we must make. Aunt Penelope perhaps makes a bridge between us. Some kind of stepping-stone is needed.'

'So my appearance has its use, and my brother's has not,' said her aunt. 'It might hardly be the natural conclusion.'

'It has indeed. And the conclusion might not be so unnatural. Ah, that nameless touch about you might be worth any handsomeness to some minds. Not to mine, as the father and daughter feeling stands in the way. But I can put myself in the other place. In my nature I am more drawn to a woman's quality than a man's.'

'I have never been jealous of my sister,' said Hereward. 'I hope I may not be now. You must not find a way of coming between us.'

'There could be no way. And I shall not seek one. I shall strive heart and soul to cement the bond. It is too great and precious a thing to be lightly assailed and weakened. You may trust me. In such a matter I am worthy of trust.'

'In all matters,' said Hereward, in a lower tone. 'I will stay no longer to-day. I feel I should take no more. And indeed there is no more to take. I have gained the whole.'

'You are wise, my dear?' said Alfred, when they were alone. 'You had little time to think. And only under other eyes. And there is need for time and thought. The change is for your life.'

'I am wise, Father. Indeed I am more. I am fortunate. I see it as a signal chance. I should not attract so many. I see myself as I am. And Hereward sees me as I am too. I shall not have to edit myself. There is no idealization, and that is the line of safety. I am not in doubt.'

'I think it would be better if there was some,' said Emmeline. 'I hope there will be for me.'

'I daresay there will. I believe there might be now, if you had come to the age. I half-think I saw there would. If it was a few years later, I don't know how things would be.'

'The years will pass,' said Alfred. 'You must see the matter from all its sides.'

'Oh, I don't believe in roundabout views, Father. I look straight at a question, and feel that is enough. Aunt Penelope, let me have a word from you. What do you feel about having Hereward for a nephew?'

'For myself what goes without saying. As regards you I feel with your father.'

'And a fair degree of feeling too. Not too much and not so little. A kind that may last and grow, when another might fade away. I am not a person for any strong romance. And I would not disturb the brother and sister relation, that I have viewed from a distance as something beyond myself. Now I am to be near to it, I shall go gently and keep a light touch. I shall not rush in where angels fear to tread.'

'I would rather have something myself than be careful of it for other people,' said Emmeline.

'I daresay you would. It is the difference between us. There is a strong vein of veneration in me. I am a person who tends to look up. I have looked up to one brother and sister, and now shall look up to another. They will feel they are safe with me, and it is a trust I value in them. And they will value my own trust. I also feel I am safe. I could hear their talk of me without a qualm.'

This talk was proceeding, as the latter brother and sister went home.

'You are sure, Hereward? It was the work of a moment. It is to last to the end. It will change your daily life. You need to be sure, if you will ever need to.'

'Yes, I am sure. I want to marry. I feel the urge, and it is time. Ada is good-hearted and will adapt her life to mine. She will accept our parents. She will be content with what I can give. There is much that I like about her. I need not say all that it is. She may hardly be a friend for you, but she will leave us our friendship. That is a condition I must make, and could not make with every woman. We are not asking nothing, Zillah. We can hardly ask more.'

'Should you not have more? For yourself, if not for me? More for the years ahead? More foundation for all that is to come? Is it a better future for me than for you? I see it takes less from me than any other.'

'Then it is the one for me. I will have nothing taken from you. No relation shall supersede our own. That is the one I will not do without. Only the woman to leave it to us can be my wife. I could not live with any other, would not ask her to live with me. My work is hard and never-ending. It will never end. I could not have another taskmistress. I serve only the one.'

'How will you put it to our parents? Not in that way.'

'No. You will put it for me as you please.'

Zillah led the way to Sir Michael and his wife.

'I bring you some news. You are prepared for part. If you claim to have foreseen the rest, you must prove it.'

Sir Michael spoke in a moment.

'My Zillah, I am prepared and not prepared. I knew it must come some day. And you have been going with your brother to the house. You act together, as you always do. And Merton is a good fellow and a good father. And as he has been a good husband, he will be so again. And if he was younger and not a widower, he would not be the man you choose. We cannot decide for other people, however near they may be. Joanna, come and wish our daughter all that is good. It is what she has always given.'

'No, it is I who claim your feeling,' said his son. 'That is, if you have any over for me. It is Ada, not her father, who is to join our family. She is to be your daughter as well as his. Zillah will remain with me. I could not lose her. I was startled by the picture that you drew.'

'Then my congratulations, my son,' said Sir Michael, holding out his hand. 'We rejoice with you, if you rejoice. And of course you do. Your time has come for it. I remember when my own time came. And it is a good girl whom you have chosen, whom fate has thrown in your way. We must choose from the people we meet. We hunt in our own demesne. And the long friendship is a safeguard. It atones for not breaking up new ground. Ah, it is great news, the greatest we could have. It is true to say that words fail me, as I find they do.'

'I am not quite sure they did,' murmured Joanna. 'Of course a mother's feelings are too deep for words. How sad it would be, if they were not!'

'You feel it is a humdrum marriage,' said Hereward. 'It may mean it is the one for me. It breaks no ground, as is said. I use my energy for other ends. It is safe and open and sound. It carries no doubt and no risk. It will not separate Zillah and me. We will leave you to see it as it is, as she and I and Ada see it.'

'Michael, we have failed,' said Joanna. 'Failed our son in a crisis of his life. But it did not seem like a crisis, when it depended on dear Ada Merton. What do we feel about it? Well, you have said.'

'I believe I did almost say it. I was taken by surprise. I wish I could re-live that moment. And that blunder I made about Zillah! What a thing to have said and unsaid! I wish I could undo it. Not that any harm is done. She and Hereward are enough for each other. I only hope there will be something over for the wife. Well, she will not ask too much. She is a good, unexacting girl. I hope I did her justice. I hope I did not give a wrong impression.'

'No, you gave the right one. Now all you can do is to erase it, knowing it can never be wholly effaced. I saw Hereward carrying it away with him.'

'Tell me what you feel, Joanna.'

'I could not tell anyone else. I am too ashamed of it. I am glad that Hereward can't like his wife any better than me. Because I don't see how he can. And glad that we may have grandchildren. All this selfish gladness, and then to have failed my son!'

'Well, Galleon,' said Sir Michael. 'You have not heard our news. Or have you heard? You look rather full of something.'

'Some stray words did reach me, Sir Michael. I don't know if I gained the right impression.'

'I daresay you did. So tell us what you feel.'

'Well, it was a case of proximity, Sir Michael. That is how things must ensue, as I believe was said.'

'So you listened to it all.'

'I mentioned that some stray words reached me, Sir Michael. That happened to be one of them. I could have supplied it.'

'We could not be more pleased with the marriage than we are.'

'No, Sir Michael; it is a line of safety. There is the familiarity with everything. And so no uncertainty to come.'

'Miss Ada is proud of Mr Hereward's place in letters.'

'Well, Sir Michael, it is even better, going so far.'

'You would not go to the length yourself?'

'Well, Sir Michael, I have learned to go some way. I must suppress any personal bias. Sufferance is the badge of all my tribe.'

Chapter 4

> 'Ring-a-ring-a-roses,
> A pocket full of posies,
> A-tish-a, a-tish-a,
> All fall down.'

Sir Michael Egerton sank to the ground, and assisted his wife to do the same, an example that was followed by their three grandsons, with mirth in inverse proportion to their age.

'Galleon fall down too,' said the third, observing that the butler was at leisure.

'No, Master Reuben, I have other things to do.'

'No,' said Reuben, as if seeing this was not the case.

'You can do them afterwards,' said the second grandson.

'No, Master Merton, I have no time to waste.'

'It seems as if you have,' said the eldest.

'I know what I am doing, Master Salomon. You are not old enough to understand.'

'I am not, if you are really doing something.'

'Galleon fall down too!' said Reuben, more insistently.

Sir Michael made a sign to Galleon, who complied with openly simulated liveliness, resorting to the aid of a chair, as if unconsciously.

'That is not falling,' said Merton.

'Poor Galleon!' said Reuben, looking at him.

'It must be easy to be a butler,' said Salomon. 'It would make other things seem hard.'

'Nuts in May!' said Reuben, suddenly.

'Yes, that is an idea,' said Sir Michael. 'We must choose our sides.'

'Do we have to fall down?' said Joanna.

'No, my lady. Merely move forward and backward to the jingle,' said Galleon, his choice of word shedding its light.

'Oh, what a good game! I wonder who invented it.'

'I cannot say, my lady. Or to what purpose.'

'There are not enough of us for sides,' said Salomon.

'Yes, I think there are,' said his grandfather. 'You and I and Galleon on one, and Grandma and the little ones on the other.'

'Salomon little too,' said Reuben, at once.

'Not as little as you,' said Merton.

'Yes, all the same,' said Reuben, shrilly.

'Yes, all the same,' said Salomon, in a pacific tone.

'Always all the same,' said Reuben, sighing.

Salomon was a short, solid boy of seven, with a large, round head, a full, round face, wide, grey eyes and features resembling Sir Michael's. Merton, two years younger and nearly the same height, was a dark-eyed, comely boy with a likeness to Ada's father, whose name he bore. Reuben at three was puny for his age, with a pinched, plain face surprisingly like Emmeline's, considering the vagueness of feature of both.

'There are Father and Mother,' said Merton.

'And Aunt Zillah, if Father is there,' said Salomon.

'Well, that will swell our numbers,' said Sir Michael. 'And I hear your Aunt Emmeline too. It will give us a good game.

'Why are things called games?' said Salomon.

'I don't know,' said Joanna. 'It is not the right word.'

'What would you call them?' said her husband.

'They are a kind of dance,' said Merton.

'Something handed down,' said his brother.

'Yes, they are old games,' said Sir Michael. 'Handed down to us from the past. I don't know their history.'

'I am glad of that,' said Joanna. 'So no one else need know.'

'Play again,' said Reuben.

'Yes, in a minute,' said his grandfather. 'The others are on their way.'

'All unknowing, my lady,' said Galleon, with a smile for Joanna. 'Or they might be disposed to divert it.'

Hereward and his wife and sister entered, followed by the group from the other house. Alfred looked disturbed, Penelope grave, and Emmeline sober and aloof.

'Grandpa Merton play,' said Reuben, laughing at the idea. 'One, two grandpas play. Galleon grandpa too.'

'No, Master Reuben. I have no little grandsons.'

'He means you are old,' said Salomon.

Galleon did not reply.

'No, Hereward, I can't put it off any longer,' said Ada, in a tone that did not only address her husband. 'I have tried to shut my eyes, but the time is past. I can't go on being blind and deaf and silent. I have eyes and ears, and now you will find I have words as well. You can feel you are finding it late. My father and aunt see the truth. Your father and mother see it. You and my sister know it in your hearts. Emmeline, my sister! To think what has come between us!'

'There need be nothing between you. No change has come to her or me. If there is a change, it is in you.'

'It is true. No change has come. It was there from the first, the feeling between you. The change in me is that I see it. It is strange that I did not before. But I thought of her as a child.'

'Of course the feeling was there. You were anxious that it should be. You put it in my heart. It was a thing we shared.'

'No, something else is the truth. It helped your feeling for me. It went through everything. I see it now. I should have seen it then. You hardly hid it. It could not have been hidden from yourself.'

'Why should I hide it? From myself or anyone else? I cared for you both. I do so now. What is there wrong about it?'

'We need not say,' said Alfred. 'But there is something that must be said. We know our world. We know its limits and its laws. We know they must be followed. We do not make our own.'

'You need not think of me,' said Emmeline. 'I shall not be with you any longer. I am going away. I shall live at a distance from you all. Father and Aunt Penelope have arranged it. I see myself that I must go. I believe everyone would like me to stay. It is only that someone would like it too much.'

'Oh, there it is!' said Ada, with a sigh. 'As it has been, so it will always be. It is no good to talk of it. It must simply be accepted.'

'I fear it must be,' said her father, in the same grave tone. 'And dealt with for the threat it carries, for the harm it does.'

'Play game,' said Reuben, as if matters had left their course.

'Yes, let us blow the cobwebs away,' said Sir Michael.

'Cobwebs are light things,' said Salomon, as though the word was not in place.

'And some things are not,' said Ada. 'Out of the mouth of babes! What would my sons say, if it was twenty years hence?'

'I know what to say now,' said Salomon. 'Father ought to love you, and not Aunt Emmeline.'

'And I do love her,' said Hereward. 'And I love Aunt Emmeline too. And I love you and your brothers, and your aunt and your grandparents and others. So many people are dear to me, that I don't always judge between them.'

'I think you will have to now. Mothers can't be quite the same. And you did judge in a way.'

'Do you want to join in the game?' said Sir Michael, as if recognizing evidence to the contrary.

'I would rather read. The game isn't a real one. It is only meant to hide something.'

'Oh, we are all younger than he is,' said Hereward. 'Come, my three generations. We will leave our elder to himself.'

'I want to hold Salomon's hand,' said Reuben.

Salomon put down his book and went to his side.

> 'Here we come gathering nuts in May, nuts in May,
>   nuts in May.
>   Here we come gathering nuts in May, on a cold and
>   frosty morning.'

Sir Michael rendered the words with abandon, and paused for Alfred to take him up on the other side.

'Whom will you have for your nuts in May?'
'We will have Ada for nuts in May –'
'Whom will you send to fetch her away –?'
'We will send Hereward to fetch her away, on a cold and frosty morning.'

Hereward and Ada came into the centre to engage in the contest. Hereward was the victor and drew his wife to his own side. She fell against him and broke into tears, and her second son observed them and was disposed to add his own.

Her eldest gave them a glance.

'I knew it was not a game. It was the opposite of one.'

'Well was it a success?' said Alfred. 'I am not a judge.'

'It was a success, Father,' said Ada. 'It has done its work. It has shown us things as they have to be, as we must see they are. We will leave it there.'

'We will,' said a quiet voice, as Penelope moved forward. 'I think this scene is at an end. To continue it would avail us nothing. Emmeline will go home with her father, and will not come again. If the sisters say good-bye here and now, it will be said.'

Emmeline suffered Ada's long embrace and Hereward's openly affectionate one, made little response to either, and followed her aunt.

'Play game,' said Reuben, in a tone without much hope.

'No, a tale,' said Merton. 'Father always knows a new one.'

'Not a new one,' said Reuben, with a wail.

'I can tell you an old one,' said Salomon. 'Father can tell us one out of his head.'

Hereward gathered his sons about him, taking Reuben on his knee, and threw himself into a narration that held them still and silent, and moved them to many human emotions, indeed to most of them.

'Again,' said Merton, when it ended, keeping his eyes on his father's face.

'No, that should be enough, sir,' said a voice from the door, where the nurse had stood with a dubious expression. 'They will take some time to forget it.'

'Is it only worthy of oblivion?'

'Well, that is really the best thing, sir,' said Nurse in a candid tone. 'It might prey on their minds.'

'Again,' said Merton, moving his feet rapidly.

'No, come and tell it to me,' said Nurse. 'I have only heard part of it.'

'Yes,' said Merton after a pause, a smile creeping over his face. 'I will tell you it all.'

Reuben waited on his father's knee until Nurse lifted him from it, indeed waited for her to do so. Merton followed them upstairs of his own will. It was where his treasure was, and where his heart was also. He was Nurse's favourite of the three brothers, and she was his favourite of all human beings.

Salomon sat down and opened his book, as a member of the remaining company.

'What a difficult book!' said his father. 'Do you understand it?'

'I know it is an allegory. But I think of the people as real ones.'

'Do you get any lessons from it? It is supposed to afford a good many.'

'I am not old enough for them,' said Salomon, meeting his father's eyes, as if this might not be true of everyone.

Hereward smiled to himself and went to the door.

'Well, it was a strange scene,' said Sir Michael to his wife, waiting for it to close. 'To take place before us all, as it did. I could scarcely believe my ears. I had a sense of eavesdropping somehow.'

'I had not. Being obliged to hear something is so different from being tempted to hear it. It does not remind me of it.'

'No, it has no zest about it. I don't mean the other would have any zest, of course. If we yielded to it, which we should not, of course. Well, it was an unusual scene.'

'Oh, I daresay I have cut a sorry figure,' said Ada, with another sigh. 'But I felt the time had come, and that it was then or never. In marrying an ordinary woman Hereward has involved himself with an ordinary woman's feelings. But I have talked enough about my ordinariness. You are well aware of it. You know Hereward has not married a martyr. And you see that I have not either.'

'You have not married an ordinary man,' said Zillah. 'You must meet much that is not ordinary. He can only be a rule to himself.'

'But only in his own sense. A gifted person owes as much to other people as an average one. Surely not any less.'

'You can hardly feel that Hereward has not fulfilled his human debt.'

'His debt to his wife is part of it. He has a duty to her as well as to the public. Or I am one of the public, if you like.'

'No, do not be one,' said Joanna. 'I am sure I am not, though I don't dare to give the reasons.'

'Well, I dare for you, Mamma,' said Ada. 'I dare to give many. And one of them is the way you have behaved to-day. Taking no sides, understanding everyone, condemning no one. Just there to help by being the whole of yourself. What better reason is there?'

Before an answer was necessary, Hereward returned to the room. He wore an absent air and was humming to himself.

'Still at the book?' he said to his son. 'Don't you get rather tired of it?'

'I don't read it all the time. I don't like the second part.'

'You have not been listening to grown-up talk?' said Ada, with a note of reproof.

'It was the only kind there was. Of course I have heard it.'

'Are you any the wiser?' said Hereward.

'Yes, I think I am a little.'

'Tell us what you have learned from it.'

'It would be no good to tell you. You must know it yourself.'

'Why, this is a son after your heart, Hereward,' said Sir Michael. 'Do you begin to see yourself in him?'

'He likes Reuben best,' said Salomon.

'That is a different kind of feeling,' said his father.

'I think there is only one kind.'

'I am a lover of very young children. You would hardly understand.'

'I think I am too,' said Salomon, smiling at his own words. 'I like Reuben myself.'

'My feeling for all of you grows with every day.'

'I thought it had got less for me.'

'That is because you don't understand it.'

'It might be because I do. And I think it is. There isn't much in a feeling to understand. It is just something that is there.'

'You must not argue with Father,' said Ada. 'He must be wiser than you are.'

'I can't help not thinking what he does. It is a thing no one can help. It is only he and Aunt Zillah who always think the same.'

'Ah, that is what they do,' said Sir Michael. 'And a great thing for both of them it is. Neither will ever stand alone. They can always be left to each other. Indeed they might be now. They deserve an hour to themselves. We all acknowledge their right to it.'

'Come then, my little son,' said Ada. 'We will go upstairs and give our minds to the young children. Father is leaving them to us.'

'And trusting them to their mother with an easy heart,' said Sir Michael, in a full tone, as he left the room. 'He is making no mistake there.'

'Well, it was a thunderbolt, Zillah,' said Hereward. 'I was taken by surprise. It all seemed to fall from nowhere.'

'I have wondered if it would come. And it has come and gone, and will not come again. But what will it mean? What will you do without Emmeline?'

'Think of her, and write to her, and know why I have no answer. They can't take everything from me. And they can't take you. They do not dare to think of it. Ada would not wish to have me without my sister.'

'Nor you to have her without hers. And that has to end. But she can be accepted in herself. She does not give us nothing.'

'To me it is more than that. I have a value for all that she gives. I have not lost my feeling for her. I will not lose it. I guard it more closely than my feeling for you. It is not so safe. And much depends on it.'

'I will help you to keep it. You need not fear. In a sense it is at the root of our life. It is the basis of the future and the safeguard of it.'

'Zillah, we are brother and sister. If we were not, what could we be?'

'Nothing that was nearer. It stands first among the relations. There is nothing before it, nothing to follow it. It reaches from the beginning to the end.'

'Well, I may or may not be welcome,' said Ada's voice. 'But I must assert myself once more. There are things I can and do accept. But banishment from my husband in my own home is not one of them.'

'My father's words mean nothing,' said Hereward. 'We have ceased to listen to them, almost to hear them. You must learn to do the same.'

'I know they meant nothing to him. Why, he and I are fast friends. His presence is often a help to me. To-day it enabled me to break my silence. To do what was beyond myself. And it was time it was broken. There had ceased to be a case for it.'

'Whether or no that is true,' said Zillah, 'I think there is a case for it now.'

'Oh, well, I am willing. I don't want to press things home. There is too much of the fairness of the ordinary person in me for that. Something had to be ended, and it is at an end. I shall not return to it. But I don't feel with you about your father. I like to hear his voice, sounding cheerfully about, expressing goodwill to every-one. I hear it now; and if it cannot be music in my ears, it is something that is no less welcome.'

The voice was coming across the hall, gaining volume as it drew near.

'Here we come gathering nuts in May, nuts in May, nuts in May. Here we come gathering nuts in May on a cold and frosty morning.

'A touch of frost in the nuts in May, nuts in May, nuts in May. A touch of frost in the nuts in May, on a cold and frosty morning.

'Ah, we managed to smooth it away, smooth it away, smooth it away. Ah, we managed to smooth it away, on a cold and frosty morning.'

'Oh, there you all are! How that jingle sounds in one's head! The tune that is, of course. The words have no meaning.'

'Can that ever be said of words?' said Zillah to her brother.

Chapter 5

'Well, the book is ended,' said Hereward. 'What there can be in a word! I am in a strange solitude. I seem to move in a void. I am without any foothold, any stake in life. I have suffered it before, and it is never different. I have had and done what I wanted. But I pay the price.'

'Come, what of your home and your family?' said Sir Michael. 'What is this talk of a void? You have the stake in life of other men.'

'I have lost my own. The people have left me, who have lived with me and made my world. More deeply than mere flesh and blood.'

'You mean you have finished with them? And mere flesh and blood! What are you or any of us? What of your mother and me? What of your characters themselves? They are supposed to be like real people. I thought that was the point of them. It is what is often said. Indeed I have thought –' Sir Michael broke off and glanced about him, a smile trembling on his lips.

'I don't use my family as characters, if that is what you mean. They would serve no purpose for me.'

'Well, not as characters, not in your sense I daresay. But things here and there – little touches – I have thought –' Sir Michael leaned back and smiled again to himself.

'*Mere* flesh and blood!' said Salomon to his father. 'And Grandpa before your eyes!'

'Well, I am the man I am,' said Sir Michael, modestly. 'I have my thoughts and perceptions like anyone else. Or like myself I suppose. It may come from being flesh and blood. That is, of one's own kind.'

'I daresay a good deal comes from that,' said Merton.

'Well, I return to your world,' said Hereward. 'I have lost my own. I am happy in having had it. But I would not urge another man to follow in my steps. I do not wish it for my sons. It is a hard path to tread.'

'It seems that it has its allure,' said Salomon. 'I don't feel it myself. Or perhaps feel that of any other.'

'Well, you are in a place apart. You will not have to earn your bread. Your brothers must think of the future. I shall not live and write for ever.'

'To think that I must tread a path!' said Reuben.

'And earn bread,' said Merton. 'What a hard and frugal course! It is a malicious phrase.'

'Have you thought of a way of gaining it?' said Hereward. 'What of your work in the years ahead?'

'Well, I know the main line, Father. I can put it in a few words. I want to be a writer. But not of your range and kind. I should not appeal to the many, and shall be content to write for the few. But by them, in this country and beyond it, I hope to be known in the end. And not only known; read.'

There was a silence.

'It ought hardly to have been in a few words,' said Salomon.

'But it is in those that good writers suggest so much,' said Joanna.

Hereward was silent, and his father gave him a glance.

'Why should I not speak the truth?' said Merton, looking at them. 'It was a simple thing that I said.'

'Simple in a sense you did not mean,' said Hereward, in an even tone.

'You have had a writer's life yourself. You should not feel it a strange one for your son.'

'You spoke of a different one from mine.'

'You feel I should follow in your steps? But we cannot choose our paths. They are chosen for us by something in ourselves. As yours was for you, and mine is for me. There can be no family custom there.'

'I find no fault with your path. I am glad you have chosen one. It is what I hoped for you. But what do you mean by the few?'

'You will know, if you think. I have heard you use the phrase. A small part of your books is read by them. It is they I should write for, and hope to reach; and feel I should in the end.'

'"In this country and beyond it",' said his father, as if to himself.

'Oh, you think it is too ambitious. To choose the better part, if that is what it is; and I admit I think it is. But it might be thought narrower than yours, and by some it would be. Our abilities are different, and must lead to a different end. It is not unreasonable to think it. But it is rather in the air at my age.'

'It is not only in the air. It is in your thought. And your age perplexes me. Sixteen is hardly childhood.'

'Yes, in this matter, Hereward,' said Zillah. 'It is what it is.'

'I wonder what fourteen is,' said Reuben. 'I will not talk of it, in case someone tells me.'

'Anything worth knowing is known by my age,' said Merton. 'Sixteen may be the high mark of youth. After that there can be retrogression as well as progress.'

'Father is deprived of words,' said Salomon.

Hereward was silent, as this was the case.

'Seventy-nine is not what it is,' said Joanna. 'Or it would be old age.'

'Neither is it,' said Sir Michael. 'I feel as young as I ever did.'

'I do not,' said Reuben. 'I must begin to realize my age. I have to know all that is worth knowing in two years.'

'Childhood does take us quickly onward,' said Zillah.

'So it does,' said Hereward, lightly. 'We see where it has taken Merton. Beyond his father.'

'That is the idea that troubles you, Father? But there is nothing so unusual about it.'

'Nothing. It is its commonness that strikes me. I have seen the death of hope.'

'You have also seen its fulfilment. And met it yourself in a sense. Of course I don't know what your original ambitions were.'

'We shall not say that of yours. And, as you have said, I am troubled by them. Both as a writer and a father. What are your hopes for the future, Reuben?'

'I have none, Father, only fears. And one of them is that I may be an usher. It is one that does take the place of hopes.'

'Why do we say "usher" and not "schoolmaster"?' said Sir Michael. 'It has a disparaging sound.'

'That is the reason,' said his grandson. 'We should hardly admit a note of respect.'

'Why not?' said Hereward. 'Education has its purpose and serves it. I wish I had had more.'

'You would not have it,' said his father. 'You said it would crush your creative gifts.'

'You can't be an usher without it,' said Salomon. 'So I suppose ushers' gifts are always crushed. Before we have the advantage of them.'

'I wonder we risk education,' said Reuben, 'when you think where it might lead. You will all remember that my gifts have been crushed.'

'That does not happen so easily,' said Merton. 'People are without them, because they have never had them. If they had, they would not be ushers. And the lack of talent in many writers is a part of themselves. Of course I am not talking about Father.'

'Well, I suppose you are not,' said Sir Michael. 'Why should you be?'

'I wonder he was not,' said Hereward, smiling. 'But I have a word to say of him. They are all to go to Oxford, when they reach the age. It is their mother's wish, and therefore mine.'

'Yes, my word was the determining factor,' said Ada. 'I brought in the ordinary strain. That is my accepted part. My sons cannot follow in their father's steps. They must see him as widely removed from them, as my sister and I saw mine. They must have the usual training of average men. Why should they be above them? We should not hope, or perhaps even wish for it.'

'There are cases of a literary father and son,' said Merton. 'And either of them may be the better. But it is idle to plan the future. It must take care of itself.'

'I did not find it did,' said Hereward. 'The effort fell to me. I found it a long, hard service. And you may do the same. I even hope you will. It might be better for you in the end.'

'Why are early struggles so much recommended? They may not lead to success, because they end in it.'

'Well, may you do all you hope, my boy. No one would be prouder than your father.'

'No one is prouder of you, than I am in my way, Father. Of course it must be in my way. Our opinions and aims are different. They would hardly be the same.'

'I thought aims were always the same,' said Joanna. 'And I believe they are.'

'They are more so than is thought,' said Zillah. 'They tend to meet, as time goes by. They are adapted to achievements, and those do come nearer to each other.'

'Have you found that true, Father?' said Merton.

'I think there is truth in it. But I have never been concerned with aims. We give out what is in us.'

'Is not that saying the same thing?'

'I daresay it is,' said Joanna. 'It so often is, when people say different things.'

'Let us leave our aims,' said Salomon. 'I like to forget them, as I have none. Mother, you spoke of your sister. Why has she passed from our lives? I remember so well when she was in them.'

'She lives at a distance,' said Hereward. 'And her marriage has widened it, as marriages will.'

'My Emmeline!' said Ada. 'I hardly feel I have lost her. Reuben gives her back to me. And more with every day.'

'There is a great likeness,' said Zillah. 'And it seems to grow with him. I suppose a real likeness would.'

'It is not only in his looks and ways. There is something that defies words. It is the touch I have missed myself. It is impossible to define it. I don't know if it will lead anywhere.'

'That would need something with more depth and force,' said Merton.

'I don't think Merton has a touch,' said Reuben.

'It is an elusive thing,' said Ada. 'We can't give it a place.'

'We have given it one,' said Reuben. 'It is in Aunt Emmeline and me.'

'Aunt Emmeline! How natural it sounds! How I wish we had heard it oftener!'

'Why have we not?' said Merton. 'Why do we never see her? There must be a private reason. I suppose some family trouble.'

'There is or there was,' said his mother. 'So that is enough.'

'But it is not,' said Salomon. 'Not nearly enough, as you know.'

'We can add to it,' said Merton. 'I expect it had to do with money.'

'You are wrong,' said Hereward. 'Money is not the whole of life.'

'It is often the whole of quarrels, Father.'

'It was no part of this one.'

'I am surprised that there was trouble, Father,' said Salomon. 'I remember you and my aunt together.'

'There was no trouble between her and me.'

'Perhaps it was the opposite,' said Merton. 'Ah, that is nearer the truth.'

'So it is out,' said Ada. 'Well, it had to come. Questions are asked in the end, and carry their answers. Yes, your father and my sister were becoming too much to each other. And it led to a breach that has remained. Not an estrangement, not a silence. But a parting of the ways.'

'How I long to ask a question!' said Reuben.

'Well, what is it?' said his father.

'What do you feel for Aunt Emmeline now?'

'I keep the memory. I cared both for her and your mother. I cared for them both for each other's sake and their own. We fell in with your mother's wish and parted. She married later. That is the whole.'

'My wish!' said Ada. 'No, it is not quite the whole. Both my father and Aunt Penelope advised the parting. But my sister! How I wish it had been different! I hope and feel so does she. But nothing can be undone.'

'It seems that this might be ended,' said Salomon. 'Do you need to remember the past?'

'Now that is enough,' said Sir Michael. 'Your parents have told you all they can. You should know better than to ask more.'

'Well, we will be content. It is a relief to know. I have wondered and feared to ask.'

'So have I,' said Merton. 'It has been on the tip of my tongue.'

'That does keep people silent,' said Joanna. 'It hardly seems that it would.'

'Well, the truth has escaped, Grandma. I admire Mother's simple courage. It is a thing I am without.'

'And you admire yourself for being without it,' said Ada. 'It may not be a high quality. But it is not such a common one.'

'I think it is,' said Reuben. 'I am always meeting it.'

'I have to show it now,' said Hereward. 'I am reluctant to

cloud our reunion. That is how it seems to me when I leave a book. But there is a word that must be said. Your reports are here and cannot be quite passed over.'

'Well, now they have not been,' said Reuben. 'We have met the courage.'

'Yours was no worse than mediocre.'

'That is right for me, as I am to educate others. If it was better, I should not educate them. And if it was worse, I could not.'

'There is never any fault to be found with yours, Salomon.'

'None by you, Father. I am steady and of sound intelligence. But they are things that Merton would be ashamed to be.'

'He has his own cause to be ashamed. His is hardly a report at all. It seems there was little to make one. He is said to assume he is a man before his time. He may not have to educate others. But he can hardly do without education himself.'

'So you think I could be improved, Father?'

'It appears to be what is thought.'

'Not by prolonging boyhood. Education so-called does only what it can.'

'And does idleness so-called do so much?' said Sir Michael. 'And does ingratitude so-called do any more? Things have to be known by their names. Why should your father immure himself and moil, for you to be a man before your time? "So-called" is the right word there. Why, I am ashamed of being your grandparent.'

'I am not,' said Joanna. 'I don't see how I can help it.'

'Well, I have done what I can,' said her husband, leaning back. 'No one can do any more.'

'That is good to hear,' said Merton. 'I was fearing you might go to almost any length.'

'Any length! Well, I went a certain way. I felt it was my part. It is my duty to second your father. I see it as the least I can do. The brunt of things falls on him. I take any chance to support him.'

'Well, I give you one by speaking the truth. I am not afraid of it. I can't be a slave to what is called my work. I know where my real talent lies, and what I owe to it.'

'What is called your work! Is everything to be so-called? What do you do with your so-called leisure, may I ask? Perhaps it is the word there.'

'It is. I give it to the writing that is to be my life, and to last it. And not more for my own sake than for other people's.'

'Oh, well, for other people's. Well, if that is what it is. Well, it is a thing I am used to. I am no stranger to it. This working for the world outside, and forgetting the one you live in. Like father, like son, I suppose. Well, we must not find fault with it.'

'I fear I must,' said Hereward. 'Though I may not seem the person to do it. I am troubled for Merton's future. The likeness between us is not so great. It should have a better basis than these early efforts and hopes.'

'What basis did you have for your own, Father?'

'That of a stronger brain and greater creative force,' said Hereward, in an almost ruthless tone. 'I will say the truth, as you do. It is time it was said. We are right not to be afraid of it.'

'But just afraid enough,' murmured Salomon.

'I am terrified,' murmured Reuben.

'I am untouched,' said their brother. 'If it is the truth to you, you are right to say it, Father. It is the honest thing. Indeed I admire your courage.'

'I admire Merton's,' said Salomon.

'But I have no fear. There are different kinds of brain. The one that is known as powerful, may not be the best.'

'You would not like to have written my books?' said Hereward, meeting his eyes.

'Well, to be as honest as you are, Father, I should not.'

'We are told not to be afraid of the truth,' said Joanna. 'But no one is.'

'No one who speaks it,' said Reuben. 'Everyone else.'

'The people who speak it can be the most afraid,' said Hereward. 'But at times it must be said.'

'There is nothing in Merton's feeling,' said Zillah.

'No writer goes the whole length with any other. Each of them shivers at the lapses of the rest, and is blind to his own. And the youngest shiver the most. And the greatest writers have them.'

'And I daresay the smaller ones too,' said Sir Michael. 'And a boy who would not like to have written a mature man's books, is a queer example of one to my mind. Why, I should like to have written them myself. I should be proud to have written a word. And he can think what he likes of it.'

'I think it is quite reasonable, Grandpa.'

'The less we can do a thing ourselves, the more we should appreciate it in other people. To fail is to grudge someone else the better place. We should be ashamed of it.'

'Grandpa need not be ashamed,' said Reuben. 'He tells us about it.'

'Well, I need not either,' said Merton. 'I simply want to write for a body of readers neglected because it is small. It is not an unworthy ambition.'

'I am sure it is not,' said Joanna. 'An ambition would not be. Nothing can be said against ambitions. They are worthier than anything I know.'

'Not unworthy on its narrow scale,' said Sir Michael. 'But there is something more generous about serving the larger body. It commands more sympathy.'

'It is true that it does,' said Merton.

'I can't think a son of mine would go far along either road,' said Ada. 'There is too much of myself in them. My father's gifts are of another kind, but they too have passed them over.'

'It is a habit of gifts,' said Salomon.

'But broken in Merton's case,' said Reuben.

'Not by the second kind,' said their brother. 'I lay no claim to that. The two kinds of gifts are wide apart, and the gulf is seldom crossed.'

'Well, it need not concern us,' said his mother. 'For us the gulf may be all there is.'

'Well, that may be true,' said Sir Michael, laughing.

'Gifts must be rare, of course. But to have a father and a grandfather endowed like theirs is a unique position. Ah, they have a fine heritage. Something ought to come of it.'

'Merton has come,' murmured Reuben.

'Still we can't choose the kind of people we are to be.'

'Some of us feel we can,' said Hereward.

'If you are thinking of me, you are wrong,' said Merton. 'I

know what I am, as everyone must. How can we escape the knowledge?'

'Mr and Miss Merton,' said Galleon at the door.

'Why, Father, you were in my mind,' said Ada. 'I was thinking of your having only daughters. We are facing the future for our sons. And daughters are allowed to disregard it.'

'I would have faced it for and with any sons of mine.'

'Father, you have had a disappointment! How wonderfully you have hidden it! How grateful we ought to be!'

'Father and Mother have had one,' said Reuben. 'And I suppose it could hardly be hidden. It was me.'

'Yes, I did want a daughter,' said Ada. 'But I would not change my sons. Or change anything about them.'

'Father should emulate a mother's feelings,' said Merton. 'They are much respected.'

'What about you, Aunt Penelope?' said Ada. 'Would you have liked to have great-nieces?'

'I am content with what has come to me. I have taken no steps myself.'

'And how grateful for it we should be! Ah, our unmarried women! Where should we be without them? What a place they fill!'

'It is not always so highly considered.'

'Oh, but it is. By people who take the broader view. And in this matter they are many. What would Father say about it?'

'The place I fill for him was left empty. That is how I came to be in it.'

'Honest and clear as always! How we should miss the light you shed! There will be a void one day.'

'You don't mean that she will die?' said Joanna. 'You know she will not. You must know no one will, who is here.'

'I mean that she will live on in our memories and our lives, as long as we breathe ourselves. That is what I mean.'

'It is what you suggested,' said Hereward.

'Oh, you are a sardonic, carping creature to-day. You are not fair on anyone. If the boys want to escape to their own sanctum, you must not blame them. They may have had enough of you.'

'I should not blame them. I daresay they have had too much. They can go and forget us. And we will go our several ways.'

'Well, Galleon,' said Sir Michael. 'You have heard the talk. What do you say to a second writer in the family?'

'Well, "like father, like son", as was said, Sir Michael. Or that at the moment. It is a stage that may pass.'

'And you feel it better that it should?'

'Well, one irregularity in the family, Sir Michael. It is no great thing.'

'You still see writing in that way?'

'Well, hardly Mr Alfred Merton's, Sir Michael. Involving what it does. This of ours is of a lighter nature,' said Galleon, trying to take a step forward.

'But that is not against it.'

'On the contrary, Sir Michael. It has its own purpose.'

'Well, you know, Galleon,' said Sir Michael, lowering his tone and glancing round the empty room, 'I half-feel it myself. There might be something more solid, and without the personal touch. But I am wrong you know. Utterly off the truth. I understand that now. And there is no prouder father.'

'And there is no point in a prouder butler, Sir Michael,' said Galleon, smiling. 'There would be no place for pride.'

'And we welcome the help with expenses. They grow with every year.'

'I have heard of a lady who made a fortune by the type of writing, Sir Michael,' said Galleon, with another effort to adapt himself.

'Well, I hope my grandson will make one. And in the same way. Though there seems somehow to be a doubt of it.'

The grandsons had gone to the room that was known as their study, on the assumption that it earned the name. They took their accustomed seats and leaned back in silence.

'Strength will return,' said Salomon at last. 'We have found it does. What if a time came, when it did not?'

'For me it has come,' said Merton. 'Virtue has gone out of me.'

'It has,' said Reuben. 'We saw and heard it going out. I suppose you will never smile again. I hardly feel that I shall.'

'Father will not, if I follow in his sacred steps. No one else is to tread in them.'

'Is anyone else able to?' said Salomon. 'It is on that score that he is troubled.'

'He may feel some doubt of his work, and not welcome a competitor.'

'Whom does he see in that light? His doubt takes another direction.'

'He must be conscious of his failings. He may feel that I may avoid them.'

'He is conscious of other things that you may avoid.'

'I would rather write nothing than write as he does.'

'Well, that should offer no problem.'

'I have already written, you know.'

'Nothing we may see. We could all say that.'

'Well, the future will show.'

'I can't bear the future,' said Reuben. 'Why must we always harp on it?'

'There is a past as well,' said Merton. 'We have had new light on Father's. No wonder you are his favourite, with your likeness to Aunt Emmeline. We feel how little we have known him. And feel there may be more to know. We can see that the trouble lives in Mother's memory.'

'That would not matter,' said Salomon. 'But it lives in Father's.'

'He ought to have a strange, mixed feeling for me,' said Reuben. 'Perhaps he has.'

'His feeling is mixed for all of us,' said Merton. 'It is not pure fatherly affection, as we have seen.'

'No, it is also anxiety and fear for your future,' said Hereward's voice. 'You are taking hasty steps on the path of life. I watch them with misgiving.'

'You know what it is to have taken them,' said Merton.

'And so do not want you to know it. You will be wise to move with care. The forces about us are many. We have need of a sure foothold.'

'I wish Father would not talk as he writes,' murmured Merton, looking down.

'We write from within,' said Hereward, keeping his eyes on his son. 'We write as we feel and live. It is the way to be honest and ourselves. It is as ourselves that all is done.'

'I have no doubt that I shall write as myself, Father.'

'My boy, I wish you would. I hope you will. But you may be afraid of the natural springs and deeps. If you are, you fear yourself.'

'We must know ourselves to write as them,' said Salomon. 'And that might arouse fear.'

'It means we must have courage,' said Hereward, as he closed the door.

'We often need it,' said Merton. 'I feel I have shown it to-day.'

'We feel with you,' said Salomon. 'We wondered how much you would show. We did not show it. But we had to have it.'

Chapter 6

'Well, I have a word to say,' said Merton at the table, using a conscious tone and throwing up his brows. 'It may cause some surprise.'

'It can only cause me pleasure,' said his mother. 'I wondered if we should ever hear a word from you again.'

'A voice from the silence,' said Reuben. 'With a strangely familiar sound.'

'I have had to give some thought to my own life. It is a thing that no one will do for me. And I am about to tell you the result. You can hardly guess it.'

'You have had a book accepted,' said Reuben. 'No, we should hardly have guessed it. I do feel some surprise.'

'I have not offered one. And when I spoke of my own life, I meant something that went deeply into it.'

'Your books should do that,' said Hereward. 'If they are to find a place in other lives.'

'You are going to be married?' said Ada. 'No, no, my boy, you are too young.'

'Women and their wits!' said Merton. 'How these things are true! But you are only partly right. I am twenty-four.'

'That may confirm what your mother said,' said Hereward. 'And how will you support a wife?'

'When you have not had a book accepted,' said Reuben.

'It is not a joke,' said Merton. 'I don't know why you think it is.'

'Your becoming a family man! What else can it be?'

'And the support of a family!' said Salomon. 'There is no reason for thinking it a joke.'

There was a pause.

'I am going to hang up my hat in my wife's hall,' said Merton.

There was another pause.

'I always think that sounds so comfortable,' said Joanna. 'And then you will go in to her fire.'

'Yes, that is what I should do,' said Reuben.

'Ah, ha! So should I,' said Sir Michael. 'And that is not all it would be. Let us hear about everything.'

'Yes, tell us the whole,' said Hereward. 'It concerns us as much as it does you. We are deeply involved, my boy.'

'My son, may it all go well with you,' said Ada.

'It sounds as if it is doing so,' said Salomon.

'It is going well,' said Merton, in an even tone. 'I am happier than I thought I could be. And I welcome the material ease. It is a great thing, as you all agree. She is an orphan, without near relations, and has inherited the family money. I feel no scruple in sharing it. I am taking deeper things. And we must be able to accept.'

'We most of us are,' said Salomon. 'And we must be, as you say. I have always been equal to it.'

'You earn what you take, by filling my place,' said Hereward. 'It enables other people to accept.'

'She will take something herself,' said Reuben. 'Merton will provide the relations. I hope she will find me a brother.'

'I shall have a daughter,' said Ada. 'It will be a long wish fulfilled. How it makes us talk of ourselves! But Merton knows our hearts.'

'I shall go on with my writing,' said her son. 'I hope I shall go further with it. It will be a help to feel there is no haste. It should mean work of a deeper quality.'

'Urgency is said to be a stimulant,' said Salomon. 'It seems it is not a dependable one.'

'Writing is not breaking stones,' said his brother.

'That sounds as if it must be true,' said Joanna.

'It is only partly so,' said Hereward. 'Everything is breaking stones, up to a point.'

'When are we to meet her?' said Ada. 'What a moment it will be!'

'I have asked her to dinner to-morrow,' said Merton. 'And we will ask Grandpa Merton and Aunt Penelope. And kill all the birds with one stone.'

'There are a good many birds,' said Joanna. 'I feel rather ashamed of being one.'

'Will you be living near to us?' said Zillah. 'The questions must follow each other.'

'Not far away. In the house in the bend of the hills. The small one in the curving road.'

'I don't call it small. How your ideas are enlarging! And at what a pace!'

'My son, it is a great step,' said Hereward. 'You will let us take it with you? There is indeed a place for her.'

'Would you be annoyed if I asked her name?' said Salomon. 'I don't mean it as a joke. Everyone has one.'

'Yes, even I have,' said Reuben. 'But I feel it is rather a joke.'

'You will know it to-morrow. And part of it will cease to be hers.'

'And may we ask her age? She has lived for some years, as we all have.'

'I hardly know it. That is, I am not quite sure. It is a little more than mine, and so will balance the lack in it.'

'You can now be any age you please,' said Zillah. 'It is true that everything has to be paid for.'

'Well, Merton has outdistanced you, Salomon,' said Sir Michael. 'The one of you who seemed at a standstill. That is, there hasn't been much about him of late.'

'It is no great feat, as I am always at a standstill.'

'I am not,' said Reuben. 'I take my brave, little steps forward.'

'I feel I have outdistanced everyone,' said Merton. 'I am uplifted to a height I had not known.'

'Well, make the most of it,' said Sir Michael. 'It will not last. Well, we hope it will. I mean, may it last, of course.'

'How quickly you have found a house!' said Ada. 'Have you been looking for one?'

'No, it is her own. She is living in it. I shall join her there. When I said I should hang up my hat in my wife's hall, I meant it.'

'Well, your path is smooth,' said Sir Michael. 'It might have been a rough one, as your parents feared.'

'It might. And I should still have taken it. I am not blind to my good fortune.'

'Merton is softened, like his path,' said Reuben.

'As he would be,' said Zillah. 'We must be influenced by the ways we take.'

'Well, the hour of the meeting will come,' said Sir Michael. 'It is an exciting thought. We have had no change in the family since Reuben was born. And that wasn't much, as he was a third son.'

'Fate was against me from the first,' said his grandson. 'I have trodden a hard way. It is really quite dignified.'

The hour came, and with it Alfred and Penelope to meet the newcomer. She was a tall, dark, quiet young woman, clearly more mature than Merton, with straight, rounded features, large, dark eyes, and a way of looking fully into people's faces, as if in appreciation and interest. Merton was too sure of her appeal to show more than his usual consciousness.

'Well, here is the patriarch, my grandfather; his consort, my grandmother; his son, my father; his daughter-in-law, my mother; his daughter, my aunt. Oh, and his grandsons, my brothers.'

'I did not know I was a consort,' said Joanna. 'Then I think Ada must be one.'

'I have avoided the stigma,' said Penelope. 'And have had no credit for it.'

'My maternal great-aunt, Miss Merton, my maternal grandfather, also of the name.'

'Are we not to hear another name?' said Ada. 'The one we are waiting to hear.'

'It is *Hetty*,' said its owner, in quiet, even tones. 'The only one to all of you. The other I am going to share with you. I must learn that it is mine.'

'There will be more for you to share,' said Sir Michael. 'We will give you all we can.'

'It cannot be much,' said Hetty, smiling. 'What you have can only be your own.'

'I would give all I could,' said Joanna. 'But I can't think of anything.'

Hetty laughed, with her eyes on Joanna's face.

'You make such a difference to so many people. You are making it to me.'

'It is a thing that will be true of you,' said Salomon. 'I hope Merton will let me say it.'

'I knew he would not let me,' said Reuben. 'So I had to waste it. It did come into my mind.'

'Merton's parents await judgement,' said Hereward, standing by his wife. 'We need not speak of the one we have made.'

'Neither need I,' said Hetty. 'I envy Merton the background to his life. It must mean so much to have one.'

'Well, now it will be yours,' said Sir Michael. 'With everything else that is his.'

'I feel less poor already. I see how poor I have been.'

'My brothers' names can come later,' said Merton. 'When we have had some meat and drink.'

Sir Michael led Hetty to the head of the dinner table. Merton sat by her, and the others fell at random into place. Alfred and Hereward were opposite to Hetty, and found her resting her eyes on them.

'What a pair to have before me! I am not used to people on the heights.'

'Merton does not see me in that way,' said Hereward. 'He thinks lightly of his father's place.'

'It may be too far removed from him. It is yours and belongs to yourself. He must see it from a distance, and judge it as he can.'

'You do not put him above us all in everything?'

'I put him in the place he is right to fill. The place that is his own.'

'What do you say to it, Merton?' said Salomon.

'Oh, Hetty is not versed in such things as yet. She is content to be simply herself. She never pretends to be anything she is not.'

'You are brought to this! I have no conception of your state.'

'No, I can see you have none.'

'You are my first grand-daughter,' said Alfred. 'And I am your second grandfather. I must seem to you a superfluous figure.'

'How can I say what you are? What do I know of you and your work? What can I know?'

'What of me and my work?' said Hereward, in a lower tone, as his son looked aside. 'Have you not your knowledge there?'

'Yes, I have,' said Hetty, meeting his eyes. 'But it is still only mine. Merton's time for it has not come. We don't know the whole of each other yet.'

'Would you dare to tell him the truth?'

'I have dared to tell him part. And he recognized my courage and disputed my judgement. But he will grow towards it. I am older than he is, you know.'

'Surely not much,' said Alfred.

'Five years. A good deal for a woman over a man. I should be content to go further than he does. I have gone further.'

'And you are content?' said Hereward, smiling. 'And so am I.'

'Come, come, you elderly men,' said Sir Michael.

'Is Merton to have a share of his future wife? Or are you taking his place?'

'They have their own place, as he has,' said Hetty. 'And I am learning mine.'

'She has a liking for men two or three times her age,' said Merton. 'It is a tribute to me that she accepted a younger one.'

'They may have a liking for her,' said Sir Michael. 'They can see age in their own way.'

'I would ask no one's opinion of her. I have my own.'

'My daughter!' said Ada. 'It would be safe to ask mine.'

'I might say the same,' said Hetty, meeting her eyes. 'Indeed I have said it. To myself, when I first came in.'

'I must appear another superfluous figure,' said Penelope.

'Well, luxuries may seem superfluous things. But they can be among the best.'

'What will you say of me?' said Zillah. 'I am more of a problem. Even you may be at a loss.'

'I will say nothing. What can I say? To you, to whom we owe everything, even the great man himself.'

'What is that?' said Hereward, as they left the room, seeming just to catch the words. 'Yes, we may talk to each other. We are not to separate to-night. We are all to have our share of you. And I will have mine. Tell me what the talk was about.'

'Why should I tell you what you know?'

'Well, I will understand you. And it was not Merton's voice I heard.'

'No, it was mine. I know his would be his own. I know his work is different from yours. I wish it was not. And he does not see yours as I do. I wish he did. I wish he could see it as it is.'

'Well, with you I wish he could. As much as would be of use to him. It need be no more. I would not be of use to me. And I do not serve myself.'

'He may in the end. It seems he must.'

'I think he will not. And I do not ask it. I would ask nothing to which I had no right. We have none to be looked up to.'

'Some of us have earned it. We know you are among them.'

'Not in my own family. I have earned it in many others. I am what is called a household word. It is what I wanted and have had. My son has other hopes. He has told you what they are.' Hereward smiled and then let his voice get fuller. 'My wish is to reach the multitude, to go deeper into many hearts. I think it comes from a deeper one. It meets a greater need.'

'The difference in Merton may be in himself. His aims must come from his powers, as everyone's must. They may be nearer to yours as they grow. And that will show him their distance.'

'Ah, I should have had a daughter. I have always known it.'

'You will have one now. And you will have others through your other sons.'

'I only want one. It is what I need. It is the classic relation, rooted in the past. My wife has done much for me. But now all she can do. And my sons go their distance, and can go no further.'

'It must be true of all of them. It would have to be.'

'Yes, I should remember. You will help me not to forget. I know what they have to give. They do not fail to give it. I myself can say no more.'

'You always have your sister?'

'We have gone through life together. She goes with me still. She will always go with me. I have no doubt of her. And my wife has not grudged us to each other. I have had all I could from both.'

'And now you will have something from me. On my own small scale.'

'It will be what I want, what I have not had. You will come to me often, come when I am thought to be alone. It is what a daughter would do.'

'What are you saying, Hereward?' said Ada. 'You will bewilder Hetty and ask too much of her. You have no right to ask anything yet. You are going too fast and too far. Merton is turning his eyes on you.'

'I am taking what he gives me. We do not reject a gift.'

'I have become so many things,' said Hetty. 'And I am still only myself.'

'I can't say he has given me a sister,' said Reuben. 'He might turn his eyes on me.'

'Do you feel you can say it?' said Hetty, smiling at Salomon, whose voice had been more seldom heard.

'Well, it is all a matter of Merton's eyes.'

'He is giving me a grand-daughter,' said Joanna. 'But I am not sure that he thought of it. I believe he just meant to give himself a wife.'

'So you need not show your gratitude,' said Salomon. 'And it might be a false step.'

'I shall not show any. I see no reason. And it is better not to take steps. They are so often called false.'

'The evening is too much of a success,' said Merton. 'I must appeal to you, Aunt Penelope. A great-aunt is a safe character. Will you give Hetty your protection? Mine is not enough.'

Penelope and Hetty turned to each other, the former at a loss for words, the latter at none.

The evening moved to its end. Alfred and his sister took their leave. When Merton returned from taking Hetty home, Galleon was standing in the hall.

'May I add my congratulations, sir?'

'You may. I am in a mood to expect them. I feel they are earned.'

'May I also be glad of the accompanying circumstances, sir?'

'You may. I am glad of them myself. They will mean more ease.'

'Complete ease I imagine, sir,' said Galleon, smiling. 'There will be no call for anything else.'

'My work may improve, when I have no sense of urgency.'

'Or be discontinued, sir,' said Galleon, in an almost roguish tone.

'You would hardly expect me to do nothing.'

'Well, sir, if there is no need of anything.'

'Would you like to do nothing yourself?'

'Well, sir, I appreciate my occasional leisure. Nothing further is in question.'

'But you would not like leisure and nothing else?'

'Well, sir, my life being of the opposite nature, I have no means of judging. I sometimes wish the duties were intermittent.'

'As mine are? I have to wait on the mood. It must be so with my kind of work.'

'It is not with mine, sir. Mood is not taken into account. It might lead to inconvenience.'

'I believe you think writing is not real work.'

'Well, sir, there is no great resemblance.'

'It is not like digging potatoes?'

'No, sir, or like the manual duties of a house.'

'Well, that is something.'

'Yes, sir, it is in its favour.'

'There is something I have not dared to tell you, Galleon,' said Reuben.

'Oh, the attempt at schoolmastering, sir. It is a passing phase.'

'Suppose it is a lasting one?'

'There is hardly any likelihood, sir.'

'It is little better than writing?' said Salomon.

'Well, sir, hardly as good,' said Galleon, in a serious tone. 'In writing you are master of yourself, and there are no contacts.'

'We ought to love our pupils,' said Reuben.

'It is our neighbours, sir. The term is hardly inclusive.'

'So our pupils are not neighbours?'

'Well, if their attitude was neighbourly, sir! But I gather it is not the case.'

'But we are supposed to love our enemies.'

'Well, if that is the ground, sir.'

'Their attitude does present problems.'

'Well, you will not have to solve them, sir.'

'Why not? I have no share in my brother's prosperity.'

'And prosperity need not end all human effort,' said Merton.

'It tends to end a good deal, sir. It is often its object.'

'I suppose another side of us can assert itself.'

'Our better nature, sir? There is not always any need of it. In which case it is not resorted to.'

'There is surely need of yours, Galleon,' said Salomon.

'Well, sir, my life consisting of service to others, it must at one time have asserted itself once for all.'

'But you do not remember it?'

'There is no point in recalling it, sir. It was not to my advantage.'

'You did not really wish to live for others?'

'Well, sir, it was perhaps as far as I could go in living for myself. It could not be to any great length.'

'You don't enjoy a glow of righteousness?'

'I am not subject to glows, sir. There is need of something to give rise to them.'

'I believe I could be,' said Reuben. 'And I suppose Merton is at the moment.'

'It is true,' said his brother. 'And the moment foreshadows a life.'

'Here is a man we have not known,' said Salomon.

'You are simple in your idea of me. Have you no depths yourself?'

'Yes, I have them myself.'

'Then you have a weak imagination.'

'Well, you need me to have such a strong one.'

'One would think nothing had ever happened to you.'

'Well, nothing ever has,' said Salomon.

'And this has made you realize it?'

'It may have brought it home to me. And I am affected by the change in your life.'

'And you would like a change in your own?'

'Well, I think I have become unfit for it,' said Salomon.

Chapter 7

'What is it, Merton, my son? You have something on your mind? You will not hide it from your mother. Tell her what it is.'

'I can tell the assembled family. Indeed I was about to. I will tell you first, if you will find it an advantage. I am not going to be married.'

'Not going to? No, it is not true. It is simply some passing trouble.'

'There are troubles that do not pass. You are fortunate not to have found it.'

'Come, tell us, my boy,' said Hereward. 'If it is nothing, let it be so. If it is not, say what it is. We may be of help.'

'That is often thought and said. People over-estimate their powers. Yours are great, if you can help this. You can hardly undo what is past.'

'Come, say a little more,' said Sir Michael. 'It seems such an unlikely thing. The girl would not be at a difference with anyone. We already know it.'

'I know it too. There is reason. That is what it is, or has been. How you are in the dark!'

'Well, shed some light,' said his father. 'You need not leave us in it. Let us look at the trouble with you.'

'I will shed it fully. Perhaps you will be dazzled by it. Hetty is going to have a child. And it is not mine.'

'Oh, no, it is not possible,' said Ada. 'There is some mistake. And of course it could not be yours.'

'It is not. It is what I said. In your sense it could not be. I do not know whose it is. I am never to know.'

There was a silence.

'It is sad news, my son,' said Hereward, with his eyes down. 'Sad for you and all of us. Your trouble is your father's.'

'Well, I would not have believed it,' said Sir Michael. 'I hardly believe it now. I don't know what to say.'

'It seems to be the case with most of you,' said Merton. 'And I can't be of any help.'

'You know what we feel,' said Salomon. 'You do not want our words. Have you broken off everything?'

'Well, it has come to an end.'

'Is she to marry the other man?' said Reuben.

'No, she is not. He is married. That is all I know.'

'This will not break up his marriage?'

'No, there seems to be no thought of it.'

'What will be the future of the child?'

'I do not know. It is not my concern. When I knew the truth, it ended things between us.'

'You are sure?' said Zillah. 'That it ended them for ever? Say the truth to yourself and to us. Have you lost your feeling for her?'

There was a pause.

'Such a feeling does not die at once, or ever die. I need say no more.'

Hereward was silent, his head bent as if in thought.

'What will her future be?' said Salomon. 'We are forced to question you. You are not forced to answer.'

'I am not able to. I do not know. It must be what she can make it. I hope it will not go hard with her.'

'It seems it must,' said Zillah, pausing after her words. 'If she gave up the child, and the trouble was concealed, would you forget it and marry her? Would it be for the happiness of both?'

Hereward raised his eyes.

'I hardly know. It will be months before the child is born. And how could she give it up?'

'It could be adopted. The way is not hard. And perhaps she need not lose sight of it.'

'You will help us, Zillah, if anyone can,' said Hereward.

'I had not thought of it,' said Merton. 'And neither has she. I don't know how I feel about it.'

'You hardly can, my son. You must take your time. We must have long thoughts in youth. The decision would shape your life.'

'If I made it, I should mean it to. It would be the reason of it.'

There was a pause.

'Have you not made it?' said Hereward gently, bending towards him.

'I have, Father. There can only be one. I can make no other.'

'You are sure, Merton? Sure in your heart? Sure for the years of your life?'

'I am, Father. I have no doubt. I see I could have none.'

'Then it is the best one,' said Hereward. 'There could be and might be others. But it is the best.'

'It is mine,' said Merton, lifting his head. 'I hope we can do as has been said. Then things would be, as far as they could be, as they would have been.'

'It is true,' said his father. 'And in a way and in the end they may be more.'

'It is a great difference. It is another path. But it is one I can tread. I see it plain before me. It is no longer blank and dark. And I should be willing to give. I am taking much. And I am glad to be taking it. It will give her something on her side.'

'You think and speak as yourself, my son,' said Hereward.

'It is not unusual to adopt a child,' said Ada. 'We have spoken of it ourselves. You remember, Hereward, a few days ago. We said how we should like to have a child in the house again, and almost thought of adopting one. I don't mean we could adopt this child, of course.'

'No, that could hardly be our choice,' said Hereward, gravely.

'Why could it not?' said Sir Michael. 'I see no reason against it. It would give you a child whose parentage you knew, and keep Hetty's child under her eyes. There seems a great deal to be said for it.'

'There is something,' said Zillah, after a pause. 'Merton would want to do everything for Hetty, if he did anything. It can only be everything or nothing, as he has really said. And it would give him a wife who was grateful to him, and at peace herself. And the secret could be kept.'

'Would it be?' said Salomon.

'Yes, yes, of course,' said his grandfather. 'It could be all but forgotten. We should all do our part. We need scarcely say it.'

'No, we could hardly fail in a trust like that,' said Hereward. 'But it is a serious and sudden idea. I don't know what to say

Any talk of adopting a child was casual. I only half-remember it. It was a passing thought.'

'You agreed with me,' said Ada. 'I believe you gave me the idea. If you were casual, you were serious. You meant what you said.'

'I am sure I did, if it fell in with a wish of yours. But words are only words in such a case. They must be taken as nothing more.'

'Do we know anything about the child's father?' said Zillah.

'Enough,' said Merton. 'Hetty has not been silent. He is a man of a high mental type and of our own class and kind. More I am never to know. I shall not seek to. I have seen it as the final word.'

'You are right to accept it,' said Hereward. 'It gives your course its meaning. You will be right never to question it. I feel you will be right, my son.'

'It would be a good work,' said Sir Michael. 'There could not be a better. It is one I should respect, that I should regard with sympathy and interest. I should respect the feeling that led to it. And I speak in a serious spirit.'

'I do not speak at all,' said Joanna. 'I am taken by surprise. You must all be people of the world, never at a loss.'

'What do our sons say?' said Ada. 'How do they see the idea? Are they enough ashamed of growing up to make their parents this amends?'

'Would not this child grow up?' said Salomon. 'What you need is one who would not. You would suffer the same thing.'

'Oh, it would take a long time. We need not think of it.'

'No, we are in our later years,' said Hereward. 'This would take us towards our last ones. There need be no trouble there.'

'I feel that light has broken,' said Merton. 'I will say once that I should be grateful.'

'And I will say once that that settles it,' said Hereward. 'That and your mother's wish.'

'How strange that we thought of adopting a child just at this time!' said Ada.

'The three young men in front of you are there all the time. One extreme suggests another.'

'Well, it will all work out,' said Sir Michael. 'She will leave us for a while, and return as if nothing had happened. And they will marry, as if nothing had. And no one will connect the adoption with anything. And we must cease to do so.'

'Mamma, have we asked your permission to have the child?' said Ada.

'I don't know,' said Joanna. 'I daresay you can tell me. But a noble course of action needs no permission. Only admiration. And that I give.'

'We must see it as an ordinary course,' said Hereward. 'Nothing else need be thought or said. Anyone can adopt a child. We all know cases of it.'

'The plan seems to have made itself,' said Reuben. 'We can leave it to develop in its own way.'

'What do you think of it, Salomon?' said Zillah.

'Well, I feel we are moving over rather deep waters. But it is out of our hands, as Reuben said.'

'It is Hereward who will benefit the most,' said Ada. 'We can foresee the success of the plan in his case.'

'Well, childhood makes a great appeal to me. I have always been alive to its charm. It is a mark of the mature, worldly man, and calls for no surprise.'

'Now there is a question, Hereward. Are my father and aunt to know the truth? We must make our decision and hold to it.'

'They know it,' said Merton. 'I have told them. I asked if anyone else should know. And they said I should not face it alone. And I see they were right.'

'Dear Father and Aunt Penelope! I feel they could not be wrong. I honour them equally. I have come to do so. It is good to find my son depending on them.'

'I have found I can depend on you all, Mother.'

'You must depend on no one else,' said Hereward, gravely. 'See that you do not forget.'

'My boy, may your grandfather say once how he feels for you?' said Sir Michael.

'There is no need, Grandpa. You have shown it.'

'And now must show it in another way,' said Hereward.

'Now I am going to say whom I feel for,' said Ada. 'It may be unexpected, but I will say it. I often have a sudden feeling that is just my own. I feel for Hetty; for what lies before her; for having to face us with our knowledge; for feeling she must take so much, when she herself has failed. Merton is beyond pity, with the generous part. And that his mother feels for him need not be said.'

'Perhaps none of it need have been,' said Hereward, gently. 'For the reason that his mother felt for him.'

'Now here is our recurring difference. I do not believe in hiding what we feel. It means that no one knows we feel it. I will say it again. I feel for Hetty. A sense of guilt is no help with its consequences. And we all do wrong.'

'And only the ordinary kind that does not add to us,' said Joanna. 'It hardly earns us any feeling. It is really expected of us. We might almost as well do right.'

'Ah, the poor girl, we all pity her,' said Sir Michael. 'I quite dread meeting her in a way. I shall be ill at ease, as if I had done something myself.'

'Well, perhaps you have, by not doing anything,' said Reuben.

'There should be no trouble,' said Zillah. 'The moment will come and go. She will know what is being done for her, and will do her best.'

Chapter 8

Hetty could do no more than this. She entered in her ordinary way, looked once into everyone's face, and although more silent than usual, betrayed nothing. She seemed to control what she felt by holding herself from knowing that she felt it. She was, as always, appreciative of everyone, and by listening with especial attention saved herself from the need to speak.

The need fell on other people.

'Well, we are all together,' said Sir Michael. 'Just as we shall be in the end. It brings the future near to us. And it is not so far away.'

'Grandpa knew he would be ill at ease,' said Reuben. 'He should have been prepared. Let someone talk about the weather.'

'The gales never cease,' said Merton. 'They are doing harm to the trees. I hear more than one is down.'

'The elements are against us,' said his father. 'Just when we want them in our favour. I mean, we all know people with journeys before them. I can think of several.'

'He can think of one,' said Reuben. 'But he need not say so.'

'An elm came down near a cottage,' said Salomon, 'and startled the cottager's wife.'

'Yes, poor woman, she is expecting a child,' said Sir Michael. 'It is not the time for shocks. We must hope for better things ourselves. I mean I do for any friends of mine.'

'It is said to be difficult to give our real meaning,' said Joanna to her grandsons. 'But I don't think it can be.'

'The weather has failed us,' said Salomon. 'We are supposed always to talk about it. And it does seem a suggestive subject. But I never will again.'

'Never will do what?' said Ada.

'Talk of the weather, Mother. It is unworthy of me.'

'Well, I don't know,' said Sir Michael. 'It can be a help when other subjects are forbidden – fail us in some way. It is awkward when there is a hush, and you could hear a pin drop, and everyone waits for someone else to speak, and no one does.'

'What harm is there in hearing a pin drop?' said Joanna. 'And there is little danger of it. When a pin is needed, no one ever has one.'

'I have seen Hetty's house, Merton,' said Hereward. 'And I am as pleased with it as you can be. But the men can't begin to work on it yet. So much harm has been done by the gales.'

'Well, there is no hurry now,' said Sir Michael. 'That is, they will do it in their time.'

'We can do nothing,' said Reuben. 'We must just bear it.'

'Just bear what?' said Ada. 'Speak so that we can hear.'

'We have countenanced the habit of whispering,' said Hereward. 'And now can hardly complain of it.'

'There is no reason for it,' said Sir Michael. 'We should never seem to be covering anything up. It might give a wrong impression.'

'It is more likely to give a right one,' said Hereward, smiling at his sons. 'The same as not covering it up.'

'Father surprises me,' said Reuben. 'He is simply trying to help. He almost reminds me of myself. Can it be the simplicity of greatness?'

'I could almost think so,' said Merton. 'I have nothing but the truth to suffer. Many people despise the unfortunate, and hardly hide it. He does emerge as a man by himself.'

'I wish you would include your mother in your talk,' said Ada. 'Who is man by himself?'

'Father,' said Salomon. 'We were speaking in his praise.'

'What were you saying about him? Hereward, come and hear your sons' description of you.'

'I spoke in praise,' said Reuben.

'So did I,' said Merton.

'I would have,' said Salomon. 'But the other two forestalled me.'

'It is enough, my sons,' said Hereward, in a moved tone. 'Few fathers hear as much. I am content.'

'Well, that is true,' said Sir Michael. 'Some would be wiser not to hear at all. When I think of the things I said about my father! But he did not hear them. So it was another matter.'

'Your sons did not mean you to know what they said, Hereward,' said Ada, moving forward. 'It was the outcome of their real feeling. Dear boys, how fortunate we are!'

'And they are!' said Sir Michael. 'There is the other side.'

'Well, I have not kept apart from them,' said Hereward. 'I have tried to see things through their eyes. It has helped them to see them through mine. It has given us a shared vision.'

The evening came to its end. Its minutes had been separate and slow. The hour felt later than it was, and put the scene into the past. Hetty left the house with Merton as simply as she had entered it. Alfred and Penelope entered as they left it. And the future took its meaning and its shape.

'Well, I am relieved,' said Reuben. 'Merton is not here to know. I have seen the depths, and should hardly have known they were deep. I feel I should be grateful.'

'We must feel there is someone else who might be that,' said Penelope.

'Poor little Hetty?' said Sir Michael. 'Well, I have no doubt that she is. She had her own way of showing it. She faced us bravely. I felt an admiration for her. I don't deny it.'

'There might have been other feelings. It seems there is something in her that prevents them.'

'There is. I felt it. I was alive to it from the first. I felt my heart turn over, when I saw her walk up to the cannon's mouth. I asked myself if I should have been equal to it. And I told myself I should not. I make no secret of it.'

'I make most of what I tell myself, a secret,' said Reuben.

'Many of us do,' said Penelope. 'We don't show too much of what is in us. There is an example of it in Hetty's case.'

'Ah, your strong moral sense is in our way, Aunt Penelope,' said Ada. 'But your natural generosity will assert itself. We do not fear.'

'When we talk of self-exposure, we do mean something derogatory,' said Salomon. 'It does not occur to us that it could be to anyone's credit. And as it is usually unconscious, I suppose it would not.'

'How much of himself does Grandpa expose?' said Reuben.

'More than most people,' said Salomon. 'I think almost the whole.'

'And Father?'

'I don't think much.'

'Aunt Penelope?'

'More than she means to. But nothing to consider.'

'Mother?'

'A great deal. She has less to be ashamed of.'

'Grandma?'

'No one could say. Grandpa Merton what he must. Aunt Zillah almost nothing. The three of us as much as we dare. Galleon most of himself, as he sees no fault to be found in it.'

'Some people suppress their better selves,' said Sir Michael. 'It is a known thing.'

'Then they must make it known,' said Salomon.

'You would think they would feel pride in their own goodness.'

'They do,' said Joanna. 'So much pride that they cannot face it. And feel no one else will be able to.'

'Could real goodness cause too much pride?' said Salomon. 'An instance of it amazes me, or would, if I could think of one.'

'Father's adoption of Hetty's child?' said Reuben, in a lower tone. 'Wise or not, does it serve you?'

'Well, it does enlarge him for me.'

'Is there any idea what the child's name is to be?'

'Zillah!' said Hereward. 'A name that carries so much for me. My mother and wife would understand.'

'Is the child to be a girl?' said Reuben.

'Yes,' said his father, smiling. 'I have three sons.'

'And if it is a boy?'

'Hereward,' said Ada. 'So as to be a real son. We could call it something else.'

'Is there anything to know about a child?' said Penelope.

'Oh, Aunt Penelope, a moment. Thereby hangs a tale. But this question of the name is a part of the same matter. I should have thought my own had the strongest claim, and should be inclined to assert it. But I know what it is to be called by it. So we will postpone the answer.'

'Don't you like your name?' said Alfred.

'Father, how could anyone like it?'

'It was my mother's name,' said her father, disposing of any objection to it.

'And does that make it the best name for anyone else?'

'It gives it a reason and a background. If you like, an excuse.'

'Well, I am glad it has the last. It needs it.'

'It does not need one to me.'

'Well, tell Father and Aunt Penelope our plan, Hereward. Let them know the pleasant side of the matter as well as the other. "It is an ill wind —" as we feel. I wonder what they will say to it.'

'I think it can wait for the moment. It will emerge in its time.'

'Let the time be now. There is no virtue in mere delay. I want them to know it. I feel a wish to share it with everyone.'

'It is rather too much your own affair for that. But do as you will. It is because of you that the plan is made. Tell them yourself. Your own words will be best.'

'Well, you know the dark side of the story, Father. Now hear the one that helps us to accept it. It is the moment to speak of it, as Merton is not here. It is clear that Hetty's child must be adopted. That conclusion came about of itself. Indeed it was foregone. Well, who do you think the parents are to be? You will hardly guess.'

'Then do not expect us to,' said Alfred. 'It would lead to nothing.'

'Well, I will give you your chance, Father.'

'No, it is out of my sphere. I deal in certainties. It is not you and Hereward, of course?'

'Now why *of course*? And why should it not be? *Of course* it is. It will fill a gap in our lives. We have wished for a child in the house. It is so long since we had one.'

'The last might be said of many of us. Of most of us after a time.'

'I hardly knew my own heart,' said Hereward, 'and had to be informed of it. But I want what Ada wants. And I am a child-lover, as you know. It may work out well.'

'You could have adopted a child at any time. This trouble can hardly have caused the wish.'

'It has made us realize it,' said Ada. 'And it was not a new one. We had spoken of it. The plan will serve both our son and ourselves. What is there against it?'

'Nothing in itself. But surely there are other things. It brings the matter too near for something that is to be concealed.'

'Oh, we shall forget what lies behind it. We shall impose that condition on ourselves. We shall just adopt a child in the ordinary way. We might have done so at any time, as you said.'

'As I have also said, it keeps it too close to everyone. Too close to you too, too close to your son and his wife.'

'Oh, they know we are doing it for their sakes. They will think out their course and follow it. There is no danger there.'

'Why is it for Merton's sake? How does it serve him?'

'By serving Hetty. By ensuring her peace of mind. His one wish is to be of help to her. And so of help to himself.'

'You may soon be having your own grandchildren.'

'But not a child in our own home. The grandchildren would be apart from us. We should be without a child ourselves.'

'Well, it is true,' said Hereward.

'You may come to feel a bias towards your own descendants. Will it be easy to keep a balance?'

'Yes, quite easy. Or quite possible. We shall make our resolves and hold to them. Indeed they are made. Now have I to refute any more objections? If so, let me hear them. I am ready.'

'Ada has made up her mind,' said Hereward. 'And she is true to herself, and so cannot be false to any man. We need not doubt her. I have learned that I never need.'

There was a pause.

'We are not to know who the father is?' said Alfred, relinquishing his stand.

'Not now or ever. Merton is never to know. It is the final decision, and may be the best.'

'The father is responsible for the child's support.'

'Oh, well, well,' said Hereward, moving his hand. 'That is as it may be. It is by the way. I am glad to give Ada what she needed. I had not realized her feeling. But for this I might never have done so. It has come about as she said.'

'So you will never know the child's heredity?'

'We know enough. There is no need to know more.'

'What do you know? You must forgive my pursuit of the truth. I am Ada's father and must question what lies before her.'

'I will answer as I can. On one side you know what we do. On the other, the father is a man of our own class and kind. As I said, it is enough.'

'He has hardly been true to either. And does he not know his obligations?'

'He has fallen in with our wishes and given us his trust.'

'Through Hetty you mean?'

'It could be through no one else. But question me no further. I can say no more.'

'We want to do everything for the child ourselves,' said Ada. 'So as to feel it is our own, and separate from our grandchildren. Doing all you can for someone is known to create a strong feeling.'

'Well, it is a way of putting what you want into your life,' said Alfred, smiling. 'And you might have a worse. You might indeed, my dear. It is a good scheme in some senses, a generous one in all. May all go well with it.'

'Well, I am glad to have an approving word from you at last, Father. I wondered if I should ever hear one again. I do think the scheme has things to recommend it, and things not quite to be despised. Aunt Penelope, you say nothing.'

'I say what your father said. As so often, our thought is the same. But I have a word of my own. What do Merton's brothers feel about it?'

'They have given their approval. It means they will do their part.'

'It does,' said Salomon to Reuben. 'What will it prove to be? What an odd and sudden change! And what light it throws on everyone! What light especially on Merton! I did not know he was a noble man, great enough to forgive.'

'Nor did I. I remember when he was strong enough not to have to.'

'It was a different stage of life,' said Sir Michael. 'You have come to another.'

'I have not,' said Reuben. 'I believe I should never forgive. And I am not sure that it is great. It seems to me rather humble.'

'It could be both,' said Ada. 'There is humility in all greatness.'

'There are other things,' said Salomon. 'Not always akin to humility.'

'Great people always know how little they have achieved,' said Joanna. 'It does show how much they expected to.'

'It is time for us to leave you,' said Penelope. 'We take away a great deal to think of.'

'And do not let Father think of it in the wrong way,' said Ada. 'He will benefit much more, if he takes the right one. We are all going to benefit so much.'

'Are we?' said Reuben, as his elders followed the guests. 'Or are there troubles ahead? The wise ones feared it.'

'We must avoid them,' said Salomon. 'It will become an unwritten law.'

'What will become one?' said Hereward, glancing back.

'The avoidance of troubles arising from the new plan, Father.'

'It must become a law,' said Hereward, almost sternly. 'And one that we never break. See that it is never broken.'

Galleon entered as Hereward went on, wearing a face so expressionless as to suggest control of it.

'Oh, you have heard, Galleon!' said Salomon. 'Oh, we ought to have thought of it.'

'I did not hear, sir,' said Galleon, specifying no further.

'I did not mean you could help it.'

Galleon again did not hear.

'We know you will keep your own counsel.'

'It is best as I have said, sir.'

'You will forget anything you heard?'

'No, sir, it is best as I have said.'

'It is,' said Reuben. 'We can only look up to you, Galleon. I suppose you look up to yourself.'

'Well, I have my share of self-respect, sir,' said Galleon, as he moved away.

'I can have none,' said Salomon. 'I almost gossiped with a dependant about our private family affairs! I have no respect for myself, and I have lost Galleon's. How his virtue has to be its own reward! When it is the only thing that deserves another.'

'We will follow his example and forget everything,' said Reuben. 'But I feel we might be reminded.'

Chapter 9

'Does Henry love father?' said Hereward.

'No,' said his adopted son.

'Oh, Henry loves good, kind Father,' said Hereward, suggesting grounds for the feeling.

'No, Father love Henry,' said the son, using the name that had come about through his own rendering of *Hereward*.

'Oh, why must we only love you?'

'Because,' said Henry, looking at him with grave eyes.

'Don't you love anyone else?'

'Father and Nurse,' said Henry, sitting up on Hereward's knee. 'Always very much.'

'Father does more for you than Nurse does.'

'No,' said Henry, surprised.

'When you are big, you will know it.'

'Big now; very big boy.'

'Yes, very big. You have lived nearly three years.'

'Five,' said Henry, erroneously. 'Seven, five, eight.'
'You will be more than that one day.'
'A hundred,' said Henry, with force.
'Even Father is not as much as that.'
'Oh, no,' said Henry, compassionately.
'How old do you think Father is?'
Henry raised his eyes in silence, unequal to the demand.
'It was Father who brought you a toy to-day.'
'Broken,' said Henry. 'Poor horse!'
'Oh, how did that happen?'
'Break it,' said Henry, illustrating the movement with his hands.
'Oh, that was not very wise.'
'Very good boy,' said Henry, in a precautionary tone.
'Let me see if I can do anything. Why, the horse is without a head.'
'No,' said Henry, putting the head and body together to remedy the position.
'You would not like your head to be apart from you.'
Henry broke into mirth at the idea, and took his head in his hands as if to safeguard it.
'So you did not like the horse?'
'Love it,' said Henry, stroking the head.
'You are not very kind to your toys.'
'Not put them away,' said Henry, in agreement.
'Not when Nurse tells you to?'
'She could spare herself the trouble,' said Henry, reproducing more than the words.
'She does not make you do it?'
'No good when they are young. A waste of breath.'
'Why, here is Mother coming. Show her how pleased you are to see her.'
'Always see Father.'
'Oh, you have the child, Hereward,' said Ada. 'What a difference he makes to you!'
'Do you?' said Hereward, putting his face against the boy's. 'Ah, you make a difference.'
'One, two, three,' said Henry, as his grandparents and aunt appeared. 'Poor Grandpa has a stick.'

'Yes, poor Grandpa,' said Sir Michael. 'You would not like to walk with one.'

'Yes,' said Henry, holding out his hands.

'No, it is Grandpa's stick.'

'No, Henry's,' said Henry, getting off Hereward's knee and advancing to the stick with open purpose.

Sir Michael gave it up, and Henry walked about the room, imitating his use of it, and appearing to find it an employment that could not pall. When he caught his foot and fell, he waited to be picked up and resumed it.

'Give the stick to your big brother,' said Salomon.

'Not big,' said Henry, looking at him.

'Yes, we are bigger than you are.'

'Men,' said Henry, in a somehow baffled manner.

'You are right. We are not big for men.'

'No,' said Henry, smiling at the expression of his thought.

'What do you call your horse?' said Reuben, as Sir Michael retrieved the stick.

'Horse,' said Henry, surprised.

'But hasn't it a name of its own?'

'Horsie,' said Henry, after a pause.

'Isn't its real name *Dobbin*?'

'Yes,' said Henry, smiling again.

'And what does Dobbin call you?'

'Sir,' said Henry, laconically.

'Does anyone call you that?'

'Yes, the coachman and his boy.'

'What do you call him?'

'Davis. Or Davis dear.'

'Why don't you call him *sir*?'

'Not a coachman,' said Henry. 'But the boy does.'

'Would you like to be his boy?'

'Yes,' said Henry, rather unexpectedly.

'And would you call him *sir*?'

'Oh, yes.'

'And what would you do?'

'Hold the reins and have a whip.'

'You have them both,' said Hereward, who had provided them in miniature.

'Very small,' said Henry, incidentally.

'Mr and Mrs Merton Egerton,' said Galleon at the door.

Henry alone of the company gave no sign.

'Here are brother Merton and sister Hetty come to see you,' said Ada.

Henry did not disagree.

'And will you come soon to see us?' said Hetty, stooping towards him.

'No, not soon.'

'But you want to see little Maud?'

'See you,' said Henry, as if this duty should suffice.

'Maud talks as much as you do,' said Merton. 'And she says words of her own.'

'Baby,' said Henry, seeing this as a mark of the state.

'We must ask her to come to tea with you,' said Joanna.

Henry turned and climbed on Joanna's knee, got down and returned with the horse, and settled himself with a portion in each hand.

'They both change with every day like flowers,' said Hetty, looking at him.

'Maud is at the age when it is almost with the hours,' said Joanna.

Henry turned and put his hand over her mouth.

'Not talk about Maud,' he said.

'Oh, but why not?' said Ada. 'We talk about you.

'Yes, talk about Henry.'

'We talk and think about you both.'

'Yes, think,' said Henry, as if this did not matter.

'Maud is a dear little girl. She does everything her nurse tells her.'

Henry looked up at Joanna with a light in his eyes.

'Naughty Maud,' he said.

'Now you are making a joke,' said Ada.

'Yes,' said Henry, giggling in recognition of it.

'Well, who is this coming in?'

'Great-aunt Penelope,' said Henry, glancing at the door. 'And poor Grandpa Merton.'

'Why is he poor?' said Joanna.

'Spectacles. Poor eyes! Oh, poor Grandpa Merton!'

'Would you like to wear the spectacles?'

'Yes,' said Henry, doubtfully.

'Go and ask if you may try them on.'

Henry did so, and walked about, wearing the glasses and laughing rather unnaturally. Then he suddenly threw them off and returned to Joanna.

'Oh, you might have broken them. What would Grandpa Merton have done then?'

'Not wear them,' said Henry, stamping his foot. 'Never wear them any more.'

'They did not suit his sight,' said Alfred. 'The result of the lifetimes between us. He thinks they affect me as they do him. I had better have them back.'

'No,' said Henry, trying to intercept them. 'Not wear them ever again.'

'Grandpa Merton sees nicely with them,' said Joanna.

'Oh, yes,' said Henry, standing with tears in his eyes.

'They make everything good for him.'

'Yes,' said Henry, finding her tone dependable and sighing with relief.

'He sees what you do,' said Salomon. 'And is just as happy as you are.'

'Ring-a-ring-a-roses!' said Henry, struck by the idea of happiness.

The younger people accepted the prospect, and the rite began.

'Again,' said Henry, as they rose from the ground.

It was repeated.

'Again,' said Henry.

The door was opportunely opened and Nurse appeared.

'May Master Henry come now, ma'am?'

'Not *Master*,' said Henry, with a wail.

'Come then, Nurse's little boy.'

Henry put his hand in hers and turned to the door.

'Won't you say good-night to me?' said Hetty, whose eyes had followed him.

'Good-night, sister Hetty,' said Henry, in a tone of quotation.

'And you will say good-night to Father,' said Salomon, seeing the direction of another pair of eyes.

Henry suffered the observance, and Hereward lifted him and

held him close. He disengaged himself to the point of comfort, and remained passive, awaiting release.

'The first shall be last, and the last first,' said Salomon, looking at them. 'Of all Father's infants I have been the least to him.'

'The last, the child of my old age,' said Hereward, almost to himself. 'No other has been so much blood of my blood, so deeply derived from me. We go forward, a part of each other. We join the future and the past.'

Hetty's eyes changed, and in a moment went to Merton, who had moved away. Reuben glanced at her and looked aside. Hereward continued in another tone.

'Henry's way of echoing and copying everyone gives him his own place to me. He seems to represent you all.'

'I have noticed that about him,' said Ada. 'He gets little touches from each of them. He is young to observe so much.'

'He is not always beyond his age,' said Merton, brushing down his clothes.

'Nuts in May!' said Henry, seeing the movement and accepting its suggestion.

'No, no, you have had enough. You know how it will end,' said Nurse, referring to the outbreak of violence by which the young signify exhaustion. 'You must come upstairs.'

'Horse,' said Henry, in an acquiescent tone.

The parts were put into his hands, and he was led away.

'Now we can talk to Hetty and Merton,' said Ada. 'They will feel it hardly worth while to visit us.'

'When a child is about, no one else's existence is recognized,' said Merton. 'I sometimes feel with Henry that Maud's might be ignored.'

'You are looking tired, my son. Are you working too hard?'

'All day and part of the night,' said Hetty. 'He has never had such a spell.'

'I have had a grim moment,' said Merton. 'I will say a word of myself. I never know why it is a sign of baseness. I collected and revised what I had written, to prepare it to see the light. And suddenly and finally consigned it to outer darkness. I face the world with an empty sheet, and feel it will be long before it is filled. It may be a forward step, but it feels like a backward one.'

'Which it is not, my son,' said Hereward. 'It is a man's step forward. It takes a man's strength. I would have taken it myself, if there had been need. It makes a bond with your father.'

'And I have my own good fortune. In a way I am doubly blessed. I appear to work for my wife, and I work to fulfil myself.'

'I could envy you,' said Reuben. 'I find that independence as a state is over-praised.'

'I do not agree,' said Ada. 'I should be proud of anyone belonging to me, who achieved it.'

'Then you are proud of Father and me. I hope equally.'

'Well, in proportion to yourselves, my son. And I am proud of the qualities that lead to it. It needs self-denial and courage.'

'I said it was over-praised. But it is more so than I thought.'

'Most people pretend to admire such qualities,' said Merton. 'What they really admire is the power to avoid them.'

'They don't even pretend to in my case,' said Hereward. 'They are disturbed when they hear I put effort into my work. They want to feel it is spontaneous.'

'Well, I think that is nice of them,' said Reuben. 'I can't think of a kinder feeling.'

'I am ashamed of understanding it,' said Joanna.

'Well, I understand it too,' said Sir Michael. 'To do that would be a mark of genius. And they would like to think he had it.'

'They seem nicer and nicer,' said Reuben.

'And no doubt they do think so. And I daresay he has. If they want the proof, his books give it.'

'I agree that they are nice,' said Salomon. 'They don't think that genius is an infinite capacity for taking pains. It is a grudging and heartless theory.'

'And a false one,' said Merton.

'Well, we ought to appreciate them,' said Sir Michael. 'They are Hereward's readers, and we can't have too many of them.'

'His work would always create readers,' said Zillah.

'Yes, of course. It has created me. I feel I now belong to them.'

'I have not been created,' said Joanna. 'I enjoyed the books from the first. And I am not at all sure I enjoyed them for the wrong reasons.'

'Well, I must go and work for the readers,' said Hereward. 'If it is a humble position, it is.'

'And I must go and work to gain some,' said Merton. 'And it is a humble position.'

'And we must go home,' said Penelope. 'It has been good to have an hour with you.'

'And to us to have one with you, Aunt Penelope,' said Ada. 'You don't know what these flashes of you and Father mean to us. They hold all the echoes of the past for me. My girlhood and my sister seem to be carried in them.'

'Well, your girlhood and motherhood are in the hours for us,' said Alfred. 'It is no wonder that we seek them.'

The older people went with the guests to the hall, and Salomon and Reuben were alone.

'You heard, Salomon? I saw you heard. Hetty heard too, and Merton did not. Don't pretend you don't understand. We both know you do.'

'Would it be best not to understand? Best to forget?'

'We shall not forget. No human being could. And we must speak of it. No one could be silent.'

'Well, words may be a safeguard. It is the suppressed things that escape. "Blood of my blood, so deeply derived from me". It is a warning. We are Father's sons.'

'Things fall into place,' said Reuben. 'There are a number to be explained.'

'Yes. Father's sympathy with Hetty. The way he saw other people's feeling for her. His acceptance of the news of the child. His wish to adopt it, and his contriving to represent the wish as his wife's. I was struck by that at the time, but could not explain it. His caring for Henry more than his own grandchild. The touches in Henry supposed to be copied from us. What a story it is! It should not belong to real life.'

'It would be better in a book. I am sure I wish it was in one.'

'It would. It is a pity Merton cannot use it. It is hard to be the victim of it, when he might find it useful. And the light on the character of Father! It is a pity he cannot use him too. He may be short of material. His progress seems in doubt.'

'Hetty must live on the edge of a precipice,' said Reuben.

'She was prepared. And she keeps her foothold. Father is on it, and is growing unwary. He should be warned, and we cannot warn him. We are in peril.'

'I suppose Mother has never suspected?'

'Why should she? We did not suspect. She would not think it possible. And in a sense it was not. A father's having that relation with his son's promised wife! What man would have come to it?'

'This one,' said Reuben. 'He yields to all his feelings. He does more; he fosters them. That is how he gets them on to paper. If he subdued them, they would lose their force. And releasing them sets them free in his life. I understand it all.'

'You have great understanding. Take care that it does not betray you. And remember that other people are without it. If this came out, they would see it through their own eyes.'

'How do you see it?' said Reuben.

'Through mine. I cannot help it. I should not have thought it of him. What man would of his father? I resent being forced to think it. It is not a lapse we can condone. If he was helpless, he should not have been. We are masters of ourselves.'

'Perhaps he was not. He is not a man who would always be. He can be carried away. Think how he is affected by his books.'

'This was actual life. He knew it for what it was. The truth is what it is. It must not escape. It proves what we think of it, that we fear it so much. And Mother and Merton do not know. Remember they do not. If they do, the guilt will be ours. And it is a guilt that no man should incur.'

'Why, what a solemn pair!' said Hereward. 'What serious matter is on foot?'

'Henry and his story,' said Salomon. 'You will not be surprised.'

'No, he makes a strange appeal to me. There is wonder in every child. And in this one I find so much. I feel that my love for him will remain and grow, instead of changing to another, as with all of you. It may be so with a late child. And to me he is the last of my sons. It is strange that so great a good should arise from what might be called a wrong.'

'It must be called one,' said Salomon. 'What else could we call it?'

'It might have been almost unconscious.'

'What led up to it was not.'

'Well, well, we will not judge,' said Hereward, as he turned away.

'We can't all arrange for our wrong-doing not to be judged,' said Salomon. 'The weak point about it is the judgement.'

'It is what there is to trouble us. We don't find anything else. Anyhow Father does not. And people feel a zest in judging. I am glad I never do wrong.'

'I never do either. "Not anything the world calls wrong." And I think the world must know. Indeed we see it does. But if we cannot speak without referring to the matter, we are bound to betray it. I feel the deepest misgiving.'

'And Father feels none. The danger is there. What has happened can happen again.'

'The words may escape at any moment. They are on the edge of his mind. But are we quite sure of their meaning? Were they used in a literal sense? He has been fond of us all as children.'

'He has,' said Reuben. 'And here is one of us.'

A cry came from an upper floor, and the brothers' footsteps joined the others on their way to it.

Henry was sitting up in bed, looking small enough for any trouble to be large for him, and Nurse was standing, remonstrant and unruffled, at his side. He spoke in an accusing tone.

'Poor Grandpa Merton wear them! Hurt him very much.'

'No, no, he is not wearing them now,' said Ada.

'Yes, Henry see him. He always wear them. Oh, dear Grandpa Merton!'

'No, he left them behind,' said Hereward, with a glance at his wife. 'He will never wear them again.'

'No?' said Henry, relaxing in a doubtful manner.

'There is a pair on the table in my room,' said Hereward, in a rapid, incidental tone that eluded Henry. 'Let someone fetch them.'

This was done, and Henry looked at them in recognition. 'Yes,' he said in relief.

'So that is all right,' said Ada. 'You can go to sleep.' Henry kept his eyes on the glasses.

'You don't want them, do you?' said Nurse.

'Yes,' said Henry, holding out his hands.

'What will you do with them?' said Salomon.

'Not wear them. No. But very nice spectacles. Henry's.'

'Look how well they suit me,' said Reuben, putting them on.

'Yes,' said Henry, smiling at the sight. 'But Henry's spectacles. Grandpa Merton give them.'

'Oh, are you sure that is true?' said Nurse.

Henry nodded without looking at her.

'Put them in their case,' said Ada. 'Then you can have them under your pillow.'

Henry manipulated the case with interest and appreciation, laid it on the pillow by his own head, and prepared to sleep in its company, having an equal regard for its accommodation and his own.

'Henry is a person of a great compassion,' said Salomon.

'He shows many qualities,' said Hereward.

'He is a person of a great acquisitiveness,' said Reuben.

'Not more than any other child,' said Nurse.

'And of a great self-complacence.'

'Not more than you were at his age. All children are alike.'

'I wonder who thought of the innocence of childhood. It must have been a person of a great originality.'

'But how innocent a child is, compared to ourselves!' said Hereward. 'We have only to think to know it.'

'It hardly needs thought,' said Salomon.

'Well, well, we can hardly go through life without a stumble.'

'We all do wrong, sir, it is true,' said Nurse, accepting the current theory, though she was herself an exception to it.

'And the wrong is great more often than we know,' said Ada.

'Well, if it was great, we should not know,' said Salomon.

Chapter 10

'I am surprised at myself,' said Reuben. 'I am just like everyone else. I am sure you will all be surprised. Of course I think you are all thinking about me. I said I was like everyone else.'

'One moment, my boy,' said Ada, who did the family carving and was engaged on it. 'Let me hear when I can attend.'

'You will not hear until you do. I take myself very seriously. I am exactly like everyone else.'

'Well, what is it?' said his mother, with her eyes on a plate that Galleon was taking from her.

'I am treading in the usual steps, and thinking I am the only person who has done so.'

'You yourself?' said Ada, in a different tone. 'You are going to be married! Or you think you are. Another of you. And at your age!'

'It would not be unnatural, if it was all of them,' said Hereward. 'They are at the normal age.'

'But it is me, Father. That is not natural. I am sure you can't think so. Anyhow no one will agree. You see that Mother does not.'

'Well, I am glad,' said Sir Michael. 'I find it good news. I don't believe in postponing everything and prolonging youth until there is none of it left. I did not do it myself, and it has turned out as you see. Where would you all be, if I had? I congratulate you, my boy. I am glad to have lived to see the day.'

'So am I,' said Joanna. 'I am sure we all are. That is what we do live for. To see days.'

'I must know a little more before I am glad,' said Ada. 'Where did you meet her, my son?'

'At the natural place, the scene of my life. Where else should it be?'

'At the school? You met her there? She has not anything to do with it?'

'Yes, she has a minor position there. I share the general view of that. We are all like everyone else.'

'You want to rescue her from it,' said Sir Michael. 'It is another reason for marrying. I sympathize with you. It would be my own feeling.'

'It hardly sounds quite what I wished for him,' said Ada. 'But I have not heard the whole.'

'Well, I suppose it does not,' said Reuben. 'It would be a strange wish for a mother.'

'Tell us everything, my son,' said Hereward. 'You know we are waiting to hear.'

'I have told you most of it. And the rest you seem able to supply. But I need not keep anything from you. Her name is *Beatrice* and she is called *Trissie*. She has nothing, and to me she is everything. It somehow sounds rather clever.'

'It sounds as if cleverness might be needed,' said Salomon.

'What a very nice name!' said Joanna. 'Of course she would not have anything. *Beatrice* means "*blessed*", and naturally, blessed people would not. They would be ashamed to.'

'And it is more blessed to give than to receive,' said Reuben. 'And she finds it is, and so would never have anything.'

'Come, come, money is not everything,' said Hereward. 'It plays its part, and I am glad to have and use it. I may be able to help. Reuben may be thinking of it.'

'I was not, Father. But I am glad if you were. I have no reluctance to be under an obligation. I should like to be under one. You know I am like everyone else.'

'How good human beings must be!' said Joanna. 'I don't think they have the credit of it.'

'How long have you known her, my boy?' said Ada.

'Since she came to the school, a year ago. We met on a common ground of grievances.'

'But when they pass, your feeling may pass with them.'

'They will not pass,' said Joanna. 'He spoke of grievances.'

'What does she teach?' said Zillah.

'Something to the younger boys.'

'Don't you know what it is?'

'I know what it is called. The name is *English*.'

'What does she call it?'

'*English*. I said that was the name.'

'Does not she know what it is?'

'No, or she would be teaching older boys.'

'Are you serious, Reuben?' said Ada. 'This is not a joke to us.'

'Yes, I am. It is only the little way I have.'

'Has she a little way too?' said Salomon.

'Yes, people will smile at the sight of us. We shall be such a quaint little pair.'

'Well, I smile at the talk of you,' said Sir Michael. 'I am amused by it, whether I should be or not. And I think it will all turn out well. I have a feeling that it will. And my feelings are usually sound.'

'My feelings are mixed,' said Ada. 'May it be the right thing for you, my son. When are we to meet your Trissie?'

'Next week. I have asked her to stay. You are right that she is mine. She did not want a single, great occasion. She felt an ordinary visit would be more in accordance with her.'

'What does she mean?' said Sir Michael.

'You will soon know,' said his grandson.

This was not to be wholly true. Trissie came in without embarrassment, and with a simple acceptance of what was to become her own. She was small and spare without being fragile, with light eyes, a pale, freckled skin, a small, alert nose, and an almost covert look of something that was akin to humour. A certain ease and confidence lay under a subdued exterior.

'Now you are to be my second daughter,' said Hereward. 'I am in want of daughters, and grateful to my sons for providing them.'

'I am glad I am to be the second. I am never first in anything.'

'Oh, come, you are first to Reuben in everything,' said Sir Michael.

'Yes, but he is a third himself. He would never be first either. Of course he is better than I am.'

'You will be sorry to give up your work,' said Zillah, after a pause.

'No, I shall be glad to. Before I am found out.'

'Found out? In what way?'

'In not being equal to it. And so in being dishonourable in doing it.'

'Why did you take it?' said Sir Michael. 'I mean, how did you come to make the choice?'

'I had to do something. And there was nothing I could do. So there was no choice.'

'Of course there was not,' said Reuben. 'It was the first thing we had in common. And it led us to see that we should have everything.'

'Do you like the head master?' said Ada. 'Reuben does not very much.'

'No. I am afraid he will ask me how the boys are getting on.'

'And can you not tell him?'

'Well, I can't say I don't see how they can be. He would only be surprised.'

'You could make up something that would satisfy him,' said Salomon.

'I think he would be able to tell. A schoolmaster would be so used to it.'

'I suppose it is dreadful to work? I am the one of us who has never done it.'

'Yes, it is,' said Trissie, soberly.

'My son knows quite well what it is,' said Hereward. 'He does the work I should do, if I had the time.'

'You do not call that work?' said Salomon to Trissie.

'Well, it is just looking after what is your own.'

'You will have a house to look after, if you marry Reuben.'

'Yes, and that will be the same.'

'A poor thing but our own,' said Reuben. 'That is what you feel it will be. I have found it. That is what it is.'

'I daresay no one else would want it,' said Trissie. 'But I always like what is mine. It isn't very nice when nothing is.'

'Where is your home?' said Zillah.

'In a country village. My father is the clergyman. That is why I had to work.'

'And you were busy in the parish as well?' said Sir Michael.

'Well, we did sometimes take things to the poor.'

'That must be a pleasant thing to be able to do.'

'Well, we really weren't able to. A clergyman has to do it, even when he isn't.'

'Is your father pleased for you to marry?'

'Yes. It lessens his anxieties.'

'I hope you don't mind all these questions,' said Ada.

'No. Not if you don't mind the answers.'

'We find them very interesting.'

'I don't think they are,' said Trissie.

'Have you ten brothers and sisters?' said Joanna.

'Well, I have a great many. How did you know?'

'Well, a clergyman in a country village! He does have eleven children. It comes in the great books. I think it is so dignified.'

'It is not. It is different.'

'And I am afraid your mother is dead?'

'She is. But how do you know? And why should she be?'

'She should not. It is sad that she is. It is in the books. All human life is in them.'

'You must have great knowledge of that,' said Sir Michael.

'No, we couldn't have any. Or only one kind.'

'Well, you can support yourself,' said Hereward. 'That is a thing to be proud of.'

'No one has been proud of it.'

'I am sure your father must have been.'

'No, he seemed rather ashamed that I had to.'

'Well, I am proud of it for you.'

'I don't think anyone else is.'

'People are not proud of the right things.'

'They are proud of the same ones. It doesn't seem they can all be wrong.'

'Most of them are wrong about everything,' said Merton.

'I don't think they are about this. Why should they be proud of what does no good to anyone?'

'Well, you look things straight in the face,' said Hereward. 'And there is something in what you say.'

'There must be in what ordinary people say. They don't invent it, because there is no need.'

'Reuben will live with a fount of wisdom.'

'It is the kind I have had to get. It is only knowing what some people don't have to know.'

'You are young to be married,' said Sir Michael.

'I am nearly as old as Reuben. I know I shall never look mature. It does not matter now. It will be different when I am middle-aged.'

'Well, he will not mind how you look. He likes you to look as you do. And he is not much to look at himself. I mean, it does not matter for a man. I have never found it did.'

At this moment Henry entered, flushed and disturbed, followed by Nurse in a similar state.

'Naughty dog! Nurse run away. Henry did too.'

'A dog ran after him, ma'am, and I had to follow them,' said Nurse, in an incidental tone. 'The young dog from the stables. It was only in play.'

'Bark at Henry! Bite him!'

'No, no. You know he did not bite.'

'He want to. Breathe at Henry. Look at Henry with his eyes.'

'Bring the dog in here,' said Salomon. 'He must learn not to be afraid of it.'

The dog entered in a friendly spirit, and Henry looked at it with a reverent expression.

'Dear, dear doggie! Wag his tail. Look very kind.'

'Yes, dear doggie. Stroke him,' said Nurse.

'No,' said Henry, recoiling with his hands behind him.

'He does not want to bite any more than you do.'

'Not want to,' said Henry, in a shocked tone.

'You never bite, do you?' said Ada.

'Yes, poor Nurse! Only once. Never any more.'

'Come and say how-do-you-do to sister Trissie.'

'Not sister,' said Henry, looking at her. 'Come to see us.'

'No, not sister yet,' said Trissie.

'No,' said Henry, nodding.

'Well, say how-do-you do?' said Nurse.

Henry looked up at Trissie, smiled and turned away.

'What a darling!' she said.

'Yes,' said Henry, glancing back.

'You must come for your walk now,' said Nurse.

'No,' said Henry, going up to Joanna.

'I can't do anything. I am too afraid of Nurse.'

Henry went on to Trissie, as someone less likely to have developed this attitude.

'Don't you like going for a walk?' she said. 'I don't like it much.'

'No,' said Henry, sympathetically.

'Does walking make you tired?'

'No. Very big boy. Yes, very tired. Poor Nurse carry him.'

'You are getting too heavy for that,' said Ada.

'No, he is not heavy yet, poor little boy.'

'He is like you,' said Trissie to Salomon.

'He is an adopted child. But he copies us all. And that gives him a likeness.'

'You are fond of children?' said Hereward to Trissie.

'Yes. But not of teaching them what I don't know myself.'

'You felt you were sailing under false colours?'

'I don't think I have any true ones. Or I don't know what they are.'

'Do you always speak the truth?'

'If I can. Then there is nothing to remember. And words mean something.'

'Your true colours are clear to me. I shall be envious of Reuben.'

'With all the people in your life?' said Trissie, looking round.

'I would not be without them. But there is something that is not there. Perhaps you will give it to me.'

'I don't know what it is.'

'You need not know. I can take it for myself. You may not understand what you give.'

'Then it will not matter. It will have no meaning. But it must not be much, because of Reuben.'

'It will not be much to you. If it is more to me, he will not mind.'

Chapter 11

Reuben did not mind at first. But there came a time when he did; another when a sense of danger dawned and grew; and one when his feelings rose and carried him beyond himself.

He spoke to his father in front of everyone, as though meaning openness to ease the moment.

'Father, I must say a word to you.'

'As many words as you please. The more, the merrier,' said Hereward, who was in the mood of stirred emotions.

'You will not misunderstand me?'

'Why should I? You can be plain.'

'Or read more than you must into what I say?'

'Why should I again? You are able to say what you mean.'

'I must be. The time has come to say it. These hours alone with Trissie. They are so many, and they are somehow surreptitious. I feel they should cease.'

'Oh, come, she is to be my daughter. I am her father as well as yours. I am to care for you both.'

'You are to help us, and we are grateful. But it should not lead to anything further.'

'It will add to our relation. That is as it must and should be.'

'It should only add certain things. If it means others, I would rather not take the help.'

'That is natural, as many men would not need it. As you do, you must accept it for your own sake and hers. And accept what must go with it.'

'I did not know you wanted return. And return of this kind. I suppose I might have known.'

'Say what you mean, if you mean it. There is no need to talk in riddles.'

'I don't think I do to you.'

'There is no reason to do so to anyone. Put your thought into words. I suppose you are not ashamed of it?'

'I am in a way. You are my father. My thought is not only on myself. There may be reason to be ashamed.'

'You are young and ready to judge. I cannot help you there. You cannot help yourself. And you are the son of a man who lives in his imagination. If you are living for the moment in yours, it is no great wonder.'

'Is there to be an end of what I mean, or of what I imagine? That is all I ask?'

'There can be no end. There is nothing to be ended. In your sense there has been nothing.'

'Then I must make an end,' said Reuben, in a deeper tone, seeming another and older man, as he lost his command of himself. 'I have no choice but to force one. What has happened can happen again. What sort of man should I be, if I took the risk? There is Henry before my eyes. And before any other eyes that are not blind. The daily reminder of the truth, the daily proof of it. Do not think you have not betrayed yourself. You have done so all the time. And once it was in open words, in Salomon's hearing and mine. We had the proof of what we knew, and realized that we knew it. Yes, you can all hear me. I have betrayed the hidden thing. What was to remain hidden, what should have been hidden to the end. I was driven to it. I was helpless. And what have I betrayed? Only what you have known. You will find you have known it. And you will see the danger that I saw.'

'There was no danger,' said Trissie, with tears in her voice. 'There was not anything. There would never have been. With him and me how could there be?'

'There was already something. My father was using his power. You were feeling it. You might not have withstood it. It had done its work before. Perhaps he cannot help it. He is not made up of strength. But does that lessen the danger? You must see it was too great. I could not face it. I would not. I could only force it to an end.'

'Salomon, what have you to say?' said Hereward. 'You hear what Reuben says.'

'Father, it is a case for the truth. I cannot support both you and him. And the truth is on his side. It is true that your words betrayed you, that they were plain and meant one thing.'

'Well, of course they betrayed me. They would always have done so. I have come to see Henry as my son. I have spoken of him in that way often and of set purpose. You will see there is nothing there. When I adopted a boy, I resolved to be his father. I have tried to keep the resolve. I hope I have not failed. I think we can say I have not. I may have kept it too well, or in too literal a sense. But to my mind that does not matter, and could hardly be.'

'It could not,' said Reuben. 'But you have not kept another. You meant to be always on your guard, and it was a thing beyond yourself. It would have been beyond most of us. Always is a long word.'

'A good many words are long,' said Hereward, with a faint smile. 'But the end of all words comes. I have forborne to hasten it. But I hope it has come.'

'It has. And it is more than the end. The meaning and the memory remain. They will never be unsaid.'

'Well, that would be a waste of time and energy and invention. And it is a shadowy edifice, built out of fancy. It would shatter at a touch.'

'It is built out of truth and reason. It can be left to its life.'

'Are these your own words, Reuben?' said Hereward, looking full at his son. 'Their ring is not a true one. It is unlike you to be fluent and high-flown. Unlike you to use prepared speech. It is not hard to explain it. It is this moment in your life. It puts everything out of scale. Small things loom large, and chance words take another meaning. That is what has happened to mine. And it is said that the words of genius hold more than the author meant. I am thought by some to use such words. It may be that it chanced then.'

'These were not words of genius. I don't say that words of yours might not be. These were words of simple emotion, honest and deeply felt. In themselves they did you no discredit. But they betrayed the truth.'

'I will not ask you what they were. It would give reign to your fluency, your fancy, whatever it is. It would lead you further astray.'

' "No other of my sons has seemed so much blood of my blood, so deeply derived from me". They are not words of my fancy. They were not of yours. They came from your heart.'

'Salomon, what is your real feeling about this?'

'What I have said, Father. I cannot unsay it. The truth has gone beyond disguise.'

'Hetty!' said Merton, in a voice no more his own than Reuben's had been. 'So this is why you were silent, why you would not acknowledge Henry's father, why you determined you never would. The man was my father. You and he fell to that. You were right not to tell me. It was better that I should not know. It would be better if I did not know now.'

'I did not mean you to know. I thought you never would. But I am glad you do. It ends the thing that lay between us. And I did not feel it was falling. At the time it was something else. I looked up to your father. I still look up to him. You look up to him yourself, or you should. I thought his feeling was an honour. I still think it was. I forgot he was your father. To me he was simply himself. I was lost to everything, and I know he was too. And then I was glad for him to take the child, for it to have its true father. I was its mother, and I could not be. And it has turned out well. I think it was not a wrong thing. I think I did right to consent to it, right to be silent. You say you wish you had not known. And what else could I do? What would anyone have done? What would have come from revealing the truth? What has come from it now?'

Hetty's words had a sound of having been prepared, as though they were held in readiness in case of need.

'One thing has come,' said Merton, looking away. 'One that there must be, that cannot be gainsaid. I cannot see my father again. This is the last time that I speak of him as my father, to him as another man. Henceforth to the end of our lives there will be silence between us. My wife says she looks up to him. It may be that I never have. Something seemed to hold me from it. Something holds me now. It is a sad word to say and hear. And it cannot be unsaid.'

Hereward turned away, as if accepting what was out of his power, and Salomon moved towards him.

'Father, is this wise? Is it a thing that should be? It would mean mystery and question. It might lead to the escape of the truth. It would bring trouble into our family life. It would help no one and harm us all. Is it not a case for thought?'

Hereward made a gesture towards Merton, as though the words should be for him.

'Merton, I need not say it again. You have heard it, and know its truth. The natural feelings of a moment are not those for a life. You have reason and judgement. I beg you to use both.'

'Then I will use neither,' said his brother, turning away. 'I will neither think nor feel. I will keep my eyes from everything. I will forget I am alive. You speak of my reason. I will forget I ever had it. I must learn to have none. That is what you ask of me. I would ask it of no one. As you do so in the way you do, I will obey in the way I can. I have said what it is.'

'Merton, I am grateful,' said Hetty, going to his side. 'I care for you more for this. I care in that way for no one else. The moment in the past is dead. I can hardly believe in the memory. I can't wish that Henry was not with us. There is no one here who can wish it. But that is all that is left.'

'We know who Henry is,' said Merton, almost to himself. 'We thought we should never know. It seems strange that we thought it. He will come to think in his time. When he asks who he is, who will answer him?'

'The time is not yet,' said Salomon. 'Is not the present enough?'

'My wife, it is,' said Sir Michael to Joanna. 'It is much for us at our age. We must not judge, and will not; we must still look up to our son. This does not alter what he has been to us and done for us. But I wish we had not known. I wish I could have spared you at the end of your life.'

'There was nothing to spare me. It is what I have thought. It is too late to say it now. It would be seen as wisdom after the event, and make people unkind. But not much wisdom was needed. I saw and heard and knew. And I am glad to be sure, and to see Henry as our grandson. And as I am glad, I will not complain, though I see that perhaps I should. I see how nicely you complain for me. But you need not talk of the end of my life. I like to feel I am in the middle of it.'

'Am I utterly alone?' said Ada, standing apart. 'Does anyone think of me, of my place in the grievous story? Is it only my son who has been wronged, and left to live under the wrong? I have to see the truth for myself, to face the difference. Henry has belonged to us all. Now he is Hereward's son and not mine. The same change goes through everything. This house is my home no longer. It has always held a life without foundation. I have felt the emptiness underneath. I forgave the trouble with my sister. But I cannot always forgive. It becomes a weakness and an indifference to wrong. And this wrong was deliberate and furtive, and the deception was to last my life. And further wrong was on the way. I cannot live in dishonour, with a husband I cannot trust. I will return to my father, to rectitude and strength, to a man who can rule himself. I feel I am under an alien roof. My younger sons have left it. My eldest must make his choice.'

'I hardly can, Mother,' said Salomon. 'This house is at the root of my life. It is bound up with my being, with my boyhood, with all I have ever had. It is the scene of the only life I have known. I will be honest: of the life I have wearied of, but would not leave. My brothers have lives of their own. This is the whole of mine. The choice is made for me. Or rather I have no choice.'

'Well, your mother believes in honesty,' said Hereward, keeping his eyes from his son. 'She will not find fault with that.'

'I find none, Hereward. I see it is straight and clear. And I see its truth. And I can keep in touch with Salomon. You would not put trouble in the way. You would not fail us there.'

'You will think again, Mother,' said Salomon. 'What will you lose, if you leave us? Your life with your husband and sons, your place as a wife, as a woman who has done well, and won return. These things are not nothing to any honest woman, or in the eyes of any honest man. And in themselves they are much. You have lived with the wrong for years. It is no greater than it has been. What would you gain but loneliness and a sense of being revenged? Are these things worth so much to you, being the woman you are? We have seen what you would lose. Think of me and of your other sons. Think — I will say it — of my father. His weakness needs your strength. His kind of helplessness needs your help. This last threat shows his need. Will you not give it to him? Ask your father. We know his home is yours. But ask him if you do not need your own.'

'What do you say to it, Father? They are plausible words. But is not their danger there?'

'They might be mine,' said Alfred.

'But, Father, what of the wrong to me, and so to you? Is it nothing to you? Are you untouched by it?'

'I am touched to the heart. I am your father. But I have long known of this. When I have come, I have seen and heard what escaped those who lived with it. When I was once alive to the truth, it lay before my eyes. No one can be always on his guard. The moment when your sons heard incautious words, was not one by itself. I hoped it would not escape. I feared it would. It has, and we can only face it.'

'Aunt Penelope, what do you say? I know you will speak the

truth. I know that Father has spoken it. I must steer my way between you. Have you known what he thought?'

'No, he has been silent. I did not know. I have known only with you. When I knew, I felt at first with you. I saw myself in your place. And then I felt with your son, and then with your father. Their words convinced me. I feel they should convince you. It is a poor account of myself.'

'No, it is an honest one. One that few people would have given. So you all advise me to accept the truth, and to begin my life again?'

'No, to go on with it,' said Alfred. 'There has been no change.'

'There has been a hidden one. And there might have been another.'

'My dear, it is all the same thing. Your husband has his powers and his weakness. You are faced with one; you are still dependent on the other. I am grieved and angry. I did not wholly like the marriage. But it is late to undo it; we know it is too late. For your own sake, for his, for your sons', for your father's, you must take it as it is.'

'Well, I will be guided by you, Father. I have lived by your guidance and never found it fail. I will stay with my husband and my son. It may be the better thing.'

'Do not stay for my sake,' said Hereward. 'Do nothing that is not for your own. I will fall in with either course.'

'I suppose it is for my own sake, Hereward. It is taking what is left. I will be honest; it is keeping what I have. There would be nothing in its place. And it is better for my sons. And I feel it is better for you, though you may not say it.'

'I should not say what does not need to be said.'

'And shall I do and say likewise?' said Merton, in a tone of self-mockery. 'Am I also to retract my hasty words? "I will try to be a son to you, Father. Better perhaps than I have been. If I had not failed you, you yourself might not have failed. Let us learn from each other".'

'I am glad, Merton,' said Hereward, as if accepting the literal words. 'I will not say more. Again it need not be said.'

'Zillah, how much have you known?' said Ada. 'Hereward keeps nothing from you.'

'Nothing. He did not keep this.'

'And you accepted and condoned it?'

'He is himself, as we are all ourselves. He too may have had to condone. He too may have wished for a difference.'

'You mean I have not been the wife for him?'

'I mean you must accept him as he accepts you. The demand is the same on you both.'

'To you that is fair,' said Ada, sighing. 'It would not be to everyone. It is not to me. What we are and what we do are separate things. We can control the one and not the other. I shall have to try to forget.'

'It is not fair,' said Alfred. 'You have done your part. And Hereward has not done his. And you will not forget. But a wrong is better suffered as it is, than carried beyond itself. That you must suffer is no reason for suffering further.'

'How wonderful everyone is!' said Joanna to her husband. 'I did not know they were all like this. I know that some troubles bring out the best in people. But I should not have thought this was one of them. I suppose, when there is so much quality, anything does to bring it out. I am so proud of everyone.'

'Well, I am proud of everyone but Hereward,' said Sir Michael in a low tone. 'I can't reconcile myself to this. I had had no thought of it. I am not a person who suspects such things. I can't understand the excuses made for him. Though of course as his father I am grateful.'

'Oh, but isn't it better to be proud of him too? We should not like him to be left out. And a mother has to forgive everything. It has always been recognized.'

'I suppose a father should too.'

'I don't think it matters about a father. Anyhow there is no rule. Perhaps we only have rules that can be kept.'

Chapter 12

Henry ran into the room and paused with his eyes on Trissie's face.

'Poor sister – !' he said, at a loss for the name. 'Come to stay with us and then cry.'

'I can't help it,' she said, speaking to anyone who heard her. 'It is all through me. You were happy, and you will never be again. And I have not done anything. I never have. I am not a person who could. When people are kind to me, it is because I am less than they are. I did not want to be. I wish I was not. How could I think it was anything more, when it has never been?'

Henry waited for her to pause, placed a doll on her lap, and went on to Hereward. He was not taken up as he expected, as his father was conscious about showing his feeling for him.

'Dear, dear doggie!' he said, looking round. 'Not run after Henry any more.'

'So you met the dog again?' said Ada.

'Oh, yes, met him.'

'No, you know we did not,' said Nurse. 'You must say what is true.'

'Oh, yes, always say it.'

'You only thought about the dog?' said Hereward.

'Yes, think about him. And he think about Henry.'

'What a nice doll it is!' said Trissie.

'It is mine, you know,' said Henry, glancing back.

'Will you give it to me for Maud?' said Merton.

'Oh, yes, he will.'

'Are you quite sure you don't want it?'

'New one,' said Henry.

'Oh, you are a spoilt little boy,' said Nurse.

'Yes, he is. Not Maud; just Henry.'

'Well, you can buy a doll to-morrow,' said Hereward, his voice seeming to assume a return to normal life.

'To-day,' said his son.

'No, the shop is shut,' said Nurse.

'No,' said Henry, whose disregard of truth was equalled by his suspicion of it.

'It will be open in the morning.'

'Very nice shop. Very large. Buy a train.'

'No, no. You are to buy a doll.'

'A kite,' said Henry, with humour in his eyes.

'No, a doll. You must not be greedy.'

'Oh, no. Give one to Maud.'

'Will you give her the new one?' said Merton.

'No, Maud like this one better.'

'Well, let me have it for her.'

'No, one, two. Henry have them.'

'So there is not one for Maud after all?'

'Yes, poor Maud!' said Henry, offering the doll.

'You had better seize the moment,' said Hereward, smiling at Merton, and going to the door.

'Well, what a scene!' said Salomon to Reuben. 'What power we had, that we thought we should not use! I suppose people always use it. The sense of having it leads to one end.'

'I was driven to it. And no wrong is done. We were living over a morass. The surface was already broken. Uncle Alfred and Grandma knew.'

'I can say nothing,' said Merton. 'There is nothing that can be said. What is unspeakable must be unspoken. It will be in the end. It is not that it throws Father off the heights. He was never on them to me. It has done something that will never be undone.'

'But he is to return to the heights,' said Reuben. 'You are to find you have never liked him so well. You gave your own hint of it.'

'And it is what happens when wrong-doers are exposed,' said Salomon. 'I always feel I should like them less. But it seems to be unusual.'

'You must go, Aunt Penelope?' said Ada. 'It has been a strange day for you. You will come in future with a new knowledge. You will know what lies under the surface of our life. Well, we shall talk with a full understanding. And Father will not carry hidden thoughts.'

'It seems that a good deal of good has been done,' said Joanna.

'Of course we know that truth is best. But sometimes it hardly seems it would be. I am rather surprised that it is.'

'You feel the moment is a light one, Grandma?' said Merton.

'What a word for a writer, Merton! Surely you know about the melancholy that underlies all humour.'

'It now underlies everything for me. Nothing can be set apart.'

'There may be little outward change,' said Zillah. 'We shall know what we do, and never mention it. The subject will protect itself.'

'Then it is not like other subjects,' said Joanna. 'But then I suppose it is not. There would not be any subjects, if we had not developed the power of speech. They are not really natural!'

'It does not seem the word for this one,' said Salomon. 'And the guests will be gone and leave us with it. How will Father meet the occasion? He may be equal to it. He must have carried off a good many.'

Hereward carried off this occasion by at once ignoring and accepting it. He joined in the talk as it arose, neither alluding to the disclosure nor avoiding what it involved, and as soon as it was natural, spoke of his work and left them.

Sir Michael had sat by himself, hardly glancing at his son, and speaking barely enough to avoid the effect of silence. He leaned back with an open sigh.

'Well, this is a relief. It is a chance to sort our thoughts. We have to get used to the truth. I admit I find it much. I feel I shall never see Hereward without remembering it. And perhaps we ought not to forget. It is sad knowledge for his sons. And my Zillah has had to carry it alone. She could not turn to her father.'

'Hereward and I shared it, Father, as we have shared everything.'

'You were nearer to him than his wife,' said Ada. 'It was as it had to be. I suppose it is how it has always been.'

'His wife was hardly the person to share this secret,' said Salomon. 'It was largely because of her, that it had to be one.'

'I am a wronged wife,' said Ada, almost musingly. 'It is a strange thought. And that I accept it is stranger. I wonder how I shall feel to Hereward, how I shall manage our life together. It will be a test.'

'Ah, you will be equal to it,' said Sir Michael. 'I have no doubt of you, my dear. I am as proud of my son's wife as I am of my son. She is as much above him in one way, as he may be above her in another. And her way may be the better. To me I admit it is. This is a grief to me. I can't deny it.'

'Grandpa feels it more than anyone,' said Reuben, resuming his usual tone. 'He must be a very good man.'

'Grandma has always known,' said Salomon. 'And she has not felt it at all. What a good thing she is not a very good woman!'

'I admire goodness,' said Sir Michael. 'I can't say I do not. I don't mean I am good myself. I admire it wherever I meet it. Hereward has been a good son to me. He has not failed his father. It is not for me to judge.'

'It is for us all to judge this,' said Reuben. 'There must be some moral standard in human life.'

'Standards seem to be based on the likelihood of their being violated,' said Joanna. 'I suppose my son is a man like other men. Though I am not sure that so many men are. You see your grandfather is not. I don't think there is such a thing as a woman like other women. Perhaps there are no other women. Or not enough of them to count.'

'There is a child who may be like other children,' said Merton. 'But in this house it would not be believed.'

'Let us go and look at him,' said Trissie. 'Children are so pretty when they are asleep. And he will grow into a boy and be different.'

'And boys are so often awake,' said Reuben. 'And we have noticed the difference.'

'I will go home,' said Hetty. 'Merton can follow me later.'

'As you will,' said her husband. 'I shall not be very long.'

'Hetty lives up to herself,' said Joanna to Sir Michael. 'She will not stand with Merton by Henry's bedside in Hereward's house.'

'Ah, it was a natural feeling. It was a sensitive thought. I sympathize with it.'

'So do I. How nice it is that we both have wide sympathies!'

When they reached Henry's room, a figure was in their path. Hereward was bending over the cot, his eyes on its occupant's face.

'Hush; he is asleep,' he said.

'That is why we are here,' said Salomon. 'It is our object to view him in that state.'

'Do not wake him, sir,' said Nurse, whose instinct had brought her to the spot. 'He is disturbed by any sound.'

'What of the deep sleep of childhood?' said Reuben. 'Is it another of the illusions about it.'

It seemed that it might be, as Henry stirred and murmured.

'Henry. Not Maud. Just Henry.'

'I might come to say it in the opposite way,' said Ada to her husband. 'Do I begin to feel it?'

Henry's eyes wavered over her face, and he made an effort to speak.

'Yes, yes, always just Henry,' said Hereward.

'Oh, no, poor Maud!' said Henry, in a reproachful tone, and succumbed to the kind of sleep expected of him.

'He has held us together, Hereward,' said Ada. 'Will he now come between us?'

'No, you are yourself, and he is helpless. I will trust you, as I know I can. It is you who are proved worthy of trust.'

Nurse moved away, as though as unconscious of their presence as they were of hers.

'Well, we have the hours before us,' said Salomon, as they left the room. 'We can't take refuge in sleep like Henry. And even then Father might come to look at us.'

'Not at me,' said Reuben. 'It could only be at you. For Merton he must have the awkward feeling we have towards someone we have wronged. What has Merton to say to me? I meant to be silent to the grave. I was driven beyond myself.'

'The truth was there,' said his brother. 'It has lain between my wife and me. The change is in my feeling to my father.'

'What an hour he has lived!' said Salomon. 'Could anyone have deserved it? His guilt exposed and discussed before him! And judgement and mercy meted out! To him, the head of the family, and destined to remain so! The way he did remain so showed the man he was.'

'He had already shown us that,' said Reuben. 'I don't regret that I betrayed him. Why should I control myself? I am his son.'

'Not wholly,' said Hereward's voice behind them. 'I may not always be master of myself. But I have never betrayed another man. Any other man's secret is safe with me. If you would not have my actions on your conscience, I would not have yours on mine. You may come to the first, as your life goes by. I shall not come to yours. That is my word on the matter. I shall say no more.'

'But I shall,' said Reuben. 'Your secret was safe. It would have been safe to the end. But it was leading to another. That is my word. I too shall say no more. It is enough.'

Hereward passed them in silence, and Salomon spoke in a low tone.

'It seems I can never be married. My wife would be in the house. I should live under a dangling sword.'

'You would not,' said Hereward, glancing back. 'Your talking in that way shows you know it.'

The brothers were silent until their father's door closed, and then went down to their mother.

'Well, you know it all, my sons. You knew when I did not. In knowing your father's life you know your mother's. You see her wrongs and her forgiveness of them. And you do not see her exalted by either. I can put myself in your place. You feel she is humbled by both.'

'Well, I did feel reluctant to take similar risks,' said Reuben.

'You are not cast for a heroic part,' said Salomon. 'It is Mother who is.'

'I did not know that anything could happen in a family,' said Joanna. 'I thought it was always outside them. And wild oats used to be sown in youth. Now it seems to be different.'

'And they ought to be,' said Sir Michael. 'It is the right time for them. I mean, if they must be, it should be at that time. At the natural, excusable one. Or at any rate more excusable.'

'You must not excuse it, Grandpa,' said Reuben. 'You must live up to yourself.'

'Where is Trissie?' said Zillah. 'I hope she is not still in trouble. She should be with us.'

'She is in her room,' said Reuben. 'She will go to-morrow, and will not come again before our marriage. And I daresay not often after it. This must leave its trace. Father will never forgive me. And I am hardly inclined to set him the example.'

'How you are meeting life!' said Joanna. 'If I have not lived, I am glad I have not. I don't even like to see other people living. And they don't seem to like it very much.'

'Ah, Joanna, you have a simple old husband,' said Sir Michael. 'He did not see what you did. He saw nothing. He took things to be what they seemed.'

'It is what they generally are. It is conceited to say they are not. And it is really what they were.'

'Well, the truth has come out,' said Salomon. 'And few of us are wiser, and no one better for it. Shall we have to treat Father in the same way? We should not dare not to. But is it a moral duty?'

'Yes, it is,' said Sir Michael. 'He is your father, and you owe him everything. You take from him more than you return. Nothing else can be said.'

'Many men have secrets in their lives,' said Zillah. 'It is by chance that this one has escaped.'

'It was its destiny,' said Salomon. 'Henry could only be its betrayal. And he will be the reminder of it. I wonder Father was not prepared. He knew the risk he took.'

He paused, as Hereward stood on the threshold, upright and calm and in possession of himself.

'Yes, I knew the risk and faced it. I knew what I owed, and to whom I owed it. That debt will not soon be paid.

'You have all given your account of me. I will give you my account of myself. I am not afraid of it, and you need not be. I do not speak to hurt.

'I am a man of great powers, swift passions and a generous heart. You have met them all, benefited by most, suffered from some. You will not cease to benefit. You will not suffer again. I am an ageing man. My vigour fails. This last approach was a light thing.

'But I still have a word to say. I am a man, as not all men are. If I have lived a man's life, what other life should I have led? I have carried a man's burdens, given up a man's gains, done the work of men. It is my nature that enables me to do it. It is the force in me that carries me on. All force may at times go astray.

'I have cheered the homes of thousands. I have served our family home. I have judged easily, pardoned much, helped others to fulfil their lives. I will help them still. I will still understand and give. Would some men ask a return?

'I will ask nothing. I have never asked. I find no fault with what has been. But am I not too simply judged? Should a stumble be so hardly forgiven? I will leave it to you. My word is said. I shall not say it again.'

The door closed on a silence.

'Suppose he did say it again!' said Reuben. 'How would things be then?'

'Well, I suppose it is true,' said Sir Michael. 'There is truth in it, of course. But I can't go the whole length. I feel we should keep our human laws. I am carried away at the moment. But I can't alter myself.'

'I am really carried away,' said Joanna. 'So I must alter myself. I am going to try to be worthy of Hereward. You see I am already trying. And I think you must feel I am succeeding.'

'I may disturb you, my lady?' said Galleon at the door. 'It is already later than usual.'

This was true, as Galleon and Nurse had met and talked in the hall.

'Well, when something should be safe with me, Nurse, that is what it is.'

'Silence is my watchword, Galleon. It is natural to me, my tendency being to reticence.'

'I am myself a man of few words,' said Galleon, sighing in remembrance of large numbers.

'And this might befall any gentleman. It is not a loss of dignity.'

'When he addressed the family, Nurse, dignity was the word: I shivered as I heard.'

'I should have done the same. A gentleman justifying himself! It is not a thing that should be.'

'Well, he did not lower himself. It marks him as what he is. And the writing cannot alter it.'

'No, he keeps above it. It is a call for quality. Few would be equal to it. And I cast no stone. As regards me he has not failed.'

'Ah, well, you know your time of life, and so does he.'

'You can hardly be aware of it, Galleon. You go beyond yourself. And you are light in your talk of those above you. To fall is not to condescend. And you should not broach the subjects. It does not sit well on you.'

Chapter 13

'I am resolved, Aunt Penelope,' said Ada. 'I have made up my mind. I will not let my heart be troubled. I will not let it be afraid. Whatever happens, I shall have my sister. We shall bridge the gulf of years and re-live youth. It will be as if the parting had not been. The reason for it is dead. And if it is not, I will not see it. I will keep above what is beneath me. I will pay the price that must be paid. Who should have learned that lesson, if not I? I look forward with an easy heart.'

'There should be no danger,' said Alfred. 'The memory will be a safeguard. And time has passed.'

'It is true, Father. I will feel it is. We turn to you for truth. I will take full joy in the reunion, in the future that must hold so much of the past. My sister will be with me. My sister who has lived in my thought, who returns as a widow to my care. I envy you, Aunt Penelope. I grudge you the task of preparing for her. For her and the adopted daughter we are to see as her own. I long to be making ready for them. But I respect your prior claim. We shall all be with you to welcome her. My sons know her only as a name. So much has been forbidden to us, and to Hereward is still forbidden. To him it is a matter for silence. But I can forget it and go forward. This my sister was dead and is alive again, and was lost and is found. I feel I could break into song.'

'You have not fallen so far short,' said Alfred, smiling.

'Oh, Father, think what it is to me. Even more perhaps than to you. I have watched her growth as I have watched that of my sons. And now the years of our parting fade away. They will never mean nothing. We shall not atone for the loss. But I shall have something of what I might have had.'

'Watching my growth has achieved as much as watching anything else,' said Reuben.

'You should be grateful,' said Salomon. 'Only a mother would have done it. Most people express surprise when growth attracts their notice.'

'Even my father forgot about mine,' said Trissie. 'Of course there wasn't much to remind him.'

'Oh, forget yourselves and your growth,' said Ada. 'It is someone else who is in our minds to-day. Our growth can take care of itself. We can all see how much of it there was. In my case there was a good deal. But I have no thought to spare for it.'

'You have words to spare, as we had,' said Merton.

'Oh, I make no claim to be consistent. My mind is too full for me to watch my words. I shall not be in command of myself until the moment comes. If only the days would pass!'

The days did not fail, and the family gathered in Alfred's house to await the arrival. The meeting seemed to come and pass before they knew. It seemed there was something wanting, to which they hardly gave a name.

Emmeline greeted them without emotion, and with an ease that was more in accord with their memory than their mood. She was heavier and soberer, and her charm revealed itself at once as more intermittent and ordinary. Her eyes went often to her adopted daughter, and her thought seemed to be on her more than on herself.

'My sister!' said Ada. 'After the years of thought and memory. How I have lived in this moment!'

'My daughter!' said Alfred. 'The other words can be the same.'

'Your niece, Aunt Penelope!' said Emmeline, smiling and passing to the third embrace.

'My sons!' said Ada. 'Your nephews whom you have not seen.'

'And my daughter!' said Emmeline. 'For that is how you must see her. It is what she is to me.'

'And will be to us,' said Penelope. 'You did wisely to choose a girl. Your father is rich in grandsons.'

'She has always been needed. She came to me when I was alone. And my husband was glad to share her. We never felt we were childless. You will not think of me in that way.'

The daughter came forward, a comely girl of about twenty-two, seeming rather mature for her age. She had pleasant, straight features, large, hazel eyes, and an expression at once amiable, confident and resolute. Emmeline was always aware of her, and when interest turned to her from herself, seemed to expect and wish it.

Hereward moved towards them and spoke for every ear.

'So we meet at last. With much to remember and forget. We can do both. It is a clear way.'

'It is,' said Emmeline. 'And it is more. It is to be a new one.'

'I am a minor figure on the occasion,' said Sir Michael. 'But as Ada's father-in-law I can feel a part of it.'

'I feel it might be the same without me,' said Joanna. 'And I believe it would.'

'I feel you are my relations as well as Ada's,' said Emmeline. 'As we are sisters, it seems to be natural. But there is so much to know about you all.'

'I will give you my account,' said Hereward. 'I am still the slave of the pen. And still by some held to be its master.'

'I am one of those,' said Hetty. 'And I am Merton's wife. That is all I need to say.'

'There is that about Hereward's books,' said Sir Michael. 'They can be read by people of any age or kind. To my mind it is the truest strength.'

'One of them could be read by Grandpa,' said Reuben. 'I saw it admitting of it.'

'So did I,' said Salomon. 'And the true strength was Grandpa's.'

'I am hardly a slave of the pen,' said Merton. 'That implies too much. But I remain its servant.'

'I am a useful member of society,' said Reuben. 'I should hardly be a member, if I were not useful. And that may show it is not society.'

'I am nothing but myself,' said Salomon. 'So that is enough about me. There can hardly be any more.'

'So am I,' said Viola. 'And I feel it is quite enough. Why should we be more than ourselves?'

'I am the person who provides Viola,' said Emmeline. 'Nothing further can be asked of me.'

'Oh, I belong to myself, Mother. But I am glad to be with you in your home.'

'She will belong to someone else one day,' said Sir Michael.

'Not any more than he will belong to me. Things will be equal between us.'

'Now there is another meeting,' said Ada. 'Viola, here are your grandparents. I see my aunt as a sort of parent. She has filled the place.'

'I make no bid for attention,' said Alfred. 'There are many stronger claimants.'

'Oh, you are still our show specimen, Father. None of us can hold a candle to you, though Merton owes you a debt. I am happy to be like my mother, but the prize for looks was yours. She would have been the first to assign it to you.'

'I did not ever wish her different.'

'No, and you would not wish me so. We do not want change in the people we care for. It would mean they were not the same.'

'I daresay it would,' said Salomon.

'It might be the outcome,' said Merton.

'Now do not sneer at your mother. Any chance word can be taken up like that. It is too obvious a line to follow. Now who is this come to see us?'

Henry entered the room by himself, having been brought to the house by Nurse and left at the door. He kept looking back, as if at a loss without her, and paused to gaze at the newcomers.

'Now who are these dear people?' said Ada. 'Can you guess?'

'Two,' said Henry, finding the number unusual.

'Yes, Aunt Emmeline and Cousin Viola. Are you not pleased to see them?'

'Very nice house,' said Henry, looking round.

'Nicer than ours?'

'Oh, yes it is.'

'It is smaller,' said Alfred.

'Yes, dear little house.'

'You know it is not small,' said Merton. 'Did you walk to it or let Nurse carry you?'

'Yes, poor Nurse very tired. Henry read to her.'

'What do you read.'

'Little Bo-Peep,' said Henry, incidentally.
'You know it by heart,' said Merton. 'You don't read from a book.'
'Yes, have a book and read.'
'Well, read to us out of this one.'
Henry took the Bible and proceeded with his eyes on it.

> 'Little Bo-Peep
> Has lost her sheep,
> And doesn't know where to find them.'

> 'Leave them alone,
> And they'll come home,
> Bringing their tails behind them,'

said Merton, exposing the method.
'And does Nurse listen?' said Hereward, disregarding his second son.
'Yes. Not tired any more. Show her the picture.'
'And what else do you read?'

> 'Ride a cock horse
> To Banbury Cross,'

said Henry, looking down with the negligence of modesty.
'Would you really like to read?' said Merton.
'No, he is too young yet.'
'You know you can't read, don't you?'
'Oh, yes, he knows,' said Henry, with the air of a conspirator.
'We don't want Maud to pretend to read. We will wait until she can.'
'Yes, pretend,' said Henry, as if accepting the word.
'She has forestalled us,' said Hetty. 'She pretends already.'
'Oh, no, not pretend,' said Henry, in a tone of disapproval.
'He is getting rather spoilt, Father,' said Merton.
'No,' said Henry.
'Do you know what it means?'
'No,' said Henry, easily.
'I don't think you are spoilt,' said Viola.

'No,' said Henry, smiling into her face.

'Have you a message for Maud?' said Merton. 'You love her, don't you?'

'No, her,' said Henry, indicating Viola.

'I have no little boy,' said Emmeline. 'Only a girl.'

Henry looked round for the latter.

'Here she is,' said Emmeline, putting her hand on Viola's shoulder.

'No,' said Henry. 'Lady.'

'I think it is long enough, ma'am,' said Nurse at the door.

Henry turned and ran towards her, ignoring the farewells that followed him.

'You are honoured among women,' said Salomon to Viola. 'And indeed among men. We all strive for Henry's favour.'

'Were you glad when your father adopted him?'

'I was surprised. But I like a child in the house. My brothers are married and provided for.'

'You could marry yourself, if you wished.'

'I would only marry whom I wished. And another point of view is involved.'

'Is it strange to have a famous father?'

'I am used to it. It has become a part of our life.'

'You do not want to write yourself?'

'The question does not arise. I am not able to.'

'If you were, would you try to write like your father?'

'Would anyone try to do anything like anyone else? If I produced anything, it would be my own. But my father's work looms large to us. We depend on it for much of what we have. We can only be grateful for it. And there are parts of it, that I can be proud that he has written.'

'Does he know how you feel about it?'

'He has two sets of readers, the large and the small. He knows I belong to the second, and is not concerned. He sees his work with his own eyes.'

'Both may be right in a way. The larger need not always be wrong.'

'It contains many honest people. I am not going to pity it, if it includes you.'

'What of your brother's work? Has he also two sets of readers?'

'He writes for one. And it remains small. His work has not so far found a place. Of course my father's always did. But it is easy to judge such things, and difficult to do them. I have no right to speak.'

'It is such a change for me to be with a family like this.'

'It is not to me. But something else is a change. Something I have imagined and given no name. I can hardly give it one now.'

'There may be things that have no names.'

'There are. They are outside the sphere of words. If you had lived in that sphere, as I have, you would know it. They have their life beyond them.'

'What an earnest pair!' said Hereward. 'Am I allowed to join?'

'You hardly can,' said Viola. 'The talk was about writers, and you would have to lead.'

'What has Salomon been saying of his father? I dare to guess I was an example.'

'That you have written things he is proud of.'

'Oh, so I have a loyal son. I was not sure of it.'

'How can he not have?' murmured Salomon for Viola's ears, as he moved away. 'Things being as they are. He being as he is. His writing giving us what it does. I am what I have to be. I do what I must.'

'So you are my adopted niece?' said Hereward. 'We will forget the adoption and keep the rest. We will forget it all, and have something of our own. There is a word I have to say to you. I want to take the place of the father you have not had. You will let me try? My heart would be in it. And it could be between ourselves.'

'I wish you would try. I wish you were my father. I have thought and asked about you. But my mother could not tell me much.'

'And am I what you imagined?'

'I did not dare to go far, in case I imagined too much. But it might have been the whole. You are just what you ought to be.'

'So I have been told. And I should be what people want. They want my books, and I put myself into them.'

'And you are yourself out of them. And it is said that writers seldom are.'

'Their energy is used. As mine would never be. I say it of myself, as it is true. It is a thing that puts me apart.'

'One of the things. It is what you are.'

'And what you should not be,' said Ada's voice. 'Come and join the rest of us, and put all ideas of being apart out of your heads. Apart! Why should you be? Why should any of us? I have never had such a thought in my life. The wish must be father to it. Come and join your – betters I almost said – but I will say your equals. That should be enough for you.'

'For me,' said Viola. 'But what about my Uncle Hereward?'

'Enough for him too. In ordinary life he takes the usual part. His position with his readers is different.'

'It is,' said Hereward. 'I will not deny it.'

'Then it can be with me,' said Viola. 'I am one of them.'

'Well, so it can,' said Sir Michael. 'And he deserves that it should be. He has a right to anything that comes to him.'

'Very little comes to us, that we have not a right to,' said Zillah. 'We can accept it all freely.'

Hereward accepted what came, until a time when it was questioned. Some weeks later Salomon approached him, and spoke of the matter in a candid manner that suggested it was not a great one.

'Father, you will let me say a word? It is nothing of great significance. I am not suggesting that history is repeating itself. I know your feeling for Viola is fatherly and nothing more. It has been clear from the first. That is why you have not thought. But in a way you are trespassing again on a son's preserves. I will ask you to leave my path clear. You are too impressive a figure to be in the way.'

'What do you mean? What is it you are saying? You don't mean you are in love with Viola?'

'What else should I mean? I should be taken to mean it. I tried to make it plain.'

'You are not thinking of marrying her? No, you cannot be.'

'Why not? I am in a position to marry. You have said you wished I would, that it was time. What is there against it?'

'Oh, my poor boy!' said Hereward. 'My poor boy!'

'Why, what is the trouble?'

'Now I am an unfortunate man,' said Hereward, throwing up his hands. 'Here I do my best for my family, work for them, bear with them, make no effort for myself! And I become a threat and a danger and a despoiler of their lives! You tell me to get out of your path. There is a word for a father's ears. What if I had not been in it? If I had left it clear, as you say? It is true that I have had my temptations, and that my life has kept them at hand. But what would have happened, if it had not been so? Where would you have been without me? Where would those who matter more than you, have been? Your mother and mine would have been thrust from their place. Would you have been able to help them? Or would you have turned to me? Answer me and answer me truly. What can I be but what I am? What could I have done but what I did?'

'Father, have done. Be plain. You have said nothing yet. I feel you can have nothing to say.'

'Salomon, I speak to you as to another man. You have reached your full manhood. You know that your mother's sister left us in her youth. That a threat was seen in her remaining with me. My son, it was more than a threat. The consequence came. Neither she nor I betrayed it. We felt silence was best. She adopted the child and still said nothing. I provided for its needs, and still provide for them. I had my usual part. Viola does not know. It seemed better that she should not. But it was not better. Nothing has been. Everything has gone awry for me. I look for nothing else. But of course I was drawn to her. Of course I was in the path. Did I not see her in mine? You have my sympathy, Salomon. You deserve it indeed. But I ask for yours. And I ask something else. I can face no further exposure. I ask that there shall be none.'

There was a pause.

'Viola should know,' said Salomon, in an empty tone. 'Anything else has danger. We see the danger that it holds. And she must see the difference in me. Her own feeling may not have gone far. She welcomed your presence in the path. Well, it is clear for you now.'

'Do not be bitter, my son. I have been as helpless as you have. And my way is not clear, if this is to be known. It is not the word.'

Salomon spoke in a more natural way.

'It should be known, Father. Viola has her claims. The knowledge may affect her future. She is my grandparents' true grand-daughter.'

'My son, she is the child of your father and your mother's sister. She is your half-sister and more. Things are as they are.'

'My mother must know. She will see the change in my feeling. And, Father, it has not changed. You say I deserve your sympathy. You are right that I do.'

'Then let it all be known,' said Hereward, throwing up his hands again. 'Let them all start and stare and cast their stones. Let them do their part. It's what I am used to, what I have had. It is not what I have given, not what I will give. I will go on working and giving and suffering what I must. For I have suffered, Salomon. I am an unsatisfied man. I live with a want at my heart. You know now what that means.'

'I am learning it, Father. And I have no wish to be revenged. You have done me no conscious wrong. But these secrets should not be. They lie beneath our life to escape and shatter it. They must be revealed and ended.'

'Then end this one. Do as you will. Expose it in this house and the other. Let two families be shocked and saddened. It is your moment. They are all here. It is the usual treble gathering. Go and do your worst. Or your best, my boy. Go and do the only thing. We see it should be done.'

'Not before Viola, Father. She must hear when she is alone. I will do it when I can.'

'She is not with them,' said Hereward, looking aside. 'She is in my room. I was going to her there. She was to wait for me.'

'Then I can go and do it now. It is the moment, as you say. You will break it to her yourself. In your room, where she is waiting for you. I said your path was clear.'

Salomon almost ran from the room, paused on the threshold of the other, and stood with his hand raised.

'Hear me, all of you. I have a word to say. That is, there is a word to be said. You have heard others. This may or may not be the last. It is Viola who is involved this time. She should not have come amongst us. Do you guess what it is? Can you think what it might be? If so, I need not use the words.'

'My son, what is it?' said Ada. 'Surely there can be nothing more. Surely there has been enough.'

'I think I can guess,' said Alfred, coming forward. 'This time I have felt I knew. At the early one I had no thought of it. Am I to say it, Ada? It is for you to judge.'

'Say it, Father. Say anything that is true. Nothing is too much for me now. Too many things have been too much. It is silence that I cannot bear. It has covered too much. Let it not cover any more. It is the thing I cannot face.'

'Then here is the truth. The last to come on us. This time I see it as the last. Viola is not the stranger we have thought. She is what she might naturally be. It is simply what might have been.'

'I see, Father. You need not say it. We all know what it is. She is the child of Hereward and Emmeline, of my husband and my sister. We will say no more.'

"My daughter, you have had much to face. But this is no new thing. Its place is in the past.'

'My poor son!' said Ada, turning to Salomon. 'This is not in the past for you. It is your trouble more than mine. For me the truth has been there, in a way a part of my life.'

'Yes, it is so, Ada,' said Emmeline. 'There is nothing new. It is all so long ago. It has come to mean nothing. I felt it was best to hide the truth. Best for you and me and the child. I was going away, and it was easy to hide it. I thought I should never come back. And then it all seemed to be over, to be sunk in the past. And so it is. It is as you said. I did not think of this. How could anyone have thought of it?'

'There was a risk,' said Alfred. 'There is danger in hidden things. We see they have their life, that they do not die. There may be many of them. We do not know. We will not add to them. It is well that this has come to light. I have nothing to say of it. It is late to judge. It must join the knowledge behind our lives.'

'Ada, I can go, if you wish,' said Emmeline. 'Tell me the truth. Do you want me to go or stay?'

'To stay. I need my sister. Nothing new has happened. No change has come. I simply have greater need. And Father wants his daughter – his grand-daughter – all that it is. I can accept it. If I had not learned to accept, I should be a person who could learn nothing.'

'What a family we are!' said Reuben to his brothers. 'I don't know whether to be proud or ashamed of belonging to it.'

'I see no cause for pride,' said Merton.

'I do,' said Trissie, in a whisper. 'They would make anyone proud. And I am almost their relation.'

'I say nothing, Joanna,' said Sir Michael. 'Once more I wish you had not known. Once more I would have spared you.'

'I say nothing too. I should like to say something in my own vein. Even at this moment I should like it. And I cannot think of anything. And I see I don't deserve to. Alfred was more fortunate. But then I daresay he did.'

'Did you ever suspect this was the truth?'

'No, but I sometimes felt it ought to be. It fitted in like a book. And truth is stranger than fiction. So it ought to be as good.'

'You all say that nothing has happened,' said Zillah. 'And you go on talking as if something had.'

'You do not, Aunt Penelope,' said Ada. 'And I should like to have a word.'

'Then you shall. I will say one. The word that had come into my mind. That I find you brave and kind and wise.'

'Oh, Aunt Penelope, that is a help. It is just the word I need. It gives me strength to go on.'

Sir Michael moved to Ada and put a hand on her shoulder. She started and broke into tears, and at that moment the door opened and Hereward stood with his eyes on her.

'So I have come at the peak of the occasion. I hoped it would be over. I thought I had given it time.'

'It is over, Hereward,' said Ada, raising her eyes. 'And other things are over too. I shall say nothing. There is nothing for me to say.'

'There is nothing for me either. The words would have no place. They are out of their time.'

'Is this all it is to be?' said Joanna to her husband. 'It somehow does not seem enough. I suppose I can't want it to be any more. It must be that human motives are mixed.'

'So you have had a burden I did not know of, Hereward,' said Ada. 'As well as all those I know.'

'My wife, it is a good word. It was a good thought. I do not meet so many. And there is a word I will say to you. And it has nothing to do with my daughter. I am glad you have given me my sons.'

'So this has drawn Ada and Hereward together,' said Joanna to Sir Michael. 'It is always an unfortunate thing that does that. And it was unfortunate things that put them apart. I wonder if a fortunate thing could do anything. I have never heard of it.'

'Joanna, I find it too much. Do not try to help me. Do not say we have another grandchild. I am degraded by these covert relationships. I am only sure of one thing. I wish my son had been different.'

'In one way, Father,' said Zillah. 'Surely in no other. A man must be taken as a whole.'

'Oh, this whole! It is a bale and a ban. Why must we take the whole of anything, when it is both good and bad? I can't help it, Joanna. I can only be myself.'

'I don't want you to be anyone else. The standard is too uncertain. I must be able to respect my husband.'

'I wish poor Ada could respect hers. I wish I could respect my son.'

'I know you cannot, Father,' said Hereward. 'But you can take what I give. And I can respect you. Let that be the exchange between us. And this trouble is in the past.'

'And when things are there, they do not count,' said Joanna. '"It is a long time ago" people say. So nothing is really wrong. It only has to wait long enough. It is a good thing this has done so.'

'Mamma, you are what you are,' said Ada. 'I would not and could not say more.'

'And I am what I am,' said Sir Michael. 'And I do not hear such words. But I can't help feeling there is right on my side.'

'Of course there is,' said Joanna. 'There has to be right somewhere. Or there would not be such a thing. And there is not any anywhere else.'

'Joanna, have we cared for Ada enough?' said Sir Michael, lowering his tone.

'We have not. She would never be cared for enough. Just as I am always cared for too much. Don't tell anyone I am proud of it.'

'Well, you have never tried to achieve it.'

'But I have. I have tried very hard. And I can feel I have my reward.'

'Should we have a celebration to-night?' said Hereward, in an ironic tone. 'There is nothing more to come to light. Is it an occasion to be observed?'

'Let us forget it and go on in our usual way,' said Sir Michael, with something in his voice that did not exalt any other.

'Then we should send for Henry,' said Salomon. 'We have seen nothing of him since yesterday. That is not our usual way.'

Henry appeared in response to the summons, and stood inside the room without evincing any sign of interest. Nurse had an air of uneasiness and remained at hand.

'He is not quite himself to-day, ma'am. He may be a little fractious. He had better not stay too long.'

'Stay a long time,' said Henry, in a tone that supported her misgiving.

'Come and talk to Father,' said Hereward.

'No, not talk.'

'Tell us what you have done to-day.'

'No, not tell.'

'Is it a secret?'

'No, not a secret. Secret is good.'

'What has made you tired this evening?'

'Not tired. Not go upstairs. Not go to bed any more.'

'But you would be tired then.'

'Yes, he would, poor little boy,' said Henry, wearily.

'Think of something you would like to do.'

'Ring-a-ring-a-roses!' said Henry, a light breaking over his face.

The ensuing scene was a contrast to those that had preceded it. Galleon, alive to all of them, smiled to himself at the difference, while keeping in the background to avoid being involved.

'Well, I am the person to be tired,' said Sir Michael, as he rose from the ground. 'This is more for Henry's age than mine. I am three-quarters of a century too old for it.'

'Grandpa very slow,' said Henry looking at him.

'Yes, his bones are old and stiff. He can hear them creak.'

Henry looked at him and broke into a wail.

'Poor Grandpa! His bones creak and he hear them. Hurt him very much.'

'No, they are not hurting him now,' said Nurse.

'Yes, he hear them. Henry hear them too. Oh, poor Grandpa!'

'No, you know you did not hear them.'

'Not say he didn't hear,' said Henry, angrily, as he was led from the room.

Chapter 14

'Rosa, I am glad to be with you,' said Hereward. 'How long is it since we met?'

'I have lost count, as you have. Why are you with me now?'

'Does there have to be a reason?'

'No, but there is one. What has happened?'

'The one thing there was left to happen. My last secret has escaped. I must talk of it to someone. There has to be silence at home.'

'You are fortunate. There might be something else. Does Salomon want to marry Viola?'

'Rosa, you think of it at once. How did you guess?'

'Well, he is the one who is free. And she is what we know. It seems a situation for your family.'

'I should not have kept the secret. I am learning the value of truth.'

'It might not have seemed to have so much value at the time.'

'If I had married you, Rosa, these things would not have happened.'

'Other things would. They did happen. Our relation was one of them.'

'My poor boy! My selfless, dependable son! The girl is less on my mind. I almost feel I came first with her.'

'Hereward, how far did you go?'

'As far as I should, and no further. Who should have a greater care for her? And I can guard against women's feelings for me.'

'You might have put the power to better use. But you have

used other powers, Hereward. You have served many.'

'My heart goes out in sympathy and pity,' said Hereward, moving about the room. 'My strongest instinct is to ease the human way. I see it as a long, hard journey. I take no credit for it. It is my way of fulfilling myself. I ask no gratitude. And perhaps I hardly have it. It is felt it means no sacrifice. And it has meant none. I am not made up of failings. And those I have, come from my strength.'

'What a satisfactory reason for them! Mine come from something else.'

'You could have held me, Rosa. Something in you would have done it, something in yourself.'

'It would have worn thin. You would have come to the end of it.'

'But I have not done so. It is always there for me.'

'It is there when you are with me. That is not always. It is very seldom.'

'From the first I saw the whole of my wife. I do not mean there is little to see. She is larger-hearted than many. And there is other largeness in her. But she is herself and nothing more.'

'You say you saw the whole of her. How much did you see? How much did she see of you? She may have realized her largeness of heart and felt you would both need it. And it seems you have done so.'

'It is true. But her life has been a full one. And I feel she knows it.'

'I have no doubt of it. It could hardly have escaped her.'

'You and she might have had a friendship, if you had come together. But it seemed it should not be.'

'It did. You could hardly betray yourself before your marriage.'

'Would you have liked to have sons?'

'I suppose I should. I see people do like it.'

'You would not like the position of my wife?'

'The words can have two meanings. On the whole I should not.'

'On the whole Ada does.'

'Well, she is large-hearted. I think my heart must be only of average size.'

'You can't think that average is the word for you.'

'Not on the whole. No one thinks that of himself. If anyone did, we should sometimes meet it.'

'I believe we meet it in Ada. She does not see herself as above the average.'

'But she knows how rare that is. It is a way of feeling she is above it.'

'I am grateful to her, Rosa. Do not think I am not. But I might have been grateful to you.'

'I don't want gratitude. It is earned too hardly. And people do not give enough.'

'Perhaps not. But I have tried to give it. I believe my wife has found it all worth while.'

'Some of it has been so. She has taken the rough with the smooth. I should have been inclined to reject the rough. I don't know why it always has to be included.'

'Well, I have a good wife, Rosa, dear sons, grandchildren coming. But I hoped to have them through you. And to-day I feel I must imagine it. It is not often in my thought.'

'It hardly ever is. So do not put it into mine. I have no place for it.'

'So you really never feel regret?'

'You think I should imagine what might have been? We found I had not a large heart. Now you must find I have not much imagination.'

'In me it is the force of my life. And to-day it is working on you.'

'What do you mean? You don't want to use me in a book?'

'You would not recognize yourself. Would you not be glad to be of help to me?'

'I am seldom glad to be of help. The gladness would not be on my side. And we are supposed not to write about a person until the deep feeling is past. So that is what it is.'

'Rosa, I gave you a book before I was married. With a farewell poem on the flyleaf. If you have it, will you lend it to me? It would be of help.'

'I will give it to you. It is yours. It holds something for you and nothing for me. You can put it to your own use.'

Hereward accepted the book, and soon afterwards took his leave. He seemed ready to be gone, as if his thought was pressing forward. His companion let him go and did not look after him.

When he reached his house, he left the book in the hall while he changed his clothes. Ada and Salomon entered from outside, and Ada took up the book and glanced at it.

'What is this? The poem that is written here? What does it mean?'

'Yes, I see it, Mother. It means or has meant what it says. It may mean nothing now. The years have passed.'

'Your poor father! I have wondered what he did before we were married. It seems there must have been something.'

'Considering what he did afterwards? Yes, there must have been. I have wondered too. Well, it seems it was no bad thing.'

'My poor Hereward! I was not the woman for him. So I was not even then.'

'Mother, was he the man for you? Is that someone you have not known? Perhaps that was equal between you. And you have come to a fair end.'

'Other things have not been equal. And there have been things before the end. I do not forget them. I never shall. And there are others who will not forget. But we will not speak of the poem to your father. It was not written for our eyes.'

'Or it would not have told us so much. And it tells us something more. The woman it was written for has parted with it. And to the man who wrote it and gave it. Perhaps we are told enough.'

As they entered the library, Hereward followed with Henry in his arms, having met him as he came from the garden. The latter carried the book, and seemed content with his possession of it.

'Read,' he said as his father sat down.

'No, you read to us,' said Hereward.

Henry leant towards the book and appeared held by its words.

> 'Ride a cock horse
> To Banbury Cross,'

he said, as if struck by them.

'Well, go on, or do you forget?'

'Not forget. Book not tell any more.'

'No, say what is true,' said Nurse. 'You often forget just there! "And see a fine lady –."'

'"Get on a white horse",' said Henry, in a painstaking tone, his eyes close to the page.

'There is something written on the blank leaf,' said Sir Michael. 'It looks like a poem.'

'That is what it is,' said Hereward. 'An effort of my youth. Not to be regarded or revealed.'

'I did not know you wrote poetry.'

'I don't. And I have realized it. I found it was not what I wrote.'

Sir Michael made a movement to take the book, but Henry forestalled him.

'No, not Grandpa's. Take it upstairs. Henry's own book.'

'Well, perhaps you can have it,' said Nurse, with a glance at Hereward. 'But you would like to hear a story first.'

'Once upon a time,' said Henry, urgently, turning to his father.

Hereward rose to the effort, and as Henry became absorbed, received the book from Nurse and put it in his pocket.

Chapter 15

'Good-morning, Sir Hereward,' said Galleon.

'Oh, good-morning. So that is what you call me now. I had forgotten about it.'

'It will have to be remembered, Sir Hereward. The change has taken place.'

'It is only a nominal change. It will not affect myself.'

'Well, that is as you feel, Sir Hereward.'

'My life and my work will go on. The difference will only be in name.'

'Names are an indication, Sir Hereward. And this is something further.'

'You feel that work and a title do not go together?'

'Well, there tends to be a gulf, Sir Hereward.'

'This is a very small title.'

'As old as the Tudors, Sir Hereward, I am told.'

'And a writer may be a man without a background?'

'Well, it is as you say, Sir Hereward.'

'I meant it was as you would say.'

'There was no need for me to take it upon myself, Sir Hereward.'

'You would respect me more, if I did nothing?'

'On the contrary, Sir Hereward. There are duties in every sphere.'

'My eldest son represents me. He is my deputy.'

'Yes, Sir Hereward. It can only be the word.'

'We need the money that I earn.'

Galleon paused and then just inclined his head.

'You think that is not a subject for words?'

'It is not always seen as one, Sir Hereward.'

'You feel the fact is a thing to be ashamed of?'

'It is a chance circumstance, Sir Hereward.'

'We could hardly have kept things up, if I had done nothing.'

'These places have their life, Sir Hereward. It involves the power of holding to it.'

'They can lose their life. In a measure they depend on money!'

'You are not of a stock that looks to it, Sir Hereward. There are other standards.'

'But everything has to be paid for.'

'It is true that the world is run on that basis, Sir Hereward.'

'And does our corner not belong to it?'

'It is perhaps apart in more than one sense, Sir Hereward.'

'You feel that I fail it in some way?'

'Well, perhaps that you withdraw from it, Sir Hereward.'

'Won't you get tired of using my name?'

'No, Sir Hereward. The question would not arise.'

'I shall get rather tired of hearing it.'

'It will cease to strike your ear, Sir Hereward. Good-morning, my lady.'

Joanna entered the room by herself, a reminder of how seldom she had done so. She was dressed as usual, but her look was unfamiliar. Her son went to meet her and take her to a seat.

'Mamma, this is brave and wise. The first steps have to be taken. It is like you to know it.'

'It would be like most of us. How can we help knowing?'

'At the moment you wish you had no more to take.'

'No, I wish both your father and I had more.'

'I know what it is to you to be here without him.'

'Well, it is the alternative to being nowhere.'

'You are feeling he is the more fortunate?'

'No, I suppose I am. But it is not the word.'

'We all have to die in our time. There is no escape.'

'When we have had to be alive. And when the two things are so different. We ought not to have to do both.'

'It is true, my lady, if I may interpose,' said Galleon. 'The one does not help with the other. It seems to render it unnatural.'

'And in spite of that it leads to it. The position is unreasonable.'

Ada came into the room, and at once turned her eyes on her mother-in-law.

'Mamma, it is what I expected. I meet what I knew I should. May I do as well, when my time comes.'

'Perhaps you may escape it,' said Hereward. 'A man may outlive his wife. It is a thing that happens.'

'Not as often as the other thing. It is the woman who is left. Women marry younger, and on the whole have longer lives. It is no advantage to them.'

'I think it is,' said Joanna. 'And I am one of them.'

'In a sense you hardly are. You are so much one by yourself. And your courage does not deceive us. We know what is in your mind. That you have come to the end. But you are too brave to allow yourself to betray it.'

'People are always brave in trouble. How can they be anything else? It is brave of them to suffer it.'

'Dear Mamma! You are feeling there is nothing left for you.'

'I do feel there is only a little left.'

'You will live in the past. That will always be your own.'

'I have lived in it. But then it was the present. And that was much better.'

'There is the future,' said Ada, raising her hands, 'the great, unforeseeable future. With its hopes and fears, its demands and its duties. You are to have a share of it.'

'It does not sound so very good. But I daresay it would not. This was once the future.'

'Well, we are now in the present,' said Hereward. 'And we all have our duty to that. I must go and attend to mine.'

'No, you must not, Hereward,' said Ada. 'You must remain with your mother. No duty is as pressing as that to-day. An exception can sometimes be made. And Galleon is here with the breakfast. Are we to live on air?'

'You may have feared it, my lady. I have had to assert myself. Trouble is taken to mean that life has not to go on.'

'Well, it ought to mean it,' said Joanna. 'It should be allowed to prevent it.'

'Oh, that is what I am called now!' said Ada, as if taken aback. 'I am not sure that I like it. No, I find I do not. It is someone else's appellation, not mine. I had forgotten, and I shall continue to forget.'

'Other people will remember, my lady. The change cannot be denied.'

'But then there will be two of us. How is that to be arranged? If the title is mine, and I suppose it is, what of the accepted bearer of it?'

'Joanna, Lady Egerton, my lady,' said Galleon, evenly.

'I am too old to have a Christian name,' said Joanna.

'Then you shall not have one,' said Ada. 'You shall be what you have always been. And I know the thought in your mind. The name was for Papa's lips and for his alone. And so it shall be to the end. It does not matter what I am. I will be anything that comes about. I have no claim, or anyhow I make none.'

'There is no choice, my lady. And the name is not used in speech.'

'Oh, how we are all under orders! We in the land of the free! Well, we must submit, I suppose. If the change must come, it must.'

'We have made enough of it,' said Hereward. 'It is no such great one.'

'It is a mark of the change in our lives. And that is a great one. It will be a shock to Merton. I have sent the message.'

'He and his wife are in the hall,' said Hereward, who now spoke of Hetty in this way.

'Ah, he would come to his mother. My son, I had to send a sad word. Yes, go first to your grandmother. She is the claimant to-day. All our thought centres round her. We take a secondary place.'

'Now this is a relief!' said Merton. 'I looked to be without grandparents. Things are only half as bad as I expected. I did not know that could happen. I feel it is too much.'

'And so it is. She comes out high. You must see that her grandsons are worthy of her. – Father, I knew you would be here. Aunt Penelope, I looked for this. It is what we can do for each other. To be ourselves as far as we can.'

'I suppose I am being myself,' said Reuben. 'But I half-felt we ought to be different.'

'So did I,' said Salomon. 'I felt my ordinary self was not enough.'

'Hereward may not quite come up to himself,' went on Ada. 'You may find him a thought aloof and silent. I think we must look for it to-day. His mind is on the past.'

'Mine is being held to the present,' said Merton.

'Well, I will take my cue,' said Hereward. 'My wife will fulfil a double part.'

'Well, it is what my hand findeth to do. So I do it with my might. These are difficult moments at the best. And a general silence would not serve. I don't know why we feel a sort of uneasiness and guilt, when we have lost someone near to us. But so it is. There is no eluding it.'

'I know why,' said Salomon. 'We are uneasy at the proof that we can die, and guilty because we have not died, when someone else has. It seems ungenerous of us.'

'Well, we must just get through the time as best we can.'

'And that is as we see,' said Merton.

'And it might be worse,' said Salomon. 'If it were left to us, it would be. What are we doing?'

'Nothing. And it is not worse.'

'I think it is,' said Reuben. 'I am feeling ashamed of it.'

'Father, step into the breach,' said Ada. 'Someone must second my efforts. My powers are giving out. They are not unlimited.'

'Do not give a sigh of relief,' said Reuben to Merton. 'We should have to hear it.'

'I have lost an old and dear friend,' said Alfred. 'Your husband has lost his father. And his mother has the greatest loss. What else is there to be said?'

'Nothing, Father. But it is a help to hear you say it. It becomes simple and natural, coming from your lips. It seems to lose its mystery and threat. And his mother is true to herself. I cannot tell you to what height she has risen. It leaves us impressed and silent.'

'Don't say it has not done the last,' said Reuben. 'Again we should have to hear.'

'And now, Aunt Penelope, something from you. We are not to be without it.'

'I will say it to the one with the greatest loss,' said Penelope, moving to Joanna.

'Ah, right again. Your instinct never fails. You cannot do better than follow it.'

'We know no one wants us, Ada,' said Emmeline. 'But we felt we wanted everyone. So we have come with nothing to say and no help to give.'

'But with a touch of the old charm,' said Ada, caressing her cheek. 'I don't mean it is not often there. But it must become intermittent, with the other echoes of youth. We are grateful for any return of it. We are having all we can.'

'I am not,' said Hereward to Viola. 'Where is the chance for us to have anything? Our relationship is seen as a reason for keeping us apart. It is an unusual view of it.'

'It is the relationship that is seen as unusual. But in the end it will be accepted. We will go slowly and not expect too much. And gradually expect more and more.'

'And in the end expect the whole,' said Hereward, in a distinct tone, glancing about him. 'I will have what is mine.'

'People feel it strange that life goes on, when someone has died,' said Zillah. 'But does it go on? There seems to be little sign of it.'

'You notice the pause more than I do,' said Salomon. 'So much of my life is pause.'

'Now are we accepting the pause too much?' said Ada. 'Is there an element of self-indulgence in it? We must be on our guard against the temptations of grief. They exist in that state as in any other.'

'I wish I knew what they were,' said Joanna. 'So that I could yield to them.'

'Mamma, through everything you remain your original and immutable self. You are a beacon in the darkness, something to point our way. You remind me of a light-house, solitary itself, but sending forth light. Now do you not all agree with me? Is there a dissentient voice?'

'It would be a bold one,' said Merton.

'And a wicked one,' said Reuben.

'It would be both,' said Salomon. 'Of course it is noble to endure grief. Not being able to help it makes it nobler. It would be different if we chose it.'

'Zillah, you did not mind my taking the office of eulogist upon myself? It might be held to be the part of the daughter. But feeling took hold of me, and I was carried away. And I know I have your support.'

'You have. And I am going to ask for yours. I am about to adopt the character myself. Not on behalf of my mother. That has been done. On that of my brother and your husband. Is there not a beacon there, a light to point our way? Something solitary itself, sending forth light? If his failings are on the scale of himself, on what other scale should they be? Has not the time come to know him, to see him as he is? To see ourselves as we are, and in our dealings with him. I will not ask for an answer. There is none, as there is only one. I will say your own words to you. I have taken the office of eulogist upon myself. It might be held to be the part of the wife. But feeling took hold of me, and I was carried away. And I can echo you again. Is there a dissentient voice?'

'There should not be one at all,' murmured Reuben. 'Suppose it was dissentient?'

'How Father's failings add to him!' said Merton. 'I join in the respectful admission of their scale. I am ashamed of my own petty faults.'

'I don't think I have any,' said Reuben. 'Or I can't think of them. They must be on a scale too mean to gain my attention.'

'I can only think I am perfect,' said Salomon. 'People say how trying a perfect person would be. And we see they are right.'

'Well, I have my part to play,' said Hereward. 'We are grateful for tribute, and our gratitude is sincere. But I have had to thank my sister for too much, to thank her further now. It is not for me to agree with her, or to presume to disagree. I will say I have done my best. And my worst, if it must be said. I can hardly wish I had done more. I wish some things were undone. But they have brought their good.'

'Father, is your silence to persist?' said Ada. 'It may seem to you natural, even fitting to-day. But your voice is always welcome.'

'You hardly encourage me to use it.'

'Now you know what I mean. I do not think feelings should be hidden. I have never subscribed to that school of thought. Anything that is there must give its signs. Anything does, as far as I have seen. But we will accept your silence as a sign, if that is what it is. Aunt Penelope will represent you.'

'I will ask for silence to serve me in the same way.'

'I am nervous,' said Reuben. 'Lest I should be giving signs.'

'I am nervous lest I should not be giving them,' said Salomon. 'I can only half-hope I am.'

'I am nervous lest everyone should begin to give them,' said Merton. 'I hardly dare to see and hear.'

'And now, Hereward?' said Ada. 'You can't have nothing more to say.'

'There is nothing more to be said. The part of an echo is not mine.'

'Hereward, that is unworthy of you. You know what you would make of all this, if you were conceiving a book. You are an adept at letting things grow under your hand and become larger than life. It is held to be your strong point.'

'Life is enough in itself to-day. It does not need my service.'

'Oh, there it is again! My words are misinterpreted, and my thought with them, I had better be silent.'

'A safe choice,' murmured Merton.

'Now why?' said his mother, turning to him. 'Would it do for everyone to be mum and mute, and self-indulgent in the way that goes with grief? Ah, every state has its snares, and we should remember them. And saying nothing may mean that people have nothing to say.'

'Then it is hard to see how they can say it.'

'Well, they don't, my dear, as we can see. But the excuse does not apply to your father. Even this argument could be material for him.'

'You said I was expert at making things larger than life,' said Hereward. 'I should have to depend on the gift.'

'You might make it smaller than life,' said Merton. 'So that it could reach vanishing point.'

'Now I knew you could talk, if you liked. Not that your speeches had so much to recommend them. Mamma, you have not made one.'

'No, and she will not,' said Hereward.

'Of course she will not, if she does not wish to. What a tone to take over something that goes without saying! Do you suppose that pressure would be brought to bear on her? Salomon, say a word to your father to bring him to a state of reason.'

'Here is one that is workaday enough. I am doing the accounts and some of the rents have not come in. Two of the farmers', and one other. They are a good deal behind with them.'

'I know the men you mean,' said Hereward. 'I have waived the rent of one, and given the other more time. These are not easy days for them. Rosa Lindsay's rent comes through me. I must give it to you.'

'Rosa!' said Ada. 'Oh, yes, the name! Yes, of course. Rosa Lindsay. Is she not an old tenant?'

'Yes, and an old friend. I sometimes see her.'

'Why does she send the rent through you? She must know that Salomon does the accounts.'

'Must she? I don't know how or why. I have not told her.'

'You must talk about something when you are with her.'

'That is true. But there are other topics. We should not be at a loss for them.'

'No. There would be many. You must both remember the past.'

'What do you mean? Oh, the book that was in the hall! You saw it and read the poem? Well, it did me no discredit. Or none on moral grounds.'

'I suppose the relation is now a formal one?'

'No, its roots are too deep. It dates from before my marriage.'

'I wonder it did not end in it.'

'Some people thought it would. For a time I was one of them.'

'Why did you not propose to her? You had the matter in your hands.'

'I took it into them. But it was also in hers.'

There was a pause.

'I suppose I should be grateful to her. So she determined the course of my life.'

'There is no need. She had no thought of it.'

'And you turned to the second best. I wonder if I have realized it. I think in a way I have.'

'Ada, I have not regretted it. I hope on the whole you have not.'

'I wonder you charge her any rent, when there is that between you. Oh, I daresay you don't. Do you provide it yourself?'

'You seem to have your thoughts on the matter. You can decide.'

'Is the rent paid by cheque, Salomon?'

'No, I think it comes in money.'

'Then your father does provide it. Only cottagers pay in coin. Does it always come in that way?'

'You are talking to my father, Mother. I hardly remember how everything comes.'

'You remember how this does. Well, there is no reason why he should not help someone who needs it.'

'None,' said her husband. 'I have never seen any. If I had, my life would have been different. And not only mine. I am as I am. That is why you and your sons are as you are. I need not say it again. You know the truth.'

'Oh, I do, Hereward. You have not hidden it. It is not the kind of thing you hide.'

'No, do not say it again,' said Alfred. 'You are as you are, and it is why my daughter and her sons are as they are. Yes, we know the truth. I need not say it again either. I shall never say it again. I will say nothing more to-day. We will have a word with your mother and take our leave.'

Hereward gave no sign and accompanied them to the hall. And at first his family were silent.

'It is not strange that Father admires himself through everything,' said Merton. 'It is what most of us do. It is strange that he does it openly. Most of us would not dare.'

'It shows we don't really admire ourselves,' said Salomon. 'He has the courage of conviction.'

'I don't think I admire myself at all,' said Ada. 'Perhaps not even as much as I might.'

'I don't think I even might,' said Trissie, who had been silent.

'I daresay there is not much to admire. But I doubt if most people have much more.'

'I think they have less,' said Trissie.

'So do I,' said the three brothers.

'Oh, how worth while you make it seem! How worth while you make it in itself! I would not go back and unlive it. The good has outweighed the bad.'

'I felt it would,' said Hereward, in a quiet tone, as he returned. 'I meant it should. I look back without regret. I do not see myself as a god.'

'Then how does he see himself?' murmured Salomon. 'None but a god could be as he is, and remain exalted in all our eyes. Literature and legend prove it. And feeling for children is known to go with divine powers. Here is someone who illustrates it.'

'Raining,' said Henry, in an incidental tone, as he entered the room.

'We had only gone a few steps when it began,' said Nurse.

'Not a few,' said Henry, looking down at his feet, as if in concern for them.

'Anyhow you did not get wet.'

'He did,' said Henry, passing his hands down his coat.

'Only a few drops,' said Nurse.

'No, not a few.'

'So you don't like the rain,' said Ada.

'Yes, he does. Very nice rain. Henry heard it.'

'But you did not have your walk.'

'No, it rained,' said Henry, contentedly.

'Come and tell Father about it,' said Hereward.

Henry went towards him, glanced at Joanna as he passed, and came to a pause.

'Poor Grandma very tired this morning.'

'Yes, she is. You must not trouble her.'

'Play game,' said Henry, observing the size of the gathering, and suggesting a beneficial course.

'No, we want to be quiet to-day.'

'Grandpa play,' said Henry, looking round the room.

'No, Grandpa is not here this morning.'

'Grandma want him,' said Henry, in a tone of remonstrance.

'Yes, she does. But he cannot come to her. He has been too ill.'

'Henry read to him. Then quite well again,' said Henry, ending on a rising note.

'Yes, he liked you to read,' said Hereward. 'You will always be able to remember it.'

'Yes, Father play,' said Henry, finding the attitude amenable.

'No, we are not thinking of games to-day.'

'Not a nice day?' suggested Henry, seeking a reason for the blankness.

'Come and let us tell you about Maud,' said Merton.

'Very good girl. Not stamp and cry. Not at all spoilt,' said Henry, openly forestalling information.

'What shall we tell her about you?' said Hetty.

'Send her his love,' said Henry, in a tone of ending the matter.

'A letter, my lady,' said Galleon, offering a salver to Ada.

'Grandma my lady,' said Henry looking at them.

'And one for you, Sir Hereward.'

'One for you, *sir*,' corrected Henry.

'He does not miss much,' said Galleon.

'Oh, yes, he knows everything,' said Henry.

'I think they have had enough of you,' said Nurse.

Henry turned to Hereward and climbed on his knee.

'Whom do you love?' said Hereward.

'Galleon,' said Henry, with feeling. 'And dear Grandpa best.'

'You will not see Grandpa again,' said Hereward, in a quiet tone.

'Oh, no,' said Henry, easily.

'You will not forget him, will you?'

'See him tomorrow. Not forget.'

'It is no good, Sir Hereward,' said Nurse. 'He is too young to understand.'

'Only say *sir*,' said Henry, with some impatience.

'He likes the old order,' said Hereward.

'He is wise,' said Salomon. 'There seems little to be said for the end of it.'

'Ah, my dear father! We saw things and thought of them differently. But at heart we were at one. A part of myself and my life is torn away.'

'Poor Father!' said Henry, looking up at him.

'Yes, poor Father! But it is poor Grandma most of all.'

Henry got down and went to Joanna, patted her knee and looked up into her face, doing what he could to compensate her.

'Grandma better now?' he suggested, hardly confident of his success.

'Yes, you have made me feel better.'

'But not well; no. Henry tell her something.'

'What have you to tell me?'

'Once upon a time there was a little boy,' said Henry, after a pause.

'And is that the whole of the story?'

'Yes. Not any more.'

'Well, now we can go upstairs,' said Nurse.

'No. Show her the picture. Quite safe in your bag. Draw it himself.'

'Oh, yes, in my reticule,' said Nurse, accustomed to interpreting primitive speech. 'Yes, I will leave you to show it to your grandmamma.'

Henry took the sheet of paper in both his hands, looked at it for a long moment, and displayed it.

'So you have made a picture,' said Joanna. 'What is it meant to be?'

'It is still raining, my lady. It is meant to be a horse. I hardly think it will stop to-day,' said Nurse, in an even, incidental tone, without turning her head.

A GOD AND HIS GIFTS

'Why, it is a horse!' said Hereward. 'Why, so it is.'

'Yes,' said Henry, smiling. 'It has legs.'

'And is that the tail?'

'No tail,' said Henry, who had not thought to put one.

'Well, we will give him one. There it is.'

'Yes,' said Henry, smiling again. 'Henry did it.'

'Oh, what would Nurse say? You know it was Father.'

Henry turned and showed the picture to Joanna.

'Horse and tail,' he said, choosing words that did not commit him.

'Oh, how clever you are!'

'Yes,' said her grandson.

'And where is the horse's mane?'

Henry attempted to depict it, regarded the result, and suddenly tore the paper across.

'The despair of the creator!' said Merton.

'A feeling known to Merton,' said Reuben.

'It is,' said his brother. 'It will never be known to you. And it can be beyond us.'

'Oh, what a waste of your work!' said Hereward to Henry.

'The feeling is not known to Father,' said Salomon.

'No, it is not,' said Merton, and was silent.

'Would you like to be destroyed?' said Zillah to Henry. 'Perhaps the horse did not like it.'

'He did,' said Henry, looking away. 'And Henry made him.'

'The god-like spirit,' said Salomon. 'He creates life and destroys it. His father's son.'

'Draw again,' said Henry to Joanna, and receiving another piece of paper, began to do so.

'You will learn to draw when you are older,' said Hereward.

'Yes, to-morrow,' said Henry, not looking up.

'He will have to learn other things,' said Merton to his brothers. 'Things of another kind. Who he is, who we all are, and what some of us might be. There may be breakers ahead.'

'That is enough,' said Salomon. 'What a thing to talk about to-day! Father is looking at you.'

'And hearing him,' said Hereward, quietly. 'And it is true that the time is ill-chosen.'

'The truth is in our minds,' said Merton. 'It is one that should never leave them. It may bear on coming lives.'

'Not to their harm, if we have a care.'

'Some things are out of our hands.'

'This one will be in mine.'

'It is time for us to go,' said Hetty, who, as always, had been watching Henry. 'Maud and her nurse are calling for us. I hear them in the hall.'

'They can come in for a moment,' said Hereward. 'And we can see if there are signs of danger.'

Merton's daughter entered, glanced at Henry and stood in silence. Henry returned the glance and looked away.

'Say good-morning to Great-Grandma,' said Merton.

Maud remained silent.

'Come, surely you can say a word.'

'Pencil,' said Maud, looking at Henry's occupation.

The latter did not raise his eyes, and Maud's also maintained their direction.

'Let her have the pencil, Henry,' said Ada. 'She is younger than you, and she is your guest.'

Henry put it smoothly behind his back.

'Come, the house must be full of pencils,' said Hereward, glancing at his son.

Maud looked round for signs of this, and seeing none, made an advance on the pencil and acquired it.

Her host broke down.

'Come, what a way to behave!' said Ada.

'Paper,' said Maud.

Zillah produced a sheet and another pencil; the nurses assigned them to their charges; and the latter turned their backs on each other and gave themselves to their art.

'Well, there seems no need for anxiety,' said Hereward.

'None at this moment,' said Merton. 'It is one that has no meaning.'

'It bears on others. I shall watch them as they come.'

'Don't you want to see Henry's picture?' said Hetty to Maud, feeling that egotism should have its limits.

'No, see Maud's,' said the latter, in whom it had none.

'Look at Maud's picture, Henry,' said Ada.

Henry gave a glance in its direction and returned to his own.

'We should be going, ma'am,' said Maud's nurse. 'Maud come home to her pretty toys.'

Maud pursued what she felt to be her calling.

'We must take your picture home or Henry will want it,' said the nurse, putting the virtue of necessity before any other.

Maud accepted this likelihood, gathered up her acquisitions and was borne away.

'We don't make enough of Maud,' said Ada.

'You don't make anything of her,' said Merton. 'Henry fills your eyes.'

'Not mine. Maud is my own grandchild. It has been an effort to make no difference.'

'You have failed in a sense you do not mean.'

'Well, Henry is in the house,' said Hereward.

'He is, at all times and in all parts of it.'

'Merton, you are a father yourself.'

'I am, and I am reminding you of it.'

'Would you like to have Maud to tea?' said Ada, bending to Henry.

'No,' said the latter, keeping his eyes on his work.

'But you always like to see her.'

'Take Henry's pencil,' said Henry, after a pause.

'But you were glad for her to have it.'

'No,' said Henry, looking up.

'Henry has a future,' said Merton. 'Do you ever give a thought to it?'

'Oh, surely the time is not yet,' said Hereward.

'The early steps lead to others. They would be better on the right path. He will have to grow up and marry like everyone else.'

'Marry,' murmured Henry to himself.

'Have a wife to live with you,' said Hereward. 'Whom would you like to have?'

'Dear little Maud,' said Henry, in a tone of ending the matter to everyone's content.

PARENTS AND CHILDREN

Chapter 1

'I suppose my thoughts are nothing to be proud of,' said Eleanor Sullivan.

'Then they are different from the rest of you, I am sure, dear.'

'I always mean what I say, Fulbert.'

Mr Sullivan did not make the protest of himself.

'If you reveal the thoughts, I will give them my attention,' he said, leaning back and folding his arms with this purpose.

'It is the old grievance of spending my best years in your parents' home.'

'It would be worse not to spend them in a home of any kind.'

'You must turn everything into a joke, of course.'

'I should be hard put to it to manage it with that. You would have a right to your long face.'

'We should do better in a cottage of our own, than as guests in this great house.'

'No chance of it with nine children. The cottage would not contain them. And I am not a guest: I am a son of the house.'

Fulbert uttered the words with an expression of his own, as if the position were a rather surprising one. He had a tendency to unction in speaking of himself, and the death of an elder brother had given him a place to which he had not been born.

'And what am I?' said Eleanor.

'The son's wife and the mother of his children,' said her husband, completing his picture.

'That is what I am. And it is not so very little. But if you are to go abroad, I shall have to be a good deal more.'

'That will be enough. The family can get along on it.'

'Is it necessary that you should go?'

'The old man insists upon it.'

'Is that the same thing?'

'Under this roof, my dear, as you give signs of knowing.'

'Your father believes in his divine right.'

'Well, there is a certain reason in it. His position will pass to others in their turn.'

'I don't see how it can go beyond you. The money will come to an end. This place is not part of the essential order of things. And though it is your old home, it is not mine.'

'Where your treasure is, there must your heart be also,' said Fulbert, in his deliberate, strident tones.

'That is true. No woman is more fundamentally satisfied.'

'Well, the deepest experience is known to be hidden, my dear.'

'I may be a murmuring woman. But I shall not feel the house is my home while your parents are alive. And that is not a generous thought.'

'It has no claim to be,' said Fulbert, throwing up his voice.

'I must try to conquer myself,' said his wife, with the sigh natural to this purpose.

'As you only have your own power to do it with, it sounds as if it would be an equal struggle.'

'Heaven helps those who help themselves.'

'It sounds grudging of Heaven to stipulate for its work to be done for it.'

It would have been clear to an observer at this point that Eleanor held the accepted religious beliefs, and that her husband held none.

'I wish you would not take that tone, Fulbert. It shows me how poor my example is.'

'Well, you have not been recommending it, my dear.'

'I know you do not like me to talk of my religion.'

'People are not at their best doing that, and it is wise to accept that as the truth.'

'I suppose actions speak louder than words.'

'I find no fault with silence.'

Eleanor followed the hint and changed her tone.

'This is an odd little room to give us for ourselves.'

'Not according to your preference for a cottage.'

'If we live in this house, we may as well have the benefit of it.'

'The dozen rooms allotted to us upstairs constitute our advantage,' said Fulbert, spacing his words as if they had a certain merit.

'I still think we might be happier, living on our own small income.'

'A family as large as ours is nothing under such conditions.'

'After all, our children are your parents' grandchildren.'

'That is their claim upon them, which is fortunately recognized.'

'You think you have a clever tongue, Fulbert.'

'You have hinted at advantages of your own, my dear.'

'I do not dispute it. I only meant you were conscious of it.'

'I have yet to meet the man unaware of his endowments. I have met many a one sensible of some that are not his.'

'And to which class do you belong?'

Fulbert rested his eyes in quizzical acceptance on his wife. His reasons for not mentioning women in connexion with endowments was not that he thought they would not have them, but that he saw little connexion between such things and their lives. He had a full respect for the woman's sphere, but was glad it was not his own. It seemed to him that his peculiar attributes would have little exercise in it.

'I must not make claims if I do not live up to them,' said Eleanor.

'Not if you want them recognized.'

'I wish there were a little more sympathy and warmth about you, Fulbert.'

'I wish you had a husband after your own heart, my dear.'

Fulbert Sullivan was a spare, muscular man of fifty, with a sort of springy quality going through his frame, which gave him a suggestion of controlling superfluous force. As he was a man of considerable vigour and no less leisure, this may have been the case. The suggestion of pent-up energy appeared in his narrow, near-set eyes, in his long, unmodelled lips, and even in his solid brow and nose and chin. His strong, metallic voice had a sudden rise and fall, and his manner might have been self-conscious, if its deliberate confidence had been less real. There was a suggestion about him of being prepared to be criticized at sight, and of meeting the attitude with unprejudiced and rallying goodwill. His wife was a tall, angular woman of forty-eight, with large, pale grey eyes, a narrow, shapely head, a serious, honest, somewhat equine face, and a nervous, uneasy, controlled expression. Her long, gentle hands and long, easy stride and deep, unaffected voice seemed less essential to her, than such attributes to other people. To those who knew her, all her physical qualities seemed to be accidental. To a stranger she gave the impression of being indefinite in colour, but very definite in everything else.

'Mother,' said a voice at the door, 'can you bear with Graham for a moment? I am allowing him a break from work and there is no service that I require of him.'

A youth led another into the room, deposited him in a chair and remained with his hands on his collar. Eleanor surveyed the pair as if the situation were familiar, and Fulbert watched with lively vigilance.

The occupant of the seat leaned back with an almost obliging air. He was a tall, bony youth of twenty-one, with head and hands and feet too heavy for his yielding frame, prominent, pale, absent eyes, and features that were between the fine and the ungainly. He had a deep, jerky voice and a laugh that was without mirth, as was perhaps natural, as he was continually called upon to exercise it at his own expense. His brother, who was older by a year, resembled Eleanor except for his weight and breadth, and for a widening and shortening of the face, which resulted in a look of greater power. He had a ready smile and an air of having the wisdom to find content in his lot. Eleanor surveyed her sons with affection, sympathy and interest, but with singularly little pride.

'What ought you both to be doing? Are you not wasting your time?'

'It is one of his worse days, Mother,' said the elder son. 'But a mother's words may succeed when all else fails. And I can only say that it has failed.'

Graham turned his eyes to Eleanor in automatic response.

'Do you never take a holiday?' said Fulbert, his eyes seeming to be riveted to his sons.

'Their grandfather likes them to work in the morning, when they are not at Cambridge,' said his wife.

'Graham, how do you fulfil that trust?' said Daniel. 'Think of that old man's faith in you.'

'I believe it has not struck me,' said Fulbert, with a laugh. 'I wonder what will be the end of all this poring over books.'

'Some sort of self-support,' said Daniel. 'Or that is accepted.'

'You can't both be ushers in a school.'

'It is good to know that,' said Graham.

'There are good posts in the scholastic world,' said Eleanor.

'Many more poor ones, my dear,' said her husband.

'I can imagine myself that accepted butt, a poor schoolmaster,' said Graham.

>   'When land is gone and money spent,
>   Then learning is most excellent,'

said Fulbert, as if the quotation put the matter on its final basis.

'I wish we could follow in your steps, Father,' said Daniel.

'In what way, my boy?' said Fulbert, with his eyes alight.

'You toil not, neither do you spin.'

'Your father worked hard as a young man,' said Eleanor.

'I did the work I could get, my dear. That was not often the word.'

'Success at the Bar is always some time in coming.'

'And in your servant's case it delayed too long.'

'You lost your patience too soon.'

'I kept it for a good many years, though patience is not my point,' said Fulbert, speaking as though he would hardly feel more self-esteem, if it were.

'It may have been the wisest thing to give up hope.'

'It was the only thing. My income did not meet my expenses, and my family was increasing them.'

'I do not mind a little pinching and scraping to keep out of debt.'

'It did not secure the end. And it has little advantage in itself.'

'Father,' said a new voice at Fulbert's elbow, where his daughter had been standing in silence for a time, 'we should remember that Mother's income went on our needs in those days. It is not fair to forget the source of so much of what we had.'

'And who is going to do so?' said Fulbert, turning with amused and tolerant eyes.

'No one while I am here, Father. And it seemed to me that a reminder was needed.'

Fulbert jumped to his feet, took his daughter's face in both his hands and implanted a kiss upon it, and then threw himself back in his chair as if he had disposed of the matter.

Lucia Sullivan was two years older than her brother Daniel. She was in appearance a cross between her parents, but was shorter and rounder in build, with more colour in her eyes and skin and a more lightly chiselled face. There was something solemn and almost wondering in her large, steady, hazel eyes, as if the world struck her as an arresting and impressive place. Her voice was full and deliberate; her lips moved more than other people's; and her eyes seldom left the face of the person she addressed.

'Father,' she said, with these attributes in evidence, 'Grandpa is by himself in the library. Grandma is doing the housekeeping. Ought he to be alone?'

'He can join us at his pleasure.'

'He never comes into this room, Father. He leaves it to you and Mother. He always waits to be asked.'

'If I reward his delicacy by joining him, I do not see what I gain.'

'I hardly agree with you there, Father. I can't feel it would be the same thing, if he came in and out at will. It is the intangibility of the distinction that gives it its point.'

'Well, perhaps that is why it escapes me,' said Fulbert, remaining in his chair, and then suddenly springing to his feet and running to the door.

Lucia looked after him and quietly turned to her mother.

'Mother, I don't think Father much liked my saying that about your money. But it did seem a fair point to make. I should not have been at ease with myself, if I had not said it.'

'It was a case for Father's being sacrificed,' said Daniel.

'No, boys,' said Luce, turning calm, full eyes on her brothers. 'Dealt with as a normal, intelligent being. It is how I should wish to be treated myself.'

'I should like all allowance to be made for me,' said Graham, with his eyes on the window.

'It is a good thing the boy is not embarrassed by the necessity,' said Daniel.

Luce threw a swift look at Graham and turned again to Eleanor.

'Mother, there is another little doubt. Was it a welcome reminder about Grandpa? Or quite well received? But I do not feel it right for him to be too much alone.'

'Your father agreed with you, my dear. He has gone to be with him.'

Eleanor spoke with natural simplicity. She had the power of esteeming people for their qualities, and as Lucia had honesty and kindliness, she valued her for these. Moreover her daughter had the gift of appreciation, and used it especially upon herself. Many people were put out of countenance by her dramatization of daily things, but Eleanor was affected in this way by few things that were innocent.

'Luce, you might make an effort with Graham,' said Daniel. 'A sister's influence may do much.'

'Mother is here, Daniel,' said Luce, with quiet emphasis.

Graham's face did not change.

'Will you be able to look at your grandfather and say you have done a morning's work?' said Eleanor to her sons, in an almost sardonic manner.

'I acquired the accomplishment years ago,' said Graham, absently.

'Was there a hesitation in the lad, in spite of those hardened words?' said Daniel. 'Where there is any sign of feeling, there is hope.'

'I shall not support you in what is not true,' said Eleanor.

'So our mother will fail us,' said Graham, in the same absent tone.

'Both of you away to your books,' said Luce, making a driving movement. 'I want to have a talk with Mother.'

Daniel led his brother from the room, while his sister looked on with gentle, dubious eyes.

'Mother, do you think it is good for Graham to be teased and made a butt? Because I really do not feel it is.'

'I don't suppose it does him much harm. He could stop it if he liked. He gives no sign of minding.'

'But, Mother, could he stop it? And don't you think that things may hurt all the more, that they are allowed no outlet?'

'I hardly think he seems to need any sympathy.'

'Mother, do you think you are right?' said Luce, sitting on the arm of Eleanor's chair. 'Don't you think there are feelings that shrink and shiver away from the touch, just because they are so alive and deep?'

'There may be, but those of boys would not often be among them.'

'Mother, I believe a boy is a very sensitive thing. Almost more so in some ways than a girl.'

'The sensitiveness of both is generally a form of self-consciousness. It does not relate to other people.'

'But may not a thing that relates to oneself be very real and tormenting? The more so for that?'

'No doubt, but that is not a reason for fostering it.'

'Don't you think that withholding sympathy may cause it to crystallize into something very hard and deep?'

'They seem to prefer it to be withheld.'

Luce went into slow laughter, with her eyes on her mother in rueful appreciation.

'Mother, you and I are very near to each other,' she said in a moment. 'I always feel it a tragic thing when a mother and daughter are separate. And yet I suppose it is common.'

'I wonder if I shall get on as well with my other daughters.'

'You know, I think you will, Mother,' said Luce, swinging to and fro on her chair, with her eyes turned upwards. 'I think there is nothing in you that would repel the young, or send them shuddering into themselves.'

'This youthful sensitiveness seems a problem,' said Eleanor, rising. 'I cannot say how far I am equipped to cope with it.'

'I think you are qualified, Mother,' said Luce, looking dreamily after her. 'I should think there is that in you, that will carry you through.'

'Your grandmother has gone into the drawing-room,' said Eleanor, leaving the subject. 'Perhaps we had better follow her.'

'Do you know, Mother, you have quicker ears than I have?' said Luce, remaining where she was. 'I had not heard Grandma. As far as I am concerned, she might still be at her duties.'

'She never takes more than an hour.'

'I had not noticed that either, Mother,' said Luce, slipping off the chair. 'I had no idea of the time she needed. You are a sharper person than I am, more alert to our little, everyday attributes. And yet I do not think I am indifferent to people, or blunt to their demands.'

'Your grandmother would not say so.'

'I think she depends on me, Mother,' said Luce, taking Eleanor's arm. 'And as long as she does, I hold myself at her service. It makes me dependent on her in a way. Well, Grandma dear, so you have finished your duties for the day.'

Lady Sullivan appeared unconcerned by this limit placed to her usefulness. She was sitting in the chair on the hearth, where she sat throughout the year, as though her comfort depended alternately on a full grate and an empty one. She was a portly, almost cumbrous woman of seventy-six, with a broad, exposed brow, features resembling her son's under their covering of flesh, pale, protruding eyes that recalled her second grandson's, large, heavy, sensitive hands, and an expression that varied from fond benevolence to a sort of fierce emotion. Her name of Regan had been chosen by her father, a man of country tastes, and, as it must appear, of no others, who had learned from an article on Shakespeare that his women were people of significance, and decided that his daughter should bear the name of one of them, in accordance with his hopes. When Regan came to a knowledge of her namesake, she observed that the name must have been in use before Shakespeare chose it, or it would not have been a name; and did not reveal the truth to her father, who was not in danger of discovering it. When people said that the name suited her, she accepted the compliment from those who intended one, and smiled on the others, or smiled to herself with regard to them in a manner that preserved them from further risk. So the name brought her no ill result, and a good one at the time of Sir Jesse Sullivan's approach, when the name in itself and the manner of her support of it determined his desired advance. Regan was a woman who only loved her family. She loved her husband deeply, her children fiercely, her grandchildren fondly, and loved no one else, resenting other people's lack of the qualities and endearing failings of these. And it meant that she had loved thirteen people, which may be above the average number.

She looked at Eleanor with a guarded, neutral expression. She could not see her with affection, as they were not bound by blood; and the motives of her son's choice of her were as obscure to her as such motives to other mothers; but she respected her for her hold on him, and was grateful to her for her children. And she had a strong appreciation of her living beneath her roof. If Eleanor saw it as a hard choice, her husband's mother saw it as an heroic one, and bowed to her as able for things above herself. The two women lived in a formal accord, which had never come to dependence; and while each saw the other as a fellow and an equal, neither would have grieved at the other's death.

Luce sat down on the floor and laid her head on her grandmother's lap. Regan put a hand on her head. Eleanor took her usual seat and her skilled needlework. She was a woman who did not make or mend for her family. Her daughter broke the silence by throwing her arms across Regan's knees and giving a sigh.

'Grandma,' she said, putting back her head to regard the latter's knitting, 'your needles flying in and out remind me of the things that work in and out of our lives. Each stitch a little happening, a little step forward or back. I daresay there are as many backward steps as forward. But that is not like your knitting, is it?'

She continued to survey the needles with a steadiness that was natural, in view of what she derived from them; and Regan smiled and continued to knit, as if she did not take so much account of the employment.

'We have not much chance of going back,' said Eleanor.

'Not in your sense, Mother,' said Luce, not moving her eyes. 'But there is a certain progression in our lives, which we do not always maintain. It so often comes to a swinging to and fro.'

'You mean in ourselves, don't you?'

'Yes, Mother, I do mean that,' said Luce, looking at her mother as if struck by the acuteness of her thought.

'My days for progress are past,' said Regan.

'I wonder why people say that in such a contented tone,' said Eleanor.

'They may as well put a good face on it.'

'No, Grandma, I do not think it is that,' said Luce, tilting back her head to look into Regan's face. 'I think it is just that many things still stretch in front of them, though some may be behind. I think we all go on advancing in ways of our own, until some sort of climax comes, that we all look towards as a goal.' She said the last words lightly, as if not quite sure if she had made or avoided a reference to her grandmother's death, and settled herself in a better position on the floor to indicate that her thoughts were on trivial, material things.

Regan kept her eyes on her needles, which she seldom did if her thoughts were on them. She was thinking for a moment of her own end. It engaged her mind no oftener as it drew nearer, and it did this so lightly at the moment that it failed to keep its hold.

'Where is Grandpa, dear?' she said to Luce, in a tone that offered the tenderness due to a child, and the respect due to a woman.

'I don't know, Grandma; I hope he is not by himself.'

'Your father is with him,' said Eleanor. 'You reminded him to go to him.'

'So I did, Mother,' said Luce, putting frank eyes on her mother's face.

'Fulbert will find it a change to have regular work, if it has to come,' said Regan, with the thrust in her tone that seemed to be an outlet for emotion.

'And it seems that it must,' said Eleanor.

Luce glanced from one face to another, as if she would not seek information where it was not given.

'I think Father sometimes does more for Grandpa than appears at a glance, Mother. His desk is often littered with accounts.'

Eleanor did not dispute this.

'It all appears at a glance perhaps,' said Regan, with a smile of pure indulgence.

'Grandma, you are not at heart a critical parent. Your children must always have found you a refuge from the censorious world.'

Regan's face worked at mention of her children, two of whom were dead.

'You would not say the same of your mother,' said Eleanor.

'No, Mother, no,' said Luce in a deliberate tone, lifting her eyes in sincere thought. 'But we can say other things.'

A sound of singing came from the hall, and the performer entered and proceeded to the hearth, where he ended his song with his eyes on his hearers and an expression of absent goodwill. Regan looked at him with automatic fondness; Luce gave him a smile; and Eleanor did not move her eyes.

'Grandpa,' said Luce, moving hers so much that they almost rolled, 'did you feel the impulse to come to us about three minutes ago?'

'Just about, just about, my dear,' said Sir Jesse, adapting his measure to the words.

'Then it is a case of telepathy,' said Luce, looking round. 'I have noticed that Grandpa is sensitive in such ways. His response is almost consistent.'

'Well, how are all of you?' said Sir Jesse, surveying the women as if they belonged to a different sphere, as he felt they did.

'We are well and happy, Grandpa,' said Luce, in a personally satisfied tone.

Regan's face showed her support for this view, and Eleanor's face told nothing.

'How has this young woman been behaving?' said Sir Jesse, displacing his wife's cap and causing her to simulate a pleased amusement.

'She has been behaving well, Grandpa,' said Luce, turning up her eyes to Regan's face.

'And this younger woman?' said Sir Jesse, indicating Eleanor, but disturbing nothing about her.

'She has been behaving well too, Grandpa,' said Luce, in a demure tone.

'And this youngest woman of all?'

'Well too, Grandpa,' said Luce, hardly uttering the words.

'Three good women,' began Sir Jesse to the tune of a song, but broke off as his grandsons entered, and spoke with a change of tone. 'Well, I suppose it is time to eat, as you appear amongst us. What meal do we expect?'

'Luncheon, Grandpa,' said Luce, in the same tone.

'It is a pity we cannot break Graham of this way of eating,' said Daniel. 'It is such a primitive habit.'

'Do not talk nonsense,' said Eleanor, in a low tone.

Sir Jesse Sullivan was a large, strong man of seventy-nine, whose movements were surprisingly supple for his build and age, perhaps the result of his frequent mild exercise, and perhaps the cause of it. His small, dark, deep-set eyes looked out under a jutting, almost jagged brow, and his blunt, bony features seemed to mould themselves to his mood in a manner inconsistent with themselves. This element of inconsistence seemed to go through him. His solid, old hands had a simple flexibility, and his hard, husky voice had vibrations that suggested another being. His eyes were familiar and fond on his wife, less familiar and faintly admiring on Eleanor, comradely and somehow unrelenting on his son, indulgent on Luce, and sharp and piercing on his grandsons, who as males dependent on their education, and dependent on him for its cost, struck him as suitably occupied only at their books. The expense of the training that produced schoolmasters and curates and such dependent men, was so startling to Sir Jesse, who had himself had little education and no thought that he required more, that he put it from his sight; and it seemed inconsiderate and almost insubordinate in his grandsons to act as a reminder.

'Is Father ready for luncheon, Grandpa?' said Luce.

'He is, my dear,' said Fulbert, running into the room, 'and he hopes it bears the same relation to him.'

'It will be ready at the right time, Father,' said Luce, folding her arms round her knees in preparation for waiting.

'I suppose Graham must come to meals,' said Daniel. 'There ought to be some other way of managing about him.'

'We must eat to live,' said Fulbert.

'But is that necessary for Graham, Father?'

Luce gave a quick look at her second brother.

'The gong gets a little later every day,' said Fulbert consulting his watch.

'It is the someone behind the gong, Father,' said Luce, and in a tone so light and even that it might have escaped notice. 'And then the someone behind that.'

'You would think it would help the household to have things on time.'

'Such a household would be above help,' said Daniel.

'It is a tribute to Grandma's management that you can talk like that, Father,' said Luce.

'Well, I may be allowed to pay her the compliment.'

Regan looked touched beyond the demand of the occasion.

'The gong must soon sound with so much behind it,' said Graham, in his toneless voice.

'It will sound when luncheon is ready,' said Eleanor.

'It will be our last luncheon without the babies at the end,' said Luce. 'Their holiday ends today. I cannot get used to being without them.'

'Luce has not forgotten her brothers and sister in three weeks,' said Daniel. 'It must be the depth of her nature.'

'You did not remember them enough to speak of them,' said Sir Jesse.

As the gong sounded through the house, Fulbert walked swiftly to the door and held it open for the women, sending his eyes to different objects in the room, as if he felt no inclination to hurry this part of the proceedings. He rather enjoyed any duty that had a touch of the formal or official. At the table he did the carving, a duty deputed by his father, and performed it with attention, swiftness and skill, supplying his own plate at the end with equal but not extra care. Daniel and Graham were talking under their breath, and their mother threw them a glance.

'You need not concern yourself with them,' said Sir Jesse. 'They are about to address themselves to their business.'

'Isn't it a repellent trait in my brother?' said Daniel.

'So is Grandpa,' murmured Graham. 'He and I are of the same old stock.'

'Any word you have to say of me, you can say to my face,' said Sir Jesse.

Graham was about to reply, but his mother's eyes prevented him. He was dependent on Sir Jesse for most of what he had, and this was not a forfeiture it was wise to incur. Daniel took his grandfather in an easier spirit and reckoned with him in so far as he served his purposes. Sir Jesse thought him better behaved, a not uncommon result of this attitude of youth.

'Well, my boy, we must break our news,' said Sir Jesse to his son.

'Of the prospect that takes me from the bosom of my family,' said Fulbert, looking with mingled apprehension and resolution at the faces round him.

'Mother, Grandpa,' said Luce, turning steady eyes upon them, 'we should be glad to have this thing cleared up, whatever it is. We have been living for days under the sword of Damocles, and it will be a relief to have it fall. What is this threat of losing Father for some reason unexplained? We should be grateful for the truth, and we feel we have a right to it.'

'Your father has to go to South America to look into the estate,' said Eleanor. 'Your grandfather had the final letters today.'

'Thank you, Mother. That is at once a shock and a satisfaction. We had no idea what the dark hints might portend, and imagination was outstripping the truth. Now we may hope that the exile will not be long.'

'A matter of six months,' said Fulbert, with courage and ease.

'Thank you, Father. That would have been a blow not so many days ago. As it is, we chiefly experience relief.'

'You could have asked before,' said Eleanor.

'No, Mother, we could not,' said Luce, meeting her eyes. 'There was that about you, that precluded approach of the subject.'

'What led our elders to conceal the simple matter?' said Daniel, in a low tone.

'The instinct to keep all things from the young,' said Graham. 'Even a temporary concealment was better than nothing.'

'Six months is a moderate sentence,' said Daniel. 'We can hardly expect Graham to show a new son to Father on his return.'

Graham glanced at Regan in imagination of her feeling.

'I shall not live six months many more times,' she said.

'Yes, you will, Grandma,' said Luce, in an even tone. 'Probably a good many more.'

'What about me in exile?' said Fulbert.

'Poor Father! You did not expect to have to ask that question.'

'I would go myself if I were younger by a few years,' said Sir Jesse, with an undernote of inflexibility that revealed his true relation with his son. 'And it is not only for that reason that I wish I were.'

'I cannot imagine you in a stage more becoming, Grandpa,' said Luce.

'I have liked others better, my dear,' said Sir Jesse, smiling to himself as he recalled these.

'Perhaps I ought to pay Grandpa an occasional compliment,' murmured Graham.

Regan made an emotional sound, and Luce came and stood behind her, stroking her shoulders as she continued to talk.

'A great part of Father's duty must devolve on Mother.'

'And she will be equal to it,' said Fulbert, in a tone of paying the fullest tribute.

'She will have but little support in one of her sons,' said Daniel.

'I wish the time were behind us,' said Eleanor. 'And I may make other people wish it more.'

'A mother's life is not all sacrifice,' said Fulbert.

'It is not indeed,' said Regan, in allusion to her own lot.

Luce gave Regan's shoulder a final caress, and left her as if her attendance had done its work, as it appeared it had.

'Father, perhaps a word from you would touch Graham at this time,' said Daniel.

'Nothing is asked of either of you, but that you shall consider your future,' said Sir Jesse.

'Grandpa, that is rather hard,' said Luce. 'More than that must be expected of everyone. And long months spent over books may not strike young men in that light.'

'Then they are not what you call them.'

'Well, they scarcely are as yet,' said Eleanor.

'Mother, that is even harder,' said Luce, with a laugh.

'The most abandoned youth is a child to his mother,' murmured Graham.

'Mother, you are setting a gallant example,' said Luce. 'Father has not a wife who will make things harder for him.'

'We are none of us taking the line of showing him how much we are affected.'

'No, we are not engaging in that competition, Mother. But we might not follow the other course with so much success.'

412

'Those who show the least, feel the most,' stated Fulbert.

'That is not the line to take with me,' said Regan, with smiling reference to her swift emotions.

'You are a self-satisfied old woman,' said her son.

'Grandma has no need to wear a disguise,' said Luce.

'And have the rest of us?' said Eleanor.

'Well, Mothers, many people do wear one. That is all I meant.'

> 'This above all, to thine own self be true;
> And it must follow, as the night the day,
> Thou canst not then be false to any man,'

quoted Fulbert, in conclusion of the matter.

'Why is that so?' said Graham. 'It might be true to ourselves to do all manner of wrong to other people.'

'The only thing is to conquer that self, Graham,' said Daniel.

'It depends on the sense of the word, true,' said Eleanor. 'It means it would be dealing falsely with our own natures to do what degrades them.'

'I expect it does mean that, Mother,' said Luce, in a tone of receiving light and giving her mother the credit. 'No doubt it should be taken so.'

Sir Jesse broke into a song of his youth, a habit he had when he was not attentive to the talk, and sang in muffled reminiscent tones, which seemed at once to croon with sentiment and throb with experience. He glanced at the portraits of his dead son and daughter, as if his emotion prepared the way for recalling them; and sang on, as though the possession of life overcame all else.

His wife followed his look and his thought, though her eyes were not on him. She would have given her life for her children's, and knew he would have done this for nothing at all, and accepted and supported his feeling. The pair lived with their son and his family, feeling amongst and not apart from them. They saw themselves as so young for their age, that they shared the common future. They were neither of them quite ordinary people, but they were ordinary in this.

'Well, don't I deserve a word to myself on the eve of my banishment?' said Fulbert.

'You do, Father,' said Luce, 'and you would have had it, if you had not contrived to forfeit it. I cannot see how we are to live the next six months. We shall have to take each day as it comes.'

'Why is that a help?' said Graham. 'It seems to spin things out. It would be better if we could compress the days.'

'Graham, are you going to let these months be different?' said Daniel.

'I have not heard either of you say a reasonable word for days,' said Eleanor.

'Mother, let them veil the occasion in their own way,' said Luce.

'Our boyish folly covers real feeling,' said Graham, stating the truth of himself.

'Would you like to be going with your father, Daniel?' said Eleanor.

'Mother, don't speak in that cold voice,' said Luce, laughing. 'It is not Daniel's fault that Father has to leave us.'

'He can answer my question nevertheless. Your father is going partly for his sake.'

'It is a good thing that everything is easier when it is shared,' said Daniel. 'If there were enough of us, I suppose it would disappear.'

'You would think there were enough,' said Graham, dreamily.

'I am tired of hearing nothing but nonsense,' said Eleanor, with a break in her voice.

'Graham, how many young men have heard their mothers use that tone!'

'I daresay the larger number,' said Eleanor, sighing.

Sir Jesse broke again into song, and sang very low, as if unsure of the fitness of the words for the audience. Regan smiled with an indulgence that was more apposite than she knew, or betrayed that she knew; and Fulbert took up the song in a strong, metallic voice and with a certain gusto. Graham kept his eyes down, as if he could only meet the manifestation with discomfiture, and Sir Jesse flashed his eyes into his son's and turned to his luncheon.

Luce had sat with her eyes on the men, and now addressed her father, as if quietly putting behind her what she saw.

'Father, is there any writing to be done? I had better undertake it, as my hand is clear.'

'This is an awkward moment for Graham,' said Daniel.

'After my advantages,' said Graham, in his absent tone.

'I had a reminder of those only this morning,' said Sir Jesse. 'An account came with my breakfast. You had nothing at yours but what you could swallow.'

'It is impossible of Graham,' aid Daniel. 'Simply eating at the table! He seems to live by bread alone.'

'Be silent,' said Sir Jesse, with sudden harshness. 'I blush to think you have been brought up in my house.'

'We have always had to blush for that,' muttered Daniel. 'But I did not think Grandpa would ever do so.'

'Will neither of you speak again until you have something to say?' said Eleanor.

'Would you have the lads dumb?' said her husband.

'It might strike many people as an improvement.'

'Mother, you don't mind what you say,' said Luce, laughing under her breath.

'You must grow up, my sons,' said Fulbert. 'I am leaving burdens upon you.'

'I need not become a baby again to comfort Mother,' said Graham.

'It does not seem to have that result,' said Fulbert. 'Well, do any of you give a thought to my exile?'

'Many thoughts, Father,' said Luce, 'but we are not to help it. We are sad to our hearts, but we do not feel guilty.'

'That must be wonderful,' said Graham.

'We ought to feel grateful,' said Eleanor.

'That involves guilt,' said Daniel. 'It seems grasping to have so much done for you.'

'I suppose that is what it is about gratitude,' mused Luce. 'I have wondered what it is, that takes from it what it ought to have.'

'I should always be glad of a chance of feeling it,' said Fulbert.

'That is a sign of a generous nature,' said Regan, who was direct in tribute to her family.

'Father does not say he has had the chance,' said Daniel.

'He is a proud man,' said Graham.

'Do you wish you were old enough to help your father, Daniel?' said Sir Jesse.

'I should like to be considered to be so, if it would mean my going with him.'

'What is your reason for desiring it?'

'It would make a change,' said Daniel, keeping his face grave.

'That shows you are not old enough,' said his mother at once. 'That is not your father's reason for leaving us.'

'No, but it will be one of the results.'

Regan gave a laugh and Eleanor looked at her.

'You are too kind to them, Lady Sullivan. Their life in this house will hardly prepare them for the world outside.'

'I never feel that that sphere is as bad as it is painted,' said Daniel.

'You can talk of it when you are qualified,' said Sir Jesse.

'Grandpa does not set us the example,' murmured Graham.

'Your experience of it at Cambridge has not taken you far,' said Eleanor.

'No, Mother dear, but farther than you think,' said Luce. 'Cambridge would be a miniature world.'

'I am to have a good, long glimpse of a far corner of the real one,' said Fulbert.

'I shall have to be father as well as mother here,' said Eleanor.

'There goes the attention from Father again,' said Daniel, while Graham gave a glance at Fulbert.

'Hatton will be both to the little ones,' said Luce.

'Don't you know more about it than that?' said her mother. 'But that is how it would be, I suppose. The nurse who does it for a living is the one preferred. Mothers must learn that they come second.'

'My dear, do not talk without sense,' said Fulbert. 'You do not make the affairs of childhood your province. You cannot shine in a sphere where you have not chosen to function.'

'Do you want a nurse for your children, or a mother?'

'I want both, and my children have them. And I hope they also have a father. But we must not claim other people's credit.'

'I suppose I may have my own. I can expect a little recognition in the family that takes my life.'

Regan looked on without a change of expression, as though having no feeling that would cause one. She had neither pity nor blame for a woman who gave way under the demand of her family. She had never done so herself, but to her the family was the only thing that did not produce such a result.

'We know what you give us, my dear,' said Sir Jesse to Eleanor. 'You do not think we do not?'

'If feelings are always covered we may not remember them.'

'They are no less safe like that, Mother,' said Luce.

'I know they are there, my dear. I ought not to need to be reminded.'

'Father,' said Luce, turning her eyes on Fulbert's face, 'what did you mean by saying that Mother did not make the affairs of childhood her province?'

'I meant what I said, my dear, as I generally do.'

'It is true that I give less time to these children than I gave to the elder ones,' said Eleanor.

'Why do you, Mother?' said Luce, transferring her eyes.

'I seem to have less to give. You are in so many different stages. And I may have lost my knack or my zest as the years passed,' said Eleanor, who spoke of herself with the same honesty as of other people. 'And when the habit is broken, there is little to be done. My younger children are shy of me.'

'No, Mother, I don't think they are.'

'They behave as if they were.'

'Mother, I think it is better to be at your best with your elder children,' said Luce. 'It is when they are older that they need understanding. There is little that cannot be done by nurses for young children.'

'That is assumed in our class,' said Fulbert.

'You sound as if you do not approve of it, Father.'

'I don't know that I know much of the subject,' said Fulbert, with a suggestion that further knowledge would hardly add to him.

'Graham has always had his mother's influence,' said Daniel. 'It almost seems a case where nothing can be done.'

'Boys, you might be monotonous,' said Luce. 'I don't know how you contrive to be amusing.'

'I do not either,' said Sir Jesse. 'You might have the goodness to inform me.'

'Grandpa, you have had enough of them,' said Luce, with swift compunction. 'We forget we are not natural members of your house.'

'Indeed you are,' said Regan.

'Grandma has said one of those little words that will be remembered,' said Graham.

'As neither of you seems about to leave the table, I will do so myself,' said Sir Jesse.

'No, Grandpa, you will not,' said Luce, leaning forward and putting a hand on his arm. 'You will stay here and have your smoke and talk with Father.'

'A strong man is checked in his course by a woman's hand,' said Graham.

'Will you both be silent?' said Eleanor.

'Boys, you are upsetting Mother,' said Luce.

'I was always afraid that Graham would grow up to be a grief to her.'

Sir Jesse rose and walked from the room.

'Boys, look at that,' said Luce.

'I saw it myself,' said Fulbert.

'Do you hear what I say, or do you not?' said Eleanor.

'Graham, answer your mother,' said Daniel.

'You can answer me yourself,' said Eleanor.

'No, you are mistaken, Mother. I am at a loss.'

'This is one of your worse moments, my boy,' said Fulbert, with his air of enjoyment.

'He can easily put an end to it,' said Eleanor.

'Why am I not struck dead,' said Daniel, 'if that is a thing that has happened to people?'

Regan's deep laugh sounded through the room.

'I wish Grandpa had stayed to hear that laugh,' said Luce.

'I wish he had done so for any reason,' said Daniel.

'Daniel, I am waiting to be answered,' said Eleanor.

'Surely not still,' said her son.

'You have staying power, my dear,' said Fulbert.

'I forget what you asked now, Mother,' said Luce.

'Oh, you are not equal to your mother, child,' said Fulbert.

'Your brothers do not forget, and it was to them I spoke,' said Eleanor.

'Mother, when you speak in that tone, I defy anyone to face you without flinching,' said Luce.

'I do not accept the challenge,' said Daniel.

'There is no real cause for annoyance, Eleanor, my dear,' said Fulbert.

'I hope your father is of that opinion.'

'I am sure he is,' said Regan, in an easy tone.

'Yes, Grandma, so somehow am I,' said Luce.

'In case he is not, it may be as well to avoid risk in future,' said Fulbert.

'Yes, Father, I would not put it more strongly than that,' said Luce.

'I think I would,' said Eleanor.

'Mother, do thaw,' said Luce. 'Your sons are not a pair of criminals.'

'They are penniless boys, who are doing no good to themselves.'

Regan looked at her grandsons almost with compunction, as if it were a natural ground for resentment, that other people should have more than they had.

'Yes, I suppose that is an accepted handicap,' said Luce, in a musing tone. 'To be penniless. And yet I would not have people modify their actions too much because of it. I do not think I would.'

'There is no harm in young men's being well-behaved to an old one,' said Fulbert.

'No, Father. But is it a fair accusation? What exactly is the boys' misdeed? I mean essentially. Not at the moment.'

'The fact of their existence,' said Fulbert. 'The sins of the fathers are visited upon the children.'

Luce gave a series of slow, little laughs, keeping her eyes from her mother.

'Their grandfather wants what is best for them,' said Regan.

'Graham, Grandma has dropped her handkerchief,' said Luce, without a break in her tone, and hardly changing the direction of her eyes. 'Are we to expect Grandpa to take the same attitude towards the other boys?'

'The younger ones often remain the younger ones,' said Eleanor.

'That sounds a cryptic remark, my dear,' said Fulbert, 'but I recognize the truth it contains.'

'Are not the schoolroom children coming down today?' said Luce.

'I have just sent word that they need not come,' said Eleanor. 'Missing their grandfather would only lead to questions.'

'Their yoke is easy and their burden light,' said Graham.

'Mother, I will try again with Graham,' said Daniel. 'It cannot be that I shall always speak in vain.'

'It is a fact that you do so at the moment, my boy,' said Fulbert, in mingled enjoyment and apprehension.

'Mother dear, relax,' said Luce. 'It is not good for you to remain in that wrought-up state.'

'Come, come, my dear, things are not so bad,' said Fulbert.

'I cannot bear the ignorant quoting of sacred words.'

'We see that you can't, and so the lads will remember it.'

'That should not be their reason for avoiding it.'

'It should be one of them. And they know the others.'

'Father, is Grandpa by himself?' said Luce.

'I daresay he is. Indeed he must be.'

'Don't you want to go to him, Father?' said Luce, looking at Fulbert with mild amusement.

'I have never heard that the sins of the children should be visited upon the fathers. But I can't leave the old man to simmer on the hob, when he is in danger of boiling over.'

'Grandpa is not a kettle, Father,' said Luce, in a quiet tone.

Regan laughed, and Fulbert ran round the table and gave her a kiss, and then did the same to his wife and daughter, and seemed about to run from the room, but did not do so.

'I wonder if we shall realize that Grandpa is human, before – while we are all young about him,' said Luce.

'Before he becomes more than human,' said Graham.

'Yes, before that, boys,' said Luce, in an unflinching tone.

'It will be wasted when Grandpa understands all,' said Graham.

Regan rose and rustled from the room in some personal preoccupation. Eleanor dropped her eyes and remained still. Fulbert's eyes flashed with rallying apprehension round the table.

The silence held until it reached the stage at which it is impossible to break.

'Graham, I do not remember that I forbade you to speak,' said Daniel.

Graham emitted a sound.

'Cry, Graham, if you must. We shall understand.'

Luce made an involuntary sound that served as a signal, and the brothers and sister rocked in mirth, or in some emotion that bore the semblance of it.

Eleanor had her own reaction to such proceedings. She rose and appeared to engage herself with a bowl of flowers.

'You boys can go and sit with your grandfather,' she said, inserting a hand to gauge the depth of the water. 'I want your father to myself for a time.'

'Mother, do not hold yourself aloof,' said Luce, in a voice that had not quite regained its steadiness. 'Magnifying a matter is not the way to mend it.'

'That sort of laughter is very easy to catch,' said Eleanor, in a condoning manner that did her credit, considering that she had hardly found this the case herself. 'But your father and I will be left to ourselves. We have many things to discuss.'

'Well, let us begin on them, my dear,' said Fulbert leaning back in his chair.

Eleanor was silent for a moment.

'It is strange that we can get so vexed with people who are so much to us.'

'Not at all, when they give us cause. It was a good move to send the young jackanapes to their grandfather.'

'Do you think it was a mean thing to do, that I was retaliating on them?'

'No doubt you were, my dear. And it was the right thing. Why shouldn't they learn that they get as good as they give?'

'They ought not to learn it from their mother.'

'They are happy to have from anyone what is best for them. And that is what a dose of the old man will be. I hope they are not queering their pitch with him.'

This question was answered by the opening of the library door and the sound of Sir Jesse's voice.

'So I am held to be short of company. If you are engaged with your wife, I will have my own. I prefer a woman to half a man. I have sent the pair about their business, and I hope they will follow it.'

'I will fetch Grandma for you, Grandpa,' said Luce, coming forward. 'Father thought it would be good for the boys to talk to you.'

'So I shoulder the responsibility,' said Fulbert, with an amused air.

'I daresay,' said Sir Jesse to his granddaughter, without a hint of disputing the idea. 'But where is the benefit for me? I get my share of them.'

'It is not the boys' fault that they are not quite up to you, Grandpa.'

'Nor mine either, as I see it. And I put it to their account that they are so far behind. We are all of us human or should be. In their case I begin to have doubt. Grinning and chattering like apes and costing like dukes!'

'I wish you could forget how much they cost you, Grandpa,' said Luce, fingering Sir Jesse's coat.

'I wish the same, but I get too many reminders. Other people seem to bear it in mind.'

'It will not be for much longer, Grandpa. They are both in their last year at Cambridge.'

'And where will they spend the next ones? Behind bars, I should think. I hope that will be less expensive.'

'I should think it would be, Grandpa,' said Luce, in a demure tone, making a little grimace and curtsy for the eyes of her brothers.

'If we are fed by the public through a grating,' said Daniel, 'it will take our keep off Grandpa.'

'We should still carry our debt to the grave,' said his brother. 'Or to Grandpa's grave we should.'

'Why does he mind supporting us, so much more than the others? I suppose because we are adult and male. None of the others is both.'

'It seems odd that I should be both,' said Graham. 'Neither seems suited to me.'

'It is true of Grandpa and Father. And they have never earned a penny. We belong to the new generation that has to gain its bread.'

'It is a poor position not to be entitled just to that,' said Graham, with a faint smile. 'Think what Grandpa is entitled to!'

'I do not envy him,' said Daniel.

'You mean he is old and you are young,' said Graham, looking into his brother's face. 'You think he will soon die. But he sees his death as too far distant to count. So that takes away your advantage.'

'He can't think he is a god.'

'We have done what we can to foster the belief. And I have almost come to accept it.'

'He insists that we shall do so,' said Daniel.

'That is the way to make himself into one. And I feel he has succeeded.'

'He thinks that youth is a time for mischief and the concealment of it,' said Daniel. 'I expect he remembers that it is. And he knows that mischief costs money.'

'I have heard him observe that everything does that,' said Graham.

'The inheritance must vanish with so much division,' said Daniel. 'Father is the last to anticipate it. I am a poor sort of eldest son. Grandpa rightly despises me.'

'Father says he will not see the time when it is gone,' said Graham, smiling. 'By claiming extinction for himself, he puts any experience of life in a favourable light.'

'He does not think he is immortal, as Grandpa does.'

'He does not need to yet. He has too good a span of life before him.'

'The girls will share equally with us,' said Daniel. 'There is not enough for anything else.'

'I see you do not think that Father is immortal.'

'I feel that I am, and that I shall have to support myself through that eternity.'

'And you think you will do it by coming out high on college lists.'

'Well, what are your own anticipations?'

423

'They are of an uneasy nature,' said Graham. 'I tell myself that the time of reckoning will be short; and I know that is said when things are very bad. But I would not change my last three years for yours.'

'The moments to be exchanged are not yet.'

'Moments instead of years. I hold to my opinion. And when people hold to things, they have not always lost them. Most great men have failed at the university.'

'I do not miss the implication. But other kinds of men have done the same.'

'What are you discussing?' said Eleanor, coming into the hall.

'Our own prospects,' said Daniel.

'Do you think you have good ones?' said Eleanor, while Luce walked up with a noiseless step, and placing her hand on her mother's shoulder, followed her eyes.

Eleanor had ambitions for her sons, and found herself assailed by doubts whether they were justified. She felt the position to be difficult for her, but had no uneasiness lest it might be the same for them.

'If not, what have we?' said Daniel.

'You will make your mother proud of you?' said Eleanor, who saw her preference for her eldest son as simple tribute to him.

'I believe you see it as a discredit to me, that I have not won your interest in equal measure,' said Graham.

Eleanor looked at him in faint surprise.

'Do you think your ability is equal to Daniel's?'

'Yes, but different in kind.'

'Any sign of self-respect is a good thing,' said Daniel. 'The respect of others may follow.'

'I think it often comes first,' said his brother.

'Mother,' said Luce, looking after the two young men, 'do you know that you treat those boys quite differently?'

'A mother often has an especial feeling for her eldest son.'

'Isn't that hard on the second one? It does not follow that he is inferior.'

'He does not think he is,' said Eleanor, in a tone of seeing a new light on the position. 'So it has not had much effect on him.'

'It may have had the more for that, Mother.'

'I must try to be more impartial. I see that Graham has developed a good deal lately.'

'Mother, you do honestly try to put right anything that is wrong,' said Luce, looking at Eleanor with gentle appraisement.

'I know you think my heart is in the right place,' said Eleanor, with a note of dryness.

'And why is that a poor compliment? It is the most fundamental of all things, in the sense that nothing counts without it.'

'Perhaps that is why we never hear that a heart is anywhere else.'

'Mother – you are a truer parent of your sons than you know,' said Luce, going into silent laughter, with her eyes on Eleanor.

Chapter 2

'Hatton in a big bed, Nevill in a little bed,' said Nevill Sullivan surveying the scene of which he spoke.

'Lie still and go to sleep,' said the nurse.

'Hatton get up,' said Nevill, in a tone of agreement.

'Shut your eyes and try to sleep.'

'Shut his eyes,' said Nevill, keeping them shut with a trembling of the lids.

'Don't take any notice of me while I dress.'

'Watch Hatton,' said Nevill, turning on his side with the purpose.

'Now you are wide awake. You must rest until I am ready. You went to sleep very late.'

'As late as Hatton.'

'Yes, nearly as late.'

'As late as Hatton,' said Nevill, on a higher note.

'Yes, as late as that. That means you are tired this morning.'

'He is tired,' said Nevill, leaning back on his pillows.

'Here are Honor and Gavin coming to see you.'

'No,' said Nevill, in a tone of repudiating the prospect.

'Don't you want to see them?'

'No. Just Hatton and Nevill.'

'They have come to say good-morning.'

Nevill looked his question of this purpose, and his brother and sister ran into the room at a halt in their morning toilet, followed by a nursemaid baulked in her intention of completing it. The girl was a solid, lively-looking child of ten, with a fair, oval face, observant, grey eyes made smaller by the roundness of her cheeks, thick bright hair, small hands and feet, and a benevolent, interested, rather complacent expression. Her brother was a ponderous, drab-coloured boy a year younger, with blunter features and large, pale, steady eyes; and Nevill was a brown-eyed, flaxen-haired child of three, with an ambition to continue in his infancy and meet the treatment accorded to it.

'He is tired this morning,' he said, looking at the others with an eye at once pathetic and observant. 'He went to sleep as late as Hatton.'

'And what does that signify?' said Honor, giving a spring.

Gavin looked at her and followed her example, the method by which he gave the normal amount of activity to his life.

'They shake the room,' said Nevill, uneasily, to Hatton.

Honor and Gavin leapt about the floor, less damped by Hatton's indifference than spurred by the nursemaid's protests. Bertha Mullet was a freckled, healthy-looking girl of twenty-two, with eyes and hair and brows of the same fox-red colour, and something foxlike in the moulding of her face. She would sometimes push up her cheeks towards her eyes, and entertain the children with a representation of this creature, regarding the power as a simple asset, and supported in the view by Honor and Gavin, and more dubiously by Nevill, who found the performance realistic. Emma Hatton was a short, square woman of an age which had never been revealed, but revealed itself as about fifty-five, with a square, dark face, large, kind hands, deep, small, dark eyes, stiff, iron-grey hair, and a look of superiority, which was recognized and justified. She was a farmer's daughter, who saw the training of children as her vocation and therefore pursued it. Honor and Gavin regarded her as the centre of their world, and Nevill expended on her the force of a nature diverted by nobody else. Her assistant looked up to her and bowed to her rule, but found in Honor a more equal, indeed a completely equal companionship.

'Leap into the air,' chanted Honor, proceeding by this method round the room.

Gavin repeated the words and the action.

'Leap into the air,' said Nevill to Hatton, in a tone that made his words a request to be assisted to follow the example.

'No, you must rest a little longer.'

'He must rest,' said Nevill, in an explanatory tone to the others.

'Why don't you think of something to do yourself, Master Gavin?' said Mullet, who had viewed the proceedings with a serious eye.

'Because I don't want to,' said Gavin, giving an extra jump, by way of displaying a certain initiative.

'He will think of something,' said Nevill, nodding to Hatton in encouragement upon his own future.

'How old are you, Hatton?' said Honor, in an incidental tone.

'Older than you, but not a hundred,' said Hatton, automatically.

'Hatton is a hundred,' said Nevill, with pride. 'Not yet, but very soon.'

'Here is the mistress on the stairs! Here is your mother come to say good-morning to you,' said Mullet, in a rather bustling manner.

Honor began to fasten her garments, as if to be employed would give a better impression; Mullet drew her towards her and took the task into her own hands; Hatton and Nevill were unaffected; and Gavin's unconcern was so marked that it became a positive condition.

'Well, my little ones,' said the voice that hardly varied with the people it addressed, 'so you are back from the sea. Did you have a happy time? Are you tired after your journey? Is no one going to answer me?'

Nevill laid hold of Hatton's dress and raised eyes of disapprobation and apprehension to her face.

'Are you coming to kiss me, my boy?' said Eleanor.

Gavin approached and suffered an embrace, and Honor followed his example.

'It was a pity I had to be out last night. It was a dull homecoming for you. I wish I could have helped it.'

'Mother couldn't help it,' said Nevill, in a condoning manner.

'We had Grandma,' said Gavin.

'But that was not the same,' said his mother.

'No, it was different.'

'It was better, wasn't it?' said Nevill, in an obliging tone.

'Honor kissed me, as well as letting me kiss her, Gavin,' said Eleanor.

Gavin did not answer, and his mother turned to Nevill's bed, as though she felt it hardly fitting that he should receive her under such conditions.

'Is anything the matter with him, Hatton?'

'He is only tired, madam. He went to sleep very late.'

'As late as Hatton,' said Nevill.

'Was he not in bed at the usual time?'

'We were at home too late for that, madam. And he could not sleep in a strange room.'

'A strange room? It is his own night nursery.'

'Yes, but he had forgotten it.'

'He had forgotten it,' Nevill explained to his mother.

'Could not someone sit with him?'

'Mullet and I were unpacking, madam. And no one else would have done.'

'No one but Hatton,' said Nevill.

'He hardly looks as if he had been to the sea.'

'People would not look different,' said Gavin.

'Hatton did sit with him for a little while,' said Nevill, more in condonation of Hatton than in information to his mother.

'Don't cover your face, dear,' said the latter, drawing down the clothes.

'No,' said Nevill, in a sharper tone, pulling them back.

'You will not be able to breathe properly.'

'He never breathes,' said Nevill, and closed his eyes.

'Isn't he growing rather a wilful little boy?'

'He is tired, as you say, madam. He will soon be himself.'

'Mother didn't say so,' said Gavin.

'You had better keep him in bed,' said Eleanor, suggesting an uncongenial course both for Hatton and her son.

'He will get up now, madam, and rest before his dinner.'

'In his little bed,' said Nevill, and changed his tone the next moment. 'Get up now.'

'Then I will go downstairs and come up when they are up and dressed.'

'We are up now,' said Gavin.

'Will you come again to see us?' said Nevill, leaning out of the bed to take hold of his mother's skirt and raise his eyes to her face.

'Yes, of course Mother will come to see her little boy.'

'Now she has gone,' said Nevill, in a satisfied tone, as the door closed.

'Oh, and you said you wanted her to come again,' said Mullet, with reproach.

'Nevill fawns on people,' said Honor.

'He doesn't,' said Nevill. 'He won't marry Honor when he is grown-up.'

Nevill's consistent use of the third person for himself suggested a cultivation of infantine habit.

'You can't marry your sister,' said Gavin.

'He can marry who he wants to. And he will marry Hatton.'

'Hatton and Nevill are engaged!' said Honor, with more contempt for the condition than for the unsuitability of the parties.

'Hatton will like it,' said Nevill.

'Why can't brothers and sisters marry?' said Gavin.

'Because they have to start a family,' said his sister. 'If they married people in the same one, there would never be any new ones. But they can live together.'

'Do they have any children then?'

'I don't think they do so often. But they can adopt some.'

'He will be your little boy,' promised Nevill in full comprehension.

'Nevill is one of the baser creatures,' said Gavin.

'He isn't,' said Nevill, clutching at Hatton's skirt and pointing to his brother. 'He is the same as him.'

'If people knew we had a baser creature, we should be prosecuted,' said Honor.

'What is prosecuted?' said Gavin.

'Put in prison.'

'They will be put in prison,' said Nevill, in a comfortable tone to Hatton. 'It is because they don't like him to be best.'

'Why should we mind what he is?' said Gavin.

'I wish you did not mind so much,' said Hatton, causing Mullet some amusement. 'It is past the time for your breakfast. Nevill must come in his dressing-gown.'

'Not much appetite,' said Nevill, leaning back in his chair.

'You will eat like a baser creature,' said Gavin.

'He was sick in the train,' said Nevill, disposing of the suggestion.

'So was Honor.'

'But he wasn't,' said Nevill to Hatton, indicating his brother.

'No, Gavin was my choice at that moment,' said Hatton.

'No, he was,' said Nevill, clutching at her arm and speaking in reference to what had taken place.

'We were all rather uncivilized,' said Honor.

'He was too,' said Nevill, nodding.

'You are three children come back to your home after a period of exile,' said Mullet, speaking as if she were beginning a tale.

'We haven't got a home,' said Gavin. 'This home is Grandpa's. It is because we are poor.'

'You are not,' said Mullet, in a sharper tone.

'Mother said we were.'

'That sort of poorness in your kind of family is different.'

'It is better, isn't it?' said Nevill, in a consoling tone.

'It is considered superior to the money of ordinary people.'

'Why aren't we ordinary?' said Honor.

'You are, until you prove you are not,' said Hatton.

'Youngest are best,' said Nevill.

'You won't be the youngest, if there is another baby,' said Honor.

Nevill regarded her for a moment.

'He will,' he said.

'That can be his distinction for the present,' said Hatton, leaving the table on some errand.

'I do think Hatton does talk beautifully,' said Mullet, in a tone that seemed a reproach to the existing social order. 'As pointed and as finished as any lady.'

'Pointed?' said Gavin.

'To the point,' said Honor.

'Hatton does it, doesn't she?' said Nevill, looking up into Mullet's face.

'Now we must not let time steal a march on us,' said Hatton, returning and using a rather conscious tone.

'Why mustn't we?' said Nevill. 'Why mustn't we, Hatton?'

'There is a lot to be done by tomorrow, when the new governess comes.'

'Not for him is she coming?'

'Not for you as much as the others. You will go in for half an hour.'

'She will like him, won't she, when he goes in?'

'Nevill says she will like him!' said Honor.

'I daresay she will at this stage,' said Hatton. 'It is later that the crux comes.'

'Crux?' said Gavin.

'Crisis,' said his sister.

'Hatton will come and fetch him,' said Nevill.

'I have had two governesses,' said Honor. 'I know the tricks of the trade.'

'Yes, you know, we know them,' said Gavin.

'He doesn't want to,' said Nevill.

'And the nature of the beasts,' said Honor.

'And the snares of the way and the obstacles of the race and all of it,' said Hatton, in an easy, rapid tone, keeping her eyes from Mullet and her hands employed. 'But that does not prevent you from attending to your breakfast.'

'It does do it,' said Nevill, putting his hand on her arm. 'It does, Hatton.'

Eleanor's voice came again at the door.

'Well, are you happy to be at home? Have you begun to feel brighter for your time at the sea?' she said, with a suggestion that this reaction had as yet been prevented in her children.

It seemed to her that it was still delayed.

'I think they do look better, Hatton. Honor was well before, but the boys were too thin. Now tell me how you enjoyed your holiday. Did you like it, Honor dear?'

'Yes, thank you, Mother.'

'Haven't you any more to say about it than that? Why, you went to the sea, and had rooms taken for you, and Hatton and Mullet there to take care of you, and had three weeks in a lovely place by the sands and waves. Now didn't you enjoy it all, and find it a treat?'

'It wasn't a lovely place,' said Gavin. 'It was all houses and streets. And we always have Hatton and Mullet.'

'But there had to be houses, or there wouldn't have been one for you to stay in.'

'There could have been just that one house.'

'But how would you have got anything to eat, if there had been no shops?'

'There could have been one like the one in the village, that sells most things.'

'It sells string,' said Nevill.

'But you wanted things to eat like those you have at home. And they don't come from the shop.'

'We didn't have them even as nice as that,' said Honor.

'You don't know when you are well off,' said Eleanor, laughing before she knew. 'I suppose all children are the same.'

'Well, the same and different,' said Honor.

'Hatton buy him a ball,' said Nevill.

'Why, you have one there,' said Eleanor, looking at some toys on the ground.

'No,' said Nevill, in a tone of repulsing her words.

'You don't want another, do you?'

'No,' said Nevill, in the same manner, shaking his head and a moment later his body.

'What does he want, Hatton?'

'Ball of string,' said Nevill, in a tone that suggested that the actual words were forced from him.

'Oh, that is what you want. Well, I daresay you can have one.'

'There is a kind that only costs a penny,' said Gavin.

'It costs a penny,' said Nevill, in a grave tone. 'But Hatton buy it for him.'

'Well, Honor dear, tell me about the holiday. What did you like best?'

'I think the beach,' said Honor.

'That was all there was,' said Gavin. 'The lodgings weren't nice.'

'Weren't they? What was wrong with them? Were they not good ones, Hatton?'

'Yes, madam, they were clean and pleasant. The children mean that the rooms were smaller than these.'

'This home will be a disadvantage to them. It will teach them to expect too much. Now have you really nothing to tell me, but that the rooms here had spoiled you for others?'

'We didn't tell you that,' said Gavin.

'He found a little crab,' said Nevill. 'It was as small as a crumb.'

'Well, that was something,' said Eleanor. 'You played on the beach, and found crabs, and found a lot of other interesting things, didn't you?'

'Not a lot,' said Gavin. 'We found an old net and a piece of wood from a ship.'

'We weren't sure it was from a ship,' said his sister.

'From a little boat,' suggested Nevill.

'And didn't you find seaweed and shells, and wade in the sea and build castles and do things like that?'

'We did when it was fine,' said Honor.

'And was it often wet?'

'No – yes – two days,' said Honor, meeting her mother's eyes and averting her own.

'Well, that was not much out of three weeks. They do not seem to appreciate things, Hatton. When I was a child, I should have remembered the holiday for years.'

'They will do the same, madam. And it has done what we wanted of it. But the truth is that children are happier at home. And it is fortunate it is not the other way round.'

'We found one shell that was not broken,' said Nevill, in further reassurance.

'So you love your home, my little ones,' said Eleanor, making the best of her children's attitude. 'Of course you are glad to be back again. And you have Father and Mother to welcome you. You have been without them all the time. So it couldn't be perfect, could it?'

'We have Grandpa and Grandma too,' said Nevill. 'And Grandma wasn't out, was she?'

'Yes, you have Mother and Father and Grandma and Grandpa', said Eleanor, adjusting the order of these personalities. 'And your brothers and sisters, and your new governess coming tomorrow.'

'He has Hatton,' said her youngest son.

'It is the same nursery as Grandpa had, when he was a little boy like you.'

'Not like him,' said Nevill.

'Well, when he was as small as you. He used to play in it, as you do.'

'Not as small as him; as small as Gavin.'

'Yes, as small as you, and even smaller. He was here when he was a baby. You like to think of that, don't you?'

'He couldn't come in it now,' said Nevill. 'Hatton wouldn't let him.'

'Now, Honor dear,' said Eleanor, turning from her son to her daughter, perhaps a natural step, 'I hope you will try with this new governess, and not play and pay no attention, as you did with the last. You are old enough to begin to learn.'

'I have been learning for a long time.'

'It keeps Gavin back as well as you. And we should not do what is bad for someone else.'

'It is only being with me, that makes Gavin learn at all.'

'Well, well, dear, do your best. That is all we ask of you. But if you have such an opinion of yourself, we can expect a good deal of you.'

'I only said I didn't keep Gavin back, when you said I did.'

'Dear me, Hatton, girls are even less easy than boys,' said Eleanor, with a sigh.

'It is the person you are talking to, that you don't think is easy,' said Gavin.

'I daresay it sums up like that,' said his mother.

'Father likes girls better,' said Honor.

'He is a girlie,' said Nevill, recalling his father's attitude to his sisters. 'He likes Father better too.'

'You are a boy,' said Gavin. 'As much a boy as I am.'

'No, not as much. He is a little boy.'

'Yes, yes, a little boy,' said Mullet, taking his hand and speaking for Eleanor's ears. 'And now the little boy has had his breakfast, he must come and put on his coat for the garden.'

'Like a girlie,' said Nevill, in a tone of making a condition.

'Yes, like that. And when you come in, I will tell you a story about some children who had a new governess. You will all like that, won't you?'

'I would rather have one about a wrecker,' said Gavin, who had hardly done justice to the influence of the sea.

Eleanor looked after Mullet and Nevill with a smile for Hatton.

'You don't give me much of a welcome,' she said to the other children. 'Do you think of me as an ordinary person, who may come in at any time?'

'You do come in often,' said Gavin.

'You must remember I am your mother.'

'A lot of people are mothers. Hatton's sister is.'

'My honest boy!' said Eleanor, suddenly kissing her son. 'Now what is it, Honor dear? You seem put out about something. Do you know what it is, Gavin?'

'It is when you make me out better than she is.'

'Well, she does not always think people just alike, herself.'

'I do when they are,' said Honor.

'Well, I expect you are tired by your journey. Were they upset by the train, Hatton?'

'Honor and Nevill were, madam. Gavin never is.'

'I was sick almost the whole time,' said Honor.

'Dear, dear, poor Hatton and Mullet!' said Eleanor, in a bracing tone. 'Well, I must go and see if the others have anything that does not please them. We must not give all the attention to one part of the house.'

'We didn't say we were not pleased,' said Gavin, when his mother had gone.

'Neither did Mother,' said Honor. 'But she palpably was not.'

Hatton dispatched the three to the garden in the charge of Mullet, who walked up and down telling stories, with them all hanging on to her arms. When the time for exercise was over, she was the only one who had had any exercise, and she had had a good deal.

Eleanor went to the schoolroom to visit the next section of her family. She found two girls and a boy seated at the table with their governess, engaged in scanning an atlas, which could only be surveyed by them singly, and therefore lent itself to slow progress. This was their customary rate of advance, as Miss Mitford was a person of easy pace, and it was the family practice to economize in materials rather than in time. It seldom struck Eleanor or Regan that a few shillings might be well spent. Shillings were never well spent to them, only by necessity or compulsion. Two governesses came under the last head, and money was allotted to the purpose, but to do them justice in the smallest possible amount.

'Well, my dears,' said Eleanor, her tone rendered warm by her sense that these children probably differed from the others, 'you have not been to the sea. You have been at home and been bright and happy all the time. I believe it never pays to do too much for children.'

'No,' said James, the youngest of the three, making an accommodating movement.

'You would just as soon be at home, wouldn't you?'

'Yes.'

'Wouldn't you, Isabel?'

'Yes.'

'Wouldn't you, my Venice?'

'I am not quite sure. No, I don't think I would.'

'You would like to go to the sea?' said Eleanor, with a surprise that would have seemed more natural to a witness of the late scene. 'We must see about it next year. What do you think, Miss Mitford?'

Miss Mitford looked up in response, but not in response of any particular nature. She was a short, rather odd-looking woman of fifty, looking older than her age, with calm, green eyes, features so indeterminate that they seemed to change, and hair and clothes disposed in a manner which appeared to be her own, but had really been everyone's at the time when she grew up. It had seemed to her the mark of womanhood, and it still served that purpose. She was a person of reading and intelligence, but preferred a family to a school, and knew that by taking a post beneath her claims, she took her employers in her hand. She held them with unflinching calm and without giving any quarter, and criticism, after she had met it with surprise and had not bent to it, had not assailed her. Eleanor was hardly afraid of her, as she did not feel that kind of fear, but she hesitated to judge or advise her, and seldom inquired of her pupils' progress except of the pupils behind her back.

James joined his sisters on such days as a recurring and undefined indisposition kept him from school, occasions which did not involve his dispensing with education. They were actually the only ones when he did not do so, as he was a boy who could only learn from a woman in his home. The stage at which he could learn, but only under certain conditions, had never received attention. He was a boy of twelve, with liquid, brown eyes like Nevill's, features regarded as pretty and childish, and vaguely deprecated on that ground, and a responsive, innocent, sometimes suddenly sophisticated expression. His dependence on Hatton at Nevill's age had exceeded his brother's, and still went beyond anyone else's. If Hatton could have betrayed a preference, it would have been for him; and it sent a ray of light through his rather shadowed life to remember that at heart she had one.

Isabel was a short, pale girl of fifteen, with a face that was a gentle edition of Fulbert's, delicate hands like Honor's, a humorous expression of her own, and near-sighted, penetrating eyes; and Venetia, known as Venice, was a large, dark, handsome child a year and a half younger, with a steady, high colour and fine, closely-set, hazel eyes, and an amiability covering a resolute self-esteem, which was beginning to show in her expression, though only Isabel was aware of it. The two sisters lived for each other, as did Honor and Gavin; and James lived to himself like Nevill, but with less support, so that his life had a certain pathos. He would remedy matters by repairing to the nursery, where Hatton's welcome and Honor's inclination to a senior brought Nevill to open, and Gavin to secret despair. The suffering of his brothers was pleasant to James, not because he was malicious or hostile, but because the evidence of sadness in other lives made him feel a being less apart. He showed no aptitude for books, and this in his sex was condemned; and he carried a sense of guilt, which it did not occur to him was unmerited. It was a time when endeavour in children was rated below success, an error which in later years has hardly yet been corrected, so that childhood was a more accurate foretaste of life than it is now.

'So you are not at school, my boy?' said Eleanor.

'No,' said James, giving a little start and looking at Isabel.

'He does not feel well,' said the latter.

'Doesn't he?' said Eleanor, with rather dubious sympathy, as if not quite sure of the authenticity of the condition. 'The unwellness seems to come rather often. It is kind of Miss Mitford to let you be in here. Have you thanked her?'

'No.'

'Then do it, my dear.'

'Thank you,' said James, without loss of composure, having no objection to being treated as a child, indeed finding it his natural treatment.

'He is not much above the average, is he, Miss Mitford?' said Eleanor, not entertaining the possibility of an absolutely ordinary child.

'No, I don't think he is.'

'You think he is up to it at any rate?'

'Well, I did not say so. Perhaps it was you who did.'

'Do you think he would learn more with his sisters at home?'

'You mean with their governess, don't you? Well, a good many boys would.'

'But I suppose we cannot arrange it?'

'No, you must be the slave of convention.'

'I suppose most boys are backward.'

'Well, some are forward.'

'You must make Miss Mitford think better of you, James.'

'I hope you do not think I take an ungenerous view,' said Miss Mitford.

'Do you never alter your opinions?' said Eleanor, with a faint sting in her tone.

'I seldom need to. My judgement is swift and strong,' said Miss Mitford, with no loss of gravity.

'Could you not help James, Isabel?'

'Not as well as Miss Mitford.'

'Could you, Venice? You are nearer his age.'

'Is that a qualification?' said Isabel.

'It would help her to see his point of view.'

'It might make her share it.'

'You think the girls are intelligent at any rate, Miss Mitford?' said Eleanor, seeking to turn this readiness to account.

'It is a good sign that they think so.'

'Do you never praise anyone?'

'I am rather grudging in that way. It is a sort of shyness.'

Venice gave a giggle.

'Are you not going to say a word to me, Venice?' said Eleanor.

'Yes,' said Venice, in a bright, conscious tone, turning wide eyes on her mother. 'I was thinking about the sea. I should like to go next year.'

'And so you shall, my dear. I wish I had arranged it. I ought to have thought of a change for you. And I could have sent James with Hatton. It would have done him good. Don't you think it would, Miss Mitford?'

'Yes.'

'But you did not suggest it.'

'No.'

'Miss Mitford knows that suggestions cost money,' said Isabel.

'They cost nothing, my child. I am always pleased to have them. It is carrying them out that costs.'

'My suggestions are not any good, when they are not carried out,' said Miss Mitford, in a faintly plaintive tone.

'Well, I hope you will make them another time. Good-bye, my dears; I will come up again and see you. James, do you forget again to open the door?'

James could not deny it.

'Does he generally, Miss Mitford?'

'Yes.'

'Does he not open the door for you?'

'No.'

'You must remember you are not a baby, mustn't you, James?'

'Yes,' said James, who had little chance of thinking he was, as the family steadily combated the supposed conviction.

'Could you remember to tell him, Miss Mitford?'

'Well, my memory is no better than his.'

'Then the girls must remember. Will you think of it, my dears? Now, my boy, if you are to be at home today, you must have tea in the nursery and go early to bed. When we are not well, we must not behave quite like well people, must we?'

'No,' said James, who had no great leaning towards the routine of the healthy, which he found a strain.

'Why is he to have tea in the nursery?' said Miss Mitford, as the door closed.

'The tea there is earlier than ours,' said Venice.

'Mother hasn't a favourite in this room,' said Isabel.

'I somehow feel it is not me,' said Miss Mitford. 'And my instinct is generally right in those ways.'

'I don't want to be one of her favoured ones,' said Venice, who had a familiar sense of meeting too little esteem.

'She only likes two people in the house, Daniel and Gavin,' said Isabel.

'And I like so many,' said Miss Mitford. 'I must have a more affectionate nature.'

'She likes Father and Luce,' said James, just looking up from his book.

'That is true,' said Miss Mitford. 'I hope it is the history book that you are reading, James.'

'Yes,' said James, who was perusing a more human portion of this volume, indeed an intensely human one, as it dealt with the elaborate execution of a familiar character. When any trouble or constraint was over, he allowed it to drift from his mind.

'What is the time?' said Venice.

'Two minutes to your break for luncheon,' said Miss Mitford, in an encouraging tone.

'You like your luncheon too, Mitta.'

'You must not call me Mitta except in a spirit of affection. And it is not often affectionate to tell people they like their food.'

'Here it comes!' said James, throwing his book on the table and himself into a chair.

'I am punctual today,' said Mullet, entering in understanding of the life she interrupted, and viewed with sympathy as inferior to that of the nursery. 'And Hatton says, if Master James has a headache, he may ask Miss Mitford to excuse his lessons this morning.'

James at once rose, selected some biscuits and a book and arranged a table and the sofa for the reception of them and himself. He did not look at Miss Mitford nor she at him. Hatton's word was law in the schoolroom, as Miss Mitford chose to accept it as such, pursuing with it the opposite course to that she took with other people's.

'Miss Isabel, look at your hair,' said Mullet, as if the vigour of the enjoinder rendered it possible.

'Hatton said I was not to touch it myself, because I tear at it.'

'Then you should come upstairs to have it done. I wonder the mistress did not notice it.'

'How do you know she did not?' said Miss Mitford.

'She would have sent her up to have it done,' said Venice, who managed her own with care and competence.

'Perhaps that is why it is shorter than Venice's, because you pull it,' said James, turning a serious eye from the sofa.

'You pull it often enough yourself,' said Isabel.

'I never pull any out,' said James, in defence of his own course, returning to his book.

'Why should we go down to dessert twice a day?' said Venice.

'Just to make the household as odd as possible,' said Isabel.

'You get twice as much dessert,' said Miss Mitford.

'Will you have tea or coffee after your dinner, ma'am?' said Mullet.

'I think coffee is more sustaining, as I don't have dessert.'

Mullet laughed, and the children did so with more abandonment, taking the chance of venting their mirth over Miss Mitford's practice of broaching private stores while they were downstairs. It merely made her meal correspond with theirs, but they thought it a habit of a certain grossness and never alluded to it to her face.

'Shall I tell Cook to send up the things you like?' said Mullet.

'It might be suspected that we had asked,' said Isabel.

James raised his eyes in survey of the situation.

'The little ones are going down before their dinner, so you

won't have them,' said Mullet, in encouraging sympathy with intolerance of the creatures to whom her own life was given. 'The nursery dinner is late. And now I must take my tray.'

'I will go up to Hatton about my hair,' said Isabel.

'Don't put off your lessons longer than you must,' said Miss Mitford, in a tone of rejoinder.

'There is only one book,' said Isabel, implying a sacrifice of opportunity to her sister.

'Why don't they do different lessons at the same time?' said James, without moving his eyes.

'We might find it a strain,' said Miss Mitford.

Mullet went to fetch the children from the garden, and Eleanor met her coming up the stairs, with the three of them clinging to her.

'Dear, dear, can't any of you walk alone? Mullet will need to have several pairs of arms and legs.'

'Mullet help him,' said Nevill, with a note of defiance.

'She seems to be helping the others too. I think you must all have a rest this morning.'

'Hatton sit on his little bed,' said Nevill, as he entered the nursery.

'I have not time this morning. Mullet will stay with you for a while.'

'Mother likes us to be alone while we go to sleep,' said Gavin.

'Her standard is too high for Nevill,' said Hatton. 'And I notice it sometimes is for you.'

Honor broke into mirth.

'Don't you mind what she says?' said Gavin, with a note of respect.

'Hatton doesn't mind,' said Nevill, with tenderness and pride.

'The mistress said they were all to rest,' said Mullet.

'Well, that is not beyond us,' said Hatton. 'And there need be no delay.'

Presently Gavin awoke with a cry, and Eleanor came to his bedside. She found him sitting up, in the act of receiving a glass of water from Hatton, his demeanour accepting his situation as serious, and this view of it in others.

'What is it, my boy?'

'I want Honor to wake.'
'Did you have a dream?'
'No.'
'Tell Mother what it is.'
'It is nothing.'
'Is it burglars?' said Honor, suddenly sitting up straight.
'No, Gavin has had a dream and wants to tell you.'
'I don't,' said Gavin, turning away his head.
'What is it?' said his sister, in a rough tone that cleared his face.
'It was a sort of a dream.'
'Were you afraid?'
'No.'
'Will you tell me after dinner?'
'Yes.'
'It was kind of Honor to wake,' said Eleanor.
Gavin did not reply.
'Don't you think it was?'
'She thought it was burglars,' said Gavin, and turned on his side.
'What is wrong with them, Hatton?' said Eleanor.
'Only the journey, madam. They will be themselves tomorrow.'
'I wonder the human race has been so fond of migrations, when the young take so hardly to travelling,' said Eleanor, with her occasional dryness.

Mullet fell into laughter and hastily left the room, as though feeling it familiar to meet an employer's jest with the equal response of mirth. Honor looked at her mother and laughed in her turn, and Gavin surveyed them with a frown.

Chapter 3

Eleanor went downstairs to the dining-room, where her husband, his parents and his three eldest children were assembled for luncheon.

'Hatton continues to manage the little ones in her own way. I suppose it would do no good to interfere.'

'What is wrong with the method?' said Fulbert, seeming to gather himself together for judgement.

'A good many things that only a mother would see.'

'Then we cannot expect Hatton to be aware of them.'

'Nor the rest of us, Mother dear,' said Luce. 'You must not look for sympathy. I am always thankful that I had the same nurse when I was young. It takes any anxiety for the children simply off me.'

'Hatton will rule the house in the end,' said Eleanor.

'A good many of you seem to be doing that,' said Sir Jesse. 'But if too many cooks spoil the broth, the right number make it very good.'

'It is a real achievement, the way you all work together,' said Fulbert. 'I mean to pay you a serious compliment.'

'You talk as if you were a creature apart,' said Eleanor.

'Yes, you do, Father,' said Luce.

'Have you two lads forgotten your tongues?' said Fulbert.

'I had a hope of it,' said Sir Jesse.

'I don't think I forbade you to speak, Graham,' said Daniel.

'Did you change your room, Luce, my dear?' said Regan.

'Yes, I am having Graham's, Grandma.'

'What is this about changing rooms?' said Eleanor. 'It is the first I have heard of it.'

'Luce wants more light,' said Daniel. 'So we are arranging for Graham to do without it.'

'Well, what use is it to him?' said Sir Jesse, who resented any aspersion on his house. 'To look at himself in the glass? He can give way to his sister there.'

'I was the natural person to consult,' said Eleanor.

'Well, Mother dear, Grandma seemed just as much so,' said Luce. 'Perhaps more, as the house is hers.'

Eleanor was silent, submitting to the place she had accepted, and Regan gave her an almost sympathetic glance.

'The children are on the stairs,' said Daniel. 'They will have their dessert at an odd time today.'

'They had better dispense with it,' said Eleanor.

'That is seldom a happy solution,' said Fulbert. 'Things in the wrong order won't hurt them for once.'

Nevill ran into the room in the manner of a horse, lifting his feet and head in recognizable imitation.

'So you are a horse today,' said his mother.

'A charger, a little charger.'

'Chargers are big,' said Gavin.

'No,' said Nevill, shaking his head in a manner at once equine and negative; 'a little charger.'

'A pony,' suggested Daniel.

'A pony,' agreed Nevill.

'Ponies are always small,' said Regan.

'Always small,' said Nevill, on a contented note.

'Do you want me to go on with the tale?' said Luce.

Nevill trotted to her side and stood with his hand on her knee, and his eyes on her face.

'I don't remember if I like it,' said Gavin.

'It is Nevill's tale,' said Honor.

'But you can all listen,' said Eleanor.

'His tale,' said Nevill, throwing them a look.

'Can you tell me where we left off?' said Luce.

'No,' said Nevill, rapidly moving his feet. 'Don't let Gavin tell you. Luce tell Nevill.'

'Don't you remember yourself?'

'No.'

'And it is your tale,' said Eleanor.

'He doesn't remember,' said Nevill, striking Luce's knee.

'Read us a piece out of the book,' said Gavin.

'Well, get it and find the place,' said Luce. 'We have only a few minutes.'

Honor obeyed with speed and success, and Gavin waited while she did so, and joined her to listen.

'Why do you leave it all to Honor?' said Eleanor, who was not happy in the child whom she singled out for achievement.

Gavin kept his eyes on his sister's face. Nevill turned away and resumed his imitation of a pony, trying to distinguish the movements from those of a horse.

'Well, is no one coming to talk to me?' said Eleanor. 'Why did you all come down?'

Gavin did not allow his attention to be diverted, and Luce

read on, as if she would not undertake a thing and not accomplish it.

'I must ring for Hatton to fetch you, if you haven't any reason for being here. Luce can read to you upstairs.'

'She never does,' said Gavin, in a parenthetic tone.

'We can't have your mother left out in the cold.'

Nevill paused in his prancing and glanced at Eleanor; Sir Jesse and Regan remained aloof, claiming no part in the separate family life; Fulbert beckoned to Honor and lifted her to his knee; Gavin did not move his eyes and frowned at the interruptions.

'Now we don't want any fallen faces,' said Eleanor, putting her arm round Nevill, and looking for the change which she described, or rather suggested. 'You will know how to stay another time.'

'Go with Hatton,' said Nevill, in an acquiescent tone.

'We should have had to go soon because of our dinner,' said Honor, in a confident manner from Fulbert's knee.

'Don't you want to go, my boy?' said Eleanor to Gavin.

'I don't mind.'

'Well, run away then.'

Gavin looked at her and sank into tears.

'Honor, is Gavin quite well?'

'Yes, I think so, Mother.'

'Then what is the matter with him?'

Honor met her mother's eyes.

Daniel and Graham picked up Honor and carried her round the room. She put her arms round their necks and laughed and shouted in reaction. Eleanor looked on with an indulgent smile, and Gavin with an expectant one. Nevill beat his hands on his sides and moved from foot to foot; and when his brothers took Gavin in Honor's stead, broke into wails and maintained them until they came to himself, when he repulsed them and stood abandoned to his sense that nothing could wipe out what had taken place. When Eleanor and Luce had expostulated in vain, and Regan explained with some success, he raised his arms and allowed himself to be lifted, leaning back in his brothers' arms with an air of convalescence. They tightened their hold and quickened their pace, and he held to their shoulders and accepted this compensation for what he had borne, while Honor watched with bright eyes, and Gavin with a smile of gentle interest.

'Give Gavin one little turn, and then that is enough,' said Eleanor.

Nevill stood with his arm on Regan's knee, and his eyes on his brothers with a watchful expression. Hatton arrived in response to the sounds that had reached her ears.

'Say "Thank you", Gavin dear. You heard Honor say it,' said Eleanor.

Gavin did so.

'And look at Daniel and Graham while you speak.'

Gavin turned his eyes on his brothers, content with fulfilling his obligations separately.

'It was him that ran,' said Nevill, with a sigh.

'I suppose it is still the journey, Hatton,' said Eleanor, with another.

'It was best to cry it out, madam, whatever it was.'

'He cried it out,' said Nevill, in information to Hatton.

'Come and give me a kiss, and then run away,' said Eleanor.

Nevill went to her with a trotting step, took Hatton's hand and proceeded in this way towards the door.

'So you are a horse again. Daniel and Graham have been your horses, haven't they?'

'Pony, little pony,' said Nevill, seeming oblivious of his brothers.

'Isn't the little pony going to trot to say good-bye to Father?'

'Only to Grandma,' said Nevill, and trotted past Regan and then through the door.

Honor and Gavin kissed their parents and frolicked from the room, their voices sounding high and continuous until they reached the upper floor.

Regan had witnessed the scene with interest, and Sir Jesse without attention. The latter seldom noticed children, rather because it did not occur to him to do so, than because he disapproved of the practice.

'Their new governess is coming tomorrow,' said Luce. 'I do trust she will be a success.'

'Why doesn't Miss – Miss who teaches the others, teach them?' said Sir Jesse.

'Grandpa, you must know Miss Mitford's name after all these years,' said Luce. 'I expect she knows yours.'

'Why, so do I, my dear. And in that case she does the better, as you say.'

'I don't know who would dare to make the suggestion,' said Eleanor.

'Why, is there any risk?' said Sir Jesse. 'If so, I beg no one will take it. But isn't teaching her business? What she does – what she chooses to do, I should say?'

'I doubt if there is so much choice about it,' said Regan.

'In so far as there is, she exercises it,' said Eleanor. 'Her pupils must be in a certain stage. James had to go to school, because she found him too young.'

'I daresay the girls give her less trouble,' said Sir Jesse. 'If she has the right to choose, let her use it. But wouldn't one woman for the lot cost less?'

'We should have to increase her salary by as much as we are to give the other,' said Regan.

'So the other has not much choice,' said her husband, with amusement and no other feeling. 'Have as many as you like, if it is all for the same expense. I would rather be in a place where I got it all. But as you say, or as Miss Mitford says.'

'Grandma does not shrink from exposing the whole of her mind,' said Graham. 'That is a very rare thing.'

Regan smiled at her grandson before she resumed the subject.

'Miss Mitford would never take a hint,' she said.

'I hardly like to do so myself,' said Daniel.

'She is quite right,' said Luce. 'If we are ashamed of what we ask, there is no reason to help us. And it would be more strain to teach three extra children.'

'I don't think Miss Mitford suffers much in that way,' said Regan. 'She takes great care of herself.'

'There is nothing wrong in that, Grandma.'

'We do find the habit unengaging,' said Fulbert. 'But in Miss Mitford's place I should recommend it.'

Regan gave her son a look of admiration for his freedom from her own failings.

'Isn't the little fellow too young to learn?' said Daniel.

'Why can't you call your brother by his name?' said Eleanor. 'He would not forget yours.'

'We have not had him long enough to get used to him.'

'It is not good for him to be actually kept young,' said Luce.

'He seems all in favour of it,' said Daniel.

'Gavin has the most in him of the three,' said Eleanor.

'You mean you think so, my dear, or perhaps that you hope so,' said Fulbert. 'And he has his own ways, I admit. Or rather he has not any ways, unless that constitutes one. But I put my Honor down as the highest type.'

'Girls are more forward than boys. Gavin has more to come.'

'I am only talking of what is there. I find that the most good to me.'

'You are a partial parent, Mother,' said Luce. 'It is a good thing Hatton is free from the failing, a serious one with children.'

'It was I who chose Hatton.'

'Fortune favoured you, my dear,' said Fulbert.

'My own sense and judgement did so.'

'Well, we cannot find a ground for disputing it.'

'You sound as if you would like to do so.'

'Well, I hardly support you, my dear.'

'Isn't that one of them crying?' said Regan.

'It is only Nevill,' said Luce. 'It does not mean much with him. And we can rely on Hatton's ever-listening ear.'

'If you begin on Hatton again, do not rely on mine,' said her mother.

Fulbert and his father laughed, and Eleanor looked rather gratified. She was unusually sensitive to approval or appreciation. The schoolroom children entered the room, in accordance with the custom that allowed or required their presence at dessert. They came to established places at the table. Only the nursery children were expected to stand, and they would presumably continue to do so, as there was no further provision of seats.

'Who came in last?' said Eleanor, almost at once.

'James,' said Daniel. 'He has reached that stage.'

'Then go back and shut the door, my boy. Doors do not shut themselves, do they?'

James was enabled by experience to agree.

'It is a pity they do not,' said Isabel. 'It is absurd not to invent one that does, considering how often the process takes place.'

'Well, you have done a good morning's work,' said Sir Jesse, disposing of this question for his grandchildren, and pushing a dish towards them, before withdrawing his thought.

'Grandpa means you to help yourselves,' said Eleanor, in almost disapproving congratulation.

'They are old enough, Mother,' said Luce.

'If they were not, I should not allow it, my dear. That was a needless speech. James, don't you want any?'

James hesitated to say that the delicacy in question upset him, and helped himself.

'Venice looks well, doesn't she?' said Eleanor, willing for notice of her daughter's looks.

Venice turned her eyes to the wall and struck the ground with her foot.

'What is there on the wall that interests you?' said her mother.

'I am looking at the pictures of Aunt Lucia and Uncle Daniel.'

'You must know them very well,' said Eleanor, forgetting that Regan would be moved to emotion, and Sir Jesse to consequent concern, and averting her eyes as the scene took place.

The portraits of the dead son and daughter were rendered with the simple flattery of mercenary Victorian art, and Regan accepted the improvement not so much because it had come to her to be the truth, as because nothing seemed to her to be too good for the originals. That a portrait of Fulbert had a less honourable place, was due less to its obvious discrepancy with truth, than to the fact that he was not yet dead. Regan carried the loss of her children as she carried her body, always suffering and sustaining it.

'James,' said Eleanor, taking any chance to end the pause, 'you must not put things in your pocket to take upstairs. That is not the way to behave. Take what you want and no more. Grandpa did not mean that.'

'Isn't that the thing that makes him sick?' said Graham.

'Is it, James? Then why did you take it? You must know when you do not want something. What was your reason?'

James had several reasons, a reluctance to appear to fuss about himself, a fear lest allusion to his health should in some way expose his morning's leisure, a purpose of transferring his portion to his sisters, and a hesitation to meet his grandfather's kindness with anything but gratitude. He did not state them, though some were to his credit, but some of his experience, of which there was enough and to spare, welled over into his eyes.

'You are not crying!' said Eleanor, honestly incredulous. 'Crying because you have too many good things! Well, what a thing to do.'

'He has had one thing that is bad for him,' said Graham.

'If good things bring tears, he is better without them,' said Eleanor, giving James a sense that a general impotence did not preclude a mental advantage. 'And I think they had better go to the schoolroom. Perhaps there are fewer there.'

'There are fewer bad ones anyhow,' said Venice, under her breath.

'What did you say, dear?' said Eleanor.

'I said we had not been down here very long.'

'No, you have not, dear child,' said Eleanor, changing her tone. 'But luncheon is dragging on very late. That is why I am asking you to go. Not for any other reason.'

'Why do you state other reasons, if they do not hold good?' said Fulbert.

'Because I am a feeble, querulous mother. So my good children will leave us. I am afraid Grandpa will be getting tired of us all.'

'Door for the girls,' muttered Graham, without moving his eyes.

'What a little gentleman James grows!' said Regan, as this warning took effect.

'He is really a dear, well-behaved little boy,' said Eleanor, as if evidence had been accepted for another conclusion.

'A nice, mannerly lad,' said Sir Jesse.

James lingered at the door, prolonging his only moment of enjoyment, and free from any sense that he was not responsible for his own success.

'If James could purr, he would,' said Daniel, and sent his brother from the room.

'You are up very soon,' said Miss Mitford, raising her eyes from her book.

Her pupils dispersed about the room without replying.

451

'A good dessert?' said Miss Mitford.

'For Venice and me,' said Isabel. 'That thing that James does not like.'

'And what did James have?'

'Oh, nothing,' said Venice, turning her back before she answered.

'I ended up in favour anyhow,' said James, throwing himself on the sofa and taking up his book.

'It is no good to settle down,' said Miss Mitford, speaking as though she must reduce him to hopelessness. 'We have to go for our walk.'

'It is a completely fine day,' said Isabel, in the same tone.

James did not move his eyes, for the reason that he was not yet obliged to.

Eleanor appeared at the door.

'Isabel, don't you remember anything about this afternoon?'

'No, Mother.'

'Surely you will, if you think.'

'You were going out with your father,' said Miss Mitford, turning away her head.

'Oh, I was going out with Father!' said Isabel, in glad recollection. 'Of course I was. He promised to take me for a walk. I will go and get ready.'

'It was a strange thing to forget, when he has to leave us so soon.'

'Oh, I had not really forgotten,' said Isabel, on her way to the door, affording her mother satisfaction on her mental process, though no impression of it. 'I will be ready in a few minutes.'

'Would Venice like to go too?' said Eleanor, speaking as if this would be almost too much at her daughter's stage.

'It would be nice for us both to go,' said Venice, as though this would be the normal arrangement.

'Oh, would it?' said Eleanor, in half-reproving sympathy, as her daughter left the room.

James remained upon the sofa, hesitating to draw attention to his recumbent position by relinquishing it.

'And James? What about him?' said Eleanor, using an almost arch manner, as she made this unparalleled suggestion.

'Yes,' said James, sitting up straight, and using the movement to hide his book under the cushion. 'All three of us.'

'Well, run away then. Don't keep Father waiting. What is that book?'

James took it up and surveyed it as if for the first time; and indeed it presented a different aspect to him, seen under his mother's eyes.

'Is it a book to be about in a schoolroom?' said Eleanor, in a rapid, even tone to Miss Mitford, handing the book to her without seeming to look at it.

'I can keep it in my own room,' said Miss Mitford, in her ordinary manner. 'If there is any harm in it, you will not mind it for me.'

'Either schoolroom stories or instructive books are best. But you weren't reading it, were you, James?'

'Oh, no,' said James, with so much lightness that he hardly seemed to grasp the idea.

'You were reading it, my boy,' said Eleanor, in a deeper tone, taking a step towards him. 'There is your penknife in it, keeping the place.'

James took up the knife, propped it against the book, and moved a piece of cardboard up and down against the blade, as if the arrangement were necessary to his purpose.

'Oh, that is what you are doing,' said Eleanor, without more idea than James of what this was. 'But you will spoil books if you do that. Did Miss Mitford know you were doing it?'

'No,' said James, with an habitual movement of nervous guilt that came in well.

'Give it back to her, and go and get ready to go out with Father. Ah, that sends you off like an arrow from the bow.'

Eleanor smiled after her son, whose movement did suggest this simile, and turned to the governess.

'He is developing better now, isn't he, Miss Mitford?'

'Yes, he is, in his own way,' said Miss Mitford, meaning what she said.

'It is a pity he is not better fitted for school,' said Eleanor, unaware that some of her son's tendencies stood him in good stead there. 'I wish I understood children as you do. It would be such a help to me.'

Miss Mitford smiled in an absent manner, thinking of the shocks that Eleanor would sustain if this could be the case, and wondering if she had forgotten her own childhood or had an abnormal one. Eleanor saw her children's lives as so much fuller and less constrained than her own, that her own early temptations could have no place in them.

'Well, I must go down to my husband. I seem to spend my life in moving from one department of my family to another,' she said, smiling at Miss Mitford with a suggestion of the difference between their lots. 'I hope you will do as you like this afternoon, Miss Mitford.'

Miss Mitford did not reassure her, though she might have done so. She settled herself with a book which she did not leave in the way of her pupils, and a box of sweets which she dealt with in the same manner. She was a fairly satisfied person, with a knowledge of books which was held to be natural in her life, and a knowledge of people which would have been held to be impossible, and was really inevitable. She had a carelessness of opinion which protected her against the usual view of her life, and had pity rather than envy of Eleanor, whom she saw as a less contented being. Her influence over her pupils was not much the worse, that she accepted life as it was, and allowed them to see it. She would not speak to James of his duplicity, but he would derive some discomfort from her silence.

Eleanor went to the study she shared with her husband, and waited for the latter to join her. He was still at the luncheon table, whence Regan had departed and her grandsons been dismissed. An allowance of talk without boys or women was Sir Jesse's acknowledged right, and was daily accorded him. When Fulbert left his father for his wife, he was reminded of his promise to his daughter and informed of the extension of the scheme. He took his stand in the doorway, with his watch in his hand, possibly having faith in the theory that the memory is stronger in youth.

'They should not keep their father waiting,' said Eleanor, moving to the bell. 'They must not take your attention as a matter of course. Why should you think about them?'

Fulbert could produce no reason why he should give a thought to his offspring, and the summons brought them running downstairs in a manner that suggested that this was not a mutual attitude.

'Why are you so late?' said Eleanor. 'I should have thought you would be anxious to start, when you were to go out with Father.'

'We have been ready for some time,' said Venice. 'We did not know when we were to come down.'

'Oh, that is what it was. Well, another time it will be better to be in the hall. Then there will be no question about your being ready and waiting.'

The capacity for waiting assumed in the children, perhaps without much attention to heredity, was proved for some minutes longer; and then the party set off, with the girls on their father's arms, and James capering about them in a manner that baulked their progress and brought him steady reproof, but was the only means by which he could join the talk.

'Well, so you are glad to be rid of your father,' said Fulbert.

'No,' said Venice, with the strong protest suggested.

'No,' said Isabel, in a weaker tone and with the tears filling her eyes. She depended on her father and dreaded the house without him.

'No,' said James, in a tone that seemed an echo of the others.

'We shall write to each other, you and I,' said Fulbert, pressing Isabel's arm. 'Every week a letter will come for you, and nobody else shall read it.'

Isabel appeared as gratified as if this were a possible prospect, and her sister looked baffled by the comparative failure of her own more normal effort.

'You shall share the letter,' said Fulbert, with no feeling that his first promise was affected. 'I shall write a letter to my two middle girls, and it shall be just for themselves. Unless they like to show it to Mother.'

James curveted in the consciousness evoked by being left out of the attention, which indeed was becoming general.

'It shall be for my boy too,' promised Fulbert, with a sense purely of further magnanimity. 'My schoolroom party shall have their own letter, and show it to everyone else at their own discretion.'

A tendency to frolic indicated the view of this prospect.

'Don't be always under my boots, my boy,' said Fulbert, throwing up his feet to render this position untenable, and also slightly painful.

'What is it like in South America?' said Venice.

'Now you are putting the cart before the horse. This is the wrong occasion for that question. I like to give you that sort of information at first hand.'

'Grandpa knows,' said James. 'He said that the trees and flowers were quite different.'

'It can hardly be as it was when he was there,' said Fulbert, not surrendering the position of coming authority, though the changes might hardly extend to the vegetation. 'You must wait for my return.'

'Don't walk in front of me, James,' said Venice, in an amiable tone.

'Nor of me,' said Isabel, speaking with more sharpness.

'Keep to the side, my boy,' said Fulbert. 'What exactly do you want to know? Tell me and I will remember.'

James was obliged to return to his place to make this clear, and Fulbert paused and listened with patience, before he allowed the party to proceed.

'What does Isabel want to hear about South America?' he said, in a gentle tone. 'That the whole continent is at the bottom of the sea?'

'Yes,' said Isabel, quickening her pace.

Fulbert bent and whispered in her ear, and Venice suffered from her failure to produce feelings on the unknown continent on this scale.

'Do countries have the sea underneath them?' said James. 'Or does the land go right through?'

'It is the sea above them that Isabel wants,' said his father.

'But do they really, I mean?'

'People's thoughts and feelings are just as real, my boy.'

'Yes,' said James, in a lighter tone.

'Now we will all race to that tree and back,' said Fulbert, deciding that interest and entertainment should remain in his children's memory. 'Take your stand and start fair. We must all run right round it.'

The children braced themselves for the effort, James in a

serious spirit, Venice in a semi-serious one, and Isabel with an appearance of sprightly interest which she could hardly feel, as she was of weaker build than the others, and though unconcerned for success in the contest, counted the cost of her father's sympathy.

'Well done, Venice!' said Fulbert, as he reached the goal, second to his daughter and a tie with his son, but prevented from yielding a place to his other daughter by the transparence of the manoeuvre. 'Well done, my boy. And so my Isabel is last, and tired into the bargain.'

'I am a poor athlete, Father.'

'Are you, my dear?' said Fulbert, putting his cheek against hers. 'Your strength has gone into other things, better ones for your father.'

Venice again had a feeling that she met the more ordinary kinds of success. It was hardly weakened when Fulbert gave a shilling to each of them, in reward for their respective achievements. When the walk was over, it was found that it had occupied an hour. Fulbert and James would have guessed it an hour and a half, Venice somewhat longer, and Isabel had lost all count of time. Eleanor came into the hall to receive them.

'Why, Father looks quite tired, and so do you, Isabel. He has some reason, with the weight of two of you on him, but you seem to tire very easily.' Eleanor was at once moved and vexed by sign of weakness in her children; it seemed to threaten her possession of them. 'Venice looks as fresh as when she started. I think Isabel is depressed by the thought of your going, Fulbert.'

Isabel turned at once to the staircase; Venice followed in a rather disheartened manner; and James gave a jump and looked up at his mother.

'We had a race, and Venice won, and I was second, and Father gave us all a shilling.'

'That was a treat, wasn't it? But all this running and jumping for a little boy who cannot go to school! What does that mean, do you think? And now you had better all be off to the schoolroom. We don't want tears and tiredness on Father's last days.'

The children, uncertain of their mother's exact leanings, went upstairs, and Fulbert entered his study and threw himself into a chair.

'You know, Eleanor, or rather I suppose you do not, that you treat your children as if they were men and women.' Fulbert had a right to make this criticism, as he did not fall into the error.

'I am simply myself with them. It is best to be natural with children.'

'You overdo it, my dear. You prevent them from being the same. And each child needs a separate touch and a separate understanding.'

'I doubt the wisdom of making any sort of difference.'

'It needs to be done in a certain way,' said Fulbert, feeling that there was an example before his wife.

Eleanor gave a little laugh.

'I wonder you like to leave them with their feeble mother.'

'You are not without support, my dear.'

'I feel I could not leave them for any reason.'

'It is a good thing I can do so for the right ones. I am going for their sakes. I am sure you will give yourself to them. I can only put you in my place.'

'There is no one whom I could leave in mine,' said Eleanor, believing what she said. 'No one else would have the nine of them always in her thoughts. I ought to be saying good-night to the three youngest at the moment.'

'That is a duty I shall be pleased to share with you. And I do not pity you for being left with it.'

They mounted to the nursery and found its occupants nearing the end of their day.

'You will soon be in your little bed,' said Eleanor to Nevill.

'By Hatton.'

'Yes, unless you would like to begin to share a room with Gavin.'

'By Hatton,' said her son, looking puzzled and uninterested.

'Yes, for a little while you can stay with her.'

'All night. Stay with Hatton all night.'

'How soon are you going away?' said Gavin, to his father.

'In about seven days.'

'That is a week,' said Honor.

'All night, all night,' said Nevill, beating his hand on his mother's knee.

'Yes, yes, all night. Honor, talk nicely to Father about his going. Tell him how you will miss him.'

Honor began to cry; Fulbert put his arm about her; Nevill gave her a look of respectful concern; Gavin surveyed her with a frown.

'There, dry your eyes and don't lean against Father,' said Eleanor. 'He is as tired as you are, at the end of the day. She was hiding her feelings, poor child.'

'She didn't hide them,' said Gavin.

'She tried to; she did not want to upset Father. You mind about his going too, don't you?'

'If we say we mind, he knows,' said Gavin, who was successfully hiding his own jealousy of his sister's interest.

'Father will be gone away. Gallop-a-trot,' said Nevill, illustrating this idea of progress.

'Nevill doesn't know much,' said Gavin.

'Well, he is only three,' said Eleanor. 'Neither did you at that age.'

'Father come back soon,' said Nevill, showing his grasp of the situation.

'I think I knew more,' said Gavin.

'We shall expect good reports of your lessons, if you talk like that.'

'It is boys at school who have reports,' said Gavin, mindful of James's experience.

'Mother meant a verbal report,' said Honor, causing her parents to smile.

'You will soon be able to go to school,' said Eleanor, to her son. 'You won't always have a governess.'

'James sometimes has Miss Mitford. I could always have her.'

'Do you mean you want to learn with Honor?'

'No,' said Gavin, true to his principle that real feeling should be hidden.

'Good-night, Mother,' said Nevill, approaching Eleanor with small, quick steps.

'Good-night, my little boy. So you are a horse again.'

'Puff, puff, puff,' said Nevill, in correction of her idea.

'He has passed to the age of machinery,' said Fulbert.

'Is that age three?' said Gavin.

'Father means to a different date,' said Honor.

'The boy may be right that he can be educated at home,' said Fulbert.

Eleanor made a mute sign against such reference to Honor, which she believed to be lost upon her daughter, though the point at issue was the latter's intelligence.

'I don't feel I have a great deal in common with Mother,' said Honor, as the door closed upon her parents.

Mullet looked at her in reproof and respect.

'In common?' said Gavin.

'You have had enough education for tonight. There must be something left for the governess to teach you,' said Hatton, producing mirth in Mullet. 'Now I am taking Nevill to bed. You must not stay up too long.'

'Will you tell us about when you were a child, while you do Honor's hair?' said Gavin to Mullet.

'Yes, I will give you the last chapter of my childhood,' said Mullet, entering on an evidently accustomed and congenial task, with her eyes and hands on Honor's head. 'For I don't think I was ever a real child after that. You know we lived in a house something like this; a little smaller and more compact perhaps, but much on the same line. And I was once left behind with the servants when my father was abroad. Not with a grandpa and a grandma and a mother; just with servants, just with the household staff. And I found myself alone in the schoolroom, with all the servants downstairs. I was often by myself for hours, as I had no equal in the house, and I preferred my own company to that of inferiors. Well, there I was sitting, in my shabby, velvet dress, swinging my feet in their shabby, velvet shoes; my things were good when they came, but I was really rather neglected; and there came a ring at the bell, and my father was in the house. "And what is this?" he said, when he had hastened to my place of refuge. "How comes it that I find my daughter alone and unattended?" The servants had come running up when they heard his ring, when his peremptory ring echoed through the house. "Here is my daughter, my heiress, left to languish in solitude! In quarters more befitting a dog," he went on, looking round the rather battered schoolroom, and saying almost more than he meant in the strength of his feelings. "Cast aside like a piece of flotsam and jetsam," he continued, clenching his teeth and his hands in a way he had. "When I left her, as I thought, to retainers faithful to the charge of my motherless child. Enough," he said. "No longer will I depend on those whose hearts do not beat with the spirit of trusty service. People with the souls of menials," he went on, lifting his arm with one of his rare gestures, "away from the walls which will shelter my child while there is breath within me." And there he stood with bent head, waiting for the servants to pass, almost bowing to them in the way a gentleman would, feeling the wrench of parting with people who had served him all his life.' Mullet's voice changed and became open and matter-of-fact. 'And there we both were, left alone in that great house, with no one to look after us, and very little idea of looking after ourselves. It was a good thing in a way, as the crash had to come, and I think Father felt it less than he would have in cold blood. He was a man whose hot blood was often a help to him.' Mullet gave a sigh and moved her brows. 'But I think his death was really caused by our fall from our rightful place.'

'So then you were left an orphan,' said Gavin.

'Yes, then came the change which split my life into halves.'

'Would your father have liked you to be a nurse?'

'Well, in one sense he had the gentleman's respect for useful work. In another it would have broken his heart,' said Mullet, hardly taking an exaggerated view, considering her parent's reaction to milder vicissitudes.

'What happened to the house?' said Honor.

'It was sold to pay debts. My father was in debt, as a man in his place would be.'

'He really ought not to have kept all those servants.'

'Well, no, he ought not. But he could hardly change from the way his family had always lived.'

'Were they all paid?'

'If a farthing to a dependant had been owing, Miss Honor, I

could never have held up my head,' said Mullet, straightening her neck to render further words unnecessary.

'You told us you had a maid of your own. But you didn't have one then.'

'My last nurse was on the way to a maid. But I was quite without one on that day when my father came home; absolutely without,' said Mullet, with evident attention to accuracy. 'I was entirely at the mercy of all those servants downstairs.'

'Is Grandpa in debt?' said Gavin.

'Now if you talk about what I tell you, I shall only tell you the tales I tell to Nevill.'

'You ought to say Master Nevill.'

'Well, so I ought in these days. But the old days drag me back when I talk about them. Now remember these things are between ourselves.'

'Wouldn't people believe you?' said Honor.

'I daresay they would not,' said Mullet, with a little laugh at human incredulity.

'I don't think Mother would.'

'Sometimes I can hardly believe myself in my own early life,' said Mullet, fastening Honor's hair with a rapid skill acquired in a later one, and using a sincere note that was justified.

'There are Daniel and Graham on the stairs,' said Gavin.

'Your big brothers have come to see you,' said Mullet, in a rather severe tone. 'And you can put things like stories out of your head.'

This was hardly the purpose of the newcomers, who had found their study occupied by Luce and a friend, and hoped to find the nursery free at this hour of its occupants.

'You are going to bed, I suppose?' said Daniel.

'When we do go,' said Gavin.

'Well, that is now,' said Daniel, supplanting him in his chair.

Gavin recovered it; his brother displaced him and he returned; Graham and Honor enacted the same scene; the struggle resulted in screams and mirth, and in the course of it Honor knocked her head and wept with an abandonment proportionate to her excited mood. Hatton arrived with her fingers to her mouth, and Nevill under her arm, and made warning movements towards the floors beneath. Gavin was checked in a disposition to maintain the sport in spite of the consequences to his sister, and Nevill from under Hatton's arm made a hushing sound and raised his finger with the appropriate gesture.

Hatton became oblivious of her late anxiety, and directed Mullet's attention to Honor.

'If you put on a handkerchief soaked in water, there won't be much of a bruise in the morning.'

'Then Mother won't know, will she?' said Nevill, in a comforting tone.

'Why do you hold that great child?' said Honor, seeking to counteract the impression she had given.

'Hatton carry him,' said Nevill.

'Honor will have a pigeon's egg on her head tomorrow,' said Daniel.

'Not pigeon's egg tomorrow,' said Nevill, in a troubled tone. 'A nice handkerchief wet with water.'

'We will come and rock you to sleep,' said Graham.

'Hatton will sit on his little bed,' said Nevill, in a reassuring manner.

'Be a pony and trot away to it.'

Nevill agitated his limbs in rebellion against his bondage, and on being set down, trotted round the room and out of it, accepting the opening of the door as necessary and natural.

'Will Honor have a headache in bed?' said Gavin to Mullet.

'If she does, you must come and fetch me.'

'She can fetch you herself, when she has only knocked her head.'

'The nights are not cold yet.'

'I like cold; I like even ice.'

'He is afraid of the dark,' said Honor, stooping to gather her belongings. 'He is almost as afraid as I am. But my head doesn't hurt any more; I can dispense with this handkerchief.'

'You can dispense with it,' said Gavin, with more than one kind of admiration.

'Open the door for me. Because I am carrying so much,' said Honor, indicating that she did not require it on other grounds.

The pair departed without taking leave of their brothers, who neither noticed nor offered to remedy the omission. They were succeeded by the schoolroom party, who entered the room without any sign of interest as if the change meant nothing to them. They were marshalled by Luce, with the air of a benevolent despot.

'Can we be of any use to you?' said Daniel.

'Luce said the schoolroom must be aired before supper,' said Venice.

James went to a chair and resumed his book.

'Is Miss Mitford proof against chill?' said Graham.

'She has gone to her room,' said Isabel.

'I have been wondering if Graham ought to be handed back to her,' said Daniel.

'Well, she likes her pupils to be of advanced age,' said Graham.

Venice laughed.

'Now why is it amusing?' said Luce, leaning back and locking her hands round her knees. 'Miss Mitford is older and wiser than Graham. Why should he not learn from her?'

'She is a woman,' said Venice.

'But knowledge is no more valuable, coming from a man.'

'It is held to be,' said Isabel. 'Men are more expensive than women.'

'Isn't Mitta expensive?' said Venice, surprised.

'She still seems to me in her own way a person born to command,' said Luce.

'Few of us can so far fulfil our destiny,' said Graham.

'I wonder if anyone is born to obey,' said Isabel. 'That may be why people command rather badly, that they have no suitable material to work on.'

'I wonder if we are a commanding family,' said Luce.

'I expect Isabel is right that most families are,' said Daniel.

Venice came up as if wishing to join the talk, but at a loss for a contribution.

'So James has learned to read,' said Graham.

'You are less forward for your age,' said Daniel.

'Mitta forgot to put that book away,' said Venice.

'Isn't James supposed to read it?' said Luce. 'Let me see it, James.'

James passed the book to his sister with disarming obedience.

'An instance of the normal reluctance to obey,' she said, raising her brows and returning the book.

Miss Mitford opened the door.

'I have had to come up for you,' she said.

'True, Mitta,' said Daniel.

'Supper has been brought in.'

'What is it?' said Venice, while Isabel turned in milder interest.

'Something made with eggs,' said Miss Mitford, on a plaintive note.

'It seems that Mitta is old enough to dine downstairs,' said Graham, as the door closed, or he thought it did.

'The bread of dependence is generally eaten upstairs,' said Miss Mitford.

'So your speech could not wait for a moment,' said Daniel.

'It is a pity it did not, Graham,' said Luce.

'It is not so long since we were Mitta's pupils,' said Graham.

'Does that make it better to see you turning out so awkwardly?' said his brother.

'It may have prepared her for it.'

'And you have been other people's pupil since.'

'But no one ever taught me as much as dear old Mitta,' said Graham, in a tone of quotation.

'It will soon be recognized that you have not made suitable progress since.'

'Oh, you and your coming school success!'

'Now why do people despise that kind of achievement?' said Luce, again with her hands about her knees. 'Why belittle any kind of gift?'

'We certainly never have any other kind,' said Graham, as if he were speaking to himself. 'People who have that sort of success never do anything in after life, but neither do the other people. No one does anything in after life. I see that my only chance has been missed.'

'Be quiet for a moment, boys,' said Luce, raising her hand. 'I want to listen to the wheels of the house going round. Yes, Mother is going into the schoolroom to say good-night. That means that the dinner gong will soon sound.'

'And Graham will be indulging his vice,' said Daniel. 'Can nothing at all be done?'

Eleanor had entered the room below.

'Well, my dears, have you had a happy day?'

'It has been much as usual,' said Isabel.

'Well, that is happy, isn't it? Could you have any more done for you? And you have been out with Father. Surely that prevents the day from being ordinary.'

'Yes, of course it does.'

'And has James had a good day at school?'

'Yes,' said James. 'No, I have not been to school.'

'Then weren't you to have tea in the nursery and go early to bed?'

'Oh, yes,' said James, in a tone of sudden recollection.

'You must not forget what we arrange, my boy. Your eyes look tired. What have you been doing?'

'Nothing,' said James, in an almost wondering manner.

Eleanor left the subject. Her son's recent practice of reading had escaped her. She thought of him as a child, to whom a book was a task, a thing he had been long enough for her to form the habit.

'You had better run upstairs, as you don't seem to have much appetite. Are you too tired to eat? Why, you are sitting on a book.'

'Oh, that chair always seems lower than the others.'

'There are plenty of other chairs. Why choose one so low that you have to put something on it? And surely a cushion would be more comfortable than a book.'

James looked as if this were a new idea.

'What things boys do! Now kiss me and be off to bed.'

James embraced his mother with zest, and ran from the room with the lightness of one with no interest behind.

'He is a dear little boy,' said Eleanor, in the tone of voicing a recent conclusion, which marked her approval of James. 'Did not anyone – did not either of you girls remember that he was to go to bed?'

'We all four forgot,' said Miss Mitford. 'That seems to show it was not an easy thing to remember.'

Eleanor smiled only to the extent required.

'He is young to remember everything for himself, with several people – with two sisters older than he is, in the room.'

'I am older than he is too,' said Miss Mitford.

'This is a thing that only concerned himself,' said Isabel.

'My dear, the little boy's health is a matter of equal concern to everyone. I am sure Miss Mitford agrees with me.'

'Not that it is of equal concern,' said Miss Mitford.

'So you will remember another time, my dear,' said Eleanor, not looking at the governess. 'Come now and say good-night, and then have a happy hour before you go to bed.'

'What is to make our happiness?' said Isabel. 'I wish Mother had told us.'

'She could have done so,' said Miss Mitford.

'I don't wish she had told us anything more,' said Venice.

'There are no books I have not read,' said Isabel.

'You must fall back on your old, tried favourites,' said Miss Mitford. 'There is no pleasure equal to it.'

'You don't think so yourself. You know you would rather have new ones. You have them from the library every week.'

'Yes. One of my few extravagances.'

'One of her two extravagances,' murmured Venice.

'Mother says she wonders you have time to read them all,' said Isabel.

'Does she?' said Miss Mitford, gently raising her eyes. 'I never forget the claims of my own life.'

'You would not like to be a child again.'

'No, not at all.'

'I would rather be a woman, even if I had to be –'

'You will be able to be one, without being a governess,' said Miss Mitford, in an encouraging tone, beginning to cut the leaves of a volume that required it.

'Didn't you want to be a governess?'

'Why is it said that people judge other people by themselves? It is the last thing they do.'

Isabel was silent and Venice drew near to listen.

'Of course I am different,' said Miss Mitford, keeping her lips steady.

'I meant there were other things you might have been,' said Isabel.

'I do not see what they were.'

'I should think there are worse things.'

'Yes, so should I, but I believe it is not generally thought.'

'What would you have liked to be?' said Venice.

'What I am, with enough money to live on.'

There was silence.

'Just my plain, odd self,' said Miss Mitford.

'You would not have liked to be married?'

'No, I never wanted a full, normal life.'

'I don't think I do,' said Isabel. 'Do you, Venice?'

'I don't know; I am not sure.'

'You would pay the price of full success,' said Miss Mitford, in a tone of understanding.

'I don't see why spinsters have any less success,' said Isabel.

'Well, they have no proof that they have been sought,' said Miss Mitford.

'Have you ever been sought?' said Venice, in a tone that recalled Honor's when she asked Hatton her age.

'You must not probe the secrets of a woman's heart,' said Miss Mitford, putting down the knife and taking up the book.

The door opened and James entered in his dressing-gown, and leaving the door ajar to indicate a transitory errand, began to collect his possessions. He picked up his book, put it under his chin and piled other objects upon it, and using it in this way, went from the room.

'He will think about it more, if he does not finish it,' said Miss Mitford. 'It is better to fulfil the spirit than the letter of your mother's wish.'

'James is fortunate in getting the first,' said Isabel. 'There is nothing in the book that I did not know.'

'James will not understand it,' said Venice.

'People do understand things when they read them for the first time,' said Miss Mitford.

'Yes,' said Venice, who had been struck by this herself.

'In a year I shall read what I like,' said Isabel. 'When we are sixteen, we can choose from the library.'

'You will browse on the wholesome pastures of English literature,' said Miss Mitford. 'Browse is the wrong word. But it is right to tell us they are wholesome.'

'Well, they are,' said Isabel.

'Yes, that is why it is well to know.'

'I wonder if Mother knows,' said Venice, laughing. 'I hope she will not go up to see if James is all right.'

Miss Mitford raised her eyes.

'Won't he think of it himself?' said Isabel, meaning that there were precautionary measures.

'You are as afraid of Mother as we are, Mitta,' said Venice.

'Not quite. She has no affection for me, and that puts me outside her power. But I am afraid of her, of course. I am a sensitive, shrinking creature at heart.'

'Would you mind if she —?'

'Dismissed me? Yes. This is to be my last post. I shall retire when Honor grows up.'

'What will you do then?' said Isabel.

'I can live with my relations, if I pay them.'

'But you don't like being with them. You are always glad to come back.'

'And yet I think I shall enjoy living with them. What an odd incalculable person I am!'

'You ought not to have to pay relations.'

'Well, the English have no family feelings. That is, none of the kind you mean. They have them, and one of them is that relations must cause no expense.'

'Perhaps they are poor, said Venice.

'Not as poor as you think, considering that I am a governess.'

'Perhaps they are not near relations.'

'Yes, they are. It is near relations who have family feelings.'

'You might as well live with friends,' said Venice.

'Well, there is the tie of blood.'

'What difference does that make, if people forget it?'

'They know other people remember it. That is another family feeling.'

'I shall not let Isabel work, when I am married. She will always live with me.'

'I may be married myself,' said Isabel. 'I am not quite sure that I shall not.'

'You will have enough money to pay your sister, without working,' said Miss Mitford.

'I should not want her to pay,' said Venice.

'People with families often need money the most,' said Isabel. 'You might be dependent on my contribution to the house.'

'That is another set of family feelings,' said Miss Mitford.

There was silence.

'We know things we should not know, if we had not had you, Mitta,' said Isabel.

'That is the purpose of my being with you.'

'I meant things apart from lessons.'

'Well, you know them sooner,' said Miss Mitford.

Chapter 4

'We have not tidied the nursery,' said Honor, in a nonchalant tone to the new governess. 'Hatton told us to do it, but we took no notice.'

'Then you had better do it now. The room is not in a suitable state for lessons.'

The pupils exchanged a glance over this unforeseen attitude.

'Why don't you do it?' said Gavin, in a just audible tone.

'I did not make the room untidy.'

Honor kicked some toys towards a cupboard, and Gavin idly seconded her. Both had an air of putting no value on the objects that had engaged them.

'Why were you playing with the toys, if you do not care about them?' said Miss Pilbeam.

'We didn't say we didn't,' said Gavin.

'We have nothing else to play with,' said Honor.

'Will she give us some more?' said Gavin, with a nudge to his sister.

'I am here to help you to work, not to play. Why do you use your feet instead of your hands?'

Miss Pilbeam was a large, pale woman of twenty-seven, with rather solid features, small, honest eyes, large, white hands, a sober, reliable expression, and a smile that seemed a deliberate adaptation of her face. Her qualification for teaching was her being presumed to know more than young children, and she was required to produce no others.

'That will do for a summary clearance,' said Honor, drawing Miss Pilbeam's eyes.

'Yes, it will do,' said Gavin.

'Now come and show me if you can use your hands as well,' said Miss Pilbeam, putting a smile on her features and some copy-books on the table.

'We don't begin with writing,' said Honor.

'What do you usually do first?'

'Spelling or history or French or sums. That is all we learn, except a little Latin,' said Honor, in an easy tone that forestalled a possibly slight opinion of these studies.

'Well, we will begin with writing today.'

'Why should it be different?' said Gavin.

'Because I wish it to be.'

'Is that a reason?'

'You will have to learn that it is.'

Honor thrust her pen into the ink so sharply that it spluttered.

'The poor, old cloth!' she said, indicating another slight opinion.

'It is a pretty cloth. It is a pity you have made it so dirty.'

Honor took up a corner of it and wiped her pen, in further suggestion of her attitude.

'It is really to protect the table,' she said.

'Well, it must save it a good deal,' said Miss Pilbeam.

Honor laughed.

'Haven't you a pen-wiper?' said the governess.

'No.'

'A thing to wipe pens?' said Gavin.

'Of course,' said his sister.

'I will make you one,' said Miss Pilbeam.

'Oh, you don't have to buy them,' said Gavin.

'They have them in shops, but I can make you one quite well.'

'Why don't you buy one?' said Gavin in rough tone.

'Because it is not necessary.'

'We always buy things,' said Honor.

'I will teach you how to make some.'

'What will you teach us to make?'

'Pen-wipers and needle-cases and blotters and several other things.'

'Is she supposed to teach us that?' said Gavin, aside to his sister.

'I am not obliged to,' said Miss Pilbeam, 'but perhaps you would like to learn.'

'I don't want to learn things I don't have to,' said Honor.

'Would she be allowed to teach us them in lesson-time?' said Gavin, in another aside.

'I should not let you do it then,' said Miss Pilbeam making the necessary adjustment. 'We will remember at some other time.'

'Do you know how to make a bow and arrow?'

'Yes, I can teach you that.'

'I only asked if you knew.'

'A bow and arrows,' said Honor.

'Would you like to make them too?' said Miss Pilbeam.

'Yes, I think I should.'

'Then we will make some one day after lessons.'

'Don't you go home then?' said Gavin.

'Yes, as a rule. But sometimes I can stay with you for a little while.'

'Do you have to?'

'No, but sometimes you might like me to.'

Honor and Gavin looked at each other, and broke into laughter at the assumption of welcome.

'You can go on with your writing now. We shall not talk so much another day.'

'It is you who are talking,' said Gavin.

'Well, I must stop now.'

'Are you going to stay today?'

'No. I must go home this morning. My father wants to see me.'

'Oh, has she got a home?' said Gavin, to his sister, turning his thumb towards Miss Pilbeam.

'Yes,' said the latter, smiling. 'Where should I live, if I had not?'

'You might live in the streets.'

'Do you know many people who do that?'

'No, but we don't really know you.'

'Do you have to do what your father tells you?' said Honor.

'I like to when I can. So do you, I suppose.'

'Why does he want to see you?'

'He will like to know how I have got on.'

'With us, do you mean?' said Honor, surprised at this question's having any interest outside.

'Yes, and that reminds me that we are not progressing very fast. Let me see your copies.'

Honor slapped her book down in front of Miss Pilbeam.

'It is not very good, and you have smudged it.'

'It is as good as I care to do it,' said Honor, leaning back.

'Haven't you got to see mine?' said Gavin, thrusting it forward.

'Yes, I want to see yours too. This is not good either. I think you can both do better.'

'We might with an effort,' said Honor.

'Then you must make the effort in future. Now we will go on to history.'

'Do you want ordinary string for a bow and arrow?' said Gavin.

'No, a special kind. We might have to buy that. How much pocket money do you have?'

'Oh, about threepence a week,' said Honor, casting a vagueness over the insignificance of the sum.

'That is what we have,' said her brother.

'You can do a good deal with threepence a week,' said Miss Pilbeam.

'Did you have as much when you were a child?' said Gavin.

'Yes, that is what I used to have.'

'Could your father afford to give it to you?'

'Yes, he used to manage that.'

'Then why do you have to be a governess?'

'Well, I want more than that now.'

'How much do you have?' said Honor, with her eyes and her

473

hands engaged with her pen, and her voice sounding as if it barely detached itself.

'You know you should not ask that question.'

'You asked us how much we had.'

'That is quite different. Get out your history books.'

'We only have one book. Nevill will have to share it too.'

'Is that your little brother? He looks such a dear little boy.'

'He isn't,' said Gavin. 'He keeps doing the same thing.'

'Well, I shall judge for myself. Now I will read you a chapter and ask you questions afterwards.'

Honor rose and threw herself on the sofa.

'You must not sit there, Honor. Come back to your place.'

'I always do when I am being read to.'

'This is not a story book. Sit up and pay attention.'

'Is reading teaching?' said Gavin.

'Yes, when I am going to ask you questions. It is all a part of our work.'

'But we shall be telling you; not you us.'

'I hope that is how it will be.'

'Is teaching work?' said Honor.

'Yes, and learning too, when they are both done as they should be.'

'Will her teaching be done like that?' said Gavin, to his sister.

'I hope it will be; I shall do my best,' said Miss Pilbeam, choosing to use a simple, sincere tone, as she sometimes chose to wear a smile. 'Now will both of you listen?'

Miss Pilbeam read, while her pupils occupied themselves with the only thing in front of them, the tablecloth, Gavin plaiting the fringe, and Honor drawing out threads and weaving a string. When Eleanor entered, Miss Pilbeam was the only one who continued her employment, and she pursued it as if unaware of interruption, until the visitor spoke.

'Well, how do you find the new little pupils, Miss Pilbeam?'

Miss Pilbeam raised steady eyes.

'I hardly know what to expect of them yet.'

'What lesson are you doing?'

'We are beginning history.'

'They have done a good deal of that, I think.'

'I shall soon find out what stage they are in.'

'She has to read it out of the book herself,' muttered Gavin.

'What did you say, dear?' said Eleanor. 'What did he say, Honor?'

'He said Miss Pilbeam was reading from the book. We are to answer questions afterwards.'

Miss Pilbeam glanced from one of her pupils to the other, without raising her eyes. She was perhaps the first to begin to make progress.

'That is a good way of using the book,' said Eleanor. 'I will come in another day to hear how they acquit themselves. How is your father, Miss Pilbeam? He must miss your mother very much.'

'Yes, he does. He is in better spirits, but he is very dependent upon me.'

'You are a useful person in two households. I hope this little woman will grow up to be like you.'

Honor looked surprised.

'Don't you hope you will, dear? You would like her to, wouldn't you Gavin?'

'No, I don't think so. If people are useful, it is only nice for other people, and not for them.'

'She is safe with her brother, isn't she, Miss Pilbeam?' said Eleanor, smiling as she left the room, and unconscious of any implication upon Miss Pilbeam's lot.

'Has your mother gone away?' said Gavin.

'She is dead. She died over a year ago.'

Gavin and Honor looked at each other and broke into awkward mirth.

'Then why don't you wear black?' said Honor, as if this excused their outbreak.

'I have just gone out of it.'

'Then you don't mind any more.'

'Of course I do. Clothes do not make any difference.'

'Then why do people wear black? Isn't it to show that they mind?'

'It is just a custom.'

'Does your father wear black?' said Gavin.

'He wears a black band on his arm. That is what men do.'

'Then he minds more than you do?'

'Yes, I am afraid he minds even more than that.'

'Would he rather you had died?'

'Yes, perhaps he would.'

'I should hate anyone who wanted me to die,' said Honor.

'Is he glad you have stopped minding?' said Gavin.

'You know I have not stopped. Now we will go on with the lesson. I hope I shall not have to tell your mother that you are inattentive.'

Honor and Gavin shared the hope to the point of allowing the lesson to proceed to its end. Then Gavin resumed the talk.

'What is your father, Miss Pilbeam?'

'He is a veterinary surgeon.'

'What kind of a surgeon is that? An ophthalmic surgeon is one who cures people's eyes.'

'Yes. A veterinary surgeon is one who cures animals.'

'Animals? Just horses and cows?'

'All kinds. Hunters and hounds and everything,' said Miss Pilbeam, carrying the subject into its higher sphere.

'Then your father is not a real doctor?'

'He is something different and something the same as well,' said Miss Pilbeam, in a tone of throwing full light on her pupils' minds.

'Then he is not a gentleman?'

'He is an educated man. He passed very hard examinations.'

'As hard as those for people like Daniel and Graham?'

'Yes, I should think nearly as hard.'

'But he doesn't earn enough for you not to be a governess.'

'He likes me to do something useful.'

'But teaching isn't useful unless you know enough to teach.'

'I know enough to teach you.'

'But you had to read the history out of a book. You didn't know it in your head.'

'I could not make a second book, could I?'

Honor broke into laughter.

'You will soon cease to expect duplicates in this house,' she said.

Miss Pilbeam looked at her in silence.

'Then we can answer out of the book,' pursued Gavin.

'We will see what your mother says.'

'We do sums now,' said Honor, recognizing the end of the matter.

'Give me the arithmetic book.'

Gavin handed it with a look at his sister, and a snake wriggled out over Miss Pilbeam's hands.

'What a babyish toy to play with!' she exclaimed, as she realized its nature, and her pupils' faces showed the fulfilment of their hopes.

'It is Nevill's,' said Gavin, in explanation. 'I just put it inside the book. I thought that, as your father was a surgeon of animals, you might like it.'

Miss Pilbeam laughed before she knew, and general mirth ensued.

'It is a realistic object,' said Honor.

'Yes, it is very simple,' said Miss Pilbeam. 'Now take down this sum.'

'We always have our sums put down for us.'

'And I don't do the same as Honor,' said Gavin. 'She has harder ones. Farther on in the book.'

'Well, show me the ones you do have.'

Honor did so, and Miss Pilbeam dictated the examples, and worked Honor's herself, to be ready with her aid. Honor soon gave the correct answer.

'Let me see your book.'

Honor tossed it forward.

'Yes, that is good. You have been very quick. How about you, Gavin?'

'I only do one sum. Honor does three.'

'And there are only eleven months between you. You must catch up, Gavin. Do you ever help him, Honor?'

'No, I don't teach people,' said Honor, implying a difference between her experience and Miss Pilbeam's.

'She is a year older than me,' said Gavin. 'Her birthday is on the second of July, and mine is on the last day in June. It is a year all but two days.'

'I think you must be better at mathematics than you seem,' said Miss Pilbeam, smiling.

'We are the same age for two days,' said Honor, hardly doing herself the same justice. 'This sum is wrong, but I see where. I always find my own mistakes.'

'You are good at arithmetic,' said Miss Pilbeam.

'Better than you are, isn't she?' said Gavin.

'I think she is for her age.'

'She is apart from that. You have not done the first sum yet.'

'I have not been trying. I saw she did not need my help.'

'You seemed to be trying.'

'Appearances are deceitful,' said Miss Pilbeam, with a pleasant note that was only fair on appearances, as she had this point in common with them. 'I shall expect Honor to get on very fast. I can always prepare the lesson, if necessary.'

'You will have to do that at home, and your father will know that you can't do Honor's sums.'

'Well, that will not matter,' said Miss Pilbeam, laughing amusedly. 'I think this is your luncheon.'

'It is your luncheon too.'

'Yes, I think we are to have it together.'

'Does she have to pay for it?' said Gavin, aside to his sister.

'Master Gavin, that is very rude,' said Mullet. 'Miss Honor must be quite ashamed.'

'I am not,' said Honor.

'Can I get you anything else, miss?'

'She would not dare to say "Yes",' said Gavin.

'Now I shall tell Hatton,' said Mullet.

'I can talk to Honor, if I like.'

'Hatton would wish to know.'

'Then she will be pleased about it.'

'I think he is not himself,' said Miss Pilbeam. 'He may be shy. Perhaps we might pass it over this time.'

'Now isn't that kind of Miss Pilbeam?'

'She is trying to curry favour.'

'You can leave him to me, Mullet. We will see what your mother says presently, Gavin.'

Mullet took her tray, and Gavin swung on his chair to show

his indifference, a state which certainly could not be deduced from his expression.

'Mother does not like to be worried about little things,' said Honor.

'Rudeness is not a little thing.'

'Pretence rudeness is,' said Gavin.

'Why do you pretend anything so babyish and silly?'

'Honor and I always pretend.'

'Well, if you pretend rudeness again, I shall ask your mother what to do about it.'

Gavin ceased to swing, the purpose of the process being over.

'She can't stand on her own legs,' murmured Honor.

Miss Pilbeam fixed her eyes on Honor's face, kept them there for some moments, and withdrew them with an air of ruminative purpose.

'We have Latin now,' said Honor, in a pleasant tone. 'We are doing a book called Caesar. We have only read one page.'

'Well, in that case we will not go on with it today. I will take the book home and read it to myself, so that I can tell you the story. That will make it easier.'

'Graham has a translation of it,' said Gavin. 'But Miss Mitford reads Latin books without.'

'Oh, we won't talk about translations,' said Miss Pilbeam, justified in her protest, as she was going to make no mention of one she had seen at home.

'Why can't we just read the translation?' said Honor. 'We should know what was in the book.'

'Because that is not the way to learn Latin,' said Miss Pilbeam, who meant to use it only as a way of managing without having done so. 'We will do some Latin grammar this morning.'

'We don't much like doing that.'

'But think how useful it will be in reading the books,' said Miss Pilbeam, with earnestness and faith.

'Latin is a dead language,' said Gavin.

'Yes, it is not actually spoken now,' said Miss Pilbeam, confirming and amplifying his knowledge. 'But it is nice to be able to read it. It is the key to so much.'

'The key?'

'Yes, it opens the gates of knowledge,' said Miss Pilbeam, laying her hands on the table and looking into Gavin's face.

'Miss Pilbeam is speaking metaphorically,' said Honor.

'Yes, I was; I am glad you understood.'

'I didn't,' said Gavin.

'We must make allowances for those twelve months,' said Miss Pilbeam, smiling. 'Here is your little brother.'

Nevill left Hatton in the doorway, ran twice round Miss Pilbeam, paused at her knee and raised his eyes to her face.

'He is the youngest, miss. These are his first lessons.'

'Hatton teach him,' said Nevill, on a sudden note of apprehension.

'No, Miss Pilbeam can teach better than I can.'

'Not as well as Hatton,' said Nevill, his tone changing to one of resignation and goodwill; 'but very nice.'

'I will leave him, miss. If he is not good, send one of the others to fetch me.'

'We can ring for Mullet,' said Honor.

'No, Mullet has other things to do.'

'We might refuse to go,' said Gavin.

Hatton left the room in a smooth manner, suggestive merely of concern that Nevill should not notice her going.

Miss Pilbeam bent towards the latter.

'Can you say A, b, c?'

'A, b, c,' said Nevill, looking up.

'He doesn't know anything,' said Honor.

'He does,' said Nevill, not taking his eyes from Miss Pilbeam's face.

'Well, I will teach you four letters, and show you how to make them,' said Miss Pilbeam, lifting him to her knee.

'A chair like Gavin.'

'No, a chair would not be high enough.'

'Shall he paint?' said Nevill, who sat on Mullet's knee for this purpose.

'Well, you may colour the letters.'

'A paint box,' said Nevill, to Honor.

'No, I can't go and get one. Here are some crayons.'

'That is better,' said Miss Pilbeam. 'There will be no mess. And you can make the letters coloured from the first.'

'He will make them all coloured,' said Nevill, looking round.

'Let me hold your hand and make an a.'

'A red a,' said Nevill, putting his eyes, his mind and a good deal of his strength on the crayon.

'A red a, a blue b, and a green c,' said Miss Pilbeam, guiding his hand.

'A is red, b is blue, and c is green,' said Nevill, in a tone of grasp and progress.

'It does not matter which colour each letter is.'

'It does,' said Nevill, suspecting an intention to smooth his path.

'You can make each letter in any colour. You can have a green a, and a red b, and a blue c.'

'But always coloured,' said Nevill.

'No. Letters can be black.'

'No, not black.'

'Yes, that is what they generally are.'

'Black,' said Nevill, looking for a crayon of this kind.

'You will never teach him anything,' said Gavin.

'It would have been better not to have colours,' said Honor.

'I shall teach him easily. He is very quick. You try to get on with your declensions,' said Miss Pilbeam, implying that her confidence did not extend indefinitely.

'Quick,' said Nevill, pushing his crayon rapidly about.

'No, that is not the way. You must make the letters as I showed you. Now we will make d.'

'D is – pink,' said Nevill, after a moment's thought.

'Yes, d can be pink.'

'A is red, b is blue, c is green, and d is pink,' said Nevill, in a tone of concluding the subject, preparing to get down from Miss Pilbeam's knee.

'No, I want you to make them all again.'

'He will make them all again,' said Nevill.

The lesson proceeded until Eleanor entered with some friends. She was accustomed to conduct her guests round the departments of her house, as she felt that in these lay the significance and the credit of her life. Nevill left Miss Pilbeam's knee and ran to meet her.

'A, b, c, d,' he said, looking up towards her, as if he were not quite sure of the position of her face.

'That is a clever boy. I am very pleased. So he has made a beginning, Miss Pilbeam.'

'A, b, c, d,' said Nevill, in a sharper tone, indicating the superfluity of the question.

'You know it all, don't you?'

'He knows it all,' said her son, with a faint sigh.

'There are a lot more letters,' said Miss Pilbeam, addressing her words to Nevill, and her tone to everybody else.

'There are four,' said her pupil.

'No, there are a great many. You have learnt the four first ones.'

Nevill looked up with comprehension dawning in his eyes.

'What are you doing?' said Eleanor, to the other two.

'Latin declensions,' said Honor, not taking her eyes from her book.

'Aren't they almost too wonderful?' said a woman guest. 'I thought it was only backward children who ever fulfilled any promise. But these have fulfilled the promise already, so it is all right. I always find it a test to be with a woman with nine children. I find I am inclined to feel that she has more than I have. Of course one ought not to feel it, but I almost think she might agree. It somehow seems nice of Miss Mitford to have that small one on her knee, so unembittered.'

'This is Miss Pilbeam,' said Eleanor.

'Of course, I felt I knew her face. I knew it was a different face from Miss Mitford's. It is much younger, isn't it? And Miss Mitford's face is quite young enough.'

'I think we sometimes pass in the village,' said Miss Pilbeam.

'Yes, that would be it,' said Mrs Cranmer, shaking hands. 'When we learn faces, it is in the village. There don't seem to be so many outside. You knew my face was not Miss Mitford's. Of course all our thoughts might be hers. And I hope they are. Miss Mitford would have such deep thoughts.'

Hope Cranmer was a small, vital-looking woman of sixty, with strong, grey, springy hair, a straight, handsome nose, clear, brown eyes, an openly curious and critical expression, and a voice so strong and sudden and deep that it took people by surprise. Her stepdaughter stood behind her, a tall, slightly awkward woman of thirty-six, with pale, hazel eyes, a long, stiff nose and chin, an oddly youthful expression, and an obstinate, innocent, complacent mouth, which did not open as much as other people's, when in use. The husband and father was a short, solid man of sixty-eight, with a heavy, hooked nose, bright, dark eyes with a look of benevolence and scepticism, and an air of humorous content with part of life, and gentle regret for the rest of it.

'Paul is always with me now,' said Hope. 'He has saved some money and inherited some more, and he is going to devote himself to leisure, because he likes it so much. He has even given up the work he loved, because of it. And he has not aged or soured or gone to pieces or anything.'

'I think he deserves a rest now, Mother,' said Faith.

'But then he would be one of the people who are lost without their work. Or who would those people be?'

'I enjoy leisure the more for not deserving it too well,' said Paul. 'People who have hardly earned it, are past its use.'

'And I can't help thinking we ascribe too much to leisure,' said his wife, 'that even if people do spend their lives in useful effort, they may age a little sometimes. It seems hard, when they have done all they can to prevent it. Up with the lark, a hard day's work, and going to bed healthily tired; what more can people do?'

'We confess to a suspicion of your good faith, Mrs Cranmer,' said her stepson, who completed the family.

'We should follow the golden mean,' said Faith.

'I dislike the mean,' said Paul, 'and anything else that prevents our going the full length with things.'

'You will follow that principle in your pursuit of leisure, Father,' said Ridley.

Ridley Cranmer was a tall, large, almost commanding-looking man of forty-three, with a broad, full face and head, large, expressionless eyes, whose colour could not be determined, and cannot be recorded, a rather full and fleshy, but not ill-modelled nose and chin, and a suave, appreciative, and where possible chivalrous manner. He was a lawyer in London, as his father had been before him, and spent his spare time at home; where the spectacle of Paul's freedom chafed him with its reminder that his inheritance might have been increased, an attitude which his father found unfilial, which he did not mind, and unreasonable, which he did.

Ridley and Faith were on terms of inevitable intimacy. Ridley understood his sister, and neither liked nor disliked the character he accepted; and Faith, who was used to vague conceptions, had a feeling that it was as well not to understand her brother. Hope said it was absurd that she and her stepdaughter should be called Hope and Faith, and that she admired Paul for not betraying embarrassment, and sympathized with Ridley when he did. Ridley treated his stepmother with formally affectionate concern, and Faith tried to be a daughter to her; and these efforts increased her tendency to admit acid undertones into her apparently inconsequent and genial speech.

Faith's name had been chosen by her own mother, in spite of, or perhaps because of, her father's lack of the attribute. It was said to suit her, and she had been heard quietly to observe that she hoped it did. Paul viewed his daughter's religion with a smooth consideration, and Hope with an indifference changed to impatience by Faith's conscientious concern for herself. Whether or not Ridley had a religion was not known, as he evinced one or not according to his company, a course which he pursued with many things.

'Fancy having to sit on someone's knee to learn!' said Hope.

'You mean, Mrs Cranmer, fancy learning when you have to sit on someone's knee!' said Ridley.

'I am sure the lessons are very interesting,' said Faith.

'They are bad things for the young,' said Paul. 'We don't choose the right time for them.'

'They will come to appreciate them later, Father.'

'You both seem to think the same,' said Hope. 'And that happens so seldom that I am sure you must be right. But we are supposed to see them appreciating them now.'

'You must be very gratified, Mrs Sullivan,' said Ridley, in an almost emotional tone.

'Haven't we any more rooms to see?' said Hope. 'I look

forward to going from floor to floor, and seeing people younger and younger on each. Isn't there anyone smaller than that little one? I am sure there used to be. I do hope this house is not going to be that depressing thing, a home without a baby.'

'The person smaller than Nevill was probably Nevill himself,' said Ridley.

'Yes, he is the last,' said Eleanor. 'This is the first day he has had lessons.'

Ridley shook his head with no change in his eyes, and his sister gave him a glance with one in hers.

'Do you remember me, Honor?' she said.

'Yes, you are Miss Cranmer.'

'Yes, my name is Faith Cranmer.'

'Isn't she Miss?' said Gavin to his sister, with a gesture towards Faith.

'Yes, that is what you would call me,' said the latter.

'She is only Miss, isn't she?' said Gavin to Honor, in a more insistent tone.

Faith gave a smile to Eleanor, with reference to this childish view.

'No one thinks it better to be Mrs, dear,' said Hope.

'I think I do,' said Honor.

'Why do you think so?' said Eleanor, with a smile.

'Well, it is better to have a house and a husband and children, than not to have anything.'

The laughter that greeted the answer mystified Honor.

'Why isn't it better?' she said.

'It is in some senses, of course,' said Faith.

'I think it is difficult for Honor,' said Hope. 'I am almost finding it so myself.'

'Do you think you are an advantage?' said Eleanor, to the child.

'She does sums better than Miss Pilbeam,' said Gavin.

'That settles it,' said Paul.

'Now isn't that a little bit of an exaggeration?' said Faith.

'No, it really is not this morning,' said Miss Pilbeam, in a tone of full tribute. 'I was very pleased.'

Eleanor laid a hand on Honor's head.

'Now what about the question of the advantage, Mrs Sullivan?' said Ridley.

'We have seen a rare caress,' said Hope. 'And it is true that it means more than frequent ones. Though perhaps the frequent ones together may mean more still. But of course it means enough.'

'Some more letters,' said Nevill, striking Miss Pilbeam's knee.

'No, you have had enough for today. I am afraid you will forget them.'

'There are a lot,' said Nevill in recollection.

'He thirsts to learn,' said Hope. 'You need do nothing for your children, Eleanor. And people say you do so much.'

'I do nothing for anyone else, I suppose they mean.'

'Well, if they do, it is not nice of them, dear. I shall know what they mean, another time.'

'Some more letters,' said Nevill, with increasing urgency.

'How many do you think there are?' said Miss Pilbeam, bending towards him.

'A hundred.'

'No, there are twenty-six.'

'There are twenty-six,' said Nevill, in an impressed tone. 'And he will learn them all.'

'The next one is called e.'

'A white one,' said Nevill, looking about for the crayon.

'Yes, if you like. The letters are called the alphabet.'

'They are called letters.

'Yes, they are called that too.'

'He calls them that,' said Nevill.

'He is the first person I have met who really said "Let me know all",' said Hope. 'And at his age too! I suppose the others do know all by now.'

'They are just beginning Latin,' said Miss Pilbeam.

'Well, isn't that knowing all? People don't begin Latin until then. And now we go down and meet those who have been learning even longer. I see it is true that the whole of life is education.'

'That is a happy thought,' said Faith, as she turned to follow. 'It makes me feel less regret that so far I have learned so little.'

'I am sure you mean you have had no advantages,' said Hope. 'And I believe they were equal to Miss Pilbeam. And you have only just begun to want to know all. I don't know how it is you are so late.'

'Would you prefer this chair, Mother?' said Faith at the table, suggesting that she harboured no ill feeling.

'No, guests always think everything is perfect. Isn't it nice of her to go on calling me Mother? I always think it is so daughterly.'

'You are the only mother I can remember.'

'I appreciate your not recalling other examples of what I am. Your father and Ridley both do it, and it seems such a double course.'

'Ridley does not do you the same honour,' said Fulbert.

'It is a little different,' said Faith. 'He is older and a man.'

'It seems to be quite different,' said Hope.

'How was Nevill managing his first day in the schoolroom?' said Luce.

'Managing is the word,' said Hope. 'He was giving directions and having them followed.'

'Is Miss Pilbeam a success?'

'Yes, indeed. They were doing Latin and the alphabet. And those are the foundations of all learning.'

'I am so glad,' said Luce. 'I suggested Miss Pilbeam, because I knew she really needed the employment. It is a relief that the arrangement is a success.'

'You are unPlatonic, my child,' said Fulbert. 'The work does not exist for the man, but the man for the work.'

'I know nothing about Plato, Father,' said Luce, illustrating the methods of education in her family. 'But I do know when a kindness needs to be done. And this was a clear case of it.'

'I am so glad Miss Pilbeam has a post that suits her,' said Faith. 'I have been so sorry for her and her father since Mrs Pilbeam died.'

Fulbert threw his quizzical glance from one young woman to the other.

'You need not worry about your children's education, Fulbert,' said Hope. 'I saw it going on on every floor. There is a room on each on purpose. I am glad we never go round our house; the difference would strike us too forcibly. I daresay Paul and Ridley go sometimes, to hear the echo of a voice that is still.'

'Mrs Cranmer, there is room in my heart for more than one person,' said Ridley.

'Yes, that is what I was saying, dear.'

'And I am sure I may say the same of my father.'

'No, you may not,' said Hope; 'I forbid it.'

Faith turned grave, neutral eyes on her stepmother.

'You will miss the hunting this winter, Fulbert,' said Paul.

'I shall, and other things as well.'

'Yes, that would not be the first thing on his mind, Father,' said Faith with a smile.

'We do not talk of the things that go too deep for words,' said Hope. 'I suppose it would really be no good.'

'Will you be hunting, Daniel?' said Paul.

'There are other things that he must do,' said Eleanor at once.

Regan turned eyes of troubled sympathy on her grandson.

'It is a thing he should not have begun,' said Sir Jesse.

'You forget, Paul, that they do nothing but learn,' said Hope. 'A person has only to need a post, to be accommodated as a teacher here. I think it is wonderful of Luce to lift weights off people's minds. If we had not provided for Faith, it might be such a relief.'

'I am far from regarding myself as fit for such important work as teaching, Mother.'

'But Luce would regard you as fit, dear. That is what I mean. I said it was wonderful of her.'

Regan laughed in enjoyment of the joke, quite free from uneasiness about her grandchildren's advantages.

'I don't think you hunt, Faith?' said Fulbert.

'No, I do not,' said Faith, in a quiet, pleasant tone.

'You are like Luce and uncertain of your nerve?'

'Yes, I make no claim to that kind of courage, Father,' said Luce, smiling and saying nothing of other kinds.

'It is not the highest sort,' said Fulbert.

'I wonder if there is any other,' said Graham. 'I felt it was the lack of the whole of courage that prevented my hunting.'

'My nerve is quite good,' said Faith, in the same tone.

'She thinks it is cruel to the fox,' said Hope. 'Isn't it imaginative of her? She puts herself in his place.'

'We must set the pleasure to human beings on the other side of the scales,' said Sir Jesse.

'She thinks the fox doesn't count that, or not enough to find it any compensation. She believes he only thinks of himself. And yet she thinks of him. She is a wonderful character.'

'She thinks of the fox and not of men and women.'

'No, she thinks of them too. She says that hunting degrades them, that they should get their pleasure in other ways. She wants them to have pleasure.'

'Hunting takes a lot of qualities,' said Sir Jesse.

'Grandpa speaks after a lifetime's practice of it,' said Daniel.

'A way you will never speak,' said his grandfather.

'Is this being cruel to be kind?' said Hope. 'Or is it just being cruel?'

'It is being honest,' said her host.

'It is showing moral courage,' said Graham. 'In other words yielding to temptation.'

'The qualities might surely be put to better purpose than hounding to death an innocent creature,' said Faith.

'Hounding is a good word,' said Hope. 'It seems such a right use of it.'

'I do think, Mrs Sullivan,' said Ridley, bending towards Eleanor, 'that there is something repellent in the idea of a little, terrified creature being driven to exhaustion and death. How would any of us like it?'

'The fox has his own chance,' said Sir Jesse.

'He would prefer the one that we have,' said Daniel. 'Not that I consider his preferences.'

'You may do so,' said his grandfather.

'You are hunting as usual, Paul?' said Fulbert, regarding Faith's scruples as things to be necessarily passed over.

'More than usual, now that I am my own master.'

'Can I pass you the sugar, Father?' said Faith.

'Isn't it selfless of Fulbert to take an interest in what he will miss?' said Hope. 'It is people with emptier lives like mine who ought to go away.'

'It is because of what my life holds, that I am going.'

'Yes, it would hardly be worth while for me to go.'

'Take what you can get out of it, my boy,' said Sir Jesse, almost harshly. 'You are not a woman.'

'Father knows that, Grandpa,' said Luce, in her demure tone.

'I think he is one of those men who do,' said Graham.

'Do men get more out of things than women?' said Faith. 'I should hardly have thought so.'

'I would not exchange my life for a man's,' said Regan.

'You would be an odd person if you would, Lady Sullivan,' said Ridley, in an earnest tone.

'I always think I should have been more of a success as a man,' said Eleanor.

'Mrs Sullivan, you do not wish for the change?' said Ridley, in an almost stricken manner.

'Well, not at this stage, I suppose.'

'Would you be rid of us all, Mother?' said Luce.

'Well, I might prefer to be your father.'

'That would be giving up a good deal of us.'

'It would be gaining some more,' said Fulbert. 'I admit no belittlement of fatherhood.'

'We must acknowledge the woman's part as the deeper and fuller here,' said Ridley.

'In most cases,' said Faith. 'And exceptions prove rules.'

'They seem to break them,' said Graham. 'But what does it matter?'

'Would you be a woman or a man, Luce, my dear?' said Regan.

'A woman, Grandma,' said Luce, simply, turning her eyes full on Regan's face.

'Which would you choose to be, Father?' said Faith.

'Well, I think a man gets more and gives less.'

'You have not answered my question, Father.'

'He has in his own way, Faith,' said Luce, in a low, amused tone.

'It would be no advantage not to give,' said Faith. 'One would not wish to give that up.'

'It would be shocking to ask Faith what she gave,' said Hope to her husband. 'She can only give intangible things, and no one can speak of those. And I did feel the impulse.'

'Few normal people would wish to belong to the opposite sex,' said Daniel.

'It would mean they were different,' said Graham. 'And that would seem to them a pity.'

'A human being is a wonderful thing,' said Faith.

'Then of course it would be a pity,' said Paul.

'A human being is in some ways a melancholy thing,' said Ridley, glancing at Eleanor.

'People often make their own troubles,' said Faith.

'Well, it does seem shallow to be fortunate,' said Hope.

'We don't all have to make them,' said Regan.

'I wish I had had as much sorrow as you have, Lady Sullivan,' said Hope. 'I am really ashamed of having been through so little.'

Regan laughed.

'I don't know anyone with such an infectious laugh as Grandma, when she really gives it,' said Luce.

'I daresay the experience behind it only adds to it,' said Faith.

'Can't we even laugh properly without having trouble?' said Hope. 'Then it is true that laughter is near to tears. Is this six or seven children coming in?'

'You know it is six, Mother.'

'I knew it ought to be. But it did seem to be more. And surely these children ought to count more than one.'

Nevill ran up to Regan and stood by her knee.

'A, b, c, d,' he said.

'What a clever boy! I did not know you could learn so fast.'

'A is red, b is blue, c is green, and d is pink,' said Nevill watching her face for the effect of this knowledge.

'Does Miss Pilbeam colour them?'

'No, he does. There are twenty-so.'

'Twenty-six what?'

'Twenty-six a, b, c, d,' said Nevill, rapidly moving his feet.

'Letters,' said Honor.

'Letters,' said Nevill, a calm overspreading his face.

'And you will learn them all?' said Regan.

'He will learn twenty-six.'

'And what colours will they be?'

'White, purple, brown, crimson lake,' said Nevill, with very little pause.

'Does it confuse him to have the colours?' said Eleanor. 'I should have thought it would make it harder.'

'It does make him think each letter has its own colour,' said Honor. 'But he asked to have it like that. He really wanted to paint them.'

'Aren't they wonderful to have to have things made harder?' said Hope. 'And to ask for it too. I have never heard of it before.'

'You must have heard of children who wanted to colour things, Mother,' said Faith. 'I always did myself.'

'Yes, dear, but I thought it was to make them easier.'

'We can't catch my stepmother out, Mrs Sullivan,' said Ridley.

'That was the last thing I wanted to do,' said Faith, in a quiet tone.

'We know quite a lot about Faith,' said Hope. 'Most people are so secretive about themselves.'

'I hope I do not talk about myself,' said Faith. 'Not that there is anything I wish to hide.'

'I want to hide almost everything,' said Hope. 'Some of it must leak out, but I do trust not all.'

'Did you like your lessons with Miss Pilbeam, Gavin?' said Eleanor.

'I didn't mind them.'

'Did you, Honor?'

'Yes, thank you, Mother.'

'He liked it too,' said Nevill, turning his eyes rapidly from face to face.

'Don't they think or talk of anything but learning?' said Hope.

'This is an exceptional occasion,' said Eleanor. 'They have a new governess.'

'Yes, the one that was not Miss Mitford. Have you got rid of her? I mean, have they grown beyond her? Of course they would have.'

'No, they are not up to her yet.'

'Who is up to her?'

'These two,' said Eleanor, indicating Isabel and Venice.

'And does James have someone in between?'

'No, James goes to school.'

'The school is between Miss Mitford and Miss Pilbeam. And Daniel and Graham are at Cambridge, and there is no more for Luce to learn. I see I denied my stepchildren every opportunity.'

'Have you little ones finished your dessert?' said Eleanor. 'We don't want much of you today.'

Nevill forced the remainder of his portion into his mouth and prepared to leave.

'The child will choke, my dear,' said Fulbert.

His son ran towards the door, with a view to dealing with his situation in his own way.

'Honor, tell Hatton to see that Nevill does not choke,' said Eleanor.

'Is that what Hatton does?' said Hope. 'And the other nurse and Miss Mitford and Miss Pilbeam all do their own things. Suppose something unforeseen should arise? I suppose you would have someone else. I am so glad this was not unforeseen.'

'Civilization has its weaker side,' said Fulbert.

'It seems a strong side, so well supported,' said Graham.

'It is more difficult to make other people do things than to do them yourself,' said Eleanor.

'It seems a foolish way of arranging matters,' said Daniel.

'What a family for liking difficult things!' said Hope. 'Always choosing the harder part.'

'You would not suggest, Daniel, that your mother should be a slave to all the departments of her house?' said Ridley, in some consternation.

'Yes, I would, if it would save her any trouble.'

'Isn't anyone going up with Nevill?' said Eleanor. 'I am so afraid he will choke.'

'Are you really?' said Hope. 'I do sympathize with you. You make me very anxious, myself. Can't we send for the person who deals with it? You would want to get that off your mind.'

Sounds came from the hall that disposed of the question, and Venice hastened to her brother's aid.

'That is a good sister,' said Eleanor, as her daughter returned, leading Nevill, who capered forward in open relief. 'Is there anything to be done out there?'

'Mullet heard and came down,' said Venice.

'It was Mullet, was it?' said Hope. 'Not Hatton; you were wrong, Eleanor; but it is a good deal to keep in your head.'

'You are laughing at us as a family, Mrs Cranmer,' said Luce.

'I am only jealous of you for being one, dear.'

Nevill ran up to Regan.

'He ate it all at once,' he said, looking at the table. 'But not do it another time.'

'No, no more today,' said Eleanor. 'People who are sick have had enough.'

Nevill turned and ran to the door, the purpose of his presence being over. A maid opened it and he went out.

'You should say, "Thank you",' called Eleanor, who though providing attendance as a matter of course for her children, did not approve of their accepting it in the corresponding spirit.

Nevill ran back and up to the maid, and taking her apron, looked up into her face.

'Thank you,' he said, and dragged her from the room.

'He did want someone else,' said Hope. 'And they say that children left to scramble up anyhow, do better.'

'Honor and Gavin can run away too,' said Eleanor. 'The elder ones at the table can stay.'

'Why don't they all do the same?' said Hope. 'Because it would be easier?'

'They would not like it. The same things are not suited to them.'

'Do you understand them like that? And I thought that parents always misunderstood their children.'

'The very strength and possessiveness of a parent's feelings may prevent easy understanding,' said Luce.

'Is that what I said?' said Hope. 'I am glad. It sounded like something not so nice.'

'Is James at home today?' said Eleanor, looking at her son.

'Do a parent's feelings render a child actually invisible?' said Graham.

'But is he at home? You know what I mean. Is he not well?'

'It seems that children understand their parents,' said Paul, laughing.

'Sons understand their mothers, we know,' said Hope. 'But is it a thing we talk about?'

'There is a holiday at the school,' said Isabel, while Faith gave a glance at her stepmother.

'Oh, that is what it is,' said Eleanor, as if this were a more venial circumstance than indisposition. 'But the holidays seem to come rather often. It is early in the term.'

'It is the schoolmaster's wife's birthday,' said James.

'Is it?' said Paul. 'Or is it out of the Bible or the grammar?'

'Either is very suitable for a school,' said his wife.

Faith gave another glance at her.

'Would the master give a holiday for his own birthday?' said Daniel.

'He never does,' said James.

'It seems a reversal of the usual theories with regard to ladies' birthdays,' said Ridley.

'It is nice of him to choose his wife's,' said Hope. 'It makes him seem so glad that she was born.'

'I don't know why the rest of us should rejoice,' said Regan.

'It is James who is doing so, and he knows her,' said Hope. 'One sees what the master means, and I think it is very nice.'

'I never see her,' said James.

'Well, that does make him seem rather absorbed in his own point of view. But it is pleasant to keep birthdays, Lady Sullivan, and he will give James a holiday on yours, if you wish.'

'James takes a holiday on mine anyhow,' said Regan, smiling.

'Well, that is the birthday to be kept,' said Sir Jesse. 'That, if no other.'

His wife looked deeply moved.

'I think you are even better than the schoolmaster, Sir Jesse,' said Hope.

'Now, Isabel and Venice, let us hear your voices,' said Eleanor.

For a moment no sound at all was heard.

'Do you have a holiday on Miss Mitford's birthday?' said Paul.

'We don't even know when it is,' said Venice.

'An unjust distinction between educationists,' said Daniel.

'We should not despise people who are employed in the house,' said Hope.

'Miss Mitford is a very well-read woman,' said Faith.

'Yes, that is not at all like despising her, dear.'

'Books seem to come for her by every post,' said Regan.

'I think that is rather like it,' said Paul.

'Miss Mitford has been with us for seventeen years,' said Luce.

'I hope it is not a tragedy in a phrase,' said Graham, his tone not betraying that he really hoped it.

'She would be well-read by now,' said Isabel. 'The books do come twice a week.'

'Grandma was not exaggerating as much as I thought,' said Daniel.

'Ninety-six times a year, if we do not count her holidays,' said Isabel.

'I do not wonder you wanted them to talk, Eleanor,' said Hope. 'It would have been a great pity to miss it.'

'Now we know the length of Miss Mitford's holidays,' said Daniel.

'I do not,' said Paul, while Fulbert rapidly and openly calculated on his fingers.

'Four weeks,' said Faith, in a slightly breathless tone, outstripping him by a tense and covert effort.

'You see I did have her educated,' said Hope.

'Now I think Miss Mitford will be expecting you,' said Eleanor to the children.

'Let them stay for a while,' said Fulbert. 'I will have them while I can.'

'Yes, I am to lose my son, Cranmer,' said Sir Jesse, who was inclined to refer any subject to himself, and to address his words to men. 'I ought to say I may never see him again. But somehow I feel I should not mean it.'

'People would think you did,' said Regan.

'I should not,' said Hope; 'I am sure he is immortal.'

'I am seventy-nine,' said Sir Jesse.

'There, I said you were.'

Regan laughed.

'But I must not depend on my father,' said Fulbert. 'And I should make my plans to meet the event of anything's happening to me. The one thing's happening, of course I mean. I only have the normal chance.'

'I daresay there are plenty of risks out there,' said Regan.

'Someone must break it to my mother and my wife,' went on Fulbert, with the faint unction that marked his utterance of anything that bore on himself. 'Someone must share the guardianship of my infant children. My sons are young, and younger to my wife than they are. I am dependent on someone outside. Paul, will you face the risk of another man's burdens?'

'I am no good at other people's affairs. I don't take as much trouble with them as I do with my own. I don't even take enough trouble with those.'

'Then, Ridley, I must turn to you,' said Fulbert, doing as he said. 'We have never been close, or even perhaps congenial friends; but I depend on your character; you have our affairs in your hands; you would work well with my wife. Will you undertake the trust?'

Ridley rose to his feet.

'I will undertake it, Fulbert. And from the bottom of my heart will I regard it as a trust.'

'It is not as if it would ever happen,' said Regan.

'Lady Sullivan,' said Ridley, turning quickly to her, 'do you think we should be calmly discussing it, if we thought it would?'

'I don't know what else you could do.'

Ridley looked round, allowed his face to relax into a smile and resumed his seat.

'Well, there is an end of that,' said Fulbert. 'I can return to my own character. There is something unnatural in making plans for one's own end.'

'It is too necessary for us to like it,' said Regan.

'It is very brave,' said Graham. 'But people think so, and that is something.'

'I think we ought to go, Mother,' said Faith.

'You mean we are constraining their last hours?'

'I have not seen any sign of constraint.'

'We are happy to be helped over them,' said Sir Jesse. 'It is hard to talk to my son, with this in front. And most of what I have to say can wait for his return. He must have heard it many times.'

'He will not be in the same position, Sir Jesse,' said Ridley, speaking with easy confidence in the future. 'He will have much to relate, that is entirely unfamiliar.'

'We know he will come back, if he is alive,' said Regan. 'It will be a good thing when he is gone now.'

'What are you children doing, listening to grown-up talk?' said Eleanor.

'You have stated our occupation,' said Isabel. 'And it is hard to see our alternative.'

'You can all run away to the schoolroom.'

'You do mix the sexes,' said Hope. 'I was wondering if I had been wrong in keeping Ridley and Faith together.'

'Brothers and sisters are separated soon enough.'

'Ridley and Faith were not. We only found it out when they were.'

'Ridley was always a very masculine type,' said Faith. 'And he was some years older than I was, and I think more developed for his age.'

'You must remember you are speaking of your brother, dear,' said Hope.

'I said nothing against him, Mother.'

'You were damning him with faint praise; I think with almost no praise at all. I believe you were just damning him.'

'I am not always thinking of praising people or not praising them.'

'It would be nice to think of the first, dear.'

'You don't often do it yourself, Mother.'

'Well, I so seldom see any cause for praise. And when I do, I am so often upset about it. So it is not very easy for me.'

'I shall be quite an important person for the next months,' said Fulbert. 'I daresay you all think it will be a change.'

'It had not crossed my mind, Father,' said Luce, with a smile.

'Other things will be that, my boy,' said Sir Jesse. 'My advice is to make the most of them.'

'Away, away, you children,' said Luce, gently clapping her hands.

'Yes, Miss Mitford will be expecting them,' said Eleanor.

'Miss Mitford's heart must grow sick with hope deferred,' said Graham.

'You have taken a weight off my mind, Ridley,' said Fulbert.

'There is happily no need to regard it as transferred to mine.'

'I wish I could sometimes meet a mark of confidence,' said Hope.

'Different people are suited to different things,' said Faith.

'I don't think that is a better way of putting it, dear, or anyhow not nicer. I ought to go away like Fulbert, and let absence make the heart grow fond.'

'Such a step would be fraught with danger for many of us,' said Ridley, shaking his head.

'I don't mean I should dare to go.'

'Ridley does not mean in Mr Sullivan's case,' said Faith. 'He was thinking of ordinary people like ourselves.'

'Being coupled with you, dear, makes up for everything,' said Hope.

'I think the gap must tend to get a little narrower,' said Fulbert, in an unflinching tone.

'It is a good thing if it does,' said Regan; 'I am sure I hope it will.'

'What should we talk about, if it disappeared?' said Graham.

'Do you think you will miss your father less, as time goes on, Graham?' said Eleanor.

'I hope my elders are right. I want to be saved all I can.'

'Do you, Daniel?'

'I will take Grandma's word for it.'

Eleanor looked round in an instinct to pass on to James, but realized that he was gone.

'You ought to bear your own testimony, my dear,' said Fulbert, 'if you require it of other people.'

'I think you ought, Mother,' said Luce.

'I shall miss your father more with every day.'

'I am sure that is the truth, Mother. And very few people could say it unflinchingly like that.'

'I am glad Grandma set the fashion, and not Mother,' said Graham.

'This is excellent for the gap,' said Daniel. 'Father may have been getting anxious about it.'

'How wonderful heroism is!' said Hope.

'I think we ought to leave them, Mother,' said Faith.

'To wallow in our family miseries,' said Regan, in a tone of contempt for the prospect.

'I have never seen the courage of despair before,' said Hope.

'I can quite understand it,' said Faith. 'It does not show any lack of feeling.'

'We shall be outstaying our welcome,' said Paul.

'And doing other things to it,' said his wife. 'Good-bye, Fulbert; we shall meet you again before you go, and again when you come back; it will be nothing but meeting. I am hiding everything under a cheerful exterior, as that seems to be the kind that is always used.'

'You put rather a strain on our patience, Mrs Cranmer,' said Ridley, as they left the house.

'But not too much for it, dear. You mean that too.'

'You can talk with more sense, Ridley,' said Paul.

'I do see what Ridley means, Father,' said Faith, in a tone so quiet as to be almost an undertone. 'I cannot say I do not.'

'Then we won't expect it, dear,' said Hope. 'I wonder if I shall be the means of binding you and Ridley together.'

'Do you ever show your true self, Mrs Cranmer?' said Ridley, who was proceeding in a state of exaltation produced by the trust reposed in him.

'I hope not often. I do my best to conceal it.'

'Our true selves should not be anything to be ashamed of,' said Faith.

'I don't think it would be nice not to be ashamed of them,' said Hope. 'I am ashamed and terrified of mine, and even more of other people's.'

'Other people's are the thing,' said Paul.

'There are people in whom I would place an absolute trust,' said Faith.

'We won't ask you to mention them, for fear they are not us,' said Hope.

'I think one of them is Mrs Sullivan.'

'Oh, so they are not us,' said Paul.

'I confess that the inner truth of people tends to elude me,' said Ridley. 'Penetration may not be one of my qualities.'

'Well, that was not mentioned,' said Hope. 'But I daresay it does not matter. You are able to think the best of everyone; and as people live up to our conception of them, that would improve them.'

'Here we are at home,' said Faith, in a bright tone, as if welcoming an end to a conversation she regretted. 'It is nearly time for tea.'

'I am glad to hear it,' said Paul. 'A woman's life is giving me a woman's ways.'

'That may not be the explanation, Father. I also feel ready for it,' said Ridley.

'And your life is a man's, a hero's really,' said Hope.

'That is perhaps an exaggeration, Mrs Cranmer.'

'Talking to the old man is a tax,' said Paul. 'He is like a volcano that is quiet at the top.'

'Then he is like a real one,' said Hope, 'and that must be alarming. I sympathize with him, if he has to pretend to be better than he is. I know what a strain it can be.'

'Did you adopt the course today?' said Paul, laughing.

'No, I was dreadful, wasn't I? Absolutely myself. To think that Fulbert will have to remember me like that!'

'It is better to be oneself, whatever impression one gives,' said Faith.

'But we are told to conquer ourselves,' said Hope.

'The process was perhaps incomplete, Mrs Cranmer,' said Ridley.

'Well, we are not to mind about success. It is only the effort that counts.'

'To disguise one's real nature seems such a second-rate instinct,' said Faith.

'I suppose all instincts are,' said Hope. 'That is why they have to be overlaid by reason. I know I am inconsistent, but it upsets me to visit the Sullivans. It is because their house is so much better than mine.'

'The Sullivans have a place, Mother. This is just a comfortable home.'

'I know you do not mean to be unkind, dear.'

'I do not indeed; I was only speaking the truth.'

'There isn't much difference. Brutal frankness is an accepted term.'

'I think this is a very restful room.'

'Yes, you know just what I mean.'

'We should not be any happier in a better one.'

'Well, it would not be true happiness. But I like the other kind. And having a dozen children would be the first kind, wouldn't it?'

'You know Mrs Sullivan has nine children, Mother.'

'Yes, but easy exaggeration glosses it over, and makes it seem more trivial and vague. I could not bring myself to say nine; I am such a coward.'

'Have you not found two stepchildren enough?' said Ridley.

'Oh, of course, dear. You have given me the duties and responsibilities of motherhood. I ought not to want any more.'

'We know it has not been the same, Mother,' said Faith, in a quiet tone.

'Oh, well, dear, I am not one of those women who have never heard themselves called Mother.'

'I wonder how much feeling those youngsters have for their parents,' said Paul.

'Paul, that is kind. I do feel that perhaps I am making a fuss about nothing. Faith and Ridley think I am. Now I have had some comfort, I will show my better qualities for the rest of the day. I will be one of those rare people who keep them for their families. I am glad I have not expended them on anyone else.'

'Are you jealous of the whole brood?' said Paul.

'I am jealous of Nevill,' said Faith, lightly.

'The one who choked?' said Hope.

'You know that was Nevill, Mother.'

'There is my worse nature again. It really seems the only one I have.'

'I should like him to stay always as he is now.'

'Why, he would be bound to choke sooner or later, if it went on.'

'Venice will grow up a handsome girl,' said Ridley.

'The one who prevented the choking? But wouldn't she have to remain in the same stage too? Because it couldn't be allowed to happen. Eleanor saw it herself.'

'There are seven more,' said Paul.

'Are there?' said Hope. 'There it is again.'

'I should like to see more of the girls,' said Faith.

'Surely a wish you can gratify,' said Paul. 'That is the best thing to do with wishes.'

'I think I like girls better than boys.'

'Then you need only be jealous of four,' said Hope. 'But of course you are too young for such feelings. People would be jealous of you. Where is Ridley going?'

'To London,' said her stepson, slightly drawing himself up.

'Of course, you are indispensable there. And here too, as we know. You are not without honour anywhere.'

Faith glanced at her parents, and as they made no movement towards the hall, accompanied her brother herself.

'Do you like Faith the better of your children?' said Hope, to her husband.

'Oh, well, yes, a father takes to his daughter.'

'I like her better too. And you would expect me to be a woman who never preferred her own sex.'

'I should have said you generally did so.'

'Most people do. It is a thing that has not been noticed. People know too much about their sex, to think it possible to prefer it, when really they find it familiar and congenial.'

'Faith seemed to feel that she preferred it,' said Paul.

'Yes, but Faith knows nothing about it. And I could pay her no greater compliment. Self-knowledge speaks ill for people; it shows they are what they are, almost on purpose. And I am not speaking against her the moment her back is turned. I am not at all what I am supposed to be.'

'That would perhaps be the safest moment to choose,' said Faith, returning and speaking with a smile. 'But it is better to be open and above-board with everybody.'

'But we could not speak evil to their faces,' said Hope.

'Well, it is not a thing we are obliged to do, Mother.'

'I like my friends best when they are doing it. It makes them so zestful and observant. Original too, almost creative. You see I am speaking good behind their backs. And you don't seem to like it much, but I suppose no one likes to hear other people always praised.'

'I think that would be very pleasant,' said Faith.

'Well, let us all praise Ridley.'

'He has met a great mark of confidence today.'

'That is not praise. You must say you think he deserved it.'

'I think that trust often makes people worthy of it.'

'Faith, I like to hear people speak evil. You know I have admitted it. But you must remember that Ridley is your brother.'

Chapter 5

'Sir Jesse says we must continue to practise economy,' said Priscilla Marlowe, lifting her eyes without warning from her book. 'He says it need not interfere with our comfort. I could see he knew it prevented it.'

'People used to talk about elegant economy,' said her sister, also looking up from a book. 'I suppose they meant unobtrusive expenditure.'

'Sir Jesse says our interests lie in things of the mind,' said Priscilla, in an absent tone that suggested that this was the case. 'And they do cost less than other things.'

'I wonder why he chose such interests for us,' said the third member of the group, relinquishing the same occupation as his sisters.

'Because it would be an economy,' said Priscilla; 'perhaps an elegant one in this case.'

'I hope he is not thinking of reducing our allowance,' said her brother, in a shrill, anxious voice. 'Because we have cut things to their finest point.'

'It was in his mind, but it did not come out. He would have found it too embarrassing. We hardly know what we owe to his dislike of discomfiture. I wonder why I have to see him alone. I suppose so that he may have only one third of the discomfiture that is rightly his. I ought to be sacrificed as the eldest sister, but it seems that I have three times as much as is mine.'

'It is awkward that I am assumed to earn so much more than I do,' said Lester. 'My last book brought in sixty pounds, and it took two years. And I am ashamed to confess how poorly my work is paid. It would make him think it was poor work and despised. And so he believes I spend money on myself, a thing I should never do.'

'It would be a selfish course,' said Priscilla. 'But Susan earns a good deal at her school, and he does not separate our incomes. He assumes that you earn the most, as the man.'

'I do not mind being helped by my sister. I must grant her the superior place, when it is justly hers. But I wonder why Sir Jesse despises me for earning so little, when he believes it is really so much.'

'He is used to thinking in large sums,' said Susan.

'He breaks the habit when he comes here,' said her sister. 'Perhaps that is why he never seems at ease. He does think in very small ones then.'

'We ought to be grateful to him for saving us from penury,' said Susan. 'And giving us an education that makes us self-supporting.'

'In your case,' said Lester, gravely. 'I could not be a schoolmaster because of my voice and manner. The boys would be amused by me.'

'And we are grateful,' said Priscilla. 'I never know why people say they ought to be. Of course they ought.'

'It is hard to be beholden to him,' said Lester.

'We have been glad of the chance,' said Priscilla. 'And it is one that people always take.'

'We had no alternative,' said her brother.

'None but perishing of want,' said Susan. 'Three orphans from South America, the children of Sir Jesse's friends, but having no other claim. That is what we were.'

'And see what we are now,' said Lester, with a crow of laughter. 'Still orphans, but having established a claim.'

Priscilla, Lester and Susan Marlowe were aged thirty-five, thirty-four and thirty-two. They had pale, oblong faces, tall angular frames, round, grey, short-sighted eyes, peering through cheap, round glasses, and seeming to peer considerably beyond, heavy, shelving brows, from which curly, colourless hair receded, and in Lester's case had disappeared, and features so little conforming to rule, that they differed equally from other people's and each other's. Priscilla's voice was slow and apparently serious, Lester's shrill and uneven, and Susan's rapid and deep.

Sir Jesse gave them a cottage on the place, the services of an old couple whom he wished to support, and did so in this way, and an allowance to eke out what they earned. He never asked them to his house, seldom visited them and passed them abroad with acknowledgement but without a word; a course which people attributed to embarrassment at his generosity, though the feeling arises more easily from the consciousness of other qualities. They were used to his ways, hardly knew his wife, unaware that her hostile indifference embraced others besides themselves, had an almost surreptitious acquaintance with Daniel and Graham; and lived in their interests and anxieties and each other, with as much satisfaction as most people and more enjoyment.

'I have a month at home,' said Susan, looking round the low, cramped room with an expression that hardly suggested its character. 'How did we get all that wood for the fire?'

'We collect it in the park,' said her sister. 'We go after dusk, so that we shall not be seen. We are not ashamed of our poverty, but we know Sir Jesse is; and it might look as if we were short of fuel.'

'It would look so,' said Lester. 'And we do not want to suggest that he might provide it, when he does so much for us.'

'It is a good method of making him do so,' said Susan. 'Do you suppose he knows you get it?'

'He must know that the coal he sends is not enough,' said Priscilla. 'And I expect he would know if we were cold. He seems to know everything about us.'

'He must know that we have thin walls and no damp course,' said Lester, in a serious voice. 'He may think we don't feel the cold.'

'What could you do with the cold but feel it?' said Susan. 'How else would you know there was such a thing?'

'People seem to think other people don't feel cold or grief or anything,' said Priscilla. 'I don't think they mind their feeling the heat. It seems a more comfortable thing, and it does not require any fuel.'

'Why are we having so much to eat?' said Susan.

'I am afraid not because it is your first day at home,' said her sister. 'Mrs Morris has to nurse her husband, and cannot cook tonight.'

'It is only old age,' said Lester, with simple reassurance. 'Nothing infectious.'

'Well, not immediately,' said Priscilla.

Lester gave a laugh.

'I am thankful to be at home,' said Susan. 'We can never be at ease except with each other. No one would understand our life, who had not lived it. A past without parents or a background is as rare as being brought up in an orphanage.'

'Is that rare?' said Priscilla. 'The papers always say how many thousands of inmates are admitted every year. It shows how few people behave as well as Sir Jesse.'

'That is why we have to contribute to such institutions,' said Lester.

'Do you?' said Priscilla, astonished. 'How you prevent the left hand from knowing what the right hand doeth!'

'Not I myself,' said Lester, opening his eyes. 'I never spend money without saying so.'

'We are the last people to support orphanages,' said Susan. 'They are fortunate in not having had to support us.'

'I suppose Sir Jesse has been father and mother to us,' said Lester, as if the thought amused him; 'though no one would think it, who saw him pass us without a word.'

'Family life seldom gets to that,' said Priscilla, 'or not with both the father and the mother.'

'We have never lisped our prayers at our mother's knee,' said Susan. 'What can be expected of us?'

'Hard work and reasonable success,' said Lester, in an almost wondering tone.

'Criminals are always told to look back on the time when they did that,' said Priscilla. 'It does not seem to be an auspicious beginning.'

'Our parents were friends of Sir Jesse's,' said Lester. 'And they lived in South America. I do not want to know more about them.'

'It seems to stamp them,' said Priscilla. 'I should not dare to ask. If it were anything that could be borne, Sir Jesse would have told us. And he would not mind our bearing a certain amount.'

'He seems to avoid contact with their children,' said Susan. 'We should never forgive ourselves, if we exerted any untoward influence on him. I wonder he allows us to mix with each other.'

Lester raised his eyes at this train of thought.

'It is the cheapest way of disposing of us,' he said. 'He gives us a house and a little money, and we provide the rest.'

'You would not think we had such large appetites, to look at us,' said Susan.

'I should have thought we were rather hungry-looking,' said Priscilla. 'As though we hardly knew where our next meal was coming from. And we do know. From Sir Jesse and our own hard earnings.'

'Well, Mrs Morris,' said Lester, 'I hope Morris is better.'

The housekeeper closed her eyes and kept them closed, while she placed the teapot with her usual precision.

'He must have a very good appetite.'

'What makes you say that, sir?' said Mrs Morris, performing an action that seemed unnatural to her, and looking at the speaker.

'You cook so much for him, that you have no time for us.'

'I hope to give you your usual dinner, sir.'

'If we have this tea and our usual dinner, Morris must be very bad.'

'He could not eat what I cooked, sir,' said Mrs Morris, arranging the table for those who could.

'Would he like anything special?' said Priscilla.

'He is not used to having what he fancies, miss.'

'There he is, going down the path,' said Susan.

'He can get about, miss.'

'He is going to the inn.'

Mrs Morris just cast a glance after her husband, as if his errand meant too little to warrant attention.

'Not used to having what he fancies!' said Susan, as the door closed. 'He gets more and more used to it.'

'Well, it means we can do the same,' said her sister.

'I am glad Morris has his own life,' said Lester, gravely.

'Lester talks quite like a man to Mrs Morris,' said Priscilla.

'Mr and Mrs Cranmer,' said Mrs Morris.

'Well, my dears,' said Hope. 'Are you expecting friends to tea, or is this your ordinary standard?' Her tone had a slight difference from the one she used to the Sullivans.

'It is Susan's first day at home,' said Paul, whose tone was always the same.

'I do respect the power to spend on things that did not meet the eye of outsiders. I don't believe they are even glad we have come on them in their luxury. And I should think it such a happy coincidence.'

'We are glad you are to share it,' said Lester.

'And now you do not pretend that you take it as a matter of course. I can't tell you what I think of you. I almost wish Faith were here; Paul will never appreciate the position.'

'Did she know you were coming?' said Lester, simply.

'What insight you have into our family life! No, I did not tell her.'

'I expect she is just as happy at home.'

'No, she likes nothing better than a little change, and she really needed it. But I needed it more, because compared to her as a companion I am a Cleopatra in my infinite variety. How few people would dare to say that!'

'How many of us think it of ourselves?' said Paul.

'Do not be foolish, Paul. Very few of us.'

'Very few,' said Priscilla.

'Have you been to the big house to say good-bye to Fulbert?' said Hope.

'No, his going makes no difference to us,' said Susan. 'We see none of them but Sir Jesse and the two elder boys.'

'Has Sir Jesse been to see you lately?'

'He came this afternoon.'

'And you were not going to mention it! I should take the first opportunity of bringing it in. Why did he come to see you? I must ask, Paul. They don't mind my knowing, and it would never occur to them to tell me.'

'Partly because a visit was due,' said Priscilla, 'and partly to hint that we might be more economical.'

'Even more than we are,' said Lester, seriously.

'Well, there is always something that can be cut off,' said Hope. 'But I wonder how Sir Jesse knew.'

'He didn't; he only hoped so,' said Priscilla. 'And when he saw the cottage, he thought he was wrong and took his leave.'

'But what about the tea? Did you expect him to stay?'

'To tea here?' said Lester.

'Yes.'

'And have it with us? Sir Jesse?'

'Yes. Is it impossible?'

'All things are possible,' said Susan. 'It is unthinkable.'

'We thought Mrs Morris could not cook tonight, because Morris is ill,' said Lester.

'Thank you so much; I am glad you do not always live like this. I don't like to think I am a stingy housekeeper. I am mean in so many matters; all the others, I think; and I hoped I made an exception of little, material things. The larger ones just can't be helped.'

'They never can,' said Lester, gravely.

'Sir Jesse said that he would miss his son,' said Priscilla. 'It seemed odd that he should have ordinary human feelings.'

'I shall have to do my best for him,' said Paul. 'He must have men about him, and he will not suffer his grandsons.'

'He does too much for them,' said Susan. 'Even what he does for us, makes him think we are on a different level.'

'Well, the things he does, giving us a cottage and a small allowance, keeps us on one,' said Priscilla. 'But isn't it wonderful that he does it?'

'Sometimes I feel I am an able-bodied man, accepting help from another,' said Lester, expecting and meeting sympathy for this trick of his imagination.

'We are told that giving has the advantage over receiving,' said Paul.

'We should have to be told,' said Priscilla. 'Whoever said it, must have thought so.'

'You don't find it so in your experience?'

'We never give,' said Lester. 'It would not be fair on Sir Jesse.'

'I always feel that being here is a lesson,' said Hope.

'In rising above disadvantages, do you mean?' said Susan.

'Well, dear, I suppose I did. But I also meant in depending on your own qualities.'

'We are not going to disclaim them,' said Priscilla. 'It would be less awkward to mention them.'

'Do mention them, dear,' said Hope. 'I don't think anyone else has done so.'

'Intellect, individuality, our own kind of charm,' said Priscilla, with her lips grave.

Her sister laughed.

'Why is it amusing?' said Hope. 'I call it almost solemn. I feel inclined to rise. And now anyone could just rattle them off.'

'We could all have done so,' said Paul.

'I am glad you are a gentler creature than I am, Paul. I should hate you to be as hard as a woman. A husband ought to have some masculine qualities.'

'We are quite content,' said Lester.

'I see you are,' said Hope; 'and though I can't understand it, it makes me appreciate my easier lot.'

'I should have thought it was more difficult,' said Lester.

'I don't know whether to be annoyed or flattered by that. I like to feel I am in a hard place, but somehow any kind of difficulty seems a humiliation.'

'I believe you look down on us,' said Susan.

'Well, one does despise poverty and dependence,' said Hope, in a sharper tone. 'You did not speak in praise of them yourselves. But I pity them too, and I never feel that pity is such a dreadful thing. It is absurd to say it is the same as contempt. It even leads to kindness, and contempt never does that.'

'People even pity themselves,' said Priscilla. 'So the two feelings must be quite separate. People call contempt pity. That is how the confusion arises.'

'What is that parcel, Priscilla?' said Lester.

'Oh, I had forgotten. Sir Jesse brought it this afternoon. It is a photograph of our mother. He said he came across it. It seems strange to think of Sir Jesse going through his odds and ends. One would think that sort of thing would be done for him. It must be one of those wrong ideas that the poor get about the rich. I did not dare to open it by myself.'

'No, of course not,' said Lester, looking at the parcel as if he would hesitate under any circumstances.

'What are you afraid of?' said Hope. 'I know it is an insensitive question, but nothing brings out my better qualities today. If your first meeting with your mother fails to do so, nothing can be done.'

'It seems strange that most people know their mothers from the first,' said Priscilla.

'Now we shall be able to trace our odd physiognomy to its source,' said Susan.

'We shall have to,' said her sister.

'I don't mind what she is like,' said Lester.

'We see the strong feeling of the son for the mother coming out,' said Hope.

'I am sure Lester is not a man who would ever be ashamed of his mother,' said Priscilla.

'I have always thought it silly to say that photographs seem to be looking at us,' said Susan. 'But it does seem that this one would have the impulse.'

'I am glad it sees us with the condoning eyes of a mother,' said Priscilla, holding the photograph out of her own sight.

'I am sure her ugly ducklings are swans to her, dears,' said Hope.

'She is tall,' said Lester.

'I don't know why,' said Hope, 'but I suddenly feel inclined to cry.'

'And as plain as we are,' said Susan. 'Or not quite.'

'No, not as plain,' said Lester.

'Of course a mother is always beautiful to her son,' said Hope. 'There was no reason for Lester to be afraid. It was different for his sisters.'

'It is a good face and a good head,' said Paul.

'I do congratulate you all,' said Hope. 'And her as well, of course. I have never seen such a family.'

'I wonder why she made a friend of Sir Jesse,' said Lester.

'Is that the only thing you know against her?' said Paul, laughing.

'It is all we know about her,' said Susan. 'Perhaps she felt he would be a friend to her children.'

'We see where Susan gets her practical side,' said Priscilla. 'From Mother. This is the first homecoming when she has been here to welcome her.'

'So Sir Jesse did not bring a photograph of your father,' said Paul.

'I am rather glad,' said Priscilla. 'These family reunions are rather a strain.'

'We must have the photograph framed,' said Susan.

'Don't go yet, Paul,' said Priscilla. 'Sit down here by Mother.'

'I feel ashamed that the meeting has been witnessed by our idly curious eyes,' said Hope.

'I think you ought to share Mother with us, Lester,' said Priscilla. 'Mothers are not quite indifferent to their daughters. Perhaps Mother would not change me for all the sons in the world.'

'How much does a frame cost?' said her brother.

'There is Mother coming out.'

'It depends on the quality,' said Susan.

'In both of you,' said Priscilla. 'But ought the first economy we make after we have known Mother, to be on her? Though of course mothers do not like their children to spend their money on them.'

'I will subscribe to the frame,' said Lester, who could not always take this course with the family expenses.

'There are Ridley and Faith,' said Susan. 'How did they know you were here?'

'Just what Mother would have said!' said Priscilla.

'Something must have told them,' said Hope. 'It was not me.'

'We guessed you would be here,' said Faith, as she entered with her brother. 'We thought we might as well walk home together.'

'Need you have walked home at all, dear?' said Hope.

There was a pause.

'We have had tea,' said Faith, as if they would not impose this demand on the house.

'I hope we are not intruding,' said Ridley, with a smile for his suggestion.

'I hope not, dear,' said Hope.

'Have you been turning out old albums?' said Faith, looking at the table. 'I think the old-fashioned photographs are often so interesting.'

'They certainly throw a vivid light on the past,' said Ridley.

'Who is the lady?' said Faith, with the sprightliness that does not suggest high or serious anticipations.

'It is our mother,' said Lester, handing her the photograph. 'Sir Jesse brought it today. We had not seen it before.'

'Oh, I did not know,' said Faith, taking a step backwards with her eyes on his face.

'I think that was natural,' said Paul.

'It shows that one should be careful what one says,' said Faith, lightly. 'But I did not say anything derogatory, did I? And I had not looked at the photograph.'

'Your opinion would not have been of value,' said Paul.

'It must be quite a significant occasion,' said Ridley. 'I can picture the flights of imagination that the sight must produce.'

'It seems to render them for the first time unnecessary,' said Priscilla.

'Do you see any likeness in her to any of you?' said Faith. 'Or in any of you to her, I should say?'

'I think Lester is a little like her,' said Susan.

'They say that sons take after their mothers,' said Faith.

'We shall be four instead of three in future,' said Priscilla, putting the photograph on the chimney-piece.

'There is a photograph at home that I shall destroy,' said Hope. 'I want Faith to be sincere when she says I am the only mother she has known.'

'I have always been so,' said Faith. 'It is not my habit to say things I do not mean.'

'Then I hope we have never been five.'

'I think that photographs are chiefly useful for recalling people to those who knew them,' said Faith.

'Then they are not of great use,' said Paul.

'They are better than nothing for those who did not,' said Lester.

'As you say, Lester, nothing is not much to depend upon,' said Ridley, in a tone of sympathy.

'Has Sir Jesse a photograph of your father?' said Faith.

'Not to our knowledge,' said Susan.

'Have you not asked him?' said Faith, with a smile for this indifference.

'We don't often ask him questions.'

'I don't think he would mind one on that subject.'

'It might not be the exception,' said Paul.

Faith gave her father a glance, as if perplexed by his attitude.

'Would it help you if I were to ask him?' she said to the Marlowes. 'I could just put a casual question, and pass on to something else, and give you the result later. I think I am at the house rather oftener than you are.'

'We are never there,' said Lester.

'I expect that is just a custom that has grown up.'

'It is, dear, no doubt,' said Hope.

'You don't want to go,' said Paul, his bright eyes scanning the Marlowes' faces.

'We don't wear their kind of clothes,' said Susan. 'And we should feel we were dependants.'

'Then wouldn't the clothes be all right?' said Hope.

'I think that dress is very becoming to Susan,' said Faith.

'She has to have things for outsiders,' said Lester.

'People look themselves in whatever they wear,' said Faith.

'It is a good thing they don't know that,' said Hope. 'And I am not going to believe it.'

'We should have to look like other people,' said Priscilla, 'and that costs money.'

'I think you would find it a little change to go now and then,' said Faith.

'Daniel and Graham come here sometimes,' said Susan.

'Do they? I did not know that.'

'I wonder how it escaped your notice, dear,' said Hope.

'I expect Mrs Sullivan is glad for them to have the break, Mother.'

'It is their own feeling that brings them,' said Paul.

'Yes, they come to see us,' said Priscilla. 'It is one of those cases of people's finding their happiness in humbler surroundings.'

'I don't suppose they even notice the surroundings,' said Faith, showing that she was more observant herself.

'We owe too much to Sir Jesse for our intercourse with him to be natural,' said Lester.

'That does not argue any lack of generosity on either side,' said Faith.

'It does not on Sir Jesse's,' said Priscilla.

'I know that the little discomforts of any unusual position are often very hard to get over,' said Faith.

'They must be,' said Hope, 'because any embarrassment is bad enough.'

'We have got away from the subject of your father's photograph,' said Faith.

'And now you have led us back to it, dear,' said Hope.

'Very few people never have their photographs taken, Mother.'

'We have never done so,' said Priscilla. 'Perhaps it runs in the family.'

'Your mother's was taken,' said Faith.

'Well, people do sometimes take after one side.'

'Do people have their own photographs taken?' said Paul. 'Other people want a record of them.'

'And then they have to be told to look pleasant,' said Hope. 'If anyone wanted one of me, I could not subdue my elation.'

'I am touched by people's wanting a record of Mother,' said Priscilla. 'It says so much for them and for her.'

'I do not believe I have ever been immortalized in that way,' said Ridley.

'But think of the other ways, dear,' said Hope. 'I have not been taken since I was married. Your father was in the mood for wanting a record of me then. People do want them of people when they are about to spend their lives with them, though it is difficult to see what use they will be.'

'Sir Jesse will miss his son very much,' said Faith. 'It will make a third empty place in the house.'

'Are there any others?' said Hope. 'I know there are a great many full ones.'

'Lady Sullivan has lost two children, Mother.'

'The house never strikes me as empty somehow. There are

plenty of little, pattering feet. I mean there are eighteen.'

'I suspect it has its own emptiness for her, Mother.'

'Well, you would understand. Our house must have its own for you.'

'You have your own place, Mrs Cranmer,' said Ridley, with a note of reproach.

'Yes, it is mine now.'

'Sir Jesse's is the perfect place,' said Susan.

'I think I would vote for Eleanor Sullivan's,' said Ridley, looking about with a grave eagerness. 'All the advantages of a married woman, and none of the care and contrivance.'

'I thought those were dear to a woman's heart,' said Hope.

'I am sure I do not want any place but my own,' said Faith, contracting her brows at the thought of other people's.

'I want any place that is better than mine,' said Hope.

'Do people's places mean their endowments?' said Paul.

'No, our characteristics in their places,' said his wife. 'Everyone is content with his own endowments. The Marlowes' are things one could hardly speak about. I have never heard anyone but them do so.'

'I have heard many people.'

'You need not pounce on the one touch of meanness in my speech.'

'I am afraid I am not content with my endowments,' said Faith, with a wry little smile.

'Don't you think there is something about you that no one else has?' said Hope. 'Because I am sure there is.'

Faith raised her eyes and looked into her stepmother's.

'I know you think I cannot meet your eyes,' said the latter. 'And that being so, why do you put me to the test?'

'I think we had better be going, Mother.'

'We were all to go together. But as Priscilla cannot spare your father and me, the rest of you must go by yourselves.'

'That is only Ridley and me, Mother.'

'Is that all, dear? Then there are not any more.'

'I think that is a hint of whose breadth we need not be in doubt,' said Ridley, rising and going into mirth. 'We have no choice but to withdraw with as good a grace as possible.'

Faith stood for a moment, irresolute, and then went from one Marlowe to another in quiet and pleasant farewell, and led the way from the house.

'Of course stepmothers are cruel,' said Hope, 'but then so are stepchildren, though they don't have any of the discredit. We all have a right to survive, and only the fittest can do so, and it seems that a struggle is inevitable.'

'I wonder why we are all entitled to life,' said Susan. 'But I am glad Sir Jesse accepted it in our case.'

'We have a right to work for our bread,' said Lester, almost wonderingly.

'We have so many rights,' said Priscilla, 'but they don't seem such very good ones.'

'Will you come home with us, now that we can't overtake the others?' said Hope.

There was a silence.

'Well, it is Susan's first day at home,' said Priscilla.

'She would have to walk back,' said Lester.

'You know you would have the carriage,' said Hope. 'You should not stoop to falsehood to avoid an invitation.'

'What alternative is there?' said Paul.

'Are you so fond of your life in this cottage?' said Hope.

'Yes, we are,' said Priscilla. 'Our odd, isolated experience has drawn us so close.'

'The cottage is our home,' said Lester. 'Sir Jesse gave it to us.'

'I have always felt a little sorry about that,' said Hope. 'But there is never any need to worry about people. They are always so satisfied.'

'A poor thing but our own,' said Susan.

'I quite agree, dear. But why put it in the form of a saying? They don't contain the truth.'

'They call attention to it,' said Priscilla. 'Of course it is there without them.'

'I am glad it is there,' said Lester, with great content. 'Of course people do not see the cottage with our eyes.'

'Books and a fire,' said Priscilla, looking at these things. 'What more could we have?'

'I see you haven't any more,' said Hope, with some exasperation.

'But does that prevent your having dinner with a friend? You could have that as well.'

'We know about the other things,' said Susan. 'Cushions and flowers and things that shimmer in the firelight.'

'We like the firelight better by itself,' said Priscilla.

'I can see you do,' said Hope. 'And I like the things that go with it. I don't even want a mind above material things; I enjoy having one on their level.'

'I have never seen better firelight,' said Paul.

'It is the beech from the park,' said Lester.

'Does Sir Jesse send it to you?' said Hope.

'No, we have his tacit permission to gather it.'

'Are you proud of the mark of intimacy? Or humbled by being in need of fuel? I must remember that beech makes a fire like this. I want one to play on my possessions. I don't care if it is a nasty use for it. I don't want it for anything else.'

'It is a mistake to make the lily gild other things,' said Susan.

'If you liked me a little better, I should not be so petty,' said Hope. 'What is the good of striving to be worthy of your friendship, when I have no chance of it? You know how I long for your affection; people always know the things that add to themselves; I expect you exaggerate my desire for it. Of course I don't show it in public, when you are so neglected and eccentric. You could not expect it of a petty person, or what is your reason for thinking her petty? But you might save me from spending all my evenings with the family. I love to do it for Paul's sake, but I like to have things for my own sake as well, and I believe you know that I do.'

'Well, Susan only came home today,' said Lester.

'And I came thirty years ago. I do see she doesn't need a change so much. And of course I like her to be considered first. So I will leave you to look at the firelight playing on nothing. Though if you won't exert any influence over me, I don't see how I can improve.'

'We like you as you are,' said Lester.

'That is a crumb of comfort for me to take with me. I do hate going empty away. Would you like me to send you a load of beech?'

'Yes, if you will,' said Lester.

'How people do jump up and pin one down! Now we are committed to it. Well, it will come with love from us both, and I hope it will be all right by itself.'

'We know it will,' said Paul.

'Hope does not respect us as much as if we had the usual position,' said Susan, when they were alone. 'Her referring to it openly does not alter it.'

'Is it one reason why we do not respect ourselves?' said Lester, in simple question.

'The only one, I think,' said Priscilla.

'Ridley and Faith seem to respect us,' said Lester.

'Faith respects her fellow-creatures,' said Susan. 'And Ridley is a lawyer, and knows how common it is to be penniless; and he respects us for having a little money from Sir Jesse, and being able to earn a little more.'

'How I respect us!' said Priscilla.

'Do we respect other people?' said Lester.

'I do very much indeed,' said Priscilla. 'They seem to have so much of everything. Think of Faith, and her charitable nature and her comfortable home and her life of ease. I think a human being is remarkably well equipped. Kind hearts are more than coronets, but so many people seem to have them both.'

'A good home is not a coronet,' said Susan.

'Well, I should have said it really was.'

'It is odd that we cannot ask Sir Jesse about our parentage,' said Lester.

'It is because he has never told us,' said Susan.

'It seems a pity that one should preclude the other,' said Priscilla. 'One does not see what can be done. He hardly spoke of the photograph when he left it.'

'Perhaps he was thinking of what it could tell us, if it could speak,' said Susan.

'He was quite sure it could not do that. And I should hardly dare to listen. And I don't suppose it would.'

'We ought to imagine things about ourselves.'

'If they were true, Sir Jesse would not have had to bring us up,' said Lester.

'He never seems proud of what he has done,' said Priscilla. 'He almost draws a veil over it.'

'Over us, I think it is,' said Susan. 'He does not require us to go to church, because he would have to recognize us.'

'It would be a great waste of our Sunday,' said Lester, in a startled tone.

'I wonder if we are as odd as we think we are,' said Susan.

'We can only hope so,' said her sister, 'and continue to do our best.'

'There is Daniel's voice,' said Susan. 'And I expect Graham is with him.'

'That would not mean a voice,' said Lester, in a tone of stating a fact.

'You do not mind my bringing Graham,' said Daniel. 'I find it best to keep him under my eye.'

Graham took a seat.

'Has your father gone yet?' said Susan.

'No, or I should be at home, taking his place,' said Daniel.

'I wish I had just enough money to live on,' said Graham, looking round the room.

'Why do people wish that?' said Priscilla. 'Why not wish to have enough and to spare?'

'They mean they do not ask much,' said Graham. 'But of course they are asking everything.'

'A thing is more desirable when it is unattainable,' said Daniel.

'And how reasonable that is,' said Priscilla, 'when nothing comes up to expectation!'

'This would,' said Graham, 'to anyone brought up as an obligation.'

'We have been brought up like that too,' said Susan, 'but it has sat on us more lightly.'

'Sir Jesse seems to have formed the habit,' said Priscilla. 'And it is a very useful one.'

'I wish you could sometimes come to the house,' said Graham.

'Sir Jesse is ashamed of us,' said Susan. 'We never quite know why.'

'We will not pretend to see any reason,' said Priscilla.

'I wonder if we shall ever know,' said Lester.

'Grandma is the person to ask you,' said Daniel, 'and she never welcomes outsiders.'

'Then how do your friends get to the house?' said Susan.

'They do not,' said Graham. 'We have no friends.'

'The iron has entered into the boy's soul,' said Daniel.

'Graham and Lester both have a squeak in their voices,' said Susan.

'Lester must unconsciously try to catch a note from a different and more spacious world,' said her sister.

'I have very simple tastes,' said Graham.

'You have had little chance of acquiring others,' said Daniel.

'That is said to give people expensive ones,' said Priscilla.

'Has it in your case?' said Graham.

'No, but we are unusual. It is no good to say we are not.'

'Is that why Hope is uneasy about knowing us?' said Lester.

'It is only because we are not known,' said Priscilla. 'It is nothing personal.'

'There is something second-rate going through Hope,' said Susan. 'She thinks she makes it better by joking about it.'

'And so she does,' said her sister. 'She makes it very good indeed. You don't mean you do not like it?'

'I wish the next six months were over,' said Graham.

'I do not,' said Lester. 'It would mean that all three of us had six months less to live.'

'It would mean it for us too,' said Daniel, 'and for everyone.'

'I suppose it would,' said Lester, after a moment's thought.

'Oh, let me introduce Mother,' said Priscilla, taking up the photograph. 'My long struggle to take her place is over. She is here to fill it herself. I almost feel jealous of her, but I suppose that is usual with eldest daughters. Sir Jesse came this afternoon and filled the blank in our lives.'

'Grandpa did not say he was coming,' said Graham.

'Is it the first time you have not had his confidence?' said Daniel.

'I am so grateful to Mother for my existence,' said Priscilla. 'I believe that is very unusual, but I enjoy existence very much. I do agree that life is sweet.'

'You are more like your mother than you are like each other,' said Graham.

'She must be in all of us,' said Lester.

'So she has really been here all the time,' said Priscilla. 'That makes me feel rather foolish.'

'Who will miss your father the most?' said Susan.

'Grandma,' said Graham, 'and then I suppose Mother, and then one or two of the girls. But no one will like the house without him. He seems to lift some blight that hangs over us.'

'I hardly know him,' said Lester.

'You must feel you are beginning to do so,' said Priscilla. 'And you must find it a privilege?'

'We shall have to settle down,' said Daniel. 'We can't remain in a state of tension for six months.'

'It does sound dreadful,' said Priscilla, looking at Graham's face. 'To settle down for six months, when youth is such a sad time. Not that I did not find it very pleasant. I always wonder why people cling to it, when they find it so uncongenial. I get to like it more and more. You see I still think I have it.'

'I could like it,' said Graham, again looking round the room.

'Books and a fire,' said Priscilla. 'You can have nothing more. I am not one of those people who belittle the things they have. I daresay you think I do the opposite.'

'People pity us,' said Lester to Graham, in a tone of information.

'Because we have the bare necessities of life,' said Priscilla. 'And that is foolish, when necessities are so important. They would hardly pity us any more for not having them.'

'They pity you and not me,' said Graham, in an incredulous tone.

'Well, you live in Sir Jesse's house, and we live here,' said Susan.

'I have a seat at the table and a room on an upper floor.'

'And what do you do at the table, Graham?' said Daniel.

'You cannot have pity as well,' said Priscilla. 'And it would not be much good to you.'

'We know about it, though we do not mind it,' said Lester.

'You know nothing of self-pity,' said Graham. 'And that is the only sort that counts.'

Chapter 6

'Does no one want to say good-bye to Father?' said Eleanor, in a high, incredulous voice from the hall, with her face held towards the upper landings. 'Do you not want to see the last of him? Or have you all forgotten he is going?'

'Our minds may be so weary of the image that they have yielded it up,' said Isabel, as her feet kept pace with her sister's on the stairs.

'Are you just going on with your life in your ordinary way?' said Eleanor, in the same tone and with her brows raised. 'Is this day just the same as any other to you?'

'It is an odd person who can suggest that,' said her daughter. 'We thought you might want to say good-bye to Father by yourself, that that was perhaps why he came to see us last night.'

'Oh, that is what it was. But I do not want to keep him to myself at this last stage. He will want to remember us all together,' said Eleanor, with her querulous honesty. 'I am not the only person he has in his life. Run up and see that everyone is here. He will be going in half-an-hour.'

Isabel mounted a flight of stairs and raised her voice in a message to Hatton.

'From the way Isabel moves, you would think your father had a month to be here,' said Eleanor.

'He has almost,' said Isabel, in a low voice to Venice, as she returned. 'Thirty minutes, and we have had one!'

'Shall I go and fetch Luce and Daniel and Graham?' said James, hovering near his mother.

'Yes, tell them all to come. I cannot understand this lackadaisical attitude. You might not have a father. I simply do not feel I can explain it.'

Eleanor was released from this effort by the appearance of her sons and daughter from their study, with Luce holding her father's arm, and her brothers wearing the look of the final advice and farewell. Sir Jesse and Regan came from the library, the former resolute and almost urbane, the latter ravaged and fierce. Hatton appeared on the landing with the children, put

Nevill's hand into Honor's, and withdrew round the balusters to await events.

'So we are here to get all we can out of it,' said Regan. 'It shows it is not too much for us; that is one thing.'

'It ensures that it shall be,' said Graham.

'Trouble shared is trouble halved,' said Fulbert, in a cheerful tone. 'It will be disappearing amongst a dozen, and I shall leave dry eyes behind.'

'Grandma, Luce, Daniel, Grandpa,' said Nevill, seeming to follow out his father's thought. 'Venice, Father, Graham, Isabel. And he is here too, and Hatton. And Mother and James.'

'Father is the important person today,' said Eleanor.

'We are all Father's,' said her son, supporting her view.

'And he is obliged to leave us.'

'No,' said Nevill, in a light tone. 'Father is not going away any more.'

'He has heard too much of it,' said Fulbert.

'We have all done that,' said Regan, rapidly blinking her eyes.

Luce put a chair for her grandmother and stood stroking her shoulders, and Nevill ran to another chair and climbed on to it, and keeping his eyes on Regan, pulled out his handkerchief and retained it in his hand.

'Why are you in out-of-door things, Luce?' said Eleanor, surprised by any sign of personal pursuits.

'Because I am going to the station, Mother.'

'As well as the boys?'

'Yes.'

'Will there be room in the carriage?'

'Yes.'

'Won't it upset you?'

'Yes,' said Luce, smiling, 'but that need not be taken into account.'

'But won't that be depressing for your father at the last?'

'No, Mother, he will not be conscious of it.'

'But is there any point in your going?'

'Yes,' said Luce, now with a note of patience. 'Father will have a woman to see him off, as well as young men.'

'I should find it too much.'

'I am in my way a strong woman, Mother.'

'And I am a weak one, I suppose.'

'It is the first time I have heard a woman make that claim, without any sign of satisfaction,' said Graham, who had been watching his mother.

'I have no fault to find with the strength or the weakness,' said Fulbert. 'They are both after my heart.'

Luce moved her hands more rapidly on Regan's shoulders, as if to stave off any impending emotion.

'I hope the occasion may prove a turning point in Graham's life,' said Daniel.

Venice laughed, and Eleanor glanced at her in mute question of such a sound.

'Mother,' said Luce, in a low tone, 'let Father leave us in a happy atmosphere.'

'It can hardly be that, my dear, when he is going for six months.'

'Not after he has gone. But while he is here, let us stand up to the test.'

'Isabel looks as if she were at a funeral,' said Eleanor, as if this were going beyond the suitable point.

'She may be right,' said Regan.

'I don't want her father to remember her like that.'

'Why is it assumed that people forget all moments but the last?' said Daniel.

Isabel broke into tears; Fulbert put his arm about her; she could not control her weeping, and it became almost loud. Hatton came round the staircase and stood with her eyes upon her, as if debating her course.

'Isabel dear, if you cannot control yourself, Hatton must take you upstairs, as if you were one of the little ones,' said Eleanor, speaking as though her daughter were nearer to this stage than she was.

'She will come and sit by Grandma,' said Regan, using the same manner, but also the gift for doing so.

Isabel sat on the floor at Regan's feet; the latter began to stroke her hair, and Luce noted the action and glided away, seeing her own ministrations rendered unnecessary by this transference of thought to another.

'What are you doing, Gavin?' said Eleanor.

'Drawing,' said her son, continuing the occupation.

'Isn't that rather a strange way of spending your last half-hour with Father?'

'No.'

'What makes you do it just now?'

'Nothing.'

'Let me see what you are drawing.'

'No,' said Gavin, pocketing the paper.

'That is not nice behaviour. But I expect you are upset by Father's leaving us.'

'No, I am not.'

'He will draw,' said Nevill, throwing himself off his chair and running to his brother.

Gavin turned aside.

'Let him do it, Gavin,' said Eleanor.

Gavin pursued his way.

'Let him have a piece of paper.'

'I only have the one piece.'

Nevill stood with his feet apart and his arms at his sides, on the point of surrendering himself to a lament of frustration.

'Will my good, useful girl get him a pencil and paper?' said Eleanor.

Venice recognized herself in the description, and was in time to prevent Hatton, who had partly descended the stairs, from coming further. Nevill put the paper on a chair, and stood, pushing the pencil rather violently about it, as if he were unfitted by emotional stress for normal application.

'What is the mystery about Gavin's drawing, Honor?' said Eleanor.

'There isn't one, Mother.'

'What is he drawing?'

'A portrait of Father.'

'Oh, that is what it is; that is very nice,' said Eleanor, as though finding herself wrong in some surmise to which this adjective could not be applied. 'That was the right thing to think of, wasn't it?'

'I didn't think of it. It was Honor,' said Gavin.

'Poor little girl, she wanted a portrait to keep,' said Eleanor, making a statement that was natural to the circumstances, but caused her daughter to fall into such violent weeping, that the services of Hatton were called upon and she was led from sight.

'Here is a dear, bright face for Father to remember!' said Eleanor, taking Venice's cheek in her hand.

Venice stared before her and struck her side, and Eleanor turned to her sons, baffled by her daughters' various responses to the occasion.

'Have you asked your father if you can do anything for him, as the eldest son?' she said to Daniel, with her vague note of reproof.

'Yes, I have, and been answered.'

'And you, Graham?'

'Yes, with the same result.'

'I am sure I can depend on my two tall sons.'

'A conviction that seems to be born of the moment,' said Daniel.

'Mother, you haven't much hope of your children, have you?' said Luce.

'I am so used to training and guiding them, that I forget the time has come for results.'

'The results do not remind you, Mother?'

'I wish they could sometimes be allowed to appear.'

'Graham need not be self-conscious about his little efforts at improvement,' said Daniel.

'Let me see your portrait of Father, Gavin,' said Eleanor, simply passing from her elder sons.

Gavin took the paper from his pocket and handed it to Graham, as if in a near enough approach to obedience, and Eleanor looked at it without moving, seeming to accept this method of putting it at a convenient level.

'Anyone can see it is a man,' said Graham.

'That halves the number of people it may represent,' said Daniel.

'It is a grown-up man,' said Gavin. 'It has wrinkles.'

'Perhaps that quarters them.'

'Let me see myself in my son's eyes,' said Fulbert. 'I admit the wrinkles, both here and in the original. There is a framed photograph in my dressing-room that may pass into Honor's possession, if she so desires.'

Honor, who had been led back in a state of pale calm, raised a lighted face.

'It has the advantage of having no wrinkles, as the less honest artist took them out.'

'If the frame is silver, Honor could sell it for a lot of money,' said Gavin.

'But she will want to keep it,' said his mother. 'It is a picture of Father.'

'Can I have it even after Father comes back?' said Honor.

'It is your very own,' said Fulbert, 'and the lack of wrinkles will become a more and more distinguishing feature.'

'Now you feel quite cheered up, don't you?' said Eleanor.

'Yes,' said her daughter, agreeing that this was a natural result.

'You will feel you have a little bit of Father always with you.'

'It is all of him down to his hands,' said Gavin.

Nevill, who had been making rapid but considered marks on the fair side of his paper, now approached and proffered it for inspection.

'It is Luce; it is Grandma,' he said.

'It is differentiated to about the same extent,' said Daniel. 'It indicates age and sex.'

'It does, Daniel,' said Luce, as if this were an all but incredible circumstance.

'It is Hatton,' said Nevill, in a settled tone.

'Poor Father!' said Luce, half to herself. 'He stands amongst his family on a day when he should be the hero, and everyone seems more in the foreground than he.'

'He is the basis that everything is built upon,' said Graham. 'Surely that is enough.'

'Well, it cannot go on much longer, boys.'

'If there were any reason why it should stop,' said Graham, 'surely it would have operated by now.'

'The train will become due,' said Luce.

'I suppose it has always been expected at a certain time,' said Daniel. 'Was no account taken of it, when we assembled for the final scene?'

'We could have acted a play in the time,' said his brother.

'We have done so, Graham,' said Luce.

'Father's wrinkles can hardly be getting less,' said Venice.

'We have stood and striven faithfully,' said Graham; 'we have jested with set lips; two of us have wept. Have we not earned our release?'

'We will act no more,' said Sir Jesse, suddenly striding forward with a scowl on his face. 'We will cease to parade the tears of women and teach young men to make a show of themselves. My son can go to his duty without that. I have left my family in my time, and without exposing them to this. Does no one think of anything but disburdening himself? Let him think of other things.'

He drew back, breathing deeply. Fulbert looked up with an expression that made his face a boy's; Regan surveyed them both with a look that also came from the past; and in the silence that followed, Luce approached her mother.

'Mother, I am going to end the scene. For the sake of Father and ourselves. It is losing weight and meaning. It will be less significant, not more, for being prolonged. I take it upon myself to say that time is up.'

'Time, is it?' said Fulbert, turning and beginning on the round of his farewells, as if seeing the mistake of prolonging them. 'Time for me to enter on the months which are to restore me to you. I am like a criminal anxious to begin his sentence; I am one, in that I should have served it years ago.'

He went the course of his family with a sort of resolute ease, embraced the women and girls with a suggestion of an especial meaning for each, and left before emotion could be manifest. Regan stood and stared before her with a face that was suddenly blank and old, and Sir Jesse was silent and almost absent, as if withdrawing from further part in the scene. Eleanor was pale and controlled; Isabel and Honor were lost in the struggle with their tears; Venice and James were conscious of themselves and nervous of the attention of others; Gavin appeared to be unaffected; and the two young men devoted themselves to the duties of the moment.

Nevill ran up to Fulbert as he reached the door, and thrust his paper into his hand.

'A picture of Father,' he said.

'Nevill has made the supreme sacrifice, that of Hatton,' said Graham, and brought a smile to Regan's face.

Luce stood in the hall and motioned her father onward in a manner that gave no quarter, and as Daniel held open the carriage door, entered almost with alacrity and took her seat. Fulbert followed with his usual springy gait; the brothers sat at the back; Fulbert raised his hand to his mother and his wife, or to one or the other, as each took the salute to herself. Of the group in the hall Regan was the first to speak.

'Well, the children will be back, I suppose. There is no danger of our losing them.'

Sir Jesse turned and walked to the library, with a lack of expectance about him, that sent his wife after him with an altered face. Eleanor was the next to utter her first words.

'James, I do not believe you uttered a syllable during the whole of Father's last half-hour with us.'

James looked at his mother and maintained this course.

'Why did you suppose you were here?'

'Hatton told us to come down.'

'Then did you not want to say good-bye to Father?'

'Yes, but we did it last night.'

'But wouldn't you have liked a last word?'

'Well – but we had it last night – it was better – then we had it by itself,' said James, in a barely articulate tone.

'Oh, that is what it was. Well, I can understand that.'

James simply relaxed his body and his face.

'You did not speak to Father, either, did you, Gavin?' said Eleanor, in an almost expressionless tone, as if she hesitated to commit herself on her son's motives.

Gavin looked at her in silence.

'Of course you were making a picture of him,' said Eleanor, seeking his corresponding justification.

'He was too,' said Nevill, beginning to look about for the paper, which he knew his father had not taken.

'We can't help Father's going to America,' said Gavin.

'No, but it is because of you in a way,' said Eleanor, at once. 'It is because he wants to make the future safe for us.'

'Then it is because of you too.'

'Of course, it is especially because of me. But I did not think it was not.'

Gavin considered for a moment and then left the subject.

'Isabel, you seem in a state of utter exhaustion,' said Eleanor, in a sharper tone. 'How you are upset by any little strain! Everything seems too much for you.'

'The last half-hour has been,' said Isabel, for her sister's ears.

'Venice, take her upstairs, and tell Miss Mitford that I said she was to go to Hatton and lie down.'

Isabel proceeded to her rest; the circuitous method also disposed of Venice; James stood with a sense of personal justification; Nevill ran up to Eleanor and offered his paper.

'A picture of Mother,' he said.

'My dear, little, comforting boy!'

'A picture of Mother; Father come back soon; all gone away, but come back tomorrow,' said Nevill, rapidly enumerating grounds of consolation.

'Luce and Daniel and Graham will come back in a few minutes,' said Gavin.

'Come back in a few minutes,' said Nevill, passing on this information to his mother before he left her.

'Honor, hadn't you and Gavin better have some game?' said Eleanor, looking at the silent children.

'He will be a horse,' suggested Nevill.

'Would you like to get that photograph from Father's room?' said Eleanor, seeing the need of another solution.

Honor and Gavin sprang towards the stairs, and Nevill gave them a glance and continued his exercise.

James made a movement of sudden recollection and ran up after them, producing in his mother the impression that he had some object in view, and no curiosity concerning it, which were results that he had intended.

Nevill suddenly realized that he was alone with his mother in the hall.

'Go with Hatton,' he said, in a tone of giving the situation one chance before he despaired of it.

'I will take you to her,' said Eleanor, offering her hand.

Nevill accepted it and mounted the stairs with an air of concentrating all his being on one object. When they reached the nursery, he looked up at his mother.

'Father come back tomorrow, come back soon,' he said, and ran through the door.

Eleanor satisfied herself that Isabel was asleep, and paid a visit to Venice and Miss Mitford as she passed the schoolroom.

'Are you standing about doing nothing, dear? Is she, Miss Mitford?'

'Yes.'

'Is that the way to keep up her spirits?'

'I do not think she is in spirits.'

'Cannot she find some occupation?'

'Girls of her age have no pursuits.'

'Could she not make something to do?'

'That is beneath human dignity.'

'Is it so dignified just to stand about?'

'It is more so. And she is accustoming herself to the change in the house. Surely that is quite reasonable.'

'I think we shall have to let time do that for us.'

'Well, that is what she is doing. Half-an-hour cannot do much.'

'Is James anywhere about?'

'He is with the children in the nursery. He had a holiday because his father was going.'

'He will no doubt have one when he comes back. I don't know how he makes any progress. I don't suppose he does make much. Are the girls resting too today? Isabel is asleep.'

'I hope that is resting,' said Miss Mitford. 'I hope it is not one of those heavy, unrefreshing sleeps.'

'Can Isabel and I have a photograph of Father, like Honor and Gavin?' said Venice, in a sudden tone.

'Yes, of course you can, dear child. I will put one out for you. There is sure to be a frame that will fit it.'

'Is there?' said Miss Mitford, seeing this question in Venice's eyes. 'I should think that is unusual.'

'I don't know of one, certainly. But we shall find one.'

'I should not know where to look for such a thing.'

Eleanor's face revealed that this was the case with herself.

'I have a pair of frames that I do not want,' said Miss Mitford.

'Whom have you had in them?' said Venice.

'My father and mother. But I am inclined to take them out, because they stir the chords of memory.'

'Venice dear, do not ask questions,' said Eleanor. 'Just say you will like to have the frames, if Miss Mitford has no use for them. And then you may come and get the photograph.'

'Whom will you put in the second frame?' said Miss Mitford. 'I could give you a photograph of myself, to balance your father's.'

Venice hesitated with a half-smile, and Miss Mitford suddenly gave a whole one.

'Come with me and I will give you one of my own photographs,' said Eleanor. 'Then you can have your parents on either side of your fireplace. It is kind of you to amuse them, Miss Mitford. She is quite cheered up.'

Isabel awoke to find her sister disposing the photographs on the mantelpiece.

'What are those?' she said, and heard the account. 'I would as soon have had Mitta as Mother,' she said.

'We could not put her to correspond with Father,' said Venice, not criticizing the view on any other ground.

'I think I shall say I am too tired to come down to dessert.'

'Can you be as tired as that, after your rest? Mother saw you were asleep.'

'I can after these last days.'

'Well, if you want to explain that!' said Venice, causing her sister to rise from her bed.

'Now remember,' said the latter, as they left the schoolroom later, 'I am quite myself and not at all depressed, and I wanted to come downstairs. I was only tired and upset by Father's going.'

'And what if I am asked what you ate at dinner?'

'Oh, just tell a fib,' said Isabel, as if her previous injunctions had not involved this step.

'Well, my weary girl,' said Eleanor, 'are you quite yourself again?'

'Yes, thank you, Mother.'

'Did she have a good luncheon, Venice?'

'Yes.'

'And James? How is he? Doesn't he think he might go to school this afternoon, and do some hours of work? It would be a little thing he could do for Father.'

'When we have a holiday, we are supposed to have one,' said James in a faint voice.

'Do you mean you would find it embarrassing to go back?'

'No,' said James, who would have found it even more so to admit this.

'What does he mean, Isabel?'

'Well, he is not expected, and they are supposed to keep to what they say.'

'Mother, I think Father has unwittingly put enough on the children today,' said Luce, with an unconscious glance at Sir Jesse.

'The boy is right that he should do one thing or the other,' said the latter, with a suggestion of seeking to counteract his outbreak. 'If he has begun the day in one way, let him finish it.'

'Then he must have a walk and a rest,' said Eleanor, who seemed to consider widely varying courses adapted to her son. 'He is not having a holiday in the ordinary sense.'

'James would not dispute it,' said Graham.

'I don't think he ever has one,' said Isabel. 'Does he know what an ordinary holiday means? To him a holiday must be a sort of tribute paid to other people's experience.'

James gave his sister a look of seeing someone familiar passing out of his sight.

'Wouldn't any of you like to hear about your father's last moments?' said Eleanor.

Her chance use of words with another association caused some mirth.

'What an odd thing to laugh at, if you really took the words as you pretend!'

'It is their bearing that interpretation that constitutes the joke,' said Daniel.

'Joke!' said his mother, drawing her brows together.

'We had an ordinary little talk,' said Luce, in a tone unaffected by what had passed. 'We found ourselves discussing the best time for leaving England. The last moments' – her voice shook on the words – 'tend to lack vitality and interest.'

'Why did you insist on being present at them?' said Eleanor.

'To prevent them from being worse for Father than they had to be, Mother.'

'Sit on Grandma's knee,' said Nevill.

Regan lifted him and he settled himself against her in dependence on the effort to support his weight, and closed and opened his eyes.

'He has missed his sleep,' said Venice. 'It was because of saying good-bye to Father.'

'Sleep, school, everything missed,' said Eleanor, with a sigh.

'Good-night, Grandma,' said Nevill, meeting Regan's eyes with a smile.

'The child will be a burden. Can't somebody fetch him?' said Sir Jesse, seeming to find no fault with a burden, if it were suitably disposed.

'Let him lie down, Grandma,' said Luce, with her eyes on the pair.

'No,' said Nevill, struggling to his former position.

'Hatton can carry him without waking him, when he is once asleep,' said Venice.

It was decided to rely on this power, making a temporary sacrifice of Regan, and Eleanor turned to her sons.

'Have you your father's directions clear in your minds?'

'Yes. Habit has not yet overlaid them,' said Graham.

'I wish he had told you to learn to answer a serious question. It grows wearisome, this taking everything as an excuse for jauntiness. It will become a recognized affectation.'

'We will not look at Graham at his hard moment,' said Daniel.

'I am glad to bear it for us both,' said Graham.

'Mother, that is too severe,' said Luce, laughing. 'It is natural to the boys to be as they are.'

'We cannot always leave our natural selves unmodified, and expect other people to bear with them.'

'It is about what most of us do,' said Sir Jesse, with some thought of his own illustration of the point.

'I suppose it is,' said Eleanor, with a sigh that seemed to refer to herself.

'Are our natural selves so bad?' said Isabel.

'More petty and narrow than bad,' said her mother. 'Not that that is not poor enough.'

'Mother, you have your own opinion of yourself and other people,' said Luce.

'Do you show your natural self, James?' said Eleanor, with one of her accesses of coldness.

'No; yes; I don't know,' said James, looking surprised and apprehensive.

'Do you pretend to be different from what you are?'

'Oh, no,' said James, suddenly seeing his life as a course of subterfuge.

'Do you, Venice?'

'No, I don't think so.'

'Do you, Isabel?'

'I don't know. I have not thought. And I do not intend to think. Probably most of us do the same thing.'

'That is not a gracious way to talk.'

'It was not that sort of question. It was one to make people admit what they had better keep to themselves.'

'You have answered it more plainly than you know.'

'Well, I suppose that was your object in asking it.'

'You think people do disguise themselves?'

'Up to a point, of course. We should be sorry if they did not. I should be grateful if you would resume your disguise.'

'Isabel, you must remember you are speaking to your mother.'

'It is not a moment when I should choose to do so.'

'My dear, I know you are tired and upset, but there is reason in everything. Do you think it is nice to take advantage of Father's going at once like this?'

'No, not at all, but you were the first person guilty of it. And in James's case you wreaked your feelings on a helpless child.'

Graham rested his eyes on Isabel, as if he thought these words did not only apply to James.

'Isabel, I shall have to ask you to go upstairs,' said Eleanor.

'I have not the least wish to remain.'

'Then do not do so, my dear.'

Isabel rose and, bursting into tears, ran out of the room. Luce rose at almost the same moment and went with a movement of her shoulders after her.

'Well, what a lot of smoke without any flame!' said Eleanor, not looking into anyone's face.

'There was a certain amount of flame,' said Daniel. 'And you put the match, Mother.'

'It was very inflammable material.'

'That did not make it wiser.'

'Venice, go and see what is happening,' said Eleanor.

Venice went out and found her sister weeping on the stairs, with Luce standing over her; and not being inclined to return and describe the scene, she simply joined it. The same thing happened to James, who was the next emissary, and to Honor, who succeeded him. Gavin was the first to report on the situation.

'Isabel is sitting on the stairs, crying, and the others are standing near.'

Nevill struggled to the ground and ran up to Eleanor.

'Isabel is crying, but stop soon, and Father soon come back and put his arm round her.'

Eleanor stroked his hair.

'Do you think you can go to Isabel, and try to bring her back to Mother?'

Nevill ran to the door, waited for it to be opened without looking at the operator, mounted the stairs to his sister, took her hand and tried to drag her to the dining-room. Luce came behind, as if not yet relaxing her vigilance, and Venice and James and Honor rather uncertainly followed. Sir Jesse put some viands on a plate and pushed it towards his granddaughter, who was moved to uncertain mirth by this method of encouragement, and Nevill took his stand at her side, with his eyes going from the plate to her face.

'Now you had better go upstairs and enjoy your good things there,' said Eleanor. 'Here is another plate for the nursery children.'

Honor took it and Nevill ran by her side, openly yielding himself to the occasion. Hatton appeared in response to a summons, took both the plates in one hand, and Nevill's hand in the other, and led the way from the room. The other five children followed. Luce lay back in her chair and gave a sigh.

'Dear, dear, the miniature world of a family! All the emotions of mankind seem to find a place in it.'

'It was those emotions that originally gave rise to it,' said Daniel. 'No doubt they would still be there.'

'What a thing to be at the head of it!' said Eleanor.

Sir Jesse looked up, but perceived that the reference was not to himself.

'I think it is the place I would choose,' said Daniel.

'I would not,' said his brother.

'Isabel has a very deep feeling for Father,' said Luce, looking round the table. 'It seems to be something altogether beyond her age.'

'It is unwise to imagine the months ahead, if that is her trouble,' said Graham.

Regan covered her face and sank into weeping. Luce left her chair, and with a movement of her brows in reference to the consistent nature of her offices, went to her relief. Sir Jesse beckoned to his grandsons to follow him in Fulbert's stead, and left the women to their ways, as his expression suggested. Luce stood a little apart from Regan, as if the moment to officiate were not yet at hand, and touched her shoulders from time to time in token of what was in store. Eleanor looked at her mother-in-law with guarded eyes, and Regan felt the gaze and returned it almost with defiance.

'Don't try to control yourself, Grandma. Let yourself go; it will do you good,' said Luce, taking a sure, if unintended method of inducing recovery.

'So your grandfather has gone,' said Regan. 'Men don't feel things like women.'

'Well, perhaps they don't, Grandma,' said Luce, giving her hands a regular movement. 'Do you know, I think Isabel is very like you in some ways?'

Regan's face and Eleanor's responded to this suggestion in a different manner.

'Mother, I don't believe you like people to show their feelings,' said Luce.

'It depends on their age and other things.'

'Age hasn't much to do with it, if we are to judge from Isabel and me,' said Regan, with a smile.

'Grandma, you are yourself again,' said Luce.

'Shall we go to the drawing-room?' said Eleanor. 'If we are to support each other, we may as well do it at ease.'

As Regan led the way into the room, Hope sprang from the hearth.

'I told them I would wait for you. I know I ought not to have come. We do not intrude upon family privacy at such a time. But I know what such a condition can be, and it did seem I ought to prevent it, if I could. If I only annoy you, it will take you out of yourselves. That always seems to have to be done in some unpleasant way. I do want to sacrifice myself for you. I have sacrificed the others by leaving them at home. No sacrifice is too great.'

'You have made Grandma laugh, Mrs Cranmer,' said Luce, in the tone of one pushing up with an assurance.

'That shows I have forgotten myself, for I was really out of spirits. I see why the jesters of old were such sad people. If their profession was cheering people who needed it, it would have been unfeeling not to be. They couldn't have had enough sadness in their own lives to account for their reputation.'

'Comic actors and writers and all such people are said to be melancholy,' said Luce. 'And they do not come in contact with the people they cheer.'

'Well, it may just be the contrast of their professional liveliness with their normal human discontent. We might say that wrestlers and acrobats are lazy, because they sit on chairs at home. People do give their spare time to complaining. Well, I saw you and your brothers driving with your father to the station, and I said to myself, There are those dear children facing the hardest moments, and here am I, just running the house, that is, giving spare time to complaining. So I have come here to be rejected and unwelcome, because that will give me a hard moment, and I really cannot go on any longer without one.'

'Mother is laughing now,' announced Luce. 'And I did not think that would be contrived today.'

'I have been a sad, sour woman for a good many hours,' said Eleanor.

'Well, you have not been yourself,' said Hope. 'So that shows how different you really are.'

'There is not much in my life that I can look back on with pride.'

'What an odd thing to think of doing! I thought people looked back with remorse, and thought of the might-have-beens, and how it was always too late. I should never dare to do it at all.'

'I have had such sad, little faces round me today, and I have not done much to brighten them.'

'I am quite above minding the number today, my dear.'

'They will all be six months older before their father sees them again.'

'Yes, they will, but does that matter? It is not like being ill or an anxiety.'

'Nevill will be three and a half,' said Luce, in the same regretful tone.

'Will that be a disadvantage to him? Is there something about age that I don't understand?'

'Their childhood is slipping away,' explained Luce.

'Yes, but it won't do that any more quickly because Fulbert is gone. I expect every day will drag. And doesn't time always stand still in childhood? I thought it was always those long, summer days.'

'It has been a chill enough day today,' said Eleanor.

'So I have come to bring it a little ordinary warmth. I know it is ordinary; I am not making any claim. I enjoy having a talk with women, and I know you will like to give pleasure to another in your own dark hours, because that would be one of your characteristics. I will begin by saying that Faith is so forbearing that it is impossible to live with her.'

'You go on managing it,' said Regan.

'Another laugh, Mrs Cranmer!' said Luce.

'I do it by being always in the wrong. And though that is not much to do for Paul, it is the little, daily sacrifices that count. They are so much more than the one great one.'

'I wonder if people would recognize that one, if they saw it,' said Eleanor.

'There, see how much good I am doing you! It is a healthy sign to see the inconsistencies in others. It seems fortunate that it is almost universal.'

'Does Ridley make any sacrifices?' said Regan.

'Well, he may be waiting for the one great one.'

'I hope we are not putting too much on him,' said Eleanor.

'I don't think you could have thought I meant that, dear,' said Hope.

Regan went into laughter and Eleanor looked puzzled for a moment.

'Fulbert may come back to do his own work,' said Regan, with a return of grimness.

'And Ridley will go on waiting,' said Hope. 'And I like my stepchildren to be frustrated. I can say it today, because it is to do you good.'

'Do you know, Mrs Cranmer, it does have that effect?' said Luce, bringing her brows together.

'Where is Sir Jesse?' said Hope. 'I keep being afraid he will come in.'

'He is with the boys in the library,' said Eleanor.

'I always say people prefer their own sex. It is such a tribute to everyone, when they understand it so well. It means they don't even mind being understood. I am glad Faith is not here, to look as if I were really saying something uncharitable.'

'Faith is here, Mrs Cranmer,' said Luce, in a just audible tone, glancing out of the window and trying to suppress a smile.

'I suppose she would be by now. So she has come to put me at a disadvantage.'

'I hardly think that is fair.'

'No, dear, but I am here to do you good. Being fair would achieve nothing, and being put at a disadvantage may. We will wait for Faith to do her part. If it is for your sakes, I mind nothing.'

Faith looked with gentle inquiry from face to face.

'I am afraid it is the last of all days to call.'

'I don't think you can be, dear,' said Hope.

'I feel I must be an unwelcome visitor.'

'I don't think you can feel that either.'

Faith brought her eyes to rest on her stepmother.

'You see it is happening,' said Hope, fidgeting. 'But I am only too glad to be of use.'

Faith's expression became one of inquiry.

'You must have some errand that you have not said,' said Hope.

'I did not like the idea of your walking home by yourself, Mother.'

'But when we walk together, we can't keep in step.'

'I will try and take shorter steps.'

'And if I do the opposite, we shall meet each other. It is quite a little parable for our daily life.'

'I am afraid I am rather tall,' said Faith, looking round with a deprecating smile. 'But I do not think it at all fair for the shorter person to adapt herself. It is for the taller one to do that.'

'It must be nice to give out of abundance,' said Hope.

'Or bearable anyhow,' said Regan.

Luce exchanged a glance with Faith, in smiling reference to the attitude of the older women.

'How are the children?' said Faith, turning to Eleanor.

'They have had a sad day, I am afraid,'

'Perhaps I may go and see them.'

'Well, it would be very kind.'

'Do let us go from floor to floor,' said Hope, incurring a glance from Faith, who had wished to go alone with Eleanor. 'I should not feel I had been here, if I had not done that. And it would be a pity not to take advantage of my unembittered mood. I must always have seen the children with a jaundiced eye.'

'I must just look in on my husband,' said Regan, as they crossed the hall.

'I see I have no conception of a true union.'

Sir Jesse was engaged on some game of his youth with his eldest grandson, while the second looked on. He had lost his skill with years, and Daniel was being hard pressed to give him play, and at the same time cover his lapses. Graham was pale with the effort of following and supporting the contest.

'Youth and Age,' said Faith, looking round with a smile. 'It makes me wish I were a painter.'

'That was a picture in words,' said Luce.

'Not a very elaborate one, I am afraid,' said Faith, looking down as she turned to the stairs.

'We see the older children first,' said Hope. 'The higher we go, the younger they get. It seems odd that the smaller ones should have to climb further. We read about little, sturdy legs toiling up the stairs, but why does it have to be like that?'

'The nurseries are always furthest from the lower floors,' said Faith.

'Yes, that is what I said, dear. But why?'

'We don't want too many nursery sounds,' said Eleanor.

'I thought they were the most beautiful sounds in the world. I don't seem to understand the things I have missed. But I daresay that is natural.'

The schoolroom children were lying back in their chairs, listening to Miss Mitford reading aloud. They rose, looking rather conscious of their self-indulgence.

'So they are in spirits again,' said Eleanor, who took any form of recreation as a token of this.

'How do you know they are?' said Hope. 'Miss Mitford may be trying to distract them.'

'I hope she has met with a measure of success. They are themselves again, are they, Miss Mitford?'

'No.'

'Are they not? Why?'

'Because their father has left them.'

'But they are up to enjoying a book.'

'Anyone is equal to something done by someone else.'

'Well, I hope your time is not being quite wasted. What are you doing, James? You don't seem to be listening.'

James did not say he was sunk in the lethargy of exhaustion. He sat up and alertly indicated a box at his side.

'I am tidying my case of curiosities.'

'They do not look as if they had had much attention,' said Eleanor, smiling in the belief that a boy could pursue such an occupation without result. 'You had better ask Venice to help you.'

'Why Venice?' said Hope.

'She is our obliging little woman.'

'Miss Mitford said she would help me to put labels on the things,' said James.

'Well, that would bring order out of chaos. Why do you prop up the box on a book? I never knew a boy put books to such odd purposes.'

'It goes down without it,' said James, drawing out the book so that the box dropped with a crash, and taking the box into his arms as if to protect it.

'Where did you get the book?' said his mother.

'From the dining-room,' said James, in immediate, cordial response.

'I saw a space on the shelves. Did you take more than one?'

'Three all the same,' said James, holding the box with his chin, while he adjusted his hands beneath it. 'Two of them are in my room.'

'Then run and fetch them, my dear. They are not books you want to read.'

James looked for someone to whom to entrust his box, yielded it to Faith's ready hands, and scampered upstairs.

'What is the book?' said Hope.

Eleanor met her eyes, while she addressed a casual remark to Miss Mitford, and everyone knew that the subject was not one for Isabel and Venice, including the pair concerned. James returned and put the books into Eleanor's hands without looking at them, and carefully retrieved his box.

'Why did you take them?' said his mother.

'They looked as if they were interesting,' said James, in an almost confidential tone. 'They have covers like Miss Mitford's German fairy tales. And there were nine all alike. But perhaps the leaves wanted cutting.'

'And can't you do that?' said Faith, at once.

'I always tear them, if I do it,' said James, looking at her with frankness in his eyes, if in no other part of him.

'That would not do for the dining-room books,' said Eleanor. 'They must be left alone in future.'

'Would you like to have a paper knife?' said Faith.

'Is that a knife for cutting pages?' said James, with his customary unawareness of the purposes of things.

'Yes. I will bring you one next time I come.'

'Then I shall have one like Miss Mitford,' said James, betraying that he had seen this one in use.

'Isabel looks tired, Miss Mitford,' said Eleanor. 'And she has had a sleep. She cannot spend her life resting.'

'Certainly not, on such a day as this in her family.'

'Everything possible has been spared her.'

'I am sure it has. But that could hardly be much.'

'They would be better in bed,' said Eleanor, taking an accustomed outlet for her anxiety and other feelings.

'You need not stand, children,' said Luce. 'We know you have had a long day.'

'Need they sit either?' said Hope. 'I think they like to lie down. Are they prostrated by their father's going?'

'Yes,' said Miss Mitford.

'I expect they would like to be rid of us,' said Faith, going with decision to the door. 'After all, they did not invite us in here, did they?'

'You seemed to have a standing invitation, dear,' said Hope.

'What an open expression James has!' said Faith, when she gained the landing.

Luce touched her arm and her own lips, and motioned towards the open door, and Faith nodded and smiled in suitable dumb response.

'Well, that wasn't a very gracious welcome,' said Eleanor, to her children. 'It is kind of people to come and see you. Don't you think it is, Isabel?'

'I don't suppose so, or they would not come so often. People are not so fond of being kind.'

'I don't think you have any reason for saying that, my dear. You have had great patience today.'

'Oh, so have you,' said Isabel, raising her hands to her head.

Miss Mitford made as if to resume the book, and Eleanor left the room without requiring James's offices at the door, indeed shutting it herself with a certain sharpness. Her expression for the moment resembled Isabel's. Her daughter was at the end of her tether, and so was she.

The party went upstairs to the nursery, where Honor and

Gavin were employed at the table, and Nevill was sitting on Hatton's lap, looking flushed and rumpled.

'Too tired to sleep,' he said, as he turned to the guests.

'Is he, Hatton'?' said Eleanor, with a certain weariness in her own manner.

'He missed his rest, madam. He will be all right in the morning.'

'But not go to bed yet,' said Nevill, in a sharp tone.

'I hope he isn't sickening for anything,' said Eleanor.

'You must hope so,' said Hope. 'I am sure I do too. Indeed I hope no one is.'

'What are the others doing?' said Faith.

'We are painting arrows for our bows and arrows,' said Gavin. 'Miss Pilbeam helped us to make the bows. The arrows were in the shop.'

'He has a bow-and-arrow,' said Nevill, pronouncing the last three words in one, and indicating a production of Mullet's on a chair.

'That is not a real one,' said Gavin.

'A little bow-and-arrow,' said Nevill, in a contented tone.

'What will you shoot with them?' said Faith, with some misgiving in her tone.

'Oh, birds and animals and things,' said Gavin. 'They are not toys. They could give a mortal wound.'

'I don't suppose we shall hit much,' said Honor. 'And they are not poisoned arrows.'

'He will shoot a bird,' said Nevill, his voice rising with his thought. 'He will shoot a chicken; he will shoot a cock.'

'A duck would be easy to shoot,' said Gavin.

'A duck,' agreed Nevill, settling down on Hatton's lap.

'They must not make havoc among the poultry, Hatton,' said Eleanor.

'Then how are they to manage?' said Hope.

'Why don't they have a target to shoot at?' said Faith.

'What is a target?' said Gavin.

'A piece of wood made on purpose for shooting,' said Faith, with mingled eagerness and precision. 'It has holes or marks on it, so that people can aim.'

'I would rather shoot at something alive. I expect I shall shoot at wild birds.'

'He will too,' said Nevill.

'But suppose you hit one and hurt it?'

'It wouldn't know it was hurt; it would be dead,' said Gavin. 'Grown-up men shoot birds.'

'And animals too,' said Honor. 'They shoot big game.'

'What would you do with a dead bird?' said Faith.

'Cook it and eat it,' said Gavin.

'Or have a funeral,' said Honor.

'And say prayers, said Nevill, in a lower tone, with a movement of his hands towards each other.

'But it might be hurt and not dead,' said Faith.

'Then I would shoot it again and make it dead,' said Gavin.

'Well, if you can depend on your aim like that!'

'He doesn't,' said Honor, defending her brother from this charge. 'If he shot a bird once, he could do it again.'

'We might stuff a bird, to give to Father when he comes home,' said Gavin.

'How would you do that?' said Faith, believing the process to involve objections.

'Take out the inside and fill it up with something else. Fred knows about it. He is the gardener's boy.'

'Fred is a nice boy,' said Nevill.

'Wouldn't a live bird be better than a stuffed one?' said Faith, looking at Nevill with disagreement.

'It wouldn't be your own,' said Honor. 'It couldn't belong to anyone. It wouldn't be different from other birds.'

'Father likes stuffed birds. There is one in his dressing-room,' said Gavin.

'A little, red bird,' said Nevill. 'He will shoot a robin for Father.'

> 'A robin redbreast in a cage
> Puts all Heaven in a rage,'

quoted Faith, with rising feeling.

'Faith does have points in common with Heaven,' said Hope.

'Not a cage,' said Nevill. 'A nice, glass *case*.'

'We needn't kill a robin,' said Honor. 'Father kills other birds.'

'All hang down,' said Nevill. 'Poor birds!'

'Yes, that is what I mean,' said Faith. 'Poor birds!'

Nevill beat his hands together and uttered the sounds he made when chasing the fowls.

'The bird couldn't run, if it were stuffed and dead,' said Gavin.

'It sings,' said Nevill. 'Father's bird sings in its case.'

'I don't think it can do that,' said Faith.

'Tweet, tweet,' said Nevill, in disproof of this, assuming a listening air.

'I don't think they are very cruel to anything,' said Eleanor.

'Well, only to Faith,' said Hope. 'I think they are to her. It is three against one.'

'I do not feel that at all,' said Faith.

'We only don't think the same as she does,' said Honor.

'We can't all think alike, can we?' said Faith. 'But I hope we shall agree about this some day.'

'Some day he will shoot a little bird for you,' promised Nevill, in vague amendment, as Faith bent to bid him good-bye.

Chapter 7

'Have you all read Father's letter?' said Eleanor. 'It is meant for us all. There is a note for me, that I have taken.'

Regan put aside a note for herself, with a look of promise at her husband.

'Here is a letter addressed to Isabel,' said Eleanor, turning out the envelope. 'I had better see if there is anything in it, before it goes upstairs.'

'No, Mother,' said Luce, putting out a restraining hand, 'that is not the way to deal with letters. Let Isabel have it intact, as she would expect. That will teach her how to treat correspondence.'

'Does she not know?' said Daniel. 'Has she never seen any letters?'

'I daresay not addressed to herself,' said Graham. 'As she has no friends, she can only hear from her family. And they generally share one's life. In her case they always do.'

'Your father may have put in something as an afterthought,' said Eleanor, still handling the letter.

'Then Isabel will tell you of it,' said Daniel.

'I don't know that she will. She is a strange, independent child. And her father may not have thought to give a definite direction.'

'He would put any message for you into your own letter,' said Graham.

'Not certainly. Things so often occur to him at the last. He may even have written this note on purpose to include something, and thought he would give Isabel pleasure at the same time.'

'There is no ground for that assumption,' said Sir Jesse, in an easy tone.

'More than anyone would think, who did not know Fulbert.'

'Would you say that, Mother?' said Luce. 'I think it is more like Father to have his own message for each of us. I can often tell to which one he is speaking, by his voice and words.'

'But not by his notes,' said Eleanor, smiling. 'You have never watched him write them, if you think that.'

'We generally communicate by word of mouth, as we share our home,' said Daniel.

'But he has to deal with people outside,' said his mother. 'His family is not the whole of his life. He has a good deal of correspondence.'

'Then I suppose he addresses his letters to the people who are to read them. And this one is addressed to Isabel.'

'A letter written by my own husband to my own child and enclosed in a letter to me, is not a secret from me,' said Eleanor, tearing the envelope.

'We see it is not,' said Graham.

'You talk as if we all lived in a state of estrangement.'

'Two of us will now do so.'

'No, my boy, Isabel will hardly notice that the envelope is broken.'

'Father seems anyhow to have wasted an envelope,' said Daniel.

'A weak yielding to curiosity, Mother, that is unworthy of you,' said Luce.

Eleanor looked surprised by the charge. She had felt no interest in Fulbert's word to his daughter, and had given the true account of her motives.

'You don't keep the children apart in your mind, as Father does, Mother.'

'They don't need all that differentiation. I am tired of hearing about it.'

'It is well that they should not need it,' said Sir Jesse.

'It teaches them to be touchy and exacting.'

'You do not expect those qualities in Isabel,' said Daniel. 'I trust that your method will prove its success.'

'There is nothing in the letter,' said his mother, putting it down. 'Isabel can have it when someone goes upstairs.'

'Who will be the bearer of it?' said Graham.

'None of you need be. I will take it myself when I go to the schoolroom. For the matter of that, the girls will be passing in a minute.'

'You might put it in a fresh envelope,' said Graham.

'I am not ashamed of anything I do,' said Eleanor, raising her brows. 'I should not dream of hiding it. I have opened Isabel's letter, and she may know I have done so.'

'I am sorry for that,' said Daniel.

'I never know why revealing baseness makes it better,' said Graham.

'People do not reveal such a thing,' said Sir Jesse.

'Isabel,' said Eleanor, raising her voice, as footsteps sounded in the hall, 'come in and say good-morning to us. Are you all there?'

Isabel and Venice and Miss Mitford entered the room.

'Good-morning,' said Miss Mitford, looking at Eleanor and using a tone of compliance with an injunction.

'Good-morning, Miss Mitford; good-morning, my dears. I want to read you Father's letter. Come and hear it.'

The two girls listened to the letter, put the normal questions and comments, and were about to go.

'Here is a note put in for you, Isabel,' said Eleanor, handing it to her daughter.

'Thank you. Father said he would write to me,' said Isabel, turning to show the letter to her sister.

'It came inside my letter,' said her mother.

'Who opened it?' said Isabel.

'Now, who had the right to do that?' said Eleanor, stroking her hair. 'No one touched it, who had no business with it. I should not have allowed that. I wanted to see if there was any message for me. There is one for all of you in my letter.'

Isabel looked at her mother's note, as it lay on the table.

'You have not let anyone see that.'

'Well, naturally not, my dear. Father would not have liked it.'

'Would he have wished you to see mine?'

'Think for a moment and tell me.'

'It is a pity you do such second-rate things,' said Isabel, in a slow voice. 'It is a mean way of using power.'

'What other second-rate thing have you known me do?'

'You do not deny the term. And these things are never isolated.'

'Come, come, my child. You would have shown me the letter, would you not?'

'I might have had no choice. But I should have read it myself first. There would have been a semblance of free will. Decency would not have been outraged.'

'What a term to use of a mother's overlooking her child's correspondence!'

'The thing's being between a mother and child, or rather its coming from a mother, adds to the ugliness.'

'Do you think it so important that a little girl's letter should be private? It clearly cannot be so in itself.'

Isabel deliberately took up her mother's letter and tore it open.

Eleanor took no notice, as if regarding such an incident as too trivial to heed.

Isabel glanced down the letter and then opened her own. A faint smile crept round her lips as she scanned it, and she put it in her pocket and relinquished the first. Fulbert's attitude to writing was as his wife had suggested. He had done the duty amid a pressure of work. It had been convenient to him that his sentiments as a husband and father should be the same. The two letters were identical in wording, except for the beginning and end. Isabel looked round the room.

'Father draws no distinction between Mother and me,' she said, with a touch of satisfied pride. 'He has copied one letter from the other. I don't know which was the original.'

Eleanor took up her own note and found that this was the case. Regan tore open hers and looked in appeal at her granddaughter. Isabel yielded her own letter, and Regan made a swift comparison and smiled her relief. Graham, who had been watching his grandmother, relaxed his expression.

'You meant to sacrifice me, and you have sacrificed Father,' said Isabel to her mother. 'You thought I should look childish and foolish, and you have contrived that he does. You can deal as you will with people who are away. He and I were both in your hands.'

'I did not think how you would appear,' said Eleanor. 'It is not a question that would enter my mind. I thought there might be a message from Father, as I said. And you must see that the letter did not apply especially to you.'

'You see the same about yours. And you would not have let me read it, if you had not read mine. You only did that to make the whole matter seem nothing.'

'Well, I am glad it has come to seem so,' said Eleanor, finding that she matched her power against her daughter's, as she could not otherwise withstand her. 'It did not take much to make it.'

'You know you will not mention to Father that the two letters are the same.'

'I should hardly think of it. And you give the message to yourself too much of a place. He wrote it separately to give you pleasure. He had no idea it would be pushed into this sort of prominence.'

'Doubtless he had not,' said Sir Jesse.

'None at all. That is clear,' said Isabel. 'He meant it to be private.'

'I have written the same letter to different people,' said Daniel. 'But never to people under the same roof. Separation struck me as the first condition.'

'So an idea came to you,' said his grandfather.

'Your father was very much occupied,' said Eleanor.

'A very disorganizing circumstance,' said Graham, sighing.

'Well, Isabel will be able to write him a nice, long, amusing letter in exchange,' said Eleanor, with a hint of revenge on her daughter. 'She has no duties and she can give plenty of time to it. Will you see that she does it, Miss Mitford?'

'Well, it is nothing to do with me.'

'That seems to be the case,' said Sir Jesse.

'Then she can attend to it herself,' said Eleanor. 'She is old enough to write her own letters.'

'And also to read them. The one thing follows from the other,' said Isabel. 'People's correspondence is their own affair.'

'Is that quite the word for this little message?'

'You used it yourself. And you talk about a long, amusing letter in return. If I describe this scene, I might write one. Perhaps I shall.'

'I don't think you would like to make Father feel even a little uncomfortable. It was not a very unnatural thing to model a letter on one already written, when he was pressed for time.'

'I think I could give the scene without referring to that. That does not seem to me the point of it.'

Eleanor gave a glance almost of apprehension at her daughter, and turned to the governess.

'So James is at school today.'

'Yes.'

'He could find no excuse for staying at home. If he had known that Isabel was to have a letter from her father, he might have used that.'

'It seems to be an event of a portentous nature,' said Sir Jesse.

'Venice must write a letter to Father, and then perhaps she will have the message next time,' said Eleanor, smiling at her daughter.

'Father might have some copies of a note printed off, so that we could all have one,' said Graham. 'Then he could reap a good harvest in exchange.'

'What a lot you make of the little circumstance of the notes being worded in the same way!' said Eleanor, in a wondering tone.

'It is true that they do so,' said Sir Jesse.

'You were led further by your assumption that they were different, Mother,' said Daniel.

'Oh, don't let us go on harping on one little point. Pray let us change the subject. Do you feel that you have lived these weeks since Father left us, as he would like? Do you feel that, Isabel?'

'I have no choice how to live them. The question is more pertinent for you. What do you feel about the weeks, including this morning?'

'I have done my best,' said Eleanor. 'I daresay he would like me to do better.'

'Shall we stamp off a dozen impressions of a creditable letter, and all sign it?' said Daniel. 'Nevill could put a cross.'

'You have been helped to a subject for a jest,' said Eleanor. 'And between you, you will make the most of it.'

'They generally share such things,' said Sir Jesse.

'I hope Father will not stay away long,' said Isabel.

'What an odd little speech!' said her mother. 'You would surely not hope the opposite. And you know that he must stay for six months.'

'Mother, Isabel is younger and more helpless than you,' said Luce, in a low tone.

Eleanor looked at Isabel, and suddenly covered her face in her hands and broke into tears.

Sir Jesse rose and walked from the room, holding the paper before him with an effect of being absorbed in it. Regan smiled on the family in simple affection. She thought little of the opening of the letter, and assumed that trouble had arisen because the moment was ripe. Her son had left his family, and it was brought to this.

Miss Mitford sat down to await the end of the scene. She did not leave it, because of its human appeal. She was the happiest person present, as she was more often than was suspected. She did not let pity for her employer or pupil mar her interest. Pity had come to be the normal background of her mind, and other feelings arose irrespective of it.

'Did we know what Father did for us by his mere presence?' said Luce. 'We think of service as coming from definite action. This is a lesson.'

'He will come back and find himself a god,' said Daniel. 'That will make a hard demand on him.'

'I only want him as he is,' said Eleanor, raising her eyes. 'Miss Mitford, you must think this is a strange scene to arise out of nothing.'

'I don't know how it could do that.'

'Well, to develop from a trifle, or to have the trifle made the reason of it. No doubt the emotions were there, and had to come out.'

'I hope it has been a relief,' said Miss Mitford.

'Yes, I think it has. I believe I feel the better for it. Do you, my Isabel?'

'No, I don't think so. I had no emotions until the scene made them. I think I feel the worse.'

Regan gave a kind laugh.

'I don't expect you understand yourself,' said Eleanor, gently. 'Your father is the person who understands you. Poor child, you are one of the greatest sufferers from his absence.'

Isabel naturally began to cry. Venice glanced about in some discomfort at having no ground for tears. Miss Mitford rose from her seat.

'Yes, run out into the air,' said Eleanor, as if the movement suggested a solution of all questions. 'Take your letter, Isabel dear. You will like to have it.'

Isabel looked at the note with an uncertain smile.

'Yes, it is funny, isn't it?' said Eleanor. 'Poor Father! He must have been very busy. Well, he meant to send you your own message. You know that.'

'And Mother will know it in future,' said Isabel, as she left the house. 'I think she has had a lesson, and one she needed.'

'I wish it were time for me to give your father an account of my stewardship,' said Eleanor, to her elder children. 'I dread the prospect of guiding you all for so many months. You do not respond to the single hand.'

'A good deal is to your credit, Mother,' said Luce.

'You make an exception of this morning. But I only ask that there should be honesty between us.'

'I would ask rarer and better things,' said Graham.

'People take perfection as a matter of course,' said Daniel. 'Anything else affronts and enrages them.'

'I have learnt not to look for it,' said Eleanor.

'You make your own demand, Mother,' said Luce.

'Miss Mitford and the girls are coming back,' said Eleanor. 'Of course it has begun to rain. It is to be one of those days when every little thing goes wrong. Perhaps they would like to sit with us until their lessons.'

'Is that a risk, if the day is of that nature?' said Graham. 'It has so far been true to itself.'

'Come in, my dears, and take off your things,' said Eleanor. 'You can stay with us for a time. It will make a change for you. I expect Miss Mitford would like an hour to herself.'

'Do I not also need the change?' said Miss Mitford.

The laughter that greeted the words showed that it did not even now occur to anyone, and Miss Mitford went to the door, striking everyone as a mildly ludicrous figure, with the exception of Graham, who saw her as a sad one. It would have been cheering to him to know her view of herself.

'Well, what is a subject fraught with no danger?' said Luce.

'Hardly that one perhaps,' said Daniel.

'Let us talk in our own way,' said Eleanor. 'The subjects will arise of themselves. We are seldom at a loss for them.'

The minutes passed and this did not come about. Eleanor took up her needlework, as if it were a matter of indifference. When Venice giggled she looked at her with a smile.

'The five of them ought to be photographed,' said Regan, surveying her grandchildren.

'We ought to have a group of them all, to send to their father,' said Eleanor. 'They have not been taken together since Nevill was born.'

'How sincerely they speak, considering that they do not consider spending the money or the effort!' said Daniel, to his brother.

'We must be grateful for the thought,' said Graham. 'I see how real a thing it is.'

'Father will no doubt appreciate it when it reaches him,' said Isabel.

'It is a photograph of Mother that Father would want,' said Luce.

'He took one of me with him,' said Eleanor.

'And one of Grandma too, I suppose.'

'No, I did not load him up with one,' said Regan.

'He asked me for one of myself,' said Eleanor. 'Or rather he was packing a clumsy one, and I gave him another.'

'He will not forget us,' said Luce, in a peaceful tone.

'No, dear, but that is not the point of a photograph,' said Eleanor. 'It gives a sort of companionship, an illusion of the presence of the person.'

'The real presence must be a shadowy one in that case,' said Regan.

'Is it better to have a photograph of oneself packed or not?' said Graham.

'I see it as a tribute,' said Daniel.

'It is in a sense, of course,' said Eleanor.

'I expect there was one about the room,' said Regan.

'There were photographs of all of us,' said Eleanor. 'Of everyone in the house.'

'Mother said a subject would arise, and it has arisen,' said Graham.

Regan laughed and went to attend to her housekeeping.

'It does not often occur to your grandmother that I may like to be left with my children,' said Eleanor.

'It strikes few of us that people want to be rid of us,' said Daniel. 'I do not remember having the feeling.'

'I feel a temptation to mark time until Father returns,' said Luce.

'The house is even duller, the house seems duller than it was,' said Isabel. 'And that produces a sense of waiting for something.'

'You cannot be dull when there are so many of you together,' said Eleanor, with simple conviction. 'You have your own rooms and your own interests. And Miss Mitford gives all her time to you, and you seem to find her amusing.'

'Another subject has arisen,' said Graham.

'I am not going to have any more of them,' said Eleanor, shaking her head. 'We must not make Father's absence an excuse for complaint and indolence. I see the rain has stopped, and there is time for a run before lessons. I wonder if Miss Mitford has noticed it.'

'She does not notice anything when she is reading,' said Venice.

'Does she do nothing but read? I hope she will not teach you to be always poring over books. There are other things in life.'

'Not in every life,' said Graham.

'That is what she does teach us in our lesson hours,' said Isabel. 'We thought she was supposed to, and so did she. At other times she does not interfere with us.'

'I should think Isabel is the last girl to be dull in herself,' said Eleanor, looking after her daughters. 'She is always amusing and amused. And Venice is the easiest child. I should think no schoolroom could be happier. It is nice for James to come home to all of it.'

'So it all works round to James's advantage,' said Graham.

'You talk as if he were a pathetic character,' said Eleanor. 'He could not have more than he has.'

'Graham dear,' said Luce, in a low tone, 'things can only be done by us according to our nature and our understanding. It is useless to expect more. We can none of us give it.'

'That does not take from the pathos. Indeed it is the reason of it.'

'It is partly the ordinary pathos of childhood, Graham.'

'Of childhood in the later stage, when it is worked and confined and exhorted. For its weakness the burden is great.'

'James has his own power of throwing things off,' said Luce.

'Of course all my children are tragic figures,' said Eleanor.

Chapter 8

'Two for Mother, and four for Father,' said Faith, distributing the letters at the breakfast table. 'And three for Ridley.'

'And how many for you?' said Paul.

'Seven, Father,' said Faith, in an unobtrusive manner.

'And were they less worthy of mention?'

'Well, there was no need to speak of them, Father.'

'Why not as much as the others?'

'Well, one does not want to draw attention to one's own things, when they are more than other people's.'

'I did not know that,' said Hope.

'Faith had a fair method of attracting the general interest,' said Ridley.

'They are only to do with oneself, after all,' went on Faith, as if her brother had not spoken.

'I wish I had more than two letters,' said Hope. 'It makes it seem as if only two people were thinking of me.'

'It was very nice of seven people to be thinking of me,' said Faith, in a light tone.

'It is even better to be the sort of person to be in their thoughts.'

'I did not mean to suggest that, Mother.'

'Well, it was not necessary, dear.'

'Faith is an inveterate correspondent,' said Ridley.

'Letter writing is not a vice,' said his father.

'I think in this case it has become a habit. And people are obliged to write letters in answer to those they receive.'

'I see. It is a good idea to put oneself in their thoughts,' said Hope.

Faith looked down at her letters, as if she would like to make a protest concerning them, but was silent.

'Faith keeps up with everyone who has crossed her path,' said Ridley.

'I see no reason for dropping people, when once I have known them,' said his sister.

'I can't understand people's not seeing those reasons,' said Hope.

'I never lose my interest in anyone I have known.'

'I like to hear about them, and the different ways in which they have gone downhill.'

'They have not always done that, Mother.'

'Then I think I correspond with them. Two people write to me, to every seven to you. That shows the proportion.'

'I think Faith's correspondents are often a good way down the hill, when she first meets them,' said Ridley, laughing.

'I see no reason for only being interested in fortunate people,' said his sister.

'You are not good at seeing reasons, dear,' said Hope.

'I like people for their personal qualities.'

'If they have many of those, they are not objects for letters,' said Paul. 'They would have their own way about them.'

'I suppose Faith won't tell us who her correspondents are,' said Hope.

'Well, I see no point in doing that. It is not quite the sort of atmosphere in which I should choose to reveal them.'

'I am sure they would be very uncomfortable, dear,' said Hope.

'What is that letter, Ridley?' said Faith, looking past her stepmother. 'You look as if you had had bad news.'

Ridley kept his eyes on the letter and did not speak. His parents turned their eyes on him, and he remained as still as if he were on the stage. Something about him suggested that he felt he was on it.

'Mrs Cranmer,' he said, partly rising from the table, 'may I ask you for a moment of your time?'

'You may have it all. I cannot do anything with it until I know the subject of that letter.'

'I would willingly postpone your knowing.'

'But do not do so, dear.'

Ridley sat down again and appeared to be lost in thought, and his father rose and read the letter over his shoulder.

MY DEAR RIDLEY,

I must depend on you to fulfil your word. I am so sick a man that when this reaches you, I shall be a dead one, unless a cable has come to you earlier. There is no need to hasten hard news to innocent people, and the word of my death can come to my family through you. All to be told will follow by a later mail. I have written this letter with my own hand. I know you will serve my wife to the limit of your power. And I will end to you, as you are to be to me,

Your friend,
FULBERT SULLIVAN.

The family stood in silence. Paul was sunk in thought. Faith put her handkerchief to her eyes. Hope rose with an almost energetic movement.

'Well, someone has to be the first to speak. And I can see you expect it to be me. I am the one whose feelings don't have to be too deep for words.'

'We can't help having the feelings, Mother,' said Faith.

'What have you to do, Ridley?' said Paul.

'To go to Mrs Sullivan, Father, to go to Eleanor Sullivan, and break to her the truth. And from my heart do I wish that this cup might pass from me.'

Faith looked at her brother with open eyes.

'I must not delay,' went on Ridley, as if unconscious of his last words. 'I can only make the blow as swift and merciful as possible. I can only do my best.'

'Do you think that perhaps a woman might do it better?' said Faith.

Ridley turned and looked into her face.

'It was not so that Fulbert left it. And it is not so that it shall be. I do not break my faith with the dead.'

'I only made the suggestion for what it was worth.'

'And Ridley has told you what that was, dear,' said Hope.

Ridley looked at his stepmother as if he thought she misused the occasion.

'Of course all the best in people will come out now,' she said. 'It is true that the accompaniments of grief are the worst part. I am always uneasy when people show the best that is in them. I am not talking about Ridley's best, as that is indispensable, but on the whole I prefer people's dear, faulty, familiar selves.'

Faith looked up as if she hardly saw herself in these last words.

'It is something that we don't seem to be drawn closer,' went on Hope. 'That is what is done by the most distressing things. I am glad we don't feel it to that extent.'

'There seems no urgency to break the news,' said Paul. 'But Ridley will have to get it behind.'

'I can hardly face the family, Father, with this between us. Even my lawyer's training in inscrutability does not prepare me for that.'

'You will tell me if I can be of any use to you, Ridley,' said Faith, in a gentle tone, after a moment's communing with herself.

'Faith's best seems to improve with every moment,' said Hope. 'And Ridley has only to use his as it is. He will have to decide when to do it.'

'That was not left to me, Mrs Cranmer. If it had been, I fear I might have taken some way out. As it is —' Ridley straightened his shoulders and made his way from the house.

'Ridley's best is rather unfitted for daily life,' said Hope. 'This is the first time I have seen it in thirty years. It might be better to have one that came in oftener. But I suppose it is meant for an emergency.'

'We must hope it will do its work on this occasion,' said Faith. 'After all, Mr Sullivan depended on it.'

'I am sure it will,' said Hope. 'You see that my best is as good as yours.'

'Are we not rather running this idea to death, Mother?'

'My best is better than yours. It is never used for people's embarrassment. My worst is used for that. I am right not to like the best in people. Why should I, when it is put to a mean purpose? And I believe it generally is.'

'I hope my worse side did not creep out for the moment,' said Faith, in a lighter tone.

'I don't think so, dear; I am sure you were at your very best.'

'Father,' said Faith, 'I think Mother is much more upset by this news than she shows.'

'She has shown it to me,' said Paul.

'The best in you both is better than I have ever imagined,' said Hope. 'I am really comforted by it, and I did not know it ever did that. If Ridley's is doing the same for Eleanor, I see what Fulbert meant.'

'Well, now don't you think we might consider if there is anything we can do, Mother?'

'I think we might; I should agree with anything you said. If we don't put ourselves forward, and don't fancy we are the sort of people who could be tolerated at such a time, I think we might do what we can. But I don't quite see what that is.'

'Need we be quite so unsure of ourselves? If we took that line, we should never do anything for anyone.'

'And that is too high a standard for us. So we will go and do the womanly duties that are borne at these times. I suppose people do put up with them. It is known that the well-meant offices aggravate sorrow, so no doubt they must. And we will leave your father to suffer in a man's simplicity. I feel rather anxious about him, and it is the irritation in anxiety that is the worst part.'

'I am coming with you,' said Paul.

'Now I can throw myself into serving others. I will make it all as easy to bear as possible. Ridley must be breaking the truth by now. I have heard that that is harder than hearing it, but I do not agree.'

Ridley had reached the Sullivans' house and asked for Eleanor. He was shown to the drawing-room, where she was with Luce and Regan. He had depended on seeing her alone, and had to adjust his words. He met her eyes and then advanced and laid a hand on her shoulder. She looked up, alarmed, but her voice was forestalled by Regan's.

'He is dead, is he? He has gone after the others. Well, I can live in peace now. There is no one else.'

Eleanor was standing, pale and still, heedless of those about her. Luce took the letter from Regan's hand, and went and put her arms about her mother. Regan spoke again, neither to herself nor the others.

'It wasn't much good to have them, for my husband to be left without a son. We have wasted it all, our time and our feeling. All our feeling has gone. And we have only each other at the end.'

'Lady Sullivan,' said Ridley, in a low tone, 'we have to tell your husband.'

Regan made a movement that would have been a spring, if she had had youth and strength, and was gone from sight. It was not from Ridley's lips that Sir Jesse would hear of the death of his son.

Daniel and Graham came from their grandfather, with the truth in their faces, and the thought in their minds that they were tied to Sir Jesse now. They gave their attention to their mother, while they imagined their own future; the full manhood, the loss of their father, the service to two generations; and saw the truth of their father's life, which they had deemed so easy.

Eleanor looked up and spoke in her natural tones.

'We had better send for the children. It is no good to put off their knowing.'

Her words revealed herself, and her children confronted their knowledge of her. She felt real grief, made no pretence of despair, tried to face her loss and her duty, could not follow children's suffering. Luce looked in mute appeal at Ridley.

'Mrs Sullivan,' he said, bending towards her, 'would you not leave them a while in their happiness? That is the way to spare yourself.'

'I must not think of that. The thing will have to be done.'

The schoolroom children were summoned. They caught the threat in the message, and came with fear in their eyes. Their mother put her arms about them.

'My little son and daughters, there is a great sorrow come to us today. Father will not return to us. We are to be alone.'

The children broke into weeping, at first without character or difference. James was the first to recover, and to try to realize his new life. Venice looked at her mother, as though with an instinct to help her. Isabel stood as if she were alone. Ridley remained with his eyes on Eleanor, and wore a look of venerating sympathy.

Regan returned to fetch the letter for her husband, took it from Ridley and went from the room. As she passed, she cast on the group a glance without hope or gentleness, almost without pity, a glance of hard resignation to the helpless suffering.

'My children,' said Eleanor, 'will you do your first thing for your mother? Will you break it to the little ones for me? Will you begin to help?'

Venice went to the door, as if to fulfil the request. James made a movement to follow her, glancing at his mother. Isabel met her eyes, but seemed not to hear what she had said.

'Is it too much for you, my dear?' said Eleanor, looking at Isabel. 'Then I will do it myself. Why should I put my duty on to those weaker than I? It is for their mother to spare them. James, will you bring them to me?'

James began to run from the room, checked himself and subdued his pace, and looked in appeal at his brothers.

'I can go and tell them, Mother,' said Graham.

'No, Graham,' said Luce, moving forward with her eyes on her mother. 'It is natural for them to hear the truth amongst us all. It will make one shock and one memory, and will spare them the meetings afterwards. We must think of the things that make children suffer.'

'We cannot save them the one thing,' said Eleanor, with a faint smile. 'I should not think those will count beside it. But do as you will, my dear. I am grateful for any help.'

A message was sent upstairs. Hatton entered with the children, and remained in the room, as though she would not withdraw the protection of her presence. James seemed to drift towards her, and stood at her side, suggesting the sphere with which he identified his life. Eleanor drew the children to her, and said the words she had said to the others. Honor wept in startled despair and grasp of a changed life; Nevill in abandonment to the general sorrow, and sympathy with it; Gavin did not weep, and looked at the older faces in resentment and question. Daniel put a hand on his head and said an encouraging word. His mother looked up, unsure of this line, but let her eyes fall, as if offering no judgement. Sir Jesse and Regan entered and went to their chairs by the hearth, acquiescing once again in the old customs in a different life. Sir Jesse laid his hand on Eleanor's shoulder as he passed, and Regan gave her grandchildren a smile that did not touch her own experience beneath. Luce waited for the tension to relax, and then moved towards Daniel, who knew that she put him in his father's place.

'We must make an effort, Mother,' he said. 'It is the only thing. We must leave this moment behind. Life will not wait for us.'

'When life has done what it has, it might have the grace just to do that,' said Graham.

Gavin gave a loud laugh, and his mother turned her eyes on him. She did not know that he was hailing the first break in the oppression. Nevill left Hatton and went up to Daniel.

'He won't cry any more,' he promised, and looked round the room. 'All stop now.'

Venice took his hands as if in play, but he seemed to feel some lack in her, and returned to Hatton. Eleanor gave Venice the smile of approval that she gave to this child's courage.

'Did Father have an ordinary illness like an English one?' said Gavin. 'Or are the illnesses different there?'

'We do not know yet, my boy,' said Eleanor. 'I think it was different. We shall hear soon.'

'How do we know he is dead?'

'He is not dead, my child. He is more alive than he has ever been.'

'But how do we know he is what we call dead?' said Gavin, with a faint frown.

Eleanor explained and Gavin listened until he understood, and then moved away.

'What is the good of his being more alive, when he is not with the people who belong to him?' said Honor, in a tone that seemed to anticipate a mature one of the future. 'And he is always more alive than other people. He ought not to be even what we call dead; he ought not to be.'

'Mrs Sullivan,' said Ridley, as if the words broke from him, 'what a duty you have to live for! We see how much your husband had.'

'I am not a person fitted to carry such a burden.'

'I have my grandchildren,' said Sir Jesse's voice from the hearth. 'I do not go empty to the grave.'

Nevill looked in the direction of the voice, and going to a vase on a table, drew out some flowers and thrust them towards his grandfather.

'They are all for Grandpa.'

'Won't you bring me some flowers too?' said Regan, turning more slowly than usual, as if her response were feebler.

Nevill returned to the vase, looked back at the flowers in Sir Jesse's hands, and ran and transferred them to Regan's.

'All for Grandma,' he said, wiping his hands down his garments, as though the office were distasteful.

'Isabel dear, sit down and try to stop crying,' said Eleanor. 'You know you do not help us by making yourself ill.'

Isabel obeyed as if all things were indifferent, and her mother gave a sigh as she withdrew her eyes.

'I wonder when I shall be able to get to my own sorrow,' she said to Ridley, with a faint smile.

Ridley met her look and swiftly touched his eyes, and Nevill ran up to him and looked up into his face.

'All stop now,' he told him for his guidance.

Ridley gave a smile at Eleanor.

'"*O sancta simplicitas*",' he said.

'What does that mean?' said Gavin.

'It means that childhood is sacred,' said Eleanor.

'You don't think it is, do you?' said her son.

'What will happen when they have all stopped?' said Graham to Daniel. 'Is there anything left?'

'Is there?' said Eleanor to herself, in a tone only partly designed for the ears of others.

Daniel led her to a seat; Ridley looked at him with a change in his face; Regan turned her eyes from the hearth, and rested them for a moment upon Ridley.

Gavin detached himself from the group and went towards the door.

'Where are you going, my boy?' said Eleanor.

'Upstairs.'

'But you will be alone up there.'

Gavin continued his way.

'Wouldn't you rather stay down here with all of us?'

'I don't much like seeing people when they are like this.'

'We cannot help being sad for Father. But we are going to do our best to be brave.'

Gavin waited as if to weigh the evidence of this, and then proceeded.

'Don't you mind being alone?'

'I shouldn't be alone, if Honor came with me.'

'Do you want to go up, Honor?'

'I don't mind.'

'It is all too much for them,' said Luce.

'Of course it is, my dear,' said her mother, with a sharper note. 'How could it not be?'

'Always cry now,' said Nevill, sadly. 'It is because Father goes away.'

'Mother, I think we must release them,' said Luce. 'It is all beyond their age.'

'If release is the word, let them go, my dear, of course. But Nevill is the only one who is too young to understand.'

'That does not make it better for them, Mother.'

'It is him that is young,' said Nevill.

'We are so glad you are what you are,' said Eleanor, smiling at him.

'So better now,' said Nevill, in a tone that lost its cheerfulness as he looked at Regan. 'But not poor Grandma.'

'Can't you go to her and do something to make her better?' said Luce.

Nevill went up to Regan and paused at her knee, while he considered his course. His earnest eyes fixed on her face made her smile and finally give a little laugh, and he ran back to Luce to report on his success.

'Grandma laugh now. All laugh now,' he said, looking round to witness the change.

Sir Jesse beckoned to him and lifted him to his knee.

'What should we do without our little lad?'

'Grandpa loves him too,' said Nevill, in some surprise.

'Hatton, I think you can take them,' said Eleanor. 'I am not being much help to them.'

Nevill ran towards the door with a feeling of achievement; Gavin walked out of the room and towards the stairs; Honor looked round as if she hardly realized what was happening, and got off her chair in a dazed manner and followed.

'Come and kiss your mother, Gavin,' said Eleanor, as if this observance might be omitted with the others.

Gavin returned, took a passive part in the embrace, and retraced his steps.

'You will like to think of Father when you are upstairs.'

Gavin paused at a distance and looked into his mother's face.

'We don't any of us seem much to like it.'

'Of course it will make you sad. But we can hardly remember him unless we are that.'

Gavin paused for thought.

'I think I can.'

'Well, remember him in your own way. Good-bye, my Honor; you will think of Father too.'

'I shan't ever think of anyone else now.'

'You will think of your mother too, and remember that she is alone.'

'We are all alone now. Father was the person who held us together. It is the father who does that.'

'I know your father did. But you still have your mother.'

'And you have Luce and Daniel and Graham. And Grandma has Grandpa. We all have someone. But it doesn't make it different. Father was the person who protected us.'

'Take her upstairs, Hatton,' said Eleanor. 'I can feel they are safe with you.'

'Hatton will take care of her,' said Nevill, running at Honor's side. 'He will too.'

James, with an almost capering movement, came to take leave of his mother, with a view to establishing a precedent of following Hatton himself.

'Are you going with them, my boy?'

James made another movement.

'Do you want to go?' said Eleanor, in a gentle, condoning manner.

'No,' said James, in a light tone.

'You would rather stay down here with me?'

'Yes, I would.'

'Then stay, my little son. I shall like to have you. You can leave him with me, Hatton.'

'I should like his help with Honor, madam. She needs to have one of them older than herself. She can't take the lead today.'

'Then go up, my boy, and comfort your little sister, and remember that you do it for your mother.'

James withdrew with a sense of having satisfactorily and even with credit laid the foundation of his future.

Mullet was awaiting the stricken group, and began at once to talk, as if she had been summoning her powers for their benefit.

'Now here you are, safe and sound. And you have your home and Hatton and me. Some children lose it all when their father dies, but it is different with you.'

'Why is it different?' said Gavin.

Hatton withdrew to liberate Mullet's gifts, and James quietly followed and went to his room.

'Because this house belongs to your grandpa, and you will still live here with him. You won't have to move into a small house and face a changed life.'

'Why do people do that?' said Gavin.

'A dear little house,' said Nevill, coming up to Mullet.

'Dear, dear, the collapses and crashes there have been in my family! You would hardly believe the tale of them. First prosperity and luxury and leisure, and then downfall and poverty and trouble. Poverty in a sense of course I mean; all things are comparative. And desertion by friends is always part of it. I am thinking of a cousin of my father's, who was a well-known physician and lived in Harley Street, which is an address for people of that kind. And they kept a butler and a cook and the usual complement of under-servants. And they did much as the mood took them. Yes, their lot was cast in pleasant places. And then the curse that was hanging over them gathered and fell. There has always been this something ill-fated about our family. My uncle died, and the end of it all came. They had to take shelter under a humble roof, and keep one servant; well, one good servant from the old days, and one or two young ones it really was, though to hear the family talk, you would have thought it was a state of penury; and move out of society and face a different future. Yes, I often think of them, moving in their shabby gentility about their second-rate social round, always with that air of having come down in the world, which a truer dignity would lay aside. A morning of trivial shopping, after an interview with the rather tyrannical cook; a dose of cavalier treatment from the tradesmen instead of the accustomed respect, for that class of person is the first to show a sense of difference; an afternoon over a dreary fire, missing the friends who used to attend their frequent functions; that is my cousins' life. I often think I have been wise in cutting right adrift from the past, that I have chosen the better part.'

'I don't think you have,' said Gavin. 'You don't have even as much as they have. And perhaps that is why they don't write to you.'

'It may be; there are more unlikely things. I often think of those people who used to cross our threshold and accept our hospitality. How many friends have I from my old life? None. But I would not thank them to darken my horizon. They were fair-weather friends.'

'How do you pronounce horizon?' said Gavin, Mullet having put the emphasis on the first syllable.

'Horizon,' said Honor, in a mechanical tone, placing it on the second.

'Well, there are different pronunciations in different circles. And my education was broken off too soon for me to have the usual foundation. And my father never did believe in much learning for girls. It was one of those old-fashioned ideas he had inherited from his ancestors. I was never to do anything, and what was the good of so much training? And there it was.'

'But you might have been a governess instead of a nurse,' said Gavin.

'It would have been all the same to him,' said Mullet. 'A dependent position is a dependent position. That is what it would have been.'

'I think your father was a rather foolish man.'

'He had his vein of foolishness, according to modern ideas. But I could not help loving him for it,' said Mullet, bearing out the theory that people love their creations. 'And, after all, I owed him my being.'

Honor got off her chair and came up to Gavin with a faint smile.

'Perhaps it is the other way round,' she said, as if feeling that the day broke some bond upon her tongue.

Gavin seemed puzzled, and at that moment Hatton returned to the room and at once looked at Honor's face.

'Well, now,' she said in a cheerful tone, while her eyes met Mullet's, 'it is time for you to have your dinner. I expect Mr Ridley is staying, and you will see him when you go downstairs.'

'We have seen him,' said Gavin.

'I don't want to go down,' said Honor.

'It will make a change for you,' said Mullet.

'It won't,' said Gavin. 'We go down every day. It will be the same as usual.'

Honor raised her eyes to his face, dumbfounded by a knowledge that went no further.

'Well, you will soon come up again,' said Hatton. 'Now Gavin will have some meat, won't he?'

'Yes.'

'That is my sensible boy.'

'He will eat it all up,' said Nevill, in a vigorous tone.

'So I have two sensible boys.'

'But he will eat the most.'

'I shall see which of you does that. Now Honor will come and have her dinner on my knee.'

Honor went at once to Hatton.

'Sit on Hatton's knee,' said Nevill.

'No, Honor is my baby today.'

'No, he is.'

'You are my baby boy, and Honor is my baby girl.'

'He is a girlie,' said Nevill, holding his knife and fork idle.

'Poor Gavin can't be anything,' said Mullet.

'Not anything,' said Nevill, sadly surveying his brother.

'Honor is going to sleep,' said Gavin, in a rough tone.

'She is tired out,' said Hatton.

'He is tired,' said Nevill, laying his head on the table.

'I am not,' said Gavin, loudly.

'You are a brave boy,' said Mullet.

'He is brave,' said Nevill, leaning towards Hatton, 'a brave soldier boy.'

Honor sank into weeping, cried to the end of her tears, and stood pale and barely conscious while she was made ready to go downstairs. Hatton took them to the door and stood outside, with her ears alert. Mullet remained with her, as if any demand might arise.

'Miss Luce will be a second mother to the children,' she said.

'They will be the better for another,' said Hatton.

'Don't you think the mistress does her part by them?'

'She does all she can, but children hardly want what she gives them. In a way they need very little. They want at once more and less.'

'Master Nevill will hardly remember his father.'

'He has not been able to do much for them lately,' said Hatton, with a sigh. 'And he can do nothing more.'

The children entered the room and stood aloof and silent. Nevill looked about for some employment. Honor was exhausted and Gavin in a state of inner tumult. Eleanor was talking to Ridley, and Regan was lost in herself. Honor sent her eyes round the faces at the table, and went and stood by Isabel. Fulbert's absence of the last months saved his family an empty place. Sir Jesse made a movement from habit towards the things on the table.

'Can they eat them today?' he said, in a voice that simply implied that the day was different.

Gavin came up to the table.

'Yes,' he said.

Sir Jesse pushed a dish towards him and seemed to forget his presence, and Nevill came to his brother's side. Eleanor turned her eyes on them.

'You are having dessert, are you?' she said, in a tone that added nothing to her words.

'Yes,' said Gavin.

'Yes,' said Nevill, standing with his eyes and his hands at the edge of the table.

'Would you like some, Honor?'

'No, thank you.'

'Have it, if you like, dear.'

Honor did not reply.

'James, did you try to take care of Honor?'

James looked at his mother, with a wave of recollection sweeping over him.

'Did you do what you could for her, my boy?'

James met his mother's eyes, and moisture came into his own.

'She – I don't think – she didn't seem to want me.'

'Never mind, dear,' said Eleanor, kindly. 'She could not help it. I am sure you did your best.'

James looked at Honor, saw that she had hardly heard, and realized that even a fatherless boy might continue to have escapes.

'Gavin, tell Hatton when you go upstairs that Honor is to lie down,' said Eleanor.

Gavin made no sign.

'Do you hear me, my boy?'

'Honor can tell her herself.'

'But I asked you to.'

'He will tell her,' said Nevill, to his mother.

'Gavin, do you want to be less useful than Nevill?'

'It is not useful when she can do it herself. And lying down doesn't make any difference. You always think it does.'

'Not to Father's having left us. But it will make Honor's headache better.'

'Have you got a headache?' said Gavin, to his sister.

'No.'

Nevill looked round the table over his hands.

'Poor Honor!' he said, in a rapid tone. 'Poor Isabel! Poor Grandma!' He returned to his plate and looked up to add an afterthought. 'Poor Luce!'

'Nevill admits only feminine feeling,' said Daniel.

'He has met more of it,' said Graham. 'And there may be more.'

'Poor Graham! Poor Daniel!' said Nevill, in an obliging tone.

'Poor Mother!' said Eleanor, gently.

'Poor Mother!' agreed her son. 'But Father come back after a long time, and Mr Ridley stay till then.'

'He must not eat too much,' said Venice, in a lifeless tone.

'Not much today,' said Nevill, in grave tribute to the occasion.

Hatton opened the door and stood with her eyes on her charges. Nevill looked at her and back at the table, supplied his mouth with a befitting moderation, and went to her side; Honor slowly followed; James glanced from Hatton to his mother; Gavin continued to eat.

'Go with Hatton, my six poor children,' said Eleanor. 'She can do more for you than your mother. Go, James dear, if you want to.'

James could only hesitate at this imputation, which he realized was to be a recurring one.

'Have you had your dessert?' said his mother, misinterpreting the pause.

'Oh, no,' said James, with a lightness that disposed of the idea.

'Did you not want any?'

'No.'

'Would you like some now?'

'No, thank you.'

'You weren't thinking about it today?'

'No,' said James, as if his thoughts were still absent from it.

'Then go, my little son. You will be safe with Hatton.'

Ridley waited until the door closed, and bent towards Eleanor.

'There is something particular in our feeling for these old attendants, who have spent their lives in our service. They, if any, have earned our affection.'

'My children have much more feeling for Hatton than they have for me.'

'Mrs Sullivan!' said Ridley, a smile overspreading his face at this extension of the truth.

'Hatton is not so much older than Ridley,' said Daniel.

'He is not an attendant,' said his brother. 'Attendants may age earlier. There are reasons why they should.'

'I was older than most of these children when my feelings transferred, or rather extended themselves to my parents,' said Luce.

'And we must not say that was long ago,' said Ridley.

Regan left the room, as if she could sustain her feeling only by herself. Ridley hastened to the door and stood, as she passed through it, with an air of putting the whole of himself into his concern.

'There seems a hopelessness about the grief of the old,' he said, as he returned to Eleanor. 'In proportion as it lacks the strength of our prime, it is without the power of reaction and recovery.'

'You none of you think you do anything like the old,' said Sir Jesse. 'You feel things in the same way as they do, just as you feel them in the same way as the young. We suffer according to ourselves.'

Ridley gave an uncertain glance towards the end of the table, where he had believed Sir Jesse to be sitting, lost in his grief.

'All real sorrow must last to the end,' said Eleanor.

'Mrs Sullivan, you do indeed think so now,' said Ridley, in earnest understanding.

A message was brought and delivered to Ridley.

'Mrs Sullivan,' he said, with a rueful smile, 'my family seek admittance, but are prepared to be denied.' His tone suggested that he also was ready for this climax.

'Let them come in, Mother,' said Luce. 'The boys would be better for a change. And we need not repel kindness.'

'If anyone will benefit by it, my dear, let them all join us.'

'It is a case of pure friendship,' said Daniel, 'for it is clear that the advantage will not extend to the guests.'

'Why are we the ones not satisfied with the situation?' said Graham. 'Would the others ask nothing better?'

Hope went in silence to her usual place; Paul walked to Sir Jesse and sat down by his side; Faith stood apart, as if she would put forward no personal claim, even for a seat.

'I hope it does not look as if Paul were trying to take Fulbert's place,' murmured Hope.

'There would be no possibility of his doing that, Mother.'

'No, dear, that is what I meant.'

'Mrs Cranmer is ill at ease because of our trouble,' said Luce, for her mother's ears. 'It must be accounted to her for friendship.'

'I hope no one is looking at me,' said Hope. 'I am so ashamed of not being dead. It is the valuable lives that are cut off, but one does not like to acquiesce in it. How does one seem as if one really wished one had died instead?'

'How are all the children?' said Faith.

No one answered her, as she addressed no one in particular.

'I knew you would come, Mrs Cranmer,' said Luce. 'I don't know how, but I did.'

'I think Luce had grounds for expecting it,' said Daniel.

'And you did not give orders that we were not to be admitted,' said Hope. 'I know now that I have never appreciated anything before.'

'No, Mrs Cranmer, we omitted to do that,' said Luce.

'How are all the children?' said Faith.

'It is something to feel we have friends in the stretch of darkness before us,' said Graham.

'I know that nothing equals the despair of youth,' said Hope. 'I am almost as much ashamed of being middle-aged as of being alive, and no doubt you see less difference than I do.'

'Faith, are you not going to sit down?' said Daniel, who with his brother was standing by his seat.

'No, I don't mind standing,' said Faith.

'But I do,' muttered Graham.

'Faith dear, sit down and let the boys do the same,' said Luce. 'The main trial is enough, without little extra ones.'

Faith gave a slight start and walked to a seat, and at once looked round, as if her mind had not left the question on her lips.

'How are all the children?'

'My dear, would you ask again?' said Hope. 'Perhaps they are all so stunned by grief, that it is not referred to.'

'They are in different states, Mrs Cranmer,' said Luce. 'It is asking about them together that precludes an answer. James and Gavin and Nevill are not giving anxiety; Honor and Isabel are; Venice is in a state between. That is all I can tell you. It is all I know.'

'Poor little things!' said Faith.

'I can see Ridley being a support to your mother, and Paul to your grandfather,' said Hope. 'I don't think I need be ashamed that they have not died.'

'Mrs Cranmer,' said Luce, as if speaking on a sudden impulse, 'would you go and do the same for Grandma? She is alone in the library, and I don't feel I can undertake it.' She gave a little smile. 'My strength is giving out.'

'I am sure that is the bravest smile I have ever seen,' said Hope, hurrying to the door. 'It is shocking of me to have any strength left, and I will go and expend every ounce of it. The sooner it is used up, the better.'

'Luce seems to be different,' said Graham, looking at his sister. 'We ought none of us to be the same again. I hope I shall not be found to be the only one unchanged.'

'I hope you will be among them, Graham dear,' said Luce.

Hope crossed the hall and found Regan sitting by the library fire.

'Don't take any notice of me,' she said. 'You would be hardly conscious that I have entered. I know that all real experience has passed me by. But I have heard that a mother's feelings are the deepest, and so I have come to you.'

Regan raised her eyes.

'I heard you all come,' she said.

'Don't talk in that unnatural way; it makes me feel even more inferior. I have never been in an unnatural state; I have never had the chance of getting into one. I suppose this is the third time for you.'

'The third time,' said Regan. 'I only had three.'

'I am not being of any use at all. My words ought to have brought a flood of tears.'

'Crying does no good.'

'And I thought it was an outlet and a safety-valve. I thought, if people cried until they could cry no more, the worst was over. How do all these wrong reports get about? Is there no healing power in tears?'

'I ought to know,' said Regan, with a faint smile. 'The worst comes to stay, when it comes. But I expect you think I can live in the past, like other old people.'

'I have heard that report about them. Is it another wrong one?'

'They live more in the present, which is sensible of them; and in the future, which perhaps is not, though it is the only share they will get of it.'

'Then it is simply a mistake about their living in their memories?'

'Memories only have a meaning, if they lead up to the present. This sort of thing takes the life and heart out of them.'

'Is there no satisfaction in the dignity of deep experience? I should really like to know that.'

'Depth is no help in trouble. And why is it dignified to be battered? It might be more so to get your own way.'

'I am doing you a great deal of good. I call that quite natural. But you look down on me for my superficial life.'

'Some people seem to skate on the top of things,' said Regan, in a tone of agreement.

'I think I have done you enough good now. There is reason in everything. People can be too natural. I suppose most people are.'

Regan laughed.

'You are not one of those people who see nothing and hear

nothing and know nothing,' she said. 'I never thought you were.'

'That is the word I needed. To think of your fulfilling my need at such a time! You have come out of your own sorrow. And that must show the worst is over. Or is it another error?'

'The worst comes back,' said Regan.

'But gradually with less force?'

'Well, it gets dulled.'

'But isn't that an improvement in a way?'

'A great one. People who don't think so, have not been through much.'

'But I think so; I said it of my own accord. I need not be so ashamed of my easy experience, if it hasn't done me any harm.'

'Well, there is no good in weeping here alone,' said Regan. 'I may as well put myself on my family. It is better for me, if not for them.'

'Well, Grandma, I was waiting for you,' said Luce. 'It is not in you to remain at a standstill. I knew you would move forward.'

'Not a useful habit at this stage. It won't come in very well.'

'Mrs Cranmer, I am grateful,' said Luce. 'You have restored to us the real person and the real voice. We are all taking our first steps on our new path. It is more difficult for us in a way, that we shall not have the usual observances. They make a barrier between the first shock and the beginning of the future. It will be left to us to help ourselves.'

'That is a good way of saying there does not have to be a funeral,' said Graham.

'I agree,' said Daniel, 'now that I know what it is.'

'So do I,' said Hope. 'I will never call a funeral gruesome and obsolete pageantry again. No wonder the custom survives. Now I will take my family away. I suppose Ridley is not going to live with you now?'

'I believe Nevill did suggest it,' said Daniel.

'He has been here long enough for you to judge of his presence. And I can see you have done so. Paul, we must go. We have done all we can; I mean, no one can do anything.'

'May I see the children?' said Faith.

'No, Faith,' said Luce, in a quiet, almost ruthless tone. 'They have borne enough today. I mean' – she gave a smile without moving her head – 'even the most well-meant and careful touch might be too much. I want them to face nothing more at all.'

'I hope Faith is really one of those people who forgive anything,' said Hope. 'Or even one of those who forgive big things and not small. That would do.'

'I would not touch on anything sad,' said Faith, hesitating near the door.

'Faith, will you accept what I say?' said Luce. 'Whether you agree with it or not? I know it is one of those things that do not carry their evidence, but I will rely on your understanding.'

'Of course, I see what you mean,' said Faith.

'Dear me, does she really?' said Hope.

'Thank you, Faith,' said Luce.

'The children always take the initiative with me,' said Faith. 'I am never the instigator of the proceedings.'

'Can it be that Luce's words have had no effect at all?' said Hope.

'Well, go and do your worst, Faith,' said Luce, with another smile.

'I did not know that people spoke true words in jest, on purpose,' said Hope.

Faith left the room with a smoothness that seemed to draw a veil over the proceeding, and mounted the flights of stairs to the nursery, her expression becoming resolute as her breath failed.

'Well, what are you all doing?' she said, putting her head round the door, as if to surprise and engage the occupants.

Isabel and Venice and Honor were doing nothing; James was reading on the sofa; Gavin and Nevill were playing on the floor, at a similar game but separately.

'Boys should get up when a lady comes into the room,' said Hatton. 'James, bring a chair for Miss Cranmer.'

James did so, placing his open book on a table in readiness for his return.

'So you are not painting arrows today,' said Faith, taking the chair as if it were her due.

There was silence.

'You are not, are you?' said Hatton.

'No,' said Gavin, 'we are playing at soldiers.'

'He is too,' said Nevill, placing one in position.

'And what are the soldiers doing?' said Faith. 'Are they having a great battle?'

'Say what they are doing,' said Hatton, who did not know what this was.

'They are having a military funeral,' said Gavin, not moving his eyes from the floor.

'Bury a general,' said Nevill, in a solemn tone, with his arm poised for another adjustment. 'Bury a tall, big man like Father. Poor Father is all buried in a far land. But he is like a soldier now.'

There was silence.

'Do you have a coffin?' said James, in an awkward manner.

'No,' said Gavin. 'Just his martial cloak around him.'

'Just his cloak,' said Nevill, picking up a soldier and beginning to wrap something about it.

'And what are the rest of you doing?' said Faith.

'James is reading – was reading,' said Hatton, 'and the others are not up to much today.'

'There is a difference between boys and girls, isn't there? This seems an illustration of it.'

'You should not talk about children as if they were not there,' said Gavin.

'Gavin, that is rude,' said Hatton.

'Not any more rude than she was.'

'He is not himself today, miss.'

'I am,' said Gavin.

'He is too,' said Nevill, in an absent tone.

'One does not know what to say to them,' said Faith.

'She needn't say anything,' said Gavin, addressing Hatton.

'You will excuse him today, miss.'

'I don't care if she doesn't. Then I needn't excuse her.'

'Well, I think I must say good-bye,' said Faith, as if she were uttering a threat.

'Come again soon. Good-bye. Come again to see him,' said Nevill, glancing up from the floor.

Faith looked at the three girls, and after a second's hesitation walked towards them and stooped and gave a kiss to each, smiling gently and fully into their faces. Then with a slightly heightened colour she turned to Nevill.

'Are you going to give me a kiss?'

Nevill sat up and raised his face, and when Faith had knelt down and embraced him, resumed his game.

As Faith closed the door, Honor uttered her first word since her coming.

'Not a high type,' she said.

James gave Honor a look he sometimes gave Isabel, and returned to his book.

'I was not very proud of any of you,' said Hatton.

'Well, no one would be proud of her,' said Gavin.

'I was quite ashamed of you, Gavin.'

'I am glad.'

Faith went down to the drawing-room, and spoke in a cheerful, satisfied tone.

'Well, I was glad to get a glimpse of them. I remembered the instructions to make it no more than that.'

'That was understanding of you, Faith,' said Luce.

'We had better go,' said Hope. 'I simply don't know what Luce will say next.'

'Did you think that they seemed themselves?' said Eleanor.

'I would hardly say that of the girls. The boys seemed in better spirits.'

'I hope they weren't too unkind to you,' said Hope.

'Why should they be, Mother?'

'There is no reason, dear. That is why I hope they were not.'

'Nevill was very friendly, and so was James. The girls were not equal to so much; things go deeper with them. Gavin is a rougher diamond altogether. I have promised Nevill to pay another visit soon.'

'Were they all together?' said Eleanor.

'Yes, in the nursery with Hatton.'

'I suppose they cannot bear Miss Mitford's touch in sorrow,' said Hope.

'I wish I had gone in and said a word to Miss Mitford,' said Faith.

'Why should you do that?' said Hope.

'Well, it is always nice to see a friend, Mother,' said Faith, her tone somehow making a point of the equality and friendship.

Sir Jesse and Paul came from the fire, continuing to talk. Paul went at once from the house, giving his family no chance to linger. Ridley bent over Eleanor's hand, and followed his father with an expression of controlled feeling.

'I wish we had only to sustain grief,' said Graham, when the family were alone.

'So do I, Graham,' said Luce. 'But we have to support many burdens. I cannot say I don't see them as such, that I would not rather sorrow in peace. But there is no choice before us.'

'And not much else,' said her brother.

'No, Graham, not much else.'

'The way you dealt with Faith gave me a gleam of comfort, Luce,' said Daniel.

'I could hardly put my mind on her. I see what people mean by the selfishness of sorrow.'

'I take exception to the phrase. It suggests some personal advantage.'

'If it means that people who are sorrowing, should give their attention to those who are not, it is a wicked thing to say,' said Graham.

'And why shouldn't we be absorbed in our own trouble?' said Luce.

'If we were not, we should be called shallow,' said Daniel.

'People are indeed wicked,' said Graham.

'Mother,' said Luce, as Eleanor passed them, 'had you not better sit down and rest?'

'I am not tired, my dear.'

'Honest, as usual, Mother. But it may be the false energy of exhaustion.'

'I wish exhaustion had that effect on me,' said Graham.

'I don't even feel it,' said Regan, in a tone that did not bear out her words.

Luce sat down at her grandmother's side, as though without the power to aid her further.

'We have all to move forward,' said Sir Jesse. 'Some of us can only go slowly, but our direction is the same. And my son left sons behind him.'

'You talk as if women did not exist, Grandpa,' said Luce.

'It is a pity men do not manage to do so,' said Regan.

'They are more exposed to risk than women, Grandma. It is a thing that has its brighter side.'

'For them perhaps.'

'Yes, only for them, Grandma.'

'I belong to the sex that encounters perils,' said Graham. 'That does not seem very suitable somehow.'

'It does not, Graham dear,' said Luce.

'We must manage to keep him from them,' said Regan, in a tone that did not grudge her grandson the life her son had lost.

'He does not strike me as a person who will incur them,' said Sir Jesse.

'It is a pity that Grandpa has ever had to meet us,' said Graham. 'The mere idea of us seems to be satisfying to him.'

'Ridley has done a great deal for us today,' said Eleanor. 'I dare not imagine what things would have been without him.'

'We should not have known what had happened,' said Graham. 'I shall always see him as the bearer of ill tidings.'

'I wonder if we shall,' said Luce.

'I am afraid I am very restless,' said Eleanor, who was moving about the room. 'I suppose I am in an unnatural state. I hope I shall be able to do my duty by you all. I don't seem to be able to reach my own sorrow. I am simply oppressed by a fear of the future.'

'We all tremble a little before that, Mother,' said Luce.

'It was good of Hope to come at once,' said Regan.

'Grandma, you don't often say a word in favour of anyone outside,' said Luce.

'She is a deal better than most people.'

'I like her very much, Grandma, but is she *better*? Is that quite her word?'

'It does as well as any other.'

'Grandma, I should never have suspected you of making a woman friend.'

'I have to do what I can with the people left. And it seemed to me that I had one.'

A silence fell on the family.

'Mother,' said Luce, 'shall we give ourselves a little help on this first day? Shall we have Nevill brought down to say good-night?'

'Ought we to make a sacrifice of him?' said Graham.

'We shall not do that, Graham. We will not take him beyond his scope.'

Hatton obeyed the summons and led Nevill into the room. She had an air of disapproval and gave him no injunctions. He seemed preoccupied and stood waiting for what was required of him, before returning to his own sphere.

'So you have come to say good-night,' said Eleanor.

'Good-night, Mother,' said Nevill, going up to her to get the first step over.

'He has come to give us a glimpse of him,' said Regan.

'Good-night, Grandma,' said Nevill, doing the same to her, and then sending his eyes round the room and speaking more quickly. 'Good-night, Luce; good-night, Grandpa; good-night, Graham; good-night, Father; good-night, Daniel.'

He turned and looked up at Hatton in inquiry as to the moment of withdrawal.

'Father is not here, my little one,' said Eleanor.

'Yes, he is here,' said Nevill, in an absent tone. 'Father has come back today.'

'No, he cannot come back to us, my little boy.'

'Good-night – Grandpa,' amended Nevill, looking about for a substitute for Fulbert.

'How strange that he should say that, on this day of all days!' said Luce.

'He has heard his father's name a great deal,' said Regan, in simple explanation.

'That is all of his father he has left,' said Eleanor, sighing.

'When people accept the death of someone, are they always staggered by the general results of it?' said Graham.

'Well, what have you been doing upstairs?' said Eleanor to Nevill.

'He played at soldiers. And Gavin did too.'

'Did you play together?'

'No, he did it all by himself.'

'What did the soldiers do?'

'Bury a general,' said Nevill, in a deepening tone. 'Bury a soldier man like Father. Beat the drum and make a thunder noise.'

There was a pause.

'How did he think of that?' said Eleanor, to Hatton.

'I don't know, madam. We can never tell how ideas come into their minds.'

'It came into his mind,' said Nevill, with a pride that protected his brother.

'Was Gavin playing too?' said Eleanor, in a sudden tone.

'No,' said her son, 'Gavin played all by himself.'

'Was Honor?'

'No, poor Honor sat on a chair.'

'And James was not playing either?'

'Oh, no,' said Nevill, in a virtuous tone. 'Not talk to James when he is reading.'

'Well, good-night, my little son.'

Nevill accepted this sign of release, but on his way to the door he returned to Regan.

'Not a drum was heard,' he began, and paused as his memory failed him, and turned and ran from the room.

'It is a good thing some amusement can come out of it,' said Regan.

'We do not realize the gulf between children and ourselves,' said Eleanor.

'We do now,' said Daniel.

'That is true of Mother,' said Graham.

'Well, Father used to say so,' said Luce.

'What used your father to say?' said Eleanor.

'That you did not realize the gulf between yourself and your children, Mother,' said Luce, in an open, deliberate tone. 'What you say of yourself. What no doubt he often said to you.'

'I shall have to do so now. I daresay it will be borne in upon me.'

'Why will it be different?' said Regan.

'Well, I shall have to fulfil two characters.'

Regan was silent.

'Say what is in your mind, Grandma,' said Luce. 'That is not a fair way to deal with anyone.'

'If we could be other people as well as ourselves, it would not matter what happened to us. And a loss does not give us other qualities.'

'I suppose the days will pass,' said Eleanor, as though to herself.

'There is little suggestion of it about this one,' said Graham.

'Would it be better if we were apart for a time?' said Daniel.

'Why should it?' said Eleanor, with a change in her eyes.

'We shouldn't have each other's feelings on us, as well as our own.'

'I should have yours. They wouldn't be off my mind for a moment. You could all forget mine, could you?'

'We might have more chance of it, if we were separated. We shall have to learn to spare ourselves.'

'Well, I will go to my room and give you a rest,' said Eleanor.

'And have a respite from us, Mother dear,' said Luce.

'You can put it as you like, to hide the truth from yourselves. You do not hide it from me.'

Luce stood still with her eyes down, as her mother left the room.

'It has to be,' she said, lifting her eyes. 'It is no use to disguise it.'

'We might have postponed it,' said Graham, with a look of trouble.

'It would have done no good, Graham. The little, subtle miseries of sorrow have to be faced. I don't think they are the least part of it.'

'I think they should be,' said Graham.

'Go after your mother,' said Sir Jesse, roughly, to his grandsons. 'What do your personal pains matter, since they only do so to yourselves? Go and do what you can to help a burden heavier than yours. What else should you do? What is your opinion of yourselves and your use in this house?'

His grandchildren left the room, Daniel with an expression of almost amused submission, Graham with a look of relief, and Luce with an air of resigning herself to service. Regan looked after them with compassion.

'There is nothing you want of them, is there?' said Sir Jesse, with a note of excuse in his tone.

'I want nothing that anyone can give me; I could do with my three children.'

An almost humble expression crossed the husband's face.

'Things are not the same to men,' said Regan. 'Their family is only a part of their life.'

'I would have given my remaining years to save my son.'

'Why should you?' said Regan. 'They are all you have left. He had no more to lose than you.'

A note was brought in, addressed to Eleanor, and put on a table to await her.

'From Ridley,' said Regan, looking at the envelope. 'He will always be thrusting himself in now.'

'There was no other way. I might not have been alive. We could not foretell the future.'

'It seems that Fulbert did so.'

'He provided against its risks.'

'What does Ridley want to say to Eleanor? He has been with her half the day.'

'You cannot see through the envelope,' said Sir Jesse.

Regan took up the letter, as if she were inclined to do her best.

'I have a good mind to open it.'

'So I see. But must you not come to another mind?' said Sir Jesse, with a smile that suggested that he and his wife were both in their youth.

'If Ridley wrote me a letter, I should not care if Eleanor read it.'

'You would be surprised if she did. And you know she would not.'

'It must be in a way a message to us all.'

'In that case we shall hear the gist of it. It may be to say that he cannot come tomorrow.'

'I am sure it is not that. It is probably a piece of palaver.'

'You do not seem to need to open it. And it sounds as if it might be awkward if you did. He has to explain Fulbert's affairs. They are not much, as I am still alive, but she is new to such things.'

'It is a good thing Fulbert lived long enough to have a family,' said Regan, again at the end of her control. 'Or it would have been as little good to have him as the others.'

'We have our memories,' said her husband.

'Yes, you can add them to a stock of those.'

Eleanor came into the room and looked about for the letter.

'They said there was a note for me.'

'They should have taken it to you,' said Sir Jesse, seeming to welcome another subject.

'Luce and the boys were with me,' said Eleanor, as though to counteract the last impression given by her children. 'The servants would guess we did not want to be disturbed.'

Regan met Sir Jesse's eyes, but the latter's face told nothing.

Eleanor opened the letter and sat down to read it.

MY DEAR ELEANOR,

I could not let this day pass without expressing to you what I could not say to your face, my deep admiration for your selfless resolution and courage. Much will depend on your strength and wisdom, and I shall work with you with a growing sense of privilege.

Yours in sympathy and gratitude,
RIDLEY CRANMER.

'Does Ridley call you Eleanor now?' said Regan, in comment upon the only part of the letter she had seen.

'He does here. I always use his Christian name.'

'He is a good deal younger than you.'

'Only about five years.'

'Is there any message for the rest of us?'

'No. It is just a word about our working together.'

'Why couldn't it wait until tomorrow?'

'I suppose some things are better written,' said Eleanor, going to the door with the letter.

'Well, there wasn't room for much more than that,' said Regan. 'It hardly went down the first page. I wonder why she kept it to herself.'

'She seems hardly to have done so,' said Sir Jesse.

Chapter 9

'You did not expect me today,' said Sir Jesse, entering the Marlowes' cottage.

'No,' said Lester, 'or you could have seen Priscilla by herself.'

'I am glad to see you all. I should be happy to have young friends. I am now a childless man.'

There was a pause.

'Your son had a happy life,' said Susan.

'You see that a reason for his losing it? People state it as if it were.'

'We have to think of reasons,' said Priscilla. 'It is too shocking that there shouldn't be any. When people have had a sad life, we say that death is a release. It is to prevent things from being without any plan.'

'It is unwise to criticize one of you in the presence of the others.'

'And we do not spoil it by criticizing each other to our faces, in the accepted way,' said Priscilla.

'You hardly knew my son.'

'We met him a few times.'

'I should have liked you to know him better, and him to know you.'

'We did not realize that,' said Lester, looking surprised.

'We did our best to know him to the extent you desired,' said Priscilla.

'I wish I had died instead of him,' said Sir Jesse.

'Why do people wish that?' said Priscilla. 'Instead of wishing that no one had died.'

'I should have liked to see you all together. I believe I never did.'

'It could have been arranged. I think you could not have wanted it very much.'

'You have your son's children,' said Susan.

'Susan does offer conventional comfort,' said Priscilla. 'But what other kind is there? She does not like to offer none at all.'

'There is none,' said Sir Jesse.

'That is where she is in a difficult place.'

'You take my trouble lightly.'

'We do not feel close enough to take an intimate view of it,' said Lester, at once.

'I have not done much for you. You might have asked much more.'

'We should not have expected anything,' said Priscilla. 'But we have been the more glad to have it.'

'You are a generous girl, my dear. And not without knowledge of life.'

'Then we have some points in common.'

'That may be,' said Sir Jesse, looking into the fire. 'That may be.'

'I wish he would not keep gazing at the fire,' said Priscilla, aside to the others. 'People are supposed to see faces in it, but I am so afraid he will see wood.'

'You are not afraid of me,' said Sir Jesse. 'You would ask me for anything you wanted.'

'Does that mean he knows we take it without asking?' said Priscilla.

'We are not in need of anything,' said Lester.

Sir Jesse gave him an almost gentle look, that seemed to make some comparison.

'You do not see much of my family?'

'Daniel and Graham come in sometimes.'

'Luce does not come?' said Sir Jesse, on his suddenly harsher note.

'No, she never does,' said Lester, in simple assurance.

'Why are we pariahs?' said Susan, looking Sir Jesse in the eyes.

'It is your own word,' said the latter.

'It is yours,' said Priscilla, 'though you have not used it. And we have no right to object to it. We know nothing about ourselves, except that you knew our parents.'

'That is my reason for concerning myself with you.'

'It was a fortunate friendship for us.'

'That is for you to say.'

'That is what I must have felt,' said Priscilla.

'I must go,' said Sir Jesse. 'I am glad I have seen you. I hope you don't think hardly of me. I have had your welfare in my mind.'

He left the house with his head bent, as though feeling he would not be seen by those whom he could not see, and raised his head as he passed into another road.

'What would he have done, if we had not been grateful for bare necessities?' said Susan.

'He knew just how much he meant to do,' said Lester.

'He knows why people dislike their benefactors,' said Priscilla. 'It is because they expect them to share equally with them, when of course they do not. That is why he expects us to dislike him.'

'We are never to know our story?' said her brother.

'I feel that is confirmed today,' said Susan. 'Something made him go as far as he would ever go. It may be a good thing.'

'It gives us a feeling of security,' said Priscilla. 'I daresay it would be too much for us to know. We might not be able to forgive Mother.'

The housekeeper entered the room.

'Sir Jesse spoke to me today, miss. He has never done it before. He said he hoped I was taking care of you all.'

'Why does he break his records all of a sudden?' said Susan.

'His son has broken one by dying,' said Priscilla, 'and that has put him on the course.'

'How shall we behave when Sir Jesse dies?' said Lester. 'Shall we have to go to the funeral?'

'You will have to represent us,' said Susan.

'What a good thing Susan knows these things!' said Priscilla. 'I could not answer such a question.'

'I hope he will leave us as much as he allows us,' said Lester, in an anxious tone. 'He must know he will cause us great trouble if he does not.'

'It is wonderful of people to think of other people's needs after they are dead themselves,' said Priscilla. 'I always feel it is too much to expect.'

'People don't find it so,' said Susan.

'And we must not talk as if people were about to die, because they are old.'

'There is something in the view,' said Lester gravely.

'It is too ordinary for us,' said Priscilla. 'We have tried to get our own touch, and we must not dispel it through carelessness.'

'It does not sound as if it were natural,' said Susan.

'Well, things must often owe as much to art as to nature. I dare say the best things do.'

'Does Sir Jesse respect or despise us?' said Lester.

'It is possible to do both,' said Susan.

'One feeling must get the upper hand,' said her sister. 'And though it is extraordinary, when he supports us, I believe in his case it is respect.'

'He has quite an affection for you,' said Lester.

'Well, I have done much to earn it. They say that a conscious effort is not the best way to win affection, but it seems a fairly good way, and often the only one.'

'We cannot deal only in the best methods,' said Susan. 'What would be the good of the others? And now they are so much good.'

'We have got Sir Jesse's visit over,' said Lester. 'He won't come again for months.'

'This is an extra visit, caused by the death of his son,' said Susan.

'You need not see him when he comes,' said Priscilla.

'It gives us a feeling of strain,' said Lester. 'We know we are in his power.'

'I see how real the trouble has been, that I thought I had taken off you. But Sir Jesse does not resent our being alive when his son is dead. He seems to think he has something left in us. He must love us better than we deserve, or his grief draws him closer to us. It is strange to see these things really happening.'

'Especially between Sir Jesse and us,' said Lester.

'Would he mind if one of us were to die?' said Susan.

'He would wish he had made things easier for us,' said her sister. 'People always wish they had given more help, when people are beyond it. Wishing it before would mean giving it. One does see how it gets put off.'

'We shall never have to wish we had given help to Sir Jesse, said Lester, in a musing tone.'

'If one of us were to marry, would he reveal our parentage?' said Susan.

'I could not support a wife,' said Lester, in a startled manner.

'If we cannot find out by less drastic means, we will leave it,' said Priscilla.

'If only the photograph could speak!' said Susan. 'Sir Jesse never looks at it. It is not of much interest to him.'

'He is careful never to look at it,' said Lester.

'Why are inanimate things supposed to be so communicative?' said Priscilla. 'It might tell us nothing. And it may be on the side of Sir Jesse.'

'To think what we could tell the photograph!' said Susan.

'Well, not so much,' said Lester.

'There isn't so much to be told,' said Priscilla. 'Photographs would find that.'

'Mr Ridley Cranmer,' said Mrs Morris at the door.

'You are satisfactory friends to call upon,' said Ridley, pausing inside the room, as if its size would hardly allow advance. 'We can rely on finding you at home. It is not easy for an occupied man to appoint his time.'

'I wonder if Mother likes to hear that about us,' said Priscilla.

'You still find that your mother's photograph adds an interest to your life,' said Ridley, resting his eyes on the chimney-piece. 'I can understand that it suggests many pictures of the past. I wonder Sir Jesse did not grant it to you before.'

'He only found it by accident,' said Susan.

'Is that the case?' said Ridley. 'I believe Sir Jesse has paid you a visit this afternoon?'

'Yes, he has just gone.'

'I saw him coming away from the house.'

'Then you would believe it,' said Priscilla.

'Does he often honour you in that way?'

'No, very seldom,' said Susan.

'It is sad to think he is now a childless man.'

'He said that of himself,' said Lester.

'Did he?' said Ridley, with a look of interest.

'Does it strike you as a curious thing to say?'

'I can hardly imagine our friend, Sir Jesse, making such an intimate statement.'

'The news had leaked out,' said Priscilla.

Ridley threw back his head and went into laughter.

'I wish I could have relied upon that process for making it known to the family. But it fell to me to reveal it by a more exacting method, by word of mouth.' His tone became grave as he ended.

'It must have been a hard moment for everyone,' said Susan.

'But I had my reward in the courage and resolution displayed by them all,' went on Ridley, 'especially by the chief character in the scene, Eleanor Sullivan. She indeed rose to the heights. No yielding to personal feeling or thought of self. A calm, firm advance into the future. It was an impressive thing.'

'She will have a difficult life,' said Lester.

'Lester, it seems almost too much,' said Ridley, turning in sudden feeling. 'It seems that something should be done to ease so great a burden.'

'She has three grown-up children.'

'And the word relegates them to their position, points out how much and how little they can do. To her they are her children. Nothing can make them less; nothing can add to their significance. Nothing alters the deep, essential, limited relation.'

'She has her husband's parents.'

'Rather would I say, Lester, that they have her.'

'So that is how Mother feels to us,' said Priscilla. 'I feel half-inclined to take her away from the chimney-piece.'

'Leave her,' said Ridley, in a rather dramatic manner, resting his eyes again on the photograph. 'Nothing was further from me than to belittle the relation. She is your mother. You bear the traces of her lineaments. She is in her place.'

'People say we are like her,' said Susan.

'That is what Ridley meant,' said Priscilla.

'I must leave you now,' said Ridley, seeming not to hear the words, and perhaps not doing so in the stress of his feelings. 'My duties call me. I have more in these sad days. I hardly know why I came in. I happened to be passing.'

'Why do people give that reason for calling?' said Susan. 'They can't drop in on every acquaintance they pass.'

'They imply that they would not call at the cost of any trouble,' said Priscilla. 'They mean to give the impression of not wanting much to come. And really they give one of wanting to come so much, that they are embarrassed by the strength of the feeling. Sir Jesse called because that was his intention. We will always call in that spirit.'

'It is not like Ridley to call by himself on people of no place and parentage.'

'He had his own reasons,' said Lester.

Chapter 10

'Well, my boy, I must solicit your help,' said Ridley, entering the Sullivans' hall. 'I have come to seek a moment with your grandfather.'

'I don't know where he is,' said Gavin.

'Can you find out for me?'

'We never do find out things about him.'

'Grandpa is in the library,' said Honor, coming up. 'Couldn't you go and see him?'

'So I am to beard the lion in his den.'

'Grandpa is a big lion,' said Nevill, pausing by the group. 'He can roar very loud.'

'He can at times,' said Honor, making a mature grimace, and glancing to see if Ridley had had the advantage of it.

'Do you often play in the hall?' said the latter.

'Sometimes when it is wet,' said Gavin.

'Shall I play at lions with you?' said Ridley, looking at a skin on the floor, and seeming to be struck by an idea that would serve his own purpose.

'Yes,' said Honor and Gavin.

Nevill turned on his heel and toiled rapidly up the staircase, and paused at a secure height in anticipation of the success of the scene. Ridley put the skin over his head and ran in different directions, uttering threatening sounds and causing Honor and Gavin to leap aside with cries of joy and mirth. Nevill watched the action with bright, dilated eyes, and, when Ridley ran in his direction, fled farther upwards with piercing shrieks. Hatton descended in expostulation, and Miss Mitford in alarm, the latter not having distinguished between the notes of real and pleasurable terror in Nevill's voice. Regan hustled forward in the same spirit as Hatton, and smiled upon Ridley in a rare benevolence.

'I plead guilty, Lady Sullivan,' said the latter, standing with outspread hands, and the rug in one of them. 'I am caught red-handed.'

'You have had a good game,' said Regan, to the children.

'We did while it went on,' said Gavin.

'I fear we do not receive encouragement to prolong it,' said Ridley.

'Grandma could hide behind the staircase,' suggested Gavin.

'He will kill the lion,' said Nevill, coming tentatively down the stairs. 'He won't let it eat poor Grandma. He will kill it dead.'

'There, it is dead,' said Ridley, dropping the skin on the floor. 'You see you have killed it.'

'It is quite dead,' said Nevill, in a regretful tone, descending the rest of the stairs and cautiously touching the skin with his foot, before trampling freely upon it. 'But he will make it alive again.'

'It was dead before,' said Gavin.

'But once it was alive. It was in a forest and could roar.'

'It was in a jungle,' said Honor.

'A jungle,' said Nevill, in reverent tone.

'It is a lioness, not a lion,' said Gavin. 'It has no mane.'

'It is really a tiger,' said Honor.

'Which is more fierce?' said Nevill.

'A tiger,' said his sister.

'Then it is a tiger, a great big tiger. No, it is a lion. A lion is more fierce.'

'I fear I am in disgrace, Lady Sullivan,' said Ridley. 'And it is not a day when I should choose such a situation. I am here to make an appeal to your favour.'

'He is a lion,' said Nevill, thrusting his head under the rug and making a charge against Ridley as vigorous as possible, considering its weight.

'I wish I could say the same of myself,' said Ridley, gently repulsing the attack. 'I am feeling the reverse of lion-hearted. I had come to ask a word with your husband, and my attention was distracted by these would-be inhabitants of the jungle. I fear I helped them to realize their ambition.'

'It sounds as if you were easily distracted,' said Regan.

'So much did my errand mean to me, that I found myself postponing the risks that it involved.'

'And how long do you want to keep on that line?'

'No longer, if you will make it easy for me to do otherwise.'

Regan met his eyes in silence, not fulfilling this suggestion, and suddenly turned and led the way across the hall.

'Poor Mr Ridley has to go and see Grandpa,' said Nevill, with eyes of concern.

'He wants to,' said Gavin.

'No, he didn't like it.'

'He said he did.'

'Hints are in the air,' said Honor, swinging one leg round the other. 'Hatton and Mullet are big with them.'

'What?' said Gavin.

'Hatton is big,' said Nevill. 'But not as big as Mullet. Hatton is rather big.'

'A cloud no larger than a man's hand,' said Honor.

'Why do you talk without saying anything?' said Gavin. 'It makes talking no good.'

'All in its own time,' said his sister.

'You think you are grand,' said Gavin, and ended the conversation.

The schoolroom party came down the stairs. James took a seat on the lowest step and opened a book; Isabel leaned against the balusters; Venice came up to Nevill with a view to his entertainment.

'Why have you all come down?' said Gavin.

'We are to play in the hall, because we are not getting any exercise,' said James, just raising his eyes.

Isabel laid her head on her arms, in personal discharge of the obligation.

'There is something heavy in the atmosphere in these days,' she said.

'You have said it,' said Honor, nodding.

'Play at lions like Mr Ridley,' said Nevill, struggling under the rug.

'So that is what the noise was,' said Isabel.

'It sounded as if someone was hurt,' said James, in an incidental tone.

'The screams of the damned,' said Honor.

'Don't let her talk like that,' said Gavin, with a note of misery.

'There are breakers ahead,' said Honor.

Gavin walked up to her and gave her a kick.

'Gavin, that is very unkind,' said Venice. 'And you should never kick a girl.'

'Ought I to kick Nevill then?'

'No,' said Nevill, flying into Venice's arms.

'You must never be rough with girls, or boys younger than yourself.'

'Then I can be rough with James.'

Honor went up to Gavin and returned the kick. He took no notice beyond rubbing his leg, and they resumed their normal relation.

'They didn't mean to hurt each other,' said Nevill, withdrawing a long gaze.

Sir Jesse and Regan and Ridley came from the library, continuing their talk. They gave no attention to the children, who did nothing to attract it.

'I shall always be grateful, Sir Jesse, for the hospitality of your house.'

'You did not come here for your own purposes.'

'I have confessed that I began to do so, as time passed. How many months is it since the death of your son?'

'We know,' said Regan. 'And no one who does not, needs to be told.'

'I do not forget what is due to the memory of a man who was my friend.'

'He depended on you to be his,' said Sir Jesse, in a grave manner.

'And to the end of my power did I fulfil that trust,' said Ridley, in a suddenly full tone. 'If feelings arose to the overthrow of a simple spirit of duty, I was helpless as a man and a friend.

The emotions of manhood carried me away. I regret if my words are crude; I have no others.'

'Why are they so?' said Sir Jesse. 'Things are not that, because they are simple. They need no doctoring.'

'Eleanor was the wife of your son. She is the mother of your grandchildren. I have come to you and your wife, as those who stand in the place of her parents. I feel I have not been wrong.'

'She has had no family since we have known her,' said Regan. 'There is no demand on her, or on her family means.'

'We have not come to the discussion of such things.'

'A fact does not need discussion. No doubt you know it.'

'You came here in the service of our son,' said Sir Jesse. 'We continued to think of you as here in his interests. But I will leave our personal feelings; you are not concerned with them. I am prepared to wish you well. I desire no ill to befall you. I have been blind. I have not had my eyes on your life, but on my own.'

'I am glad the last half-hour is over,' said Ridley, speaking as if Sir Jesse's words had been lighter than they had. 'I have felt like a schoolboy making an awkward confession.'

'A schoolboy does not often have to confess a thing like this,' said Regan.

Ridley went into laughter, as though to propitiate Regan by appreciation of her words.

'What do you think of having nine stepchildren?' she said.

'I hope I shall never forget they are your grandchildren.'

'It would hardly matter if you did, as they will not.'

'I suspect they will not indeed,' said Ridley. 'I should be the last person to recommend their doing so. Not that they would appear to me to be the greater loss. And that brings me to the point of asking permission to fetch the other person most concerned.'

Eleanor was with her three eldest children in their study, and came out, accompanied by them.

'Well, my dear, we are to lose you,' said Sir Jesse. 'How much are we to lose with you?'

'I knew that would be the point,' said Eleanor.

'We have our lives,' said Regan. 'You have given your minds to yours.'

'They feel we have had them,' said Sir Jesse. 'But we have to get through the days we have left. We have a right to ask what remains to us.'

'There is a good deal that needs discussion,' said Eleanor.

'It has had it,' said Sir Jesse. 'Let us start where you left off. That is what we shall have to do.'

'We thought of several plans and discarded them.'

'Is there one you have not discarded?'

'The one that seems to us best,' said Eleanor, with an open, cold simplicity, 'is that Ridley and I should have a house in the village, and leave the children with you, on the understanding that I have daily access to them. We could not afford what you do for them, and it is best for boys to be guided by a man bound to them by blood. I would make the contribution to their expenses that I have always made. This seems best for the interests of us all.'

Regan drew a hard breath and sank into tears.

'Sir Jesse,' said Ridley, keeping his eyes averted from her, 'I should like to say how earnestly I will do my part under the new order; with what sincerity I will further the welfare of those to whom I stand in a semi-fatherly relation. If honest effort is of any avail —' He stopped as he saw Regan's face.

'Such a thing is never useless,' said Sir Jesse.

'I wonder what they will all have to say,' said Regan.

'We are all here, Grandma,' said Luce, in a low, clear tone.

'Our elders must soon have become conscious of the nine pairs of eyes,' said Daniel.

'They would have had that feeling that someone was looking at them,' said his brother.

'Lady Sullivan,' said Ridley, 'I do not desire to hear what that may be. I doubt if it will be for my ears.'

'What is your real word to us?' said Regan, suddenly to Eleanor.

Luce came forward and took her mother's hand.

'That I have felt myself unfit to be alone with my burden. I have never had faith in myself as a mother. My children will not suffer from not having me in their home. I wish in a way that they would. And I shall be at their service. I see no good in postponing a change that is resolved upon, and I am not troubled about making it so soon. I am marrying in distrust of myself, in despair at my loneliness, and in gratitude for a feeling that met my need. I was not in a position to reject it.'

'We wish you all that is good, my dear,' said Sir Jesse. 'You are doing your best for yourself and for others, and many people stop at the first.'

'And so may we say that the meeting is adjourned?' said Ridley, with a smile and a hand on Eleanor's shoulder. 'Or rather dissolved, as the business is concluded.'

Regan gave Eleanor a look of such helpless consternation at her acceptance of this caress for another's, that Sir Jesse took a step between them.

'You have other things to say to other people. You have done what you must by us.'

'It will be the same thing,' said Eleanor, 'but it will have to be said.'

'No, Mother dear,' said Luce, 'why will it? We know what there is to know. We do not need it repeated. We can bear to see you recede a little from us, if it is to result in your going forward yourself.'

'You have always made things easy for me, my dear.'

'And in this case you do so for me,' said Ridley.

'I don't think they are finding it very difficult themselves,' said Eleanor, looking at her children.

'It is not for you to see our problems, Mother,' said Daniel. 'They would not be any help to you.'

'No, do not ask for them, my dear,' said Sir Jesse.

'I should almost like to feel they were greater,' said Eleanor. 'Daniel, have you a word of your own to say to your mother?'

'I welcome anything that is for your happiness. And the feeling is not only mine.'

'So do I indeed,' said Graham, his eyes passing over Ridley.

'You are kind and just to me, my children.'

'He does too; he is too,' said Nevill, coming up to his mother.

'I did not notice you were all here,' said Eleanor, looking round the hall.

'It is a wet day, Mother,' said Luce, 'and you sent word that lessons were to be suspended.'

'Mother passed over six of her nine children,' said Venice.

'You are always in my mind, my child,' said Eleanor. 'I did not know you had come to the hall. Perhaps that is typical of my dealings with you.'

'We are in a way grateful to Ridley,' said Graham.

'Graham,' said Ridley, impulsively, 'I see that as an unspeakably generous thing to say. I hope I shall never forget it.'

'What has my Isabel to say to me?' said Eleanor.

'Simply what the others have said. We have not had time to prepare our speeches. You are spared an awkward opening to your new life.'

'The awkwardness would not have been chiefly Mother's,' said Venice.

Ridley looked at Eleanor in amusement, and with an air of being about to share the charge of the sprightly young of her family.

'Well, James, what have you to say to your mother?' said Eleanor.

James looked up from his book with a start.

'Have you not been listening, my boy?'

'No,' said James, rather faintly. 'Not to grown-up people's conversation.'

'That is a good rule on the whole, but you could have made an exception today. We have let you stay away from school to hear what we have to tell you.'

'If our family life were more eventful, James would face his future without education,' said Daniel.

'I think the strain on him would be as great,' said Graham. 'He, if anyone, must understand that life is one long training.'

'So you do not know what we have been saying, my little son. Well, something is going to happen that will make me happier. Can you guess what it is?'

'Father is not dead!' said James, jumping to his feet and standing ready to spring with joy.

'No, that is not it. You know that is not possible. But someone is going to take his place, is going to take care of me for him. Can you guess who it is?'

'It is not Mr Ridley?' said James, in a tone of getting through a step on the way to the real conclusion.

'Yes, it is he; it is Mr Ridley,' said Eleanor, looking past her son.

'He has been taking care of you for some time, hasn't he?'

'Well, now we are going to live together, so that he can do it better. You will be glad to feel I am not alone any more.'

'Is he going to live here?'

'Not in this house. He and I will have a house of our own quite near.'

'Where shall we live?' said Venice.

'Here, as you always have, with Grandpa and Grandma. And I shall come and visit you every day. You will see me as often as you do now.'

'But you won't be here in the evenings,' said James.

'I shall often be late enough to say good-night. You need not be afraid you will lose your mother.'

'Will it always go on like that?'

'For as long as we need look forward.'

'Shall we come to your house too?' said Venice.

'Of course you will, my dear. As often as you like.'

'Then we shall really be the same as we are now.'

'Yes, except that you will be happier, because you won't feel that I am alone, while you are enjoying your work and your pleasures together.'

The children were silent, as these points were revealed in their life.

'And I hope I shall be a not unwelcome figure in the background,' said Ridley.

'Yes. No,' said James, with a caper. 'No.'

'What do you mean, dear?' said Eleanor.

'Not in the background,' said James, in a hardly audible voice.

'Of course not. That was a nice thing to say. And true and sensible too. And now my girls will come and kiss their mother, and show her they feel the same in their hearts, though they may be too shy to say so.'

'Perhaps I may myself make a similar claim,' said Ridley. 'I think I see signs of the acceptance of me in my new character.'

Isabel and Venice received his embrace, Venice glancing aside as his eyes dwelt on herself. James hovered in a half-expectation of a similar salute, and was rewarded by a pat on the shoulder.

'What are you thinking of, Isabel?' said Eleanor, catching an expression on her daughter's face, which she wished explained, or rather contradicted, before she left her.

'Nothing,' said Ridley, smiling as he quoted the coming reply.

'Isabel has got beyond that stage. Answer me, Isabel dear.'

'You should not want to know the things in people's minds. If you were meant to hear them, they would be said.'

'Do you often think of such things as are not said?' said Eleanor.

'Not in your sense. Though if I did, it might not be unnatural in a child of yours.'

Eleanor looked into Isabel's face, and walked towards her youngest children. Ridley followed, as if he had not observed the encounter. Mullet had brought the luncheon and was dispensing it. Hatton was aware of the scene in progress, and had directed that the children should remain downstairs.

'Is the whole of our family life to be enacted in the hall?' said Daniel. 'We only want the beds, to make things complete.'

James carried his book to his stair, and settled himself upon it. He had an air of entering upon a life in which this sort of thing would be easier. Isabel went to a window and stood, throwing the blind cord over her finger, taking no notice when the tassel struck the pane. James raised his eyes and rested them on her, and withdrew them in aloofness from what he saw, rather than misapprehension of it. Graham also observed her, and did not free himself so soon. Nevill, seated on Mullet's lap, surveyed his mother over the rim of a glass.

'Is it a nice luncheon?' she said.

'It is the same as usual,' said Gavin.

'Well, that is nice, isn't it?'

'He likes it,' said Nevill.

'Well, what do you think we have come to tell you?'

'Don't let Honor guess,' said Gavin, rubbing his feet quickly together.

'I have some news for you about myself. You don't often hear me talk about myself, do you?'

'You have done it since Father died,' said Gavin.

'Well, I have had myself in my mind. There has been no one

else to think much about me. Have you ever thought about my being alone?'

'You are not,' said Honor. 'Not any more than we are. We have other people and not Father, and so have you.'

'Well, now I am going to have someone who will think of me as Father did, and will not feel I must only have the same as other people. Can you guess who it is?'

'It is Mr Ridley,' said Honor, at once. 'But you have him now.'

'Well, I am going to have him in a different way. We are going to belong to each other.'

'Are you going to marry him?'

'Yes, I am, my little girl.'

'It is not allowed by the law,' said Gavin.

'I think, young man, that I may be the judge of that,' said Ridley. 'The law happens to be my profession.'

'But you can't be Mother's real husband.'

'That is what I am going to be.'

'But a woman can't have more than one husband in a civilized land. It is only in savage countries that they do that. And then it is usually more than one wife.'

'In some countries polyandry is practised,' said Honor, in an easy tone.

'And you feel we are starting the custom in this country?' said Ridley, smiling.

'Say to Mother that you hope she will be very happy,' whispered Mullet.

'Why will you be happier, married to Mr Ridley, than just always being with him?' said Honor.

'An observant pair of eyes, Nurse,' said Ridley.

'We don't call her Nurse,' said Gavin.

'He calls her Mullet,' said Nevill. 'And sometimes he says, dear Mullet.'

'Here is a successful household character,' said Ridley, indicating Mullet to Eleanor.

'You shouldn't say things about her when she can hear,' said Gavin.

'I think I have upset him,' said Eleanor. 'I shall not leave you, my little son. I shall be coming to the house every day.'

'Won't you be in the house?' said Honor.

'No, I shall be in another house quite near.'

'With him?' said Gavin, with a gesture towards Ridley.

'Yes, he will be my husband then.'

'Is it because of the law?'

'What do you mean, my boy?'

'Is it because of the law, that he can't live here like Father?'

'The law has nothing to do with it. It seemed a good plan for us to have a home of our own.'

'I expect it is because of Grandma,' said Honor.

'What do you mean, dear child?'

'Grandma wouldn't have anyone here instead of Father.'

'The charm of childhood!' said Ridley to Eleanor, with a smile.

'You don't think that anyone is ever instead of anyone else, do you?' said Eleanor to Honor.

Honor raised her eyes and kept them on her mother's.

'I think that so it must seem to her in a way,' said Ridley, gently.

'He will have him instead of Father,' said Nevill, nodding his head towards Ridley.

'My poor little man, I fear you will have no choice,' said Ridley bending over him. 'No other father will have a place in your memory.'

'Honor won't cry any more, now you are instead of Father. Honor doesn't like Father to go away.'

'Does she cry?' said Eleanor, to Mullet.

'Sometimes when she is in bed, ma'am.'

'I should have been told.'

Mullet did not say that Honor had repudiated the idea with violence.

'Honor doesn't like people to talk about it,' said Gavin.

'I don't mind,' said his sister.

'Well, how are you enjoying your holiday?' said Eleanor, as if it might be realized that there was another side to life. 'I thought that, as I was happy, I should like you to be so too; so I said you were to have no lessons.'

'Lessons,' said Nevill, in a tone of glad anticipation, getting off Mullet's knee.

'No, Miss Pilbeam is not coming today,' said Mullet.

'She is.'

'No, today is a holiday.'

'This attitude does Miss Pilbeam credit,' said Ridley.

'He says all he can in favour of people,' said Gavin, to Honor.

'Not coming today,' said Nevill, in a doleful tone that cheered as he ended. 'But come again tomorrow.'

'He gets on very well,' said Eleanor.

'B, a, t, bat; c, a, t, cat; h, a, t, hat,' said Nevill, in support of this.

'He is forward for a boy. It is hard to judge of a young boy's promise,' said Eleanor, thinking of James and Gavin and postponing the difficulty.

'And yet I expect the boys rejoice in their sex,' said Ridley.

'What do they do?' said Gavin.

'They are glad they will grow up into men,' said his mother. 'Would you like to be a woman?'

'I would as soon be one.'

'I would rather be a man,' said Honor.

'He will be a lady,' said Nevill.

'You all seem to want what you cannot have,' said Eleanor. 'The children belong more to the mother, you know. Men don't have so large a share in them.'

'Father did,' said Honor.

'Well, but think for a moment. You were very sad when Father died, but you would have been even more sad if I had died.'

There was a pause.

'She couldn't have been more sad,' said Gavin.

'I shouldn't have minded so much about anyone grown-up,' said Honor, causing Gavin to turn aside with a flush creeping over his face.

'No doubt we are leading them out of their depth,' said Ridley.

'We are understanding everything,' said Honor.

'Not the things that lie underneath,' said Eleanor, in a musing tone, unconscious that she was taking her daughter on equal terms.

'Are there things like that, when people marry another man?'

'Now you are out of your depth indeed.'

'You only pretend that I am.'

'Of course one's children think one belongs entirely to them,' said Eleanor.

'You haven't ever done that,' said Gavin. 'Not like Hatton and people who really do. But you are supposed to belong to Father.'

'You know your father is dead, don't you, my child?' said Eleanor, in gentle bewilderment.

'You know I do. You couldn't be marrying someone else if he wasn't.'

'Well, well, we will begin to look forward. It is natural for you to be disturbed at first. But you are not going to lose me. You will hardly know I am not in the house.'

'Will you be there at dessert?' said Gavin.

'Not always, but I shall when Grandma asks me.'

'Will she have to ask you?'

'No, but I think she will like to sometimes.'

Nevill looked up with an arrested expression.

'Mother won't be there. Only Grandma and Luce,' he said, mentioning the other two who exercised supervision.

'Yes, as a rule, but you will come and have tea with me in my house.'

'Honor and Gavin will too,' said Nevill, in a tone that assured general goodwill.

'Will he be there?' said Gavin, glancing at Ridley.

'Yes, of course. It will be his house as well as mine. We shall share it.'

'They will share it,' said Nevill, in a tone that approved this course.

'Will you have any more children?' said Gavin.

'No, I don't think so,' said Eleanor.

'Why don't you?'

'Well, people don't generally have more than nine.'

'Queen Anne had eighteen.'

'Yes, but I am not a queen.'

'Do queens have more than other people?'

'It seems sometimes as if they do,' said Eleanor, smiling.

'If you had any more, would they live with you or with Grandma?' said Honor.

'With me,' said Eleanor, obliged to continue on the line.

'Would Hatton go to your house to take care of them, or would she stay with us?'

'She would stay with you. You will always have her.'

'Hatton will always stay here,' said Nevill. 'Not with those other children.'

'Here is Hatton coming to fetch you,' said Mullet, in the conscious tone of one whose presence has been forgotten.

'Perhaps with a true instinct,' said Ridley, smiling at Eleanor. 'I think our ordeal did not become less, with the age of those who sat in judgement.'

'Mr Ridley always take care of her, and Father coming back soon,' said Nevill, glancing behind Hatton's hand at his mother.

'Doesn't he understand any more than that?'

'He understands everything, madam. He gets into the way of saying things.'

'Father never come back any more, but Mr Ridley always stay with her,' said Nevill, with his ready proof of what was said.

'Well, you will all give me a kiss and tell me you are glad I am going to be happier,' said Eleanor, with a note of welcome for the end of her task.

'I will make the same request, as the congratulation applies to me,' said Ridley. 'And I hope to become a welcome nursery guest.'

Honor and Gavin bowed to circumstances, and their brother gave another backward glance.

'He will kiss him another day,' he promised.

Hatton let him mount the first flight of stairs, and then picked him up and carried him to the nursery, his expression undergoing no change. Honor and Gavin were in some discomfort at the end of the scene, and followed with high, conscious talk. Nevill ran round the nursery two or three times and paused at Hatton's knee, as if by chance.

'Go down to Grandma soon today. Mother won't be there any more.'

'Yes, Mother will be there. She is not going away yet. She will not be married for some time.'

Nevill cast his eyes over Hatton's face and resumed his running.

'Just fancy this change in the family!' said Mullet, in a low tone to Hatton. 'Who would have thought it, when the master died?'

'That would not have been the moment for picturing it, certainly.'

Gavin burst into a loud laugh.

'Did you have this kind of thing in your family, Mullet?' said Honor.

'Well, perhaps in a way I did,' said Mullet, in a constrained tone.

'I will go and get on with my mending,' said Hatton. 'I am not sharing the holiday.'

'Well, what was it?' said Honor, after waiting for the door to close.

'Well, something like this did happen to my relations,' said Mullet, folding up garments, as if fluency were more natural when her hands were occupied. 'It was a family of cousins who lived in London; well, an aunt and cousins it really was, but my aunt was a colourless sort of person, who attracted little attention, and it is my cousins whom I always think of as the victims of the stroke of fate.'

'Well, what happened?' said Honor.

'It is a little hard to describe,' said Mullet, with a natural hesitation, as she did not yet know what it was. 'I was never at close quarters with it. It was one of those things that cast their shadows before and aft, and no one could escape the repercussion of it. Well, after my aunt's bereavement there ensued a period of calm. My aunt was disconsolate, of course, but she maintained the even tenor of her life. And then the change came. The man destined to be my uncle loomed into view.' Mullet's voice deepened at the mention of this destiny. 'A tall, sinister-looking man he was, with thin lips and a scar stretching across his face, and twisting in an odd way round his mouth. Handsome in a way, of course, with a kind of sinister charm, but a man whose very presence seemed to cast some primitive spell.'

'How did he get the scar?' said Gavin.

'It was never spoken of, Master Gavin. There seemed to be a sort of unwritten law that no word of it should pass human lips,' said Mullet, her voice gaining confidence. 'And none ever crossed my father's or mine. I daresay he thought it was hardly a subject for my ears.'

'He knew about it then,' said Honor.

'Well, Miss Honor, these things pass from men to men. I suspect he had his shrewd suspicions. He was a shrewd man in his way.'

'Well, what happened to the family?'

'In a way nothing, in a way everything. That is the best way to put it.'

'But what was it?' said Honor, not taking this view.

'A strange, uncanny atmosphere brooded over that house. Laughter never seemed to sound, and the sun never to shine in those rooms. And in the place of those happy children, who used to shout and play in that deep-vaulted hall, there were tall, grave men and women, with haunted eyes, and lips that had forgotten how to smile. And my aunt crept in and out, a sad, silent being, who seemed to have more in common with another world. That is how things were in that household.'

'But what did he do, the man with the scar?' said Gavin.

'You may well ask, Master Gavin. He did what he did. It is best not to say any more.'

'One of those things that children are not told,' said Honor.

'And those purposes needed money, whatever they were,' went on Mullet, hastening her words. 'In those days all the wife's money belonged to the man; and he used to dole her own income out to her in pence, or in pounds I expect it was, or in low banknotes, but in small enough sums, considering her worldly estate. Yes, she must have felt she had come on evil days.'

'And how are things now?' said Honor.

'As far as I know, as they were. I have no wish to hear. It could be no good news.'

'I should think it is better here than in that house.'

'Oh, so should I,' said Mullet, with a little laugh. 'And now we must remember that you are to be punctual downstairs today.'

Honor turned to the door, expecting to see Hatton, and confirmed in the anticipation.

'We shan't have to be so punctual when Mother is not here,' said Gavin, simply stating a fact.

'And why not, Master Gavin?' said Mullet.

'She will be with us often enough to keep us up to the mark,' said Hatton.

'It is funny that Mr Ridley and Mother should both want to live together,' said Honor. 'It is a coincidence.'

'A frequent one in marriage, I hope,' said Hatton.

Mullet laughed.

'This isn't a real marriage,' said Honor. 'The Queen wouldn't see Mother now. She wouldn't see either of them.'

'Don't talk nonsense, Miss Honor; of course she would,' said Mullet.

'Mr Ridley is the worst, because it is the man who asks the woman to marry him.'

'A woman is not allowed to,' said Gavin.

'Neither the mistress nor Mr Ridley is doing anything wrong.'

'Not so that they could be put in prison,' said Honor. 'But some of the worst wrong things are not like that.'

'You must have heard of people marrying twice. It is not like you to talk in such a silly way.'

'It is a thing that only unusual people talk sensibly about,' said Hatton.

'Honor is unusual,' said Gavin. 'Father said she was.'

'Well, she wants other people to think so too,' said Mullet.

'I don't care if they don't,' said Honor; 'I don't want them to think the same.'

'James doesn't mind if Mother marries Mr Ridley,' said Gavin. 'I don't mind either, if they like to do it.'

'That is a good reason,' said Hatton.

'He doesn't mind,' said Nevill. 'He is the same as James.'

'I know why Mother wants to marry him,' said Honor. 'I always understand things. It is because she hadn't anyone to think so much of her as Father did, when she had got used to it. But I shouldn't ever marry a second person, when the first one had done that.'

'I daresay the people won't ask you,' said Gavin. 'You are not allowed to ask them yourself.'

'He will marry her,' said Nevill, nodding at Honor.

'You won't be allowed to,' said Gavin. 'You are her brother.'

'He isn't allowed either,' said Nevill, pointing at Gavin.

'Now none of this talk downstairs,' said Hatton. 'Don't say a word about it, unless other people do.'

Her injunction was heeded by one of her hearers, who ran up to Regan as he entered the room.

'He won't talk about it,' he promised.

'What is the forbidden subject?' she said.

Nevill looked at her, as if he would explain, if he had the words.

'Mother and Mr Ridley marrying,' said Gavin, in a ruthless tone.

'A nurse's idea,' said Sir Jesse. 'We may have our own.'

'I have not avoided the subject today,' said Eleanor.

'Least said, soonest mended,' said Honor.

'There is nothing that requires mending,' said her mother.

'Nevill reminds me of James at that age,' said Luce, as if she had not heard what had passed. 'He has no touch of Gavin.'

'Not him and Gavin,' said Nevill. 'Him and James.'

'None of you seems like another to me,' said Eleanor. 'Perhaps Daniel and Gavin are a little alike.'

'And Isabel and Honor, Mother,' said Luce.

'Well, not so much alike, as with a good deal in common.'

'Soundly observed in a way, Mother, but Father used to say they were alike,' said Luce, her tone setting the example of continued easy reference to her father.

'Have you settled on a house, Eleanor?' said Regan. 'I suppose you have made a search for one.'

'We have done everything but sign the lease. I think we cannot do better.'

'It is a nice house,' said Nevill.

'What do you know about it?' said Gavin.

'Mother will live there with Mr Ridley.'

'What house is it?' said Honor.

'The square house near the church,' said her mother. 'It is called the Grey House.'

'Isn't it very small?'

'Not for the two of us. It has six bedrooms. This house has given you a wrong standard. I have always foreseen that you will have to modify your ideas.'

'It is a sort of grey,' said Gavin.

'No, not grey,' said Nevill.

'It has a green lawn,' said Luce.

'Where is the lawn?' said Gavin.

'In front of the house,' said his mother.

'I don't call that a lawn.'

'What do you call it?'

'A patch of grass.'

'You will all have to live in a castle.'

'A great, big castle,' said Nevill. 'He will live in one with soldiers in it. It is called a fort.'

'I must get you some toy cottages,' said Eleanor. 'I saw some in London.'

'When will you get them?' said Gavin, coming nearer.

'Ridley will bring them. They will be a present from us both. Perhaps he will bring them tomorrow.'

'No, today,' said Nevill, with rising feeling. 'Today.'

'Tomorrow will soon be here,' said Luce.

'It won't,' said Nevill, in a tone of experience.

'Is there anything joined to the cottages?' said Gavin.

'There is a little garden with a patch of grass,' said Eleanor, with a smile.

'A cottage with a hen,' said Nevill.

'Miss Pilbeam might help us to make a pigsty,' said Honor.

'The ideas for future establishments are suitably modified,' said Daniel.

'Mother dear, your scheme is crowned with success,' said Luce.

'We shouldn't want to live in the cottages,' said Gavin.

'He will live in a cottage,' said Nevill. 'With Hatton.'

'What would you have to eat?' said Daniel.

'A hen would lay an egg,' said Nevill, without hesitation.

'Who would eat the egg? You or Hatton?'

'One for Hatton and one for him.'

'But would one hen lay two eggs?'

'One, two, three, four, five, six, fourteen.'

'But you would be sick, if you ate so many.'

'Give them all to Hatton,' said Nevill, in a tone of suitably and generously solving the problem.

'Now you three can go upstairs,' said Eleanor. 'No one else can speak while you are here. Now, James, let us hear your voice.'

'Will you often be at luncheon after you are married?' said James, recalled by his predicament to the time when it might be less frequent.

'I shall be there when Grandma asks me. Now see if you can open your mouth without asking a question.'

'There is a monkey-puzzle tree in front of your house. On the piece of grass, on the lawn.'

'Do you think you will ever have a house of your own?' said Eleanor.

'Yes. Everyone is paid enough for that. Even a labourer has a cottage. And if he can't earn, he can go to the workhouse.'

'Constant stimulus has not been in vain,' said Daniel. 'Witness the gulf between James's ideas and those of the other.'

'With the children reconciled to cottages, and James to the workhouse,' said Graham, looking at the window, 'Mother need not be distressed about the notions of her family.'

'But it would be sad to be brought to the workhouse,' said Eleanor to James, fearing she had made such a prospect too natural.

'It is better than it was, more comfortable.'

'James has carried his concern to the point of investigation,' said Daniel. 'He can pass on to Graham anything that Graham needs to know. So all Mother's sons are provided for.'

'You will step into my shoes yourself?' said Sir Jesse.

There was silence.

'With their father in his grave, it is no wonder if it seems the natural place for his parents,' said Regan.

'There is no problem about our final accommodation,' said Graham. 'We have no anxiety there.'

'People in the workhouse can have a pauper's funeral,' said James.

'I think that is enough about the workhouse,' said Eleanor.

'What can a man do to earn the most?' said James, as if going as far as possible from the subject.

'We have reached that estate, and do not know,' said Daniel.

'Has Grandpa earned a great deal?'

'He has never needed to earn,' said Isabel. 'Things will be different for you.'

'Did Father earn very much?'

'Heredity seems to justify James in his perplexity,' said Daniel. 'And it throws no light for any of us.'

'The first thing to do is to work and get to Cambridge,' said Eleanor.

'But Daniel and Graham are there, and they don't know about earning. And that is the only thing that matters, isn't it?'

Eleanor was silent before this result of her admonitions.

'You have to be an educated man before you can do anything.'

'That does not seem to James the sequence of affairs,' said Graham.

'No,' said James, in a light but unshaken voice.

'Perhaps we will leave these problems to the future,' said Eleanor.

'You had better have done so, Mother,' said Luce, in a low, amused tone.

'James would never have objected to that arrangement,' said Isabel.

'If Ridley does not come to a meal, he loses no time afterwards,' said Regan, as she heard a bell.

'He is welcome,' said Sir Jesse. 'He comes to see one who has been a daughter to us.'

'Grandma, we shall dread to hear your voice,' said Luce.

Some minutes elapsed before Ridley's entering the room, and then he advanced in the wake of Hope, and spoke without emerging from this shelter.

'I am come to proffer another plea on my own account. I should have said it was a thing I seldom did, but I must seem to be making up for lost time. You will think it never rains but it pours. I have to beg that my marriage may be hastened. I find that the effect of delay on myself, on my work, and on my clients, will be such that it becomes imperative to avoid it. Some waiting correspondence has brought my position home to me. I have no choice but to beg permission to bring matters to a climax.'

'He does not know whose permission should be asked,' said Hope, 'and I do not either. I am glad he is so ill at ease. It may be one of those times when we feel we have never liked people so well.'

'Have I the sanction of the person who should give it?' said Ridley.

'It is your own affair,' said Regan.

'Thank Lady Sullivan, Ridley,' said Hope.

'I do so indeed,' said Ridley, 'for the freedom of action implied in the words.'

'Eleanor goes from our home, and shall go when and how she wishes,' said Sir Jesse.

'The condition of a honeymoon seems to be our taking it at once,' went on Ridley, in a more ordinary and open manner. 'And I confess to a natural reluctance to forgo one.'

'Well, there is not much gained by putting it off,' said Regan.

'I think there is not, Grandma,' said Luce.

'You would not like to have me for a little longer?' said Eleanor.

'We are depending on your assurance that we shall not lose you,' said Daniel.

'I suppose no one makes a success of the transitional time.'

'We are not criticizing you, Mother dear,' said Luce.

'I had better yield to the general opinion,' said Eleanor, with a touch of bitterness.

'I hope your own is not an exception,' said Ridley.

'Is it any wonder that I did not see what was coming on us?' said Daniel, in a low tone.

'I shall never prove that I saw it,' said Graham. 'It seemed that speaking of it would establish it. Luce did not say a word.'

'Somehow I could not, Graham.'

'We cannot yield to our instinct to rescue our mother,' said Daniel.

'It does not seem that she would give you much trouble,' said Isabel.

'Hush, boys, hush. Not before the children,' said Luce.

'Well, shall we put the marriage in a fortnight?' said Sir Jesse, trying to help his daughter-in-law.

'I am afraid I must press for it earlier, even in a matter of days,' said Ridley. 'But I thank you, Sir Jesse, for generously furthering my cause. I wish I could rid myself of the idea that I am carrying off my bride.'

'Why does one dislike the term, bride, as applied to one's mother?' said Luce.

'There are several reasons, and none of them can be mentioned,' said Graham.

'Not before the children,' said Venice.

'We seem to be giving rise to a good deal of confidential discussion, Eleanor,' said Ridley.

'Are you going to be married as soon as on Friday?' said James, in a high voice.

'I thank you, James,' said Ridley, 'for putting into words what I did not dare to myself.'

'Will you just go into the church and come out again, married?'

'I thank you again, James.'

'And then Mother will be Mrs Ridley Cranmer?'

'I thank you once more, my boy.'

'So you have thought out all the steps,' said Regan, in a cool tone.

'I fear that I stand exposed,' said Ridley.

'Shall we all come to the church?' said Venice.

'No, dear child,' said Eleanor. 'You will say good-bye to me here, and I shall come to see you on the day I come back from my honeymoon.'

'And then you will come every day,' said James.

'In this atmosphere of reconciliation I will take my leave,' said Ridley. 'I must betake myself to the duties that beset my remaining hours.'

'I will come to the door with you,' said Eleanor.

Regan gave her a swift look.

'It is strange that we resent Mother's treating Ridley as she treated Father,' said Luce.

'Surely it is not,' said Daniel.

'She does not do so,' said Isabel.

'That is true,' said Graham.

'How you all suppress your personal feeling!' said Hope. 'It is wonderful when you have so much. I somehow feel ashamed of

Ridley, and yet he is only doing what your father did, and that must be a great and good thing, I suppose. I wonder if your mother knows her place in my life. I have only just found it out myself. Luce is too young to want me for a friend, and your grandmother would not be able to bear one.'

'You come nearer to it than anyone, Mrs Cranmer,' said Luce. 'Grandma does not shrink into herself or take the defensive when she hears your approach.'

'No, dear, but is that the test of real friendship? I feel it is generous of you to welcome Ridley. And it is a sensible idea to keep him in a house apart. I wonder I never thought of it. They say it is never too late to mend, but in this case it is. Your mother will be one of those people who really have two homes.'

'I wonder whom they will lose next. Their grandfather or me?' said Regan.

'The loss of your son has not killed you, Lady Sullivan. We must face facts,' said Hope.

Regan was laughing as Eleanor returned to the room.

'What is the jest?' said the latter.

'It was not one, Mother,' said Luce, 'and as far as it was, it would not gain by repeating.'

'What was it, my dear, nevertheless?'

'It was about Grandma's dying.'

'Not dying, dear,' said Hope.

'I warned you not to have it revealed, Mother.'

'But that is such a terrible solution,' said Graham.

'It is odd that old people think so little of their death,' said Regan.

'They make a good many false claims, in that case,' said Isabel.

'They would look foolish, if they forgot it,' said her grandmother. 'Other people never separate them from it.'

'I think they feel stoic and heroic when they talk of it,' said Graham.

'So it is true that human motives are mixed,' said Hope.

'I warned you not to have it revealed, Mother.'

'I must apply myself to my duties for the next days,' said Eleanor. 'There are things to be done for the children, before I leave them, I must take them into the town on Thursday, to get them some things that Hatton wants for them.'

'Don't they want them for themselves?' said Hope. 'I thought the child was father of the man.'

'I don't know how these duties get put off.'

'You had every excuse, Mother,' said Luce.

'Who is going into the town?' said James, in a casual manner.

'You and Honor and Gavin,' said his mother. 'Nevill can do with what is handed down.'

'I should think he can,' said Hope. 'I wonder it does not overwhelm him.'

'That means a holiday for James,' said Eleanor, sighing. 'And I suppose the wedding day does too.'

'I shall have to say good-bye to you,' said James, going on quickly to the next words. 'You won't mind living in the little house, will you?'

'No, not at all. It will be my own.'

'That will be a change for the better,' said Regan, in an almost cordial manner.

Chapter 11

'What is the matter, Gavin?' said Eleanor, as she returned to the house with her children. 'Why are you staying in the carriage? You seem in such an odd mood.'

Gavin got out and walked up the steps without a word.

'What is wrong with him, Honor?'

'He wanted you to stop and listen to him in the street. And now he wants to go back again.'

'He must know he can't do that. We are later than we ought to be already. Grandma is waiting for us. It is tiresome of him to make my last day so difficult.'

James frolicked up the steps in the manner of a different and easier boy, and Honor followed in a neutral manner.

'Why do people speak to each other, if other people don't listen?' said Gavin, without looking back.

'I heard what you said,' said his mother. 'You remember that I answered. But you must know you made a mistake.'

'I know that I saw him,' said Gavin. 'All my life I shall know.'

'Children do fancy they see things, when they have them in their minds. Going where Father sometimes took you, reminded you of him, and you thought you saw him. That was all.'

'I wasn't reminded of him; I wasn't thinking about him. I haven't thought much about him for some time.'

'Honor, can't you persuade him that he must be wrong?'

'He really thinks he saw him. You can't persuade a person then.'

'Well, run upstairs and try to forget it.'

'I shan't ever forget it,' said Gavin, going heavily from stair to stair. 'I shall remember it every minute. I shan't ever remember other things.'

'Honor, tell Hatton what he thinks, and ask her to explain to him.'

'I shall tell her,' said Gavin.

'Perhaps you had better say nothing about it,' said Eleanor.

'I shall tell her,' repeated Gavin.

'No, you had better not, my boy. Do you hear what I say?'

'If I didn't hear, I couldn't answer.'

Eleanor sighed and went her way, prevented from pressing the point by the thought that it was her last day with her children.

Gavin went to the nursery.

'I saw Father,' he said.

'No, you are making a mistake,' said Hatton.

Gavin sat down to take off his boots, and wasted no further word.

'You have fancied it,' said Hatton, looking at his face, while Mullet, also observing it, came to his aid.

Gavin leaned back and accepted the latter's ministrations without attention to herself.

'Poor Gavin is not well,' said Nevill, glancing at his brother.

'He really thinks he saw him,' said Honor, to Hatton.

'Of course he does, or he would not say so.'

'He does do that sometimes,' said Nevill, in shocked condemnation of his brother's practices.

'It is easy to imagine things,' said Mullet, falling into the error of judging other people by herself. 'When he has had his dinner, he will see how it was. When we are hungry, our minds are out of our control.'

'I wasn't hungry,' said Gavin. 'We had things to eat at a shop. I am not hungry now.'

'Did he tell the mistress about it?' said Mullet to Honor.

'Yes.'

'And what did she say?'

'Something like what you and Hatton have said.'

'Did she mind his saying it?'

'Yes, I think she did rather.'

Gavin took no notice when his plate was set before him, but presently took up his knife and fork, to forestall the inevitable pressure. As he ate, his colour returned, and he went through the meal with his normal appetite. When his sister talked, he answered with his usual directness, and he followed the others down to dessert, as though neither expecting nor desiring anything else. Nevill ran into the room and spoke at once.

'Mother will be gone tomorrow,' he said, and rapidly corrected his tone. 'Poor Mother will be gone away very soon.'

'They like the constant holidays,' said Eleanor, with a smile and a sigh.

'It was a chance to give Miss Pilbeam a day to herself,' said Luce.

'I thought we need hardly trouble,' said Eleanor. 'Nevill had his lessons alone.'

'Just him and Miss Pilbeam,' said the latter.

'It was not worth Miss Pilbeam's while to come for half-an-hour,' said Luce.

'He had an hour,' said Nevill. 'Then Hatton came for him.'

'I should like to die,' said Gavin, looking round the table.

'Why would you?' said Regan and Graham at once.

'Because as long as you are alive, things can happen that you don't like. Even if you couldn't bear them, they would happen.'

'A good description of life,' said Isabel.

'It is too one-sided,' said Eleanor. 'And in your case it would be absurd. No children could be more fortunate.'

'We haven't any father,' said Honor. 'So they could be.'

'We could have one, if we liked,' said Gavin

'Does he mean Ridley?' said Luce.

'He thinks he saw Father today,' said Honor.

'I did see him,' said her brother. 'In the town, when we were there with Mother.'

'It is a fancy he has had,' said Eleanor.

Gavin's face did not change.

'What makes you think so, my boy?' said Sir Jesse. 'Why did you not speak to him?'

'Grandpa, don't press it,' said Luce, in a low tone. 'It is not a matter to push to its logical conclusion.'

'He didn't want me to,' said Gavin. 'He didn't want us even to see him.'

'I should think that is very likely true,' said Eleanor, gently. 'So he would like you just to forget it. And that is what we will do.'

'Did you know he was there?' said Gavin, meeting her eyes.

'Of course she didn't,' said Honor. 'Or she wouldn't be going to marry Mr Ridley.'

'Then she won't be able to forget it. She says things that are not true.'

'So that is what you think of me,' said Eleanor.

'He will think of Mother always when she is gone away,' said Nevill.

'I seem to have chosen the right course,' said Eleanor. 'People have no trouble in adapting themselves to it.'

'I don't think I could ever come to a decision,' said Graham. 'I hope my life will not afford much power of choice.'

'I should say the hope is grounded,' said Sir Jesse.

'You are not going to live far away,' said James, to his mother.

'No, of course not, my boy. I could not bear to do that.'

'I should think you could,' said Gavin.

'My dear, I have just said I could not,' said Eleanor, in a tone of speaking to a much older person 'You must let people give their own account of themselves. You can't know as much about them as they do.'

'You can think you do. You can be sure.'

'Then you should remind yourself that you are likely to be wrong.'

'I never remind myself of things. If I don't think they are true, why should I?'

'It is an office we do tend to reserve for other people,' said Isabel.

'Why does this luncheon feel like an anniversary?' said Graham.

'It is my last luncheon as a member of the household,' said Eleanor. 'I think I shall try to forget it.'

'You do forget things,' said Gavin.

'What kind of things?'

'Not little things.'

'So I forget big things, do I? Would you all say so? Would you, Luce?'

'No, Mother dear, I should not.'

'Would you, Daniel?'

'No, it seems to me an unwarrantable assertion.'

'Would you, Graham?'

'No, I should have thought you would have them written on your heart.'

'Would you, Isabel?'

'No, I should have thought the opposite.'

'Would you, Venice?'

'No, I shouldn't,' said Venice, opening her eyes.

'Would you, James?'

'No, I should have thought you would remember them.'

'Would you, Honor?'

'No, I shouldn't myself, but Gavin only means you forgot that you saw Father.'

'He wouldn't either,' said Nevill, excitably. 'He wouldn't let them say it.'

'My little boy,' said Eleanor, lifting him to her knee.

'He would kill them,' said Nevill, sitting compliantly on it.

Gavin appeared to be paying no attention.

'Are you all going to say your own word to me on my last day?' said Eleanor.

'You would not think Mother was a person in whom hope would die so hard,' said Graham.

'I should like to have one from each of you to carry with me.'

'Surely we have all said one,' said Daniel.

'And they will be easy to remember, as they are all the same,' said Isabel.

'It isn't our fault that it is her last day,' said Gavin.

'The boy is upset in some way,' said Sir Jesse.

'Yes, of course that is what it is,' said Eleanor.

'Come, let us all disperse,' said Luce. 'There is no need to make it a melancholy occasion. Mother has things to do before tomorrow. She and I are going to do them together.'

She left the room with her arm in her mother's. Isabel and Venice and James took the chance to disappear. Sir Jesse withdrew with his grandsons, as was his habit since the loss of his son. Mullet came to fetch the children and led Nevill from the room. Gavin appeared to follow her, but in a moment fell behind and walked up to his grandmother.

'I saw Father today,' he said.

'You are thinking of him, because Mother is leaving you. I am thinking of him too. So you and I are feeling the same.'

'You are not thinking of him because of that, are you?'

Regan laughed, and Gavin's face flushed and his eyes filled with angry tears, but he spoke in a simple, controlled manner.

'Perhaps he will come to the house.'

'It would seem quite natural, wouldn't it?'

'Are you saying what you think is not true?' said Gavin, looking into her face.

'No, I am not. I shall never get used to being without him.'

'This house is his home, isn't it?'

'Yes, of course it is, or was.'

'It is now,' said Gavin. 'He hasn't any other. I could tell he hadn't another one, like Mother.'

'How could you tell?' said Regan.

'By the way he looked. And by the way he looked at Honor.'

'Didn't he look at you too?'

'Not as much. He never does. That is how I first knew it was Father. And then I looked and saw that it was. And I called to Mother, and she went on. And when I looked back, he was gone.'

'Where did you see him?'

'In the dark street that goes from the big shops to the little ones. You know there are two inns there. Mother and Honor were in front of me, and Father came out of one of them. And he saw me first, because I was behind, and then he stood and looked at Honor.'

'Did he know you saw him?' said Regan, feeling it wise to draw out the child's impression.

'No, I don't think so. If people who are back from the dead, are the same as other people, Mother ought not to marry Mr Ridley. It is against the law. But perhaps this is different.'

'People can't come back from the dead, my child.'

'I think Father has. He looked like that. And he wouldn't be the very first, would he?'

'How did he look?' said Regan, in a gentle tone.

'Thin and pale, with a smaller face than he used to have. And his hands were small and pale, coming out of the sleeves of his coat. They looked like Mother's or Luce's. And he must be smaller himself, because his coat was so large. But I daresay he wouldn't be quite the same. It must have been cold where he was, because the coat had fur on it; and he had worn it often, because it was mended down the front, and one of the fur cuffs was partly gone.'

Regan's eyes were fixed on her grandson, and she kept them on his face as she slowly rose to her feet.

'Where did you say you saw him?'

Gavin told her again, hardly varying his words, and she suddenly took his hand and hurried to the door. In the hall she snatched the first garment she saw, and almost ran out of the house. She was like a person who feels she must get something over, before she can settle to her life. As they drew near the stables, Gavin dragged at her hand and spoke in a weaker voice.

'I don't think I need go with you. Father doesn't want to see me the most. Honor would be better, but one person is enough. It is best to be all together, when a person comes back from the dead.'

Regan threw a glance at his face and then at his house clothes, released his hand and pursued her way. He walked back to the house and mounted to the nursery.

'Grandma has gone to fetch Father. So Mother will know that I saw him. Everyone will.'

'What are you saying, Master Gavin?' said Mullet.

'Things will be like they used to be. Father will be here again, even if he isn't the same. And we shall get used to his being different. And I don't think he is so very. I don't know if Mother will be here. She may go with Mr Ridley. But Grandma will love Father, whatever he is like. And one person who really loves him, is enough.'

'I would rather have a father than a mother,' said Honor. 'I think all this family would.'

'He would rather have Father,' said Nevill. 'But he would rather have poor Mother too. And she won't come every day.'

The carriage was heard to pass the house on its way to the gates.

'It is Grandma going to the town to find Father,' said Gavin. 'I told her where I saw him, and what he was like. And she knew it was him.'

'You did not, Master Gavin!' said Mullet. 'It was a cruel thing to do. You don't mean her ladyship believed you? That you have sent her by herself to find him? It is a dreadful thing to happen. Whatever can we do?'

'I didn't send her. She went of her own accord. Children don't send grown-up people. You know that. She was glad that Father had come back. No one could have been more glad. She didn't mind going by herself. She didn't mind even if he was back from the dead.'

'Grandma loves people, doesn't she?' said Nevill.

'Well, you must play quietly this afternoon, if you really think what you say,' said Mullet.

'We ought to be glad he has come back,' said Gavin.

'Of course you would be. But it would be a solemn occasion.'

'Why should it? Solemn things are sad. We were solemn when he was dead. We ought not to be the same when it is the opposite. And Nevill is not being quiet.'

'He is a coachman,' explained the latter, handling imaginary reins and also impersonating the horse. 'He will drive Grandma to find Father. He will drive her fast.'

'He is too young to understand,' said Mullet.

'But if it isn't true, there isn't anything to understand.'

'And you pretended you thought it was true,' said Mullet, with reproach.

'He didn't pretend,' said Honor, in a tone that made Hatton turn and look into her face.

'People only pretend ordinary things,' said Gavin.

'They can make a mistake about the others,' said Hatton. 'And the cleverer people are, the sooner they see they have made one. And it is easier to see that out of doors.'

'I am going to stay in,' said Honor. 'Then I can go down, if Father comes back and sends for me. He will want to see me, even if he is back from the dead. If he is so very different, he wouldn't remember enough to come home. And I want to see him, whatever he is like. I don't mind if he is a ghost.'

'He is not a ghost,' said Gavin, in his ordinary voice. 'He is like he always was. Only he is pale and his face is smaller.'

'He couldn't be smaller, if he is the same.'

'He could, if he had got thin.'

'Would you like to go out, Gavin?' said Hatton, in an easy tone.

'I don't mind. I can see Father when I come in.'

'He will stay in,' said Nevill. 'No, he will go for a walk and hold Mullet's hand. He will find a little nest.'

Honor waited until Mullet and her brothers had gone, and then threw herself into Hatton's arms in a passion of tears.

'I don't want it to be a mistake. For a minute I thought it was true. I thought Father would come back.'

'You know he can't do that. You must know, if you think. But you have a great many people to love you.'

'I haven't. Only Grandma and Luce.'

'You know how Gavin loves you.'

'Does he?' said Honor, lifting her head at the idea.

'More than anyone else in the world. And you know that I love you.'

'Yes,' said Honor, relaxing her body against Hatton's.

'And Nevill loves you too.'

'I don't count Nevill. And James doesn't like people much

better than they like him. I don't think people do. And that isn't very much.'

'You can't think that Isabel does not love you.'

'She would, if I were as old as she is. But I never shall be, shall I? Because she will get older too. And Venice only loves Isabel.'

'And there are your big brothers.'

'Do you mean Daniel and Graham?' said Honor, as if Hatton were hardly likely to mean these.

'And Mother loves you. You know that.'

'She feels I belong to her. Gavin is the one she loves. But Mother does her duty by her children.'

'Would you like me to read to you?'

'If you read a book I know. Then I can half-listen to the reading, and half to hear if Father comes back.'

'Which is a book that you know?'

'I know them all,' said Honor. 'You won't read in a loud voice, will you?'

Hatton read, and Honor divided her attention as she had said, and presently slipped from Hatton's knee and stood with an air of intense listening.

'Father has come back,' she said, with a sigh of simple and great relief. 'Gavin did see him. I don't mind if he is back from the dead. I can hear his voice, and it is the same as it used to be. I don't mind anything as long as he is here.'

Hatton went on to the landing, and stood suddenly still, her face growing white.

'I shall go down,' said Honor. 'No, I shall wait until they send for me. No, I shall go down now. I have heard his voice, and now I have heard it, I must want to see him, mustn't I? I shall run straight up to him; I don't mind what he is like. He will lift me up as he used to, and if he can't do it like an ordinary man, if it is like a ghost, it will be the ghost of Father.'

She ran down the stairs and broke into the library, where Fulbert was standing with his mother. He turned and came to meet her and lifted and kissed her in his old way, and after the first onset of tears, she subsided in simple content.

'You are the same,' she said; 'you are not a ghost; you don't look so very different.'

'I am grateful for the assurance,' said Fulbert. 'I hardly know how to explain myself on any other ground. I must be prepared for people's coming to the opposite conclusion.'

'You will always be here now. It will be like it used to be,' said Honor, as she heard the old note. 'But if you were alive why didn't you come before?'

'Father has been ill,' said Regan, who was leaning back in her chair, pale and still but hardly spent. 'So ill that he could not remember anything. But he will soon be well now.'

'But that doesn't make him a ghost. He is only like other people who have been ill.'

'You tell people that,' said Fulbert, 'if they throw any doubt on my authenticity. I am of flesh and blood like themselves, even if a little less of them.'

'Do the others know?' said Honor, beginning to jump and quiver in anticipation. 'I will go and tell them; I am the one to know first. They won't think it is true at first. Only Gavin will believe it.'

'Gavin will have his own position in future,' said Fulbert.

Regan smiled as if she were apart from words.

Honor encountered Graham in the hall, and crying the tidings, went on to find Daniel. The young men entered, half-braced for the truth, half-prepared for some travesty of it.

'Honor should be here with her assurance,' said Fulbert, as he shook hands with his sons and then drew them into his embrace. 'She protested that I was not a ghost.'

Graham turned aside, white and shaken, and Daniel stood ready to give his support to any who required it. He glanced at his grandmother, but Regan had what she needed.

Luce entered, driven by Honor, started and paled, took some steps towards her father, and threw herself on his breast. Regan surveyed the scene in sympathy, almost at ease. Regan's tears had been shed.

'Grandma,' said Luce, in a hardly audible tone, as if compelled to the words, 'does Grandpa know?'

'Yes, he knows. He has seen your father. He will soon be here.' Regan needed to say no more of Sir Jesse's meeting with his son.

'Father,' said Luce, in a gentle tone, 'would it be too much for you to have Isabel and Venice and James? They are having needless moments of feeling they are fatherless.'

'It is too much, and it is not enough. Let them all come. It is the healthy and natural way.'

Honor rushed upstairs with the summons, and her sister went to the door.

'Children,' she said, 'your life is going to be whole again. The cloud is lifted. Honor has told you the truth.'

She led them to their father, Isabel white and trembling, Venice crimson and with staring eyes, James uncertain and almost afraid. Fulbert embraced them in a natural way, keeping his old manner with each. Isabel staggered and nearly fell, but recovered and sat with her eyes on her father, almost in the manner of Regan. Venice's face relaxed and her eyes began to glow instead of stare. Daniel gave them seats and treated Graham as one of them. James fidgeted round his father's chair in his old way, until, also in the old way, enjoined to be still, and the natural words seemed to break the tension and set on foot the old life.

'The chief actor must bear the heaviest part,' said Daniel. 'May we hear the tale to be told?'

'In a word,' said his father, while Regan's unmoved and satisfied face showed it had been put in many to herself. 'You read the letter I wrote to Ridley, and the other from my servant, confirming my death. I had no equals about me. The second was written and sent while I lay unconscious; they thought I was near enough to my end. I lived for months, remembering nothing, and when I came to myself and found that no letters came, I questioned the men and found how things had gone. They were in awe of your father and had not dared to confess. They had even sent my effects to your mother. I wrote and told Ridley to prepare you for the truth, followed the letter myself, and waited at the inn to recover and to hear that the way was clear. I dreaded the shock for your mother, for mine, and for you all. That letter cannot have reached him.'

'Grandma,' said Luce, in a desperate whisper, as if the words were wrung from her, 'does Father know about Mother and Ridley?'

Regan nodded almost with indifference, as though this were a secondary thing.

'I can face the natural results of my disappearance,' said Fulbert, turning on his daughter his old unflinching gaze. 'I should wish no one to go through life alone. But I hope my wife will find it a relief not to replace me after all.' He turned and put his arm round Isabel, as though here was someone who would never have done so.

'Father,' said Luce, in a faltering manner, 'Mother had her hard time after you had gone.'

'That was the trouble, no doubt,' said Fulbert. 'I wish I could have spared you all. But our life may be better, that we know what it is to lose it.'

'It is a method of enhancement I can only deplore,' said Daniel.

'You are yourself again, my son. You have had some hard months. Your own work must have suffered. I shall be thankful to take up my duty again and leave you to yours.'

'I hope that disgrace for failure will be balanced by credit for feeling,' said Graham.

'There is greater credit in the greater feeling, that made you go on as if I were here,' said Fulbert. 'I am touched by the signs of the unbroken life in my home. It has held as though my eyes were on it. I find no change in any of you. There is no gulf to be bridged. James does not open doors and he is remaining away from school. And I would have had it so. I have no sense of missing steps in my family history.'

James gave a little jump, uncertain whether he had met success or not.

'Grandma,' said Luce, in a low tone, 'the little boys have come in. Is it better for them to be prepared?'

'Gavin does not need preparation,' said Fulbert. 'He has done his best to perform the office for you all. And no doubt he has done so for Nevill. Let it happen in its own way. I ask nothing that is not spontaneous and natural.'

Nevill ran into the room and towards his grandmother, caught sight of his father, paused and rested his eyes on him, and then ran on and laid something on Regan's lap.

'A bird's nest,' he said. 'Where the little birds used to live.'

'What will they do without their home?'

'All fly away,' said Nevill.

'The little birds had a father and mother bird,' said Regan, guiding his head towards Fulbert. 'And the father bird has come back to the nest.'

Nevill cast his eyes about in quest of this visitor, and dropped them to the nest, in case Regan's words might be true.

'Where?' he said, bringing them back to her face.

'Look and see,' said Regan, turning his head again in the right direction.

'Outside,' said Nevill, as some sparrows chirped by the window. 'He has come back. Hark.'

'Nevill is showing to the same advantage as James,' said Daniel.

'Do you see who is standing by Isabel?' said Regan.

'Father,' said Nevill, in a light tone, as if he would not emphasize what might be in doubt.

'He would like to see his little boy.'

Nevill detached himself from Regan, as if this would aid his father's view.

Fulbert came forward and picked him up, and he sat in his arms and laughed and whimpered alternately, touching his cheek and withdrawing his hand, as though uncertain whether he caressed the authentic person.

'I have congratulated myself that my family has not changed,' said Fulbert. 'I must remember to wonder if the same thing can be said of myself.'

'Dear Father!' said Luce, for the guidance of Nevill.

'Dear Father,' he agreed, using a more confident hand, and allowing himself to look definitely into Fulbert's face. 'Dear Father has come back after a long time. He won't go away again today.'

'He will never go away again,' said Luce.

'Yes,' said Nevill, struggling down from Fulbert's arms and nodding his head. 'He will. But Mr Ridley will always stay.'

'I can't live down my bad name all at once,' said Fulbert. 'And now where is my son, who helped me to get to my home?'

Gavin approached and raised his face, as for a daily greeting.

'You knew I should come back one day, didn't you?'

'No. We thought you were dead.'

'You did not seem so very surprised to see me.'

'Did you know that I saw you?' said Gavin, lifting his eyes to his father's.

'I realized you had, after you had passed. You did not come back and speak to me.'

'You didn't speak to us. And it would be for people back from the dead to speak first. They might not still understand.'

'You were an observant boy to recognize Grandpa's old coat.'

'I didn't know it was his. It was Grandma who knew. I thought it was yours.'

'Father may get tired of this changelessness in his sons,' said Daniel.

'Poor Father is very tired,' said Nevill, casting a look at Fulbert. 'He won't be able to come back another day.'

'Grandma dear,' said Luce, 'Grandpa is crossing the hall. But I suppose he knows what he can bear.'

Sir Jesse entered and came up to his son, and taking both his hands, stood thus for some time, and then passed on to his chair and sank into it.

'Now I can say my "Nunc dimittis",' he said to himself, or rather to the assembled company.

There was a pause.

'What did Grandpa say?' said Gavin.

'They are Latin words,' said Honor.

'Grandpa can say them,' said Nevill, with pride in his relative.

'Would you like to be able to?' said Luce.

'Yes, but he will some day.'

'Ask Father if he will teach you,' said Luce, hoping to make a bond where one was needed.

'No, Miss Pilbeam will teach him.'

'Has Grandpa seen Father before?' said Gavin.

'Yes, but not for long,' said Luce.

'Grandpa is glad that Father has come back,' said Nevill.

'Grandma,' said Luce, in a shaken tone, 'it is on us, the desperate moment. Mother and Ridley are in the hall. What are we to do?'

'We can do nothing,' said Regan, seeming almost to repress a smile.

'One of you go and prepare your mother,' said Fulbert to his sons, in his old manner.

'We should have thought of that, if we were not petrified,' said Daniel.

'I will go, Father,' said Luce, and went swiftly from the room.

'The occasion of Ridley's discomfiture is spoiled by its tragedy,' said Daniel.

'It is hard on us,' said Graham. 'But nothing can spoil it for Grandma. And she has had few pleasures of late.'

'Hope and Paul are there as well,' said Regan, again with an unsteadiness about her lips.

'Another circumstance of our life unchanged,' said Fulbert.

'It is a good thing that the family is not any larger,' said Isabel.

Regan laughed with noticeable heartiness, almost as though to cover some other cause for mirth.

'Faith is not there,' said Venice.

'She will remedy the matter,' said her sister.

'Will Mother be able to marry Mr Ridley now?' said James.

'Of course not,' said Isabel. 'Father was glad to see no change in you, but he will alter his mind, if you don't take care.'

Hope entered and began at once to talk, as if to give time to those who followed.

'Fulbert, I wish I could say I knew this would happen. But I did not know. I am afraid you will see signs of it.'

'I have found so few in my own home that I can hardly believe what is before my eyes.'

'I suppose I meant in our home. There are not so few there.'

'I know, I know,' said Fulbert; 'I am prepared.'

'And Ridley is not. Well, it is right that you should have the advantage of him.'

'I hope it is. For I have it.'

Hope sat down as if her limbs gave under her. Regan looked at her easily. The awaited group came into the room, Luce leading her mother. Eleanor walked forward with her usual step, and Ridley was drawn to his full height to face what was upon him.

'Fulbert!' he said, moving in front of the others. 'My friend.'

Fulbert accepted his hand, but went towards his wife, and it was not until they had exchanged an embrace that he turned his eyes on his face.

'My friend,' repeated Ridley. 'I trust that nothing will alter that for you. It will not for me.'

'It need not,' said Fulbert. 'A dead man cannot expect to be treated as a live one.'

'You left your affairs in my hands. If in the course of dealing with them, I was led further, you will understand.'

'Who should, if not I? You wanted what I chose for myself. How can I say I am surprised?'

'You might say other things. I am grateful for your forbearance.'

'I have too much restored to me, to dwell on what I may have lost. And somehow I feel it is not much, and will soon be mine.'

Ridley took a step aside and stood with his eyes averted, while the husband and wife approached their children.

'I find that I miss nothing,' said Fulbert. 'If life would have gone on after my death, that will happen to us all. And if it went on too soon and too far for my choice, I was not there to choose.'

Sir Jesse touched the ground with his stick, and Paul, who was standing absorbed in the scene, obeyed the summons. The resulting movement revealed Faith, standing just inside the room, with her hands held apart from her sides, and her eyes wide and unwinking, as though to avoid dwelling on the intimate scene.

'I forgot Faith was with us,' said Hope, 'but it seems she did the same.'

'Faith looks as if she were at church,' said Venice, in a clearer voice that she intended.

'I suppose we do all feel rather like that,' said Faith, in a low, quick tone.

'No doubt we ought to wish we were not here,' said Hope.

'I wish we were not,' said Faith, with a further withdrawal towards the door.

'I see why you stayed in the hall, dear. But why did you change your mind?'

'It is not much good for one of us to adopt a measure when the others do not follow it.'

'Where did Faith get the impression that her family follow her lead?' said Daniel.

Ridley turned from his place, and with a step that suggested that eyes were on him, walked to the window and stood with his back to the room.

'Ridley's eyes are resting unseeingly on the familiar landscape,' said Graham, his voice betraying that this was not the whole of his thought.

'I am glad he has got out of his place in the middle of the floor,' said Daniel. 'It was hardly his best at the moment.'

'You make me feel he is in the pillory, and that you would like to throw rotten eggs at him,' said Hope.

'How did people come by their supplies of eggs in that state?' said Isabel. 'Did they carry a stock of them, as if they were snuff or tobacco?'

'Perhaps they were on sale near the pillory,' said Daniel, 'as buns and nuts are at the Zoo, so that people could be helped to their natural dealings with captive creatures.'

Faith looked at the laughing group with steady eyes.

'Faith thinks we ought to be in low spirits,' said Isabel. 'I am sure I don't know why.'

'I know you are seriously thankful in your hearts,' said Faith.

Regan watched her son's reunion with his family, without jealousy, emotion or desire. She would have asked what she had.

Fulbert saw Ridley's solitary figure and went towards him.

'Well, Ridley, let us take our next steps over this strange gulf between us. I have much to thank you for, and I trust you do not resent my rising from the dead. I would have done it at a better moment, if I could. I did try to rise a day or two earlier, but fate was against me. And it is a good thing it was not a day or two later. I don't understand how my letter miscarried. It was an unfortunate lapse, when they occur so seldom. I will have inquiries made. You had the two letters some months ago, and then no other?'

'Fulbert,' said Ridley, lifting his eyes, 'I have had no letter from you or concerning you, save those two you name. I dealt with them as you directed. And so would I have dealt with this one, had it reached me.'

'I wished to spare my family a shock. And I wrote instead of cabling, to save them the weeks of waiting. I may have been right or wrong, but I have reached my home, and I cannot regret the manner of my coming.'

'Fulbert,' said Ridley, looking round with an emotional expression, 'I could not wish you more than this.'

'You are wise not to tell me your real feelings. And I will never ask you for them.'

'You spoke of the gulf between us,' said Ridley, in a painful manner. 'If you will come to meet me over it, I will do my part. More I cannot do.'

'Do let us gloss over this moment,' said Graham, as if he could not suppress the words. 'It will become too much.'

'Father and Ridley might have had their encounter without arranging themselves as the cynosure of every eye,' said Daniel.

'Well, nothing need be explained to us later,' said Isabel. 'And I trust nothing will be.'

'Well, you have been present at a scene that would be unique in anyone's life,' said Fulbert, looking round on his children. 'You will live to be glad you have witnessed it. You will carry the memory to your graves. And you will be the wiser. Nothing could have thrown more light on human nature.'

'I call that almost a personal remark,' said Hope.

Graham looked again at Ridley, whose eyes were on the ground.

Honor came up to Gavin.

'Shall we say our "Nunc dimittis"?' she said, with a gleam in her eyes.

Gavin met the look in silence.

'I mean, shall we find a chance of going upstairs?'

'Don't you want to stay with Father?'

'I don't mind, as long as he is here. I want to enjoy my ordinary life, feeling he has come back.'

Gavin gave the matter some thought.

'We should only be sent for,' he said.

'Now let me do something more for you all, than work on your feelings,' said Fulbert, who had been unfastening a package. 'I have not come home for that. Let me show you these photographs of the places I saw, and should have seen, if I had been a sound man instead of a sick one. Now put yourselves so that you can see.'

He settled himself in an armchair. Luce leaned over the back. Isabel and Venice sat on the arms, and Honor on her father's knee. Daniel and Graham stood at the sides, and James and Gavin knelt on the floor in front. Nevill took his stand at a distance, with his eyes on the photographs. Ridley slowly advanced and stood within sight of them, as if he would take a natural part. Eleanor kept her gaze on the group of her husband and children. Regan and Sir Jesse watched it with scarcely a movement of their eyes. Faith stood as if nothing mattered, as long as she did not occupy any space round Fulbert.

'Here is the house where I lived,' said Fulbert. 'There is the window of the room where I lay. For months I saw nothing except through that square of glass.'

Nevill approached and placed his finger on the point.

'It is where Father was,' he said.

'The glass is not square,' said Gavin.

'It is oblong,' said Honor.

'Father painted the picture,' said Nevill.

'It is a photograph,' said James.

'It is a picture of a house,' said Nevill, who knew only photographs of people.

'Couldn't you even speak?' said Honor to her father.

'Not so that people knew what I meant.'

'Then they couldn't do what you wanted?'

'That was the worst, my little woman. You would have found it out, wouldn't you?'

'He would too,' said Nevill.

'She couldn't have, if she didn't know what you said,' said Gavin.

'Ah, the eyes of love can divine a good deal,' said Fulbert.

'Then didn't the people who were with you – didn't they like you very much?' said James, in a high, hardly articulate tone.

'Not as much as my own girls,' said Fulbert, putting Isabel's arm about his neck, and a moment later doing the same with Venice's.

'Not as much as him either,' said Nevill.

'The voyage must have done a good deal for you, Father,' said Luce. 'You are thinner and a little older, but you are yourself.'

'If I were not, you would not see me. I would not have offered you a ghost or a scarecrow for a father.'

'If Honor couldn't see you until you were well, she couldn't have done what you wanted,' said Gavin.

Fulbert lifted Honor's hand to his cheek.

'I wish Father would arrange some caresses for himself from me,' said Graham. 'He lets me seem so cold-hearted.'

'My Isabel can't look at her father enough,' said Fulbert.

'He looks at Father too,' said Nevill. 'He *likes* to look at him.'

'Now you may have these photographs for yourselves,' said Fulbert. 'Would you like to divide them or share them?'

'Share them,' said James, at once.

'That is always a good way.'

'I should like that one with you in it, Father,' said Isabel.

Fulbert withdrew it and put it into her hand.

'Mother gave me a photograph of you on the day you went away,' said Venice.

'Well, here is another on the day I come back.'

'You gave me one of yourself on that day,' said Honor, bringing about a similar result.

James's eyes rested on the photographs in some doubt of the fate of his suggestion.

'He would like a little picture,' said Nevill.

'Come and sit on my knee like Honor, and I will show them to you,' said Fulbert.

Nevill moved forward and started back, gazed at his father, and after a moment ran to Ridley and climbed on his knee, as though he were the person interchangeable with Fulbert.

'Now I must see what I can find in my pockets,' said Ridley, holding to his line of playing a normal part. 'Here is a purse and a notebook and a cigar case, and a gold pencil case with lead in it.'

Nevill looked from the objects to Ridley's face.

'It is better than a picture, isn't it?'

'Is the pencil real gold?' said Gavin. 'Did somebody give it to you?'

'Yes, it was a present,' said Ridley, not mentioning that the giver was Eleanor. 'You can make it longer if you pull it.'

'It moves,' said Nevill, in a slightly uneasy tone, putting his hand towards it and drawing it away.

'Pull it and see how long it is,' said Ridley.

'He will pull it,' said Nevill, looking round before gingerly doing so, and breaking into nervous laughter as it yielded to his touch.

'There is a loose leaf in the notebook,' said Gavin. 'I can read grown-up writing now; I can read it as well as Honor; I even like reading it. What is the matter? I can't hurt a piece of paper. It doesn't belong to the book.'

Ridley had started and grasped at the paper, but as Gavin moved away, he changed his manner and smilingly held out his hand.

'I must ask for my property,' he said.

'Gavin, give it back at once,' said Luce. 'We never read papers belonging to other people.'

'It is only a list like Mother takes into the town. It isn't even a long one.'

'It is a memorandum,' said Honor.

'And as such, it fills a place in my life,' said Ridley, still with hand extended.

'I shan't make any mistakes,' said Gavin. 'It is sometimes two or three words and sometimes more. What is the matter? You hurt me with your great hand.'

'The moment has come for me to claim what is my own,' said Ridley, in a tone that addressed the company.

There was a stir and murmur of protest, and eyes were turned to the man and the child.

'"Arrange licence. Take house. Train and hotel",' read Gavin. 'It is quite easy. There are only a few more lines. Each one is called an item. The word is printed on the page. I shan't keep it a minute. Let me just read to the end.' He eluded Ridley's grasp and slipped into a space where he could not follow. '"Fulbert at Crown Inn from tenth to fifteenth. Keep paper as letter destroyed. Write from abroad, as if it were delayed and forwarded. Read and send lease." Leave me alone. What harm can I do to a loose page?'

Ridley was leaning over the desk, his hand clutching the air above the paper. There was a silence that became a hush and then a stir. Fulbert rose and came towards Ridley and stood waiting for him to turn. Eleanor approached the group, and finding herself between the two men, moved nearer to her husband. Regan rustled forward, simply and fiercely accusing. Sir Jesse stood with his eyes shooting from under his brows, but so far reserving his word. Luce stood with a simply startled face. Faith watched from her place, her gaze fastened on her brother. Hope and Paul remained in their seats, now and then meeting each other's eyes. Daniel came and stood by his parents, Graham and Isabel looked at Ridley, as if they could not hold themselves from following his experience. The children watched in different stages of comprehension, Gavin awaiting the reproach that was his due.

'What is it?' he whispered to Honor.

'Nothing to do with you. It is not you who have done anything.'

'Gavin didn't mean to do it,' said Nevill to his mother, feeling this to be an unlikely view.

'So, Ridley,' said Fulbert, speaking with his head lifted, and his eyes almost covered by their lids, 'I have had this kind of friend.'

Ridley appeared to be preoccupied by the notebook and some loosened pages.

'I didn't tear the book,' said Gavin.

'If you will pardon me, you did,' said Ridley, smiling at him in an absent manner.

'Be quiet, and you will be forgotten,' said Honor, to her brother.

'So my letter arrived to time,' said Fulbert, not changing his attitude.

Ridley kept his eyes on the book, carefully replacing the leaves.

'The notebook is useful,' said Regan. 'And not for the first time. What would have happened when my son came home? His wife would have been his own.'

'In name,' said Ridley, in a gentle tone, his fingers still employed, and his eyes on them. 'But we should have remained together. Your son would have had ground for any step he chose. Eleanor would have been happier in her own home with me.

This house is no home to her. Why should I not think of her and myself?' He seemed to keep his voice to its even note by an effort, as if he would not work himself up for his hearers. 'Why should I only think of a man, whose sole thought of me was to put me to his service? Why should I serve him? Why did he think that I should? Why is he so much better than I?'

Sir Jesse thrust himself between Ridley and Regan, his hands falling at his sides, as if his emotions took all his powers.

'You may cease to talk to my wife. Why should she hear and answer you? You may be silent in my house. And as you are the son of my friend, you may leave it at your own will. I will not speak to you of my son; I could not do so.'

Ridley turned as if to do Sir Jesse's bidding, but as he passed him, paused and opened the notebook and drew something else from the back. He held it under Sir Jesse's eyes, and then moved on and held it under Regan's.

'You are right that the book is useful. It proves to be so once again. It has served several of my purposes.'

Sir Jesse was not in time to find his glasses. Regan had hers in her hand and looked at the photograph. She looked also at Ridley's hand, saw that its grasp was firm, threw one glance at her husband and returned to the hearth.

Ridley moved on and held the photograph under the eyes of Fulbert, his wife and his three eldest children. Hope left her place and came and looked at it; Paul followed her example; Isabel summoned her courage and did the same. Sir Jesse, who by now had guessed its character, came up and confirmed his suspicion and moved away. Regan kept her eyes down and wore an inscrutable expression. Faith glanced at her parents and turned aside, as if she would not yield to curiosity.

The photograph was of a man and a woman, sitting in a lover-like attitude, with their arms entwined: Sir Jesse and the mother of the Marlowes.

Ridley's voice was heard again.

'You see I am not the only man who can go astray. I found that photograph amongst some business papers. It was taken years ago in South America, and it tells us what happened there. I took it with the intention of destroying it, but you set me another example. I will show that I am not the only person with the temptations of a man, and not the only one who can yield to them.'

'Why did you not fulfil your intention?' said Regan from the hearth.

Luce beckoned to Isabel and Venice and James, and led them to the door, bending to say a word to Regan.

'Grandma, some of us are too young to understand. And some of us are of an age when we must understand. These three are in between.'

Regan nodded and smiled, her face almost placid.

The three children left the room, Isabel at once startled and satisfied, James too puzzled even to be curious, Venice baffled and tormented, but encouraged by the promise in her sister's eyes.

'If you judge me, so do I judge you,' said Ridley to Sir Jesse. 'And I say you are worse than I.'

He turned and went with bent head to the door, and seemed to thrust his way through it, as though it offered some tangible resistance. As he moved his hands the photograph fell; he groped for it, and Gavin, still angry and watchful, darted on it and surrendered it to Fulbert. Faith watched her brother go, and then moved slowly and as if hardly of her own will to Daniel and Graham, and revealed the subject of her words by a sudden glance at Sir Jesse. Fulbert returned to his children and the photographs scattered on the floor.

'Well, which picture would you like?' he said, resuming his seat and bending towards Nevill.

Nevill gathered up the photographs and poured them over Fulbert's knees.

'They are all Father's,' he said.

'He may see a photograph as a sinister object,' said Graham.

'I didn't tear the paper,' said Gavin.

'We know you did not, my boy,' said Eleanor.

'Gavin took great care,' said Nevill.

'I feel grateful to Gavin,' said Daniel. 'He has ended the necessity of feeling pity for Ridley.'

'I don't know, Daniel,' said Luce. 'Is our pity any less? Of course we have other feelings.'

'Which picture do you like best?' said Fulbert, to Nevill.

'He will have that one Mr Ridley had.'

'Father has it in his pocket,' said Gavin.

'Perhaps he has a pencil too,' said Nevill.

'I will find you one tomorrow,' said Fulbert.

'Grandpa spoke in a loud voice,' said Nevill, 'loud and angry. Mr Ridley did too.'

Sir Jesse sank into a chair at the sound of his name, as if it gave him some sort of release, and sat with his head and shoulders bent, with a suggestion that he was a broken man.

'Who will live in the new house?' said Gavin. 'Now that Mother is not going to marry Mr Ridley.'

'Mother will marry him,' said Nevill, 'and have a nice house and not this one.'

'Other people will live in it,' said Honor.

'Not other people,' said Nevill. 'Mr Ridley wouldn't let them.'

'Perhaps he will live in it alone.'

'No, not alone. He would be very angry.'

'Which do you like best, Mr Ridley or Father?' said Gavin suddenly to Eleanor, seeking to remedy his own situation by bringing forward hers.

'Father is my husband,' said Eleanor, without hesitation, 'and we have always loved each other, and we always shall. But Ridley was good to me when I thought Father could not return, and I shall always be grateful to him. Some day you will understand.'

'I understand now,' said Honor. 'He kept it a secret about Father's coming back, so that he could marry you before people knew. He yielded to temptation.'

'Now I think you may run away,' said Eleanor, stroking her hair.

'What did Mr Ridley do?' said Gavin, in a low tone to his sister.

'I will tell you when we are upstairs.'

'Now you may run away,' said Eleanor again. 'You will always feel kindly to him.'

'I haven't said I shall,' said Gavin.

'I have no antipathy to him,' said Honor.

'Now I said you could run away,' said Eleanor. 'You may kiss Father before you go.'

'He will kiss Mother too,' said Nevill, coming up to her. 'And Mr Ridley come back soon, and never go away again.'

'Now I said you could run away.'

'Do you think you were right, dear?' said Hope.

'Tell Hatton and Mullet that I will come up later and see them,' said Fulbert, as he parted from his children.

'He will tell them,' said Nevill, and ran before the others from the room.

'I think I ought to go home, Mother,' said Faith. 'I have a feeling that someone should be with Ridley.'

'I am glad you take the noble course, dear. It improves our family average. And it seems to need it.'

Faith went with a grave face towards the door. Sir Jesse rose and without looking at anyone did the same, as if he found it easier to follow a lead. Regan got up a minute later and, putting her knitting easily together, smiled on the company and followed. Paul came from the back of the room, as if released from some bondage.

'Well, I am going to take my wife away,' said Fulbert. 'I have a leaning towards my own armchair. It is many months since I have sat in it. And if I leave her, other people form designs upon her. I have been happy in having my friends to welcome me. And I wish you joy of your gossip; it should be a good one.'

'It should be wonderful,' said Hope, coming quickly to the centre of the group. 'And as we all have a relation disgraced, it will not be spoiled by personal embarrassment. I have not dared to dwell on our own family dishonour.'

'Perhaps we never shall,' said Paul. 'Then we shall be saved a great deal. Poor boy! Poor boy!'

'The exposure of two people upon one occasion must be very rare,' said Daniel.

'We so seldom get any exposure at all,' said Paul.

'It is better for it all to happen together,' said Graham. 'Better for the exposed people, I mean.'

'They are saved from that sense of loneliness,' said Hope. 'Men's lives are evidently what they are supposed to be. And some have the misfortune to be found out. It is all true.'

'People should keep their darker times to themselves,' said Daniel.

'They are certainly not well advised to be photographed at one of them,' said Paul.

'Would it be better not to talk about it?' said Faith.

'Nothing could be so bad,' said Hope. 'And it is because you think so that you have not gone to Ridley.'

'I thought we should all be going soon, Mother.'

'No doubt he has taken the late train to London,' said Paul.

Faith turned grave eyes on her father, in reference to his silence on this matter.

'I wonder if he has anyone to welcome him there,' said Hope.

'Grandpa was rather mature when he sowed his wild oats,' said Daniel.

'They don't seem so very wild,' said Graham. 'People must be fairly established, when they are in a position to support two families.'

'Poor Grandpa!' said Luce. 'I daresay he was very lonely out there. Not that I want to make excuses for him.'

'There is none for the various foolishness he has shown,' said Paul. 'It comes of a life without criticism.'

'How did he manage about leaving the woman, when he returned to England?' said Graham.

'It is no good to find out about it, Graham,' said Daniel. 'You will never go as far as your grandfather.'

'He told her the truth about his life,' said Paul. 'And he lived with her again, when he went out a second time. She died when Susan was born.'

'And I pitied you for having to sit by him!' said Hope. 'To think of the freemasonry among men!'

'I suppose she was not equal to him,' said Faith.

'I daresay not, to our ideas,' said her father. 'Social and other differences would count less out there.'

'And when he heard of her death, he sent for the three children,' said Faith. 'I am glad he did not shirk his responsibilities.'

'Are they to know who their father is?' said Graham.

'No, it is to be always kept from them,' said Paul. 'He feels it is better for them and for him. I am quoting his words.'

'He must be afraid of its leaking out, now it is not his own secret,' said Graham.

'It is to be the secret of us all.'

'Well, that is the least aggravating kind of secret,' said Hope.

'Poor Grandma!' said Luce, in a soft tone.

'Yes, poor Lady Sullivan!' said Faith. 'She is the really tragic figure. I think she showed a great heroism, the greater that it was quiet.'

'I think heroism is only mentioned when it is that,' said Hope.

'She has known for years,' said Paul. 'She saw Sir Jesse's interest in the young people, and saw a likeness to him, and guessed the truth.'

'To think she has carried the burden for all this time!' said Faith, slowly shaking her head.

'It is Grandpa's affair,' said Daniel, 'or it should have been.'

'Did she tell you, Paul?' said Hope.

'She said a word to him.'

'Did he mind?' said Graham.

'Well, I think he had a shock.'

'He can hardly expect not to suffer at all,' said Faith.

'It seems like Grandpa to sin for years and suffer for a moment,' said Graham, as though he were glad if this were the case.

'It is good that there is no longer that between them,' said Faith. 'And I daresay Lady Sullivan knows men.'

'I did not know you did, dear,' said Hope.

'All women must in a way, Mother.'

'Well, I don't see how, in some cases, dear.'

'There would not be definite ways, Mother.'

'Oh, well, perhaps we think the same. Now can we dwell on Sir Jesse's lapse, and hardly mention Ridley's?'

'That is what we will do, if you please,' said Paul. 'But I should not have thought the boy would be so bold.'

'I have been feeling an unwilling respect for him,' said Hope. 'And as in me respect is generally that, perhaps the rest of you feel a proper one.'

'I cannot do that,' said Faith, in a quiet tone. 'But of course I have other feelings.'

'I can't help thinking of Grandma's tragedy,' said Luce. 'It has not come today, but there must have been a day when it did come.'

'There must,' said Faith.

'When the expedition involved what it did, no wonder Grandpa thought us too young for it,' said Daniel.

'Did Father find any traces of what had happened?' said Graham.

'He did not say,' said Paul.

'Perhaps Grandpa had prepared him.'

'Does the freemasonry extend to father and son?' said Hope.

'I suppose a long period away from home does mean all kinds of things for a man,' said Faith.

'Ridley has done well enough in his own village,' said Paul. 'I hope he will not go further outside. For he will now remain away.'

'Yes, I suppose he will, Father,' said Faith.

'Is there any likeness in the Marlowes to Grandpa?' said Luce. 'And is their real name Marlowe?'

'Yes, it was their mother's name,' said Paul.

'Of course, illegitimate children are called by their mother's name,' said Faith. 'I have always seen likenesses in them, but I have never been able to place them.'

'I have always thought the resemblance was to each other,' said Graham, 'and I think it chiefly is.'

'The likeness to your grandfather would not strike people when no one looked for it,' said Paul. 'If the relationship had been known, there would have been no need to fancy it.'

'The Marlowes are our uncle and aunts by half blood,' said Luce, in her musing tone.

'You had better forget it,' said Paul. 'If things are in our minds, they come to our lips.'

'This thing does seem to,' said Hope.

'Now how are we to face Grandpa?' said Luce.

'Yes, that is how it will be,' said Daniel, 'when surely it should be the other way round.'

'Poor Grandpa!' said Luce.

'I do admire you all,' said Hope. 'You have none of the severity of youth. I should hardly have expected Faith to be so tolerant; I might not even have approved of it. I think people must be better with each generation.'

'I can hardly be accused of youth, Mother,' said Faith.

'And poor Grandma!' said Luce, as if she could not in honesty give up this idea.

'Yes, it is Sir Jesse's career of deceit that is hard to forgive,' said Faith. 'That long course of deception of his wife. It goes against the grain.'

'But you do forgive it, dear,' said Hope.

'He meant to die with that between them, Mother.'

'It is there now,' said Graham. 'That is what he did not mean. He was just keeping his own counsel. He has never meant to die at all.'

'He will never get over my being Ridley's father,' said Paul. 'It may be a release for me in a way.'

'And how about his own varied fatherhood?' said Daniel.

'I have already recovered from it. I am not the man he is.'

'Yes, I do forgive it,' said Faith, in a quick, low tone that rose as she continued. 'Poor Eleanor Sullivan is in a sad position.'

'It is greatly improved,' said Daniel. 'She prefers Father to Ridley.'

'Well, in a position of peculiar difficulty.'

'The worst is already past.'

'It was a hard homecoming for your father.'

'It was a sound instinct that led him to prepare us,' said Luce, smiling.

'He was fortunate, considering he failed to do so,' said Graham. 'He did not find his very name forgotten, or anything like that. And he seemed to be a little surprised.'

'Why do we joke about it?' said Luce.

'I have not done so,' said Faith, rising from her chair. 'Now it is not a day for lingering.'

'My heart fails before the prospect of our first family gathering,' said Graham. 'To think that Grandpa and Grandma and Mother must all be there!'

'And this on the day when Father is restored to us!' said Luce. 'This is the thing I do not incline to forgive Grandpa.'

'It must be difficult for you,' said Faith, as if there were no question of the actual forgiveness.

'It is fortunate that Father's heart is stout enough for it all,' said Daniel.

Chapter 12

'Father has come home!' said Honor, bounding into the schoolroom. 'He was ill and unconscious, but he was never dead. Mother can't marry Mr Ridley, and things will be like they used to be.'

'I am so thankful for you, dear,' said Miss Pilbeam, stooping to kiss her. 'I heard last night and I rejoiced from my heart.'

Honor drew back with a look of consternation, and Gavin who was behind her, came to a sudden pause.

'We should have had a holiday, if Mother had thought of it,' resumed Honor, in an almost more than ordinary tone. 'But she said, as you would have the trouble of coming, we were to have lessons.'

'I think you would please your father by doing your very best.'

'I don't think he minds,' said Honor, turning round on one foot.

'Don't you wish your mother could come back?' said Gavin, with a simple air of superiority.

'I do indeed,' said Miss Pilbeam.

'I don't suppose she ever can, because she died in the house, didn't she?'

'No, I know she cannot.'

'But I daresay you don't mind her being dead as much as you did at first,' said Gavin, revealing his own experience of the effect of time.

'I mind quite as much. But I have had to get used to it.'

'I call that not minding so much,' said Honor, still turning round.

'You went on minding about your father.'

'I minded less; I had to. Everyone does. And other people get tired of your minding. Even Mother did. But if he really died now, I should mind more.'

653

'And you have not worn black since we knew you,' said Gavin to Miss Pilbeam.

'We do not stay in black for ever.'

'We do for a year, unless there is something to prevent it,' said Honor. 'We went out because Mother was going to marry again. The children can't look as if they still minded, when the mother has proved that she doesn't.'

'I don't think you quite understand your mother. She had to make the best of her life as it was.'

'If you really still minded, you wouldn't think there was any best.'

'You wouldn't think your father minded, if he was going to marry someone else,' said Gavin.

'I hope I should try to understand it. Indeed I do try to,' said Miss Pilbeam, in a lighter tone.

'Is he going to marry someone else?' said Honor.

'Yes, he told me last night,' said Miss Pilbeam, with an open, easy smile.

'It is funny that your father decided to marry someone else on the day when our mother knew she couldn't.'

Miss Pilbeam did not dwell upon the coincidence, though it was to be explained on the ground that her father had found the news an opening for himself.

'Does it make you hate your father?' said Gavin.

'No, not at all. You did not hate your mother, did you?'

'Well, she went down in my estimation,' said Honor.

'You would not have wished her to be lonely.'

'I should have thought it couldn't be helped.'

'The new woman will be your stepmother,' said Gavin, with a threat in his tone.

'Yes, she will. But she is an old friend.'

'Perhaps your father always wanted to marry her, even when your mother was alive,' said Honor.

'No, I am sure he did not.'

'Do people generally marry someone else, when their own wife or husband is dead?' said Gavin.

'No, only sometimes. I think men do it oftener than women.'

'Can they go on doing it as often as they like?'

'Yes, if they continue to lose their partners,' said Miss Pilbeam, with a touch of facetiousness.

Nevill came into the room in an absent manner, his eyes on a ball of string in his hands.

'Why, what a muddled ball!' said Miss Pilbeam.

'It is in a tangle,' said Nevill, with quiet resignation.

'I will soon put it straight for you.'

'Mullet said, do it himself,' said Nevill, with a sudden burst of tears.

'Oh, I think Mullet must have been busy.'

'Mullet was busy,' said Nevill, in a cheered, relieved tone. 'Poor Mullet was very busy. She wouldn't say it another time.'

'Miss Pilbeam's father is going to be married,' said Honor.

'Not to Mr Ridley,' said Nevill, instantly.

'Of course not. A man can't marry another man.'

'He can't have Mr Ridley's house.'

'He doesn't want it. He has a house of his own. I suppose he will still live there.'

'Yes, he will,' said Nevill. 'That is a nice house too.'

'You don't know anything about it.'

'Miss Pilbeam likes it,' said Nevill.

'Do you like it?' said Gavin, to Miss Pilbeam. 'I don't think it is at all nice.'

'I have not thought how it appears to other people. It has always been my home.'

'Perhaps your stepmother will turn you out,' said Gavin.

'No, I don't think she will do that,' said Miss Pilbeam, with a smile.

'You would laugh on the other side of your face, if she did.'

'Miss Pilbeam would live here with Hatton and Mullet,' said Nevill.

Honor and Gavin looked at each other, and burst into laughter at this estimation of Miss Pilbeam's place.

Miss Pilbeam looked towards the window.

'I am "he"; you are "she"; Miss Pilbeam is "it",' said Gavin, to his sister, seeming to receive an impetus from Nevill's words.

Miss Pilbeam turned sharply towards him.

'I suppose your father will like your stepmother better than you,' said Honor, quickly.

'He will have a different feeling for us.'

'No, he will like Miss Pilbeam best,' said Nevill.

'I see you are determined to waste your time this morning.'

'Well, it is natural,' said Honor.

'Yes, I think it is. Perhaps I had better read to you.'

Nevill at once ran to a book that lay on the sofa, brought it to Miss Pilbeam, and stood waiting to be lifted to her knee.

'We don't want that book,' said Honor.

Nevill put it on Miss Pilbeam's lap, turned the leaves until he came to his place, and began to read aloud to himself.

'No, no, that is not the page,' she said, putting her hand over it. 'You are saying it by heart.'

Nevill turned the pages again, reached one that he actually recognized, and resumed his recitation.

'No, you are not doing it properly. I will read a chapter of *Robinson Crusoe*. We are coming to the part where he sees the footprint on the ground.'

Nevill carried his book to the sofa and continued to read, resorting to improvisation when his memory failed.

'Now this is an exciting part,' said Miss Pilbeam.

'Sometimes you miss things out,' said Honor. 'I know, because I read the book to myself.'

'It would be better not to read the book I am reading to you.'

'I like reading things a lot of times.'

'Well, this book is certainly worth it.'

'Then why did you tell her not to?' said Gavin.

'I thought it might make my reading dull for her. But nothing could make *Robinson Crusoe* dull, could it?'

'I think something makes it dull sometimes,' said Gavin, in such a light tone that Miss Pilbeam missed his meaning as he half intended.

Miss Pilbeam began to read, and Nevill raised his voice to overcome the sound, and remained absorbed in the results of his imagination. Neither Honor nor Gavin appeared to be conscious of his presence.

When things had continued for some time, Eleanor and Fulbert entered.

'Well, Miss Pilbeam,' said the latter, 'I have come to give you proof of what you have heard. We don't want you in danger of thinking a ghost has sprung on you.'

'I am rejoiced to see the proof, Mr Sullivan,' said Miss Pilbeam, as she shook hands.

'Show Father what you are doing,' said Eleanor, to the children.

'They are hardly in a state to apply themselves. I am just reading aloud. That will steady their nerves.'

'Poor little things! They will be more themselves tomorrow. And what is Nevill doing?'

Nevill just glanced at his mother and maintained his flow of words, drawing his finger down the page with an effect of keeping his place.

'Are you reading, dear?'

'Yes, him and Miss Pilbeam. Honor and Gavin aren't.'

'What is the book about?'

'Don't talk to him while he reads,' said Nevill, and resumed the pursuit.

'It is a very good imitation,' said Fulbert.

His son gave him a look, and turned the page as his finger reached the bottom of it.

Hatton entered the room, and he looked at her and hesitated, and then took the open book in both his hands and came to her side.

'It is time for your rest,' she said.

'He will read in bed,' said Nevill.

'No, you must go to sleep in bed,' said Eleanor, at once.

'He will read first,' said her son.

'He is still a little shy of me,' said Fulbert.

'Come and say good-bye to Father and me,' said Eleanor.

Nevill approached her, keeping his eyes from Fulbert.

'Mr Ridley will come back soon. Not stay away a long time like Father. And then Mother will have a nice house.'

'He tried to comfort me after you had gone. He has got into the habit of saying all the comforting things he can think of,' said Eleanor, hardly giving enough attention to her words.

'Miss Pilbeam's father is really going to marry again,' said Gavin.

Eleanor turned inquiring eyes on Miss Pilbeam.

'Yes, I heard the news last night,' said the latter, in a conversational, interested tone. 'And I shall not have my father so much on my mind. I can look forward to a time when I can think more of myself. I have not been able to be quite selfish enough in the last year.'

'A healthy resolve, Miss Pilbeam. See that you hold to it,' said Fulbert.

'Miss Pilbeam's stepmother won't turn her out,' said Gavin.

'Of course she will not,' said Eleanor. 'Why should she?'

'Well, it would hide the fact that she was not the father's first wife,' said Honor, with a slight spacing of the words. 'I wouldn't marry a man who had had a wife before me. If I had been Mr Ridley, I shouldn't have liked to marry you.'

'But Mr Ridley will marry her,' said Nevill, in a reassuring tone to his mother.

'I am the man married to Mother,' said Fulbert.

'No, Father didn't marry her. He didn't come back for a long time. But Mother will come and see poor Father.'

'Mr Ridley is not coming here any more.'

'No, because he has a house. This one is Grandma's.'

'Mother doesn't want the house now,' said Fulbert.

'Father can live in it too,' said Nevill, struck by a solution of all the human problems.

'Mother and I are both staying here.'

'Yes, until tomorrow.'

'No, we are staying here for always.'

Nevill met his eyes.

'Yes, dear Father can stay here,' he said, and ran after Hatton.

'Nevill wants to get rid of me,' said Eleanor, her tone showing that she did not believe her words.

'He doesn't know what the word, marry, means,' said Honor.

'I hope he will know some day,' said Fulbert, putting his arm in his wife's.

Honor looked after them, as they left the room.

'What is it like to have a father and no mother?' she said to Miss Pilbeam. 'But you liked your mother better than your father, didn't you?'

'I think perhaps I did.'

'You would think so now, because your father is marrying someone else,' said Gavin. 'That does make people think they don't like the person so well.'

'Well, it doesn't argue any great depth of nature,' said Honor.

'We cannot lay down rules in these matters,' said Miss Pilbeam.

Gavin looked at his sister.

'Do you like Father as much as you thought you did, when you believed he was dead?' he said in a natural tone.

Honor hesitated, or rather paused.

'Well, I don't think so much of him; I thought he was a more remarkable man. But I am quite reconciled to his being of common clay. I think that is better for those in authority over us.'

'Would you mind as much, if he died now?'

'I shouldn't think it was as great a loss. But I should mind more. I couldn't ever bear it again.'

'Would you die?' said Gavin, in a grave tone.

'If that is what people do, when they can't bear the things that have happened.'

'Come, don't forget you are children,' said Miss Pilbeam, who believed that his conversation had been unchildlike.

'Our experience has gone beyond our age,' said Honor, who shared the belief.

'Something has,' said Miss Pilbeam, smiling.

'Well, go on reading,' said Gavin in a rough tone.

'That is not the way to ask.'

'I am not asking; I am telling you to go on.'

'And something has not,' said Miss Pilbeam, deciding to continue to smile and resuming the book.

Eleanor and her husband went on to the schoolroom.

'Well, Miss Mitford, I have come to see you,' said Fulbert, 'and to give you proof that I am flesh and blood like yourself.'

Miss Mitford rose and shook hands.

'It is kind of you to say so,' she said.

Fulbert laughed though his tone had hardly been without the suggestion.

'The situation puts you at a loss, does it?' he said observing or rather assuming that this was the case, and accordingly regarding her with eyes of enjoyment.

'Well, it is quite outside my experience.'

'An experience need not be so narrow, that it does not include it,' said Fulbert, giving encouragement, where it might be needed. 'Yours has taken place within four walls, but some of the deepest has done that.'

'Mine has not been of that kind,' said Miss Mitford.

'Well, well, some of us must deal with the smaller things of life.'

'Education is not among those,' said Eleanor.

'Indeed it is not. These youngsters owe you a great deal, Miss Mitford.'

'I am sure they realize it. Don't you, James?' said Eleanor, appealing to her son from force of habit, as his debt was less than his sisters'.

'Yes.'

'Why are you not at school, my boy?'

James felt that all the difficult moments of his life culminated in this one. He had accepted his father's return to family life as too solemn an occasion for the personal interest of his own education to have a place, and had remained at home in a grave and quiet spirit, and was reading a book to which these terms would apply.

'It is Father's first day at home,' he said, in a low, uncertain voice, that awaited his parents' interpretation.

'But not James's,' said Fulbert, in an amused, rallying tone, that gave his son his answer.

'And how are the others spending their time?' said Eleanor. 'I see that lessons are not in progress.'

'I am doing nothing,' said Isabel, at once.

'Is that the way to make the most of your holiday?' said her mother, her last word showing James the extent of his misapprehension.

'I daresay it is,' said Fulbert, resting his eyes on his daughter. 'People must relax when they have been wrought up too far.'

'Well, what is Venice doing?' said his wife.

Venice revealed a piece of embroidery, or rather took no steps to hide it.

'You need not be ashamed of it, my dear. I am not such an advocate of doing nothing. Let me see it.'

Venice laid it out, appearing hardly to see it herself.

'Sewing,' said her father. 'Another way of resting.'

Venice's face cleared, and she looked at her mother for her opinion.

'You are improving very much. I wish Isabel would learn to do a little needlework. As Father says, it would do her good.'

'Did I say so?' said Fulbert. 'Well, if it would, I hope she will take to it. And how is James passing his time?'

James handed his book to his mother with a smile, feeling a reluctance to show it to the parent responsible for it.

'That is a very nice book for today. I think James is developing, Fulbert.'

'This continual process in James should take him far,' said Isabel.

'I won't put him through his paces this morning,' said Fulbert, looking at his son with his old, quizzical air.

'The world is a different place to all of them,' said Eleanor.

'And to me it is the same place, and I would ask no more. Well, good-bye, Miss Mitford. It is good of you to let us intrude on your province.'

'Now you will settle down to a life where you have nothing to wish for,' said Eleanor, addressing her children at the door. 'That is a pleasant thought for your mother and for you.'

There was silence after she had gone.

'Nothing that could conceivably be realized,' said Isabel.

Her sister looked at her, and for a moment they held each other's eyes; then they suddenly rose and staggered to a distant sofa and fell on it in a fit of mirth.

James glanced up from his book, for once completely at a loss. Miss Mitford made a survey of her pupils and looked down with curiosity essentially satisfied. The two girls leant towards each other and spoke in tones audible to no one else.

'Our imagination ran away,' said Isabel. 'It is so rarely put to the proof. People have never lost what they think they have. And if they recover it, the moment comes.'

'Do you mind much?' whispered Venice.

'Not now the shock is over. In a way it is a relief. I can be at ease with everyone in the house. There is no one superior to me.'

'I am not like you,' said Venice.

'I can always protect you,' said Isabel.

'Mother will always be here as well as Father,' said James, closing his book.

'It is a small price to pay for Father's coming back,' said Isabel, causing Miss Mitford to raise her eyes. 'And she will be a great deal with him.'

'She will at first,' said James, and took up another book, as if he could leave the future.

'We can't have Father without his wife. And Mother has nothing contemptible about her.'

'You talk like Honor,' said James, in an absent tone.

'She and I are said to be alike.'

'I don't think you are,' said Venice.

'No one is really like anyone else.'

'That is true,' said Miss Mitford. 'We are struck by a little likeness because it is imposed on so much difference.'

'Venice is not like anyone. She is almost a beauty,' said Isabel, as if this precluded resemblance.

Venice fixed her eyes in front of her, while a great pleasure welled up within her, and James looked almost troubled by such an idea in connection with anyone so intimate.

Eleanor returned to the room.

'Father is worried about you, Isabel. Are you really exhausted?'

'No, only feeling a slight reaction, Mother.'

'That is my good girl,' said Eleanor, with surprised approval. 'I heard all that laughing, and I did not think it sounded much like exhaustion.'

'It was a schoolroom joke, Mother.'

'I expect you have all sorts of nonsense among yourselves,' said Eleanor, little thinking how much more worth her while such jests might be, than those she pursued downstairs.

'Is Venice really a beauty?' said James.

'Who has been saying she is?' said Eleanor, giving a deprecating look at Venice and suspecting Fulbert of the indiscretion.

'Isabel,' said James.

'Oh, Isabel,' said Eleanor, as if this testimony hardly counted. 'Why, what a flattering sister to have! What has Venice to say about her in return?'

'She often says she is clever,' said James. 'A lot of people do.'

'Well, so she is,' said Eleanor, thinking more easily of tribute along this line. 'And what of James? Are people going to say the same thing about him?'

James was taken aback by this result of his generosity, though he should have been learning that most things gave rise to it.

'Yes,' he said, in a light tone.

'And what grounds are they going to have for saying it?'

James could not refer to his choice of books for an occasion, as it had already been forgotten; or to the poems which to himself were proof of it, as he had revealed them to no one, and was postponing publication until his maturity; and merely made uneasy movements.

'Well, we won't talk about it on Father's first day,' said Eleanor, allowing that it was an awkward subject.

James returned to the book he had been reading when his parents entered.

'I should not read while your mother is in the room, my boy.'

James kept his eyes on the page until he seemed to reach a climax, put in his marker and smiled at his mother, while he put out his hand to the other book, whose appearance might need explanation.

'You were just reading to a place where you could stop.'

'Yes.'

'And now you are going to have a change,' said Eleanor, with a condoning smile and a sense of relief, as solemn spirits on seriously joyful occasions affected her as they did most people. 'And now I hear Father calling me. I must remember who has the right to my time. I may not be able to visit you again today.'

She descended to the hall and came upon Fulbert and Luce engaged in talk. Her daughter turned to meet her.

'Mother, the Cambridge results are out. They really came some days ago, but they have only transpired today. Daniel has a first, and Graham a low third. It is what they expected, so do not let us make a disturbance.'

'Was anyone showing any tendency to do so, my dear?'

Fulbert jerked his thumb towards the door of the library with an air of giving an answer.

Sir Jesse emerged and walked in to luncheon, looking at no one. His grandsons followed him and paused to join their parents.

'Well done, my boy,' said Fulbert, bringing his hand down on Daniel's shoulder. 'Some people belittle this kind of success, but I am not one of them. This is a happy chance on my first day with you all.'

'We were keeping the news for an opportune moment,' said Daniel, not mentioning that they had postponed it until after their mother's marriage. 'And then we forgot it in the excitement of your return. It was in the *Times* on Tuesday, and Grandpa scanned the lists this morning and found our place. Somehow it seems an odd thing for him to do.'

'There is no limit to what he is capable of,' said Graham. 'But I suppose not even he will think it a moment for dwelling on people's weaker sides.'

'Have you already forgotten that some things are not to be mentioned?' said Eleanor.

'I will remind myself of it, Mother. I am all for following the course.'

'You shall have my support, my boy,' said Fulbert. 'I have not come back to expect great things of you. I have done little myself but survive. I ask nothing but your welcome.'

'He has it,' said Graham, in a fervent undertone.

'You could not make an effort for your mother, Graham?' said Eleanor.

'Graham, some day you may tell people what was the bitterest moment of your life,' said Daniel.

Fulbert signed towards the dining-room.

'Is it wise to keep the old man waiting for his luncheon?'

Luce tiptoed to the room and back again, with a smile spreading over her face.

'We have not done so, Father.'

'We may as well go and catch him up,' said Fulbert, walking through the open door.

Sir Jesse gave no sign while his family took their seats, but presently turned to Graham.

'I mentioned to you that I saw those lists in the *Times*. I asked you if I was to believe the evidence of my eyes. You did not answer my question.'

'Well, I wish you would not do so, Grandpa.'

'Am I to gather there is some mistake?'

'Things in the *Times* tend to be true. And the same must be said of the testimony of people's senses.'

'Are you speaking to me?'

'I am answering you, Grandpa.'

'Would you prefer to be apprenticed to a shoemaker or a shoeblack?'

'The first; I should say there is no comparison. The work would be more skilled and more remunerative.'

'Good reasons, my boy,' said Fulbert, under his breath.

'Why are unsuccessful sons supposed to apply themselves to callings connected with shoes?' said Daniel.

'No wonder good boots seem so very good,' said Graham. 'A great deal of good blood must be behind the making of them.'

'If you cannot apply your sharpness to your work, I want none of it,' said Sir Jesse.

'Miss Mitford was so pleased about your place, Daniel,' said Luce. 'She also saw the lists in the *Times*.'

'The *Times*?' said Sir Jesse, Regan and Eleanor at once.

'Not the family copy,' said Luce, laughing. 'She has her own.'

'How like her!' said Regan, her tone almost giving way under her feeling.

'Why, Grandma, she may want to know the news of the day.'

'And no doubt does what she wants,' said Regan, in the same tone.

'You appear to be eating your luncheon, Graham,' said Sir Jesse, seeming to view ordinary proceeding in his grandson, as his wife did in the governess. 'What are your ideas about your ultimate provision?'

'If only Graham could be cured, what problems it would solve!' said Daniel.

'You have never needed to have any on the subject yourself, Grandpa,' said Graham.

'You need not compare yourself with me. I have done many other things.'

'Yes, I know you have,' said Graham, drawing his mother's eyes.

'Do you feel no gratitude to me for your home and your education?'

'You make me pay too heavy a price for them.'

'I hope that sort of payment will stand you in stead with other people.'

The three children ran into the room in outdoor clothes.

'They have just come in to see us,' said Eleanor. 'I thought they would be too much for their father today. He is not strong yet.'

'Come and have a piece of my chicken,' said Fulbert, to his youngest son.

Nevill came up and waited while a spoon was supplied, not standing very close or looking at the process.

'Did you like it?' said his father.

'No, it burnt his tongue,' said Nevill, and turned away.

'How shall I pay for my future portions of chicken?' said Graham.

'I should be glad to know,' said Sir Jesse.

'Why can't Graham just be a man like Grandpa and Father?' said Gavin, who had grasped the nature of the conversation.

'He has no money, said Eleanor. 'You will all have to earn your living.'

'Shall we? I thought it was only James.'

'No, of course not. You are all in the same position.'

'Then I shall be a traveller.'

'You would not earn much like that.'

'If I confronted great dangers, I should.'

'Who would pay you for doing it? It would not be much good to other people.'

'There are societies who pay,' said Honor. 'People like things to be discovered.'

'Graham's occupation is the immediate point,' said Sir Jesse.

'I thought you had arranged it, sir,' said Graham.

'He will call Grandpa, sir,' said Nevill, in an admiring tone.

'Shall we say a word about Daniel?' said Fulbert. 'We may as well dwell upon our success.'

'He knows how glad and proud he has made us,' said Eleanor. 'We do not need to talk about it.'

'I also have grasped the general feeling,' said Graham.

'I suppose Graham will be a tutor,' said Sir Jesse, in a tone that did not exalt this calling.

'I should be the first of Miss Mitford's pupils to follow in her steps.'

'Why isn't it nice to be a tutor?' said Honor. 'Royal people have tutors, and their names are put in the papers.'

'So are the ladies-in-waiting,' said Sir Jesse.

'Grandpa spoke to Honor,' said Nevill, impressed by this equal answer.

'Does Hatton also have the *Times*?' said Fulbert.

'Hatton has it all,' said Nevill.

'What are you going to be when you grow up?' said Fulbert, catching his son and lifting him to his knee.

'He will be a king,' said Nevill, reconciling himself to his situation.

'Then you will be above your father.'

'Yes, Father is only a man.'

'Why do you want to look down on us all?'

'He will take care of you. And he will take care of Hatton and Mullet too.'

'And what will Hatton be?'

'She will be a lady when he marries her.'

'But then she will be a queen.'

'No, he will. There is only one. Hatton likes it to be him.'

'What will the rest of us be?'

'All stand round him and wear long clothes. Not a king, but very nice.'

'And what will you wear?'

'A crown.'

'He has seen a picture,' said Luce.

'He will sit on a throne,' said Nevill, raising his arms, 'And a man will kneel down on a cushion with his gold stick.'

'I am going to leave the table before that office is suggested for me,' said Graham, to his brother. 'It seems to have points in common with that of a shoeblack. You can come with me to cover my retreat.'

'Where are you going?' said Daniel, when they gained the hall.

'To visit the Marlowes. That is a thing that Grandpa would dislike. You can come and scan their faces for signs of their parentage. That is what you want to do. I am glad I am not so nearly related to Grandpa.'

'We must keep a stern hold on our tongues.'

'Oh, I will keep Grandpa's guilty secrets,' said Graham, relapsing into his usual manner. 'And in future I will commit errors base enough to be hushed up.'

'He feels you have caused him to waste his substance. And I see there have been drains upon it. A second family is not exactly an economy.'

'He has rendered it as much of one as possible,' said Graham, looking at the cottage. 'Why did he establish the fruits of his sin at his gates?'

'Because he could do it most cheaply there,' said Daniel, hardly realizing that he spoke the simple truth.

Priscilla came at once to meet them.

'Well, there ought to be a bond between us. We all thought we were fatherless, and we all find we are not.'

'So the truth has escaped,' said Daniel, 'and with its accustomed dispatch.'

'And we find that our feelings do not go beyond speech. And we are glad of that. The speech will be a relief. We are looking forward to it.'

'Mother and Sir Jesse decided to set conventions at nought,' said Susan.

'And there is one law for the man and another for the woman,' said Priscilla. 'That makes it braver of Mother. And she has to be coupled with Sir Jesse. And that does seem a credit to her.'

'How has it got out?' said Daniel.

'Hope thinks Ridley spread it abroad,' said Susan. 'Out of revenge on your family.'

'Revenge for what?' said Graham. 'For patience and hospitality and welcome of him in our father's place? If a word was wrung from us, when his full plan emerged, it is surely to be understood.'

'He is angry at having fallen from his pedestal.'

'So Grandpa is to do the same. Well, he will not do so,' said Daniel. 'No one can speak of the truth to him, and he will die in ignorance that anyone knows. He has already forgotten that we do.'

'So you know the whole,' said Graham, to Priscilla.

'We hope we do. We have done our best. The full story may never come to us. But the bare facts are enough. We are quite satisfied.'

'It should go no further,' said Susan. 'In our case it hardly can. But James goes to school.'

'James does not know,' said Daniel.

'No doubt the boys at the school do. And James will give his own evidence. And soon know himself.'

'He cannot bring his friends home. We escape that risk,' said Graham, leaning back. 'He might be put to have tea in the nursery, or have to obey the governess, or be asked how his lessons were progressing.'

'Anything might happen,' said Daniel; 'anything would; anything did, when we were young.'

'I wish Ridley's crime had not a tragic side,' said Graham.

'It does spoil one's full enjoyment of it,' said Priscilla. 'But people's reasons for crimes always make one want to cry. Think of Sir Jesse, lonely in a far land and needing Mother. And think of Mother, prepared to face anything for Sir Jesse's sake. Between ourselves, it does seem rather odd of Mother.'

'Think of Ridley,' began Graham, and broke off.

'I am glad Sir Jesse need never know that we know,' said Lester. 'It would make it awkward for Priscilla to show him our accounts. It would seem too businesslike a relation.'

'Surely you do not owe him your confidence to that extent?' said Daniel.

'We owe him everything, even life,' said Priscilla. 'And we might have known that it is only owing people that, that leads to owing them other things.'

'It is a good thing he is the father of all three of us,' said Susan. 'It would be a poor exchange to gain Sir Jesse and lose each other.'

Lester raised his eyes.

'Have you ever suspected the truth?' said Daniel.

'We shall think we have, unless we check ourselves in time,' said Susan. 'I have thought of it, but it seemed that Sir Jesse had not enough feeling for us.'

'I have no excuse to make; it simply never occurred to me,' said Priscilla. 'That is what my woman's instinct has done. I hope it means that I am a masculine type. And I believe Sir Jesse has sometimes looked at me with a parent's eye. I have had every chance.'

'It seems almost too obvious a solution,' said Susan. 'And a good many things did point the other way. Sir Jesse's lack of affection, his putting us so near his house, his not disclaiming interest in us. But no doubt he knew they did.'

'Did Hope tell you?' said Daniel.

'She said nothing until she found we knew,' said Susan. 'No one told us in words, but something in the air was too much.'

'Hope knows where to draw the line,' said Lester.

'I had no idea of that,' said Priscilla. 'I was quite self-reproachful when I knew.'

'It is a great thing to feel we have a claim on Sir Jesse,' Lester said in a grave tone.

'No legal claim after you are fourteen,' said Daniel.

'Well, people are always children to their parents,' said Priscilla. 'And it does not seem that Sir Jesse has a great regard for rules.'

'When our origin is what it is, why is not Luce allowed to visit us?' said Susan.

'That is the reason,' said Daniel. 'It is the blood relationship. Lester might fall in love with his niece. So might you with your nephews, but Grandpa would think that was unlikely.'

'The difference in age would be supposed to prevent it,' said Susan.

'Something has done so,' said Graham.

'I wonder Sir Jesse never thought we might suspect the truth,' said Susan.

'I think he had almost forgotten it himself,' said Priscilla, 'until the loss of his son reminded him, and he saw himself as childless except for us. I see it all now. Of course people always say that, but why shouldn't they, when it is true? What is the good of their having the help, if they don't take advantage of it?'

'I wonder if he had a family anywhere else,' said Lester, as if struck by a new idea.

'He has only lived in two places,' said Daniel, 'and he was provided for in both of those.'

'I should have liked to be there when the truth came out,' said Susan.

'You little know,' said Graham.

'I am not afraid of saying that I feel with Susan,' said Priscilla. 'Women may be tough, but falsehood does not make it any better. I wish we had been present, and I almost feel we had a right to be.'

'Did you ever suspect, Lester?' said Graham.

'I cannot claim that I did,' said Lester, with a laugh. 'I once hinted to Sir Jesse that we should like a photograph of our father, and that disposes of the question. But on that day when he paid us a visit to talk of his son, I knew.'

'Why did you not tell us?' said his sisters at once, neither of them throwing doubt on his word.

'I thought it might be disturbing for you to know.'

'It is disquieting news,' said Priscilla, 'but I am glad we have such a respectable father. Sir Jesse will still be esteemed.'

'Ridley will have to live in exile, and Grandpa will remain the head of the village,' said Daniel. 'And I feel it is right.'

'If it were not for the art of photography, Grandpa would still be held a perfect man,' said Graham, in a tone of sympathy with his grandfather.

'Mankind is known to use his inventions for his own destruction,' said Priscilla.

'Suppose there should be a great deal of talk about it,' said Lester.

'Only Ridley would want that,' said Daniel. 'And he can hardly cast the first stone.'

'Grandpa can take that initiative,' said Graham. 'I can bear witness to it.'

'No doubt many people have guessed,' said Susan. 'Now that the truth is out, the position will hardly be different.'

'It is a good thing Grandpa is a man who can carry off anything,' said Daniel.

'I always wanted to meet a person like that,' said Priscilla. 'And now I am the daughter of one. I hope we have inherited the quality. It should be useful to us.'

'Perhaps it has always been so,' said Lester.

'People will have a tinge of respect for us for our descent,' said Priscilla. 'And we shall share the feeling.'

'You cannot bring your lips to utter the word, Father,' said Daniel.

'No, no,' said Lester, almost before the words were out, 'there is no need for that.'

'Here are a note and a book from Hope,' said Priscilla, as a parcel was brought to her. 'She left them herself. I can see her going down the road. I wonder if she has any more news for us.'

DEAR PRISCILLA,

I meant to come in, but I caught sight of your guests, and I could not be the only person among so many, not related to Sir Jesse. I still hope it will be found out that I am, but meanwhile I just offer my love and congratulations.

HOPE CRANMER.

'Someone else is approaching,' said Susan. 'That is why Hope did not wait. She wanted to meet Sir Jesse. He is going to that lane where he walks by himself, and he seems not to see her. Someone get in front of the window. He will be passing in a moment.'

'It seems odd that he should be following his usual course,' said Priscilla. 'But no revelation has come to him. To think what pictures of the past must be crowding through his mind! Perhaps they have always done so, and that explains his absent ways. But I daresay we are judging by our own minds.'

She moved to the window and stood with her figure shadowing the room, and Sir Jesse gave her a glance as he passed, and raised his hat and walked on.